SHADOW'S RISE

CHRONICLES OF THE FISTS

JOSEPH J. BAILEY

CONTENTS

MAP

Dharia

To Far
Aruene

The Ayle'ine Sea

Tol Aeron
Keep
of
Tarnakoor

Empen
Wastes

The Plains
of
Kadoor

Doeja

Var'Kera

Kervon

Q'shar

The Green Run

Loenia

Northlands

Shady Vale
Yildel

Uridisen

Dunmiffalien

Amaron

Aliman

The Drake Spires

Ithil'alen

Emerald Jungle

Jenyuan
Shulin

Fay Leng

The K'un Lun

Chang Sen

Liao
Huang
Qia

Lanrei

Tuoma

Luecine Sea

Landir

Lueciane Sea

Qia Shan Sea

To Far
Maeron

To Far
Kilaeron

© 2011 Joe Bushey

W

N

S

E

AUTHOR'S NOTE

For terms that are not strictly imaginary in nature, the Wade-Giles and Pinyin Romanization systems are used interchangeably, loosely, and not entirely accurately.

Transliteration devices were chosen mostly based on whichever sounded better at the time.

A glossary of terms is included at the book's end to help the reader fully engage in, understand, and explore the world of Ea'ae.

Forgive my errors for they are numerous and I am not.

DEDICATION

*To the original Four
who were, in reality, Five.*

*To the new Four
who now number Eight.*

Dare to realize your dreams. Dare to dream your reality.

- Master Wei
Priest of the K'un Lun

FLAMES IN THE NIGHT

Travel worn satchel—
how many lands have you seen
on your journey home?

A priest should not have to run.

Thoughts flitted on the surface of Yip's awareness—sea foam dancing on the shores of consciousness.

How had the Cabal found them?

Where would he run next?

Would his foe ever allow any quarter?

Were any of his fellow initiates alive?

Would the K'un Lun ever flower again?

Mirroring his thoughts, his soul shimmered in the evening light. The energy of life danced in and around him and shifted in the breeze.

Not that he was special. In fact, he was like everyone else. The only difference, well the primary difference, was that he had been taught to see…to touch…and to feel the essential in and around him.

Apparently the Cabal thought that he was, or rather those like him were, special—the dark ones had gone to grave lengths to single out members of his order.

As his eyes adjusted to the evening gloaming, the light of stars provided a gentle relief to the soft luminescence of the trees swaying in the breeze—every one utterly unique and beautiful; each in a varying state of health and repose. A single glance told him the story of the tree, the song of the forest, the light and glory of life.

As his awareness extended through and around the trees, his wandering mind kept coming back to a simple thought, his gravest concern.

Why would the Cabal want to destroy him and his kind?

Why ruin all this?

He ran beneath the tree boughs without a glance behind—a single shadow flitting through the gloom. Flowing like a thought from one moonlit glen to the next, he moved quickly from his past toward his new future.

REMEMBRANCE

Rainbow haloed moon,
occluded by clouds,
reflects on falling snowflakes.

Haunted by the memory of the horrors of the night past, phantasms ran their course unhindered and unobstructed through the bounds of his consciousness, each difficult step away from home a recollection of the terrors endured by his brothers.

The clamant call of his teacher, Master Wei, yet reverberated through his psyche.

"Run, Yip! Flee while you can!"
Master Wei's voice echoed in his mind with an urgency not to be denied.

With his master's warning, a brief glimpse from his teacher's view etched itself irrevocably within the expanse of his mind's eye: his monastery, the cradle of the K'un Lun aflame, her walls broken and breached; once noble bodies wracked and scattered throughout the grounds; priests, initiates, and acolytes engaged with seething, implacable tendrils of Darkness; his once peaceful brethren locked in mortal combat with vile hellspawn from the darkest nether realms; his past, his order's future on the brink of destruction.

"*Go now, Yip!*"

With his Master's last urging, a command to abandon all he had known, a dictate that could not be ignored, the visions ended along with any hope of reunion with his order.

He chose not to let the visions go, for he was not yet ready to surrender his past.

Nor was he ready to surrender his future.

MAGIC

Mountains touched lightly
by a tawny setting sun—
the day fades in light.

Days and nights passed in a blur, a nightmare of anticipation.

Dogged by fear, chased by an enemy he could not see, any mistake could be his last; any sign of his presence could be his undoing.

The source of his strength, his *chi*, was also his greatest weakness.

His living energies a glittering nimbus emanating outward into the surrounding energy streams, a target for any who could see, he could only hope no one noticed his swift passage.

So he ran.

There was no safe harbor for him throughout the realms of Chang Sen.

Sooner or later, despite whatever protections friends and allies may afford, agents of his enemies would find him out. His best option was to keep moving; the farther away from the world he knew the better. His instincts told him that even this was a futile gesture, that his traces would eventually be found out—physical distance was largely meaningless in a world where magical tracking and travel were possible, where traces of his essence rippled outward in cascading waves of potential—but his determination lent no credence to concerns contrary to his need to survive and assist those in his order better able to respond to the fall of his monastery, his *guàn*.

The K'un Lun range, where his order had held its seat for ages beyond reckoning, formed the northwestern barrier of the storied realm of Chang Sen. If he had fled to the East and descended along the other side of the base of the great K'un Lun Mountains, he would have eventually made his way into Chang Sen proper, first passing through small, scattered villages before reaching one of the ancient seats of power in a kingdom whose dynasties spanned millennia.

Weeks of all-consuming travel westward, however, had taken him out of the mountains of K'un Lun, the only home he had ever known. Skirting the great icy crests of those peaks, through untouched alpine forests, past glacial lakes and tarns, he pressed downward from the heights toward a region of lush forests, home more to creatures of magic than Man.

After the cool refreshing breezes he had known in the soaring mountains and the hidden valleys of the K'un Lun, the day's gradually increasing heat and haze as he descended were something of a shock to his system. Pausing to girdle his robes, his *zhiju*, tightly about his legs to ease his movements over the rocks, he breathed deeply, appreciating the fresh air as it filled and restored his lungs and weary muscles. Standing slowly to stretch, he continued his way down the mountainside to his destination below.

Late in the afternoon, after a long day spent bouldering, clambering over loose rocky scree, gradually but resolutely picking his way downward toward the feet of the range, he paused to survey his surroundings, scouting for a suitable spot to end the day's descent before continuing anew in the morning, a cycle of repeated effort without apparent end. Scrabbling along a loose rocky ridge looking out from the fall line along the slope's spine, he gazed outward toward his new future in the lush warm forests below.

Stretching to the horizon as far as the eye could see in all directions lay Jenyuan Shulin, the Forbidden Forest, the western boundary of

Chang Sen. The forest formed an impenetrable barrier that, when coupled with the lofty peaks of the K'un Lun to the east, protected Chang Sen from any armies invading by land. The forest also provided a strict demarcation to Chang Sen's western frontier for it curtailed the Empire's expansion westward as much as it protected the Empire proper.

From the stories he had heard as a child, only a righteous man could pass its borders unharmed.

Blue skies untouched by clouds soared above all the way to the horizon. An irregular carpet of verdant green stretched just as far ahead, lost in the haze from the transpiration of countless trees and other growing things. Myriad specks of small flying birds and animals could be seen coasting above the canopy, intermittently lost among the steaming reaches above the jungle's limits.

To his mind's eye, through senses cultivated by years of practice and intense meditation, the world ahead was entirely different.

The energy of life unbounded blazed beneath the sun in his inner vision. On and within his skin, countless individual microscopic organisms shimmered—a universe of radiant diamonds strewn across his body, luminous in the clear sunlight. Beneath his feet, subtle energies coruscated and gleamed faintly like foxfire along the rocks as lichens, moss, microbes, and small insects struggled to make a home in the harsh, xeric subalpine habitat along the barren slopes. Beyond, in the verdurous wilderness below, towering trees rose in a luxuriant, nutrient rich environment shining like great torches burning in the night.

The potential, interrelationships, interconnectivity, and individuation all commingled in a great sea of light scintillating beneath the sun.

These same energies washed over him in an iridescent tide, emanations he felt through his being, pulling at his core, informing his actions and intent, guiding his mind and eye.

Awash in impressions, he read and felt the patterns of development and succession in the forest below, the presence of pockets of irregularities and disease, the subtle response of potential prey to predators, the life history of a tree along the canopy's edge, the efforts put into survival in a world of extreme competition, all with a single glance. To him, the magic, the potential, the spirit, of life burned like a fire beneath the sun—the land overflowing with energies and stories few could see or comprehend.

Interwoven within this tapestry, other forces he could not identify moved, coruscating with unknown purpose.

He knew from the lore of his tradition and the experience of his subtle senses that even these impressions were not a complete reflection of the moment. True, the land ahead was lush and held many plants and animals in abundance. However, given its bounty, there must be powerful forces at work to keep it free of the touch of Man, Elf, or Dwarf.

He would have to face those obstacles as he encountered them.

Picking his way slowly downward along the ridge, the heat of the sun gradually lessening as the day approached evening, he found a flat spot beside a precariously situated boulder to lay out his bedroll for the evening. Sitting down on a nearby flat rock, he chewed slowly on a few dry, nutritious medicinal herbs. Although he felt pressed to keep moving for he might sense his pursuers only when it was too late, his system would function better after a sound evening's rest, a commodity he had been running short on for too many days. After drinking some herbal tea, he laid down on his worn bedding admiring the first of the evening stars to unfold sparkling in the sky above.

As an initiate in his order, he was well-trained in the arts of survival—foraging, trapping, reading signs and weather, land navigation, construction of shelter, dealing with extreme environments, finding and purifying water, herbal and medicinal plant identification and application, among other skills needed to exist alone in the wild. Additionally, due to his training in the secrets of his order's arts, he had almost complete control of his physical processes and metabolism. Even in the face of extreme exertion, his needs for sustenance were negligible. With assurance in his abilities to eke out a living in almost any situation ahead, he would soon make his way into a world of green, wherein bounty, not parsimony, would be the norm; a world he hoped would shelter and protect him beneath its mighty boughs and branches.

Soft as the evening breeze alighting upon his shoulders, watching the stars above, he fell into a deep sleep.

As somnolence overtook his system and his conscious mind lost touch with his body, he slowly, ever so slowly, cast his mind homeward in search of those of his kin who may be listening. After these past few harrowing weeks of flight, the time to contact those of his order who may be of help had finally come.

If any yet remained.

As if caught on that evening breeze brushing his shoulders, his thoughts floated outward along currents none could see.

Adrift in the ether, in a land of formless consciousness, time passed unbidden and uncounted. Finally, a soft voice in his ears gradually coalesced into a face, the lustrous visage of his teacher—Master Wei!

"I am so glad to sense you are safe, Yip!"

"And I you, Master!"

He felt his Master's presence as an echo of memory in his thoughts.

"Master where—?"

Reading his thoughts, Master Wei responded, *"We have restored the veil."*

He did not know what to say.

Would his order retreat so quickly after only recently reemerging into the world at large? What about the work they had only just begun? How would they retake their place in the world if they retreated so swiftly? How would they adopt an active role combating the Cabal hidden in the shadows of the world's periphery?

Gathering himself in hope, he asked, *"Are there many who are safe, Master?"*

"Master Shi gave himself to protect the students, Yip. Others were lost as well, Masters Liu, Chang, Loquan, and Wuping among them." He could feel his teacher's loss even across all this distance. Master Wei and Master Shi had often shared lessons and were both very kind to the young aspiring acolytes. Until his passage, Master Shi had been the T'ien-shih, the celestial master, of the K'un Lun. Ea'ae and the K'un Lun both lost a guiding star. The other masters were no lesser losses. Each had

contributed a breadth and depth of wisdom that would be forever missed.

"Though our walls have been breached and many broken, those that remain are safe. Almost all others have returned or are on their way."

"Of that, I am happier than you can know, master. I will miss Master Shi's wisdom and humor just as I will miss those lost. Their Light will brighten the days."

"And spread Light through the heavens." He could feel his teacher's bittersweet smile brightening his face.

"Master, I...I do not know what to do."

"You must do what you feel is right, Yip. We are still here for you. You can return to us if you will."

"I cannot yet walk the veil, Master." This was one of so many things he had yet to learn.

"I will aid your passage."

"Are there any who still walk this land?"

A pause. *"You are the last, Yip."*

"Then I will remain."

"Is this your counsel?"

"There is much to be done here. I cannot abandon all that we stand for when there are so many who may need us and our aid, especially with the return of the Liúxīng Làngrén!"

Across all this distance, he felt his Master's pleasure with his decision, a steady warmth radiating through his thoughts. *"Your heart rings true, Yip. I am glad to hear its peal."*

As the reality and import of what he had decided upon sank in and this steady reassurance from his teacher faded, he entreated, *"What shall I do, Master? There is so much I do not yet know, so much to learn!"*

How could he hope to cope with the might of the fallen priests and their unholy allies?

Anticipating his thoughts, Master Wei said, *"I will be here for you when you need me. I will lend what guidance and tutelage I can in dreams. You will not be alone."*

"Where shall I go? How shall I proceed?"

"Continue on your journey westward, Yip. Find what friends you can.

Trust your impressions. There may be those who are willing to help. Experience will be your teacher as you progress onward."

"You must learn of your enemy before you confront him. They are many, Yip. You must use caution!"

Sensing something he could not, he felt an urgency come to his master's voice, *"Yip! You must be careful in your wanderings! Ours are not the only eyes here!"*

Trying to respond, his mind suddenly lost focus. A great Darkness seemed to pass through his consciousness as if a cloud had wiped away the stars above.

A voice that only knew terror pierced to his very heart, sibilant and cold as the reaches between the stars.

"A youngling ready for harvest! Yours is an end that will bring great pleasure to my masters!"

Through an extreme effort of will, he broke off contact with the creature, his mind shrinking from its presence. With a start, he awoke dripping sweat, his heart beating rapidly in his chest.

Master Wei was gone.

With him went any chance of immediate security.

Jumping to his feet, casting away his bedroll, Yip sensed a gathering of energy, the rapid movement of force. In his mind's eye the shifting, swirling mass of living energy that normally emanated all around was rapidly coalescing, densifying, and taking form.

The air popped with sudden force as wind rushed in to fill the void left by a jagged tear in space.

Standing before him, silhouetted in the starlight, stood the crooked caricature of a man. The caster's robes were black and frayed and his eyes rolled around in his head as if trying to anticipate some invisible blow. His form was hunched and broken—a body that had been long used, ill-treated, and neglected.

"I have been watching for those of your kind who would talk through dreams, youngling," the twisted form hissed. "You are the first I was fortunate enough to find. I will be dearly rewarded for my efforts it seems!"

Across the clearing in the evening's subtle light, he sensed the gathering of power and movement of energy as the caster muttered the beginnings of a hoarse, throaty incantation while his gnarled hands spasmed through the motions of some heinous arcane ritual.

Much like a deranged painter expressing his will and lurid imaginings on canvas, or like a twisted mandala made real and vivid full of hostile meaning and implied intention, he watched the caster mangle and mutilate the energy of life itself—creating and realizing some dark and sinister purpose.

Yip's training and development allowed him to see this process unfold where others could not.

He had only the merest seconds to react before the possible became real.

Now was the time for action.

Time slowed...

The cool breeze on his shoulders stopped, his robes paused in mid-rustle, the clouds moving across the sky waited briefly in front of the moon, and the jubilant chorus of rock crickets ceased mid-stanza as the caster froze in place. In the time between seconds, he leapt into action.

Before the muttered incantation had finished, before the ritual gestures were completed, he stood over the caster's fallen form, the adulterated energies of the wizard's spent spell released as the evening returned to motion.

GREEN DESCENT

Sunlight flits upon
the dew-laden canopy—
birdsong fills the air.

He had been lucky.

That his foe had been mortal was a blessing beyond counting. His skills were not yet such that he could hope to fight against any super-mundane foes.

That his opponent had acted rashly, perhaps in eager anticipation of his reward, and not prepared adequate defenses was just as fortuitous.

Looking down at his foe, Yip muttered a brief prayer for the wizard's lost spirit, wishing him better fortunes in the next world than he had enjoyed in this one.

He had to move and swiftly. Even if this agent of the Cabal was acting alone, his absence would be noted and tracked soon enough. Even in defeat, his opponent had brought his pursuers even closer. If he had been beneath the Cabal's notice or concern before, that situation would change quickly even if he had only dispatched one of their lowest servants.

The Liúxīng Làngrén would now believe that at least one priest walked the lands of Ea'ae.

Even though he was not yet one.

He packed up his bedroll with a skill and alacrity brought on by long practice. He did not have time to try to hide his presence, and, even if he did, his foes would be tracking his essence, not his physical signs and marks. He did, however, take the time to burn the wizard's robes and other items so that tracking the wizard would be more difficult.

His only hope now was that the preponderance of greenery below would conceal his essence, lost among the signs and energy of so much life.

Mentally scolding himself, he needed to learn to mask his presence before contacting his Master in dreams. But his need had been great and he thought himself safe.

Now he knew better.

There was so much he did not know! So many things he knew of but had never done himself and so many techniques he was far from mastering. Without guidance, learning would be a struggle. His skills may fall behind where he would hope to be with a specified training program, but those techniques he did master would be based on an intuitive understanding that he could rely on with certainty, forged in the crucible of life or death struggle.

Putting thought to action, he covered the distance to the base of the last hill, the last remnant of the once mighty K'un Lun, within an hour of hard scrabbling over the largely barren hillside.

As he reached the bottom of the slope, he was struck by how abrupt the transition to the jungle at the bottom of the hill really was. Looking back up the incline toward the soaring mountains, the land-scape was largely devoid of vegetation and any real signs of life. Ahead, practically leaping up from the ground in a formidable wall of greenery, stood the boles of great trunks whose crowns were lost in mists above, whose roots anchored soundly within a mantle of magic.

The world was full of mysteries beyond counting.

Taking a deep breath, he started forward. Within a few paces into the jungle almost all sights and sounds of the world he had just left behind had faded into a tangled green profusion. All around, the buttresses of great trees formed chapel-like pillars, supporting a canopy of green mosaics—hanging plants, bromeliads, vines and lianas, various orchids, palms, and ferns all scattered among plants he had never seen, more types than he could imagine—coming together to form a cathedral of life whose vast limbs were lost amidst the canopy reaching for the sky above.

As he hurried forward, his movements slowed by the dense vegetation, he marveled at the complexity of the world around him. To his inner vision, countless webs of interaction laced the air like great spider's webs that knew no end or beginning to their weaving, tingling upon his skin in limitless abundance. His mind was lost amid the complexity and could not follow the beginning of one relationship to its terminus. The inner light of so many existences blurred together in a profusion unlike any he had ever known. Closing his eyes and holding his head in his hands amidst the flood of sensation, he stopped to recover himself and take stock of the situation.

That was when he noticed something was amiss.

He cast his mind outward into the profound silence, into the gray mist hanging indolently between the trunks.

What he found was as striking as it was disturbing.

He could find little signs of life besides plants! What should have been home to countless flying and scuttling invertebrates, myriad birds calling out to each other, boisterous primates foraging for food, reptiles lying in wait for prey, amphibians hiding under the leaf litter, was almost completely absent. All he could pick up that was remotely normal were the tiny organisms in the soil that kept it functioning and developing, continually recycling and digesting nutrients along with a smattering of hardy insects.

Why?

Moving forward, at the limits of his perception, he could make out other things, creatures the likes of which he had never encountered, but their impressions were too indistinct, too far, and too different from what he knew to make sense of without further study and observation.

Perhaps this place was home to magical creatures that could mask their presence from him, or that existed only partially in this world. He could not say.

Whatever the cause, there was a veil surrounding the jungle though one of an entirely different sort than the one surrounding his *guàn*.

Lost in his musings, he picked his way carefully forward. As the only one of his type here, this jungle would be a good place to learn to mask his essence and blend it with his surroundings. If he could develop that skill, then his pursuers would have a much harder time picking him out from amongst the vegetation. Obscuring his essence could also help hide his presence from any predators this place may harbor.

Taking a deep breath, he hoped that he had put enough distance between himself and his old campsite to confound his pursuers. If not, he would have to be ready for a fight he could not hope to win.

After another deep breath, he noticed the change.

In tune with his breathing, his respiration, and his metabolism in ways that even the most astute could not hope to comprehend, he found out why the forest edge was so still, home only to memories.

The mist all around him, the rich energies within, had a soporific effect, dulling his senses, making his motions torpid and without vibrancy, his thoughts were gradually becoming more and more turgid.

He sat down beneath a forest giant.

The dawning realization was as weighty as his limbs currently felt. Anything that ventured into this forest without protection was subject to mind numbing, physically incapacitating magical gases put out from the trees all around him. Through some bizarre, but highly effective, mechanism, the forest protected itself with a dense haze of arcane neurotoxin.

Although stunned and quite impressed with the forest's adaptation, he was not ready to become plant sustenance.

Now was the time for him to use some of those skills that he actually possessed and could rely on for critical situations. Maintaining his calm, he gradually slowed his respiration. The first step would be to decelerate and, if possible, stop the toxin's advance.

Focusing inward, he could sense the gradual numbing from the poison moving along his limbs even as his respiration and heartbeat dropped almost to nothing. Waiting patiently in the face of the poison's slow advance, he watched to see if his body's natural defenses could counteract the poison as its progress was gradually arrested.

As his thoughts slowed with his respiration, he could feel that his current efforts were not enough. If he had controlled his respiration earlier and lessened his intake of the enchanted soporific, then this approach might have worked.

He would not find any solution or counter in the limited store of medicines in his pouch, nor could he hope to find any herb in the surrounding forest that would negate the poison's effects in time. And, even if he had the proper herbs, he did not have time to make an antidote.

He had only one other choice available.

He would have to purge his system and, for as long as possible, keep his system clean. He could not go back out from under the forest's cover for then he would be found for certain, an easy target for creatures that could fly or teleport while tracing his essence as he scrambled along rocky slopes or ran along the forest's edge.

Gathering his internal energies in his *tan t'ien*, he let a burst of life-giving *chi* rush through his system. As the energies surged along his meridians, he could feel his vivacity and clarity of mind quickly returning.

Sighing with relief, he opened his eyes and stood up from the forest floor. He kept his respiration and heart rate reduced significantly to lessen the amount of air he needed to breath. The main drawback of his solution was that his rate of progress would be slowed correspondingly as he could not tax his system while in an almost anoxic state. Given his slow advance, he could only hope that any initial pursuers were either slow to respond or were mortal men like him. If so, they would be in for a nasty surprise should they venture into the forest after him unprepared.

In order to protect himself as he moved forward, he consciously guided his *chi* along the meridians around his lungs to keep them clean and free from contamination. Such efforts were almost intuitive for him, as he had spent much time first learning to see, then follow, and later guide his intrinsic energies as they traveled naturally through his microcosmic orbit and along the energy meridians to his organs and extremities.

He sincerely hoped that those trees closer to the center of the forest had less need for such defenses and had therefore not expressed them to such a degree, for he would need to be ready for any other challenges that might arise as he moved forward through the green wild.

All the while, he proceeded forward with his senses extended, probing the undergrowth and canopy nearby for any other hidden dangers.

At least the trees themselves do not reach out for me! His thoughts were half jest and half real concern.

Time apparently was all the trees and other plants needed to harvest the nutrients from anything unlucky enough to get lost in their shade.

As he picked his way forward, Yip began to encounter more signs of life, creatures that had adapted to this strange toxic environment. He saw tree frogs that apparently sweated the poison out directly through their skin, also leaving a protective covering should something try to ingest them in turn; a few hardy insects that could metabolize the poisons in various ways after intaking air through their spiracles; some brightly colored snakes that might have internalized the poison as a type of venom instead of relying on their own biological production; among many other creatures that grew more numerous the farther inward he progressed. Beyond metabolizing the poisonous air, there were creatures that appeared to use the ambient energies of the forest to protect themselves and thrive in an environment relatively free of predators and competition.

By mid-day, the air was noticeably cleaner and he felt the faintest traces of a breeze. If the air freshened much more, he would be able to breathe normally within a few hours' time.

Continuing forward through the leafy undergrowth, he reached a stream silently meandering through the flat forest bottom. The vegetation around the stream was so thick, in fact, that he would have stumbled right into the water had he not smelled it first.

Looking into the water's clear, shallow depths, he could see very little signs of discoloration from tannins leaching into the water from all the surrounding vegetation. Apparently, the trees and soil in the forest broke down and incorporated organic matter very rapidly and efficiently. Bending over by the stream's edge, he was very happy to find the water was clear and pure, drinkable, and home to several species of aquatic organisms. Should the need arise then and he burned more *chi* to protect himself than he could intake, he could have fish for meals as an energy supplement.

After refreshing himself at the stream, he continued onward, knowing that he would have several weeks' worth of travel to cross the jungle if his views from the mountainsides were any indication. As he crossed the stream, he also began to note the presence of the myriad unique magical creatures he sensed in addition to those specifically adapted to the environment. He was quite curious to find out what types of creatures would call such a remote, safe haven home, creatures whose innate defenses could easily deal with the disturbed air.

Or anyone foolish enough to come looking for them, he added silently to himself.

Using his senses as a precaution against encountering any potential magical predators, he steered clear of the most vibrant expressions of energy he sensed from these creatures as soon as he perceived them in the distance.

Based on what he could tell from afar, there were in fact a wide variety of magical creatures in the forest, almost to the exclusion of every other type of organism. Fey creatures like these lived on magical energies or had innate magical abilities and constitutions much different from other more mundane organisms. These creatures' intrinsic abilities made them very different from other beings like Men who, although magic in a sense by their nature, generally had to discover, usually through formal practice and training, how to use those capabilities in order to learn to harness the energies within and around them. Unlike Men, the creatures around him now were born to their magical heritage.

As he walked, he passed more and more supramundane creatures, beings that lived and relied upon magical energies to survive. Although photosynthetic organisms and species dependent on the productivity of plants still abounded, the aeryasynthetic creatures relying directly upon the energies of life and magic to survive drew the preponderance of his attention.

There were tree-like structures with diaphanous gauzy sails in lieu of leaves billowing loosely in the still air—capturing and metabolizing the ambient energies all around, competing only for canopy space with the trees, not for sunlight. There were mosses and fungi that appeared to soak up and absorb magical energies instead of light. Bromeliads and hanging mosses glowed like lanterns from the dense growth of limbs above, converting the *chi* he felt all around into light and metabolic energies. Lianas and vines that channeled water between the upper story and the ground also served to channel magical forces throughout the forest top.

Synergistic relationships became more and more the norm. Iridescent lichens coated the trunks of a few trees, apparently forming a symbiotic relationship, providing a magical supplement to those trees' growth. Softly glowing rhizomes sprung from the forest floor, meshing with the roots of trees and plants, fueling their dizzying growth. As he moved inward, the mutualisms between magic and mundane plants and animals heightened to such a degree that the eldritch and ordinary, the photosynthetic and *chi* dependent ecosystems intermingled and coexisted in an inseparable whole, stimulating diversity and growth beyond his ability to comprehend or resolve.

He could also sense varying degrees of sentience in the forest creatures, some actually had extremely highly evolved intelligences, although he did not encounter any signs of habitation or constructs reflecting the need to impose any will upon the environment.

In fact, as he moved forward, the impression that he was moving more and more from a land dreaming into a highly alert reality became more tangible, as if the soporific gases around the forest edges not only caused any intruders to sleep, but also invoked a deep slumber on the trees and other jungle denizens. More and more frequently, he encountered bright sparks of sentience in the distance.

As he cast his mind out, all he could tell at first was that the most vibrant of these intelligences were deep and vast, unlike any he had ever encountered. He had no idea what a creature with such a mind would look like should he encounter one, but the more his awareness brushed across them, the more he stopped in awe at their wonder.

The deeper into the jungle he traveled, the closer and more numerous these sentiences became. As he moved farther in, he realized that the sentiences he had encountered were in fact largely stationary, and, sooner or later, he would have to pass one.

Within an hour, as the land ahead finally showed its first bit of topography in the form of a few large, seemingly discarded lichen covered rocks, he gazed skyward in sheer joy and amazement.

At the center of a great clearing, a colossal silver-barked tree trunk lifted to the heavens. In a forest of giants, this tree was enormous, towering over its neighbors like an adult standing watch over children, forming a super canopy of many small golden-hued, coppery leaves that shimmered in the sunlight.

More amazing than its sheer size, was the enormity of its presence.

As soon as he first laid eyes upon the forest giant, he knew joy, as his heart soared upward along its branches reaching ever upward for the clouds. For these creatures, whose sentience filled the forest more than the very air he breathed, were the true guardians of the land. Although he could barely fathom the vastness of their beings, his mind's eye told him that this tree, and others like it, were Powers the likes of which he had never encountered. Even though their intelligence was beyond his ability to envisage or dream to comprehend, he knew that he was safe in this realm so long as continued onward with care and respect.

His enemies would not dare touch him in such a place.

A DARKER SHADOW

Stardust strewn loosely,
sprinkled across the ether.
Where do the stars call home?

The chill evening air laid still and full of the silence born of isolation. No crickets chirped, no cicadas sang. The stars scattered freely throughout the heavens left the moon in peace as it made its solitary journey across the sky.

Below, highlighted by silvery moonbeams, the bloated corpse of the fallen wizard lay cold and abandoned, left to an uncertain future on the rocky hillside, clearly marking the spot where he had met both his end and final release from servitude to his dark masters.

Several days on the hillside undergoing the slow process of decay had not helped the wizard's already unwholesome appearance.

The air warped and shimmered, bending and stretching the subtle light of the moon and stars where it landed on the blotchy, swollen form of the dead wizard. Space became malleable for the merest second, bowing outward and fluctuating violently before immense forces ripping through the fabric of this small section of air.

With a loud *pop* and the whooshing rush of once still air over the dead body, dust and debris flew through the night as a black hole, darker than the void between stars, tore open next to the wizard's still form.

Out of the darkness, a shadow emerged, even darker than the emptiness from whence it came. Its essence seemed to drink the light of the stars and moon, the figure's outlines implied by the points where light no longer lost itself in its depths.

Its gaze briefly passed over the wizard's still form.

It drank in the night and read its patterns, its past, and its potential.

The one who had done this was gone.

The one who had done this was not a priest, though he had their foul taint.

The one who had done this could not yet mask his essence.

The one who had done this would die.

GREEN MANTLE

Images glimpsed in dewdrops—
the world refracted.
What wonder waits next?

Approaching with cautious reverence, Yip carefully crossed the clearing and ever so gently placed his hand upon the tree's argent trunk.

What he received was a shock to his system unlike any he had experienced.

He fell to his knees, completely overwhelmed, totally unprepared for the gift he was given.

Images flashed through his mind faster than thought. Lost amid sensations and perceptions that spanned millennia, his only remaining connection to his world was the distant feel of his palm on the smooth bark of the tree. With an intensity he did not know that he possessed, he clung to that fragile impression, that soft sensation, to protect himself from being cast adrift in a deluge of experiences that spanned times before his race first trod upon the surface of Ea'ae.

With a sudden mental release, after he knew not how long, he let go and allowed the impressions to wash over him. Here was wisdom and patience unlike any he had ever seen. Here were ideals expressed and actualized through time—forbearance in the face of the selfishness of races that crossed the ages; endurance through never-ending competition; stewardship of a land held graciously and fostered through epochs; insight into the workings of the world—magical and mundane, spiritual, ethereal, and physical; compassion and concern freely given and unguarded; persistence through time unending; love and dedication for the land from the smallest soil microbes to the ever-changing clouds in the sky. Here was a teacher unlike any he had known.

Here were the Aeryn D'al, legendary teachers of the Elves, a race lost in antiquity, beings from the times before his order's seclusion.

Shocked, sweating, and incredulous, he collapsed to the ground as tears of joy flowed freely, the only gifts he had to offer a being of such majesty.

All around he sensed the comfort and reassurance that only a being that exists without regard to time could give and share. Struck by his own limitations, he wished to continue his tutelage in the forest, communing with these majestic presences, taking in the realizations, insights, and freedom their perspective could offer a temporal being like himself. Fresh tears marked his cheeks as he realized that he must leave these beings too soon in his journey onward if he were to ever reunite with his order and bring down the Cabal.

Holding his head in his hands, letting the tears fall unhindered to the ground, he knew that he would come back, that a sacred place and an opportunity such as this would not be squandered. Until that time came, he would learn what he could now before moving on. Emotionally torn, he also knew that his time was short, that he must move on and find those who could help restore his order. At the moment, if he could, his best option was to learn whatever he could that may help the K'un Lun bring down the Cabal.

He stood slowly and turned, facing the tree. Bowing deeply from the waist in respect, he offered a token of his appreciation. Mentally and physically exhausted, he gathered up his bedroll and kit and settled down for the evening on a flat spot by the clearing's edge opposite the boulders.

Before his head rested on the ground, he was lost to slumber and the worlds known only to the exhausted and psychically spent.

Even in sleep, his mind yet alert, he could feel the surrounding trees' presence, their care and vigilance. Enervated after his first meeting, he did not reach out to them on this first evening. He was, however, quite glad to discover that they knew the ways of dream yoga for their refulgent attendance remained unbroken in his mind. So, even from a distance while asleep, he could communicate, should they be willing.

As he slowly stirred from slumber, the sunlight from a new day bright on his closed eyelids, urging him to wakefulness, he awoke in wonderment to a new world. What had once been a green haze, largely hidden by fog, now gleamed resplendent in refracted sunlight as dewdrops cast sunlight into miniature rainbows throughout the canopy. The air was alive with birds of all colors. Small primates with wet, tousled hair cavorted in the tree limbs as Fairy Dragons flitted about the large trunks busily welcoming the new morn. Joining the birds, a symphony of insects sang in discordant choruses. Sprites, brownies, pixies, dryads, nixies, hamadryads, faeries, and nymphs were occupied by as many tasks as their variety implied; some danced and sang with the sun and trees, some chatted with the forest creatures and each other, some ran busily from branch to branch and between ferns absorbed in errands privy only to themselves, and only a few took the time to stop and take in the newcomer. He sensed an unbelievable array of other magical creatures out of sight welcoming in the day as well.

Here was a paradise the likes of which were only told in stories to children—all hidden and protected by the ever-watchful trees growing all around!

Privy to the forest's inner mysteries, he knew he had made peace with the forest.

Utterly amazed that all this activity and vibrancy had been hidden from him, he once again looked in awe toward the stately giant sharing the clearing. He had much to learn, and it seemed he needed to learn more with each day's passing. He quickly cleared the look of chagrin that had crept onto his face. If given too much thought, his own shortcomings would overwhelm him.

Better to know too little than feel he knew too much! For then how would he learn and who would teach him?

"Master, what does chi *do?"*

He stood with Master Wei before one of the monastery's many still reflecting pools. Undisturbed by wind or object, its placid surface captured the full depth of the heavens—an azure circle plucked from the sky and placed on the temple grounds.

Gazing upon its expanse, he felt as though he stood on the brink between two worlds.

If he fell forward, would he fall into the blue void or plunge into the black depths of an artfully arranged pool?

This point of transition, this space between worlds, was exactly where the Priests of K'un Lun resided, the domain initiates came to know, and teachers mastered.

Thus, it was to these places his young mind always wandered.

"Chi sustains our world as it does for all living things. We are of it and it us. We give to it and it gives to us. We breathe it and it breathes us."

"It is our bridge between the subtle and the universal, the absolute and the sublime, the yuan-chi *and the mind."*

After a silent stretch, his memories returned to the stillness that birthed them, he sat down on one of the large rocks in the clearing for a time of silent meditation. Calming his mind, he let the sounds of the busily unfolding day wash over him. He watched quietly as his internal energies flowed along the subtle energy channels throughout his body, gradually taking in and collecting energy from the ground and sky passing through his *tan t'ien*, commingling with his own bodily energies before passing back out heavenward through his crown. As the birdsong quieted through the morning, so did his mind. His awareness drifted silently without form for a time, directionless and intentionless, bathed in stillness, floating above and within his sensory impressions, the only content in his mind. When the day felt warm on his cheeks, he finally stood and moved over to the tree.

First bowing to the forest patriarch, he then took two steps forward directly in front of the tree trunk to begin his Zhan Zhuang *chi gung* exercises. Firmly establishing his root, he placed his feet shoulder-width apart and brought his hands slightly forward and out, fingertips close but not touching, in front of his *tan t'ien* as if holding a small barrel or ball. As he inhaled softly, slowly expanding and retracting his stomach, he began to gather *chi* in his *tan t'ien* in preparation for greater energy circulation. Over a period of half an hour, he gradually added more and more energy to his *tan t'ien* before letting the energy flow down his right arm between his hands and back up his left arm. Lifting his arms slightly, palms facing the tree to complete the circle, he then let his *chi* gently flow through the great bole in front of him, sharing his life, his energy, his essence, with that of the tree.

With the first pass, a vast wave of warm vitality coruscated up his left arm and surged around his small *chi* circuit before reentering the tree, leaving him shuddering in place. Vibrant and awash in vivacity as he had never known before, he continued the cycle, bringing energy up from the ground through his feet upward along his spine and out the crown of his head toward the tree. After the energy passed from him and into the tree, the force returned as a prodigious surge passed upward through him. The tide was so great he felt as if his body were floating, lifted skyward as the energy reentered through his feet from the roots below and rushed upward along his meridians. When this power finally reached his crown, his consciousness exploded upward and outward from his *pai-hui* dissolving into the heavens, unifying earth and firmament in a blazing light of golden energy.

After a time that seemed an eternity, he gradually became aware of himself again, still completing the energy circuit in partnership with the tree through his hands, feet, and head, but his experience was now wholly and entirely different. Where once his internal energy had been passive, flowing gently throughout his system like a small mountain brook gurgling quietly over smooth, age-rounded rocks, now a golden liquid essence cascaded through his system in a raging torrent, almost with a mind of its own as the *chi* worked to reinforce and restructure his energy pathways, heal old injuries, and strengthen his overall etheric and physical systems.

Gently breaking contact with the tree, he found that by letting this newfound energy flow upward through his spine along the governor channel of his microcosmic orbit that the current reinduced ecstatic states as it gathered at his crown or as he let it pass upward out his *paihui* energy gate to the heavens. By consciously recirculating the power downward through his functional channel, running along the front of his torso, the energy cooled and induced the healing and strengthening effects he had felt without the accompanying exaltation. Once he reestablished the complete etheric circuit, the energy rushed through all of his meridians in a somewhat natural, if overwhelming, flow.

Practicing energy manipulation for years on end had barely prepared him for the power surge from the tree the first time. Had he not been an experienced practitioner, well-accustomed to the rigors and spiritual demands of inner work, then his neural net could have been completely and utterly burnt out—a moth unprepared for flame.

With a few hours of practice, experimentation, and exploration, he felt comfortable enough with the new energy currents that he was both somewhat accustomed to the strengthened flow and willing to consider further practice. Given his prudent nature, however, he felt that the new wellspring of energy within should follow its own course along his open meridians naturally for a time before continuing onward with any further directed practice or exposure to the tree's power.

Going to his cot, the sun still bright in the sky above, he decided that rest was in order and would be the best course of action for his tired nerves and etheric channels as his body effectively rewired itself.

He awoke once again with the birds celebrating a new day feeling buoyant and relaxed, charged and limpid, perfectly clear.

During his small breakfast, one spent largely watching his body continually adjust and reform to his newly heightened energy state, he decided to spend the day in observation—internally and externally.

The first question he wanted to answer was how trees as large and majestic as these could survive through time untouched and so vibrant. How did they absorb the living energy around them and utilize it so efficiently for growth and development? If the greater energies of the *k'an* and *li* were any indication, then their robust internal energy states must constantly rebuild and restore their physical and etheric structures for greater and greater viability.

He also wanted to know how such powerful beings masked not just their presence but that of almost an entire forest from physical and psychic senses trained since birth to detect and comprehend the unseen.

Learning to utilize both of these skills, masking his psychic presence and learning to subsist more and more on the ambient energies around him, would go a long way to furthering his independence and effectiveness in his quests. He could see a twofold benefit: by disguising his presence from the Cabal and learning to survive on ambient energies, he would be able to function alone indefinitely while at the same time being able to hunt the Cabal and their agents with much greater impunity.

Any other potential changes wrought by the enhanced flow throughout his system would remain welcome discoveries.

Throughout the day he sat calmly on the rock watching the tree.

Serene observation showed him many things.

He could sense the tree drawing energy from the ground in the same way it drew water and nutrients from the soil. Never acting solely for itself, the tree in its patient generosity gave the water it drank back to the sky to make more rain and clouds, thereby benefiting all creatures and their environs. Absorbing energy from the sun to nourish its leaves, provide energy, and grow, the tree gave of itself in the form of leaf litter that later decayed, that the soil and its organisms could flourish. Taking in the waste air of other organisms' respiration, the tree gave its own breath that others could live and breathe. Absorbing the ambient energetic potential of life pervading the land, air, and water all around, the tree developed and protected the larger community that all could prosper. Giving of itself, the tree provided a home and haven encompassing all the forest creatures, magical and mundane.

Trees such as these were paragons, the very model for Chih-jen, the perfect realized man—immovable, unyielding, but free and at peace, beings whose wisdom spanned the heavens.

His thoughts, his marveling, and his appreciation, however, were no match for the reality before him.

Going further, he could see how his internal energy systems closely resembled those of this lord of the forest and how their two lives were tied together as intimately as branches intertwined. Just as he took in energy from the heavens and earth in his practice, gave of his breath and waste, and offered safety, protection, and comfort to those around him, he, too, aspired and acted very much like these trees.

Utilizing the tree's gift, watching the newfound self-reinforcing energy system awakened by the tree's power flow along his open channels, he began to see how he could, through diligent practice and effort, emulate some of the tree's abilities. If he could learn to manipulate his internal energies as effectively as this tree, his life would be long, effectual, and vibrant, filled with wisdom and generosity.

After a full day sitting, he once again lay down to sleep.

When he slept, he dreamed.

He dreamt he was in this forest, sitting by this very tree, communing with its essence. The tree, through some rapport beyond his understanding, reached out and granted him a brief glimpse of clarity.

He saw a brief vision of a tree growing in a sunlit clearing, striving for the sky and prosperity. Charging through the shadows at the clearing's edge, he saw the hunched mottled greenish shape of an Orc, a wickedly curved axe brandished in hand as it brazenly ran toward the sapling.

All the tree's effort and strivings at growth would be in vain without luck and a strong forest community to prevent such encroachment.

Waking up, looking deeply into the stars, he knew the tree had read much of him and his concerns during their rapport and had reached out to offer him yet another gift—a gift granted from the generous steward's perspective. Imagining his strivings as those of the small tree determinedly searching for its own place in the world, working against foes who either through their own self-interest, blatant disregard for its welfare, or conscious efforts directly pitted against it seeking to undermine its welfare, he realized the fundamental relationship that he had with his foe, complementary and interpenetrating, and how to resolve it.

Just as good matures in the light, so does evil fester in the dark. He must bring the Light of Life to bear against the Cabal to bring its downfall. He must learn and expand upon the ways of his spiritual forebears and mentors to harness the energies of creation to bring his foes' collapse. Light, love, and hope guided with wisdom would be his weapons.

Content but spent, he fell back into a sleep as deep as the stars above and as sound as the earth below.

He awoke refreshed after the third day of his work in the clearing, ready to move on, comfortable that he could take many lessons with him from the forest to occupy his time and efforts in the weeks and months to come. Shifting his balance to stand, he felt a weight on the covers between his feet. Looking downward, he saw a small iridescent purple and green lump nestled in the sheets. Chest rising and falling evenly, a small Fairy Dragon had bedded down with him for the night. Through sleep so sound, he had not even noticed the presence of his guest. Slowly gathering his feet under himself as he sat at the top of his bedding, he watched in joy as the small Dragon-kin woke with him as comfortably as an old friend, first taking several deliberate, sleep-clearing blinks as it stood and shook itself quickly to help restore circulation before flying upward into the branches on wings as clear as the heavens barely visible through the overarching limbs.

Smiling ruefully, he wondered, *With sights and sensations such as these, how could I ever leave the forest?*

He was not quite as quick to get up and move on as the Dragon, but he did get about his business with purpose and focus as the time of leave-taking had come. He must be on, indebted as he was to this place, before the forest's protection brought in elements he would rather not see visit such a sacred place.

After gathering his few belongings, he reverently approached the tree and bowed as he offered it and its kin, along with all the forest's creatures, his blessing, respect, and promise of protection.

Looking upward, following the noble trunk heavenward one last time, his eyes taking in the tree's majesty, its golden leaves scintillating in the breeze, the air abuzz with birds and fey creatures alighting on the currents, he noticed a brightness on one of the great limbs held aloft well above the surrounding trees. At first he thought the sun's reflection had caught the leaf's metallic surface at just the right angle to send a beam of sunlight directly down into his eyes. That is, until the light began to slowly descend—a small star adrift from the vault of Heaven. Staring upward in wonder, he watched as the tiny constellation drifted down, light and quavering as a dandelion's seed gliding in the breeze. Instinctively, he held his hand out as the minute star slowly, ever so slowly, floated downward and settled on his palm of its own accord.

Squinting his eyes closely together against the brightness, he could see a small nut resting gingerly on a golden leaf through the halo of surrounding light. Radiating from the seed, warmth suffused his arm with a feeling of lightness and surety. As the seed settled on his hand, he placed his palm delicately on the trunk one last time, thankful for its show of trust and gracious for its gift. Wrapping the fragile nut carefully in the shimmering leaf, he gathered up his bundle and placed the small package in his medicine pouch, one more treasure to guard and ensure it found a safe place in the world at large.

He left the clearing with a reluctant heart, torn between his need to go and his desire to stay.

His passage through the forest took several weeks. As he traveled, the very air sang with vibrancy and presence with every step. Surrounded as he was by trees, by beings, of such majesty and forest organisms too numerous to count, the world was a kaleidoscope of energies, effulgent, radiant with life unbounded. Swimming through their shining depths, he floated lightly without need for breath.

However far he traveled, he would always carry a bit of the forest's wonder with him.

WESTWARD

> Tannins dye the stream
> a deep coffee-black.
> Blinking, I turn from the sun.

Ahead, sunlight streamed through the vegetation, not from above, but at eye level. Well before he could see the light, however, the air felt cool with moisture and filled with the sounds of moving water.

Moving cautiously ahead, pushing fronds out of his way for a better view, he looked down on a slowly moving river that marked the western edge of the Jenyuan Shulin, a forest he now knew was forbidden for its own protection and for the protection of those who would venture there.

Dark waters moved slowly over rocks as vegetation scrambled for a foothold on the downward slopes. Trees and vines leaned over the waterway, reaching for light and moisture. The only ground visible in either direction was a rich, orange clay seen intermittently on the hillside where mudslides had fallen into the river. Even those openings were being rapidly swallowed by encroaching vegetation.

The forest on the other side of the stream appeared much the same; however, he could feel a difference. Although lush, brimming with life, and home to ancient trees, he could sense that the forest did not house the type of overarching sentience of Jenyuan Shulin, his constant companion and guide these joyous days past.

Where the forest on the other side of the river was suffused with life, Jenyuan Shulin burned.

He made his way carefully down the slope lest he lose purchase and slide into the river. Looking across the dark currents, he could see the clouds above moving along with the river, adrift in the air, mirrored below. He sensed no imminent danger as he peered through wispy layers of evaporation from the mid-day heat, only a river teeming with fish and invertebrates, reptiles, and the occasional eldritch tortoise, nymph, or river spirit.

He lashed his bundle tightly across his back, secured his robes, and took a few deep breaths before diving in, only to emerge gracefully to view the water at eye level in mid-current. Strong, sure strokes taken diagonally with the water's flow brought him to the far side of the river within a few minutes.

Looking back to the far shore, he wished he did not have to cross. Feelings of loss and homesickness quickly disappeared with the moisture in his clothes as the heat of the day evaporated his personal concerns and he pressed onward.

After scrambling up the overrun slope, he entered the forest proper. Bird calls and animal cries seemed lost in the fog of so much transpiration and humidity, muffled by greenery and the stillness of the air. Regulating his breathing and blood flow along the surface of his skin to allow for a cooler exterior and core body temperature, he instinctively adjusted to the increased heat.

He could sense in the fabric of the forest's interactions that there were creatures here that he would have to be wary of as he continued. He might not know the exact types, but he could feel how magical predators altered the patterns in the forest's interactions. At the same time, he could discern no trace of Man. Perhaps this area was too dangerous or remote for human habitation, if a world wherein magical travel between points could be said to have isolated areas, he thought a bit remorsefully.

Taking a bit of time to wring his clothes, he stopped to ponder briefly the orientation of human land use patterns when individuals could travel immediately between points they were familiar with via teleportation, between established locations via far stones and portals, or by floating with the clouds in air ships powered by magical contraptions of every variety. Besides outposts, isolated natural resource extraction activities, the occasional individual or community seeking privacy and seclusion, and areas too dangerous to populate, humanity and the other Crafting races tended to cluster in well-established areas, leaving much of the land wild and open. For that, at least, he was quite grateful.

With Jenyuan Shulin providing a protective barrier behind him, he considered his next course of action without resorting to mindless flight away from home and all he knew.

As much as he would hate to risk the safety of others, if he were to have any luck tracking down and ultimately undermining the Cabal's newly emergent activities on Ea'ae, he would have to rely on the help of others. Cautious progress toward populated areas would be his best hope, although at this point given the risks of detection to himself and others, he could not stay in any one area for any length of time. He could at least hope that the *li*, the intrinsic energy patterns, of other people would help hide his presence from any pursuers should his own continued efforts at masking and blending his manifestations with the ambient energy expressions prove ineffectual.

Mentally recreating the orb of Ea'ae in his mind, its continents and oceans, cities and provinces, he tried to determine the best path westward over Dharia to the larger cultural centers that could be found several hundred leagues to the west of his homeland. Most of the preeminent options laid far to the northwest, across another vast range of mountains in lands much cooler and less diverse than the one in which he found himself presently.

Unfortunately, although magical travel had opened the world and even the heavens and other planes to human exploration and population, it did not bring those communities or people any closer. If anything, it pushed them farther away with waves of human diaspora. And, although he was gifted, he did not have access to any form of magical transport or spell. Squeezing a bit of water from his blanket as he resituated his kit on his back, he decided that his life ahead would involve quite of bit of walking.

A day's travel to the north and west brought him farther into the jungle—through swamps and past streams, around tangles and thickets, past ancient trees and orchids of every color in the rainbow. Given the dense profusion, he was not as concerned about his progress forward as he was about finding an open clearing to bed down for the evening. In an area of unknown dangers, he would need the relative advantage of an open area to give himself time to react should the need present itself. He was willing to stop early should he find a suitable spot.

As he moved, he constantly read the tone of the ambient environment, checking for disturbances and the presence of any potentially hidden dangers. As much as his forward progress was slowed by the thick undergrowth, he did not lose focus on any dangers that may lie in wait.

With the day starting to darken and the gloom beneath the canopy growing more striking, he noticed the change.

At first, he thought his impression of a subtle difference in the environs may be mistaken, but as time passed, he sensed a lightness, an overarching tension in the air, as if in expectation of a sudden outburst or the coming of a storm. He had never felt anything like this before. Everything seemed to continue as normal; birds fluttered, monkeys howled, insects hummed, but he could tell that he was not the only one that sensed danger. As close as he could ascertain, there was an acceptance in the air of some impending doom, as if there was nothing to be done, that something would be taken.

After another hour's travel with no clearing in sight, he knew that he was being stalked. He could not yet sense his adversary, but somewhere out there amid the gloom or perhaps above in the canopy there was something coming for him.

After another half-hour, he happened upon a potential stopping point for the night. Despite his fatigue, he would have to make a stand here instead of taking an evening's rest. He had found a clearing where a forest giant had recently fallen, opening a ragged gap in the tangled canopy of vines, lianas, and branches as it fell while leaving an open space on the ground as new growth struggled to take the old tree's place.

His best defense against a supernatural predator would be his own guile, his ability to seize on opportunity. Unlike his teachers, he could not yet use his *chi* as a weapon for his defense against preternatural foes. He would be relatively helpless against an enemy whose nature was intrinsically magical and could only be harmed by magic.

Surprise would be his weapon.

He started camp preparations as normal, clearing a small spot to lie down, brewing an herbal tea, and eating some dried vegetables. After his brief meal, he repacked his kit. He did not bother to unpack his bedroll. Adopting an attitude of repose while leaning against the fallen trunk, he began to wait and gather himself. Calm descended over him in ever deepening waves as he prepared for his adversary.

When the sun finally set, leaving the clearing in an almost absolute dark, he began to sense the beast's approach. Using the cover of darkness, he sensed the thing circling slowly above the clearing, high in the canopy, assessing its quarry.

Only then did he realize the nature of his foe.

The thing was some kind of psion. Although he was learning to mask and blend his essence into the background patterns around him, he could not yet hope to completely hide his thoughts or the functioning of his brain from a creature born to read them. He did not know what it hunted in him or how it fed, but he knew it was after his thoughts, perhaps his fears, something of his mental essence.

The vorath circling above looked down upon its prey, already feeding on its thoughts, so rich, of such breadth and depth, so full of life compared to the other forest creatures it normally hunted.

It had never tasted something so full and vibrant.

Its animal cunning relished the hunt. Its shrewd intelligence savored the human's preparations and deliberations to avoid it. Instinctively the creature kept its mind shielded so that it could not be read or anticipated.

Sensing its prey relax below, with a suddenness belying all reason, the thing coalesced from the gloom and swooped down, silent as the shadows, into the heart of the clearing.

With a start, Yip realized his time had come. Bilious, fluid, and deadly, the thing closed the distance between them with a speed that was unnatural. Only visible as shifting darkness, he could feel the beast's presence and its impending attack before his mind could register it.

Relaxed and calm, seated directly beneath the creature's thrust, he waited just the briefest of instants as he watched his doom descend on wings of mute shadows.

Intent and baleful, the vorath exploded onto its prey, engulfing its quarry in tendrils of darkness as it prepared to feed, taking the energy and vibrancy of its victim's life as its own.

With a firmness of resolve unknown to the vorath, the human clung to its life essence in a gesture as futile as it was determined. Reaching deeply inward, the vorath sucked the last of its essence from its human prey.

Despite its tenaciousness, its prey seemed strangely empty and unfulfilling.

Only after the feeding frenzy subsided did the vorath realize its mistake, and by then Yip was long gone.

Heightened senses told him the time had come. Moving with a speed and focus unknown to all but the most uncanny, he leapt from beneath the vorath, quick as a shadow, quiet as thought.

In his place, he left only a ghost.

Holding his bundle tightly, he took the briefest of seconds to glance back as he stole from the clearing to watch the vorath feed on his *chi* ghost—a duplicate of his essence meant to buy him time and a safe distance.

By the time the vorath had understood its error, he was lost in the evening's darkness, moving away and out of its range, forcing it to look elsewhere for food.

THE AL'MARR

A sheer cliff face soars
proudly from the jungle floor,
memory of mountains past.

He had been lucky once more.

True, he had been trained from a young age to manipulate his chances for success while maintaining a positive frame of mind in all circumstances so that he could respond most appropriately, naturally and at ease, to situations given his limitations, but he knew deep down that he was ill-prepared to deal with the magical foes he would encounter when facing the Cabal. Even if he did not know yet how to do it, he would have to try to find a way to defend himself against supernatural foes.

He would have to figure out how to more fully mesh his physical abilities and martial training with his *qigong* talents in order to survive. As soon as he felt safe and able, he would also have to try to contact Master Wei for guidance.

Running through the forest, away from a beast that would steal his mind and heart, he had little time to address his worries as the exigencies of his current situation overrode any other concerns.

Living in a world of essences as much as the mundane, he did have the benefit of being able to see how to progress by darkness as his internal vision was not dependent on light as much as it was on life in the larger sense and the fundamental energies around him.

Tapping internal energy reserves to counteract the effects of muscle fatigue and intramuscular microtears, he ran on through the night.

As the jungle slowly began to lighten with the coming of a new day— the jungle floor would never be fully light beneath the many layers of competing foliage assembled to soak every mote of light and energy— he began to travel uphill over loose wet soil covered in a deep layer of leaf litter. Relieved, he hoped that he had finally reached the first signs of the slopes approaching the mighty Drake Spires.

By mid-morning, he could no longer stand completely upright on the steep incline as he scrambled on his hands and knees beneath an ever thickening tangle of vines and lianas. The hush of the morning fog, a cool drape laid full and damp over his shoulders, slowly gave way to the tumbled rush of running water.

Pushing his way through a last profusion of vegetation brought him to the foot of a curtain waterfall falling from the sky through a sheet of white sunlight. Careful to avoid slipping on the stream's mossy rocks, he stepped down for a cool, refreshing drink. Savoring the sweet freshness of the brisk water, he took the time to wash his face and hands in the newly minted stream. Looking up the swirling currents, water dripping down his face and shoulders, he sighed in anticipation of the difficult climb up the sheer, water-laden, fern-covered cliffs.

Placing his palm on the first moss-covered rock, water ran through his fingers as he gripped the stone in preparation for another grueling day. He could only hope that his trip westward would be easier as he moved forward.

Within half an hour, he had cleared the treetops. For the first time in weeks, he could look back over the ground he had covered since leaving the K'un Lun. A wave of lightness passed through him as his thoughts flew eastward toward home. Continuing upward past many glistening streamers of water falling through the air and over small rivulets dribbling between the coarse, cold rocks, his mood quickly turned as he refocused, realizing how far upward he had to go before reaching the top of the cliff. He would have to climb many times the height of the tallest trees to reach the top of the mountain's first foot.

Sweating profusely without the leafy barrier to shield him from the hot midday sun, he was at least grateful for the ready supply of water available at hand.

A full day's climbing brought him past nesting birds, scrambling insects, and basking lizards, but no closer to the end of his efforts. Behind and below him, the deep green foliage of the forest deepened from a lush, full green to a deep purple, marking his progress up the slope.

As the moon rose in the east and lit the rocks beneath his hands and feet in a pale, white-gray hue, he finally found a small, sheltered nook where he could perch through the rest of the night.

Another day's hard climbing brought him to the crest of the plateau.

As he pulled himself over the slick ledge, anticipating a view looking out on the peaks of the Drake Spires or rolling hills leading to their base, he stood instead at the edge of a large, rocky green plateau covered in erosion gullies, deep pools, mosses, and low, windswept plants able to withstand the strong winds and constant runoff and rain birthed by the jungle below.

The cliff he hoped would lead to the foot of the mountains was actually a tepui, a mountain island of sandstone, a jungle plateau standing tall and forlorn amidst the steaming forest vegetation below. Hidden beneath the trees for so long, he had severely misjudged his progress. Hoping to reach the end of one phase of his journey, he was still at the beginning.

Turning to the east, beyond the rough green treetops, the peaks of the K'un Lun were lost in the haze of humidity and distance. To the west, past another vast stretch of jungle broken only by the jutting masses of other green and brown tepuis akin to the one on which he now stood, barely distinguishable from the horizon, he could see the faint summits of the great Drake Spires several week's journey away.

With an exhausted sigh, he collapsed on the rough, wet rock and did not wake until midway through the next day.

Lost in the darkness of deep, absolute sleep, he heard the faintest of sounds—a voice!

"*Yip…*" Softer than a whisper, from a space far away and seemingly worlds apart, he heard the voice again.

So tired that he hardly listened even to his own dreams, he answered, "*Is that you, Master Wei?*"

"*Yip!*" Now he recognized his teacher's voice. "*I have been looking for you.*"

"*I have not had much time to rest of late, Master,*" replied Yip, tired even in sleep.

"*Are you safe?*" He was glad to hear the concern in his teacher's voice and feel its reassurance. "*After our last conversation, I was unsure of your health. Since I did not feel your passing, I could only hope that you were well.*"

"*I am more than well, master! I have met with the Aeryn D'al and have learned much from them in the ways of* qigong! *They will be excellent partners for us. We have much to learn from one another I feel.*"

"*That is excellent news, Yip! We will need all the allies we can find in the time to come. I am glad that you are serving as an ambassador of goodwill in your journeys just as I am glad that you still have your health.*"

"*I fear that I may not be up to the challenges ahead, master.*" His budding worries about his inability to protect himself surfaced. His teacher always seemed to bring out his deepest concerns. "*There are many foes beyond me even now and my journey has just begun. What shall I do? How will I defend myself?*"

"*Do not fear, Yip. Take what you have learned from the Aeryn D'al along with your training and practice. Just as with your forebears, experience shall be your teacher. Channel that energy and the Light you project will daunt even the stoutest foe.*"

"*I will do my best, Master.*"

"*Take heart, Yip. We all must confront our doubts and fears, lest they rule us and dictate our circumstance. Awareness of our shortcomings is the way to strength.*"

"Your words do much to lighten my heart, master."

"And that levity lightens mine, Yip, just as it always has." His teacher paused before continuing. *"Seek me out to the west, Yip. I will be there to help when I can. There is much yet to be done here."*

"Where shall I go? What shall I do next?"

"The Cabal had a stronghold in the Drake Spires of old. Perhaps you can learn something there."

"I will be there within the next month, I think."

"The Spires are vast, Yip. You may need help before you attempt to search them. Allies will be your strength should you find danger there."

"I will do what I can."

"I will contact you again when I am able, Yip. Do not doubt your talents. Your Light burns as bright as any."

"Thank you, master."

"May the light of a new dawn guide your steps, Yip."

"May your steps know no shadow, master."

And with that, he drifted back into darkness, once again alone but feeling the weight of his burden was much lighter.

When he at last awoke, his muscles ached and his eyes hurt from all the bright light streaming on his face after the unceasing gloom of the jungle. Turning his creaking neck to the left, he opened his eyes and saw the source of the waterfall he had first discovered in the jungle seemingly so long ago. Standing carefully to ease the burden on his sore muscles, he closed his eyes and moved easily through the motions of a *qigong* set while the crisp wind whipped his robes, circulating his internal energy as he drew more *chi* in from the ready elements around him to help heal and restore all he had lost on his journey to this point. As he finished, his *tan t'ien* full of swirling energy, he slowly dropped his hands as his breath sank to his navel.

Sensing something different, he opened his eyes and looked southward beyond a rocky gulley cradling another small waterfall-to-be where a small boulder had come to life.

Blinking away the sunshine, he realized that what he had mistaken for a small rock was in fact a large wyvern unfurling its leathery wings as it watched him curiously. The creature's brownish gold scales shone in the sunlight as it casually warmed itself on its roost. Watching the wyvern's deadly grace as its keen intelligence regarded him in turn, he remonstrated himself inwardly, knowing that he would have to be more careful. He had not sensed its presence for he had been too distracted. Luckily for him, the distant cousin to Dragons was unused to men and did not see him as a threat, merely as a curiosity.

He wondered what it ate, whether its prey was in the jungle below, in the air above, or on the tepui ahead, and whether it rested on the cliffs for safety or to look for prey.

Moving cautiously so as not to seem threatening to the wyvern resting just a few beats of its strong wings away, he picked his way cautiously over the moist, algae-covered rocks and climbed up a pile of loose eroded boulders to better survey the plateau and put some distance between himself and the large reptile.

Taking his eyes briefly from the wyvern, he studied the plateau stretching unevenly forward in all directions. The tepui continued ahead for several leagues to the north, south, and west. Cresting the rocks, he gave the wyvern one last look before leaving the reptile to its perch and moving farther in.

Striding onward, water greeted his every turn: algae-laden pools filled with amphibians and small crustaceans, gurgling streams rushing with reckless abandon toward their descent to the forest floor below, thick piles of sponge-like moss squished beneath his feet, while low-lying shrubs covered in bryophytes and bromeliads storing water in their lush green stems and leaves swished against his robes. Apparently these jungle plateaus served as catchments for the frequent jungle rains, helping to recirculate the life-giving waters exhaled by the jungle and showered down by the clouds that the rainforests helped create.

Traveling across the rough terrain of the tepui, he felt lost between two worlds, adrift between two times. Turning to look over his shoulder, he could see the vague outlines of his ancestral home in the K'un Lun. Ahead, floating like white-capped islands in the sky, he could see the great peaks of the Drake Spires soaring above the clouds created by the jungles below.

The lands of his past, his home in the mountain monastery, shared his uncertain future, if not his travels. He felt distant and removed from both the past and the future, detached from his own present, as aimless in his wanderings as the jungle fogs despite his strong resolve.

Picking his way carefully forward, his mind returned to his teacher's reassurance just as his attention snapped out of his reverie. Once again scolding himself, drifting was as pointless as it was dangerous, his awareness settled once again on the landscape around him as he let his thoughts flow where they would, no longer troubled or caught up by them.

He spent the whole day moving leisurely across the tepui as much to let his focus return as to let himself recover from his exertions getting here. After assuring himself that the plateau was safe, he decided to spend one more evening on the tepui, camping closer to the stars than he had been since he left his home in the K'un Lun.

Thankfully, finding a spot dry enough to safely lay his bedding was about the most difficult thing he had to do the whole day.

He awoke refreshed and renewed after a full evening of dreamless sleep. He drank deeply from one of the many clear, rain-fed streams before starting his morning meditations. More than mere rituals, the motion, the stillness, the clarity of these exercises were windows into himself, who and what he was, views into the world within and around him.

Moving through the movements of his normal energy circulation routine, consciously drawing his energy from his *tan t'ien* up through his spine and head, around the front of his torso, and down through his rooted feet and then back up through his arms and spine, he tried to increase the speed with which the *chi* moved along his meridians. As the energy flow rushed and swirled tingling through his arms and legs, he began to concentrate on his palms until with a violent motion he lashed out, projecting his *chi* toward a nearby rocky erosion feature.

When nothing happened despite his fervent desire, he let the internal energy recede and regather in his *tan t'ien* where it continued to swirl and flow unguided through his subtle meridians.

Perhaps by the time he next met Master Wei, he would have more luck projecting his *chi* and be farther along the road to personal assurance.

Moving the last few steps toward the far edge of the tepui, his spirit soared with the birds as he looked over the vertiginous drop. The verdant jungle breathed and steamed at the base of the cliffs while sunlight leapt in prism-inspired rainbows from water vapor and fog drifting in the dizzying heights as cascading waterfalls and rivulets met with clouds and mists from below.

Double-checking the straps on his kit, he found a relatively dry spot and warily dangled his feet over the hard stone edge. His destiny held tightly beneath his fingers and under his toes, he picked his way cautiously down the eroded rock surface. Unlike the trip up, the descent only took one hard day. Despite all the time he had spent beneath its leaves, he was actually glad to climb under the jungle's crown again and place his feet on the moist, downy forest floor.

Exhausted, he set up camp at the foot of the tepui he had once mistaken for a mountain.

He woke up cramped and sore after his climb and sleeping in the close quarters of the moss-draped nook in which he had hidden himself from the unknown dangers of the jungle ahead.

Taking time to soak in the environment around him, its energy and interactions, he gazed upward toward the sky he might not see again until he reached the end of his trek through the lush vegetation—that is, unless he was fortunate enough to happen upon a gap in the canopy.

He sensed the overwhelming diversity, the riot of life, the bewildering profusion of so many creatures moving through their existence around him. That so many could coexist in one place was a never-ending marvel to him. Compared to the relative dearth of the high mountains where he grew up, where each living thing encountered was a rare gem to be treasured, the exuberant jungle's overriding raucousness washed over his senses in wave after wave of stimuli. Brushing aside the first leafy fronds as he reentered the jungle proper, he knew that he had to be on guard against getting lost awash in all these patterns, the energetic profusion of so much life, lest he fall prey to a rip current lying in wait for him amidst all these swirling breakers.

Eight days of hard hiking through the wilderness brought him little closer to reaching his goal. He had skirted around another tepui over the past three days, keeping its bulk above him and to his right. He had decided to avoid the risk of another slippery climb once he recognized the sheer rocky verticality as the beginning of another jungle plateau.

During this detour, he had briefly shifted course on several occasions when he sensed the presence of powerful entities moving through the canopy above or rumbling through the understory below. He had no idea what type of creatures the jungle held hidden beneath its canopy, but after his encounter with the vorath he had no qualms about doing everything within his power to remain safe and clear of potential encounters.

The morning of his ninth day since leaving the first tepui dawned very much like the rest. He awoke covered in beads of moisture from the humid air, encased in the muffled gray morning fogs that would burn off with time as the day warmed and brightened. After rousing to ants on his first night sleeping on the jungle floor after leaving the tepui, he had taken to suspending his bedroll between trees in a makeshift hammock. As he stretched and then hung his feet over the taut cloth fabric, he cautiously wiped himself down, double-checking for pests that he may not be able to feel or easily sense. Assured that all was well and the immediate vicinity was safe, he untied and packed his bedroll after drinking a bit from his waterskin.

Setting out westward, or his best approximation thereof, he once again appreciated the silence and intimacy created by the new day's fog as he did every morning. The fog shrank his world to the limits of his mind and vision and reduced the awesome complexity of the jungle's many forms to the vaguest of outlines. Ever cautious, he was glad that the fog also stifled his rustlings as the moisture vapor absorbed and dissipated the sounds of his footfalls on the damp leaf litter. Of course, his caution held firm even as he enjoyed the morn, extending his senses in all directions, in order to avoid surprising some denizen in the hush.

As he moved through the thick vegetation, brushing aside the moisture-laden leaves and fronds, he watched the thinning wisps of fog catch sunlight and turn into golden streamers reaching down longingly from the heavens. With the fog dissipating, the sounds of life filled the void left by the moisture's passing—macaws, gibbons, howler monkeys, and others—creatures beyond naming waking up with the day.

Enjoying the morning's song, he did not notice at first that the music's tenor had changed. The quietude of the morning fog returned, gradually resetting over the forest. Out of this brief pregnant hush a vast cacophony steadily arose, building in tandem as cries of warning, fear, and alarm cawed, screeched, and howled out through the jungle.

Balanced on the balls of his feet, his head swiveled as he tried to locate any potential source of danger. As the sounds of alarm rippled through the forest canopy above and then passed him, he knew he was in trouble. Turning back toward the direction of the calls, he peered through the vegetation hoping his mind could see what his eyes could not.

Seconds before he was engulfed, he sensed a vast seething mass of living creatures rushing toward him.

As he stood calm and poised amidst the impending turmoil—the jungle exploded into motion around him.

Feathers flew under the beating of thousands of wings as the air was filled with a scintillating cloud of birds swooping through and upward beyond the canopy. Parrots, macaws, and quetzals among others lit up the air with vibrancy. Shielding his face and dropping to the ground as they passed, he watched in amazement as the avian swarm took flight through the trees and onward above them. The air still thrumming after the birds' passage, he did not have time to turn back toward the source of the clamor before the first fleet-footed jungle deer sped past in the same direction as the birds.

Head rotating to follow them, he took off into the underbrush.

Before he took more than a few steps, a variegated stampede of jungle animals caught him up within their churning sights, smells, and sounds of exertion. Sprinting among the throngs through the undergrowth, some rapidly outdistancing him, others only noticed by the sounds of their exertion and footfalls, he saw some animals he recognized like powerfully limbed flightless emus, primates of every description running on the ground and swinging through the treetops, and long-faced tapirs running shoulder-to-shoulder. Surprisingly enough, these same animals were fleeing alongside predators who might normally be hunting them, like reptilian raptors and powerful spotted leopards.

His heart dropped when he noticed the gleaming green exoskeleton and pincered legs of the mantis-like Quai-lo fleeing within the pack. If a cunning predator of unmatched physical skills like the Quai-lo were in flight, then whatever the source, he had significant cause to run.

Moving among the dispersing pack, he could sense their fear, their overwhelming desire to flee. He could see and feel the excitement running loose and unchecked throughout their *li*—flames licking unrestrained, jumping and spreading from beast to beast. He also noticed how this unchecked excitement built and burned into a fear that spread from one animal to the next, a fear that insinuated itself throughout the pack until almost every creature felt the same urge to escape.

When he saw a likely place to hide, to break free of the heaving, sweating mass of potential prey, he took it. Tucked beneath a forest giant that had finally relinquished its place among the canopy, he stilled his breath and let his energy mesh as best he could with the flora and fauna around him.

Waiting, he felt the ground shuddering beneath his feet.

Peeking out from under the smooth gray bark of the old fallen kapok tree where he hid, the ground now vibrating violently beneath his feet, ready to take flight once again, he watched in anticipation for the source of all this upheaval. Within mere seconds of settling under the tree, the underbrush and small saplings lining the tree's clearing exploded and were trampled beneath the tread of an enormous reptilian monstrosity. He could see why this beast charging through the forest in search of prey had sent the whole region in flight—it was like a reptilian avalanche rushing forward without regard to momentum or gravity.

Luckily for him, it was following the scents of other creatures. As he watched its mottled green horny bulk thunder past much faster than he could run, blood dripping from its maw where it had already snatched some unfortunate creatures, he knew he could never outpace something so quick and powerful.

Watching in mingled awe and trepidation, whatever the thing was, it had to be on the scale of an adult Dragon. He could imagine it hunting elephants as easily as tapirs. Each of its legs was over twice the height of his head. Perhaps the thing was an earthbound cousin to the masters of the skies.

Looking to the left and then to the right, he could follow the beast's progress through the formerly impenetrable jungle by the open swathe of now-trampled vegetation left in its wake. With creatures like the massive Dragonkin lumbering through the trees, he could easily see how the animals living here served as an element of natural disturbance and change shaping the forest's destiny.

Following the beast's progress, he made sure to head in a different direction.

Six more days passed without event.

He had finally settled on hiking against the current of a brown, tannin-rich stream that led roughly westward. The stream's turbid waters moved lazily to the east and south—wide, open, and unhurried after its rapid descent from the mountains. Overhanging vines and limbs covered the already dark waters in wildly intertwined shadows. At times the languid waterway resembled a cave more than a moving body of water under the thick drapery of foliage. For his part, he hoped the stream's source lay in the snow-capped peaks of the Drake Spires and not at the feet of another green tepui. He also hoped that staying by a small stream like this would provide a sure sense of direction and a ready place to hide should circumstances dictate it.

Although its borders seemed limitless, the next stage of his journey no closer, and every turn potentially harbored unknown danger, he was enjoying his time in the jungle. Its beauty, the unending complexity, the newfound wonder of discovering novel strains of life at every turn with his senses held keen and taut in ready anticipation coupled with the acute opportunity to learn and improve his skills and preparation, all fed into his intense admiration for his environs.

Moving on footfalls as silent as shadows, he wound his way through the thick, unruly vegetation, careful not to let his hand linger on any unfamiliar plant lest some alkaloid or nettle give him an unwelcome surprise. As he picked his way carefully forward, the day's passage marked only by moving shade and bands of light, he paused to take a drink from his water pouch. Refreshed and ready to move onward, he wiped his chin and cleared the sweat from his brow, and started ahead listening to sounds of the stream, the leaves' rustle, and the calls of birds and insects.

With the jungle's noises enveloping him, he hardly noticed the faint cry at first, lost and distant as it was, dampened by the vegetation and impeded by the burly tree trunks.

Stopping in mid-stride, he cocked his head to listen.

Was that the yell of a man he had heard?

Still, for fear that his movement might interfere with his hearing, he waited.

The sound came again, soft and barely distinguishable from the background hum of the forest—perhaps not the cry of a man, maybe a child. Turning his head to accurately gauge its direction, he took off toward the sound, gliding around the hanging vines and other impediments that reached out for him as lightly as a mote of dust drifting in and out of sunbeams. His breath was light and free and his feet barely disturbed the thin layer of leaves on the ground as he sprinted forward acutely aware of the fear that gave voice to the cry.

He burst into a moment suspended between instances, a gruesome scene waiting to unfold before his eyes unless he did something to prevent it. Coming quickly to a stop, he stood about fifteen paces in front of a young humanoid cat covered in the orange, white, and black markings of a tiger. Swaying back and forth like a snake charmer chanting in a steady monotone, his bright green slitted eyes were held intently upon a great beast held in abeyance before him.

Slouched between where he watched and the catman was a massive ape-like creature over twice the youngling's height. The beast's corded muscles stood out in strong relief even under its coarse black hair and overhanging brow. Its arms hung like tree-trunks, the knuckles on its boulder-like fists resting heavily on the leaf litter of the clearing.

The bright flames of fury, the marks of energetic resistance, that he would normally expect to see pluming and fanning about a creature held against its will were not in evidence to his mind's eye. He could feel the beast's all-consuming rage held somehow in check by the feline's song, almost like a candle's flame held tightly and securely within a glass bottle, while the monster stood in a stupor before him. Switching his eyes back to the feline, Yip could see his will weakening as the creature's rage strengthened, threatening to shatter the confines of the feline's refrain.

As he watched, the catman gave Yip a brief pleading glance before returning his full attention to the beast.

He would have to break the tableau before the beast did.

In the distance, rushing through the jungle toward them, he sensed the presence of several powerful beings. What these others were he could not tell, nor did he have time to give them more attention. Whatever they were, these other presences would not arrive before events here unfolded.

His only hope was to distract the beast long enough to let the youngling flee.

So he moved.

Gathering the *chi* in his legs like a coiled spring, he exploded across the ground toward the feline. He closed the distance in less than a second, grabbed the feline in his arms and leapt to the side.

Only when he reached the catman did he realize how big the youngling was. Dwarfed as the catman was by the giant ape, he had misjudged the feline's size. He stood at least a head taller than Yip and was much broader of shoulder.

He deposited the obviously mentally worn and harried feline next to the trunk of a large tree and turned just in time to watch the great ape shake its head groggily and let out a low growl as it rumbled through the trees and into wakefulness.

Dipping down while the beast recovered its senses, he snatched a handful of leaves and dirt in his palm. Pushing the cat's back to the trunk, holding his finger to his lips for quiet, he sprinted diagonally away from the feline toward the front of the mountainous ape. As he reached the groggy beast's shoulder from the back, he sprung into the air in a dive and peppered the beast's clearing eyes with dirt. Rolling head over heels and to his feet, the ape's great roar told him his throw had found its target. Turning just in time to duck, the beast's massive arm lashed out, striking the tree directly to his shoulder as bark showered down about his head. Rolling once again, he dived forward, placing the tree trunk between himself and the beast's bulky frame.

Keeping the tree between his body and the creature, there was no way he could stand toe-to-toe and hope to prevail. Balanced on the balls of his feet facing the ape, ready to move either way as the creature cleared its eyes, he waited.

He did not have to wait long.

Convulsing into motion, the creature did not run around the tree.

With one mighty stroke of its columnar arm, the tree in front of him burst into a cloud of flinders beneath an explosive swing of the monster's massive fist. Amid the showering splinters, in immediate response, he regathered his *chi* and leapt, soaring over the beast's head, turning weightlessly above it, twisting and flipping in mid-air, his head close enough to the beast's unkempt fur to smell the creature's foul rank. Howling loudly at him, the beast turned and beat its massive chest in a display of power and anger, flinging dirt and debris into the air.

Outwardly cool and ready, he waited, hoping he could last long enough for the beast to tire before he did.

Luckily for him, his endurance was not put to the test.

Before he needed to react again, the air in the clearing shattered as several deafening, all-encompassing roars brought him to his knees. His eardrums burst into small, burning shards of hot glass beneath the sonic assault. Just as stunned as Yip, the great ape let out its own howl in response, turned, and lumbered noisily on all fours through the undergrowth, crashing away from the clearing.

Blinking through vision made hazy by eyes streaming tears, he watched as several huge tiger-like cats entered the clearing. Ranging in color from orange and black to white and gray, the great felines claimed the clearing in a way that acutely evinced their dominance of the forest and its environs. Astride their backs, easily ten feet off the ground, sat several more catmen each like larger versions of the one he had rescued from the giant gorilla.

Wearing manes interwoven with small bones and talismans, well-crafted, elaborately decorated leather armor, and ornate staves strapped across their backs, these felines appeared at ease in their role as lords of the forest. All told, he could see three of the giant cats holding sway over the clearing and sensed none immediately beyond. Mounted on their backs sat humanoid felines resembling a black panther, another, spotted like its kindred jungle cat, had the markings of a gold and black jaguar, and finally, in the center, astride the white tiger, relaxed in his position above the forest floor, sat a tiger-like feline almost as massive as the cat he rode.

An aura of power hung around these three in a haze as thick as their air of command.

As he unsteadily recovered his feet, still wiping the tears from his eyes after the thunderous entrance, the feline in the center, clearly the leader, yelled out to the youth, *"Jin toth!"*

Unfamiliar with their tongue, he could feel a cloud of rage commingling with concern swirling around the ferocious tigerman. More guttural words followed as the regal feline gesticulated tersely at the youth who dropped his head disconsolately in response.

He could only imagine the scolding the youngling was receiving.

He only hoped it was warranted.

Temporarily assuaged after the youth offered a lengthy response, the tiger man directed his attention to Yip.

Placing his palm flat on his chest, he said, *"Jentara al* Uuraja." He then turned at the hip and gestured broadly including his companions and their mounts in the motion, *"Jentaro al* H'era Al'Marr." Then, apparently directing his introduction to the great tigers, he said,

"Jentaro al H'era D'ur." The cats rumbled a low growl in response to the introduction.

To his inner vision, there existed an almost tangible silvery mantle between the mounts and their riders, tied together by a deep bond or united by kindred spirits.

Bowing his head slightly as a show of honor and respect, he offered the gift of his name in return. "Yip Chi Chuan of the K'un Lun."

Gesturing toward the smaller tigerling who kept his gaze on the ground, the leader waved toward the embarrassed youth. Stepping forward, the smaller version of the feline leader placed his hand on his forehead and bowed slightly, holding his chin firm with pride despite the other's apparent displeasure. He, too, offered his name, *"Jentara al Uuraru."*

While Uuraru gave his name in a show of respect to Yip, his father, Uuraja, gesticulated and uttered beneath his breath. Watching the energy of his spell move forward, he felt a cool wave fall over his ears.

Then, bowing deeply, showing Yip his appreciation, Uuraru said, "The honor of the H'era Al'Marr is yours, child of Man."

Astride the unharnessed war cat, the formidable man-tiger then added, "You do the H'era much honor, Yip Chi Chuan of the K'un Lun." Cocking his head to the side slightly, he said, "Uuraru did not dance in honor of his forefathers on this day. Perhaps he will tell you something of our people as you enjoy the hospitality of our tribe."

Turning to the youth again, his tone softened, "The time of your testing will come *ja'lal*. Do not seek the day before you are ready."

To Yip he said, "The blood of my people now flows through your hands. Uuraru owes you much. The debt will be repaid." With a light tug on the mane of the white and gray-striped cat on which he rode and a slight shift of his hips, Uuraja turned and disappeared silently into the jungle. Following suit, the other two mounted H'era left just as quietly.

He watched in awe of the great cat's physical majesty and elegant economy of motion as the last glimpse of the fearsome war cats disappeared with their riders into the jungle. He then turned toward Uuraru who walked toward him as gracefully as the cats who had just departed. "I owe you a life-debt now, Yip Chi Chuan of the K'un Lun.

For your efforts on my behalf I will dance in praise beneath the heavens until the day my shadow no longer cools the earth."

Placing a hand on the youth's furry shoulder as he neared, he said, "If your footfalls lead you toward truth and wisdom, then the debt will be repaid." Then, smiling, he added, "And you need only call me Yip, Uuraru of the H'era."

Letting out a rush of air he could only guess was the equivalent of a sigh for the H'era, Uuraru replied, "Now we need only convince my father."

Walking through the jungle forest together, the rays of sunlight diffuse and softened after the passage through multiple layers of vegetation, Uuraru's feelings of melancholy and his concerns over the nearly deadly encounter with the great ape quickly evaporated under his exuberant youthful curiosity and enthusiasm.

Carefully inspecting Yip from head to toe as they walked, Uuraru inquired, "Tell me of your people, Yip." Uuraru's eyes glimmered in the sunlight, capturing Yip's reflection in the dark depths of the slits in his pupils. Sharing in Yip's earlier humor, he added, "And why you don't have any fur."

Yip laughed. "In the mountains where I come from, we certainly could use a bit more hair! With the wind whipping down the mountainsides, running over hidden glaciers and snowfields, a nice layer of fur would help reduce the necessity for *qigong*!"

Uuraru's head tilted and his round tufted ears rotated backward in confusion upon hearing a term for which the magic lingering between them had no translation into his tongue. "What is *qigong*? Is this a type of clothing or shelter? A magical practice?"

Yip laughed again, for these were direct questions very much like the ones he had often asked the monks of his home when he initially came to live with them and learn of their ways. "*Qigong* is working with the energy of life."

"Like magic?"

"Life gives rise to magic. The two are as intertwined as the lianas about these trees. *Chi* is the vital energy or life force that enlivens and pervades all things. So, just as life gives rise to magic, *chi* gives rise to life."

Nodding his head in appreciation, Uuraru replied, "An excellent symmetry. You would make a wonderful Maer'Din."

Now it was his turn to be confused. "Maer'Din?"

"A loremaster of the H'era. Mostly they talk in riddles when they do not dance the Seura. Then all is made clear."

Mimicking Uuraru's earlier gesture, minus the tilted ears, he cocked his head, "What is the Seura?"

"The dance of dreams unborn." Uuraru stopped walking as he gazed seriously into Yip's eyes as if to say such matters should not be discussed without full attention. Yip stopped with him. "The Maer'Din help guide our collective wisdom as the world unfolds with time. They move us forward following the insights of our history and shape our shared destiny."

Yip gave a short nod. "Your lorekeepers do much. I will be honored to meet them."

Eager to share something of his people with the stranger who had so recently come to his aid, Uuraru went on, "We all have our place in the tribe. Ours is a fabric made stronger by the presence of our brothers and sisters, tied together by the waft and weave of the Maer'Din and the H'era D'ur."

A few minutes passed in silence as they picked their way through the trees following the trail of the mighty H'era D'ur who had preceded them.

Yip was the first to speak.

"The forest you live in certainly is exceptional, Uuraru." Even after the weeks he had spent in the jungle, the complexities and tangled interactions of all the living beings around him still overwhelmed his senses.

He had to mute his inner vision and feelings, to avoid losing his sense of separation and individuality, apart from all that he saw and felt of everything that surrounded him, lest he become entirely overwhelmed and surrender his sense of identity. Otherwise, the patterns, the *li*, of so many things existing in one place would appear very much like a multicolored wash with one object indistinguishable from the next. His own feelings, too, could become overwhelmed amidst the unending complexity.

"There is much that does the H'era honor here. There is also much to challenge our continued prosperity." Following up on his earlier question, he asked, "What brings you to the Land of Twin Skies, Yip? For my people only have tales and memory of your kind here."

"The Land of the Twin Skies?"

"We H'era call ourselves the Children of the Twin Skies because we live beneath the green canopy of one 'sky,' one whose trees and vegetation give us shelter and shade, under the blue skies of the world above." He paused, as if making sure the magic had translated his sentiments correctly before continuing, "We call this forest the Al'Marr, the Green Sea, after our homeworld. Taking our name after our homeland, my people in particular are the H'era Al'Marr. There are other tribes of our kind scattered throughout the jungle who also find their way beneath the twin skies of Ea'ae."

Yip nodded appreciatively. He took pleasure in learning of the places and ways he visited, even when he could not linger as he would. "To answer your earlier question, I am on a quest, Uuraru. Your forest has offered me shelter and protection from those who would seek me out and prevent me from reaching my goal. For that I am grateful."

"Are you on a rite of passage? Among my kind, we quest to achieve new knowledge and insight. When the time comes, we are tested to prove the worth of what we have learned."

"Of a sort, perhaps, but not willingly." He let out a small sigh of his own. "Given the choice I would not have left my home. But events do not always unfold as we would choose."

Nodding in agreement, for he had just endured something of his own rite of passage, if a bit prematurely, Uuraru asked, "Are you in danger?"

"Those who would seek me can read the patterns and traces of my essence. I think the energies of the forest and all its living beings may have confused my trail even from their senses. Even if the Shadow can track me here, I think their labors at least will be slowed."

Looking into the tufted orange, white-and-black-striped face of his companion, he added, "In all honesty, I am but a minor piece in the enemy's plans. No matter how I am viewed or considered, for I am largely beneath their notice at this time, I am sure they will not stop until all my kind have been eliminated."

"Who is after you, Yip?" Ready concern was evident in Uuraru's voice, for his people, too, had their own trials and tribulations they had endured and broken free from during their relatively recent past. "And what are you looking for?"

"Perhaps we will talk of my pursuers with your father. There may be time for the telling of tales then."

A good portion of the day passed as he walked side-by-side with Uuraru, talking with the young tigerling as they ventured through the forest. As the day's light began to slant and drift to shadows, Uuraru said, "We are approaching our village."

Yip had sensed the presence of other H'era as they moved westward through the forest, but he saw very little signs of their passage. Skilled in forest lore and schooled in the ways of the jungle, either their village was relatively new or the H'era made as little lasting visible impressions on the ecosystem as did the birds alighting on the tree limbs above.

Either way, he was impressed.

He saw no guards as he crested the small rise leading to the village of the H'era, but he sensed the presence of those watching their approach, silent sentinels as strong and vibrant as the boles reaching heavenward. As Uuraru brushed aside the last leafy frond and ushered him forward, his eyes alighted upon a setting as wondrous as the jungle surrounding it.

Nestled between massive, moss-covered trunks growing in the shadow of yet another monolithic tepui, resting on the sides of a small valley bisected by a clear, slow running stream, waited the village of the H'era Al'Marr.

As his eyes took in its beauty, he heard Uuraru say, "Welcome to Aluran, the village of the Green Glade."

Spread as effortlessly as morning dew upon soft spring grass, the forms of the H'era's homes and meeting places floated and rippled in the soft jungle breeze. The valley seemed alive, aflame with gossamer sails capturing and reflecting the last of the day's light, enhancing its brightness and warmth for all.

Unaccustomed to such mutable shapes and their immediate functions, he had to pause and carefully take in the beauty spread before him. At first, the lush greenness of the valley seemed to be filled with billowing sails freed from the moorings of ships that had never tethered their freedom. As he began to make sense of the vista, he could see how the streaming sails overlapped, functioning somewhat independently, but also linked to form a series of beautiful, semi-translucent structures that only served to accent the immediate wonder and vitality of the place. He could feel the way their magic held and augmented the energies of the valley and the forest around, bringing safety and security to those who dwelled within while at the same time creating an environment at once nurturing and productive to those who lived within. The forest flowed through and within these structures unimpeded and unhampered by their presence, a commingling that he could only marvel at and appreciate.

He had never seen its like.

Letting Yip survey his village appreciatively for a time, Uuraru finally said, "Come."

Walking down the spongy hillside, Yip asked, "Where are the H'era D'ur?" For the valley did not leave much room for the great cats to board.

"Our kindred live in the surrounding jungle. They know when to come."

Curious, he asked, "How do they know?"

"Our kind shares a bond—the Aurana—with our brothers the H'era D'ur. Our Maer'Din tell us that we are descended from the same ancestors long, long ago. We have maintained and strengthened our connection through all that time." Looking at Yip significantly, he added, "Although our forms are very different, our spirits are one."

Walking down the hillside, Yip could hear the sounds of the cloth-like buildings susurrating and occasionally snapping in the breeze. The billowing impermanence of the structures kept his attention rapt in wonder, seeming as fleeting as fog on a summer's day.

"What are your homes made of, Uuraru?" He could no longer contain his curiosity. He actually felt the buildings as he felt the other living things of the forest around him—complex energetic patterns contained in a material form.

"They are of the forest as are we, its essence, its energy, its song, its vibrancy, and its dance. The forest shares this shelter with us as we share in its protection, stewardship, and spirit."

Yip could feel the buildings' hum as he approached and appreciated them as the living manifestations of the forest that they were. Looking at the mutable shimmering surfaces, he could see the forest's light, its energy, its motion, and dynamism reflected in their core. Approaching, he felt surety and warmth, freedom and expansiveness, as if under the eaves of a great tree whose welcoming shadow enveloped and protected all beneath its verdant canopy.

"I would be honored if perhaps one day you would share the art of their creation, if permissible, Uuraru."

"If the Maer'Din and my father allow it, we shall see."

Arrayed before them at the base of the hill stood the bulk of the village, young and old, large and small. He could see the semblance of many jungle cats in their visages—black panthers, spotted leopards, striped tigers, and others he could not name. Of the cats from his home —lynx, pumas, and snow leopards—he could see no sign. Perhaps H'era from places other than the jungle would show different forms.

As they walked down the slope, he was impressed by the H'era's physical stature and obvious physical prowess. He was by no means a large man, but the H'era adults easily stood half again his height. Their arms were the size of his legs, their fangs appeared at least the size of his fingers, and their hands looked large enough to easily cover his chest when spread. Although at ease and in tune with their forest environs, the H'era appeared more than well suited to defending their home should the need arise.

Tall and regal at the center of the gathering stood Uuraja, resplendent in a great cloak of many dancing hues, each festive splash of color reflecting the tone and tenor of a different forest orchid, flower, or bud. "Be welcome and know the hospitality of the H'era, Yip Chi Chuan, child of Man!" Uuraja's voice boomed almost as loudly as the roars of the H'era D'ur.

He answered his host with a deep bow, hands hidden and overlapping in the sleeves of his robes. "Your Light does me welcome and soothes my spirit, H'era Al'Marr."

Flanking Uuraja on either side were two older H'era, one male and one female, both with long, intricately woven hair. Unlike the other H'era who were dressed mostly in clothes of leather or cloth, these two were dressed in full flowing robes that seemed to catch all the forest's colors and textures in their folds from the cool shadows bordering dancing streams to the bright sunlight flitting on the branches of the tallest trees. Their spirits blazed like bonfires in the sun and he knew them to be Maer'Din, the lorekeepers of the H'era Al'Marr. Based on his surmise, both the elders' robes and Uuraja's cloak symbolized their station in the tribe.

As one, the Maer'Din stepped forward in response to Yip's bow, and offered a greeting of their own, arms outstretched wide, their robes flowing as if in response to a breeze that was not there, "May your steps be free of shadow all your days, Yip Chi Chuan. Welcome to our hearts and home."

And with that ancient greeting, known to many who tread the ways of Light on this world and others, he was glad for he knew that he was among friends.

THE H'ERA

Canopy above
lost in light.

Leaf litter under old soles,
Heaven and Earth conjoined.

"You have found your way to friends, Yip Chi Chuan, and have shown yourself to be one as well by saving my son." Uuraja's stern expression split into a great, if somewhat fearsome, grin as he put his massive arm on Yip's shoulder and pulled him into the fold of his many new friends.

The crowd parted as he was lead farther into the village, the two elders and Uuraru in tow, passing a small, gurgling stream surrounded by ferns and an open clearing with a central stone fire pit until they finally reached a great, billowing semi-transparent structure that seemed as much the stuff of air as shelter.

Waving him in, Uuraja motioned for Yip to have a seat on a large embroidered pillow. "The time for the telling of histories has almost come, Yip. Your deeds have earned our trust and our tale." Uuraja sat effortlessly down on a richly woven divan covered in an array of pillows and throws. The two elders took a place to either side of Uuraja sitting directly on the gauzy floor with their legs folded beneath their robes.

Looking around the interior, the roof translucent to the light above, he was surprised at the firmness of the floor beneath his tread and the clarity of the light within. He felt buoyed by diffuse sunlight.

Shadowing Yip to a seat placed directly in front of Uuraja, Uuraru waited until Yip took the previously offered pillow and then sat directly beside him.

Uuraja addressed him directly. "You must forgive us, Yip, if our hospitality is lacking in any way. Before we begin the telling of tales, know that we have chosen deliberately to isolate ourselves here and that we seldom receive visitors. We have not chosen isolation willingly, but as a matter of survival."

"The custom of our people has always been to accept worthies into our tribe when they do us great honor. By way of initiation, we share the story of our people that our newfound allies may know us as intimately as a member of their own family. However, since coming to this land, we have not afforded this honor to anyone. As will be made clear in due time, we have taken this course as much for our own protection as a direct consequence of our isolation. By inviting you here and telling you our story, you not only have our confidence, but our future in your hands. When you leave and journey out into the world at large, I ask you to keep us and our story in your deepest trust. Do I have your word that you will hold our history to your heart?"

He bowed. "Your honor is mine and I will uphold it as my own."

"Then let us begin." Uuraja inclined his head and the two elders stood slowly amidst the soft swish of rustling robes.

Leaving the meeting room sedately, the elders walked once again outside, leading Yip, Uuraru, and Uuraja to the village center. Surrounding the newly lit fire pit, now dressed in robes of shimmering silks and empyreal threads matching the fey fabric of the buildings, the village formed an open semicircle ready to receive their leaders and guest. Behind the assembled H'era, H'era D'ur of every shape and color sat attentively on their haunches, their massive silhouettes providing another layer of shadow beneath the eaves of the forest giants above.

To his eyes, the spirits of these twin peoples, the H'era and the H'era D'ur, commingled like fine mist above a forest on a cool winter's day, light and effusive, but undeniably deep and strong.

As Yip and the elders broke the periphery of the tribes' waiting circle, the H'era sat silently in unison, leaving only Yip, Uuraja, Uuraru, and the two Maer'Din standing.

Uuraja gestured for Yip to be seated close to the dancing flames. As he sat down, Uuraru once again settled down beside him.

Leaning close, Uuraru whispered, "The Maer'Din will now dance the Seura."

At first, only rustling robes and light footfalls accompanied the Maer'Din's slow, undulating movements. As one accustomed to intentional movement, he appreciated the two Maer'Din's grace and poise, the focus and economy of their motion. As he watched, the flickering flames caught in small, refracted shards on their iridescent robes, reflecting the flames over and over again.

Lost in the movements and dancing lights, the susurrations of the flowing robes, the reassuring movements of the tribe, he only realized as images started coalescing before his eyes that he was starting to dream. Still able to see the flames and the surrounding H'era, images gradually began to unfold and build between himself and the Maer'Din. As he watched, the air shimmered, as if opening a portal to another world, another place and time. Moving deeper into reverie, the fire and the H'era slipped away and he was lost in the Seura as the dance of dreams unborn became the dance of dreams made real.

Vast open plains and a sky as deep as a mountain pool stretched overhead as far as the eye could see. Spread loosely throughout the rippling grass, like dandelion seeds floating in the spring breeze, the H'era moved gracefully astride the H'era D'ur, the Aurana burning between them brighter than the golden sun that lit their steps.

He did not know how or why, but he knew that while the H'era traveled across plains and through forests, separate tribes came together to trade, commingle, dance, and palaver. Spending most of their time adrift in the plains, the H'era seldom settled down in a single location.

This was the way of the H'era—moving, sharing time and stories within the family group and with other clans, hunting, and dancing for the tribe, the stars, the wind, and the sky. Bound together by the Seura, the H'era knew of their past, their common origin, and their place in the world together from times long past, times lost to other people's memory.

Despite that breadth of knowledge and experience, despite their skill in arms and in the hunt, despite their control over the elements and the strength of their song, the H'era were unprepared for the doom that soon followed.

The Maer'Din did not know why, but the spirit, life's everlasting song, began to leave the land.

Tribes met and shared resources and joined together in their efforts to renew the land without effect. No amount of song or dance was able to strengthen the once vital land's weakening spirit. Warriors were sent far and wide to find the source of this plague to no avail. The land, so abundant throughout the past, the long living memory of their people, began to fade. Through the passage of time, grass seemed less green and grew shorter. Fewer and fewer animals bred as the times of scarcity grew more dire. Birdsong and insects' humming slowly faded until silence draped the land. Tribes, once strong and proud, scavenged and slowly fell, their Maer'Din and their memory lost in the dust.

As an outsider, he felt the world growing more and more translucent, as if its essence and vitality were slowly draining away. The very air seemed so fragile, so thin, that if breathed it might tear and fill the lungs with darkness. Watching this world fail, his eyes were opened to the truth and his own world seemed to crumble bit by fragile bit.

He wanted to call out into the night in desperate anger, humiliation and disgust, but he could not. He was lost in someone else's dream, in the H'era's vision. Not only did he know the cause of the madness let loose upon this world, he could sense its source and genesis. Hardly able to breath as the revelation, as the enormity, of this discovery hit him, he watched in horror as the evils of those formerly of his order were visited upon a world without proper defense or knowledge of the source of their undoing.

In a last act of desperation, while their warriors sought in vain for a solution and for the cause of their world's end, the remaining Maer'Din came together and began to call out into the darkness between the stars for help, for succor, for a new home. As their world faded, falling apart about them, no answer came to their calls. Weeks passed, time was measured in the dying of grasses, friends, and the accumulation of dust. With no response to their pleas and almost all their warriors having returned in failure, the H'era's hearts filled with woe.

Their doom would come without knowing its source, without breaking its bonds.

When despair reached a terrible crescendo within their midst, just before their time came to an end, the Maer'Din finally heard a response to their need—a lovely song weaving through the ether that lifted their hopes and offered guidance through the darkness of the void between the stars. This chorus called them to a new land where the H'era could restore themselves and dance anew.

As their final preparations to leave neared completion, Uuraja, then but a young uninitiated brave, returned at last, weakened and frail, to his tribe with news about the source of the death of their world. Far to the east, in lands mountainous and sere, a Darkness, an emptiness, leeched the life from the land.

Treading that distant place through Uuraja's eyes, moving farther and farther from home, he could feel the origin of that evil slowly pulling at his spirit, drawing more and more of himself away as he drew nearer, weakening his heart and his resolve. Forlorn souls careened past him as he headed onward, lost, directionless constellations shorn from their orbits, straying farther and farther away from what little hope remained in the few remaining lands of the living.

Fighting the emptiness, clinging on to himself, Uuraja sang his spirit strength, sheltering his heart and the Aurana shared with his H'era D'ur Iera as best he could.

Climbing bleak peak after peak, Uuraja's resolve weakening as much as his companion H'era D'ur Iera's, Uuraja pressed on. Cresting one final blasted basaltic peak, Uuraja beheld a vast, dry valley abandoned by everything but dust and memory.

Dense, low hung clouds and a weak wavering sun only illumined the paucity of the rocks, grit, and ash. As Uuraja stood on that rise, surveying the desolation, he sensed that if he took one step farther that he would never take another step back, that his soul would be as abandoned and bereft of a home as the dust. Gazing back and forth, eyes intent on the horizon, his scrutiny could not discern what his mind and heart told him, that his people's ruin lay in wait somewhere past this point of no return—a locus of evil invisible to the eye, known only indirectly by its influence on the lives it destroyed. Finally, after a short time, he could bear no more and had to turn back understanding, if nothing else, that there was an origin to this madness, that there was a cause to his people's end, an insatiable pit that devoured all that came within reach.

Watching Uuraja's journey through lands stripped and bereft of life, Yip wondered how the agents of Darkness could disrupt the *chi* of an entire world.

How could the masters of the dark ways of the spirit siphon off the life energy of a planet?

If the energy of a whole world could be sapped, what did the knaves do with such an enormous amount of power?

How was so much *chi* utilized and channeled?

When Uuraja returned, weary as his tribe's spirit, the Maer'Din, along with the remaining H'era and H'era D'ur, greeted his story with the sadness it deserved, knowing their time in this land, the land of the Twin Skies, Al'Marr, sheltered by the firmament above and the Seura within, home to their forebears, had come to an end. Although few remained, those that survived decided to retrace Uuraja's steps for a time and do honor to the faces of their mothers and fathers before their lives on their homeland came to an end.

Retracing Uuraja's steps, the H'era left their ancestral home for the last time. Once proud shoulders slumped, once light steps heavy, the H'era Al'Marr first headed east and then beyond in a cloud of dust.

ASCENT

Flitting butterfly
on a purple columbine
holds the world under its wings.

The dancing flames slowly reappeared as the gauzy visions faded softly into memory. Feeling dry, dusty, and haggard, as if he had been breathing the sere, dying air of that faraway land, his attention gradually returned to the sound of Uuraja's voice, a small thread connecting the H'era's new home to the old.

"The Yerens guided us through the darkness between the stars with their song. For our part, our people have no Travelers—the magic of our dance, our song, our shared brotherhood, our history, and our arms both define and limit us as a culture. Without the Yerens, we would not have been able to walk beyond the lands of our ancestors. We would have perished as so many others did before us."

Here Uuraja drew a deep breath, and Yip sensed the sadness with which he continued, "The darkness that stole the blood and spirit from our native home has come to this land as well."

His striped tawny face wrinkled in displeasure and he spat. "The

Maer'Din can sense its traces creeping through the air from the mountains both to the east and to the west like the briefest scent of smoke hinting at an impending brushfire. We are surrounded and do not know how long this new land will hold."

The mighty tigerman shrugged. "There are great magics in this land that may protect this place and its people. I cannot say. The ancestral forest through which you passed to the east will certainly hold for generations, but, regardless of how long we have in this place, my people may have left one home to be stripped of another."

Turning from Yip, he glanced briefly to his son, Uuraru. "I may not live to see the day, but this time my people will not run." There were muttered agreements and growls from the H'era around him. "We will meet the faces of our mothers and fathers in battle and find our end in honor."

As Uuraja paused and his tribe quieted, Yip spoke into the evening shadows, "To know that your people have such strength and courage after all you have suffered makes my heart proud, but I would not ask you to fight or endure any more hardship. The H'era have earned peace and should keep it as long as you can. Now is the time to rebuild and restore what you can of the lives you have lost. This jungle and the lands surrounding it offer much in the way of challenge. Survival here will be difficult enough without seeking more adversity and woe."

He turned his head slowly, trying to meet as many of the slitted feline eyes glimmering in the orange and yellow flames as possible. "I know the source of the Darkness that steals away the life of man, woman, and child, that leeches the living spirit from the land, and it is my duty and my order's obligation to stop it."

He took a deep breath under the enormity of the burden laid out before him and continued with deep sadness, "I had no idea that the evil spawned so long ago in the past by my order's failings had reached so far and had grown so strong after being banished from this world."

"Such are the flaws of Man."

With the surety of his worldview, his belief in the potential for his order to right their failings and to continue to foster a world where all living things were able to achieve their utmost potentiality dissolving around him, he tried his best to offer some clarity and insight into the source of the evil that had destroyed the world of the H'era. "Long ago, in times long forgotten, there were those among my kind who eschewed the Light and the ways of peace for Darkness."

"Over time, my order, which had been dedicated to culturing the highest ideals of the human spirit, was forced to become a vehicle to fight the ills of our own kind, of our own making. As those who cast off the principles and teachings of our way of life grew stronger, my order banded together with those who would help us rid the world, your new home, Ea'ae, of this evil."

"Man and Dwarf, Elf and Dragon, along with other races too numerous to count, all worked in concert to banish the evil of the Cabal, as they now call themselves, called Liúxīng Làngrén, those fallen from the path of Heaven, by my brothers, from this world forever. In the process, many great hearts and minds were lost to this world never to be recovered. In the end, after many years of strife, those in my order along with leaders of other races thought that they had not only destroyed the Cabal forever but had protected other worlds from the threat they had faced."

Looking around him with deep sorrow, he went on, "Apparently these heroes of the past were wrong. Not only did we fail in stopping the Cabal, but they appear stronger than ever. Even now they are working to sunder the barriers that protect this world from their aggression and that of their ilk."

Shaking his head, he went on with his story. "As punishment for our failings, my order chose exile as a form of penitence and disconnected ourselves from the larger world lest we spawn another menace to be unleashed upon an unsuspecting world. Our isolation held over millennia until recently. Sadly, our reemergence has been closely timed with the Cabal's recent attempts to once again make their presence felt on Ea'ae."

"We are all here for the same unfortunate reason. The Cabal destroyed all you knew and forced you from your world. The Cabal has repeatedly tried to destroy my order and its ideals. Their most recent attack nearly destroyed our monastery and forced me to flee amid the tumult."

"I do not know what their machinations will mean for Ea'ae, its people, and its future, but I know that I cannot let them continue unhindered. The fate of your world is too poignant an example. This world, and many countless ones beyond, must not follow a similar course."

He knew not what to expect of the H'era, after coming so far to meet the face of their ultimate betrayers—his brothers, his teachers, himself.

Filled with pain and compassion, his resolve firm, he waited for the response of the H'era.

He did not wait long.

Uuraja's deep voice filled the void left by Yip's closure, one filled with the compassion of one who has seen the depths of darkness and has emerged from torment renewed. "Our pasts and futures are intertwined, our songs blend together of one chorus. Though we do not ride with you now, you have our aid should you need it, Yip Chi Chuan."

"We will await your call."

Yip's shoulders slumped. "I fear that I may have done far too much damage merely by visiting you for I am certain that the Cabal seek me even as we speak. After fleeing the monastery, I am the last of my kind to walk openly upon Ea'ae."

Holding his head in his hands, he finished softly, "I have done my best to mask my presence from those who may pursue me and can only hope that my trail has been muddled by all the energies of this jungle. I would not visit further suffering upon you."

Once again looking up at the H'era who were watching him with a mixture of anxiety and concern, their gazes simultaneously expressed fierce defiance and focus. "I must go lest the evils of my past, our past, catch up with both of us."

Uuraja grinned fiercely, his wicked teeth gleaming brightly. "Fear not for us, Yip. The doom that chases you will not be ours."

Gesturing in the direction Yip had come from, Uuraja intoned, "If any traces of your path yet remain beyond the sacred glades of the forest lords, we will mask them with our song."

After a moment's pause, Uuraja then offered, "Seek the Yerens in the mountains to the west. Perhaps they will be able to offer aid where we have not. We will be here to offer our support should you need it."

"Seek us when you have need. We will be listening."

And with that, he bowed deeply and disappeared into the night.

SHAPERS

The transition from
verdant land to azure sea—
broken by a band of gold.

A little over a week later, with the dawn of a new day, Yip found himself pressing upward as the jungle began a gradual ascent of the Drake Spires. Once he reached the peaks, the mountains would be anything but green. In fact, the mountains were taller, more rugged, and occupied much more land area than the K'un Lun. With no natural breaks, these untamed peaks divided the continent of Dharia in twain. Although the bases of the mounts were covered with jungle on this their southern and eastern face, the northwestern foothills several hundred spans away were temperate. The high peaks acted as a natural weather barrier and divided two temperate zones from one another. After all the heat and humidity in the lowlands, he was looking forward to the cool heights ahead and the mild foothills on the far side of the range.

The next several days passed uneventfully as he climbed upward through cloud forests hung in moss and lichen, draped in silence, in a land largely hidden by mist, making his way upward through the clouds. Every turn brought forth a new wonder—birds as bright and colorful as rainbows, unaus moving slower than the plants that grew past and on them, whole worlds existing in microcosm in pools of water trapped in the leaves of bromeliads and other water-loving plants—an immense green realm as diverse as the sea and just as deep. He wished he had time to linger and explore, for the land he passed held marvels that deserved further study and appreciation.

Drenched from the constant brume pervading the whole of the upper forest, he finally emerged from his climb through the jungle onto a high plateau that looked out on the great peaks to come. White-capped and gleaming in the sunlight, the green long left for white and gray, the Drake Spires' high pinnacles loomed sharp and abrupt as they reached for the sky. Many peaks were so tall that they seemed to wear the high-altitude clouds as skirts. Lowering his eyes from the heights spanning the horizon, immediately ahead he looked upon arguably the strangest landscape he could imagine.

Just as wet as the forest he had just left, but noticeably cooler, the plateau benefited from the rain shadow of the mountains above while also catching a significant portion of the run-off from precipitation and snow-melt on the peaks. Too wet for trees, too moist for normal alpine vegetation, boggy and covered in great hummocks of many species of moss, the plateau represented a rare high altitude elfin forest. Pools of water were cupped by great mounds of moss and sharp yucca-like ferns, and interspersed throughout were stunted palmate trees. Wisps of fog floated leisurely above the water and pools.

Looking slowly left and right, he surveyed a land colored in rusts, browns, deep greens, and mottled yellows.

Besides the numerous plants, insects, and the occasional bird, he could sense very little in the way of larger animal life. Slightly puzzled, he did not know what to make of that assessment.

Moving forward would be an exercise in persistence as the bogs and muck dragged him down. Even the high mossy hummocks looked as though they held water, much like giant sponges always ready to receive more and more liquid. The moisture from above and below would also make finding a suitable place to camp more difficult than progressing toward the peaks.

Looking ahead, he let out a brief sigh wishing that he could be more like his teachers, the Yu-jen, who could pass untouched and unnoticed through the harshest of places—soft as a breeze, quiet as open space, empty as the sky on a cloudless day, light as a feather, totally and completely in accord. They were as much a part of the environment as the ground and sky, the rocks, trees and minerals, and the Wu-hsing—the processes changing natural phenomena.

He hoped that he could cross the plateau in two hard day's travel.

Cinching his pack tightly to his back, he took his first soggy, lurching step into the bogs, moving forward tentatively as he sought the firmness and surety of mineral soil. Each slow, slurping step onward brought with it more muck and wet, heavier and more difficult than the last. Saving himself, he tried to maintain a steady pace, choosing the path of least resistance wherever possible even if it meant continuous swimming for short periods of time.

By the time he had lost sight of the plateau's edge and the tops of the forest trees behind him, he was almost completely covered in mud, decomposing plants, strands of grasses, and bits of moss and algae. Looking down at himself, he had the makings of a very nice garden between all the soil, seeds, and remnants of plants caked all over his body.

He would have to come back for raw materials when he was ready to start his own park.

Despite the mud and chill, the unknown risk behind him, he could not help but have fun. After all, what was more amusing as a child than playing in the mud? Making the most of a difficult situation, he tried his best to enjoy himself.

Entering yet another deep, still pool as he slogged onward, he wrenched back quickly as he felt his leg starting to burn along his thigh. With a sudden gathering of force, he leapt through the air completely free of the water as a viscous, ropy tendril detached from his leg. Looking down, he could see a hole burnt through the fabric of his robes and a small cauterized burn on the surface of his leg. Inching slowly backward, he kept his eyes on the surface of the water.

Watching the pool's edge, he saw a vague translucence floating slowly toward him. The thing gradually resolved itself into an amorphous mass of dark umber, gelatinous and fluid. Gradually oozing its way forward, the slime sent out questing tendrils for any signs of life in its path. Looking closely, he could see the partially digested remains of a bird in the thing's central mass. As strange as it was, the thing registered little more vitality than the moss or lichen all around him; picking the oozes out, should there be more, would be quite a difficult task.

Sticking his finger through the hole in his *zhiju*, he decided to avoid the pools of water at all costs. At least that way he might be able to see the things as they moved mindlessly about engulfing food.

He now knew why the area was so strangely devoid of life. With those roving acidic goos constantly scouring the landscape, the bog would be a very difficult place in which to survive.

Pushing forward rapidly and with great purpose, he was not able to reach the far edge of the bog by dusk. Sighing inwardly, he still had several hours of slogging through the mire ahead before he reached the relative safety of dry ground. As darkness slowly fell across the plateau and the tracery of living things provided a faint luminescence to the bog, his concerns for safety were soon abated. Glowing with changing shades of bioluminescence in the darkness, the slimes were readily apparent in the chill, moist night air. By midnight, based on the position of the moon overhead, he began to encounter patches of dry ground.

Before he left the bog entirely, he gathered quite a bit of the sphagnum moss in his cape to dry so that he could use it as a form of crude insulation in his clothing once it had completely dried out. After another hour or so of scrabbling over rocks and loose scree, he finally found a spot flat enough to take a much welcome rest.

As he bedded down for the night, ahead through the gloom, he could sense the impending sloping mass of the great peaks above.

Several more days of hard climbing over the ever-steepening slopes brought him within a few days of his first crossing of the lowest pass to be found on the outlying peaks of the Drake Spires. Looking longingly upward, he could see the snow shimmering in the afternoon sunlight on a large, crevasse-riddled glacier directly below the pass.

Blinking away the bright rays of the sun, the glacier was shrouded in a faint bluish glow. From this distance, he could not tell if that haze was the effect of the deep interior blues of the glacial ice on the reflected sunlight or something else entirely. He would find out in time.

Turning away from the mountains, his mind opened with the view, taking in the entirety of the sky and clouds, rocks and jungle, in one seamless glance. Before and behind him, the energy of life flowed, filling his senses with vibrancy and light, the sensation of buoyancy and limitless expansiveness.

Gazing downward, an ocean of green stretched to the horizon, framed against the mountains behind him and by the sky in the distance. The verdant plateaus of the tepuis broke the uneven surface of verdure and the low-lying clouds—rocky islands adrift in the wilderness. In both directions behind him to the north and south, the great peaks loomed ever closer. His travels upward had already brought him into a land of snowfields, glaciers, moraines, taluses, and other geologic features endemic to the cold, weather-worn high altitudes. To his regret, he had left behind the last of the low-lying, flower-covered alpine meadows and other heathy vegetation a few days before.

Taking in the view, he sent a prayer for the H'era drifting away and outward on a brisk mountain wind. He wished them continued safety, freedom, and peace and hoped that his presence had not disturbed their hard-earned sanctuary.

He marveled that snow and glaciers could exist in such close proximity to the steaming jungles below. Gazing at the summits ahead, the undeniable effects of altitude on temperature were clearly visible to his eyes and felt on his skin.

The days at this height were already quite cool with the winds that sometimes rushed downward over the snow and ice fields from the peaks. Evenings were cold. He had already stuffed his clothes with the sphagnum moss he had picked up in the bog to help regulate his core body temperature and reduce energy demands.

At this pace, his journey would take months just to pass through the mountains before he could seek assistance on the other side. Breathing in the thinning air whenever possible, he planned to reduce time and effort by traveling along valleys below the peaks in the direction he had set for himself instead of continually climbing and crossing ridge after ridge. He hoped that the Yerens could provide some direction or aid in his search for a way to overcome and be free of the Cabal, if he managed to find them.

In the evenings he did his best to find shelter whether in the lee of a large rock or boulder, in a cave, by stacking stones, or even by building up a bank of snow packed into the shape of a wall or barrier. Realistically, his efforts made very little difference in terms of temperature, but finding a sheltered spot did help protect him from the wind and elements. Instead of sleeping, he spent the evenings deep in meditation generating heat and inducing a state of temporary hibernation by reducing the amount of blood sent to his extremities while gradually reducing his core body temperature; in effect, maintaining blood flow primarily to his major internal organs.

Traveling through so many diverse types of landscapes, myriad climates, various ecosystems, and ecotones had the primary benefit of giving him the opportunity to practice the techniques he had observed from the Aeryn D'al—blending, harmonizing, and ultimately disappearing into the local environment. Without any signs of pursuit, he could only feel that thus far he had been successful in masking his trail both to his benefit and for those he had and would encounter along his journey.

On the fifth day of his ascent, the morning dawned clear and cold with steel-gray clouds looming on the horizon. Looking closely into their depths as they approached, he could see great storm giants riding the clouds' billowing gray crests, urging the storm system to an even greater pitch. A storm lashed and goaded by the fury of powerful storm giants would be more than he would care to chance.

He had camped next to a large boulder the night before, but risking exposure on a mountainside to a magical storm that could potentially last several days would require more energies than he could hope to expend. He would have to find more adequate shelter.

Looking upward regretfully, he could see the pass he sought

seeming but a short distance away. He had hoped to reach the pass later that day, but the uncertainty of facing a storm completely exposed on the ridgetop would be an extremely risky proposition. Scouting briefly around, his eyes settled on the expansive, bluish-tinged glacier that fanned out from the pass. If he was fortunate, he could find a crevasse that would provide sufficient protection to weather out the storm. Hidden inside, he would be surrounded by ice instead of howling winds and snow.

Two hours of hard climbing brought him sweating and steaming to the base of the glacier. Ahead, rising sheer and abrupt from the surrounding rock, a dirty white snow- and ice-encrusted wall loomed upward toward the crest of the pass. As the great mass of ice slowly shifted and deformed under tremendous pressures, it split and fissured, inexorably moving down the mountainside, melting and advancing, scouring the rocks and ridges it crossed. Through large cracks interspersed occasionally across the glacial face, he could see the deep blue hues indicative of old interior ice hidden within.

Glad for the sight of all those openings, he was happy to have so many options to choose from to seek shelter from the impending storm. Heading upward, he chose a large, deep blue crevasse left open to his advance after a great chunk of ice had shorn off from the glacier and collapsed to the ground in front of the opening. Skirting the slowly melting chunks left forlorn and broken before the advancing glacial face, he climbed into the sheltered chasm, looking wonderingly at the clean, smooth walls that varied in color from a glaring white as he looked up toward the sun and sky to a deep blue farther back into the crevasse and nearer to the ground. After going into the opening far enough to be covered above as well as on all sides, he could still make out the opening to the icy cave.

He could only wonder at the ice flow's age, how the world had changed during the time of its formation and passage, and at the mysteries that may lie imbedded in its depths.

He settled in as best he could, wrapping himself tightly in his robe and blanket to protect himself from exposure. When he was done, he imagined that he looked quite a bit like one of the lumpy moss hummocks from the bog below. In fact, if he were not mindful of the storm's severity, with all the moss stuffed in his robes, he might in fact serve as excellent substrate for another future hump of moss.

He sat waiting for the storm sitting *seiza*, legs and feet tucked beneath him at the ready, bent at the knees—a position that also had the advantage of helping to keep his form as compact as possible while minimizing his exposed body parts. Regulating his breathing and blood flow, his metabolic processes slowed, keeping pace with the deliberate tempo of the glacier.

Hours passed in a timeless state. During that time, he knew only peace and the quietude of inner reflection. He could sense the storm and its attendant giants raging first against the mountain and then the glacier as something far off, well removed from himself. The violent throws of wind and snow, sleet and hail, cresting over the mountainside were mere sounds in the distance, as inconsequential as the gentle sigh of someone else's breath steaming and dispersing in the cold.

Though he could still feel the storm and its attendant dangers raging in the distance, he sensed that his waiting was over. He must arouse and return to wakefulness, for something was coming. Gradually opening his eyes to a white blur, he could see drifts shifting and swirling at the entrance to his chasm as violent winds whipped the snow and ice to a fever pitch. As his eyes adjusted to the storm-induced gloom, the glacier doing much to help his vision by capturing and transmitting what little light there was beneath the roaring gray skies, he could see a great shadow looming at the entrance to his icy cavern.

Roughly twice the height of a man and at least four times as wide, he could not make out what type of beast he faced, only that it was massive, hairy, and imposing. On the top of its head were two small, forward curving horns. Remaining outwardly calm and still, his body frenetically tried to recover from the lethargy and dormancy of self-induced hibernation in order to respond to this potential emergency.

As his eyes readjusted to wakefulness, he took a deep, silent breath, letting his inward tension slide away with the wind as he assessed the creature. Although not a true psion—he could only read others' thoughts under special circumstances—he could tell much from a being's energy signatures and patterns.

This being's spirit soared.

Light flowed from the creature's essence in a soothing, peaceful aureole. Although great in physical stature and fearsome in appearance, the creature was quite calm, a quality in marked contrast to the raging storm whipping about its shaggy shoulders. Although he could be wrong, the creature seemed more curious than anything else. It probably had no idea what a small strange man like himself was doing here covered in moss, all alone and obviously unprepared for the cold.

Raising his hand in a gesture of openness, he bowed his head to the creature and said a soft, "Hello." Pausing for a moment when the creature did not respond, he continued, "If you seek sanctuary, you are welcome to share in the comforts of this cave."

The creature cocked its head to the side, as if listening to some distant music Yip could not hear as he spoke. Long seconds after the echoes of his voice had faded into the howls of the storm, it took one great, bounding step forward into the crevasse and opened its savage mouth.

The creature did not roar.

It did not bellow.

Neither did it growl or speak.

Instead it began to sing.

It sang with the voice of the snow falling, of ice melting beneath the spring sun, of the briefest flame of summer blooms, of the seamless depths between the stars on a clear night, of wind caressing the tips of the highest peaks, and somehow he knew the story it told was for him.

It did not tell him its name, as was the custom of Yip's people; it told Yip its story, as was the custom of its kind.

Tears froze in his eyes before he even had the chance to realize he was crying. He had never heard any music so beautiful.

After a time, the creature's song lost itself in the storm and he knew it was done.

Here was a being at peace with itself and its environment even under the harshest of conditions. This marvelous being must be a Yeren.

Standing slowly, letting the blood return to his legs, he bowed.

Looking toward him expectantly, he offered the creature his full name in turn, "My name is Yip Chi Chuan of the K'un Lun. I come in peace, seek only stillness, and offer amity."

Tilting its head once again as if listening not so much to his words, but to the echoes of his intentions reverberating from the cavern walls, the creature turned and then looked back at Yip as if he should follow.

So he did.

Taking great, loping steps through the snow, the Yeren's long legs keeping its torso well out of the drifts, he did his best to keep up, watching the flame of its essence float ahead of him through the white haze of the now blinding snow. Surprisingly enough, it did not steer clear of the glacier; rather it moved directly toward its center along the ice sheet's gradually advancing front. There, waiting patiently in the distance, its inward radiance a surer guide than any beacon, he could see it holding aloft a small white incandescence, signaling to him.

He knew then that the Yeren was offering him shelter from the storm.

Several minutes of hard running through waist and chest high drifts of snow brought him directly in front of the Yeren. Despite its inner tranquility, the creature was even more fearsome closer up.

Should it be angered, he could tell it would make a terrible, implacable adversary. Great curving teeth jutted from several places along its lips; long, thick gray fur covered its hirsute frame from head to toe much like a great mountain yak, two massive arms ended in hands larger than Yip's torso, and two twisted horns radiated out from its temples toward deep, ice-blue eyes that belied all other outward savage appearances and showed the true depth, warmth, and intelligence of its character.

Taking a brief pause before moving forward, he wondered how a creature so fearsome could have developed a voice so sweet. Perhaps the development of intelligence and introspection in this species ultimately led to a means of communication as deep, profound, and beautiful as their own insights.

Gently motioning for him to follow, the Yeren turned and bounded forward yet again. Following, he stepped out from the drifts into another crevasse very much like the one he had previously claimed for his own. Watching the creature disappear ahead, he admired its strength, fluidity, and economy of motion—traits that ran against any initial assessments based on its size alone. Sliding forward over the ice after the creature, he lost its light around a bend in the distance. Despite his best efforts, he could not keep up with a creature born of the snow and ice even on relatively flat unbroken ground.

As he rounded a bend behind the creature, already far into the heart of the glacier, he stopped, or rather slid, to a halt in complete disbelief. Eyes temporarily blinded, he looked out onto a world of light and splendor, all intricately crafted from flowing glacial ice.

All around a great central cavern, imposing lanose creatures like his guide walked and glided gracefully about, lost deep in song. They sang to the stone, they sang to the ice, they sang to the sky, and they sang to each other. As they sang, the earth moved, the ice shifted, the ceiling burned with constellations and brightness, and they nodded in recognition and agreement, thought and felicity.

Like the songs and the expressions of their intent that filled the air within and without, the Yerens' spirits danced and flowed elegantly and joyously around their physical forms—sails barely tethered to the masts of their beings, billowing freely in the winds voiced by their arias.

He did not know how he knew, but his presence was sung about and he was added to their story. Listening, his heart brimmed with gladness. To his eyes, the cavern gleamed with the radiance of a people at peace, making their way in the world as they should, open and responsive, filled with joy.

Bringing color to a landscape of blues, grays, and whites, plants, flowers and garlands of every color and variety hung suspended in the air in clear spherical miniature aquariums made entirely of magically created ice. Fruits, yams, potatoes, herbs, leafy greens, and other foods also floated within easy reach, sustained and warmed by the power of their song. Isolated within the ice, these creatures had created a world of their own, self-sufficient and glorious.

The light above shone brightly about his head, reflected many times over in the ice, and the walls opened to his passing as if he were at the center stage of an act's curtain call or entering a room to receive an audience with a king. Not far ahead, his guide waited patiently for him at the center of the shifting chamber beneath the crystalline ceiling lit by the songs of hundreds of Yerens, the Shapers of the True Song.

He could never expect to fully comprehend their song, convey the depth of their intent, or share the quality of their perception, but through their singing as they moved about the chamber, each adding to the other's story, he knew that they sensed something of his need and were offering him more than mere shelter from the storm. Although most continued about their business as if he had not even arrived, he could sense the depth of their feeling and the breadth of their compassion.

Bowing humbly to the room in general, showing his concern for all, he waited.

After a time, three more Yerens, each slightly older than the last, each with successively longer and more intricately braided mane-like hair, gathered with his guide opposite him in the cavern.

He bowed to them again.

Together they sang.

They spoke to him directly. Their story was different from the rest. They told of a distant place, a stable place, a land free and pure deep in the heart of the mountains. They sang of others of their race, some lost, some scattered.

They sang of home.

He could only partially understand what they told him as he was not listening with his ears or his mind but with his heart. He knew then that these people had been forced from their home long ago by an ancient evil. He knew that they were compelled to scatter throughout the mountains in order to hide and persevere. He knew then that they both shared a common enemy and similar intents.

And that was enough for them.

The oldest appearing of the four glided forward, great plaits of woven fur swaying about its neck. As it neared him, it reached into a pouch at its waist and held forth a necklace of braided hair that cupped a small reddish stone. Bound in its weavings, the stone glowed with light and warmth, inner radiance reflecting upon itself over and over in an unending chain.

At first, sensing its heat, he thought the stone was a token to keep him warm and provide illumination to help protect him from the cold, the raging of the mountain storms, and the harshness of the lofty environment. That is, until he reached out his small, steady hand and gingerly took the proffered item.

Warmth coursed through him and he knew the stirrings of hope, for here was a talisman of great power. This stone would do much to help him in his quest against the Cabal, of that he was certain. Placing the necklace slowly over his head, he bowed to each Shaper in turn.

Feeling the stone protect and reinforce his essence, the life the talisman now helped guard would be forever grateful to these gentle beings. Agents of Darkness might try to drain his essence, to steal his soul, to leach his strength, but so long as he wore this amulet, the Cabal would never sap his spirit.

And for that and for him, for his purpose and potential, the Shapers sang.

THE DRAKE SPIRES

Far away, distant,
lighter than the faintest clouds,
a lone pine stands on the ridge.

A week's journey downward over and past the first rocky crest of the great mountain chain brought him to a heavily wooded valley of ancient firs and spruce. Protected and sheltered by the surrounding ridges, fed by runoff from snow and glacial melt, saturated with minerals and sediment, the rich evergreen landscape formed a thick blanket along the feet of the soaring summits.

After leaving the pass above and behind, he seized the opportunity to enjoy the warmer temperatures and loosen his garb. With a new, thickly woven robe draped loosely over his shoulders and held securely beneath his small bundle, he was also much better prepared for the inclement weather associated with the high altitudes should he need it on his next climb.

As he trekked onward, his spirit lightened, feeling that others shared his hopes and desires for the future, offered support and aid, that he was not alone in his efforts. He carried his destiny forward with a buoyant heart even though he now bore yet another burden.

Looking upward toward the cloudy peaks, he wondered which crag held the lair of the terrible Dragon Sarugauth the Red, bane of the Yerens, usurper of their ancient home.

From what he could understand of their imagery in song, the Yerens had held their ancestral home deep in the heart of the Drake Spires, far away from other civilizations, pursuing the Shaping of their Song. After dwelling in quietude for so long, the Yerens must have been ill-prepared for the concerted onslaught of a foe as dark and insidious as the Cabal and their allies.

He did not know the true nature or extent of their power, but he could imagine the Yerens' voices raised together in song would ring to the heavens and call down powers that would daunt even the staunchest adversaries. In their telling, the Yerens lost their voices as the great drake rained fire and destruction from the sky, forcing them to scatter and flee. The ancient Red Dragon then took the Yerens' home for itself, and as far as the Yerens knew resided there still, claiming the valley and its immediate environs for itself and any of its remaining cohorts in the Cabal.

He could only conjecture how it had happened—whether Sarugauth the Red and the Cabal cast out a great cloud of silence, some noxious fog, or utilized another power or device to steal the Yerens' voices and stop their song, but whatever the artifice, the result was the same. Much like the priests in his order, the Yerens had lost their home and were forced to scatter and rebuild.

Whatever the Cabal had been after in the mountains, the true power and value in the Yeren people lay not in any artifact they may possess or the place where they dwelled but in the quality of their character and their song.

Cinching his bundle against his back, he walked forward through the thick boughs of many trees, squinting his eyes as he looked up toward the mountains above, wondering if his future would be as secure as the trees in this forest, or as uncertain as those people who scattered before the Cabal.

Looking at the lay of the valley as it curved north and slightly to the west, more peaks were in his future. Feeling the weight on his back grow a bit heavier with that certainty, he once again let his spirit brighten with the day. Birds' songs spread through the trees like strands of spider webs lightly floating in the breeze. The great fan-like limbs of the fir trees and hemlocks kept gentle time to the birdsong, needles quavering in the brisk air. Gazing intently at the deep green needles of a well-formed hemlock, he realized that these tiny leaves were slightly longer than his newly growing hair. Unused to the dark stubble under his hand after growing up in the monastery clean-shaven, he would have to let his hair continue to grow if he were to fit in as he moved to more civilized climes.

Switching his eye from his hand to the valley ahead, he could follow the contours of life through the valley as well as he could follow the lay of the land. Looking around, drinking in the day and all it contained, the halo of life's potential ran upward along the slopes of the mountainside in a shimmering curtain well beyond the borders of the forest. Like a haze of fog, wispy and diffuse, evaporating beneath the midday sun, energy interlaced the needles and boughs, surrounded the trunks and trees, and enveloped the valley in a supportive mantle.

Here, too, magic infused and fostered the growth and development of all that he beheld.

The scent of this year's fresh, light green flush of foliage strong in his nose, the soft cushion of last year's needles padding his step, he looked ahead and picked out his path up the slope for the days and weeks ahead.

BLACK HEARTS, KEEN AXES

A solitary rock
weary from its journey downhill,
rests perched on the hillside.

Given his current environs, his youth and training in the mountains of the K'un Lun were well spent. With an unending line of towering ridges between himself and the Green Run, the lower temperate mountains beyond the Drake Spires, his assorted skills in mountaineering, orienteering, climbing, risk assessment, pacing, reading and anticipating the weather, and self-reliance were all put to the test with each decision every day.

Even breathing was a danger. He had to be keenly aware of the thin air of the heights that could result in hypoxia for one without magical protections. Regulating his metabolic demands was of paramount importance not only to his health but in his ability to continue making sound decisions. Knowing that there was no one to help him should he make a poor move or should he have an accident, and further tempered by a healthy respect for the power and potential danger of the mountains, he was in no hurry to push forward without proper care.

Looking left and right, south and north, over the uncharted peaks arrayed before him as he climbed on and over open rock toward the next summit, each twist and turn affording new views of the range, he once again wondered where Sarugauth lurked and waited, biding his time for the Cabal's return. As his eyes moved north and west toward the wild heart of the Spires, he felt a slight warmth on his chest. Placing his hand on the source of the heat, he felt the firmness of the Yerens' talisman hanging on the woven cord.

Another hour of hard climbing yielded yet another beautiful snow-capped summit, his pragmatism once again realizing its own reward. Arrayed before him, gleaming in the clear spring air, row after row of peaks strove for the heavens.

The view put his journey into perspective. Despite making good time, he still had what looked like a lifetime of climbing to do even after this latest summit.

Taking a moment to relax and recover after his toils of the past and in preparation for the climbing ahead, he shut his eyes briefly to gather himself, letting his mind drift with the clouds above.

He followed Master Wei out toward the monastery's perimeter, where the long shadow of her tall stone wall cast deep pools of darkness over the bamboo, cherry trees, and ornamental gardens through which they passed.

"Where are we going, Master Wei?"

He was young, standing barely taller than his teacher's waist, and had not yet truly learned the value forbearance for curiosity tempered by patience often yielded rewards far greater than active inquiry alone.

"You will see in the fullness of time, my young one." Master Wei's knowing smile did not discourage Yip's curiosity, nor did it offer his inquisitiveness its reward.

He bowed his head in acquiescence, eager to see what adventure his teacher had in store for him next. Although young, he was bright and thoughtful.

He viewed all of his lessons as adventures, exciting challenges that were put before him by his guides. If he rose to the occasion, he moved on to the next challenge. If he failed, the same lesson; the same challenge, or one very like it, continued. Failure, and the reassurance for continual improvement that it provided, were his constant teachers as much as Master Wei.

Master Wei was the guide.

He was the arrow.

Only he could seek the target Master Wei aimed him toward.

Only he could arrive at the destination his teacher targeted.

He stopped his ruminations as his teacher's footfalls ended in front of him. Looking up, the sweep of Master Wei's arm encompassed a small open area surrounded by bamboo and cherries, largely shrouded by the shade of an ancient cedar, its massive, gnarled trunk nearly as wide as the clearing it sheltered.

In the glade's center, perched above small, loose pebbles and large, irregular walking stones were a series of bamboo poles arranged in an arch like a crescent moon. Their burnished golden brown surface reflected the sunlight above giving the clearing a warm, halcyon glow. Each sturdy pole rose a different height above the ground.

To his youthful imagination, the cool shadows and still stones below the bamboo curving upward irregularly from the ground reminded him of a small reflection pool. The bamboo appeared as lilies sprouting upward in place from the still waters envisaged in his mind, their pads the steppingstones below. His vision only lacked the beautiful flowers at the tips of the lilies' stems.

When the cherry trees were in bloom, he was sure the image would be complete, the flowers in place.

"What are these, master?"

"They are Mui Fa Jong. Plum flower poles."

He was right. They were flower poles.

This must be a meditation garden.

Sure that he had drawn the right conclusion, he asked, "What type of meditation will we do here, master?"

Master Wei smiled fully, his bright teeth now visible. "Meditations on balance."

He nodded, thinking of visualization exercises, already anticipating the direction of his practice.

Master Wei gestured toward the first and shortest pole. "Stand upon the pole, Yip."

He bowed at his teacher's request walking forward toward the plum pole. As he did so, he felt the loose, round pebbles give way and shift beneath his feet. He felt as though he were walking upon sand.

Taking one step upward as he reached the pole, he put his right foot upon the pole and stood, his balance uncertain and wavering as he moved, his center shifting irregularly as he changed position.

There was barely enough room for the width of both of his small feet to perch precariously side-by-side on the post's top. His toes hung over the front and his heels hung over the back. He could feel the corded soles of his slippers gripping the edges of the bamboo wobble, losing traction with each small compensating motion of his body.

Stretching both arms out to his side, he attempted to regain his balance. As he did so, he felt a gentle push in the small of his back. Falling, he stepped off the pole and landed on the rocks.

In his efforts to remain atop the pole, he had forgotten Master Wei.

Now holding a short staff in hand, Master Wei motioned for him to get back on the pole.

"Whether you stand on one foot or two, move forward or back, up or down, you must always move from your center. Let your balance be your guide."

When he nodded, Master Wei motioned toward the poles indicating he should try again. "Walk up the poles, Yip."

He stepped forward, letting his balance carry him forward from the first pole to the second. Before he had stopped and completely settled on the second pole, just as a smile was about to rise from the depths at his accomplishment, he felt the staff once again. Jumping down—for he was higher now—he landed softly on the loose pebbles, all thoughts of a smile now gone.

He understood then that his challenge had only just begun.

Not needing his teacher's reminder, he took to the poles again and again, each time returned to the ground by Master Wei's gentle push. He tried avoiding the staff, anticipating the staff, yielding before the staff, all to no avail.

Watching his student fall over and over in succession, Mast Wei only reiterated, "Only move from your point of balance, then right motion will follow."

As the morning passed and afternoon began, he was not so certain.

He had become very good at falling. He could not yet say the same about standing up.

Finally, after he had managed to make the fourth pole for the first time, thinking he had made quite an accomplishment in so doing, he asked, "Master, how long do I have to do this?"

Reaching up with the polished wooden staff, his teacher gently pushed him from his perch with its tip.

His face no longer brightened by a smile, Master Wei replied simply, "Until you no longer fall."

Blinking away the bright glare reflecting from the snow cupped in the cirques and hanging valleys laying below jagged arêtes, he returned from his reverie, his relaxation at an end, and began scanning the mountainside in search of the best route forward up and over the next ridgeline. In particular, he planned to look for any potential cols, mountain passes, that would safely shorten his climb over the next mountain. Looking left and right past the deeply shaded valley below, he shook his head in confusion and then rubbed his eyes for clarity at what he beheld.

As he scanned the ridgeline directly opposite, he realized that one arête horn appeared to have been hollowed out to make a rudimentary tower. Small windows dotted the sides like entrances to a termite's nest. He could see no ingress to the tower from this distance. Examining the mountain ridge with more care, he shaded his eyes with a free hand.

Peering carefully forward upon cresting the ridge, what at first he had thought were bright streaks and after-images from looking at the sun's reflection on the bright snow were now clearly laid out before him.

From his vantage point, the ridge across from his perch appeared suffused with lines of putrescent greenish yellow light, as if some glowing, malignant saprophytic fungus or mold were eating away at the veins and heart of the mountain. These lines seemed to fade in and out and pulsate with uninterpretable movement under the light of the sun. From the termini of some of these lines, what appeared to be dark smoke billowed upward in thin strands.

The smoke was not coming from fumaroles because these mountains were no longer volcanically active.

These cave entrances looked to have dark piles of rock or debris mounded beneath their entrances. These disordered heaps seemed to be the work of sentient creatures, not the basalt, rhyolite, or pumice indicative of natural volcanic flows. Interestingly, bright, ruddy red lights seemed to web or overlay the entrances to these caves. He could only conjecture that these were some form of arcane wards whether for warning or protection he could not say.

At the bottom of the valley, a vague trail or poor roadbed was clearly visible as it meandered irregularly through the center of the boulder-strewn valley. This portion of the mountains at least seemed to encounter significant use but by whom or what, he did not know.

Worse than the appearance of these putrid currents was the sensation of their actual presence. He felt the vile substance of their essence from afar, unclean and anathema. The defilement seemed to course through his veins, sullying his internal energy currents. As much as he was able, he closed himself to these energies, avoiding their unsavory taint.

Deeply troubled, for he had never seen or felt corrupted energy signatures like these, he doubted whatever created and originated such traceries was friendly. Looking ahead with revulsion, he would have to be especially careful picking his way over the next ridge for whatever could make a mountain appear sick, rotten, and decaying could look upon him as a similar opportunity to harvest. With a deep breath left steaming in the cool air, he began his cautious descent into the valley.

Two days later, carefully eyeing the path he had selected up the mountain from the far side of the sere gray valley, he was heartened at least by the fact that the streaks of bilious light only impinged upon part of his path. Although the energy currents tangled and wove their way throughout the mountain in a way much like wormholes boring and coiling inside a decaying apple, if he were careful he could minimize his crossing of them.

From this distance on the mountain, he could not yet tell what created the energy channels, but his first impressions were in fact correct. Although the mountain itself was not somehow rotten or diseased, whatever caused those lines was.

He sensed the presence of many twisted creatures ahead and was wary.

Picking his way cautiously up the steeply sloping cliff face, following the line of ascent he had previously selected, he kept careful watch as he moved forward, chary of what the future may hold on the face of the mountain. Thus far on his journey, he had happened upon his trials and adventures unsuspectingly and without warning. In preparation for this most recent ascent, he had had the better part of two days in waiting and anticipation for what he would encounter. The extra time, however, did not offer any reassurance for he still had no idea of what to expect.

The first day of his climb passed uneventfully, although quietly. There were no animal signs—no birds called, no animals left tracks or scat. Unlike other alpine valleys he had passed through that were full of grass and flowers or shrouded by evergreen trees, the vegetation here was sparse and windswept, forlorn and shriveled. The web of life normally cast so thickly and richly across the land here was threadbare and disheveled. He was left to walk up the mountain silently and alone, accompanied only by the soft crunching of rocks underfoot and the streaks of sickly green light looming above like deranged cobwebs.

That evening he took shelter under a large, rounded boulder, careful to lay flush with its dry, lichen-covered base to avoid presenting a ready profile should anyone or anything be on the lookout. His worries were unfounded, however, for his only companions that evening were the distant stars above, the rocks beneath his robes, and the cool wind running down the valley.

He woke up to a cool, halcyon morning covered in dew, sore from awkward albeit restful sleep, but ready to press on up and over the pass he had spied earlier. By his estimation, he would start encountering the noxious energy currents by sometime mid-morning.

He broke camp quietly and took care to mask all signs of his presence. After he was satisfied with his attempt, he strode purposefully up the mountainside, noting the curious rock formations that appeared above, the same ones that he had noticed with the smoky tendrils. These were now visible overhead on the rock face at the termini of the energy channels.

By mid-morning, he could clearly see that the large, unusual rock formations he had seen scattered along the mountainside were in fact great heaps of solidified slag and tailings abandoned from previous mining activities. The entrances to the caverns from which the waste was discarded were warded by particularly sinister magical webs. Without his inner vision, these wards would only be visible to those utilizing some form of magically enhanced vision.

Getting closer and closer to the energy channels as he climbed, he realized something else as well. What he had felt or interpreted as energy channels from a distance were in fact not continuous energy currents at all. Those lines appeared to be made up of thousands upon thousands of individual lights moving and coruscating beneath the hillside.

As he neared the lowest conduit, as best he could determine, there were apparently untold numbers of individual souls, toiling and moving along subterranean channels some indeterminate distance below ground. Even from this distance, he could feel the malevolence and hatred fueling their work. Instead of a putrid green, he felt that the hearts of those who labored below the mountain's dark face must be as dark as the coal and ore that they were mining.

Not only would he have to pick his way up the mountainside carefully to make the pass he had chosen but he would also need to be particularly careful in avoiding the areas around the warded piles of debris lest whatever moiled in the caves below spy him upon emerging to dump the refuse from mining. As such, his path up the mountain would be more indirect than he had first hoped.

Scrabbling over boulders and rocks, scooting across patches of dirty snow and loose scree, he made his way up the slopes trying to stay as far away from the underground caverns as possible. When he had to cross over an underground cave, he made sure to do so as far from the cave mouths and the beings working below as possible. Even though the creatures were below ground, their malevolence coated his passage like a dank, clinging fog. From his impressions as he moved far over them, he felt that whatever lay below was sentient and driven by selfish desires. Aside from vague feelings and urges, he could only tell that greed, hunger, and hatred were their primary drives.

Other than reading their distinct energy patterns, trying his best not to breathe too much of the acrid fumes filling the air, and avoiding their mining tailings, he encountered no other signs of the creatures below. He could not hear any sounds of their tools, if they used tools, nor did he see any other indicators of whatever activities occupied their days and nights below ground.

After another full day of climbing and hiking, he was ready for rest. Once again, he chose a spot isolated from both the tailings and what he interpreted as the underground labyrinth riddling the mountainside that the creatures used beneath him. After settling down, he relaxed and breathed deeply, letting all of the day's tensions subside. Within moments, he knew the peace and tranquility of deep sleep.

A thick haze of anger and tension, the froth of dark souls, accompanied by the harsh guttural sounds of an argument brought him quickly to wakefulness. He opened his eyes slowly and cautiously without any sudden movements lest he draw unwanted attention. In the distance, heated conversation flew back and forth. Looking all around, feeling for traces of any presence nearby, he was assured of his immediate safety. He sat up slowly and looked for the source of the commotion.

Above, what would appear as vague shadows to the normal eye were clearly laid out to his vision. Two large, bulky figures were gesturing at one another violently, accusations flying through the air. Dark green energy arrangements flared around them as they fought. To his ear, the din and oaths of their argument sounded more like the grunts, coughs, and clearing of the throat associated with dire illness than any language he knew or with which he was familiar.

As he watched, the being closest to the cave's interior lunged forward with a steady outstretched hand. The other arguer slouched and then slumped forward and fell to his knees in response to this abrupt movement. With a sure kick, the aggressor pushed the dying victim backward and onto the nearby jumble of slag before turning quickly and reentering the cave mouth.

Left to die lying on the heap of rocks and debris, the creature's life force slowly ebbed and faded away into the night.

He whispered a silent prayer for the creature's spirit.

If he had had any doubts as to the types of creatures he may have to deal with in his crossing of this mountain, those questions had been clearly answered.

He awoke well before dawn in order to resume his ascent with less risk of detection. From his angle below the site of the previous night's violence, he could not see the fallen's body, but, nonetheless, he wanted to clear the portion of the mountainside where any who may investigate could potentially see him before dawn. He also hoped to reach the pass by day's end, but given the fact that most of the day would be spent climbing sheer faces of rock, he doubted he would achieve his aim before sunset. Looking below, he could see the steep face of the mountainside tumble away rapidly beneath his feet. With a misplaced hand or an ill-advised step, he would tumble most of the way back down the mountain and meet the same fate as last night's victim.

As he climbed through the day, he gathered and directed *chi* to his hands to keep them warm from exposure to the face of the frigid rock. The *chi* flowing through him replenished the muscles in his arms and legs, fingers, and toes. He let the *chi* course continually through his body, lightening his mind and spirit, flesh and bones, to ease his efforts upward.

With the help of the *chi* moving in and around him, he was able to ascend at a rate as fast as most men could crawl on flat ground. Caution, ice, snow, and loose handholds, however, slowed that pace considerably, but his rate of progress was extraordinary by most standards nonetheless.

Toward mid-afternoon, he realized that, if he pushed himself, he would be able to make both the pass and the summit before day's end, but he might be unable to find a suitable spot for camping on the other side of the pass before darkness fell over the far side of the mountain. He did not want to risk both the climb on the far side of the col and attempting to find a safe place to camp in darkness. Spending another night on the mountainside would at least afford him the opportunity to scout the pass in lieu of crossing hastily in near darkness and risking potential detection as he made his way through the largely exposed expanse.

After yet another day of difficult exertion, he was quite glad to finally stop at the foot of the pass he had worked so hard to reach undetected. Above him, glimmering gold, white, and argent-blue in the light of the fading sun, a large expanse of snow gleamed as brightly as a highly polished gem—nacreous and lustrous as the ice crystals caught, reflected, refracted, and transmitted the sun's golden hues. Taking care to remain low, he nonetheless took the time to admire the beauty evinced by the snow's constant changes—melting, reforming, and recrystallizing continuously beneath the sun's rays. With the sun to his back and the gleaming snow ahead, the icy expanse stood in stark relief against the bright cerulean sky above the ridgeline and the dark, rough granitic rocks rising to either side. Thankfully, from this position, the pass was clearly hidden from view of the coarse-hewn tower lying atop the horn nearby.

Welcoming the nearness of his destination, he decided to spend the evening at the foot of the pass on relatively flat and stable ground. Given the accumulation of snow at this height on the ridge, he would be able to hollow out and pack down a depression suitable for sleeping in overnight.

After a little work, he looked down at the small cave he had dug out and shaped for himself beneath the snow pack. After breaking through the outer crust of frozen ice created from the snow melting and refreezing from the sun's rays, he had found little difficulty in digging out his small shelter. As he nestled in feet-first and looked up at his new roof of ice, he felt the warmth and reassurance of both his thick woven cloak and the talisman of the Yerens. Tonight, with any luck, he would rest under the snow as comfortable as an animal hibernating through winter in darkness.

Placing his hand on the slight but steady warmth of the talisman laid against his chest, he knew that if he were to learn more of the Cabal and find their former stronghold in the Spires, he would need significant help, not just to overcome any foe or obstacle he might face, but for insight into how best to move forward. Although he wished that there were friends to find on this side of the Spires, he would probably have to cross the entire range and reenter into the lands of civilization to find those who would be willing to accompany and aid him. After his experience looking out over the Spires a few days ago when the talisman responded warmly to his touch, he felt that when the time came, the Yerens' jewel would help guide him toward his goal.

With his hands laid upon his chest, letting the warmth of the *chi* flow through and sustain him, he began the short journey toward sleep and recovery.

Harsh winds overhead, the air whipping violently about his shelter, returned him to wakefulness some hours later. Climbing out of his small dugout and looking toward the sky, he saw that no stars were visible, only a low mat of gray clouds overhead. To the north, descending in a turbulent wall to the ground, snow was steadily wiping away the peaks as the weather front moved southward.

In preparation, he returned to his shelter, once again entering feet-first. With his torso partially out of the cave's mouth, he pulled more of the surrounding snow down and then over the entrance to his cocoon, sealing himself in as he built upon the edge of the entrance, slowly patting, smoothing, and closing out the storm and the night.

Closing his eyes to the darkness, he retreated inward to calm in advance of the raging blizzard.

Some hours later, he awoke to deep silence. Casting his mind outward, he could sense that the storm had receded and all was clear above. Digging carefully, bringing the snow down and over his shoulders, he emerged after a short time to a gloriously bright day. Checking for signs of the cave creatures on the mountainside, all appeared clear. There were no cavern entrances nearby and he did not sense anything along the ridge that might indicate a watch. Slowly making his way through the loose unpacked snow, he reached the southern rock wall sheltering the pass. With some firm footing beneath him, he made his way upward along the sloping face of the rock wall toward the summit.

After an hour's climbing, he finally made the ridgeline. Below him, the mountain swept away in a great arc. He could see the same signs of the subterranean delving, the sickening green tracery of the creatures below, and the warded cavern mouths. He would have to be just as careful going down the far side of the mountain as he had been going up. Looking along the ridgeline, the guard tower he had observed from the base of the mountain was not visible. For the time being, then, he would not have to worry about being observed from above through mundane means.

Looking forward as he turned toward his future, he saw that the next mountain stood in stark contrast to the barren peak on which he stood. Skirted in green, the base of the mountain welcomed the coming warmer seasons which came so late to the high mountains with a bright sheath of low-lying plants and grasses. About a quarter of the way up, the verdant greenery disappeared and rocks reemerged. Unlike the current peak, however, there appeared to be no signs of excavation or unwholesome energy patterns marring its surface.

Although as tall and prominent as the peak on which he now stood, the next ridge at least had a gentler slope and wider passes. He should be able to reach the summit with little free climbing.

Following the sweep of the mountain to its summit, he beheld another surprise. Perched atop the peak, an elegant alabaster tower stood opposite the coarsely formed tower atop this ridge. A single framed window was visible from his vantage. Lavender light spilled forth, silhouetting the snow and boulders along the tower's base.

He did not know if a Fang Shih had chosen this locus for its favorable exposure to the elements and to the primal Wu-hsing of creation, if a wizard had selected this spot for its isolation to pursue his studies and research in solitude, or if the location served as a sentinel against the creatures that waited in the mountain below. Regardless of the reason, he would have to be on guard yet again as he made his way over the next ridge.

Despite his caution, the energy currents he sensed from the next ridge were as clean and pure as those beneath his feet were defiled.

Not for the last time, he wondered how much more mountaineering was in his future as he journeyed westward in search of friends and allies.

He remained cautious in his descent of the ridge, taking pains to move slowly without disturbing any rocks, minimizing the sounds and signs of his passage, only occasionally glancing at the sculpted tower across the valley to wonder about its occupants and purpose. Despite being in view of the white tower, he remained out of view of the ill-formed tower above for the entire day's climb until finally, as dusk approached, he reached a level on the mountain where he could comfortably camp and look forward to a day without significant climbing on the morrow.

Laying low in the mountain's shadow beside a loose wash filled with rubble and scree, he was glad to see the mountain's steep slope subside beneath him. With a hard day's scrabbling and hiking over treacherous ground, he should be able to reach the valley bottom by the next day's end. After moving so cautiously over this loathsome mountain, he was looking quite forward to leaving it along with its distasteful memories behind.

Spreading out on his bedroll, he looked back up the mountain and retraced his path downward thus far. He could see the sickening delineations of intermittent lights moving along the pathways underground dividing the mountainside into partitions just as he still felt the unsavory energies of the place within the extent of his mind. Unlike the other side of the mountain, most of the cave entrance's appeared completely closed off and warded. He was not sure if that was in fear or for protection from the watcher in the tower on the other peak, or if the mining activities on this side of the mountain had been completed.

Either way, he was glad to see that he had almost completely passed out of the region of mining activity not only for safety's sake, but to be free of the unclean taint in the air created by the presence of those delving below.

Closing his eyes in relative content, he looked forward to at least one day's travel relatively free of worry.

He awoke once again covered in frost as he waited for the sun to crest the lip of the peaks above and bring a bit of light and warmth to the valley and mountainsides. He packed his few belongings quickly and broke camp cleanly so that he could take advantage of the long shadows cast by the rising sun for cover as he descended over the loose rocks.

He had not yet reached beyond the lengthy shadows of the slope to the bright morning sun before a harsh peal rang out and echoed shrilly across the valley.

His heart sinking, he looked up to the ridgeline where a deep bellow sounded from the crude basaltic tower looming overhead. Immediately following this second call, horn after horn began to sound along the side of the mountain. Deep drums began to thrum beneath him in the heart of the rock. Above him, a rough, guttural yell sounded from the tower overhead.

Bursting forward, he immediately began to run in response, throwing caution to the wind. As he ran, he lifted and sank the *chi* first to his *tan t'ien*, letting it build and energize his efforts. Then, letting the energy circulate and return to his extremities, he let the *chi* enliven and lighten his body. With the speed and grace of a snow leopard and the agility and sureness of a mountain goat, his feet skimmed the mountainside with the lightness of a summer breeze.

With the great sweep of the mountain's base yet before him, he chanced a look back up the mountainside.

Fear followed.

Pouring from hidden caverns and recesses, the bulky, misshapen forms of fearsome, armor-clad Orcs rumbled down the slope. The sounds of horns, drums, and harsh cries rolled before them in an avalanche of seething hatred as they brandished black axes and swords wildly above their heads. Moving among the Orcs, he could see the frightful shapes of gangly Trolls and the hulking masses of Ogres towering above their subterranean brethren.

He would stand no chance if he were caught. With the focus of one knowing he could die at any moment, that there was no option but success, he redoubled his efforts and sped away at a pace far faster than the dwellers of darkness could hope to muster.

As the distance between himself and his pursuers lengthened, he focused on the slope beneath his feet and the rhythm of his gait. He would have to pace himself if he were to both outrun his pursuers and remain far enough ahead of them to remain secure.

Rounding a massive boulder lodged in the mountainside, a castoff from another age, all thoughts of outrunning his foes faded away into happy imaginings. Barring the path before him, a massive Orc waited. Brandishing a jagged black axe in each thick, gnarled hand, dark scabrous skin covered in sweat, the steam of the Orc's breath clouded the air in an ill-omened fog.

Throwing his head back in challenge, both arms thrust out to the side, a deep howl issued from the Orc's throat.

Yip did not wait for the Orc to make a second mistake.

With single effortless leap, he sailed through the air between and above them, clearing the distance separating them before the Orc finished his fomenting yell. As the Orc brought his grotesque head back down after issuing his challenge, his savage eyes warily looking for his quarry, Yip caught the briefest look of surprise in the creature's eyes before his foot connected in a sickening *crunch* with the creature's face, snapping the Orc's head back violently.

Still aloft, the creature flew limply through the air beneath him, landing with a loose *thud*, the back of his head, shoulders, and heels leaving furrows in the gravel as the Orc's body skidded across the ground. Landing lightly on his feet beyond his fallen foe without breaking stride, he continued sprinting down the mountainside, hopeful that no more Orcs were lying in wait for him along his path ahead.

He had been fortunate that he had only happened upon one Orc as he sprinted lithely over boulder and stone, gravel and grit. If he had instead encountered a massive Ogre bedecked in full tempered plate mail, its thick hide and great, stone-grinding fists might have proven too great a foe for him as he made his escape in utmost haste. Similarly, if one of the wiry Cave Trolls had awaited him with sharp fangs and uncanny reflexes at the ready, he might not have escaped unscathed.

His time to abscond past, his time to flee dwindled with each head-long step rushing down the mountainside. As soon as an Orc shaman or a Troll witchdoctor reached the light of day, one whose magics could easily bridge the distance between them, he would have no counter to their spells, save avoidance, redirection, and guile.

With the cool mountain air caressing his cheeks and the eminence astir at his back, his only hope then was to outrun his foes.

Before his ruminations were complete, with the base of the mountain tantalizingly out of reach, unbeknownst to him, Yip's worst fears were quickly confirmed. High atop the ridge, blinking to clear the snow shimmer from eyes accustomed to darkness, just as Yip had so recently done upon reaching the summit, the shaman Gorthäk heeded the drum's call and made ready to smite the manling in his cowardly boots before he left the mountain of the dread Ar'thas Orcs.

Accompanied by deep drums and wildly blaring horns, Gorthäk began his chant.

Beating his chest, stomping his feet, and lashing his head first left and then right in time to the cadence, Gorthäk spat out the dark conso-nants of his spell in a frenzy, his words casting a pall over the bleak hearts of his retainers and guards, gathering internecine forces to his summons. As he moved, the air warped and bent around him filling with a wall of calescent air, the heat of the desert sun visiting the tops of the frigid peaks for the first time.

With a gesture of certain finality and a tremendous rush of calidity, an intense, swirling fiery orb leapt from his hand, charring the ground and melting snow as it sped down the mountain's great sweep.

Yip had only the merest seconds before being engulfed within the churning fires of the sun.

With the base of the mountain beckoning, he continued his flight. The gravel beneath his feet barely rustled with his passage. Accompanied by drums and horns, roars and yells from above, the only sounds of his flight were the soft rustlings of his robes and cape.

With only the barest of warnings, he sensed a turbulent disruption in energy careening downward toward him.

Reacting on instinct, responding before he had time to think, he leapt as far forward as he could, arching through the air in a graceful dive roll. A blast wave of superheated air caught him as he stretched upward and outward through the air in an exploding conflagration of flame and debris, flinging him far down the slope with the furious impact of the concussive explosion from the shaman's sunfire.

His robes singed, his cape smoldering, he tumbled down the hillside in a cloud of dust and detritus. Maintaining his focus, he remained relaxed, keeping his chin tucked tightly to protect his head and neck, continuing to let the *chi* flow as best he could to lessen the impact of his roll and keep his body light despite the turbulence and upset of the blast.

Remaining composed despite the duress of the moment, he let the force of the blast and his fall carry him forward, not resisting or fighting against the power that violently propelled him so savagely ahead.

Finally reaching his goal at the base of the mountain in a way he would rather have avoided, he rolled and lay prone, battered, bruised, and dusty on the ground, his spiraling, dizzying descent halted by a large, unyielding rock.

Winded, breathless, and aching, he made a rapid assessment of his condition before attempting to move, his eyes staring blankly at the sky. If injuries prevented further movement, he could remain in this position and almost completely empty his body of *chi*, letting his vital signs slip to almost nothing and enter into deep stillness so as to appear dead to his pursuers. He could not guarantee that such a ruse would work, but he would at least have the advantage of surprise should he have to fight.

After several long seconds, he was reassured that all was well, or as well as could be expected. He had several deep bruises on his thighs and shoulders and his right ankle was sprained. Given a few hours of meditation, he would be able to quickly repair the damage. Unfortunately for him, he did not have the luxury of time. Above him, the growls and calls of his pursuers were growing closer.

Despite the pain and shortness of breath from the impact of the fall, he returned to his feet, the *chi* soothing his aches and aiding in his flight across the valley floor once more, letting his breath and movement come naturally. Looking up above as he ran, the mountainside seethed as if covered by a colony of enraged army ants. Much closer, the black pit created by the shaman's explosion steamed and smoked, clearly outlined on the face of rock and snow.

Seeing all the Orcs' activity, he redoubled his pace, trying to keep as far away from the casters above as possible. Had the Orc been more skillful or more prescient, the shaman would have killed him where he stood without giving him the chance to read and react to the changes in the subtle patterns around him.

Step after jarring step crunched both with the pain in his ankle and the refrozen snow scattered in crisp patches beneath his feet. Despite the discomfort and anticipation, he ran over the harsh terrain as lightly as the breath leaving his lungs.

As he ran, he once again began to feel a slow gathering of energy overhead.

"Master Wei?"

He looked up at his teacher. Master Wei's kind face was silhouetted against the deep blue sky and the rustling limbs of old trees.

"Yes, Yip?"

"I watch the older students and they move so effortlessly, so fluidly, like the wind on a still day."

Master Wei's gaze briefly aligned with Yip's before returning to the winding loose stone path ahead.

"What should I do to move like them? How shall I manifest power so naturally? What is the secret?"

Master Wei laughed, his deep eyes twinkling. "There is no secret, Yip! Move naturally. Move how your body was intended to move."

Yip averted his eyes, downcast. "That cannot be all, master! Their motions are so much more!"

Again Master Wei laughed. "Are they? Those motions that you see as effortless are the result of countless hours of hard work. Natural motion is not expressed easily. Years of practice are sometimes required to overcome the habits that have become ingrained within us."

"What, then, is natural motion, master?"

"Ah..." His teacher smiled. "Always the deepest, most meaningful questions you seek to grasp."

He averted his eyes once more, slightly embarrassed by the indirect compliment.

Master Wei raised a hand to speak, as though beginning to diagram something in the air. "Natural motion is motion in proper alignment."

Excited to hear more, in an effort to clarify his teacher's response, he broke in, "Alignment with what, master?"

This time his teacher did not smile. "Always impatient for an answer, Yip. Truth, the answers you seek, does not come easily."

Chastened, Yip lowered his head.

Master Wei patted him on the shoulder gently, "Your curiosity will serve you well, Yip. The inquisitive mind is the one that deduces true insight."

He bowed, letting his teacher continue.

"Natural alignment is like the wind, it changes in response to its surroundings, their flow, the energy of the place."

"Alignment means proper structure and reaction across many dimensions. Alignment of the body, natural, always moving in a position of greatest strength, spine centered, one's body an unbroken bridge between Heaven and Earth."

"Alignment of the mind, at ease with one's surroundings and opponent, not separated or at odds with the unfolding present, unified."

"Aligned with the ebb and tide of events, the flow of combat, the flow of energy within and around you."

"Aligned with opportunity, countering with minimal effort, moving with greatest efficiency, striking with greatest effect."

"Alignment with the spirit, actualizing the most positive outcome, the greatest potential, the most beneficial expression of life unending."

"Alignment means motion in harmony with the greatest possible consequence, with both cause and effect, the moment and its import."

"Movement with perfect alignment means an opponent can never overcome you, for who can overcome the universe acting in accord with itself?"

When Master Wei had finished speaking, the gentle afternoon silence returned to the garden.

He bowed, thankful for his teacher's insight. "I have much to learn, master."

Master Wei laughed, his good humor and cheer washing over Yip like a cool, refreshing spring rain. "As do I, Yip! As do I!"

Humbled, he silently contemplated his teacher's words as they walked along the still garden paths, his mind tracing the wind's hushed movement as he walked.

High above, careening wildly to and fro on the hillside, the shaman Gorthäk cursed and spat as he made ready to begin another spell. Before beginning, Gorthäk glanced furtively to the tower above.

He must kill the trespasser!

The manling's survival made a mockery of the Ar'thas!

Gorthäk directed his rage, forcing it to fuel and kindle the power for his next spell—sparks of enmity and hatred inside that he would lash outward onto his loathsome quarry.

Swirling his arms more and more rapidly in concentric circles, the Orcs around Gorthäk watched as an angry gray cloud slowly began to coalesce over the valley floor, blocking their view of the fleeing human. As the shaman's ranting and gyrations began to peak, the cloud first sparked and then pulsed, backlit with ominous blue and purple flashes as lightning bolts charged downward through the ionized air and exploded in terrific peals of thunder from the shockwaves radiating out from the lightning bolts' strike path. Shockwave after concussive shockwave boomed across the valley with each tremendous bolt until Gorthäk finally fell exhausted on the ground, unable to maintain and direct the crazed energies of the storm any longer.

Yip knew that another attempt on his life was impending the moment he sensed the gathering power in the sky above.

As soon as the dark cloud began to form overhead and blanket out the sun, rapidly filling the valley bottom with charged energy, he anticipated and made ready for the violence of the coming storm. Scouting around quickly, he located a small depression away from boulders and any large projections above ground. Although there was no guarantee of safety because he could not predict the discharge path of lightning bolts, he hoped the depression would at least lessen the chance he would be struck directly or lie within the field of electric discharge once the bolts began hitting the ground. As the sky boiled and roiled above him and the hairs on his neck, arms, and head stood on end in anticipation of the impending tempest, he dove into the ravine and then squatted low, covering his head, trying to present as little of his body to both the ground and the air should the electricity discharge directly through him or through the ground nearby.

Within seconds, the earth erupted not twenty paces from where he lay huddled, showering him in a fusillade of dirt and rubble as the ground and air reverberated from the impact of the first bolts. Again and again lightning strikes landed both near and far, continually raining debris, mud, and shards of rock until finally a great blast struck and shattered a huge boulder some fifteen paces away, blowing him backward off his feet and out of his crouch, first stunning him from the concussive force and then knocking him unconscious as he hit the ground.

Some seconds later, he groggily blinked dirt from his eyes, blearily staring at the now-clear blue sky. Seconds passed interminably, the day seemed deathly quiet save for a loud ringing in his ears. Shaking his head, he heard vague noises in the distance.

Focusing his attention intently, he heard the faint sounds of drums and horns.

Why was there music nearby?

Trying wearily to sit, holding his head with his left hand, warmth on his chest brought his attention back in sharp relief.

The talisman of the Yerens at his chest was burning hot!

He was in the mountains.

He had been running.

He had been injured.

Orcs!

Turning his head sharply to look up the mountain behind him, the amassed body of the Orc tribe that had been so distant before had almost made the valley bottom just a few hundred paces away!

Now that his head was clearing, he could hear their curses and grunts, see their distorted, fanged faces, see their war masters urging the seething mass forward toward him at a fevered pace. Thickly muscled Orcs, their skin black and covered in soot, tall scraggly Trolls, loping easily behind, bright tufts of hair bobbing in the breeze, and massive Ogres, as large and solid as the boulders embedded in the hillside, were all rapidly converging on his position.

With a start, his heart racing, he leapt to his feet, keeping as low as possible lest archers come within range, and scrambled across the valley. His only hope of escape would be to outclimb the horde over the mountain ahead. That would only be possible if he could keep out of range of both archers and magic wielders.

Of that, he could not be certain.

Running at full speed, allowing the aching pain in his ankle, head, legs, arms, and back fade away with his full, deep breaths, letting the relaxed motions of his stride soothe any signs of tension, he made the midpoint of the valley basin ahead of his pursuers, the impacts of his stride now lightened by occasional clumps of interspersed patches of green grass, finally crossing the green demarcation he had seen from the peaks above.

Above and behind, the hills suddenly echoed in anguish, drums beat angrily, while the amassed Orcs and foul denizens of the depths waved their arms in impotent fury.

Turning to look at the source of the redoubled cacophony as he fled, he realized that his pursuers had miraculously quit the chase.

On the mountain top above, standing on the highest level of the ill-formed obsidian tower, his callused hands resting on the cold, carved stone merlon placed at the ready adjacent to his magma-forged black adamantium helm, the war chief Radok watched as the pitiful manling elusively avoided his reach.

Radok spat in displeasure and hatred.

He had wanted to dine on Man flesh this night.

Resting his eyes on the white tower opposite, Radok grunted. The manling had reached the safety of the Watcher's aegis.

Turning his head and grunting a terse order to one of his armored retainers, Radok's black, Hellforged armor drank in the day's sun. The war chief looked down at the cliffs below him where the shaman Gorthäk stood spent, weak, and dishonorable on the cold rock.

Failure was inexcusable.

The Black Mountain Orcs would have a new shaman initiated this night. Those shaman in the mines below who had not answered the call to arms in time would be flayed.

If there was any protest, they would be boiled in oil.

Radok's face split in a grim smile, his jagged yellow teeth making his visage even more menacing as he licked his dry, wind-parched lips.

Orc flesh would have to do instead.

Unsure why the Orcs had stopped when they had their best chance to catch him nearly at their fingertips, Yip did not hesitate to capitalize on his good fortune. Pressing on wearily, his capacity nearly spent, even augmented by *chi*, he slowly made his way through the boulders and interspersed grass to begin yet another climb through the unending peaks.

As he walked, he thought back to stories he had heard of Orcs and their kind, for until now, he had been lucky enough never to encounter them.

In a world like Ea'ae, where portals to other dimensions, other planes, and other universes were possible, the diversity and richness of creatures, good and bad, would always be a source of both wonder and potential danger.

Echoing this risk, some stories held that Orcs were not in fact native to Ea'ae, that long ago in times shrouded in memories long lost, the Orcs came to Ea'ae to pillage and ravage. But, as the stories go, they met their match in the foes they fought in arms on this world, getting cut off from their home, forced to retreat to desolate corners of Ea'ae where they are hunted and persecuted to this day, degenerating and losing strength all the while.

Other stories said that the Orcs were in fact brought in to Ea'ae for nefarious purposes, bought and bartered with for their skills at arms, to meet some wizard's or warlord's mad desires for power and conquest. Even though these original plans failed, the Orcs remained.

Still other tales averred that the Orcs' ultimate origin was not even on this plane. These stories hold that Orcs and their brethren are the fiendish hellspawn of an unholy dalliance of Man and Daemon. Although fearsome and hideous in appearance, the Orcs' limited skill in the higher arts of magic compared to other sentient races would seem to belie this line of thought.

Other tales held that Dragons of dark hearts and minds had created the Orcs after their light-hearted kindred had created the Elves. Although Elves deny the validity of this claim—both that they were created by Dragons when the world was young and that Orcs were created as an evil to counter their good—many scholars feel the two races' origins may be linked, either on this world or on another.

Whatever the Orcs' genesis, whether one of these tales or another, he was glad to be free of their pursuit, at least for the time being.

That night he camped on the upward sweeping slope of the mountain crowned by the white tower high above. He kept his back to a large, weathered rock free of snow on its eastern face, overlooking the valley in readiness should the Orcs decide to attempt subterfuge and take him in the dark of night.

Scanning the valley before sleep, he felt reassured for the only signs of the Orcs' benighted presence were the putrescent green lights underground and the dark columns of smoke issuing from the mountainside opposite.

He no longer felt the troublesome taint of their twisted essences. The slope on which he rested was as pure and enlivening as the other was foul.

His eyes heavy with fatigue and deep physical weariness, needing to heal, he slowly prepared himself to enter a profound, rejuvenating sleep, urging his body to mend and restore itself, aided by the intrinsic energies within and without. As the evening became night and his rest deepened, he was only aware that he was safe.

Under the light of a bright waxing moon, his rest not yet completed, his eyes snapped open in readiness, alert to possible danger.

He was no longer alone on the slope.

Hanging suspended in the air, its details indistinct and muted, a bright golden light hovered above him, highlighting his position on the cold stone of the mountain in a diffuse light much like that reflected off the moon above.

As soon as his eyes alighted on the hazy golden orb, a firm voice echoed deep in the chambers of his mind, easily bypassing any defenses he might have called upon. *"What do you seek on the mountain of Ilidian?"*

Scanning the light, trying to read its essence, its intent, its purpose, and power was an effort in futility. He could find nothing out about the luminescence, save that it was a projection from someone or something somewhere else. Other than that, whatever was behind the apparition was completely shielded from his senses.

For all intents and purposes whatever sent the light may not even exist as far as he could discern.

Honest by nature and intent, he spoke plainly, "I seek passage. Nothing more, nothing less." Filling in the silence accompanying his answer, his breath shone a faint silver and gold under the cool light of the moon and ethereal projection.

Almost as if he were talking with himself, the voice once again echoed within the confines of his own mind, *"Why does one such as yourself brave the Spires alone and almost completely unprotected?"*

"I seek assistance on the other side, for succor in a task of grave import."

There was a pause of several seconds after this answer and he felt rather than thought that his sentiments and motivations were read and weighed by someone far away.

"Your words ring true."

As the reply faded away in his mind and memory, he blinked, feeling a sudden surge and dislocation.

Opening his eyes, he looked out onto a lush green valley of a type that should not be present high up in the cold reaches of the Drake Spires, far removed from warm summers, cool springs, and long autumns.

Trees of every description filled the valley in a riotous profusion of green. Nearby, he could hear the sweet gurgle of a stream and, in the distance, the steady rush of a waterfall.

Looking back and up over his shoulder toward the top of the mountain on whose base he now sat, the beautiful alabaster tower he had expected was gone, its one open window left to spill forth bright lavender light on a mountain somewhere far behind in the heart of the Drake Spires.

THE TOUCH OF LIFE AND DEATH

A wild azalea
with blossoms of brightest orange,
offers rest to a tired bee.

The waterfall rushed around his bare shoulders, pounding his tingling skin, roaring past his ears as he stepped out from under the cascade and gathered his intention. Wading a few steps from the falls, he turned around slowly to look at the water droplets floating gracefully through the air around him, each brilliant and distinct, perfect in its bejeweled simplicity.

Standing framed against the falls, a golden haze of water droplets danced around him, lit by the sun above the apex of the falls.

Overhead, great hemlocks sharing space with ancient chestnuts, ashes, buckeyes, and oaks created narrow windows for sunbeams to light up the rhododendrons, laurel, birch, witch hazel, azalea, dogwood, and big leaf magnolia below, all finding room to grow around the same stream in the mountain valley. Soaring silver boled and golden leafed Aeryn, massive, overarching Senea, iridescent, heavenly Vaellorea, and firmament scraping Neana formed a super canopy of magical trees scattering light and life in luminous bands along the rich forest floor. Birdsong, insects, and the thrum of fey creatures large and small, all provided a fitting counterpoint to the soft chorus of the stream and the deep rush of the falls.

A tabernacle of green, yellows, and jewel tones around and above filled him with awe and wonder. The web of interactions, the vibrancy of the place, the life of the valley, filled his senses to the brim.

If he could call a place home, this would be it.

In a different time, under different circumstances, he might come back. But as things stood, with the Cabal hunting him and trying to destroy his fellows, to eradicate their purpose, the opportunity for the realization of such musings would have to wait.

Now was the time to remain vigilant, to practice while he had the opportunity, and then move on. Perhaps soon he would not have to run, but that option seemed a dream far distant.

Refocusing his intention, he brought his mind in from his surroundings, letting the web of energies around him fade into the distance while bringing the Light of his self to a single point in his mind.

Moving from this central point, he then quickly began to circulate his spirit, his *shen*, through his energy channels along the microcosmic orbit in his torso. Gathering more and more energy with each revolution up his spine and over the crown of his head as the *chi* moved back down to his energy center in his navel, he finally directed his spirit upward and outward from the *yin-t'ang*, the point between his eyebrows.

With a sudden thrust of his intention, the golden Light of his awareness burst from his body, guided by his hand, as he shouted, "Pai-lien!"

The world around him rushed back in along with his spirit, filling his senses with the web of life unending around him. With the return to self, he looked past the stream and over at the lichen-covered rocks he had stacked a few feet distant.

Bowing his head, he sighed.

The rock he set up as a target across the stream had barely moved in response to the forces he had directed outward.

Spiritually spent, he gathered his belongings on the shore and continued onward toward the west, directing his internal energies back to his navel.

The land he now found himself in differed significantly both from the lands he had just left and from the lands from which he had climbed on the far eastern slopes of the Drake Spires. Gone were the tropical jungles with layer upon layer of vegetation competing for light, magical energies, and space on and within every nook and crack under the canopy. Gone, too, were the sere, rocky, frozen valleys of the heights and the open, bare stone faces of the peaks.

The land here was composed of old rolling mountains covered in tall, temperate variegated forests with multiple layers of undergrowth. Mantles of mist and fog added a feeling of mystery and a sense of timelessness.

Compared to the peaks from which he just left, these mountains were mere hills. However, though time and the elements had eroded the mountains here down to gently rounded peaks, age had granted these mountains character and variety, multiple niches filled unique endemic creatures and landforms. Where the Drake Spires stood young and proud, tall and soaring to the heavens, the Green Run, hunkered down, relaxed and worn, bearded with vegetation, and were granted distinction through time.

To him, each step in his journey offered new marvels.

Following the stream fed by the waterfall downhill, he made his way to the valley bottom over round moss and lichen covered rocks, past stately maples, cherries and oaks, hemlocks, hickories and chestnuts, Vaellorea, Aeryn, Senea, and Neana, through copses of rhododendrons and ferns, azalea and red bud. Other more luminous fey species predominated as well, though he knew not all their names.

As he neared the valley bottom, the trees grew taller and straighter, spread farther and farther apart, given the opportunity to reach their full potential after fierce competition for light and energy during growth and development. The broadly branching, leaf-covered limbs of the stately trees gently caught the light of the sun, tinting its rays a soft dappled greenish yellow, the beams molded and shaped by the form of the leaves through which the light passed. Still others colored the light in various prismatic splashes of color, dependent upon the tree's nature and the presence of any magical symbiosis.

As in the jungle before, the eldritch and mundane blended together in a beautiful tapestry. Stately trees reaching toward the sun were covered in multifaceted, crystalline scales scattering the sunlight in bright prisms all the while soaking in and transmitting the ambient magical energies pervading the valley. Large, granitic rocks laid bare through time by erosion, wind, and rain were covered with profusions of coral-like carbonaceous growths—fronds and frills, polyps and filaments, spirals and whorls strained the air of *chi* in bright profusion. Long, translucent filaments danced in the breeze, akin to spiders' webs without multiple moorings, channeling energy to tiny spinnerets attached to host tree limbs and branches. Here, too, wonders abounded beyond counting.

Despite the beauty of the place and forms, he knew to keep his distance. The myriad delightful plants and creatures were not without defenses. Should he venture too close, he may be shocked, blasted by force, stunned, beguiled, or something worse.

He occasionally paused to examine the light interplaying with the shadows falling on the leaf litter from the limbs and leaves above— gently rounded and knobbed shadows from white oaks; long and sharp with serrated tips from chestnuts and chestnut oaks; slightly rounded oblongs from hickories, magnolias, and ashes; sharp, branched angles from red oaks and maples; linear, straight complex shades from hemlocks; riotous overlapping palmate geometries from walnuts; among many others—all shifting and morphing with the breeze and the swaying of the limbs and trunks above.

Walking downhill, the steady call of the rushing water muffled his steps, lending a rhythmic chorus to the songs of birds and insects, the chatter of faeries and nymphs. Caught in appreciation for the sights and sounds around him, the complex array of life and energy merging and dancing within and without, he slowly began to pick out the words to a deep song blending seamlessly with the music of the stream. By the time he finally reached the valley bottom where the brook spread out into a wider bed and a more relaxed progression, he could make out the words.

> "Far from home,
> left to roam,
> desolate as the hills.

> Heart laid bare,
> burdened by care,
> whither shall I go?"

The deep baritone carried between the trunks and leaves, over the rocks and stream in a regular refrain.

Following the runnel's progression through the valley, he would encounter the singer in short order. Taking care to move quietly, he skirted the brook and moved a bit deeper into the woods, prowling quietly through the dense undergrowth taking advantage of the moisture and light along the water's edge to grow so thickly.

Casting his senses forward, he felt for the singer's presence as he moved downstream. He sensed a strong entity ahead, full of positive energy, but tinged by a deep, pervasive disquiet.

Nearing an opening in the canopy created by the overarching limbs of a giant sycamore tree, he finally saw the source of the steady refrain.

Sitting across from him, leaning against the thick white trunk of an ancient tree, was what appeared to be a man dressed the light brown leathers of a huntsman—a loose, deep green cape thrown casually over an animal skin jerkin that was tied down over a suede doublet with well-worn suede breeches tucked into calf length leather boots. A large, well-formed bow lay propped against the tree by his right side next to a massive ironshod great staff and a full quiver of arrows.

Yip blinked, all this appeared perfectly normal to him until he realized that the huntsman's shoulders were as wide as the massive forest giant growing behind his oversized frame.

His sense of scale temporarily overturned, he blinked again. The huntsman must stand at least three times his height! The arrows in his quiver were as long as Yip was tall, more like spears than arrows. The war staff at the ready by his shoulder was more akin to a tree trunk than a walking staff.

He also recognized the giant as a being of some power.

To his inner vision, a halo of light silhouetted the giant's shoulders in a deep, earthy green. Unlike his teachers, whose regular exposure to and manipulation of *chi* appeared to become less and less localized, moving more and more generally through the whole being with practice until the entire body radiated Light, the giant's essence appeared very different. Looking at the figure closely, he could see the shimmering outlines of well-defined etheric channels laced throughout his body, as if long years of magical usage had crystallized the areas through which magic normally passed into an abiding form of magical structures and conduits—heartwood within an ancient tree. The giant's skeleton and organs, skin and ligaments, tissue and sinew, all seemed to be reinforced by this radiating energetic effect very much like some Iron Shirt *qigong* practitioners he had seen in the past.

Despite the giant's inherent might, the energy around him sparked and jumped, roiled and frothed as if he were greatly disturbed.

His weapons and items, too, displayed great, deep-seated power. They appeared ancient, the energy within established and reinforced with the passage of long years.

Taking a full breath, recognizing the potential danger, he stepped forward casually with one hand held in the air peaceably, offering, "Hello, friend."

The giant moaned softly.

Yip bowed respectfully. "I am Yip Chi Chuan."

He paused for a moment waiting for a response. When none was forthcoming, he continued, "Your song is most touching."

The giant moaned again.

Still cautious, even though all his impressions showed that the giant was of an intrinsically peaceful nature, he asked, "May I come forward?"

The giant merely stared at Yip tiredly.

"Perhaps there is some way I may be of assistance?" Compassion and concern were his natural response to one he felt was in need.

The giant sighed, bringing both hands up briefly in a shrug indicating his state of desperation. "I am lost."

Looking again at his garb and equipment, one so well-equipped and obviously experienced in woodcraft was not physically lost. Perhaps at a loss or hopeless, perhaps confused about his situation and what to do, but not lost in the usual sense.

Yip tried again, taking a different tack, "Perhaps you can help me."

The giant looked up in vague recognition, actually acknowledging his presence, gazing at him skeptically through his own cloud of confusion.

The giant's deep voice answered, "Perhaps."

"May I be seated?" He gestured to a spot opposite the giant on the ground. Even standing, he was shorter than the giant was while sitting.

The giant nodded.

He sat down lightly, letting his legs fold naturally beneath his robes, "I am uncertain as well, my future unclear. Perhaps we can find our way together."

The giant let out a deep sigh once again and his great shoulders slumped in defeat. The whoosh of air from his exhalation was strong enough to rustle Yip's now singed, well-worn robes. He felt the giant's breath directly through a number of these newly minted holes.

His clothing was in dire need of attention.

Apparently this approach would not work either. If the giant's spirit were so broken that he was not willing to work his way out of his depression with another's offer of assistance, then he would have to be more direct.

He looked the giant squarely in the eye where he sat.

"A man is never lost when he knows who and what he is."

"I am not a man."

"But you are a sentient being. You sit opposite me, your reality and presence clearly evident." He paused. "A being in full possession of his senses is only lost if he believes he is. Otherwise, he denies his place in the universe and his sense of self."

"Do you deny my reality?" An edge of anger appeared in the giant's voice. "If so, I will be more than happy to prove it to you."

His ploy was working. The giant's ire was bringing his attention back to the present and out of the quagmire of his thoughts.

"Of course not. I merely question the focus of your attention." Yip's gaze did not waver. "I am confident of my place in the universe. I believe that you, too, are all too aware of your own position. Perhaps that is the difficulty."

With that the giant offered a reluctant, "Perhaps."

The giant took a deep breath and exhaled strongly, rustling Yip's robes once more.

"I may be able to help your perspective, if not your situation, if you will let me."

The giant looked at Yip skeptically.

"May I try?"

The giant gave a curt nod. "If you try anything out of bounds, I will crush you."

He smiled ruefully. "Of that I have no doubt."

Slowly leaning forward where he sat cross-legged in front of the giant's broad form, Yip brought both hands together cupped to the giant's face. Gently closing his eyes so that his eyelids barely touched together, he brought a soft inhalation of the giant's breath inward and down to his *tan t'ien*, swirling and mixing the ambient energy taken in with his breath. After a time, eyes still closed, he then exhaled lightly into his cupped hands, slowly circling the *chi* where it swirled above his palms, commingling with the breath.

As the giant watched, a soft blue radiance twinkled faintly like stars in the night sky and began to circulate in the small man's inter-linked hands with each slow breath.

Eyes still closed, Yip felt the energy held in his hands coalesce and circulate. With a final exhalation, he blew the cupped force outward. Blue light scattered, motes of dust catching and reflecting the sun's rays as azure became green under the golden light from above.

Watching calmly, his concerns temporarily forgotten, the giant breathed in the clear light of hope.

As the giant sat in place, his hands resting lightly on his thighs, his eyes now closed and facial features temporarily relaxed, the tension released from his broad shoulders and back. Yip waited patiently in place until the giant finally opened his eyes and let out a full, deep breath.

Looking directly into Yip's eyes, the giant said, "I thank you, Yip." The giant took another deep, smooth breath. "You have given me assurance where I felt I had none and of that I am grateful."

To Yip's eyes, the light of the giant's spirit shimmering around his physical form appeared smoothed, less turbulent, significantly less troubled. "As I said, I cannot solve your problems for you, only you can do that, but I can offer you a fresh perspective on your situation."

With a short nod the giant offered his name, "I am Goran of the Indural." With a full bow from the waist, he finished, "Forgive me my troubles. My heart opens to yours in welcome."

Yip bowed where he sat in return. "Your health is my pleasure."

The giant, now at ease, looked off vaguely into the forest as if trying to see something far off.

"What troubles the spirit of one so strong?" asked Yip.

Returning his gaze to the small man before him, the giant stood smoothly, the economy of his motion belying his great size. Yip stood as well, barely reaching the giant's knees.

"Walk with me through the forest and we will talk, Yip." Looking to Yip for consent, the giant asked, "Which way does your journey take you?"

"To the west."

"Then let us be off."

As they walked, Yip marveled again at the ease with which the giant moved through the forest. Despite his bulk, the giant moved so smoothly and facilely through the undergrowth that the tree limbs seemed to almost move out of his way. He was unsure if this ability came with training, was something intrinsic, or was part of an enchantment that he was unable to detect for the power radiating from the giant was complex and not easy to translate.

His curiosity getting the better of him, he inquired directly, "Your movements belie your size. Few move as easily as you, much less of your stature. What is the source of your competence?"

The giant sighed again, although he sensed this response was not from the same fit of deep depression as before.

"Have my people diminished so that the Indural are no longer known among Men?"

Once again Yip offered a short bow, "My apologies, Goran, but I am from a land very distant from this one. I have spent much of my life in isolation as have my fellows. I am merely curious. I meant no harm."

"No, Yip, I should be the one to apologize. Your question merely hit close to the root of my depression and I responded unfairly."

Looking up from his side, Yip waited for the giant to elaborate.

"My people have been the stewards of this land—the Green Run as it is called among Men, El'alen among the Elves, or Aldael among my kind—since the world was young. Whatever the name, we call it home."

"We Indural were the first of native flesh and blood to call this world sacred and strive to protect its beauty, peace, and spirit."

"There are others who still guard the wilds of Ea'ae—the Druids, trained in the ways of the earth and spirits, our first students in ages long past; the Elves whose hearts know no separation from the land on which they tread, even though their kind is not native to Ea'ae; the Yerens whose song at one time rang to the heavens, but whose voice now remains muted in hiding; the Karadüm, brother giants of stone known to guard sacred places across the breadth of the world; among others whose duty falls along similar lines and motivations."

Goran paused, his heart heavy.

"Such obligation always comes with a heavy price. Ea'ae can be a harsh place. As you know, our world, like many others, does not brook weakness. Keeping the wilds safe allowed my people to be free and at ease in our own minds, comfortable with our place in the world, but we have made enemies, many enemies. While we protect the wilderness from those who would harm it—Orcs, Ogres, Kobolds, Goblins, Gnolls, among many others far worse—there are none who protect us."

The giant shook his head sadly.

"I now wander the land not only to protect what I hold dear, but to try to find it. For although my charge is still here to protect, those who guard it are few. I am among the last. I may, in fact, be the last."

"So, in answer to your earlier question, although I may not have gone astray, I feel at times that my spirit has, for my people may be lost to the halls of memory. I have seen none of my brethren alive for many long years."

Yip's heart went out to the giant, for his was a story much more common than one would ever expect or wish to hear. In his short journey thus far, he had already experienced other similar heart-wrenching tales. His sincere hope had always been that more and more Lights would be created throughout the world while the priests were in hiding—Lights to uphold virtue, truth, and the continued development of the human spirit in whatever form it took. Now that he was out wandering the world at large, he was finding that many such Lights were disappearing, much diminished, or forced into hiding.

While some Lights waned, others still grew, he knew. The power of Man and Elf flourished and spread on this world and many others. The reach of Dwarves was still long. So, although much endemic tradition, noetic and gnostic development, and culture was lost, more moved in from other sources to replace and fill those voids created by the passage or declining of what had been.

Goran's tale of heartache was not at an end. "The barriers protecting this world grow thin, Yip. The Shadow rises and yet we wane."

"Though I have not walked with my brothers in years counted as lives among Men, I have seen my kindred's downfall, returned their corpses to the ground, and cast their ashes to the wind."

His eyes far off and distant, Goran held his lips firm with a mixture of sadness and resolution. "The Shadows that once haunted Ea'ae's distant past have returned taking my kind with them."

"I fear I am the last of the Indural to stand against the tide."

Yip gave the giant a short bow of acknowledgement, his eyes filled with sympathy and emotion. Although there was so much he wished to convey, there was just too much to express for a single gesture to encompass how he felt. So he offered a bit of his own tale and perspective. "I, too, am the last of my kind to freely wander Ea'ae."

"I, too, stand alone against the Darkness."

"I, too, have watched my fellows fall."

Yip sighed.

Goran's patient gaze waited for him to continue.

As he talked, Goran watched him curiously. "My kind has been forced into hiding as in the days of old. I now journey alone, in search of assistance, that I may make Ea'ae safe both for our return and for all who share this world with us."

"What is it that haunts your kind, Yip?" No stranger to danger and enmity, Goran sought to know the root of the evil that he, too, may one day have to face in order to make ready, fearing that this threat may be the one he already knew, the one that had claimed his kin.

"We run from our darker shadow." Yip sighed again. "Most know of them as the Cabal. We call them Liúxīng Làngrén, those fallen from Heaven's path. My brothers thought they had destroyed the Fallen long ago."

Shaking his head with a complex mixture of emotion, he went on, "After the Cabal's defeat, my spiritual forebears chose self-imposed exile as punishment for inadvertently giving birth to such an evil. Now, thousands of years later, shortly after we reemerge into the world at large, little over a generation in the time of Men, we find that the Cabal is still strong, that they are seeking to regain a foothold on our world, and that they are weakening the barriers protecting this world from encroachment by extraplanar Powers."

"For a second time, we chose exile after the Cabal attacked us directly. This time exile was accepted as a necessity for self-preservation for we, too, are much diminished in both power and numbers by our time in isolation. Thinking the world safe, many of our great masters chose to leave their corporeal forms while we waited in exile. Their skill and knowledge would be of much use now, but such is not the way of events."

Goran responded gravely, "Many of my ken were lost ridding the world of that Darkness and their ilk, long ago. I still bear scars from those battles. I am loath to see their return."

Shaking his head, Goran added flatly, "But return they have. I would see no more lost, Indural or others."

Goran paused, asking, "Are you a priest?"

Yip shook his head. "I am an initiate, but have yet to complete my training."

Goran responded with a smile. "I thought not. There are few who would remember your kind, I imagine."

Yip nodded in silent agreement. Perhaps his kindred would be lost to the halls of memory as well.

The two walked side-by-side in silence for a time, engrossed in their own concerns, making peace with their own thoughts.

Finally, Goran broke the silence. "Yip, would that I were in a position to accompany you in your quest, but my obligations to my own people and land come first."

"Do not worry, for our purposes run parallel. I will aid you when and how I can when the time comes, if you need my services at arms or assistance. Unfortunately, at this time I can only wish you well on your journey. I will, however, try to guide you toward those who would help and ensure your safety along the way."

Musing out loud, his hand placed lightly on his chin as if to rub a beard that was not there, the giant said, "I feel that the Elves will help when and if the time comes, but they will not offer much in the way of succor until then. They would face the Cabal directly for their own reasons on their own terms without an external mediator. The Dwarves as a people are too caught in their own clannish ways to unite until the situation is most grave. They will not act preventatively unless the threat is immediate and direct to them."

"Hmm..." Here Goran paused. "Perhaps the capricious nature of Man's adventurous spirit would be most amenable to your cause."

The giant stopped, looking down at Yip where he stood by his side. "What you need, Yip, is a band of foolhardy adventurers, a group whose heart and courage come in greater measure than their pragmatism or good sense."

Goran laughed at the thought, the sound akin to thunder and the cracking of tree boles under great winds. "Walking the wilds of this land over the ages I have met more than my fair share and, I mean this as no insult to your kind, the majority have been Men."

He pointed in the direction in which they had been walking. "The one place on Ea'ae with more adventurous thrill seekers than any others is Tellanon, floating far above the western shores of Dharia, a nexus place for interstellar trade and exploration. I cannot take you there myself, but I can put you on the way toward it. I will start you on the course to the nearest human outpost. They will be able to guide you from there."

"I thank you for your help, Goran. That I may finally find assistance lightens my spirit and burden. For my part, if I can help you locate those of your kind or assure their safety, I will. Unfortunately, skill of the sort needed may be outside my realm of ability."

"And I thank you as well, Yip, both for your gesture and your kindness."

As they walked together under the boughs of massive trees, following the gently winding course of the clear stream, Goran told Yip stories from when his people were young, of times when Man first came to Ea'ae and sought the giants to learn the ways of magic and the land; of the arrival of Elves, Dwarves, and Orcs to Ea'ae; of days long ago when Dragons' wings shaded out the sun and the world knew no conflict, times when giants and drakes worked together with common cause.

The world had changed much in the giant's time and would continue to change long past it.

By that evening, Yip and Goran reached the far end of the valley and made ready to camp beneath the eaves of an enormous, straight trunked chestnut tree. Thankfully for their prospects of a good night's rest, they were too early for the tree's nuts to drop, covering the ground in spiny green burs.

"You have chosen a wondrous portion of the world to live in here, Goran."

To his senses, the land around him flowed with *chi*, bright and luminous, deep and rich as the forest blanketing the hills. As dusk laid its gentle hand over the canopy and understory, the *chi* still flowed as bright and pure as the sunlight that was steadily fading away into night.

Goran nodded. "This place reminds me of the world of my youth, before the land knew the hand of Man and Dwarf, of axes or of the will to wield them. But even here, beneath this calm, there is always danger."

"With the Cabal's return, there is yet more."

Taking his massive gray staff from where it rested by his side, Goran lightly touched it to the ground in front of where they sat. With a short incantation uttered under his breath, a small floating flame came into existence, giving off light of a brightness and quality equivalent to natural sunlight.

"Would you like anything to eat, Yip?" Goran smiled, as he looked down toward his small companion, "Or have you moved far enough along in your training to have already given up the pleasure of a good meal?"

Yip smiled and gave a short shake of his head. "I see you have spent time in the company of priests. I need harm no plant or animal to subsist."

Now it was Goran's turn to smile, "Nor I!" With another deft wave of his staff, a plate of steaming roasted quail, vegetables, and assorted fruits materialized on his lap.

Yip bowed in turn, glad of the sport.

The two traveled westward together the next day, traversing a deeply wooded, sheltered valley cut only by the passage of time and the flowing of ever-present dripping and running waters, their footsteps muffled by layers of deep leaves; crossing steep ridges strewn with mossy rocks and gnarled vegetation whose final growth and form was determined by exposure to harsh winds and winter chill.

Overhead, the leaves on the stately trees appeared encrusted with precious stones. Bright jewel tones caught the sunlight in rainbow hues, casting light from multicolored prisms along the forest floor. Yip could see both the glow of the sunlight through the inlaid crystals flecked on the greenery and the magical energy flowing through the air and into the trees as a result of their presence.

After their initial conversations on the first day, much of their time together was filled with silence, the air brimming with the sounds of the world around them and their appreciation for it.

As they descended into another lush valley, trees lined with soft moss and lichen, leaves shining with crystal adornment, Yip asked,

"How far will I have to travel before I reach the nearest human settlement?"

Staring off into the distance, Goran took some time to answer, "At the pace we have been traveling, you should arrive at Shady Vale within three to four weeks I should think."

"Shady Vale?"

"Aye. It is a small, mostly human, outpost in the heart of Aldael. Perhaps someone there will be able to guide you further toward the assistance you need."

He nodded, glad for the hope Goran's words instilled.

As they clambered down the steep slope, Goran pointed across the valley to the opposite ridge, "When we reach the heights beyond the far ridgeline, past the next valley, we will be able to see Ylldel, the Mountain Father, home of the Karadüm. If you follow the ridgeline to the south, you should be able to find your way to Shady Vale without difficulty and in relative safety. This portion of Aldael is relatively free of strife."

Yip's heart leapt with joy. Soon, if all went well, he would be able to begin his quest in earnest and start searching for a means to rid the world of the Cabal once and for all.

EMERGING SHADOWS

Darkness falls complete
on downy wings of silence.

The mind shrinks,
a limitless point unbounded.

Thrak hated guard duty.

He loathed guard duty almost as much as he despised the things he had to guard against.

Glaring past the fire where he warmed his scaly green hands, beyond the rough-hewn cave entrance, trying to glare through the snow pelting the mountain all the way to the Watcher's tower beyond, he spat.

If the fire didn't keep him warm, at least his seething hatred would.

If that miserable hairy, man-ape had not come prancing through the mountains the week before last, he might still be enjoying the solid heft of a whip in his hands and the heat of working in the mines below. Looking around furtively, lest his thoughts incriminate him, he stole a glance down the gloomy passageway to ensure that he was alone. If the war chief himself had taken to capturing the human, Thrak might not be here as well.

He could not help that one weak novice shaman had failed in killing the monkey-man. Not all shaman would have failed. Not all shaman needed to be relegated to menial tasks. That he was deep in the mines and could not reach the surface when the drums beckoned was beyond his control!

He had underlings to spurn, Orcs to whip, and work to foment!

Thrak turned away from the cavern mouth to angrily grab another lump of coal to throw on the flames. As he bent down, his eye caught the fire's shadows dancing across the coarse stone wall.

Odd.

He blinked.

One shadow seemed out of rhythm with the rest. And darker, much darker! Turning quickly in alarm while reaching for the black, rune-etched dagger at his side, the words of an incantation dying on his lips, he froze in place as pain exploded in a light brighter than the most intense star behind his eyes, molten slag burning through his mind. His legs twitched uncontrollably in reaction to the pain while his bowels relaxed and spittle flew from his mouth with each paroxysm.

Only vaguely aware of anything beyond the exploding constellations of pain, something was in his mind, something horrible! Probing, probing deeper and deeper, draining all thoughts and feelings in a relentless tide.

With a final jerk, darkness and blessed peace descended and he knew no more.

The Orc's body twitched and shuddered suspended above the floor, dangling speared from the arm of a Darkness deeper than any within the ruddy depths of the cave. With a final shake, the Shadow released the corpse, withdrawing its hand from within the Orc's still-intact skull. The Orc's body hit the floor with a soft *thud*, as if the majority of his bulk had been sucked out, black ethereal smoke snaking from his mouth, ears, and eye sockets.

The Orc's shattered corpse lay abandoned and forgotten in the cave's gloaming.

The Shadow glided off into the night, untouched by snow and wind.

The priestling had been here.

His skills had grown.

He was becoming more elusive, his traces harder to read.

He would perish like the rest.

THE CIRCLE AND THE STONE

The spring falls lightly
upon the old timeworn hills,
shrouded by sheer mists.

As they began to descend into the next vale, the deep loam cushioning each step of their descent through the rhododendron thickets, the sun's golden rays a warm welcome presence on their shoulders, Goran stopped unexpectedly, sniffing the air, his nostrils flaring. He then raised his right hand up over his shoulder, rotating his hand, palm flat, fingers together, slowly back and forth.

Yip could see energy flowing into Goran's hand, a faint tracery flowing upward from the valley below, ripples in a pond returning to the source of the disturbance.

After a time, Goran asked, "Do you sense it?"

Although Yip's sense of mind could not encompass the entire valley, he could read the currents that coursed through it. He sensed a tautness, an expectancy, as if the animals and plants living here were on guard, waiting for violence to erupt at any instant. Much of the larger animal life had left the valley as well. Only a few silent birds and squirrels made their presence visible.

"I sense that something is not right, that we need to be as vigilant as the sentient beings here."

"Aye." Goran appeared troubled. "A being of some power has chosen to make this valley its home. We should proceed with caution."

"Perhaps we should seek another way?" To Yip's mind, avoiding unnecessary risk and potential violence was always the wisest course whenever possible.

"I am no wizard, so the skills of full teleportation are not mine to use. I could translate us across the valley to a point I can see in plain sight, but I am loath to do so even if it brought us closer to your destination. Using magic may draw more attention than either of us desire."

Yip agreed. "I would not wish to leave traces that are too evident to those who would seek me out."

"Nor I." Goran nodded grimly. "Nor would I want to make our presence known to the creature that lies below."

"We could follow the ridge above or return to the other valley and continue onward until we can cross in relative safety," suggested Yip.

Goran nodded again, his eyes scanning the shadows cast by the ancient trees, looking for hints of the creature that now called the valley home. "I will return once I have set you on your path safely. This valley needs to be set aright."

The surety in his voice left no alternative.

With cautious tread and wary eyes, the two climbed back up the mountainside and began a watchful hike along the ridgeline dividing the two valleys.

Time and the elements had rounded the ridge beneath their feet as it had all the other mountains in the Green Run. Just as time laid bare the bones of the mountain—boulders of granite streaked with quartz stood as steady reminders of the passing of days—the roots of the many growing trees, ferns, vines and shrubs struggled to hold the mountain and its soil in place with their deep entangling roots, fighting a losing battle against time, the elements, and the changes brought by their own existence.

Moving solemnly through the trees, lonely shadows trailed each of their steps, entwining and merging with the full and partial shadows shifting on the forest floor—umbrae cast dark by thick trunks, shrouded by lighter penumbras from the translucid leaves swaying in the brisk wind. With thoughts suppressed by concern, attention focused outward and intent, the two carried on as quietly as the shadows they bore.

As the day's shadows began to lengthen and they began to look for a suitable place to camp for the evening, Yip addressed the concern that he had sent his mind in search of since their brief foray into the valley.

"What do you think lies in wait in the valley below, Goran?"

Goran's answer was as uncertain as Yip's, but grave nonetheless. "Something not of this world, if the traces of its pattern ring true, Yip."

Yip was quiet for a time before he nodded in response. "I feel as though we are being followed, as if the shadows we cast are the merest hints of a deeper Shadow waiting to make itself known."

Goran's brief nod confirmed Yip's feelings, but his response was still a surprise. "There is Darkness trailing us, true, but I feel Darkness from more than one source." Yip raised an eyebrow as Goran continued, "Only one Darkness is near enough to cast its shadow. The other will be seen on another day."

Resigned, Yip understood that his pursuers must be getting close once more.

After that brief discussion, the two walked onward in silence, knowing only the sound of their own footfalls, the echoes of their own thoughts.

By the time the sun had dropped beneath the crest of the western ridges, Yip and Goran had found a suitable clearing to remain for the evening. At one end of the glade, a tall chestnut oak's trunk rested against a tumbled mossy boulder, propping it up from a raucous descent down the mountain. Underneath the eaves of its furrowed limbs, the clearing was covered in ferns and wild grasses that rustled softly in the pale light of the rising moon. Luminous, filamentous plants offered a soft lavender halo to the clearing in the half-light.

"We will make our stand tonight." Goran set his travel gear down beneath the shadows cast by the gray boulder.

Goran looked at Yip grimly. "Whatever comes will be a test for us. I have gotten a taste of this thing's power, Yip. You would be better served by standing clear."

Yip knew his limits and had little illusions as to how he would fare against a supernatural being, particularly one of enough power to ruffle Goran. In time, with continued development, his bounds would change, but, until then, Goran was correct.

He nodded in response.

Goran nodded curtly in acknowledgement. "I will make ready."

After setting down his small travel kit, Yip watched as Goran drug the butt of his staff in a circle around where he and Yip stood silhouetted against the mass of the large boulder, furrowing the ground as the finely grained wood moved through the soil, pushing aside leaves and debris as the stave bit into the loam. When he finally completed inscribing the protective circle in the loose dirt, Goran took two sure strides to reach the circle's center. He then planted the base of his staff solidly into the ground. Stave standing freely in the soil in front of him, Goran deliberately raised both hands in an arch over his head while exhaling slowly.

While Goran worked his spell in silence, Yip could see the diffuse light of the ambient energies gathering and flowing around the giant's form. As Goran etched the circle in the earth, the air lit up with light, flowing upward from the circle inscribed in the soil. Planting the staff in the ground caused the energy to surge from the earth in a blazing crescent, alighting on the apex of his great staff in a shimmering bubble, finally crystallizing into solidity with the giant's exhalation.

To the eyes of the uninitiated, the clearing's still air hummed expectantly, but the glade was otherwise touched only by the soft spring breeze, ghost light from the wispy plants, and silvery moonlight. To those who could see, a shimmering dome of translucent force now surrounded the giant and his small companion.

With a deep sigh, Goran took a seat beside the lichen covered boulder.

Propping his great staff on the supple leather of his tunic, the shaft left to rest on his right shoulder, Goran said, "Now we wait."

Yip nodded, sitting patiently next to his giant friend, legs crossed, hands resting lightly palms down on his legs, letting the diffuse energies of the clearing and its creatures flow through and around him.

For a time, all they saw were fireflies dancing in the clearing, the subtle yellow-green clarity of their lights echoing the constellations above. Overhead, leaves gilded in crystalline lattices reflected the moonlight in understated luminescence—gemlike hues gathering ambient energies, furthering tree growth.

Reading the flow of *chi* around and within him, he saw no sign or indication of the Shadow descending upon them.

As a fresh gust of wind moved through the clearing, the leaves above tinkling like supple glass, Yip first noticed the transition. Remaining silent, he gave Goran a slight nudge with his elbow. Goran nodded in recognition.

The clearing began to undergo an almost imperceptible shift beneath the cool evening air. In Yip's mind's eye, the ambient energies began to take on a steady rhythm, moving first forward and back, akin to the lapping motion of water on the shore of a lake—in and out, in and out. As time passed, the motion became more aggravated, more pronounced, as if a high tide were pushing inland or a storm were building offshore, forcing the magical energies around and past them, farther and faster, building in strength and violence over time. As he watched, the *chi* seemed to shift and deviate from its natural course, as if being pushed forward and away from something, growing and intensifying from a tide into a flood.

Relaxing his muscles in readiness, the time had arrived. After all this waiting, he sensed the monster's foul approach through the evening chill, a stain on his soul that he would never wipe from memory. As the tumult of magical energies raged past him marking the creature's approach, he knew Darkness had come to the hilltop and that if he had not met Goran, this beast would surely have ended his quest before it ever began.

Even with Goran by his side, both of their futures' were still in doubt.

As a reminder to be still before the coming storm, Goran rested a massive hand on Yip's shoulder, the giant's palm and fingers engulfing Yip's shoulder blade and part of his chest. Yip, however, focused his attention entirely upon the spectacle unfolding at the edge of the clearing, gathering himself as best he could should the need arise.

Moving almost hesitantly, its motions resembling those of a praying mantis on the hunt, shifting slightly forward, slightly backward, mirroring the motion of tree limbs in the breeze, Yip first caught hint of the monstrosity's shadow beyond the clearing's edge, melding with the tree trunks and their shadows.

If not for his inner vision, he never would have sensed the creature's approach.

What he could see filled him with a staggering dread.

Dark emanations filled the void in the ambient energies around the atrocity's silhouette, an aura of wicked power unlike any he had seen, causing the magics native to this plane to flee from its very presence. The creature's head shifted back and forth, back and forth, with the same motion as its body, flecks of darkness marking the sockets of its eyes, drinking in the energy of the night in a swirling vortex. Black flames licked at lips scaled and pitted, scabrous and coriaceous. Long, clawed arms swung in time with the creature's loping, erratic gate, almost reaching the ground as it hunched forward. Hornlike scales and protrusions erupted from behind shoulders wider than Yip stood tall at full height, descending in a malefic arc to the tip of a whipping tail that slashed in counterpoint to each of the beast's lunging steps. Despite its mass and apparent bulk, the sinister claws of its splayed feet did not disturb a single leaf on the ground, its motions a silent pantomime of normality.

Perhaps half again as tall as Goran, the monster from another plane resembled a twisted humanoid Dragon, draped in power and untold menace, an abomination this world could never bear nor forbear.

The creature's motions halted abruptly upon reaching the edge of the glade. The only remaining movements about its form were the dark coruscations of force burning away the energies of the living things all around.

Letting go of Yip's shoulder, Goran stood.

Waiting for the tableau to unfold, Yip had forgotten about his friend's grasp, lost as he had been in the creature's motions. Now was the time for readiness, not stupor.

With a mind-numbing roar that he felt rather than heard, a vicious slash cutting through his attention leaving Yip struggling to focus and remain present, the creature leapt forward into the glade, covering half the distance between them in a single stride. Brandishing his staff diagonally across his body, Goran waited, his feet planted firmly in the loam beneath the ferns.

Throwing both arms back and thrusting its head forward, seething black flames erupted outward from the creature's scabrous maw, splashing and snaking around the shimmering shield protecting the pair like a toxic living sludge.

As the flames roiled forward, Yip instinctively dove to the side, rolling out of any potential harm. Recovering his feet, driblets of the creature's noxious flames still sliding down the exterior of the field of force where they bubbled and ate away at the ground upon landing, he saw that Goran had not shifted his position in the slightest, waiting as stoically as the stone resting behind him.

Before its craggy mouth snapped shut, the beast vaulted forward once more, this time swinging its massive left arm downward before it in a terrible trajectory, its jagged hand surrounded by swirling waves of dark arcana. As the creature's fist impacted with the force shield hovering around them, Yip watched the shimmering field bend and bow slowly inward beneath the impact of the beast's blow before popping with a sudden inrush of fetid air. The remnants of the shield's energy glistened in the pregnant evening air, its iridescent effervescence falling about their shoulders in a slow luminous rain. When the frothing energies came in contact with the monster, its skin bubbled and the thing reared back its head to scream.

Quicker than Yip would ever have expected, the creature's arm lashed out toward him in a deadly arc where he stood watching at the side of the clearing after his roll. Unable to move in time to avoid the blow, he focused his *chi* around the point of impact, creating a vibrating band of force about his abdomen. Despite this protection, his ribs screamed in pain as the beast's fist smashed into his chest, shattering his bones with the sound of dry boughs, sending him flying through the air toward the large boulder behind him.

Whistling through the air, unable to right his limp limbs in time to recover and prevent the impending impact with the coarse stone, he watched as Goran took the opportunity afforded by the creature's strike to mount a counterattack.

With his greatstaff held overhead, Goran leapt forward, bright emerald light scintillating down the staff's length, bringing the pole down on the creature's head in a terrific blow. Yip saw a great explosion of light as the staff shattered in flinders about the monster's head, and then, with a sickening impact, he knew no more.

YLLDEL

Through the shifting fog,
the crest of a green mountain
briefly comes to view.

Yip opened his eyes with some difficulty. Bright sunlight brought tears
to eyes used to darkness. Eyes heavily crusted with sleep, his throat
dry, he felt as though he had been unconscious for some time. Despite
the discomfort, the cool earth beneath his shoulders, back, and
buttocks reassuringly held him in place. Before moving, he quickly
took stock of his situation.

Miraculously, everything felt normal and in place.

"You took quite a blow there." He saw Goran's form limned against
the trees beyond.

He opened his mouth to speak, but only a poor excuse for a croak
came out.

"Here." Goran took two long strides over to where Yip lay on the
ground. Bending over, he knelt down and carefully poured a bit of
water into Yip's parched mouth.

"Thank you, Goran," he said, gracious both for the water, the healing, and for saving his quest before his aim was realized, his path begun.

Goran nodded brusquely.

When Yip finally recovered his voice, he gestured toward the still form of the massive beast laying splayed out across the middle of the clearing. Surprisingly, nothing showed any interest in the creature's limp form—no flies circled over its bulk, no vultures flew overhead. He could, however, see a magical haze floating around the beast. Apparently, the intrinsic energies of the place were slowly cleansing the evil taint of the monstrosity.

Then the flies would come.

"What was that creature, Goran?"

Goran chuckled, "That, my friend, was a Dracodin."

"A Dracodin?"

"Aye," he answered. "A Dracodin. And let me tell you, if that's the worst thing you encounter on your quest, you will be luckier than you know."

Shaking his head in disbelief, for the thought of creatures more heinous than a Dracodin was a bit much for his still-groggy mind to imagine, he asked, "Why was it here?"

"Dracodin are attracted to power like a moth is to flame. When the barriers between worlds thin, Dracodin and creatures like them are free to cross."

Yip's eyes widened as he imagined the evil that could follow unbeknownst in the Cabal's wake, dire consequences created by their attempts to reenter and reclaim a place in Ea'ae. The thought of creatures worse than the Dracodin unleashed on an unsuspecting populace filled his heart with dread.

As more and more episodes reinforced the dangers associated with the Cabal's reappearance, he came increasingly to realize the degree to which the Cabal's presence threatened not only his monastery's immediate future, but the future of the entire planet, everything on it, and many worlds beyond. The Cabal's constant assaults could spell his world's undoing much quicker than he had feared, leaving his planet to a violent doom well before meeting a fate similar to the homeworld of the H'era Al'Marr. "The Cabal..."

"Aye, seems like your friends are making things a bit more difficult for everyone."

"We must find a way to restore the barriers around our world!"

Goran nodded. "And you need to be about your quest, Yip, for the two are interlinked."

"How shall I do both?"

Goran smiled. "Are the two opposed? Take care of the Cabal, Yip. Stay true to your focus. Many years have passed, but perhaps the time has come to reconvene the Council of Light."

"You need not be alone."

Muttering, as if talking to himself, he heard Goran add, "Maybe it's time to ask for a little help."

"Help?"

"Aye." Goran chuckled, "I've been alone too long in these woods without company. To think, an Indural starting to mumble and mutter to himself!" Goran shook his head. "Perhaps now is also the time to overcome my own hubris and ask for help finding my people, Yip. Someone on the council may be willing to offer aid."

"What is this Council of Light you speak of, Goran?"

Goran's eyebrows raised in incredulity. "You have not heard of it? Have our selfish concerns and the relative safety we have enjoyed robbed of us the knowledge of those who have protected and sheltered us over the millennia?"

"You are correct, Goran, I have been sheltered for some time. Remember, my order has not truly existed on or participated in the affairs of Ea'ae for many, many years until recently. We have tried to forget our failings..."

"And are therefore doomed to repeat them."

Yip bowed his head, unwilling to argue for a history he bore with significant guilt and remorse, feeling the failings of his spiritual fathers as his own even if they had deemed the world safe to continue without their direct presence.

"The council is an informal league of those seeking to guard and protect the well-being of our world. We have not been active for some time, I am sad to say."

Lifting his head, he then heard Goran continue, "There are some

Powers that belong in this world and others that do not." Goran's gaze turned briefly toward the still form of the Dracodin sprawled limply across the clearing.

Making eye contact with Yip once again, he added, "Your order's time has returned."

Once Goran was certain of Yip's ability to move in comfort, the pair began their descent into the valley of the Dracodin, knowing this time their progress would remain unchallenged.

Their passage downward was marked in relative silence for the pallor of the otherworldly creature still hung heavily over the valley. Other than a shift in the subtle energies around him, Yip saw little other reminder of the Dracodin's lingering presence.

"Why do you think the Dracodin chose this valley?" he asked as he bobbed beneath a pliable young hickory limb encased in glowing crystalline dust that resembled snowflakes resistant to the warmth of the spring sun.

"I do not know, Yip. Perhaps the barriers protecting our world were thinnest here. Perhaps the ancient hills and their magical energies were enough to wet the creature's appetite. I cannot say, for I sense no objects of power in the immediate vicinity."

"What will you do for a staff, Goran?" The thought of objects of power brought back the image of Goran's staff shattering over the Dracodin's vile head.

Goran laughed, his deep rumble echoing from the quiet hills, "What I always do. Grow another!" Opening his palm, he showed Yip what appeared to be a single small splinter from among the many flinders.

Yip could see the woody fragment radiating the same emerald green energy he had seen expended when it struck the monster's head. "With a little cultivation, the staff will restore itself."

He smiled at the thought.

After another three hard days of hiking, by the third day's end, they had reached the heights of the opposite ridge. The view from here afforded much the same vista as before, wondrous as it was—row upon row of rolling green mountains spotted with iridescent hues and bands stretching away toward a humid blue horizon—with one slight difference. Yip could now see the craggy spire of Ylldel looming to the south and west backlit by the setting sun—a peak full of texture and color, shades of greens, grays, browns, and others more magical—diffuse tree canopies, rounded boulders, and rolling heaths girdled by a row of white clouds.

Goran pointed. "Ylldel, the Mountain Father, worth the journey whatever the clime."

Yip nodded appreciably. The two stood together for a time enjoying the sunset, recovering their breath after a full day of exertion.

Yip set his kit down under an old red maple tree sculpted by the winds on the ridgetop, making ready for camp. While he sat and made ready beneath the boughs, Goran remained standing, surveying the expansive view.

"Although I do not wish to admit it, our journey together is at an end, Yip." Goran continued surveying Ylldel as he finished, "As short as our time together was, I am glad to call you friend."

Yip stood slowly and bowed to the giant, his shadow lost amidst those of the tree. "And I you."

Goran pointed. "Follow this ridge for some days to the east and south. In time you will see the markings of humanity. Then you will know you have reached Shady Vale and yet another beginning on your journey."

"Your assistance and advice have been most welcome, Goran."

The giant smiled.

"As has been yours."

"I wish you success on your quest, Yip. Should the time come and you need me, you have but to call. In time, I will let you know how my efforts go with the council."

Yip bowed again.

"From here, you should be able to travel to Shady Vale in relative safety."

"Many thanks, friend Goran."

Goran smiled. "And many welcomes, friend Yip."

And with that Goran disappeared into the forest, soft as the breeze, silent as still leaves.

THE CABAL

A grass covered mound
marks the yearnings and desires
of bygone warriors.

Just as his was the power of Light, there's was of the Dark. He could sense their distant presence as a faint shift in his surroundings—a deepening of shadows, a stillness in the air, a muting and dampening in the colored shimmering of the Essence.

The Cabal's shadow walkers were vacuous, more diffuse than the softest shadow, and only the keenest awareness stretched taut throughout one's environs would ever get even the slightest hint of their presence. The Cabal mold and walk within Shadow and shape Darkness to their own ends. Masters of unlife and entropy, theirs was the power of endings.

Every beginning has an end and each new ending brings about new possibilities and opportunities for the manifold expression of life. This was a principle Yip knew well. For the Cabal, however, the ending they sought was finality itself—a goal to be pursued and realized, carved and etched out of possibility, an ending to all that lived and thrived, immutable and inscribed through time, entropy incarnate.

The Cabal's Darkness grew from Light just as life grew from Light itself. Good intentions taken down wrong paths eventually led some among the K'un Lun and their allies astray. As the differences and strivings grew greater within the order, the Cabal split from the K'un Lun to seek its own end. What started first as the hand of justice and Light within the K'un Lun, virtue's protectors and guardians, grew into the hand of dismay and turmoil—an evil let loose on the world.

Thus the Liúxīng Làngrén, the Light Fallen, were born.

Built on envy for what they lost in the old order and lust for power and accomplishment, the Cabal, once an integral part of the K'un Lun, became an implacable foe, a threat to peace and nascent human potential.

This transition, then, also began a gradual transition within the K'un Lun. What had started and evolved through the ages as a vehicle for the uplifting of man and human potential became diametrically opposed to the Cabal in all its actions and activities. An agency of peace and the unfolding of wisdom was forced to learn the harsh realities of war from those it had once counted as its own kind.

Battle became a fierce teacher and the K'un Lun were forced to internalize the true value and meaning of life.

Shaking his head, Yip returned his focus to the climb ahead. Though a Shadow dogged his steps, better to focus on the necessities of the moment than the evil and failings of the past.

Urging himself forward, he pressed ahead, his own shadow trailing each step.

THE COMING SHADOW

The rising sun's rays
warm the morning dew,
birthing opalescent fog.

Goran left Yip in the clearing carrying a heavy heart. He longed for the days of his youth when he was not bound by duty and obligation, for a time when he could have continued with his new friend and aided him on his quest.

Unfortunately, those times had long passed and now these woods and those who lived in them were his charge. He had accepted such responsibility willingly and bore the burden lightly like a well-worn kit over his shoulder, a barely noticed companion at his back.

When he sensed that his friend had moved some distance away in safety, moving forward toward his future, Goran found a suitable place to wait. His efforts to reunite with his kindred would have to abide. His personal missive to the Council of Light, too, would be put on hold, if only for a time.

Should he not be able to deliver news of the Cabal's return directly, he took the time to cast a warning to the wind, giving word to those who could help restore the power and firmament necessary to hold the world's shielding together.

With a soft breath, he whispered his words to the wind, infusing his message with the power to see it reach his intended destination safely without interception,

> "Shadows lengthen through the day
> in preparation for the coming night,
>
> If left unchecked , as in days of yore,
> the Cabal will return in might.
>
> The seals are failing and must be restored
> to prevent the coming blight."

His missive complete, Goran sat and waited, preparing himself should he die.

He had spent more time on this world than Men could imagine, his life measured in ages rather than years.

He was tired.

In many ways, he felt his time had come and passed. He wished only to reunite with his kin once more and pass on what knowledge and wisdom he could to prepare a successor.

Unfortunately, the fight with the Dracodin had made his weakness all too apparent. There was a time when he would never have needed to engage such a foe in direct combat. Nor would his friend have had to worry about coming to any harm. But that time, and his ability to rapidly regain his strength and vigor, had long passed.

Now he must pass what remained of his power on to one in whom it would grow and prosper, kindling the spirit to heights where now only his memory soared.

So Goran waited, for he knew that his battle in this wood was, as yet, not done.

By the time the sun had set and darkness blanketed the wood, he sensed the time had come.

The Shadow haunting Yip's steps, kindred perhaps to the ones that had claimed his kin, was near.

A cool chill filled the air, as if winter's winds played lightly on the warm summer breeze. Shadows, too, hung heavily on the ground at his feet beneath the old trees.

Goran sighed.

The time had come.

Within the gloaming, a Shadow moved, its essence drinking the darkness and feeding on the patterns of those creatures it passed. Such a being was an abomination. His heart screamed against its reality in the same way his world recoiled from its presence.

He sensed the creature's evil, the stench of its presence, a rotting, infected carcass needing to be cleansed.

Retribution would soon come.

One waited ahead.

It was not the priestling.

It had the taint of the priestling about its being.

It was old.

It had grown weak.

It harbored knowledge.

It harbored power.

The time to feed had come.

"Reveal yourself, Shadow!" Goran's voice boomed through the wood, bouncing from tree to tree. "You cannot conceal the presence of your taint from me!"

Only the empty susurration of the wind answered his call.

The creature moved nearer. "Reveal yourself, Shadow!" Goran's voice thrummed with power, laced with command.

In response, a sibilant hiss echoed through the recesses of Goran's mind, *"Your words hold no power over me, Indural."*

"And your kind brings me no fear, Shadow!" Goran stamped the heel of his newly restored staff firmly on the ground. Light spilled out around him in a radiant arch, illuminating the boughs and branches, trunks, and leaves all around with the fullness of a newborn dawn.

Standing in stark relief some twenty paces in front of him, the Shadow floated motionlessly in the air, so dark that light seemed to move away from its loathsome presence as if the very fabric of the world had torn and the rent opened through to utter emptiness beyond.

Waiting in a tableau, each staring motionlessly at the other, Goran could see a deeper darkness gathering and radiating about the thing's hands, a sinister wind that blew out the breaths of many souls.

Breaking the stillness, he jerked his staff up, deflecting a blast from the Shadow's hands as it lashed forward toward him, moving with a suddenness beyond Goran's ability to counter without anticipation. Its hands still sheathed in seething Darkness, the Shadow flew across the clearing toward him preparing to tear all memory and thought from his being, feeding both its hunger and its masters' desire for havoc.

Waiting, he stood at the ready, great staff held diagonally across his chest, his doom staring him greedily in the eye as it lurched in for the kill.

With an alacrity beyond the creature's expectations, Goran dropped to one knee, whipping his great staff lengthwise onto the ground as the creature's claw shredded the air where he had previously stood. Where the staff smashed into the ground, blazing incandescent white Light burst upward catching the Shadow in an inferno of holy light brighter than a thousand suns.

His hands trembling with adrenaline, another sign of his age and weakness, Goran opened his eyes to the evening's darkness and an uncertain future.

He let out a deep breath.

The Shadow was no more.

There would be others in the time to come, but for now Yip would be able to travel in relative safety without a creature of Darkness hounding his steps and undermining his purpose.

One less evil remained to haunt Aldael's future.

One more horror had been banished to his people's past.

"I'm getting too old for this," he muttered under his breath, wearily returning to his feet. Clasping his staff firmly in his hands, Goran smiled and patted his luminous staff. "At least you're not broken again."

Then he, too, disappeared into the night.

A CHANCE ENCOUNTER

Hoofbeats echo through
the still wood—forgotten,
leaves scatter in their wake.

Yip had left Goran over a week and a half ago, days counted and remembered by the rise and fall of the broad wooded ridgeline beneath his feet.

The Shadow that had seemed so close over just a week past had mysteriously vanished, its presence lost in the sudden violence of a magical detonation.

Reading the currents, he sensed that Goran had saved him once again, risking his own venerable life and purpose in so doing.

His heart was filled with gratitude each and every step.

He trod lightly on what he assumed was a deer trail, a light path perhaps occasionally used by trappers or other woodsmen as they traversed the vast wilderness of the Green Run.

Here the trees grew tall and thick and the shadows deep. As elsewhere in the Green Run, the signs of Man's presence was all but invisible. Earlier that day, he had passed an abandoned ring of stones that might have once been used to hold a camp or cookfire but now only leaves sheltered within the stone's hollowed basin.

His mind roving outward beyond the sounds of his footfalls, from time to time he sensed the faint energetic traceries of human presence as the light touch of old memories long past. But, like the campfire, the presence of those beings was long departed.

Though seldom used, he was glad for the trail, for although forlorn and abandoned by those who once may have used it more frequently, relying upon it for security and as a guide, the trail represented a faint but very real thread connecting him to his future and the people he hoped to find ahead. He was also glad for the deer and their kindred whose graceful presence and light hoof steps helped to preserve this subtle reminder that he now trod.

If Goran was right, he only had another one or two week's journey until he reached Shady Vale.

His pace was steady and could best be considered a light jog for he wished to move quickly forward but not move so quickly that he would lose touch with any dangers that may lay in wait ahead or approach from behind. Moving at a steady run, with *chi* flowing though his meridians, air filling his lungs, and oxygen rushing through his veins, he also enjoyed the benefits of steady physical exertion without the need to stop and train or sit in meditation.

Each step, each breath, was an exercise in awareness, full of mindful intent and positive motion. Feeling the fullness of life flow through him, he trained as he moved to live fuller.

As the days before, this day passed with him running along the ridgeline, as light and quick as a deer, as free and easy as the clouds above. The songs of birds and insects, frogs and other animals he did not know, pulsed around him in steady soothing waves—welcome companions on his long journey to an uncertain future.

When the day's shadows began to lengthen, he began to look for a place suitable to camp for the night, perhaps a spot from which he could view the stars above or a cool nook beside a burbling stream.

As the trail dipped down into a trough between two larger shoulders of the ridge, the path opened up onto an open, spacious heath covered in waist high grasses swaying in the light mountain breeze. Colored from green to gold, the grasses held flowers of every shape and hue in their breast as butterflies, bees, faeries, and delicate Fairy Dragons flitted from petal to petal.

More complex and varied than the flight paths of all the creatures seen flitting through the air, a web of interactions spun through the clearing in a wondrously bejeweled net cast over and through all the grasses arching in the wind, more captivating than dewdrops on a spider's web exposed to the first light of dawn.

Examining the clearing for some time, he took in not only its beauty but its measure. When he sat down on his bedroll for his evening meditations, the tall grasses would easily hide his presence should anyone cross the thin deer trail bisecting its center. Should he be detected or tracked, the clearing also afforded easy access to the cover of the ancient wood with its deep shadows.

Glad for such a remarkable spot, he headed up the bald's slope, for the trail here was slightly below the ridgeline, climbing to the top of the ridge, not only for the expansive vista of the Green Run laid out in wave after wave of verdant mountains before him, but for the added safety of higher ground. Although the slope would do little to slow any pursuers should they be Shadows or the like, the grade would slow the progress of most while giving him the benefit of a quick descent should he need to make one.

Happy with his choice in a campsite, he laid his bedroll down lightly on top of the tall grasses in anticipation of the sunset and the evening's stars.

Dusk fell in lucent hues of orange and red, the sky taking much of the brightness that had been lost to the valleys below as the sun settled behind the far ridges. With the sun's descent and the deepening shadows across the hills, the heavens, too, began the steady transition from light to dark, traveling first through yellows, oranges, and reds until finally arriving at the deep blues and purples of evening.

With this sedate transition, the depth of the night sky increased until he felt as though he were staring upward into a dark pool, the bottom of which he would never find. The multitude of stars above hinted at the pool's depths but never defined its true limits leaving him to gaze serenely in joy at an expanse far greater than he could imagine or encompass within the totality of his mind.

Feeling the radiance of the bald growing as the sky dimmed, he alternated between his contemplation of the sky and the bald in which he sat. All around him, the grasses and flowers of the heath had taken up lights of their own, shining forth in subtle resplendence no longer dimmed by the light of the full sun. Adding to the light of the fey creatures of the field, the bald was awash in the lights and energies of magical plants and creatures frolicking beneath the stars. Aureate traceries of blues, greens, argents, ochers, pinks, crimsons, and many others mingled in hues too numerous to count, bathing him in energies as varied as the stars above.

To live in such a world was a wonder beyond counting.

Looking upward and beyond to the stars above, he watched the lights of those distant bodies offer forth their brilliance to the night sky. To journey to other worlds, to see the beauty of life unfold on planets as wondrous as his own, would be a blessing beyond measure. If all went well and he was one day able to help ensure Ea'ae's security, perhaps he would have the opportunity to venture beyond her limits and see firsthand what the wider universe could teach him.

His gaze deepened as he peered searchingly upward into the heavens. Above, the silvery white arch of the galaxy's heart, the Light's Swath, spilled outward in a dizzying profusion of stars. Of these, many were not stars but galaxies unto themselves. Knowing what little he comprehended of the heavens, he understood that even in the darkness between stars, the vast reaches, were filled with yet more stars and galaxies in an endless profusion.

Staring upward, he looked backward through time toward the birth of the universe.

How far did the cosmos span?

How many times had the universe been born?

How many times would it die?

Bathed in the unseen radiance of these first stars and countless others much nearer, he was fortunate to swim through their abiding light all the while.

Closing his eyes, he let the soft radiance of the stars above and the vibrant energies of the meadow wash through him, enlivening his meridians in shades as bright as his imaginings.

Gazing into the still waters of one of the monastery's many reflective pools, he asked his teacher, "Master, what does it mean to be an individual?"

"Is anything truly unique or special?"

"Am I different from everything else?"

"What separates me from everything else?"

Master Wei smiled at Yip's questions, the curiosity of a vibrant young mind discovering its place within the world. Taking his eyes briefly from the pond, turning to Yip, Master Wei replied, "Stick your finger into the pond, Yip."

As he put his index finger in the water, his teacher said, "Now pull it out as quickly as you can."

Yip watched the water flow back instantaneously around where his hand had been. After letting Yip ponder what he had seen, Master Wei asked, "What did you see?"

Watching the ripples flow away from where his finger had been, he answered. "The water filled the space where my finger had been, remaining in constant contact with my skin."

Master Wei nodded. "Now try again…faster. As fast as you can."

Yip pulled his fingers out so quickly the cuff of his robes snapped. Water splashed upward as he retracted his hand. No matter how quickly he withdrew, the water moved with him, adhering to his finger all the while.

"What happened, Yip?"

Watching the ripples once more, he replied, "The same thing only over a shorter period of time."

Master Wei nodded sagely in agreement. "No matter how quickly you pull out your finger, the water will always rush back in."

"I do not understand, master."

"No matter how accomplished you are, how well known, or how wise you become, when you leave, the space you once occupied will be filled."

"I still do not understand, master."

"Although you may have unique gifts and perceptions, though you bring unrealized possibilities to expression, ultimately, you are no different or more

important than anyone or anything else for we are all of the same being. When you leave, something else will take your place."

Master Wei smiled then in response to Yip's confusion, his eyes filled with reassurance. "Do not fear, Yip."

Here Master Wei motioned with his finger toward the pond. "The same logic holds equally in reverse by extension. My fingers will get wet just like yours. Water will rush in to fill the space once occupied by my hand should I move it."

"The same rules apply evenly to all. This equality brings with it the true gift to which you refer. All is equal. All is interconnected and bound together, part of and reflective of the totality of existence."

"One thing, everything, is just as wondrous and dazzling as the next."

Yip opened his eyes with the birds, letting the excess *chi* passing through his meridians, his *jing luo*, drift away with his warm breath into the foggy morning air before standing to face the ruddy dawn sun. Gently shaking the excess *chi* from his limbs, he packed his bedroll and walked through the dew-laden grass to the trail below. Glancing behind him, a faint trail was visible through the grass, his passage marked by dewdrops falling from the blades and stems.

Securing his kit as he walked, he felt the moist, spongy earth giving slightly with each step, not yet exposed to the heat of the afternoon sun. A short walk brought him through the small field and back into the unbroken wilderness of the Green Run.

As before, here the trees grew tall and straight, many to truly prodigious size, competing as they had for centuries for the light of the sun above. Flower laden vines stretched heavenward as well using the boughs of the trees as trellises endeavoring for the sun. The competition for light, however, seemed secondary to the competition for energy of another sort.

Walking along the ridgeline through the morning, the trunks and leaves of many trees appeared encased in translucent crystalline lattices along with similarly covered patches of moss and lichen. To his eye, much of the wood he walked through could have just received a very light frost, except that the weather here was generally too mild for freezing temperatures in the summer and all the trees still had their bright green spring foliage. Although vaguely reminiscent of a scene from winter, the trees here benefited from a symbiotic relationship with organisms of another sort. Just as the trees' leaves captured the light from the sun above, the miniscule crystals encoating much of their surface captured the *chi* existing around—aeryasynthesis abounded.

Examining the bark of one particularly large, hoary oak, looking deeply at its flaking grayish white whorls, Yip wondered if perhaps in time the mutualism expressed by the symbiosis with the trees and the energy capturing crystals would become incorporated within the tree itself as an inseparable part of the larger organism, potentially as an adjunct and eventual replacement for photosynthesis. He had seen similar processes at work elsewhere on his journey. The world, this specimen in particular, was ripe with examples of organisms that stretched across many boundaries.

Tree species such as the Vaellorea, Aeryn, Neana, and Senea had already crossed that bound. These trees could be next.

The changes and adaptations, the stunning miracle of Ea'ae as it was and would be never ceased to amaze him.

His fingertips resting lightly on the trunk of the tree, lost in the depths of the beauty of the place, Yip jerked his head upward to the distant sound of hooves. So deeply had he been engrossed in his examination of the tree that he had lost track of his surroundings and not felt the rapid approach of riders along the ridge.

Hoofbeats echoed firmly off the ground, through the trunks, and upward into the luminously dappled canopy. The rhythmic *thuds* approached rapidly at almost a full gallop. He sensed four riders with four horses approaching, three of which shone brightly with great potential blazing brightly like torches lit within the fullness of the forest's gloom. The fourth rider, of less vibrancy and greater age than his fellows, rode within their midst huddled as if for protection. As they drew nearer, he sensed that this older rider was injured, perhaps grievously.

Sensing this rider's need, he held firm on the trail awaiting their arrival and did not seek cover.

He did not have to wait long.

Bent low over the necks of their horses, the riders thundered through the wood. Rushing headlong as if a forest fire were immediately at their heels, he was not sure if they were going to stop. The foremost rider, tall and long of limb, trailed a voluminous cloak behind him. Long red hair, the color of the sky at sunset, stood out in stark contrast to his pale skin. Noticing Yip for the first time standing motionless ahead, his eyes rose in surprise as he sat up in the saddle, pulling the reins, and motioned for his friends to stop with equal alacrity.

"Ho!" Humus and leaves scattered as the horses' hooves skidded to a quick halt bringing the riders to a stop a safe distance away should he pose a threat. Heavy saddlebags jingled, full of coin or gems, as the horses' ground to a standstill and stomped their hooves energetically before being reined in.

For a moment only the sound of the horses' heavy breathing filled the space between them.

Eyeing each other warily, it was the rider in the back, a stout, heavily armored Dwarf who spoke first. "Best run fer cover, stranger. There're Orcs on our trail. More than we can kill, although they won't soon forget us." His wicked grin told Yip that there must have been many more Orcs than were now chasing them.

Yip looked toward the injured rider. "Your friend needs assistance."

The injured man rode in the middle of the group slumped over the saddle, held in place by a man obviously from Yip's homeland of Chang Sen. This third rider kept his arms around the injured gentlemen, holding him in place as gently as was possible. His long robes showed the markings of stars and arcane symbols along the hems where they encircled the unconscious man.

A fourth horse, obviously the injured man's own, trailed the Dwarf, tethered to his horse by a taut rope.

The red-haired man approached and, as he got nearer, Yip saw how tall indeed he was. Standing by his side, Yip would have barely reached his chest. He looked at Yip directly, and asked, "Are you a healer? I have healed his wounds as best I can, but his injuries are beyond my skill. If not, I ask you to stand aside and let us be on our way. We must get him to Shady Vale for treatment before the remaining Orcs find us."

Yip nodded, remaining still so as not to present any hostility or sign of aggression. "I may be able to help give him time to recover. May I?"

When the red-haired man finally nodded, he walked forward slowly and placed his hands gingerly upon the injured man's chest where he was wrapped with hastily torn cloth. Although covered in blood, the wound had been healed, at least visibly. Letting his senses drift inward, he felt disruptions in the flow of life sustaining *chi* throughout the man's torso as if his body were a piece of pottery that had been dropped to the ground, shattering upon impact. Moving his intention carefully through the injuries, he saw how magic had been used to repair what had been broken, but not fully. The injury was not completely healed. The scattered shards of bone, the bruised and lacerated organs, seemed only crudely mended and had not been restored to their original integrity.

His head bowed, he breathed deeply and totally, opening himself up, letting *chi* move through him fully from the surroundings, his body but a door, a door to be opened to let the *chi* flow through. Following the *chi's* course through the injured man as though his body were Yip's own, he guided the energy through the man's meridians slowly, carefully through and around the injuries, working to restore the flow of vitality, of life-giving and sustaining vivacity, to the man's broken form.

Although he could not heal the man completely or cure his injuries directly, he could provide the injured man's body with the energy and ability to heal itself, steadying and bolstering his systems so that he could recover much quicker and more fully than he would have otherwise been able.

Working in silence, he let the *chi* course, giving the man the opportunity to stabilize and mend himself over time.

Finally, after almost half an hour of careful attention and ministrations, he raised his head and said, "I have done what I can. If he has the will to live, he will heal himself in time. If you reach other healers before he has recovered, they may be able to complete what I have not."

"We thank you, stranger."

Yip bowed and offered a brief smile. "Yip."

"We thank you, Yip," repeated the tall man at their lead.

The man holding the injured man spoke for the first time. "Would you like to ride with us?" He motioned to a fourth horse. "Your company would be welcome."

Yip shook his head. "Perhaps another time. I would be of more assistance to you here."

The man from Chang Sen raised his eyebrows. "How so?"

"Perhaps I can help you make up the time you have lost."

The Dwarf laughed. "Ya're a brave man indeed, Yip. I reckon a company o' fifteen ta twenty or so Orcs remain behind us, although we've killed far more than that and worse recoverin' Jenkins and his gold."

The red-haired man nodded. "We are in no position to fight off the rest if we are to get our charge to safety. Are you sure you will not ride with us, Yip?"

Yip nodded and then asked, "Do you have any rope?"

The red-haired man threw a tightly wound coil he had resting on the pommel of his saddle to Yip. "If we guess correctly, the Orcs are only a few hours behind us. Their Worgs run faster than our horses but tire quicker so we have been able to put some distance between us. They will not relent until they find us or we reach safety."

He gave a slight nod in understanding.

"May I use one of your knives?"

The Dwarf tossed a small, curved blade marked with fine Dwarven runes that he had hanging in a metal holster from his belt to Yip. With a deft movement, Yip cut the long rope where he judged the midpoint to be along its length inside the coils. Finished, he tossed the Dwarf his blade back.

Knowing the answer before he asked, he queried, "Are any of you magicians?"

When the tall redhead and the man from his own country nodded, he asked, "Are you able to cast a spell to camouflage and perhaps strengthen the rope?"

With several muttered incantations and an invocation of power, he watched energy dance along the rope's length as the man from Chang Sen carefully wove his spells. When he had finished, the rope shimmered slightly upon close inspection along the edges but otherwise blended almost perfectly with the ground below as he looked down at it in his hands.

The mage smiled grimly and said, "Do not run your hands along the rope's length, they are now sharp."

When he gave a slight nod of understanding, the mage added, "Those spells will hold for a day. May those braidings serve you as well as they have us."

"I thank you."

"Thanks are ours to give," replied the man from his homeland with a smile.

The Dwarf spoke next in farewell. "Perhaps we'll see ya in Shady Vale then, Yip."

"Perhaps," answered Yip.

"Let's ride!" Ready to be on their way, the redhead gestured fiercely with his free arm and the horses rumbled forward, quickly disappearing without a backward glance.

As the horses rode off with their passengers, Yip ran along the trail behind them, looking for a suitable spot to tie his first rope. After almost two hours of running along the path beneath the early afternoon shadows, he finally found a place that met his needs.

Under the eaves of a grove of massive chestnuts and oaks, several large, weatherworn boulders protruded from the earth, creating a natural passage through which the trail cut along the ridge. Taking the first half of rope, he tied its cords between two trunks on the far side of the lichen covered rocks, obscuring their presence even further by the cover of shade and stone. When he was done, the rope hung nearly invisible just above head height, as best he could tell the distance above ground where a rider on the back of a large wolf may cross with his head or chest.

With the remaining half of the rope looped diagonally over his head and shoulder, he ran forward looking for a second spot to lay his trap. Perhaps another hour later, at the midpoint of a large unbroken stretch of trail along the ridgeline, where the trail was open and easy to follow, a place where a rider in pursuit may see an opportunity to make up ground by increasing his pace, he strung his last piece of rope across the ground at shin height. If all went well, this would cause a few wolves rushing along the trail to trip and throw their riders while running at full stride. If not, at least his simple traps may cause the Orcs to move slower and with more caution, giving the other riders more time to take their charge to safety.

Those riders that continued forward would find another deterrent lying in wait.

Having run for another hour or so more, he found a spot to his liking where the ground was flat, the trees were thick enough to provide significant cover to his advantage, the wind direction would not give away his position to the Worgs, and a large boulder overlooked the trail. Climbing to just beneath the top of the rock, his body hidden from view behind its mass, he peered out over the cool gray rim of his perch waiting for his quarry to arrive.

Time slowed, marked by the passage of each full breath, moments counted by the linked cycle of inhalation and exhalation, until he finally sensed the approach of the Orcs in the distance. Unlike the horses that had passed before, the Worgs and their riders glided silently through the wood on padded feet, unheard even by ears that listened for their presence.

Yip, however, did not listen for their arrival. He sensed their rapid passage well before he would have heard their approach. His mind loose and ready, extended about him in a diffuse, serene net, he felt their movements, counted their number, and gauged their strength before the pack arrived.

All told, there were over ten Orcs approaching. Their progress was slower than he had anticipated for some no longer appeared to ride on mounts but instead had to run afoot. Others appeared to ride unsteadily, whether having sustained some injuries after being thrown from the Worgs' backs or from earlier battles with the riders he could not tell.

In the group's center he sensed what could only be an Orcish shaman, for the air of enchantment lay heavy about him. To his senses, no others in the pack appeared cloaked so heavily in magic or so formidable.

The shaman, then, would be his target.

Peering warily over the boulder's edge, he watched the hunched forms of the Orcs lope forward on the backs of their massive, misshapen wolves. Bedecked in cruel black armor, their breath heavy in the warm early evening air, the Orcs moved with a savage grace, natural and at ease, in perfect synergy with their mounts. Although ill-formed and brutish, their corded arms and legs told of their inhuman strength and physical prowess, if not the barbarity to which those limbs were put. In the group's center, adorned with fragments of bones and other trophies that bounced and jangled with each smooth stride, the shaman rode unarmored, a great wooden staff hanging diagonally across his back topped by what looked like a human skull.

Watching the Orcs approach, his breath slowed and deepened, becoming wider and more diffuse as his body filled with *chi* and he became more and more relaxed. With each loping stride along the trail, his *chi* quickened until the Worgs and their riders appeared to be moving protractedly through water, their motions lethargic and languid, more drawn out than his own breath.

When finally the Orcs arrived and began to pass, the press of their stench and activity marked by an almost oppressive heat, their subtle emanations dark and putrid, he leapt from his perch faster than they could register surprise. Arching overhead, he launched himself toward the shaman, his foot snapping into the shaman's neck with a sickening crunch, knocking him bodily from his mount.

The force of Yip's leap carried him through the air, past the shaman's limp form on the ground, and next to the whitish gray bark of a large oak. Before the shaman's Worg could react to the loss of its master, he dropped to the balls of his feet and spun, sweeping his leg outward to trip and entangle the legs of the next Worg, sending the giant wolf sprawling in the dirt and its rider flying face-first into the boulder from which Yip had just leapt with a squelching *thud*. Standing lithely, Yip struck a third Orc in the throat, knocking him head over heels from his mount to land loosely on the ground behind his mount, breathing no more.

The impact of the attack only now registering, the Orcs began to react in response to his accelerated attacks as he ran past them toward safety in the direction from which they had come, a quarter of their ranks decimated by his attack.

Sprinting through the woods away from the Orcs, the appearance of time and motion gradually returning to sync with the normal flow through which he moved, he hoped that some of the Orcs would follow his flight. Feeling behind him for their response, he was disappointed to see that none followed. Those Orcs who had been running without a mount merely got on the Worgs of those who had fallen, leaving the dead forgotten in their tread.

Stopping his flight, he turned around and returned to the trail, resuming his run toward civilization in pursuit of both sets of riders.

The hunters were now the hunted.

Yip ran on through the rest of that day and night, the fullness and lightness of *chi* allowing him to push forward where his body would have failed without its vibrant buoyancy. First the setting sun and then the moon overhead provided silent witness to his passage through the tall trees. Around him, the wood was aglow with the argentate light of the moon and the kaleidoscopic hues of the fey flora and fauna flitting through the night.

Before the light of dawn had brightened the sky with its touch, the shadows still dark and heavy across the land, after what must have been only a very short halt, he sensed the remaining Orcs in the distance breaking a brief camp. As he neared, creeping forward on feet as light as the rustling leaves overhead, blood curdling howls rose up from the huddled Orcs and he heard the guttural cries of alarm presaging his arrival.

Although the Orcs now knew of his approach, even their dark accustomed eyes could not see him fully advancing cautiously through the shadows in the pre-dawn light. He could, however, clearly see and feel their energy signatures ahead through the boles of the trees.

Now that they were alerted to his presence, he slowed his progress and let the *chi* flow from him into the surroundings, moving forward with extreme caution, letting them try to guess at his whereabouts. Flitting stealthily through the trees, his motions as tempered and easy as the tree limbs above, he moved forward as a ghost, letting the heat of his body cool and blend with that of the pervading *chi*.

Should the Orcs be able to see the heat signatures of his form in the darkness, he would present a target as indistinct and fleeting as the shadows that lay thick beneath the ancient trees.

Of the Worgs and their sense of smell, he would let the still air hold his scent close, moving forward faster than the odor.

Once again, time slowed with his approach as his awareness branched out, full of breath and life. Moving forward at speed, a leaf's fall to his left remained aloft as though held in the air by a gentle breeze that was not present. Although he moved ahead with great care and deliberation, to anyone watching, he would seem to be moving forward at great alacrity even though by his motions he appeared to be walking with centered surreptitiousness.

Closing the distance rapidly as his body became fully enlivened and empowered by *chi*, he had to hurry for he could not remain in such a heightened state for too long lest he burn out like a candle in the wind. By hastening his faculties as he now did, he put himself at great risk especially after having done so once already within the day without proper rest and recovery.

Ahead, the clearing lay dark and thick with Orcs and their Worgs awaiting his arrival. Another series of piercing howls cut through the short distance between them as the Orcs let their Worgs loose upon him. Fierce snarls and growls, accompanied by an eerie combination of eager barks and keens, the wails of barely reined excitement, marked the massive canines' progress through the wood, attempting to ferret him out by his scent. Still moving forward, he watched the Worgs' rapid progress through the wood by their energy signatures, their erratic track becoming more and more sure and direct with each rushing stride.

Breaking into a full run, he leapt over the seething mass of Worgs before they could react to his presence, twisting and turning in the air to land at a full run, giving him a direct, unobstructed path to the Orcs themselves. With only a few paces between himself and the waiting Orcs, he paused, letting the Worgs regroup and reorient themselves in pursuit, their abrupt stoppage and quick turn marked by the sound of sliding leaves, cracking twigs, scrabbling claws, and pained yelps as some Worgs nipped others in their haste to move forward and be the first to reach their prey. He then ran forward, the Worg's breath hot and thick on his back, as close as he dared to their snapping jaws and large discolored fangs.

With one final leap, faster than eyes could register, he jumped directly upward at the clearing's edge, watching the Orcs' eyes widen in surprise as curses filled their lips, wicked black axes held at the ready. Casting his essence outward, very much as he had done with the vorath before, he gave the Worgs the brief impression that he was in the midst of the clearing with their masters, just as they descended upon the Orcs with pining bays of fury.

The surprise registering on the Orcs' twisted faces quickly turned to deep anger and determination as the Orcs found themselves fighting for their lives with their own furious curs in the ensuing confusion as neither Orcish bloodlust nor Worgish fervor could find and quell the source of their anger.

Slipping back into the night, he left the din of battle, the sounds of pain and desperation, the curses and the growls, as the Orcs tried to restore order behind him as he returned to the trail awaiting the light of day and the opportunity to rest.

His body spent, he would need time to recover before journeying onward.

THE VALLEY BELOW

Wending my way through
the damp, leaf-strewn trail,
a flower lends me a smile.

As he crested yet another thickly wooded ridge, his heart lifted in joy as he took in the valley far beneath him. Lights scattered throughout the valley floor from a small hamlet sparked and wavered in the distance. Rooms awash in evening ritual, in the finishing of daily tasks, and the preparation for rest and rejuvenation awaited him below.

To his inner vision, the night was ablaze in light.

Constellations of sentience filled the valley with hope. Intricately threaded and varied minds marked the passing of the night with bright stars of ideation and being. He could find safety, comfort, and warmth within the soft glow of people with full hearts and stout minds.

Though perhaps granted only a temporary reprieve, the light of so many lives would hide his presence and mask him from his pursuers. His own telltale signatures would blend with those of his fellows and blur away in the greater community. Although not a perfect hiding spot, he would have time to regroup and recover before continuing his flight.

Many thought magic and the arts arcane were far out of the reach of ordinary men. He knew otherwise. Just as life is magic, magic is life. The two are inseparable. Some people learn to consciously channel power, the ways are as varied as the human soul can conjure, but all are bathed in the gifts of magic even if they do not see or feel it.

In a world so full of evils and powers beyond most men's ken, how did a small village in the wilderness survive and thrive without some form of protection? Even those gifted and learned in true power would have difficulty protecting such a place.

As he scrambled down the hillside, through the undergrowth and trees, the answer was obvious to him.

All those lives in the community, each sharing in a common purpose, helped to shield and support one another and carry on the miracle of life forward. Those with ill intent would have quite a task approaching a place so rich in shared purpose and sustained power without significant preparation, though most were unaware of the boon given by the mere presence of their neighbors.

He could see the webs of light casting strands throughout the community, linking these few fragile lives together in support and prosperity. He could feel their communal strength and interlinked intention, the vibrancy of their minds and hearts.

As he ran silently down the hillside, the valley glowed with the light of their shared purpose and the beginning of his hope.

By the time he reached the valley bottom near the hamlet some time later, his loose pants and robes were soaked from morning dew. Looking around, the early morning fog that had cloaked the valley had begun its slow march up the hillsides. The trees lining the slopes and roadway had begun to brighten with the day—dark evening greens gradually moved to shades of emerald and yellow as soft, verdant rustling filled the spring morn. Morning flowers lifted their petals from their eventide repose along the roadway and amidst fields of gently undulating crops.

A few early risers were already hard at work out in the fields, culling weeds, sowing the next crop, or gentling singing the songs of growth that helped plants burgeon strong and tall free of pests and disease. His slow approach brought little signs of concern other than an occasional wave of welcome or the cautious stare of appraisal granted a stranger.

After his long, arduous journey through the wilderness, across vast lands inhabited more by creatures of one's imagination than organized settlements, he was ready to find a safe haven to rest for a time and recover a bit of the energy his efforts had expended.

The earthen roadway leading to the village hardly marked his slight step as he slipped past the first few wakening cottages. Smoke easing gently up in the sweet breeze told of day's beginning and work yet to be done. A few doors open to the new morn told him of the relative comfort and stability found in this small wooded hamlet.

As he neared the village, he was lucky enough to encounter one resident just beginning her daily chores watering the plants along her walkway in the front of her house.

"Good morning to you kind, madam," he called out to her and gave a wave, noting her well-tended clothing and efficient manner. When she looked up after emptying her pitcher, he asked, "Perhaps there is someplace nearby where a stranger might find some repose?"

Gazing at him appraisingly, she looked Yip up and down, wondering how this strange little man had wandered into her garden as quiet as the soft wings of morning birds. "G'day to you too, stranger. What, if I may ask, brings you to our fair village as isolated as it is out here in the Green Run?"

"A long road and many steps," he began smiling. "A long journey just begun and far from finished...and one man's hope." He offered her a slight bow and then the flash of a smile. "And perhaps a chance for rest."

She looked at him rather peculiarly, more from confusion at his unusual nuances and strange use of language than his puzzling tone and indirect meanings.

"If you follow the road to the village all the way to the town center, next to the large sycamore tree, you'll find the Afternoon's Shade Inn, run by old Magnus Flintforge. It's not more than a league. If you hurry, you'll get there in time for breakfast."

"Thank you for the kindness you've shown to a stranger," he replied, offering her another bow.

She smiled and turned back to her morning's work, checking the soil moisture in one pot with her finger as she turned to water the hanging baskets beneath her windows.

Walking along the roadside taking in the morning, slowly crossing a gently arching wooden bridge over a clear stream lined with wild flowers, he could see the care and effort the community put in their village. The weavings of love and hope tied them strongly to the landscape and encouraged their village and its environs to prosper and grow.

The Afternoon's Shade Inn was the focal point of the small town center, a place where villagers found rest and repose from a hard day's work and travelers, the few that strayed to this isolated area of the continent, could find a warm bed and a refreshing meal. Across the sandy lane from the inn, set back from the road amidst the shade of two old white oaks was the Feed and Philactecary purveyor of household goods, feedstocks and crop items, natural remedies, charms, and general odds and ends brought in for barter from the outlying regions.

The sign over the inn looked as new and fresh as the day, recently painted and welcoming, depicting the large sycamore giving a weary traveler a place to lay down his hat in repose for a brief nap after a long journey. The solid oaken door turned with a slight, well-worn screech to his touch and opened into a spacious room lit by a well-tended hearth and several windows along the walls. Highly polished wooden floors reflected the combination of torchlight from the wall sconces and daylight coming in from the open windows. Tables scattered around the room were organized around the hearth in preparation for evening storytelling, entertainment, and other gatherings. Across from the door, a small bar served as a reception desk for guests and serving point for spirits.

Upon his arrival, he heard a loud, booming voice welcome him to the inn. "G'day, stranger, and welcome to my inn! What can I do for ya?"

The innkeeper was a stout, voluble Dwarf with rosy cheeks, a shock of unruly gray hair, and a beard thick enough to hide a full flock of birds. His woolen vest stretched to cover his stout chest and full paunch.

"Perhaps some tea?" responded Yip

The innkeeper spread his arms wide at Yip's approach, smiling. "Certainly, friend! Magnus Flintforge's the name. Welcome to the Afternoon's Shade Inn!"

"Thank you for your gracious welcome, good sir."

"I am Yip Chi Chuan. I come from a land far from here. Your inn is a sight most welcome to my tired eyes."

"Ya know, I'd never guess it," Magnus said giving Yip a wry smile and a wink noticing the way Yip chopped his words and spoke with a lilting accent, his voice rising up and down not unlike the distant sea far to the West beyond Var'Kera. "With your worn robes, short hair, and sharp facial features, I thought ya were a local!"

"Molly!!! We have another guest! Fire up some tea for Mr. Chuan!"

He smiled back as he took a seat at the bar. Apparently Magnus's enthusiasm only knew two volumes—loud and louder.

Evidently well-accustomed to the commotion, he heard Molly yell back, "Be right out!"

"So what adventure brings ya to Shady Vale, for an adventurer ya are. Don't deny it! For I can tell by your dress and confident step."

Magnus brought his hands down placatingly. "We don't get many folks out here lost as we are in the wilds of the Green Run—a few Tinkerers sellin' their magical contraptions, the occasional treasure hunter, traders, prospectors, or miners, but, more often than not, we get adventurers seekin' fame and fortune on the fringes, past the edges of the civilized world."

Yip smiled inwardly.

An adventurer?

Why not!

NEW FRIENDS

White clouds, azure sky
shifting with the sun.
What forms will my dreams take next?

Magnus's warm welcome, the stories of his father's adventures in the hills around the hamlet before helping to settle the valley after giving up mining with his Dwarven kindred, and the soothing tea put Yip at ease. Between the warmth and refreshment and the comfort of the surroundings, he found his tired eyes drifting ever closer to sleep.

He blinked slowly looking into his tea.

"Tell ya what," said Magnus. "Why don't ya take the room at the back of the hallway up the stairs. When ya've had a good nap, ya can come back down and regale me with a few tales of your adventures!"

"Ya have an exotic look about ya and I'm sure ya have plenty to share!"

His nod was lost in the bustle of directions and gesticular acrobatics of where the linens were stored, what time supper was served, what to do should he need any assistance, and the like. Following Magnus's directions up the stairs, he found his room at the end of the hall—quite spacious and well-appointed for such an out-of-the-way place. The furniture was all hand-crafted and very well-made. He set his small traveling kit on the bureau beside a flower pot filled with fresh water for the violets set beneath the window.

Stepping toward the bed, he took off his sandals and brushed his feet before lying down. He only had a few moments to examine the wooden beams along the ceiling before falling asleep.

He awoke to the sounds of a gentle breeze coming in through his window and the murmur of muffled voices in the commons room below. Afternoon shadows of gently swaying leaves dappled his sheets in gray. Savory smells from the kitchen also caught his attention. He enjoyed feeling free to relax without care, even if for just a short time.

Smiling inwardly at the thought of Magnus's earlier comment, he thought ruefully, *Adventurers, after all, must constantly be on guard!*

Of course, an adventurer was about as far from his reality as could be. Like an adventurer, he was a seeker perhaps, and used to hardship and goals out of reach, but what he sought was not riches in the ordinary sense, wealth, or power either magic or mundane, although they might come as part of his search.

Rather, he sought truth, meaning, compassion and understanding —wealth of character would be a closer analogy, although the restoration of his order stood firmly at the fore of his consciousness. At present, this goal was seemingly intangible and far from realization, for he had only the faintest inklings of the Cabal's plans, had not yet come to his power, and still had much to learn.

By ordinary standards, his body and skills at arms were strong, his insight and wisdom acute, his thoughts deft, his vision keen. In the ways of his teachers, however, he was a foundling struggling to reach the shores of deeper knowledge and insight into the great world around him, adrift with only his master's occasional visions and the help of those he encountered to guide him.

Wiping the sleep from his eyes, he gathered his loose-fitting robes about him and headed down the stairs. As he reached the bottom, he could not help but stop to marvel at the wonder and beauty of the human beings around him. He caught his breath in amazement as he looked on a room lit with the lights of the villagers' gathered souls.

The light of their lives filled him with joy and compassion, wonder and awe, for each spirit told him a story of the person sheathed in light. Colors and hues danced around each person, blending and merging with neighboring friends to create a general mood of gaiety and lightness after a hard day's work.

As his eyes strayed slowly across the crowd, he noted three who stood out from the rest. Their lights shone bright and strong, more vibrant than the rest of the revelers, torches amidst candles. He felt their vigor and potential thrumming in the air.

These must be adventurers of the sort Magnus was talking about, he mused.

He also recognized their *li* instantly.

This was the very same group he had encountered on the trail so recently.

He would need to find out how their friend Jenkins fared. If he were lucky, perhaps they would be able to offer some insight or guidance in his quest.

Appearing to be waiting for him at the table were the extremely tall, gangly red-haired giant from the Northlands wearing rather extravagant, if travel-worn, robes. His eyes were also very bright and excitable.

With the Northlander was the stout Dwarf with a full, braided brown beard streaked with white and chain mail glinting beneath his tunic. Bangles, symbols and totems adorned his belt and beard. His demeanor, although not unfriendly, lent a no-nonsense cast to his bearing, and the revelers gave him a wide berth.

Finally, also dressed in robes, these of a bright scarlet red, patterned with symbols for various constellations of the night sky and numerous arcane runes, sat the second much smaller man. His fine, almost Elven, facial features told Yip that he, too, was from the lands of Chang Sen, far to the east.

He sensed strong undercurrents of magic about the two humans, although their power was not made manifest by any current protections, and an elemental strength within the Dwarf.

"Mr. Chuan!" Magnus roared as he entered the room. "Ya've slept away most of the day! Anythin' I can get for ya?"

A few faces looked up at his arrival amidst the din, including the alert eyes of the three adventurers.

"You have already given me more than I could ask for in the use of a welcome bed and the refreshing tea," replied Yip as he reached the bar. "Those are gifts beyond counting."

"How about some supper? We have a nice braised rabbit, roasted quail, or a chicken soup all served with bread and the valley's finest mead!"

"Do you have any more of that nice warm tea and a few dried vegetables perchance?" His smile was as warm as Magnus's welcome.

"Well, it's a might bit early in the season for most vegetables, but we do have some turnips we stored overwinter along with some sweet potatoes and some fresh dandelion greens. Unless ya'd prefer somethin' conjured?"

"The vegetables sound wonderful! I only need a few slivers. Could I also have some boiling water?"

Raising an eyebrow curiously and shaking his head slightly as he went back to the kitchen, Magnus replied, "It'll be out shortly."

Yip pulled out a small pouch of dried medicinal herbs from within his robes and set it on the counter for when his tea arrived. The talk around him revolved around the timeliness of the spring rains, the proper quarter of the moon for planting early spring crops, and the likelihood of another banner harvest season.

He would approach the adventurers after he had steeped his tea.

Protected by its relative isolation amidst the wilderness and mountains, this pastoral village was blessed with security and enough freedom to be able to focus on the ordinary.

Much of the surrounding world would give quite a bit to trade positions, he thought.

After a few minutes, Magnus came back out with a small steaming tray of vegetables and greens, a small pot of boiling water, and a well-worn glazed mug.

"Enjoy!"

"Thank you! It looks wonderful," he replied as he opened his pouch, added a few dried stems to the tea pot, and then sprinkled a bit of the vegetable shavings in his water along with the tea leaves.

Magnus merely raised his thick eyebrows in response.

From his elbow, he heard a low, guttural voice exclaim, "What kind o' man eats like that, eh Magnus?" followed by a distinct harrumph.

Evidently the adventurers wanted to speak with him as well.

Having sensed the Dwarf's approach, Yip replied, "There are many types of men in this world, Master Dwarf, a fact of which I am sure you are well aware."

"Ya're not goin' ta have any meat? Nor ale? Nor proper sustenance? How d' ya keep up yer strength? And, fer that matter, quench yer thirst?"

"Strength comes from a man's heart and how he uses his mind and body. Right action makes a man's mind and body strong. Besides, Master Dwarf, not all that fuels a man's soul comes by way of the stomach."

"Yer talk is about as outlandish as those two woolly-headed travelin' partners o' mine," he said placing an empty tankard on the counter while motioning Magnus over to refill his mug. "I suppose eatin' like a rabbit must at least make ya light and fast?" He added, pulling at his braided beard with a faint lifting of his ruddy cheeks in the beginnings of a smile.

"And I suppose eating like a griffon must make you strong and a bit surly?" said Yip smiling back.

"Aye, and cantankerous ta boot!"

Yip laughed.

"Perhaps ya'd like ta join me and my friends fer supper, Yip? We're glad ta see ya made it out alive...and thankful," he added before turning to Magnus and saying, "Thanks fer tha refill, cousin."

Taking the favorable opportunity given to join the adventurers, Yip answered, "That would be most welcome."

Reading the Dwarf's honest, forthright character, he felt that the Dwarf could be trusted and deeply appreciated the help Yip had given. Remembering that he had not given his full name before when they had briefly met in the forest, Yip said, "My name is Yip Chi Chuan," offering a slight bow.

"And I'm Slate tha Dwarf, stalwart o' tha Flintforge clan, called Daer'Duin by my kin!" said Slate firmly while grabbing Yip's hand in his callused grip before turning to take his full tankard with him to the table.

Upon closer inspection, Slate stood about two-thirds Yip's height, his thick brownish, auburn hair level with Yip's chest. His shoulders were broad and strong, easily half again as wide as Yip's own. Besides the unusual broadness of his shoulders, the thickness of his limbs, and a distinguished, bulbous nose, the rest of Slate's body appeared in relative balance, similar in proportion to the humans milling around him. The thickness of his frame and limbs, however, gave him a sense of strength and solidity that none of the other patrons held. Despite his forbidding appearance, Slate's deep brown eyes twinkled with apparent mirth and good cheer.

Woven throughout the braids in Slate's beard were sharp yellowed fangs, tassels along with various tokens, bangles, and symbols. He assumed these items were trophies and designations of honor. Some of these items glowed with inner power. A finely wrought iron hauberk covered his chest and hung over his thighs. Strapped across his back, held in place by a large leather belt, a large double-bladed axe perched at the ready.

As they crossed the room and approached the other table, the man who was obviously from Chang Sen rose eagerly with a smile on his face opening his mouth ready to speak. Before any words left his lips, however, Slate said, "Yip, I'd like ta formally introduce ya ta my travelin' partners Wrindanneth and Aroganji. They're about as strange as ya if I don't miss tha mark by too far."

Before either of his friends had any chance to offer a greeting or rebuttal, Slate continued resolutely, "Wrindanneth and Aroganji, this is Yip Chi Chuan, ya may remember him if yer brains aren't as addled as I fear."

He paused briefly before gathering more momentum and air. "Now that we have tha formalities and conversation out o' tha way, let's eat!"

Slate finished his short introduction by pulling an extra chair up to the table.

Meanwhile, Yip, Wrindanneth, and Aroganji were left to continue the story of their journeys where Dwarven hospitality left off.

"You made it! We are so thankful for your help." Aroganji spoke first, obviously glad that Yip was with them.

"And how is your friend?" Yip hoped that he had given Jenkins the energy and desire necessary to recover.

"Jenkins is doing well and, he, too, sends many thanks. He is with the healers at a nearby outpost."

Wrindanneth eyed Yip appraisingly. "Never saw another Orc or their allies on the trip here. You have done the work of several men."

Yip shrugged off the compliment, saying, "The Orcs brought about their own downfall. I was merely a witness."

Wrindanneth laughed and shook his head. "If you say so! We could use a bit more of your witnessing then."

Yip turned the conversation away from himself in an effort to continue introductions and get to know the curious traveling companions better. "It is good to see a brother from Chang Sen so far from home," said Yip, glad for the companionship and sense of a place so distant but held so dearly.

Turning to Wrindanneth, he said, "And you must tell me of your lands, friend Wrindanneth, for I know only what I have heard in story."

Aroganji had already looked Yip up and down before his arrival at the table, having had time to give the matter some consideration on the journey to Shady Vale. Watching Yip's approach for confirmation of his suspicions, he had noted Yip's somewhat recently shaven head, flowing gait, air of introspection, and general ease.

Small and compact compared to the great hairy giants on this side of the Drake Spires, Yip was large by the standards of Chang Sen. Given what Aroganji could tell of him thus far, Yip also had an interesting story. "I always welcome the sight of a brother from the lands of my youth. Well met and welcome."

Although he did his best to hide it, Aroganji was quite excited to see someone from home. In a world full of so many differences, whether by race or culture, it was nice to occasionally see someone who shared traits and traditions common to your own—like an appreciation for good tea.

Having forgotten how obviously different and out of place he must seem, Yip appreciated Aroganji's greeting and hospitality, his link to the memory of home.

"This is all fine and well and good," said the fiery Wrindanneth, picking up the civilities where Slate's Dwarven introduction ended, "but what are you doing here and why should you join us?"

Apparently he, too, had already assessed Yip's character, abilities, and demeanor and come to his own conclusions.

"Join you?"

Wrindanneth's question had caught him off-guard. Though he had been considering finding help in his quest, he had not given any particular individuals consideration. Merely trying to survive the journey west, he had not yet even begun to truly consider how to find traveling companions much less join anyone so soon.

Apparently, they had discussed him in far more detail than he had imagined after leaving him on the trail in the woods.

Once again taking their measure, he noted the intensity and focus in Wrindanneth's green gaze. Aroganji, too, exhibited keen discernment and practicality in his comportment. Smiling, he noted that Slate exhibited little more than avid, intense focus on his plate.

His eyes resting slowly on each of the traveling companions in turn, he sensed these and many other positive attributes in their natures and was glad for their company.

While waiting for Yip's reply, Wrindanneth reiterated his question. "Tell me why you should join us."

Turning back to his companions after resuming his battle with a heaping plate of half-eaten food, Slate grinned and said, "Take it easy on him, boys. He's starvin' and, by Freyda's beard, all he seems ta want is tea, so we'd better let him regain his strength before askin' too many questions."

Reading that Wrindanneth's response only reflected his concern for his friends and his desire for their safety, Yip calmly replied, "I am here because this is where my fortune has taken me. Perhaps, if I were more fortunate, I would not have been forced to take this road and arrive at this place."

"Even though some may deem my situation unfortunate, I count myself lucky to be here among friends."

At that, Wrindanneth smacked his hand down on the table, amusement obvious on his face; Yip's answer clearly suiting his taste. "Aroganji, did you say you had a twin? Are you sure this isn't some doppelganger sent to take your place? Or does everyone from Chang Sen speak in riddles?"

"Ever the jester," replied Aroganji wryly. "Perhaps we should give Yip a chance to finish his herbal tea before asking any more questions," he finished with a disapproving glance at Yip's sad mixture of water and limp greens.

As he slowly sipped the warm tea filled with mixed herbs and vegetable slices, Yip looked past the table away from his dining companions to the animated village denizens around the room. Each seemed caught up in his or her own world, lost in their story or the tales of friends, enjoying the evening for its fellowship and camaraderie.

Sensing that the time for the sharing of their stories may have come, he questioned in kind. "So what brings you three to this fair valley? Are you this village's chosen guardians? Were you on a quest with Jenkins?"

While they gathered their thoughts, he continued, "A place as idyllic as this seems to have little need for adventurers. The valley gets plenty of sun and rain, the soil is deep and rich, and the people prosper from healthy fields and forests. I do not see the kind of adventure three such as you would seek, although not all is as the eye sees."

Aroganji cleared his throat before replying, "Valleys such as this are often safe because of the efforts of bands of adventurers such as ourselves. Oftentimes, in isolated areas, the townsfolk are not numerous enough to protect themselves from all eventualities. Most monsters may steer clear, driven away by the people's innate goodness, the magic of a few, or strength at arms, but the hearts of men are often not so kind."

"And you've already seen the kind of excitement that can find *bucolic* hamlets such as this," added Wrindanneth with a touch of sarcasm.

Slate nodded, continuing where his friends had left off, "Ya've already met Jenkins. He hired us ta ensure tha safety o' his minin' operations in tha wilds o' tha Green Run."

"We had just finished escortin' one stash o' his gems from his mine ta an outpost a few leagues distant. On our return ta tha mine, a few o' tha miners were certain that more than tha occasional Orcs who regularly plagued 'em had hidden out in tha hills not far from tha mine and were preparin' fer an assault, per'aps lookin' fer a chance ta expand their range."

"Lookin' fer tha chance ta turn a good deed and perchance garner a little extra coin, we followed up on tha opportunity. Took us tha better part o' a few days ta flush out all tha Orcs scattered through tha hills. Signs were that more were comin', so we knew it was time ta move."

"Jenkins asked fer our help gettin' tha rest o' his people and goods ta safety."

"Unfortunately, ya saw most o' tha survivors."

"A few o' tha Orcs must've survived our attack or managed ta summon more o' their fell kin 'fore we finished 'em."

Slate spat. "Unlucky fer them it seems. Shoulda kept their hides intact while they had it."

"We managed ta get most o' tha miners ta safety 'fore headin' on with Jenkins but a few stragglers kept pace."

He smiled grimly at Yip. "Ya took care o' that loose end fer us."

Leaving the darkness of loss and violence behind, Slate quipped, "'Sides, it'd been a while since I visited my cousin Magnus here now that he's decided ta make a livin' aboveground, so Jenkin's offer was most welcome."

Wrindanneth finished, "As fortune would have it, we came away with our fair share of earnings and a good deed or two in the process."

Slate grinned, alternating from stroking his beard to running his fingers along the edge of his axe.

"Sometimes law and goodness are where you create it," finished Aroganji.

As Yip sipped the last of his drink, taking care to finish everything without waste while savoring the last few drops of herbal tea, for it had been a long while since he had had anything along with his medicinal herbs, Wrindanneth took the opportunity to revisit his earlier question once more, a query he had now heard several times over the past two days. "And what brings you here, of all places, to the Afternoon's Shade Inn?"

ORIGINS

Dandelion seeds
drift in the spring breeze,
awaiting a place to rest.

Yip laughed lightly. "Could I continue forward not knowing what happened to your charge?"

When they waited quietly for more, not responding to his jest, he answered seriously, looking carefully at each Wrindanneth, Aroganji, and Slate in turn. "I am here because my past dictates that I must be."

His eyes told him that these men were honorable, worth his trust and, even if they might not be able to help him directly, they were well equipped to handle hardships of the kind he currently faced. Their past actions on behalf of Jenkins and his associates told him of the depth of their care and compassion. His insight and ability to read something of their essence told him what most other men would have taken months to assess, so, as was the way of his kind, he opened up and told the truth.

"Aroganji, you may know a little of my kind, so my story may not be as strange to you as it may be to your companions. I am a priest true, Aroganji, but not a priest of a faith practiced by more than a few. I am a priest, or at least in training to be, a Priest of the K'un Lun."

Seeing them glance at each other in confusion, he continued, "I see I have traveled much farther than I thought these last few months, memory of my kind much diminished."

"We are an order of ascetics from the mountain fastness of K'un Lun, hidden amidst the peripheral wilds of Chang Sen. Ours is an ancient order dedicated to the pursuit of truth and wisdom, insight and compassion, peace and understanding."

"In some ways, these ideals are mere curiosities in this world where self-interest dictates the actions of men; where monsters, spirits, and Daemons no longer seek the counsel of Man, Dwarf, Elf, or any of the other sentient Races; where aspirations for the heavens give rise to neglect for Ea'ae herself; where violence and petty fiefdoms choke and divide the lands. We seek to understand and relate to the very under-pinnings of the land, sky, and sea, to connect to the larger universe around us and in us, and are guided by its inherent truth and unfolding wisdom."

"Although we have lived in isolation for some time, penitence for times past, we seek to share what we have learned with those around us, to offer a path of peace and freedom to those who would seek after ideals and discernment that many neglect. Ours then is a Light that shines out in this world, a beacon that seeks nothing but itself, one that lights up those who would come to it."

He paused for a moment to collect his thoughts and to change the direction of the conversation.

"We are not perfect."

"Far from it."

"What began for us, a collection of seekers after truth, as a journey in peace has, through the ages, come to encompass the lessons of war. There were those among us, once guardians of our kind, who, guided by their own deepening insights and hunger for knowledge, began to seek not after the ways of wisdom, but for power and dominion."

"Brought up to see truth from falsehood, our eyes were well-trained to discern such developing darkness and deception. These few were cast out early in their turning, well before they came to the full-ness of their power."

"Upon being exiled from our order, those that had turned from the Light began to seek for dark alliances and ever greater power. Thus, the Liúxīng Làngrén, those fallen from the Light, more often called the Cabal, was born."

At this, Aroganji gasped, his thoughts convulsed with inner turmoil, and his tendons stood out white from reflexively gripping the edges of his chair.

"The Order of the Hooded Gaze..." He hissed, choking back the violence of emotions long pent up and held in check—undergoing an inner paroxysm. "Apparently our stories are intertwined more closely than I would have imagined. Finish your story then, Yip, and I will begin mine."

"The constellations of our destinies have been arranged in a very similar configuration."

As Yip's curiosity piqued and his hope stirred at Aroganji's response, he wondered if it would be too much to expect true friend-ship or partnership with these men.

Wrindanneth and Slate shared a look of bemused concern before motioning for Yip to continue, for as much as they bantered, seldom did they share their own histories.

Yip continued, "From there our history of monastic isolation dramatically shifted, for what had been one became two, and that one had found its opposite in an order driven by desire for revenge and an ever deepening lust for power. The time of our order's trials began and we of the K'un Lun were forced to use our powers and training more and more for defense and discernment."

"In a world as troubling as ours, we could not have survived through the millennia without some defenses, but as our difficulties became ever greater, so did our abilities in war. As our enemies' numbers grew and our numbers diminished through isolation, loss, and lack of recruitment, my order retreated upon itself, so that it could survive and continue to fight from behind the scenes, away from the frontlines where our enemies' numbers and alliances with greater Powers left us out of our depth and faced with possible extinction."

He took a deep steadying breath, for even though this history was from far before his time, it touched on emotions and concerns deeply rooted in the present and his reality, clouding his past and future.

"Hidden deep in the mountains, our elders used their powers to create a schism—a gap between their section of the world and the rest—what had been whole and seamless before was no more. Only a priest trained with eyes to see the world as it is could penetrate the separation created by their workings, for the Priests of the K'un Lun are the only mortals on Ea'ae able to unify reality when it is broken, to see past the illusion of separation and into totality."

"From the newly created safety of our mountain fastness then, my order was able to send brave priests out to help fight against the Cabal and bring those looking for answers to deeper questions and truths to a refuge where they could freely pursue their dreams and aspirations."

"As the centuries passed and the Cabal's efforts to penetrate the veil surrounding our haven by using the energies of dark sorcerers and unholy powers proved fruitless, we mistakenly believed ourselves safe from their gaze and perhaps secure."

"As time passed, our few wandering priests encountered less and less signs of the Cabal, heard less of their scheming. After a few decisive defeats of what we perceived were the last remnants of the Cabal, my elders and their allies in the outside world mistakenly thought the agents of Darkness had passed forever with their legions from our world."

"The eyes of the K'un Lun are sharp, but even our eyes can be deceived, for our priests were only partially correct. The evil of the Cabal had in fact passed from our lands, and the Cabal's blight had indeed passed almost entirely from the breadth of Ea'ae itself."

"However, the Cabal had not forgotten its origins and those who had cast them out. The Order of the Lidded Eye had passed to other, darker realms in pursuit of power. Their agents in Ea'ae, though long dormant, were still rooted in their remaining fastnesses, waiting for their masters' return, fomenting and building upon their evil. Though the protective seals around our world largely kept their masters out, these allies worked tirelessly through the ages to undermine our power and defenses."

"When we finally dropped the veil and reunited our small section of the world with the rest as it had been before, after ages of self-imposed isolation, we knew a brief time of peace—our inner harmony reflected the wholeness found in the outer world for the first time in millennia. As we began to reach out to those around us and started the process of restoration and uplifting for which we were founded, Darkness struck at our hearts again."

Now he spoke personally. "This is where my story begins."

"When the veil was first lifted and the priests of my order once more increased their presence in the outside world, many students came to our doorstep. A time of dearth ended and the priests expressed their joy by opening their doors."

"I was fortunate, if fortunate can in fact describe personal tragedy, an orphan found amidst a ruined village and later sent into the care of the K'un Lun. The order became the only family I knew. From the time of my boyhood, the priests raised me in the ways of the K'un Lun, honing my mental and physical skills, teaching me compassion and insight."

"Time does not pass for the K'un Lun as it does for other men. I am much older than I look, but in the ways of the priest I am young," he continued, composing his thoughts. "I know few of our secrets and have not had time to master many basic skills. By outside eyes, I may seem to have extraordinary talents, but in the eyes of my teachers, I have only just started my initiation."

"We spent much of our time when not training helping secure and revitalize villages surrounding our *guàn*, our monastery—planting trees, herbs, medicinal gardens, tending to the sick, teaching as much of our ways as we could, helping restore hope and balance to those within our reach."

"I was out on one such expedition, finishing a day's work in the evening gloaming, working by myself in an isolated village when the Cabal struck. I had a vision sent to me by Master Wei, one of my teachers, of our monastery in flames as the few priests on the premises fought amidst the smoke and ruin with dark creatures, abominations not fit for the most horrid nightmares. Master Wei urged me to run, to go into hiding, return when all was safe, or find friends if I could. He reassured me that all would be well, that he had sent similar messages to other priests and initiates, and that he would do his best to continue my training from afar that we could flourish again."

Yip sighed, his shoulders slumped. "I have been running for several months. Master Wei and most of the others who were at the monastery survived the attack. However, many of our venerable teachers were lost and much of our tradition with them. Those who were scattered in the assault have also returned and spend their energies at the *guàn* trying to rebuild and regroup. I am overjoyed that so many survived, but I worry that our safety and future along with all of Ea'ae are in jeopardy with the Cabal's resurgence and the weakening of Ea'ae's protective seals."

He paused to collect his thoughts. "As far as I know, I am the only priest left to move freely in this world."

He sighed. "And I am not yet a priest."

"When the all the priests, initiates, and acolytes returned, they decided to renew the veil that formerly held us apart from Ea'ae and prevented detection by the Cabal. So I am now largely alone in my pursuit of those who would destroy us."

"This isolated community is the first place where I have been at truly at ease since first climbing the Drake Spires and leaving the company of the H'era and Yeren peoples who dwell on the far side of the mountains."

"From here, I do not know where my path will take me. I have not sought to make friends during this time for risk of endangering them. My order does have a few allies who would help us, but, given the Cabal's power, secrecy, and resources, our friends wait with us for the right time to strike back while we recover."

"So I find myself here, amidst wondrous calm, security, and joy knowing these gifts will not be mine for an indeterminate time, only briefly as I recuperate from my journey and then seek to do what I can to help restore my order and assure Ea'ae's safety."

He finished with a slight bow of his head to his dining companions, a show of respect and humility, of openness and care.

Slate looked at Yip intently and with deep feeling. "I am sorry ta hear about tha trials o' yer people, but those not broken in tha forge are made stronger. That's a lessen we Dwarves have learned well and why many seek their fortunes in tha dangers o' tha outside world."

"My clan has known similar hardships and, although I would wish my past were different, I am a better Dwarf fer it."

Trying to lighten the mood, he added jokingly, "Yer travels sound more excitin' than a horde o' Dragon's gold if ya ask me!"

Slate then looked to Wrindanneth, who replied in a level voice, "Your tale may hold some promise for us as well it seems."

"We must take counsel, but, until then, I fear we have a bit more to hear before we can draw any conclusions or finish our surmise of the situation."

Wrindanneth was ever reluctant to grant trust to friends, much less strangers.

Even strangers who may have saved his life.

Once again, Yip sensed that these three had carried him forward in their thoughts on their journey to Shady Vale and that he had been the object of quite a bit of conversation after helping protect them from the determined Orcish pursuit.

Before his friends could continue their deliberations, Aroganji took a deep, steadying breath. "My past seems to have finally caught up with me...for, like Yip, I, too, am all too familiar with the Cabal. Unlike Yip, I am not on the run and do not think any of their agents are tracking me."

"I am who I am in large part thanks to the Cabal's actions and would welcome the opportunity to strike back at them."

"I am where I am by choice."

He continued, "As you already know, I, too, am from the wondrous lands of Chang Sen far to the east. My heart lights up just at the thought...the marvelous fog enshrouded mountains, deep jungles, and magical creatures found from mountain to shore. Exotic cities teeming with life—all sorts of Men, Elves, Dwarves, Gnomes, and other Races less common here in the West, each with its own cultures and customs unlike any you can imagine... Ah the beauty and joy!"

"Yip, I can tell you are as you say you are and therefore know that I am a wizard, as practitioners of magic are known in this land, or a Fang Shih as we are known at home. My magic is a learned skill, not so much an innate ability as a finely learned talent practiced and built upon since childhood."

"The type of magic I practice encompasses the Wu-hsing, the principle elements of creation, an art of blending and balancing more complex than language, as wide-ranging as human thought. We utilize symbols, visualizations, inscriptions, and invocations to conceptualize and actualize our magics, to create, understand, and invoke change and transformation."

"I actually went to school to learn magic. As hard as that is for people to understand in the countries we currently travel and abide in where most practitioners of arcane arts learn their skills either as an apprentice, as part of an enclave of like-minded individuals, or as wandering journeymen and adventurers. My parents sent me away to a school focused on sharing and fostering the magical traditions that are treated with so much more secrecy here."

Coming from a tradition that was in large part hidden from the dangers of the outside world, Yip could understand the need for secrecy, but he could also understand the desire to reach out, to branch and grow whether through practice, outreach, or an educational environment fostered by collegiality and the spread of ideals.

Aroganji, however, was unaware of these thoughts as he continued with his tale. "I come from a long line of mages tracing their lineage through several imperial dynasties. Quite often, the men and women of my family have served as advisors and protectors of royal families throughout Chang Sen. Many have served in the imperial palace and several have directly served the Emperor and Empress, those blessed by the Mandate of Heaven, the T'ien Ming."

Smiling shyly, with a touch of embarrassment, he bowed his head slightly and said, "Many count us as talented magicians. If that is the case, that talent might have skipped my generation."

"Whoa! Hold on just a minute there, young fella! Don't count yerself short!" Slate stood up from the table, thrusting his chair back quickly causing it to scrape on the burnished wooden floor as he pointed severely at Aroganji in reprimand.

"I'll have none o' that foolishness! Ya're as able a mage as I've met, this wool-headed son o' an ox turd included," he said with a grin pointing to Wrindanneth who for the nonce did not rise to the bait, "and we're proud ta include ya in our company!"

A little out of breath, perhaps unused to such long speeches, or expressions of his feelings, Slate sat back down huffing a bit in indignation as he recollected his chair. "Go on, go on!" he finished rolling his hands in a gesture to move his story along.

"Yes, go on, Aroganji," said Yip with a smile. Wrindanneth added his nod after a short glare at Slate.

"As a young boy, then, I went off to study at a school focused on the Higher Arts, learning the utilization of the human will to read and create substance from potential, symmetry from chaos, matter from energy, to understand and direct the subtle elements of Heaven and Earth. As many in my family had done before me, I went to the Xian Shi temple, a small but well-respected institution known across all of Chang Sen. My studies not only included matters of the occult, but also focused on the humanistic skills necessary to function within the Empire—calligraphy, oration, discourse, poetry, imperial law, and various martial and healing traditions native to our section of the country."

"As a formal learning institution, we had grades for various studies including novice, apprentice, journeyman, master, and instructor levels. After a student reaches the journeyman stage he elects to either continue his studies at the institution to become an instructor or strikes out on his own to realize his destiny. A few, like myself, sought to continue their research to become a master, a Fang Shih, in the arts of Fang Shu, the higher arts of Heaven and Earth."

"Graduation in our tradition is a rite of passage. One has spent the better part of sixteen years of focused study just to become a journeymen, a Yuan Ser, before continuing his journey either in formal training, exploration, tutelage, or trade. The culmination of so much time and effort truly is a time of celebrations. Families gather from all over Chang Sen to express their appreciation for the efforts of their offspring at the school before returning home to continue the festivities. Meanwhile, despite all the excitement and distraction, the Yuan Ser must take the first steps to independence."

Aroganji shook his head sadly as he got to a portion of the story he would rather not remember, much less share. "The spring of my graduation had just passed. I had met with success in the trials in the Halls of Testing and was ready to relax and regroup before moving on. I was also looking forward to spending some time talking with my teachers about how best to realize my future. Almost the entire graduating class had left for the summer in high spirits with their families to continue their revelry, either going home to rest and recover their energies after much magical exertion or to continue their studies elsewhere at another specialized institution or with a particularly adept instructor or archmage."

At this point, Aroganji paused to offer a bit of clarification. "Our school represents the fusion of our art, perfectly situated to take advantage of the intrinsic energies of the environment, the basis for our practice. Carefully placed at the base of the formerly active Hsiang Lung Mountains, bordered by ancient forests skirting the base of the peaks and rolling grasslands that gradually fall into the Q'ia Shan Sea, the school embodies a harmony of the principle elements—earth, air, water, wood, and fire. Rain and ocean, sea breezes and mountain squalls, snowstorms and sea tempests, billowing fog, cyclic variegation in foliage, mosses and barnacle covered rocks, volcanic flows high in the distant peaks, all reflect seasonal changes and interactions, evolutionary growth and the perfect blending of the Wu-hsing."

"Who could come to a place such as this and not learn or thrive?"

"As I wandered the artfully arranged grounds outside the school proper, thinking of my family on their way home after the ceremonies and my future soon approaching, my spirits floated with the clouds that daily cloaked the mountains above our rock walls and tiled roofs as the sea winds moved in off the coast. I had just finished my last consultation with Master Jia Lu on how my arcane studies should best be pursued after leaving Xian Shi with a scroll of recommendation in hand to aid in my future studies. I was a newly independent young man ready to test his wings and fly on the winds of fortune."

"Like any institution dedicated to the arcane arts, our center was a repository for great powers. So, in many ways, our school was much like a fortress, protected by solid walls and bolstered by myriad hidden spells and sigils, guardians, both human and occult, to shield its walls, and ancient talismans, *fu-lu* in our tongue, ward it recesses."

"As such, one of our instructors had brought back an item of great power on a journey to the planes—an orb much storied for its ability to find what is lost, to see into what is hidden—the Eye of the immortal Dragon Guai Lo, a Lung-wang from far in our nation's past. The instructors took great care hiding and protecting this artifact in the vaults. They also took every precaution to use it sparingly and only when needed to further their studies when seeking insight into a particularly difficult subject or scrying for a much needed piece in ritual, magical, or alchemical arts."

Again Aroganji sighed. His heavy breath caused the candle on the center of their table to flicker in the tavern's half-light. "As a magician, one of the first lessens you learn is that power attracts power. Much of the skill involved in magic is not just learning the shaping of intent, the proper incantation and ritual gesture, but the proper harnessing and release of untold power. Without caution, a caster who reaches beyond himself will burn out like the briefest of flames in the night and must therefore learn his limits, only performing spells of a level he is capable of handling. Such is also the case when using an item of great power."

"Using an object of might like the Eye requires a substantial expenditure of energy, and, despite their precautions and best intentions, this usage must have been detected by someone or something looking for the Eye. The Cabal, or as they are known amongst the students of Xian Shi, the Order of the Hooded Gaze, for their servants are but the hooded shells of what they were, dark shadows of evil cloaked in death, must have been seeking this artifact as well."

His look pregnant with meaning and emotion, Aroganji gazed around the table at his friends. "Who knows? Our adepts may have even taken the Eye from the Cabal or their agents directly and only now were they willing or able to come and retrieve it."

"Whatever the cause, the Eye led to the end of those few unfortunate enough to still be on the grounds of Xian Shi when the Cabal chose to reclaim it."

By this point in his story, Aroganji's face had taken on a look that held a mixture of terror, sadness, and disgust. He slowly clenched and released his hands amongst the folds of his robes, lost in bitter memories.

"There was absolutely nothing we could do to stop their assault. I want to make that clear. After much inner questioning, this is a conclusion I have come to feel as true deep inside. The few of us who were still at school could do little to defend against the horrors that descended upon us from the sky. Luckily for us, the dark beasts were after the Eye instead of the residents of Xian Shi or even more would have died unnecessarily."

"I remember first hearing a great rush of air that drew my attention upward. Looking into the sky, a huge rent split the firmament with an undulating fissure of darkness. Writhing horrors seemed to grab the rent's edges and tear the fabric of reality apart as vast beasts struggled to impose their will on a version of creation not to their liking. As soon as the first Daemon came through and started its descent, the sky burst into radiance as our wards exploded in arching sheets of energy around the creature."

"As the thing writhed in pain, consumed in magical fires, tendrils of Darkness swarmed from the rent, smoky appendages that lashed out and tore away the defensive spells enveloping the first creature, absorbing the scintillating energies with but a touch, leaving only a burnt and broken husk in their wake. As the smoke and light from the continued detonations of protective wards finally cleared, I could see the otherworldly tendrils teeming and writhing as they felt along the edges of the energy barrier, unaffected by the explosions though the decimated shells of many other fallen Daemons littered the ground."

"Light burst and arched at each contact with the shielding, sparks shimmered and bounced along the edges of the barrier, limning its presence over and around the school in the vivid light of the afternoon. As with the tear in the sky, the wisps of Darkness coalesced into a great seething mass that eventually plunged through the barrier, gradually separating into individual strands that tore the school's shield back allowing room for yet other monstrosities to pass through along with their darker brethren."

"After seeing this display I ran."

"I was very young and scared, confused and uncertain. I was no match for extradimensional Powers such as these, Daemons from some other realm blacker than the foulest heart."

"As I ran, I began working a spell to camouflage myself and mask my passing. In my own defense, despite all my studies, I was still inexperienced in the ways of higher magics, especially when compared with beings of true Power. Perhaps if our full faculty had been there, or if we had had the aid of more trained students, we could have repulsed the beasts' invasion along with their foul seething Shadow. As it was, with just a few students, teachers, and temple guardians remaining to face the horrors from beyond, many of those with the opportunity or ability wisely teleported away or hid."

"The first horror that came through the sparking hole in our aegis appeared to have the head of an ebony lion, with a great flowing mane hovering as of its own volition. This mane flowed over scarred black armor etched and pitted in horrid runes that turned my gaze away in fear; all born by a great muscular frame as tall as the eaves on our buildings. I knew from my studies that this was a Rakshasa, a type of Daemon from another realm that wields great sorcery in conjunction with an almost unsurpassed skill at arms."

"I could see the thing rend and tear through the remaining sigils and runes protecting our citadel from infiltration even before it gracefully floated to the ground to have its way within our main courtyard."

"Light blazed from the Rakshasa's hands as buildings exploded in fire and molten rubble while the remains of houses of learning flew through the air of the central plaza. As I turned back to look, a lurid red eye blazing on its chest plate seemed to smolder and shift as if peering around the courtyard wantonly for other eyes to see."

"Later research told me that this creature was commonly an ally of the Cabal, one whose actions were dictated by the needs of dark alliances between great Powers."

"Before the beast had fully set its weight on the ground, two of the stone statues guarding the school's entry rumbled into life. The prodigious golems surged toward the Rakshasa like an avalanche, massive stone hulks implacable and unyielding. The automatons smashed into the Rakshasa amid a billowing haze of dirt churned up from their great treads. Giant stone fists pounded the feline demon into the ground, the strength of mountains smashing the thing into the earth, their blows like claps of thunder. Before the giants could close again and follow their advantage, a rainbow-colored orb of dancing energies burst into existence around the creature rendering any further blows from the golems ineffectual."

"The Rakshasa stood slowly, dusting itself off casually as the two golems pounded on the dancing energies of the sphere, and released its counter strike. With two abrupt movements of its hands, the Rakshasa lifted both golems high into the air, before jerking its hands suddenly to the ground. As its hands released, the golems' great mass blasted into our sleeping quarters, bringing the entire building down to the ground in a dusty ruin. I could feel the earth shudder with their impact even as far away as I was outside the school grounds."

"Neither giant rose from the rubble."

"Before the golems ever hit the ground, the remaining teachers' spells had torn through the Rakshasa's barrier. Taking advantage of their opening, the temple guardians leapt toward the beast, their swords ablaze with magic energies. Fast and nimble they danced and swarmed around the creature weaving and cutting, but their blows were as ineffectual as our defenses. With hardly a glance, the beast swept our men-at-arms from its path, many landing twisted and broken yards away across the courtyard."

"Weapons of far greater enchantment than those employed by the school's unfortunate defenders would be required to harm such a fell creature."

"As I ran, I could see a few instructors and beleaguered students organizing a concerted defense against the creature from the far side of the courtyard. As they worked, their bodies shimmered behind magical shields and wards meant to keep the monster at bay. From their defensive position, bright lights and flames lashed through the air, surrounding the beast in a haze of blazing destruction. Power shimmered around the creature as great torrents of energy brightened the day. I had to shield my eyes to protect them from the expenditure of power."

"As my eyes recovered from the glare, the afterimages of magic still dancing in my sight, I looked in horror as the beast roared and continued forward, seemingly immune or unaffected by all their efforts, now joined by several kindred working foul magics in support of their leader, countering the host of spells intended to destroy their vanguard. Their actions were confident and almost casual, if beings of such power could be described in such a way, as they mowed down what resistance was put up against him, tearing through the defensive spells erected to bar their way as easily as they did with the people that cast them."

"By the time I had made my escape, the Rakshasas had shorn through a portion of the outer wall of the library, the remains a great heap of stone and tiles cast flippantly to the side. As I looked back in dismay one last time, the very Darkness of the fissure in the sky seemed to be descending as dim cloaked figures drifted down from the murk above. I felt my heart sink as a cloud of evil gripped the school in a fog of dread and despair."

"After seeing such Darkness and horror, it took all my volition just to put one foot in front of another in order to flee. By the time the smoking ruins of Xian Shi were out of sight behind me, a great weight had lifted from my shoulders, but my heart was never the same again."

Lost in distant remembrance, Aroganji's eyes smoldered with intent. "I vowed on that day to avenge those lives lost so needlessly and to discover the source of the evil that destroyed the dreams that once created my school."

Gradually regrouping, once again relieving himself of great sorrow, Aroganji continued with a deep exhale, "If I had sufficient skill, I would have teleported or far-traveled home, but those skills were beyond my capabilities at that time. After I recovered myself and gathered the necessary energy from a safe distance, I morphed into a hawk to help speed the journey home."

"Several days of hard travel brought me to my family's compound near the imperial capital. I found my home in as much turmoil as my spirit. Apparently imperial messengers had arrived ahead of me, for my parents thought me several days dead, left to terrors not fit for imagining. Despite all their love and outpourings of affection, no amount of consoling from my parents could ease the burdens on my heart."

"From that day forward, I focused on bettering myself and redoubled my efforts, seeking after knowledge and arcana, a student of higher arts with a focus that few can comprehend. Searching for new spells and artifacts, I have become over time something of an adventurer."

With that, Aroganji looked up, his eyes now bright with tears, filled with purpose and passion, directly at Yip.

After gathering himself, once again he continued, "Wrindanneth and Slate share my passion for new knowledge and the arcane, each in their own way, and our overarching passion to do right, so we are a natural fit for one another. Although our ultimate goals may be different, they respect my personal aspirations even if, until now, they did not know the true cause or extent."

Once again gazing at Yip, his eyes alight with sincerity and focus, he said, "As I said, Yip, our stories appear to be more intertwined than we know. Perhaps we should continue that tale together and see what it reveals."

At this, all three traveling companions turned to Yip expectantly, obviously moved by Aroganji's story—Wrindanneth with a firm resolve, surprised and touched by his friend's hidden story, though reluctant to show it, and Slate with a grim determination, as though hearkening his friend's call to battle.

His story told, Aroganji's face lit with the light of hope.

Yip returned their looks with the briefest of smiles.

"I have always been a lover of stories," replied Yip, reaching out and placing one of his hands over Aroganji's on the table. Although he had not come to their table expecting to find allies on his quest, merely potential insight and guidance from those who appeared to be worthy of trust, he had found more than he could have ever hoped. "Perhaps soon we will be in a position to write our own."

ONE FINGER

Practicing his sword,
with great deliberation,
the young man attacks the wind.

Shadows danced in the corners and ran along the beams of the lightly plastered inn room. Overhead, weathered eaves gradually coalesced only to disappear amidst the light smoke and gloom provided by a single wax candle. Sitting calmly in the center of the room on his bedroll, poised and light, Yip's awareness filled the space, encompassing the region in its entirety around the single candle flame flitting across from him several paces away.

As his attention focused on the lone point of light wavering across the room, his intention sharpened to a luminous bolt as he cast his hand out toward the sputtering flame.

"Pai-lien!" He shouted as his hand and mind's eye exploded toward his target.

A few feet away, glowing a soft yellow-orange, the candle continued to burn, unaffected by his intent.

BEGINNINGS

Indigo hills
shelter under clouds
in preparation for rain.

The next morning dawned cool and refreshing as Yip carefully packed away his small kit and headed downstairs to meet his new friends for breakfast before continuing on their way together. A light fog had settled over the valley, cushioning the resting spirits from the beginning of a new day. Looking out his window, he could barely see the large sycamore tree shading the inn; other farm houses were lost in the gray distance.

He made his way down the old wooden stairway and looked out upon a room empty, not yet filled with the patrons who would soon lend their vivacity and character to its charms. He chose a small table in the corner to wait for his newfound companions. In the distance behind the bar, he heard Magnus bustling around the kitchen, his wife cheerfully working at his side humming with the lively birdsong coming in from the open windows.

Before they began their descent, he could hear Slate grumbling with Wrindanneth from the top of the stairs, already at odds even before the day began, arguing over who would pay for their tab since Slate had lost some recent wager.

This was going to be an interesting trip, he thought to himself, appreciating the color that these two characters would bring to the day.

With a loud grunt and some heavy treads upon the stairs, Slate was finally convinced that he did in fact owe his cousin Magnus their evening's bill. As he entered the room, however, Yip could sense that Slate had yet another card to play.

As the party's designated purse keeper, for who kept better care of coin than a Dwarf, Slate was mollified because the tab was coming from the party's purse which had yet to be divided after their recent bandit raids. As a result, with some careful accounting, he may get his fair share of gold yet!

Able to read nuances and subtleties of gesture in addition to people's energy patterns, Yip held back a small chuckle after this deduction. As the old saying went, "A Dwarf and his gold are seldom parted."

"Brother Yip! Did ya wake up hung over from all tha tea ya drank?"

The Dwarf trundled stolidly over, amiable and filled with ready anticipation, his movements steady and sure after long years spent boosting his alcohol tolerance. He had emptied more than his fair share of tankards the night before during the telling of tales between the new friends.

"Like you, I am none the worse for wear despite my hardships," replied Yip. "Have a seat."

"Aye, think I will yet," replied Slate. "Magnus! Bring us some ham and bread and something ta quench a Dwarf's thirst!"

Slate took the opportunity to tear into a steaming loaf of bread sitting ready for serving on the bar's countertop.

Just as loud from the next room over, Magnus yelled back, "Aye, cousin Dwarf, I've got yer food a cookin' already. I do no' know if we have anythin' to quench tha likes of yer thirst, especially since ya drank it all last night!"

Magnus finished firmly, "And if ya'd be so kind as to not wake tha neighbors and patrons I might even bring yer food out to ya!"

From the landing at the top of the stairs, he heard Wrindanneth reply as he started walking down, "What's all this fuss about? Can't a man bring in the day with the ceremony it deserves?"

"I am, Wrindanneth, with a tankard o' ale and a slab o' meat!"

"Are you sure we didn't bring back an Orc from our latest expedition, Wrindanneth?" suggested Aroganji as he crested the doorway.

"Well, he is small and hairy and definitely in need of a bath. If it weren't for the beard, I'd say you're right!"

"Well a fine lot o' friends ya are! Takin' a well-groomed Dwarf so far from his home and treatin' him so cruelly. Ya should be ashamed!"

"And you should use a napkin," replied Wrindanneth pointing out the bread crumbs in Slate's beard as he approached.

With that Aroganji let out a laugh and Slate slapped his hand down on the table with a great guffaw, quite used to this banter after spending so much time together.

"What should our next plan of action be, gentlemen?" asked Aroganji.

"A gentle man I am not," replied Wrindanneth, "but if I hang around with the lot of you long enough, I might become soft enough to be considered gentle."

"Speak fer yourself ya seven foot tall scarecrow. I fer one will never be gentle. It's not in a Dwarf's constitution!"

Changing directions, Yip offered, "Based on what I can see and have heard of your capabilities, we are far from a match for the Cabal and most of their servants. Compared with some Powers, we are as children."

"Perhaps our best strategy would be to gather what information we can while offering assistance to those in need that we meet in our investigations. If we are lucky, our capabilities will grow with our knowledge."

"Aye and perhaps we will find a few treasures along tha way ta keep it interestin'. Fer a Dwarf without coin or artifact is like a mine without gold...or gems...or mithril...or adamantium...or minerals..."

Slate washed his hands eagerly with a faraway look in his eyes as his words drifted to imagining.

"Or sense," finished Wrindanneth.

"Huh?" muttered Slate collecting himself from his reverie.

Yip interrupted further banter. "The sun is breaking the horizon and the time to travel is here. Where shall we go?"

While Aroganji, Wrindanneth, and Slate looked to each other questioningly, he proposed, "These lands are new to me and I do not know them well enough to say. I can tell you this, with the Cabal tracing me, the more people around to interfere with detecting my energy patterns, the better. Until I learn how to properly conceal them, though not yet a priest, my signature is quite strong and obvious to those who would look. As I said before, I still have much to learn, and masking my auric body is one skill I am still learning."

"We have a small outpost on Tellanon, a large floating city in the sky," said Aroganji. "The city serves as a major trade center for this section of the continent. Star-faring and dimensional jumping ships also use it as a docking and recovery station. Much knowledge and opportunity comes through there. We could go back and see what information we can ferret out before choosing a desired path."

"And there's also Hoyt," added Wrindanneth with a wide grin.

"Aye. If anyone's heard anythin', it'll be him."

Yip let his excitement show. "That sounds like a wise choice. We will need to know all we can about the Cabal, their dealings, and their agents. Such a large city with all your contacts will be an ideal place to go!"

"Perhaps after we learn more of their activities, I can actively seek out one of my masters for guidance."

He paused a moment before asking innocently, "How do we get to this city in the sky?"

Aroganji shrugged. "I am not powerful enough to teleport all of us there as I can only travel interdimensionally for short distances with a group, although I could port there myself. We will have to far-travel."

Wrindanneth smiled wryly. "With that I can help too. Together, Aroganji and I can transport you both."

"'Tis an excitin' form o' transport indeed! Lookin' at tha horizon and then appearin' there as if yer steps spanned tha breadths o' tha very gods!"

Slate was eager to get started as were the rest of the companions.

"The primary problem with far-traveling is that short distance ports only go as far as the naked eye can see. In this valley, for example, we will be able to port to the top of the surrounding hills. From there, we can jump from ridgetop to ridgetop so long as the day is clear and we can make out details of our destination. In order to make the most of Traveling, we must choose our destination spots wisely so as to maximize distance per port."

"Alternating turns casting, resting in between, Wrindanneth and I can only manage about five or six ports in a day. We should be able to cover a few hundred leagues if conditions are right in this mountainous region. As we reach flatter topography, our travel distances will shorten correspondingly."

"Thank you for the lesson, professor Aroganji," said Wrindanneth laughing. "You do like to go on at times."

"Why don't you go pay our room and board, so we can move on?" retorted Aroganji.

"'Tis a good plan that!" added Slate chuckling and shaking so much that his mail jingled as much as the purse he handed Wrindanneth.

RÓUCÍ

Undulating blue ridges
lost in humid haze—
peaks floating in clouds.

After saying their goodbyes and giving their thanks to Magnus and
Molly, the party gathered outside the inn beneath the eaves of the
porch, the sun just cresting the eastern ridge as the morning's shadow
gradually receded across the valley to the west.

Before leaving the shelter of the porch, while his companions organized their packs beneath the old sycamore, Yip took a moment to take
a seat on the knotty wooden planks, open his small travel kit, and
remove an intricately carved scroll case. Carved of ivory and capped
by two tasseled bronze plugs, the artistic piece stood out in stark
contrast to the travel-worn robes he wore. Carefully withdrawing a
small quill and a single piece of rice paper from within, he began to
write.

Noticing Yip sitting, wont of something worthwhile to do, Slate
called out, "What're ya up ta? We're about ta be off! This is no time fer
lollygaggin'!"

When Yip did not respond, Aroganji and Wrindanneth took a

moment to walk over. "What are you working on, Yip?" asked Wrindanneth.

"A *róucí*."

"A *róucí*?" questioned Wrindanneth.

"You would call it a poem I think."

Interrupting, Slate barked from where he was tying down his pack, "Why in tha name o' Brendle's beard are ya workin' on a poem now o' all times?"

Not responding, Yip answered Wrindanneth's question. "A *róucí* is a short poem meant to express the immediacy, the totality and fullness, of a moment. Through three simple verses, a writer attempts to capture the essence, the truth, of an event, impression, or feeling."

"What did you write?" asked Aroganji.

Tapping his quill lightly on the rice paper, words appeared and seemed to flow across the page before disappearing again upon being read.

> "Travel-worn satchel—
> How many lands have you seen
> on your journey home?"

The party paused. A bluebird in the sycamore tree began a short melody, filling the silence.

"Hmm. Not bad," said Wrindanneth.

"Do your poems take a particular form?" asked Aroganji.

"They are usually five to seven syllables per line. I generally include only three lines, but sometimes I write four."

Slate raised his thick eyebrows. "Do they rhyme?"

"No."

"Okay. I'll have a go," said Wrindanneth as he looked at Slate busily organizing all his travel gear. "You said five to seven syllables per line?"

"Yes," answered Yip. "Most commonly the lines are five-seven-five, but there is flexibility in the variation. The name itself means, 'flexible verse.'"

"I was always good at poetry contests in the town fair," said Wrindanneth as he mused and counted out syllables on his fingers, his eyes lost in the distance.

"Imagine that," muttered Slate under his breath. "Forcin' poor innocents ta listen ta yer musin's."

Wrindanneth shot Slate a glare then paused for a moment before intoning,

> "Dwarven beard unkempt—
> Tangled, matted, disheveled.
> Is there a bird in there?"

Aroganji clapped. "I think you've got it!"

"You bring the reality of the situation to my eyes," laughed Yip.

Stroking his beard somewhat self-consciously, Slate muttered, "If a Dwarf can't be proud o' his beard and Kazzak adornin' it, then what's there ta be proud o'?"

Turning back to his friends, he cleared his throat. "Enough foolishness! We've got a journey ta start!"

Robes rustling in the crisp morning air as he left the foot of the porch, Aroganji motioned everyone close. "Gather round and look with me toward that rocky prominence!" he said pointing to a particular spot on the top of the nearest small mountain surrounding the village.

As they moved in, Wrindanneth sniffed, turned, and looked at Slate. "Slate, I thought we paid to get you a room so you wouldn't have to sleep in the barn with the other sheep."

Apparently Wrindanneth had gained some momentum after composing his verse.

"If ya keep talkin' like that, I'll shave yer woolly head with my axe, Northman! I could use a new red kerchief and I hear woolly-headed Northmen hair is o' tha finest quality fer skeinin'."

Slate looked at Wrindanneth wickedly. "Or I could claim a few o' yer teeth ta braid in me beard with tha other Kazzak."

"And if you wouldn't sleep with your mail on, we wouldn't have this discussion," Wrindanneth finished haughtily, always ready to fall back into his role of sarcastic contrarian.

"Gentlemen, if you're ready?" Muttering under his breath as much at his companions as to work his spell, Aroganji first visualized his intent along with the symbol for traveling as was the way of his tradition before intoning abruptly in the language of the Elves from whom he had learned the spell, "*Sirathok gilthanel ilduran!*"

And the world shifted.

Yip looked around in astonishment.

Just the instant before, he had been on the valley floor admiring the sunrise over the ridgeline. Now he stood on the heights overlooking the small village and outlying farms all nestled cozily amidst the trees leading up the hillsides. Turning away from the valley, he could see other small mountains, large hills really, vanishing off into a blue haze. Mentally retracing his steps back to the east, he could see much larger peaks in the distance, although the full majesty of the Drake Spires were lost in the humidity of the warm morn.

Yip did not contain his excitement. "Amazing! What a gift!"

"To live in a world of magic where the thinkable is reality and all that is imaginable is possible."

"I am ashamed to have lived in such a place, never experiencing wonders such as this, only hearing of such magics in stories secondhand."

"Okay, brother monk, I know the world is full of wonder and all that, but if you hang around with me, you're going to have to curb your enthusiasm a bit," replied Wrindanneth bluntly. "After all, I have to concentrate here. We're going to be doing this more than once."

"One must also be true to oneself, brother Wrindanneth." Still turning around slowly in excitement, eyes cast to the horizon, he finished, "Don't let me distract you. I know it is hard for you to do more than one task at a time."

And with that Yip offered Wrindanneth a bright smile.

Wrindanneth smiled back. He was going to like this true-speaking little priest. "You may call me Wrin."

Yip bowed.

He then turned to look at Aroganji who was sitting nearby on the weather-beaten rock face of the outcrop, breathing a bit heavily after his magical exertion. To Yip, it seemed as though Aroganji's fire burned a little dimmer, as if casting the spell had drained him of a bit of his essence. He could gauge based on his impression that Aroganji could only work that magic one or two more times before he would be spiritually spent for the day until he recuperated fully through a restful sleep. Perhaps in the future, he could learn to share his essence with Aroganji to help make more casting possible without the need for rest.

Sensing Yip's eyes on him, Aroganji offered, "All is well, Yip. I am just recovering myself a bit. That is a new spell to me and I have never tried it with so many."

Wrindanneth chimed in, always ready to lend a helpful, if mocking, hand. "Luckily, he taught it to me as well, else we would never get anywhere!"

"Gather round and look with me northward toward that small hilltop along the crest of that broken ridge." Wrindanneth's eyes led the party's gaze as much as his outstretched index finger.

Gesturing abruptly toward his destination, Wrindanneth repeated the phrase Aroganji had used earlier, "*Sirathok gilthanel ilduran!*"

In the space between heartbeats, in the midst of the release of power, the world paused. Then Yip was suddenly perhaps thirty or more leagues away as the Dragon flies on the other ridgetop surrounded by his new companions. Looking back, he could see a journey of several days between himself and their last overlook on the other ridge.

Now both of his new friends' flames burned a little dimmer.

"You must rest a bit, my friends, and recover. Perhaps I could offer you a nice refreshing tea?"

Before either could answer, Yip heard Slate grumbling to his left as he extracted himself gingerly from a thorny thicket.

Turning to Wrindanneth, Slate pointed his finger and said, "Ya did that on purpose ya great woolly-headed buffoon!"

Not waiting for an answer, the incident quickly forgotten, Slate turned his back on Wrindanneth leaving him to shake his head, replying to Yip while reaching for a small bag tied to his belt at his side, "Keep yer tea, Yip, it's too early in tha mornin' fer that. What we need is a nice bit o' ale!"

Watching the Dwarf with an amused grin, Aroganji intoned, "We most certainly do not need any ale, Slate. Wrin and I just need a little time to recover ourselves and regain our concentration."

"Speak fer yerself. All this work has churned up quite a thirst!"

And with that, he reached down into the bag at his waist. First his arm disappeared into the sack, then his head and lastly his shoulders. Finally pulling his head back out of the bag, he turned to Yip and said, "Hold my feet!"

Crawling in to his boots, Slate disappeared into the small bag. Holding on to Slate's feet, Yip tried to wrap his mind around the spectacle of a stocky Dwarf crawling completely into a bag no longer than his forearms while searching for alcohol without breaking out in laughter.

Snickering behind them, expressing the emotion Yip did not, Wrindanneth said, "And if you find that money you owe me down there, bring it back too!"

Turning to Yip, Wrin continued, "That bag contains a small pocket dimension we use to store all our goods, provisions, and earnings. Slate, as the official bearer and counter of our coin, conveniently loses things in there all the time."

Huffing and puffing, Slate emerged shortly thereafter holding a smoky gray flask in hand proudly. "And this, my friends, is a little nip o' tha hold's finest brew!"

Popping the top, he took a deep swill from the flask, sucking in air through his lips at the same time as he swallowed, before letting out a great belch. Wiping his beard with his shirtsleeve he quipped, "Odd, that's not quite how I remembered ole Dûnedar's brew tasting."

With that pronouncement, he let out another belch, followed by a hiccup, his features shifted, and then he turned into a chair.

"By Drothman's axe! An allomorph potion!" grunted Slate, the talking Dwarven stool.

Ever the helpful companion, Wrindanneth finished his own helpful bit of advice, "You know, we really should label these things. One never knows what some of our treasure contains. At least you look like something that would come from a tavern, Slate!"

"At least we keep things interestin', eh Yip?" finished Slate, the slats on his chair back drooping a bit disconsolately.

"Don't worry, Slate, the potion will wear off in an hour or so," offered Aroganji reassuringly.

"You know, I could dispel the magic from the potion, but we may be better served by saving our strength for the next port," finished Wrindanneth as he looked to Aroganji.

"I think that may be a good idea," acknowledged Aroganji. "Are you a bit tired, Wrin?"

"You know, I believe I am."

"Perhaps you had better take a seat."

"I think I will!"

And with that, Wrindanneth sat down on Slate, relishing the comfort of a well-worn, broken in tavern chair, perched as it was in a wonderfully relaxing spot on a high mountaintop overlooking the multicolored valleys and hills stretching off into the distance beneath a clear blue sky.

Slate could not even glower in reply.

The companions waited until mid-morning before Slate finally returned to normal, his cheeks blushing with embarrassment from his blunder. Surprisingly, he was not particularly upset, perhaps because he did not want to draw too much attention to his error.

"Even a Dwarf can make a mistake!"

"We've proven that many times over already, Slate," said Wrindanneth. "Do we need further evidence?"

Changing the subject, respectful of his friend, Aroganji continued, "Do you feel up to another round, Wrindanneth?"

"Only if you go first."

Their next port landed them directly in the thick of a dense patch of thorny blackberries.

"Yargh!!!" Slate's cry was the first indication of their predicament. "Get this mess outta my beard!"

Fortunately for the party, with Slate's help, and a heavy reliance on his thick Dwarven skin, they were able to eat themselves free of the worst of the tangles.

"Looks like you've got a bird's nest buried in your beard, Slate," said Wrindanneth.

"Humph. Tha only things in my beard are marks o' honor, North-man," Slate's irritation was tinged with humor. "Besides," he said lovingly while stroking the thick twines, "if it weren't fer this beard, all these thorns might've jeopardized my good looks!"

Wrindanneth snickered.

Slate's mail allowed him to plow through the worst of the tangles until they found a suitable vantage for the next jump.

Aroganji pointed to the next ridge. "See the series of prominences that look like a face—the browline, the nose, and the chin?"

Following his finger as he pointed, Wrindanneth said, "Aye. Let's aim for the nose in the center."

Concentrating on the same point, they made the next jump with a *pop* as air rushed in to fill the void left by their passage.

Their adventures were not yet done for the morning.

As they reoriented themselves beneath the canopy of gnarled old trees, Yip was the first to notice Slate's absence.

"Slate?" His call did not elicit any response.

"Let a master try." Wrindanneth took a deep breath in preparation to let his well-practiced lungs unleash a mighty yell.

"Slate!"

His call echoed off the hills. "…late…late…late…"

Off in the distance, they heard Slate's bellowed response. "Oy!"

Apparently Slate had concentrated on the wrong hilltop.

An hour later, Slate trundled through the undergrowth, his cheeks flushed with exertion and embarrassment.

"What in the world were you thinking, Slate?" asked Wrindanneth. "I thought we had agreed on the same spot."

"Ya said ta concentrate on tha nose and so I did," was Slate's terse, slightly exasperated response.

"You mean to tell me that you thought the chin was the nose?"

"No self-respectin' Dwarf would call this minor hump a nose! Our noses are heroic and proud!"

"You mean bulbous and protuberant?"

Inserting himself into the conversation, Yip interjected, "Enough please. Why don't we settle down and regather our energy for the next set of ports?"

Aroganji added, "In the future we will have to be more careful. There will be times ahead when we cannot risk getting separated."

Slate stalked off to the side of the clearing the party had claimed while waiting for his return. After a few minutes, Yip followed to help appease his new friend and divert his attention lest he continue to stew in his thick Dwarven temper.

Still with a large part of the day ahead of them, he asked out of curiosity, "How did you come to meet the others, Slate?"

"'Tis a long tale indeed, friend Yip, a long tale indeed. Perhaps I could have a bit o' that tea ya mentioned earlier?"

Starting a small fire on an exposed portion of rock beneath the limbs of a large old red oak, Yip listened as Slate began his tale while lightly stroking the edge of his axe.

"My immediate family, but a small part o' my extended clan, are masters-at-arms, smiths o' some renown, and guardians o' Thanes— have been as long as we've kept records. Only those o' tha Thane's blood are given tha honor o' guardin' our clan's leader, so my family has always been held in high esteem in our small thanedom."

"My father learned tha art o' tha axe from his father, who learned it from his father on back through time like tha knotted links in a beard. I reckon Brendle, Baera in our tongue, must've whispered tha knowledge o' how ta handle an axe ta tha first Dwarf who ever worked a forge. Ur'Daena, tha axe's lament, is as much in my blood as any true Dwarven Bor'Banna, our bearded axe-wieldin' Daemons. Tha heat o' tha forge still burns in tha veins o' any true Dwarven axe wielder."

Slate chuckled a bit ruefully at the thought.

"Despite our lineage, or maybe because o' our lineage," he laughed again and shook his head, "we o' tha clan Flintforge are an old Dwarven lot, given ta enough adventurin' and gold hoardin' ta make any good Dwarf proud. At tha tender age o' fifty or so, dependin' on a lad's maturity, we are required ta test our might on tha field o' battle, through strength o' arms, or by completin' a quest o' import ta tha clan."

Slate paused a moment before going on and looked a bit sadly into Yip's eyes. "My testin' wasn't exactly how I would've chosen as a lad."

"Before I go on, ya've got ta understand how isolated we were in these mountains. Our thanedom wasn't really much more than an outpost here in what tha locals call tha Green Run, what we Dwarves call tha Duuna'Dan, where Brendle first started moldin' tha world fer us ta live on. These mountains were once tha original home ta Dwarves on Ea'ae before we moved on, sad as that may seem, although thanedoms like ours can still be found throughout tha mountains."

"Our nearest neighbor was no more than a trapper's outpost and that was several days travel over mountains and forests only fit ta venture through with yer axe bared and at tha ready."

"Dwarves've always been self-reliant, as we should be, and livin' in tha wilds as my clan does only encouraged our independence. Ta be honest, our thanedom had seen better times, between constantly fightin' off Orcs and our children migratin' ta other delvin's and cities, my thanedom only had a few hundred able-bodied Dwarves left ta maintain tha hold. We had plenty o' gold in our coffers ta be sure, so we were successful in a sense, but lookin' around at tha empty homes and closed storefronts, ya could see we were losin' tha battle with time."

"Fewer and fewer younglin's want ta stay or venture out ta tha wilds and try their hand at adventure and stonecraft when their future elsewhere is more secure."

"Even though most Dwarves have since moved on ta more popu-lated climes better suited ta trade and Craft, even tha largest thane-doms still need tha raw materials places like our mines provide, so those o' us too stubborn ta move on still had a spot ta call home under tha hills along with a need ta be there."

Slate barked another short laugh. "Listen ta me carryin' on like that wool-headed excuse fer a fishmonger! At this rate, I won't finish my tale before sundown! Where was I?"

"You were describing your home and its people," said Yip.

"And if I ever try to sell fish," said Wrindanneth from the far side of the campground, "I'll be sure to sell you the day before yesterday's catch, as I hear Dwarves' taste in food is about as good as their taste in spirits."

"Humph," uttered Slate, knowing full well that only a Dwarf was stout enough to appreciate true Dwarven ale. "Let me move on a bit. If I keep wagglin' my tongue, my tale's apt ta grow longer instead o' shorter."

"Our miner's began comin' back from tha deep recesses o' tha mountain's heart with tales that would make yer hair stand on end. Dark beasts were nestlin' in tha innards o' tha mountains, makin' their home in tha mines my forefathers had first worked and then long abandoned."

"When Gründen, tha clan Thane, decided ta put together a war party, I jumped at tha opportunity ta help my elders cleanse tha distant tunnels as a chance ta prove myself and reclaim what was rightfully ours in tha name o' family and clan. After a few weeks away filled with gruelin' days o' hard fightin', battlin' fer control o' tha tunnels and darkness 'neath tha mount, we finally managed ta seal off tha crooked byways tha Orcs and Trolls had used ta skulk through ta find their way inta our mines."

"We came back from clearin' tha tunnels marchin' in step ta our great war drums, bearin' trophies o' our victory fer all ta see, jubilant and proud o' tha skill we'd shown dispatchin' tha beasts we'd found shelterin' in tha caves and chasms."

At this point Slate let out a deep sigh of remorse.

"Our pride was ill-founded."

"Our joy quickly turned ta sorrow and shock as we neared home and noticed that no guards were waitin' ta greet us in tha far tunnels, no horns stridently announced our presence as sentries spied us from their crannies hidden in tha walls, and no war drums answered tha call o' our march. By tha time we reached tha great caverns before tha gates, all doubt left our minds as ta what had happened. Tha smell o' smoke and burnin', tha stench o' decay, tha ruin left spread haphazard and unwanted along tha tunnel floor all showed tha casual disregard fer life, tha blatant disdain with which Orcs deal with their enemies."

"Such was our bitter homecomin'."

"Tha mithril gates built by my father's father were left broken and discarded, blown asunder, our temples defaced, tha homes we had carved from tha livin' rock burnt and ravaged, most crushed by powerful spells or turned ta molten slag by terrible heat. Our kin were slaughtered 'neath tha black blades o' tha twisted Orcs and their allies, their bodies left out in tha open, disfigured, only alive in our pained memories."

"Our war party had fallen inta a trap long in tha makin' o' our blood enemies—tha Gromdek Orcs."

Shaking his head, Slate spat on the ground at the thought.

"While we were gone, our hold was raided by a group of Trolls, Ogres, and Orc warrior-shaman. How they fully managed tha task I cannot say, fer our gates were strong and our defenses sound. Perhaps they had other infernal allies that they had called ta their aid, pacts wrought in blood and souls. I wouldn't be surprised."

"They lured those o' us best able ta fight deep inta tha mountain with their Craft and workin's only ta flank us in their efforts ta reach their real aim—tha gold and Craft secured in our mithril vaults. Though our gates fell, know that tha Craft o' tha Dwarves held against those miscreants and their dark magics, preventin' entry ta our vaults and forge even while largely undefended. In their anger at tha failure o' their efforts, tha Orcs razed what they could and left much o' our hold 'neath tha hills smashed and ruined."

"Workin' stone and metal are the primary Crafts of Dwarves, so our hearts were strong with tha assurance that we could rebuild our homes. But, after losing all but tha few o' our priests who had ventured out with our war party in tha attack, we knew that restorin' tha lives and health lost ta tha Orcs' hatred and greed were deeds beyond our powers."

Slate sighed bitterly.

"I vowed on that day ta hunt down every Orc, Troll, and Ogre that lived in tha hills around our hold."

"Venturin' out inta tha world o' Man aboveground with a war party from tha Flintforge Clan ta track tha beasts down was a bitter-sweet thrill ta one who had spent much o' his short life underground. We spent tha better part o' two years avengin' tha deaths o' our kins-men, hearts burnin' with righteous rage as only a Dwarf's can when facin' tha evil o' an Orc. In that time, we covered much territory and made many friends and allies among tha woodsmen and Elves who counted tha Orcs as enemies as much as we did."

"After tha last o' tha terrible shaman Grast's blood had dried on my Thane's burnin' axe and we had scorched his fetid hold back down ta tha ground he had corrupted, our task was done and it was time ta head home. By that time my heart was torn, as I had fallen in love with tha life o' an adventurer, wanderin' 'neath tha skies, rightin' wrongs as I saw fit, but my kin and clan were ready ta return home and rebuild."

"After much time discussin' my thoughts with tha Thane on tha way home, I decided ta help my clan finish at least some o' their reparations before continuin' on alone. Rebuildin' and restorin' what had been undone will be tha work o' generations, if full recovery is ever possible given our limited population. I stayed home fer another year helpin' where I may while my heart grew ever more restless with each passin' day, missin' my lost kith and kin as much as my life aboveground."

"After another year o' wanderin' on my own, I happened upon Wrindanneth and Aroganji on their way ta clean out a group o' Orcs that had been raidin' a remote village o' woodsmen. Recognizin' warriors after my own heart, I've been with 'em ever since."

"Since our first meetin', each rise and fall o' my axe has marked tha passage o' a small bit o' my anger and hatred...a bloody redemption indeed."

Stroking his beard, eyes distant, lost in memory, Slate continued, "I'll return home when tha time comes, but until then, I'm happy rovin' tha land, helpin' where I may, even if it is with this band of softheads."

And with that, he looked up, smiling fondly at his two companions in arms, content with his lot, and happy to be among friends.

MID-SUMMER DREAMS

Wind blows softly on
tender green spring leaves,
lightly caressing my cheeks.

That night, while the others slept the dreams of heroes, Yip dreamt of home.

Walking slowly up the winding gravel path through the evergreens and around the great sweep of the mountain, he could see his home, the monastery of the K'un Lun, lit up in the distance, indistinct against the clear evening sky. Rooms lit with captured starlight, tiled roofs gleaming beneath the moon, ancient trees shading the walls surrounding the central compound, the main gates held open and wide, all spoke to him of home. A short distance ahead, just before the open gates, he could see the arching bamboo bridge spanning the burbling stream that ran through the mixed gardens in front of the monastery walls. Standing on that bridge waiting for him stood a shadow silhouetted in the darkness, the edges of its robes shifting in the gentle breeze.

Master Wei!

His spirit soaring to the heavens, he sprinted the last few paces to his teacher, robes billowing behind him in the wind.

"Master Wei! What are you doing here?"

"Greetings, Yip," offered Master Wei while giving him a deep bow. "This vision brings back so many memories, briefest glimpses of what was and what will be, ages past and ages yet to come, possibilities. Much has changed since you left. Our home as you knew it is no more."

"I know, master. I know." Yip shook his head sadly.

"What has been destroyed can be rebuilt, Yip, and hearts guided by wisdom mourn for the loss of each other while celebrating the opportunity that loss and life afford. Though priests no longer walk freely across the land, our efforts will not disappear. Your efforts are a testament to that, Yip."

He looked to his teacher as moonlight limned Master Wei's shoulders, and he could feel his teacher's pride.

"Yip, I would have you meet me in the hills nearby. Seek me out. I will not be far from you. Have your Dwarf friend find the cave."

"Master, you are coming here?"

"I already am, Yip, and I wait for you. Come."

And with that, Yip opened his eyes, lost in the depths of the void above, the myriad stars matching the teeming number of his thoughts.

OF STONE AND SPIRITS

Dappled sunlight falls
softly on vernal leaves—
suffusing the wood yellow-green.

Yip awoke the next morning in high spirits, eager to share his news with his friends.

Gathered around the cookfire, each caught up in his own breakfast, he broached the subject of dreams.

"I spoke with my teacher, Master Wei, last night."

"Really?" said Wrindanneth skeptically.

"Yes," said Yip. "He is nearby. I will need your help finding him as I will be unable to sense his presence until we are close. He wished to speak to me."

"Didn't he do that last night?" said Wrindanneth sardonically.

He remained unaffected by Wrin's tone. "Yes, he did. He wishes to see me in person."

"Hmph. How in tha world would a man such as yerself, one o' yer own order, travel so far so quickly after it took ya months ta get here?" asked Slate.

"He is not as I am, Slate, nor is he like others who wield magic. He is a priest, a Yu-jen."

"I'm a priest and I wield magic," muttered Wrindanneth, half in jest, half seeking a reaction and a bit of information from his stoic companion. "How is he so different?"

"His is not a way based solely on the manipulation of magic, or of magic as it is commonly understood."

Yip looked at his newfound friend in studied concentration. "Where there is life, so is he, friend Wrindanneth. His essence is of life unending. He moves with it at ease and at leisure. He is more and less a man than you and I."

Shaking his head, looking at Wrindanneth, Slate said, "Oh that really clears things up! Ya have a way o' talkin' in riddles that confuses even tha question!"

"Perhaps what Yip means is that his teacher goes where he will like a magician, but without manipulating magic in the same way as other magicians. Perhaps his way is based on coexisting with or becoming the magic," offered Aroganji.

Looking to Yip to see if he was going to offer any further clarification, Wrindanneth finished the conversation as he stood up, "Well, I'll be going soon by myself, if we don't get started."

Gathering their few belongings, the party broke camp in preparation for their search.

"Master Wei is in a cave. He said you could find it, Slate."

Slate sniffed. "I can find a mole hole three leagues distant if it goes underground."

"Why would you need to do that?" said Wrindanneth. "Going to visit relatives?"

Ignoring Wrin's early morning joviality, Slate continued, "These valleys are mostly limestone with plenty o' runnin' water, only tha mountain tops show much in tha way o' heavier rock, at least above ground, from weatherin'. If we follow a few streams ta their source, we should have a good chance o' findin' yer teacher if he's near."

"Why in the wide world could he not just meet us here in camp like a sensible person?" asked Wrindanneth.

"Meeting us hidden in a place seldom visited or noticed, in safety, away from potential distractions and observers is exactly why he would want to meet us in private, like a sensible person," said Aroganji. "You do not have the Cabal tracking you nor is it out to destroy all you are and stand for. I can respect his caution."

Wrindanneth grinned and retorted, "At least not yet!"

Aroganji laughed and Yip shared in their smiles.

"There's no better place ta be than in a nice warm, well-lit cave, I always say," said Slate with an approving nod.

"Crawling out from under a rock?" asked Wrin.

"It is good to see that you cover our troubles with humor, Wrindanneth," said Yip simply. "A wise man keeps both his counsel and his heart positive."

Looking at Yip then Slate, Wrindanneth growled.

Slate growled back.

Then they both smiled.

Even the stoic Aroganji could not help smiling at their display.

The party picked their way slowly down the mountainside under the cover of trees, moist leaves giving way beneath their feet. Yip sensed more than saw the abundant wildlife through the looming vegetation. Senses piqued, he also noticed an unusual presence all around as they made their way downward.

If this was the spot, Master Wei had chosen an interesting valley to wait in.

As the party moved down the hillside, careful not to lose footing on the steep slopes, Yip cautiously surveyed his surroundings. Interspersed throughout the trees, great moss and fern covered rocks, boulders and monoliths jutted out of the ground, remnants of older, more durable rock formations. Some of the rock outcroppings loomed over the tops of even the tallest trees.

The tree canopy was mostly made up of widely spaced, old gray-trunked beeches, oaks, and great maples, large limbs forming a leafy yellow-green shelter over the leaf litter and ferns below. Iridescent vines laced the canopy and hung downward in luminous bands, circulating energy skyward.

The large trees were interspersed relatively uniformly along the slopes of the mountainside creating a clear understory with very few saplings or seedlings in sight. As such, the trees in evidence were quite mature with little in the way of replacement recruitment of new seedlings.

He felt that the valley's denizens were largely responsible for this lack of visible regrowth.

Keeping his voice low, he whispered, "Can you sense them?"

Cocking his head, listening to the birdsong and leaves susurrating in the breeze, Aroganji said, "No I cannot. Shall I perform a scrying?"

Reaching down to his feet, Slate ran some soil slowly between his fingers. "The ground is very compacted. Somethin' big moves through here on occasion."

Looking inward as he spoke, Yip addressed the party, "It is odd, I cannot describe it, but whatever they are—there are more than one—they seem somehow distant, not necessarily removed from the land-scape…just slow, inert, almost as if in hibernation, or operating on an entirely different time frame."

He shook his head in mild consternation. "There is much I do not know, my friends, and much I have not seen. I wish I were more help-ful. I can say that whatever the beings are that reside in this valley, they are not active and do not seem threatening. I cannot feel or see much in the way of their patterns other than to say they are deep and full."

"It is as if the creatures are far off and dreaming without thought."

"The echoes of those dreams, however, are powerful."

"Well, once again, you are a model of clarity and insight, Yip." Wrindanneth looked around the large clearing they presently found themselves in and urged them onward. "Let's go."

Before they had taken more than a few steps, Yip looked up quickly as he heard a low rumbling in the distance, cautioning, "They are no longer inactive."

The deep rumbling turned into great grinding noises followed by sloughing sounds as if the earth were shifting off itself and sliding to the ground beneath something's passage—something massive.

Slate sniffed again and placed his hand firmly on the ground. "Tha earth's movin' in several places along tha hillsides above and below us."

"Remain calm," said Aroganji as he looked around toward the

noises in the distance, trying to determine their source and if they posed a threat.

"We need to find a more favorable spot if it comes to a confrontation! Let's move!"

And with that Wrindanneth was off down the hill without a backward glance, robes billowing loosely, looking for all the world like a great red-haired scarecrow given one shot at life and the chance for freedom.

Slate harrumphed and followed closely behind, shouldering his great gleaming axe at the ready. "Flint and forge, I've never seen Wrindanneth move like that!"

Concentrating on his blade, Yip watched in amazement as Slate focused his essence into his hand and flames jumped along the length of his axe.

Noting Yip's surprise, Slate chuckled and grunted as he ran forward. "A Bor'Banna is wed ta tha flames o' Brendle's forge as much as his axe!"

As the party raced to the valley bottom, the rumbling noises grew louder and closer, coming from all sides, sounding as though the mountainside was about to come apart and fall all around them. Running from clearing to clearing, grabbing on the trunks of trees for stability as they moved down, they reached the base of the hill in a clearing beneath a large silver beech, its trunk encrusted with diaphanous crystallites.

By the time he stopped, Wrindanneth had leaves and twigs sticking out from his hair. Aroganji looked little better.

Finally, as they reached flatter ground, Yip called his companions to a halt. "Stop! We are safe. There is no need to run."

"How do you know?" asked Wrindanneth, on edge and worried that their encounter may come to a confrontation.

"I can sense it. We have moved into a place that is not ours, and those who claim it wish to see us."

Quickly surveying the clearing, Slate pointed to a great hole in the ground not far from the base of the tree, as if a boulder that had been resting in place for centuries had suddenly decided to get up and seek a new home. Roots curled and twisted along the edges of the exposed earth and a few plants lay scattered along the hole's edges, having fallen off the rock after it moved.

As he looked up from the hole, Slate's jaw dropped when his eyes moved to the edge of the clearing and alighted beneath the boughs of the great beeches. "Karadüm!"

"Stone giants!!!" spurted Wrindanneth at the same instant as he pointed to the large creatures moving ponderously through the woods toward them.

Loosely surrounding the party in the forest around the clearing, some still, some yet moving in from the hillside, were great lumbering heaps of roughly humanoid rock. Knobby, tumbled heads perched atop great shoulders looked at the party with an even intensity, great gray hands the size of small boulders rested calmly by their sides, and wide legs braced them firmly to the earth. Some were still shedding dirt from their backs as they trundled forward. Marked by lichens, fissures, and cracks, covered in moss, vines, and ferns, the great giants rumbled and grated as they moved. Each was at least the size and girth of an elephant standing on its hind legs.

Yip could see now why he had problems identifying the creatures. Their essence blended in so closely with the surrounding rocks and trees, the area's ambient energies and potentials, that the giants seemed to be little more than a slight disturbance in the overall forest community. Slow and cumbersome, somnolent and resting even while in motion, the giants blended in as well with the woods as the leaves beneath the trees. Although at rest, their hearts and minds read the currents and shiftings through the earth to the far corners of Dharia.

He sensed great power moving deep within their veins.

After the last few walked stolidly in, ground shaking beneath their feet, one giant stepped forward toward the party.

Its surface was spotted with lichen, gray and marbled in quartz. A small sapling perched precariously atop its head seeking purchase and the opportunity to grow. When it spoke, its mouth a dark fissure, its voice rumbled with the sound of an avalanche, rock grating deeply on rock as if a mountain were struggling to give voice to its thoughts.

"We are the Karadüm. Ours is the task of guarding this valley and upholding this place. Why have you come?"

The air echoed with his question.

Yip bowed to the giant who spoke from across the clearing. "We come to this valley respecting its sanctity and repose while looking for my teacher. We come as friends and mean you no harm."

"What deeds precede your arrival that show your trust? What tokens do you bring to show your worth?"

Yip took a step forward and opened his mouth to begin, but before he could start Slate placed a hand on his arm and whispered to him through his thick beard, "Careful lad, tha Karadüm are a finicky lot. Good, true, but odd."

"Then he'll fit right in!" said Wrindanneth under his breath.

Turning from his companions, Yip began, "We bring hearts pure that know the value of friends and companions. We bring the opportunity to restore what has been broken, remake what has been lost, and help those who may need. We bring trust, courage, and compassion as our aegis."

Reaching beneath his robe, he added dramatically with a flourish, "And we bear this!" as he held forth the gleaming red Yeren jewel.

Head cocked to the side, the giant looked carefully at the stone. Eyes that had seen the ages of Man pass in the blink of an eye regarded Yip cautiously. "Why does a Man bear the Heart of Yere?"

Looking downward to his feet while collecting his thoughts, he returned his gaze to the giant and answered as best he could, "I do not rightly know. I only partially grasped their song as I visited with them in the peaks."

He shrugged slightly, adding, "This I can say—we share a common burden, a similar fate, and mutual hope for a new future. The Yerens have given me their trust and shared aspirations for new beginnings. We both have suffered greatly from the Cabal."

The giant hummed thoughtfully, the air filled with the sounds of rocks grinding against one another. With the deep, reverberating sounds of its consideration as loud in his ears as his heart beat in his chest, Yip waited for the giant's decision.

After a time, the giant's voice continued with the sounds of rocks falling from the heights, "We have heard that name drift to us often through the earth, in ages past and once again in the present day. The tales we hear bespeak little of value or worth. Theirs is a Darkness that shows little regard for ought but their own need. Ea'ae suffers deeply in their wake."

"We have felt the scars they have wrought, marring Ea'ae's surface, bleeding her strength."

A few of the giant's companions stomped their feet in response. Tree limbs quivered in reply to their gesture. Leaves drifted down lazily around the party, spiraling to the ground as they each awaited the giant's judgment. Gazing deeply at each party member in turn, it intoned, "Any who have befriended the Yerens, who have shared their Song, and who would stand against those that despoil the land and its people are friends of the Karadüm."

Slate's shoulders dropped at ease in response to this declaration.

"Youngling, your friend waits a few leagues distant in the next valley, deep in a cave beneath the earth, close to the eyes and heart of the Karadüm."

Bowing again, Yip asked, "Is there anything you would have us do to repay your kindness?"

"We of the Karadüm seek little and need less, human. Continue as you have and all will be well."

"May I ask a favor before we go?" He hoped his request would not be too much.

"What would you ask of me?" The giant's deep voice held a tone of warning that Yip was loath to disrespect.

"In my journey here I came across an Indural named Goran wandering at the feet of the Drake Spires. He fears for his kin, their safety, and their future. If you hear of more of his kind elsewhere, would you send him word that he may reunite with his fellows?"

"Your concern and compassion do you merit. There is news and it will be done."

Before he had finished this last pronouncement, the other giants were already gradually disappearing back into the forest, clouds of leaves and dust billowing in their wake as the ground shook beneath their tread.

Looking to Yip, Slate moved close and whispered to him again,

"We caught a bit o' luck there, Yip. Tha Karadüm are out o' our league, if ya take my meanin'."

A few great steps and the crash of monstrous feet brought the primary monolithic giant immediately next to them where they stood beside its hole in the clearing. Bending over at the waist, it looked directly down at Slate. "Aye, Dunédâne, beyond your depth and measure and well out of your league."

Slate gulped and did his best to stand his ground bravely. The flames around his axe flickered.

With that, the giant gave them something of a craggy smile as it turned and carefully settled back into the ground, reclaiming a bed it would have rather left tended. The steady grace of its repose was such that none would have guessed it had ever moved after it had finally settled.

The party left the clearing trusting the giant's directions with a sense of defined purpose. Yip was also quite happy to hear that the Karadüm would try to help Goran reunite with his kind.

If only his own journey were so fortuitous!

Still a bit harried by their encounter with the giants, Slate was loath to let himself relax after they left the clearing in safety, their immediate goal nearly attained. As was the Dwarven custom, he kept himself worked up in a lather, even with a hard day's walk ahead. As they walked, the party was treated to a string of Dwarven insights, opinions, and humor.

He huffed a new offering with almost every step.

"If ya'd wanted a pack mule, we should've bought one before we started out!"

"'Tween this mail and all tha provisions I have ta carry fer tha party, it's only a stout heart and tha generosity o' a Dwarf that carries us through."

"Ya know that if I were tha one castin' tha spells, we'd port right inta tha next valley, safe and sound as a well-spun coat o' arms!"

His comments were so regular, Aroganji began to think he could count their steps by Slate's complaints. "Don't be so peevish, Slate. You know I have to see my target to port us. I cannot teleport us directly yet, and, even if I could, I would have to know my destination at least roughly and be able to visualize it."

Wrindanneth added, "Really, Slate, that pouch makes all of our goods almost weightless. If you were actually brave enough to ever take that mail off and put it in the pouch, you might find out how easy walking can be. The only thing bothering you right now is embarrassment that you were the butt of a giant's joke."

Slate harrumphed. "'Tis a Dwarf's prerogative ta be grumpy. Those Karadüm have been known ta take a Dwarf's hard-earned gold from right under his beard after days o' back-breakin' labor."

"You mean it took them some time to find you stealing their gold and gems after despoiling the lands they guard and hold dear?" asked Wrindanneth. "Or perhaps they value the land as it is instead of how you would like to use it?"

From then on, Slate sulked in silence.

A not so quiet day's journey brought the companions over the ridge and down into the far valley.

The next dale was much the same as the last, although there were not as many rock outcroppings. The domain of the Karadüm did not seem to extend this far, nor did it need to. All the stone giants needed to know and hear came to them through the earth, the veins of mineral and ore, and the gradually shifting tectonics. Their ways and knowledge were upheld in their lone hollows, lost amidst the wilds far from others and those who would seek them out.

Not all empires are dependent on territory, expansion, and trade for success, so it seemed to Yip. The Karadüm's vibrancy sustained itself without need for outward expansion.

After reaching the feet of the mountain in the next valley, the party quickly discovered the stream that had been described by the Karadüm. Bordered by thickets of river cane, its surface broken by old, rounded rocks, the rivulet meandered gently through the wide, wooded vale on its slow, erratic journey to the sea.

After camping for the night along the stream's lush shore, the party continued uphill toward its source along the mountain's flanks.

Enjoying the rill's song as they walked beneath the green-tinted sunlight, each lost in their own thoughts, the morning passed quickly. They reached the cave by early afternoon.

A tumbled, algae covered tangle of rocks rested beneath the overarching limestone roof of the cave. Low-hanging ferns clung to the rocky entrance's ledges drinking in moisture from the small stream as roots from trees clinging to the slopes framed the cavern's edges. The cave's irregular interior appeared lit by the subtle phosphorescence and assorted hues of magical microorganisms, their light lending an ethereal cast to the way forward.

"'Tis a welcomin' sight that. Not quite tha look o' home but welcome nonetheless. Has tha smell o' home—deep air currents, cool rock, darklin' pools. Ah..." Slate's chest expanded, taking in the cool breeze wafting outward with the stream from the cave. He let out a welcome exhalation. "Onward lads!"

"*Solas lunas!*" With those words spoken in an ancient tongue, an orb of silvery light appeared above Aroganji's hand floating at the ready to guide the party inward and down into the deeps.

Picking their way carefully over the slick stones, the party found the inside of the cave surprisingly dry. The ceiling curved away and upward under the light of Aroganji's spell. After a few dozen paces in, the cavern's walls gradually receded, leaving the party in a rather sizable tunnel only partially covered by the stream at its center. Pearlescent stalactites, visible in the distance farther in, slowly trickled calciferous water into the clear stream below. Glowing fungal forms and crystalline protrusions lent an alien tone to the grotto's widening interior, casting misshapen shadows upon the receding walls.

Continuing around a bend, the sudden clatter of batwings made them all duck beneath their cloaks as the magical light disturbed the small colony from their daily rest.

Heart beating loudly in his chest after the startle, Wrindanneth was quick to point out what he thought of their trip underground. "At least your teacher could have chosen a nicer spot to meet us in, Yip. The open air and warm sun of the valley were very welcoming."

Aroganji laughed. "I would never have guessed it by the way you were running!"

"And what's wrong with a nice, natural undercroft?" asked Slate.

"Slate is right," answered Yip. "Caves have much to offer—safety, comfort, and the perfect spot for silent contemplation. Their intrinsic beauty is no less than any other spot, my friend."

Looking to Aroganji, Wrindanneth muttered, "Why do I even ask?"

Stepping with care over the loose stones, Slate urged his companions to follow his lead. "Never thought ya'd see a Dwarf so graceful, eh? 'Tis a sight ta behold—a Dwarf in his element, free ta take advantage o' his abilities, his surety of step, his ability ta see in tha dark."

"I could find my way through this cavern blind-folded, without a torch, after spinnin' in circles!"

Gesturing grandiosely, Slate slipped on a lambent, mossy rock.

Aroganji smiled and shook his head, studiously stepping over the same stone once Slate recovered himself. With a wry smile, he said, "Hard to miss a rock like that even with Dwarven sight?"

Slate shrugged the fall off as though it had never happened. "'Twas but a minor mistake in an otherwise impeccable record o' poise and grace!"

Wrindanneth sighed. "Can we have the quiet, surly Dwarf back?"

Time passed stamped out beneath the cadence of their wary footfalls. Blending with the sounds of their tread, the looming expanse of the underground cavern echoed with the slow, steady dripping of water.

After some time wending their way downward beneath the mountain, ahead beyond the floating light, Yip and his companions could sense more than see a gradual opening of space. This far underground, the web of life that normally burned so brightly in his mind felt muted and indistinct, faded and soft, a light fog hinted at but unrealized.

He could understand why a priest would seek out such a place. Just as his senses and impressions seemed muted in the emptiness underground, so, too, would those of his pursuers. Magic relies on life for form and substance and here, underground, although still potent, the energy of possibility lay dormant and sleeping—nascent and only partially realized.

Reaching his mind far out, Yip jumped in excitement as he sensed the faintest traces of a presence much like his own—shifting, shimmering, blending with the energies around—here was a Priest of the K'un Lun!

His own training in the ways of the K'un Lun was far from complete. He had been forced to leave his monastery by the Cabal just after his novice training ended and his first initiations began. Although he had been practicing with the order since childhood, he had only just begun to learn its true secrets.

All that changed when he was forced to flee into darkness on that fateful evening. His true training just begun, he carried with him only the memories of his master's teachings to build on, many secrets of the K'un Lun beyond his grasp, understood only conceptually or through the merest practice. His few remaining training scrolls had provided more hints than answers. Although over time, with due diligence and the help of the Aeryn D'al, he had managed to piece together and become comfortable with much he had been taught and read, there was a great deal he did not know, and there certainly was no real substitute for the guidance and tutelage of a real master.

Just a short distance away, all that could change!

His heart skipped with the possibility that here in the intermittent darkness ahead, far removed from the world he knew, he may find answers to his questions, new tasks to accomplish and skills to hone, the chance to continue his training so that he may bring the Darkness pursuing him to Light.

All this and more flashed through his mind as he, Aroganji, Wrindanneth, and Slate took their first steps into the expansive cavern from the tunnel behind.

"He is near!" hissed Yip in excitement.

Across from them in the distance, he sensed the coolness of a body of water large and empty, home to water droplets, refulgent bands of algae, small schools of organisms, and little else. Bands of light arched across the lake's surface and through its depths without pattern in response to the movements of these living, magical creatures. The refulgence of the algae suspended within the water column provided a constant background to the flashes of the miniscule creatures within the water's reaches.

Slate's Dwarven senses told him that this space was natural and knew not the hand of Man. The carving of water, chemical deposition and alteration, and the settling of the earth shaped the majesty unfolding before his eyes.

Wrindanneth and Aroganji both signaled that the area seemed clear of any magical artifice lying dormant, ready to spring upon the party unaware.

Holding their light before them like the hope Yip felt in his heart, the companions made their way slowly forward.

As the adventurers wound their way around the edge of the subterranean lake, Yip gradually began to sense the subtle changes and interactions indicating light habitation—purpose and use reflecting the needs of the cave's occupant lay out of sight, only reflected in possibility. After clamoring slowly over rocks and between long-settled boulders, the cavern's air began to lighten with a shifting breeze.

Off to the right, the cavern opened into a large amphitheater-sized alcove with tumbling limestone formations—stalactites and stalagmites reaching for one another like fingers entwined, roiling masses of crystallized rock, rounded formations worn down by incessant dripping. Ahead, the shoreline continued forward amid a jumble of rocks and pools, all backlit by the diffuse magical light pervading the space.

Before they could inspect their surroundings any further, a voice burst out of the silence, ringing in their ears. "Yip!"

Aroganji and Wrindanneth looked at each other in surprise, not having sensed their quarry's sudden appearance.

"Master Wei!" Yip called back, instinctively bringing both his hands upward in a greeting reflective of his personal feelings of respect and veneration for his teacher, palms held lightly together as if in prayer, in a gesture known by some as the *anjali mudra*. Used as a greeting, the *mudra* served to actualize and crystallize his esteem for his teacher in physical reality, but, on a deeper level, when used as a hand gesture of inner intent, his palms pressed together also expressed the everpresent origin, the absolute true nature of reality—nondual, formless, beyond all concepts and distinctions, empty and essenceless.

Taken together, his seemingly simple welcome signified not just his reverence for his teacher but his reverence for reality as it is, was, and would be and, in sense, was therefore an act of ultimate compassion.

Unfortunately compassion was not at the forefront of his teacher's mind when they arrived in his camp.

"I sensed your friends' *li* moving this way for quite some time, Yip! You must be more careful!"

Yip looked down at his feet in acknowledgement and acceptance of his teacher's admonition. This was not the type of impression he had hoped to make after being away from his kindred for so long.

"Perhaps a Dragon in an apothecary's shop would have been a little more noticeable, but not by much. Yours is a Light that must be contained, Yip, lest it burn out."

"Yes, master," he kept his head bowed, unaccustomed to the reprimand after functioning so well on his own and having earned the trust and esteem of his fellow companions.

"But I am glad to see that you have learned to at least partially mask your essence, my young Yu-jen!"

Yip smiled, glad that his time in the forest was well spent. He would have to practice the blending of his friends' patterns into the larger ambient background energy streams.

So much to learn and practice! At least with time his own melding had become an almost unconscious act, perhaps once he got the knack the same would hold true for his friends.

"I am so glad to see you safe!" Yip could not restrain himself any longer after his forced flight from his home, the loss of the monastery and many of his friends, his journey through the wilds, his adventures, finding himself now standing alongside his new allies.

Master Wei smiled, seeing his pupil's energy level light up with his initial excitement. "I, too, am happy to see you well, Yip. Travel agrees with you!"

To Yip's eyes, his teacher appeared more as a being of light than a man. Energy moved into, through, and around him in a constantly renewing and replenishing flux. Small burning stars of radiance shone from each of the energy gates scattered throughout his body, each serving as a nexus for energy circulation and refinement.

The internal alchemy of life and death, rebirth and reunion, occurred with each breath, with each movement of his body, naturally and without effort. *Chi* moved around, into, and out of him in an unending cycle through the energy gates, the skin, the organs, and the major body orifices. To his eyes, his master appeared akin to a living constellation of organized energy composed of a myriad of stars, moving currents of gases, and life-sustaining, life-giving Light.

To Yip's newfound friends, although they sensed something of solidity and calm, a depth of presence about his teacher, Master Wei otherwise appeared to be a small nondescript man of indeterminate years. That is not to say they did not see anything too out of the ordinary, just that the impressions they had of him were largely beneath the surface.

Master Wei's gently slanting eyes conveyed a depth of compassion and kindness they had seldom seen outside of a mother's glance for her newborn child. His skin appeared as soft and supple as a babe's though many years older. His movements evinced the grace and poise of a dancer while his head was so clean-shaven as to shine almost with its own light even in the gloom.

Wrindanneth and Slate both thought he seemed in excellent physical condition while Aroganji felt that he appeared as one who moved always in silent contemplation.

"Master Wei," Yip began while his friends thought, watched, and tried to make sense of what they felt beneath his teacher's outer appearance. "These are my traveling companions and newfound allies. This stalwart band has taken me in as family and helped offer me safety and assurance in a time of need."

Gesturing broadly to each of his companions in turn, he continued with the humor, the warmth, and the closeness he now felt for his friends. "Wrindanneth is a Priest of Maeth Onai, an order dedicated both to bad dress and the study of divine and arcane magics. Perhaps one day his powerful magics will overcome his taste."

He smiled with the joke as he looked to judge Wrindanneth's reaction, comfortable enough with his new friends to tease them in front of his teacher.

Wrindanneth smirked at Yip's poor joke and made a deep bow. "Well met, Master Wei." Returning Yip's jest as he met Yip's eye, he added in an even tone, "I trust you have had better luck with your other pupils."

Unfazed and unconcerned, Yip continued with his introductions. "Aroganji is a Fang Shih of some substance from lands very near our own. He is akin to a long lost friend—welcome and much appreciated."

"May your Light be a beacon," Aroganji bowed as well, robes whisking loosely with the motion.

Finally, Yip introduced Slate. "Slate Flintforge is a Bor'Banna—an axe master—a Dwarf of the land who draws his will and strength from the very ground he walks on and the axe he wields, imbued with power by the remnants of the flames from Brendle's original forge."

With a curt nod and a rap of his mailed fist upon his chest, Slate addressed Master Wei. "Tha people o' Brendle offer ya their honor as I offer my axe."

Looking with pride at his teacher, Yip added, "Steadfast companions and friends through and through. They have earned my deepest trust in a very short time."

Wrindanneth looked to his friends, curiously trying to gauge their reactions to Yip's introduction. As stoic as Yip was, his feelings toward the rest of them were seldom evident. Thinking back over their short time together, Yip's expressions of outward emotion were about as frequent as his statements lasting more than a sentence. In that, at least, he held much in common with Slate.

Turning to his companions, Yip added, "Master Wei is a teacher of the Five Excellencies, master of the Moonlit Mind, and keeper of the Echoing Fist. He is a Sheng-jen in our tradition, a lore keeper and sage, a paragon and exemplar."

"Well met," said Master Wei bowing to each of them in turn. "May the light of a new dawn guide your steps," he said in the traditional greeting.

"Thank you for guiding and keeping Yip safe"—he paused—"and out of harm's way I hope?"

All four companions looked at each other quickly before looking back at Master Wei.

Slate raised an eyebrow and ran his fingers through his thick beard. "Aye 'tis a hard task keepin' this lad on tha straight and narrow. He collects trouble tha way Dragons' hoard gold..."

"Or like a Dwarf collects coin?" offered Wrindanneth, ever mindful of an opportunity to bridge any gaps in the goodwill between Dwarf and Man.

Looking around, the companions noticed the rudiments of a camp hidden amidst the rocks close to where the cave opened up to the large recess in the cavern.

"Would you like some refreshment? Tea perhaps?" asked Master Wei.

As they settled around a lightly used cookfire, letting their own magical light dim, the party's eyes began to adjust to the soft glow in the gloom. Lining the rocks along the water's edge where evaporation increased the ambient humidity, moss covering the rocks provided a diffuse greenish light. The quality of the bioluminescence grew markedly after their own illumination was extinguished.

Looking around, Aroganji asked, "What do you eat, master? There is little food here. And what do you use for fuel?"

Master Wei smiled, settling into his robes, seeming to blend into the stones around him.

"Has Yip not told you? Or is he as tight-lipped as his elders?" He said with a widening grin. "Priests of the K'un Lun do not eat. Life, the energy around us, provides us with all we need."

Slate grunted, as if he would rather give up his beard than stop eating.

"As for fuel, when I need it, dried moss smolders enough to steep tea."

Always willing to speak his mind, or break the flow of conversation depending on one's view, Wrindanneth glanced from Yip to Master Wei, then asked, "How in the world did you get here so quickly?"

Then, as if mildly uncertain how best to proceed after changing conversational directions so abruptly, Wrindanneth went on, "We talked about it before and I still don't know. I would like to learn what I can, if I may. That is the way of my order, to understand, that is."

With a little more emotion, he finished, "Yip has spent the better part of several weeks getting over the mountains, running from his enemies, and you pop in without so much as offering him a ride!"

Yip placed a light hand on his friend's arm, restraining his expression.

In answer, Master Wei gave Wrin a bright smile, appreciating Wrindanneth's dynamism, forthrightness, and curiosity. "A journey is not the destination, Master Wrindanneth."

Master Wei paused before continuing, "Had Yip not come here of his own devices, would he be the same person? Would his trip have born the same fruit? Would you be with him?"

"Well..." Began Wrindanneth, unsure how to continue or answer, hoping he had not offended Yip's teacher, unable to read him, knowing full well how mercurial his own teacher had been.

"As for how I got here, that is an interesting question, one with many answers. To say that the world we commonly see and live in is a veil, a curtain behind which we can peer to see the fullness of reality would be a simplification. As a magician, you know this, for knowledge of magic and the way the world works is your truth and trade."

Master Wei paused for a moment watching for Wrindanneth's reaction before going on. "Man is but a dew drop ready to slip back into the shimmering ocean of being. When one realizes this, however, one also comes to understand that the dew drop and ocean are never separate, that this division, too, is an illusion. If one can live with this reality and actualize its being, what is the difference between here and there, you and me?"

"Uh..." Wrindanneth looked as though he had swallowed a fly...a particularly disagreeable fly. "Um..." Were all teachers like this? He felt almost like he was back at home with Maeth!

Empathizing with his friend's predicament, having been there many times before, and realizing his teacher was finished explaining, Yip offered to help with the clarification of the metaphor, although he felt his friend's head would be far from clear after his help. "An otter slips in and out of the ocean with ease, and you can, too, once you learn how."

"Perhaps now you would like that tea?" Master Wei asked smiling.

"Yes. Yes I would," answered Wrin, also smiling.

Turning to Yip, Wrin muttered, "Are you sure your teacher hasn't trained in the ways of Maeth Onai?"

After taking the offered cup when his turn came once each of his friends had had their serving, Yip eased himself down onto the rocks, letting the warmth of the tea fill and soothe him as he drank. Steam from the cup clouded his vision in a slight fog. Breathing in the vapor, he shared warmth and a feeling of companionship with his friends.

Lost in recollection, he let his mind wander back to his early days as a young child high in the mountain passes among the K'un Lun observing the snow fall and lightly settle on the ground—each flake soft and distinct until landing, only to lose itself in a sea of white.

"Master Wei?"

"Yes, Yip?"

"Why is the snow silent? Why does snow not sound like rain when it falls?"

"Snow is as light as the thoughts flitting across your mind, Yip. When viewed from afar, snow falling does not have a sound that you or I can hear, no matter how hard we listen. A wolf or snow leopard may have a different impression than us, however."

His teacher said this last part with a smile, cupping his hands behind his ears. "But if you listen closely, even snow has a sound."

Yip sat in silence for a moment listening. The faint susurration of the snow brushing upon overhanging leaves settled about him.

While he listened, Master Wei asked, "Can you sense the snow fall, Yip?"

"Sense the snow?"

"You may not be able to readily hear the snow, but can you feel it? Its soft gentle glide floating all around? Dancing in the air, melting on your skin?"

"I can see the snow, master, all around and feel the cold through and near me."

Master Wei gently shook his head. "You can feel the cold with your skin, but can you sense it with your mind? You cannot easily hear the snow with your ears, but can you encompass it with your awareness?"

"Where does your mind end and the snow begin, Yip?"

He paused, trying to feel, relaxing as he had been taught, letting his mind settle softly, ever so gently, around him.

"Master, I do not know."

Master Wei smiled, lacing his hands through the sleeves of his robes. As he turned, gliding softly atop the snow, as light as the smallest flake, disturbing it less than the slightest breeze, he answered, "Some would say that your mind begins where the snow ends, or that your mind only perceives the snow internally as best it can through senses limited by the body and mind,"

His teacher paused. "Yip, your mind does not end where the snow begins, nor is it limited to your body or the thoughts you can encompass. Yip, your mind does not end…nor does the snow."

And with that, Master Wei glided off into the night.

Looking into his tea, lost in the steam, he heard Master Wei begin, "You must have had a long journey," implying the questions he knew he would have to answer, questions that gradually brought him back to his tea, his friends, and the cool air of the cave.

THE FIRE THAT DOES NOT BURN

The mind of a babe—
open, untrammeled, boundless.
A cloudless blue sky.

The sound of water droplets falling from distant stalactites echoed softly across the cavern. Yip's thoughts settled lightly on his surroundings, as quiet and unobtrusive as the lichen growing on the rocks.

He had worked long and hard to find his way to his master, but time was now of the essence. He could not take the time to learn all he would from his teacher, nor could he take too long and jeopardize both the safety of his party and that of his instructor. He would have to see what Master Wei deemed him ready to learn and hope he was worthy of continued development. Without the support of his monastic community, his teachers, and the resources of the *guàn*, his learning and continued development were continually tested, predicated on practicality and function.

As he walked slowly back to camp, hands folded in his silken sleeves, he looked up as Master Wei rose to greet him.

Smiling at his approach, Master Wei suggested, "Perhaps your friends would be so kind as to watch the camp while we take a short walk?"

Smiling to himself, he noticed his companions were already making themselves at home—unpacking provisions, organizing stores, and starting a cookfire. His friends were more than happy to let him have some time together with his teacher.

As they walked along the shoreline limned in the soft light of the phosphorescent lichen and water, Master Wei began, "Our time together is short, Yip, and we may not see one another for a long time. True learning comes not just from observation, but from action. I sense that you have seen your fair share of adventures since we parted and feel that experience for you has not been an unkind teacher. For that and the person you are becoming, I am glad."

"Master, you are too kind..." Yip began before Master Wei continued.

"The Way of the K'un Lun is as complex as it is gentle. Light and love are our greatest gifts and our most difficult teachers. Realization must be cultivated with patience, a clear mind, and continued guidance. I regret that I will not always be with you on this path as I should, Yip."

"Your candor brings much to consider, as always, master."

"Yip, these are things you know, just as you know that I will be with you as much as possible in your dreams when you send for me and when I cast out for you. I only regret that I will not be able to oversee your development in person. Such are the limitations of the human condition—our wants are not always our reality."

"You do me a great service, my teacher, now as you always have. The limitations of our experience are no more real than our separation."

"There is much you must learn, Yip, and much I would teach you. Unfortunately, in many ways, you will have to take the path of our forebears and discover on your own. I will continue to provide what guidance I can from afar."

"Before you and your friends continue on your way, Yip, I would show you this. Take my hand."

Master Wei held his outstretched hand toward him. Slowly, and with great deliberation, he took his master's hand.

"The Light of life is your greatest teacher, Yip, your guide, and your ultimate defense. As you learn its ways and mysteries, new vistas and miracles will unfold the likes of which you can only begin to envision."

Yip felt warmth gradually spread from the palm of Master Wei's hand into his own, suffusing his entire body. Light and buoyant, possibility seemed to stretch outward uncharted before him—awareness open and untrammeled, serene and free.

When Master Wei finally released his gentle grip, he felt the warmness of his teacher's touch yet abiding. Looking down in awe, his hands were glowing with a soft blue luminescence in the darkling shadows.

FIRE AND WATER

Calm, the central point—
concentric waves rippling
around the mind's eye.

Yip felt Master Wei's energy pass like a soft current through his hands and begin circulation throughout his energy channels—first up his arms, then around the primary meridian up his spine and down into his principal energy store in his navel. From there he felt it pulse with power, ready to move and surge though him at his direction. Looking inward, he saw a small sun glowing at his center, filling him with life, radiating out from him throughout the cavern's farthest reaches.

Enlivened by his master's touch, his greater heavenly cycle was ablaze with light running from his feet all the way up around his crown and back down again through the perineum where the front and back, the functional and governing, energy channels crossed.

After all his practice in inner alchemy, opening his energy meridians and gates, directing his life force throughout his body, learning to heal and develop wisdom, his master's touch had sparked a capacity in him he had not known before. Somehow, without even having tried to utilize his new talents, he understood with complete certainty that he could now direct this energy outside his body to heal or harm.

The touch of this vitality, though now localized about his hands, would serve as a beacon for friends and a bane for foes.

"Your energy channels are open and vibrant, Yip" began Master Wei. "The light of your life force, your *chi*, shines forth from you as the morning sun ushers in a new day. You have something of me with you now, something of my teachers before me, and yourself all commingled together, a joining synergy than will guide you to new vistas and insights beyond your imaginings."

Humbled by his master's gift, he was at a complete loss as to how to best display his heartfelt appreciation and wonderment. Hands shaking slightly, he brought both palms together to his chest and offered his teacher a deep bow from the waist.

"Your next step will be to learn to direct your life force, your *chi*, outside your body after sublimating your *ching*, your generative energy, into more and more enervating *chi*, thereby creating a permanent vessel for your spirit, your *shen*, that you may penetrate the manifold universe leaving behind the realm of *shih-shen*, ordinary consciousness, and explore the untold vastness of *yuan-shen*, the primordial essence."

"You have already opened the two major channels of the microcosmic orbit, the six special routes, and the twenty-four energy passageways corresponding to the internal organs. Additionally, through diligent practice, you have internalized and unified the five elements of the Wu-hsing through the Fusion of the Five Elements practice creating a high state of bodily harmony and beauty. Apparently, you have even begun the process of *k'an* and *li*."

"You have learned much on your own, but onward you must continue."

Master Wei's hands seemed to swirl as if circling smoke. A bright, bluish light coalesced between his palms, pulsating slowly.

"The process forward will not be easy. You will literally steam *ching* into *chi*. Your body's generative reproductive energies will transform into even more *chi*. The power of the *ching* will in turn rejuvenate, stimulate, and transform your whole body and brain. You will begin by directing your generative energies after this steaming upward through your primary energy centers starting at the navel until finally reaching the brow."

As he talked, the energy ball floated into Master Wei's *tan t'ien* where it glowed softly, still visible to Yip's heightened senses. Gathering power from his *hui-yin* at his perineum, the sphere of force slowly migrated up the functional channel along the front of his body passing from the navel through the energy centers at the spleen, heart, throat, until finally reaching the *yin-t'ang* at the brow.

"As you advance, you will learn to harness and gather ever greater energies into yourself as you progress upward along the meridians through the energy centers, continually converting more and more *ching* into *chi*. The myriad benefits of the lesser, greater, and greatest enlightenments of *k'an* and *li* will unfold before you as a lotus rises up from a still pond untouched by the water's depths."

Master Wei gestured broadly. "Now that you can see, feel, and manipulate the intrinsic energies around you, your abilities to shape, project, and redirect those forces will grow along with your talents and insight. Keep pushing forward, your body will be your guide. Let your spirit lead you for amazing destinations await an awakened mind."

Shaking his head sadly, his eyes looking briefly inward, Master Wei continued, "I will not be with you to directly guide you through this process, although my contribution to your essence should help ease your progression. Should you have the need or any pressing questions, I am, as always, available in the spirit world as you dream. Be forewarned, however, agents of our enemies can track our steps even there, so, in many ways, you will have to continue your progression as a pioneer."

Reaching into his robes, Master Wei brought out an old rice paper scroll and proffered it to Yip. "Take this ancestral scroll. It will serve as a guide when I cannot. The scroll's magic only works for the K'un Lun, so it will be safe in your hands."

"The wisdom within will provide guidance based on your present need."

"Thank you, master," Yip said with a bow, humbled by his teacher's generosity. "I, too, have a gift for you and our order. Much have you taught me and much have I learned through my travels. I am sure you have sensed that I have been touched and guided by others outside our lineage in my journeys."

Reaching into his medicinal pouch, he brought forth the seed from the Aeryn D'al wrapped in the shimmering golden leaves taken directly from the tree of life, so warm and vibrant.

"In a great valley west of our mountain fastness I encountered a forest of Chen-jen, beings of such wisdom and perfection as to bring tears of joy and happiness to the hardest hearts. Many gifts they gave me in the short time I spent with them, including the kernels of wisdom to keep me safe from the Cabal and move my practice forward."

Holding out his open palm to his teacher, his hand shining with light from the carefully protected seed, Yip went on, "Master, these trees, these Chih-jen, called Aeryn D'al by the Elves, gave of them-selves, their essence and their progeny, for us to hold in our keeping."

"We can both grow and develop together, learning what the other has to offer, benefiting from the other's protection and wisdom. Master, I think this seed and the seedling it will become can become the new heart of our order, a pillar we can rebuild around and prosper with through the future. Together, our strengths will usher in a new age of prosperity for our order in our efforts to uplift and cultivate wisdom in the world at large."

Waiting for Master Wei to take the seed from his hands, he said, "Master, I would leave this seed in your keeping."

Master Wei's face shone with delight as he gently took the nut from Yip's outstretched hand.

"I can feel the potential of which you speak, Yip. This little being, so full of life, will be a wondrous catalyst to our eventual regrowth and mutual harmony. Perhaps with time, our two ways of learning will grow together as two trunks intertwine to become one tree."

Yip bowed to his teacher who responded in kind.

Walking back toward his companions, the slow drip of water keeping steady time on the rocks, he asked what his heart wanted most to know. "How do the others fare, master? Are you and the others well?"

He could not hold back his concern any longer, his time alone and his unanswered concerns had worn his patience thin.

Master Wei shook his head. "Much has changed since you left, and not all for the bad, Yip. In many ways, this attack has given us the opportunity to return to our roots and retill the soil of our practice in preparation for a new season."

"Quite a few priests, like you are now doing, have decided that they will walk openly through Chang Sen and beyond despite the peril to themselves, sowing the seeds of wisdom and compassion, helping as needed, and reestablishing our position in this world and others. These seek to branch outward in lieu of retreating within."

"Others are repairing what was broken and restoring the monastery while working to keep it hidden should we need another safehold, all the while preparing for the next attack when it comes."

"Only a few remain truly lost, in that we were quite lucky."

His smile lit Yip with warmth. "This is another reason why I came to see you, to let you know that your path is opening as it should and to continue as you have been while remaining vigilant for those who would seek you out. Your bravery has set an example for many!"

"Do not fear for us, your danger is as real and relevant as ours. Just as I have faith that you will move forward growing in tune with the dictates of the moment, know that we will continue in your absence as you do what you can while abroad."

"When the time comes, we will be ready for your return."

He placed a firm hand on Yip's shoulder. "Unfortunately, our time together is at an end, Yip."

Master Wei's smile then turned into a brief frown. "I must leave now, Yip, lest the signs of our meeting and the repercussions of our interactions, of two Tao-shih together, serve as a beacon to those who would harm us, no matter how well we disguise our presence."

"Although I have been waiting for you here, my efforts must now shift to the East in Chang Sen where I hope to reunite with some of our lost brethren and guide them home. Continue on your path, bringing Light and wisdom to those upon whom you share your blessing. Know that the Cabal will continue to seek us out."

Bowing again, Yip briefly opened himself to his teacher. "Master

Wei, your wisdom and compassion will always serve as an inspiration in times of need. I cannot thank you for all you have given to me and our order. My prayers will be with you in your efforts to rebuild. I will do my best to aid how I may in the hopes of abolishing the Cabal and spreading the light of wisdom to those who would seek it."

Yip briefly embraced his teacher, thankful for all he had been given but wishing he had more.

"May the light of a new dawn guide your steps, Yip"

With those words Master Wei disappeared, smoke shifting into the shadows.

As his teacher passed from this world into the universal *yuan-chi*, a Shen-jen intimately familiar with the untold potential inherent in all sentient beings, a faint sigh echoed softly in the cavern. The burden of his responsibility along with his own profound limitations seemed to weigh even more heavily on his shoulders.

WRINDANNETH

Locust husk clinging
loosely to a whorled bark raft—
memory of spring past.

Yip returned to his friends by the camp in a state of confused excitement, the thrill brought on by the discovery of his newly manifested *chi* abilities already fading with his building concern. Torn between exhilaration and unrest, a mixture of thoughts, impressions, and emotions played out through his mind. Taking a deep breath, inhaling to his *tan t'ien*, his shoulders rose up then settled with the intake of air as his heightened energies found new means of expression within his body in ways that pulled and caught his attention despite the necessities at hand.

He was unsure of how to continue.

On the one hand, he now had access to new innate potentials the likes of which he had never realized. On the other, he now had to face what had only been his distant future in the immediate exigencies of the present. With the help of Master Wei, he was at least capable of attempting tasks along his journey with some possibility of success. Instead of moving forward directionless in trepidation, he could now rely on his abilities to actually make a difference to his order, those that depended on him, and help overthrow those who had taken Darkness into their hearts. Instead of focusing on mere survival, running away from his enemies, or only making it through an encounter as best he could, he could now take a direct hand in his destiny.

Although still largely alone and far from his order, he was now privy to inner mysteries long entrusted to the stewards of his cause, abilities bolstered by years of training, exploration, and practice. He had friends in whom his trust was well served, even if he had spent only a short time in their company for his mind's eye confirmed the impressions of his intuition.

After this small milestone in his development, the question then became what should he do next?

Where should they go?

How best could he go about actually starting the tasks necessary to overthrow the Cabal?

Whereas some in his order did not risk or seek out direct confrontation with the agents of their enemies at this time due to their need to heal, rebuild, and recover, he could.

How could he use that freedom to his advantage?

How much would his newfound friends be willing to chance?

Was it, in fact, fair to them to put them in danger, even with his sincere attempts to accurately portray the depths of the Cabal's evil and thereby demonstrate his companions' potential peril?

Was the party's desire to help enough to warrant the risk necessary to overthrow the Cabal?

As he walked to the small fire by the edge of the underground lake, a question brought him out of his reverie.

"Your master certainly was off in a hurry. Are we not interesting enough company to hold his attention?" asked Wrin.

Before he could answer, gazing at Yip intently, Aroganji asked, "What did he say? What did you learn?"

Yip opened his arms widely as if to show they were empty and held no tricks or obfuscation, that he was open and available for his friends. "We of the K'un Lun derive our abilities from the powers of life itself. When I was forced to leave by the Cabal's attack, there was much I did not yet know, much I had not practiced, had not been shown, or even been introduced to beyond the merest preamble or discussion. Much of what we in the K'un Lun have to learn and later pass on is dependent directly on our ability, concentration, individual study, and degree of attainment."

"Certain skills are not possible until one has reached the necessary levels of comprehension, internalized specific principles, and manifested various abilities. As such, there is much in the way of knowledge and understanding a priest, acolyte, or initiate can possess, but until they are ready, those abilities and insights will be out of reach other than as mere intellectual concepts and curiosities."

"For my own protection, and because he deemed me ready, Master Wei sought me out to show me how to direct internal energies outward around my body, my hands, in a localized field to heal or harm, destroy illusion and falsehood, tend or defend, as needed."

"He taught me the ways of Shakyamuni's Palm, the intricacies of the *chi* fist."

With that pronouncement, his hands began to glow with a soft blue light, complicating the shadows already dancing on the rock formations from the fire and bioluminescence.

"What does that do? What is that energy?" asked Wrindanneth as he came close to Yip, his face highlighted by curiosity and the azure luminescence around Yip's hands.

Yip smiled deeply with Wrindanneth's question for it brought back a memory from his own past when he had once asked the very same question.

He and Master Wei sat perched upon a grass covered hillside overlooking the mysterious, cloud enshrouded mountains of the K'un Lun. A chill wind blew down the mountainside whipping their robes about their shoulders and legs where they sat in the lotus position surrounded by swaying grass.

Without turning to his teacher, Yip asked the question he had been puzzling over for some time. "Master, what is chi?"

His fellow acolytes, initiates, and teachers talked about chi as if it were all around and readily apparent, easily accessible, able to be seen and felt. He, however, felt nothing.

"Breathe in deeply, Yip. Let the air fill your lungs, bringing life and energy to your body."

He did as his teacher instructed, letting the air swell within his chest.

"Can you feel the air in your lungs, Yip?"

"Yes, master."

"Can you feel the effects of the air filling your lungs, Yip?"

"What do you mean, master?"

"Can you feel the air enlivening your blood, giving oxygen to your body, providing the basis for the creation of energy within your self?"

He shook his head.

"In time, Yip, in due time you will."

He sat quietly, waiting patiently for his teacher to continue. When Master Wei did not add anything more, he asked, "What do you mean, master? How does breath relate to chi?"

Master Wei smiled. "Just as the air you breathe enlivens your body, so the chi you breathe and are bathed in enlivens your shen, your spirit and consciousness. Chi is the basis of life, Yip, the energy of creation."

After a time spent in silence, Master Wei added, "In time, you will come to feel and interact with chi as easily as you breathe and feel the air around you, moving over your skin, through your nostrils, and filling your lungs."

Looking at Wrindanneth, he answered, "Chi is the life blood, the essence, of life and living. With the Lion's Palm, I can touch and interact with another's essence to heal or harm, read their intentions, and react in ways I was unable to before. Shakyamuni's Palm lets a priest fight foes that would normally be immune to the mundane touch of Man while serving as a safeguard to the tenderness of flesh and blood."

He smiled, adding, "The power of the Palm grows with the priest."

"By Brendle's axe, Yip! I'd wager ya could give an Orc a right proper thumpin' with those mittens!" Slate's exclamation was accompanied by the loud slap of his hands on his thighs.

Yip sighed and let his hands return to normal. "There is much yet to be done for both Master Wei and for us. He has pressing concerns in Chang Sen and had to return as soon as possible should the Cabal try to impose their will on my order yet again."

"His concern for me, my tutelage, and well-being brought him here to help in our preparations and continued work. Since we are each left in this place with our own futures unfolding before us, now is the time for decisions, my friends, and I am torn as to what to do."

He looked at each of his companions in turn—Slate, stalwart and brave, as solid as the stone, resolute of heart and true; Wrindanneth, astute and quick, observant, a man whose volatility was often a mask for deep concern and feeling; Aroganji bright and caring, watching out for his friends' needs, remaining faithful to them above all others.

How could he best serve them?

What about their needs and futures apart from his concerns and motivations?

"Master Wei only provided me with some of the tools to continue. He did not give me directions on which path to take." He shrugged slightly again, releasing a bit of tension through motion.

"That is not our way. I, we, must decide what is best to do, but I cannot do that without your help and consideration for your desires and aspirations. We must decide if we are to remain a party, if our goals are to be shared, if we must part to pursue our own destinies, what is in the best interest for each of us individually and as a group, what we are to do, and where we are to go if we stay together. We must weigh our options carefully."

He looked to each of his friends once more in the gloom of the cave, waiting for their response. Slate was the first to answer, as was the often compulsive way of the Dwarves. True to his heart, emotions visible for all to see, Slate held table around the fire.

Smacking his hand on the face of his axe, its blade holding a greenish tinge reflected from the bioluminescence, Slate began, "By Horarum's bones, Yip! Tha only thing I weigh carefully is gold, if I'm lucky enough ta find it! Ya know I've already committed myself ta these other Cave Trolls, so if they're with ya, so am I."

"Tha great lord Brendle put me on this Earth fer adventurin'. Whether it's with ya, tha party, or someone else, that's what I'm gonna do!"

Slate scratched his beard carefully, pausing before adding, "I'll tell ya this, wherever this quest o' yers takes us, sounds like ya've got a pretty excitin' bit o' work ahead; work that could even hold a Dwarf's interest, if ya take my meanin'."

Aroganji responded then as Slate glanced around at his friends to see who would speak next. "Yip, I believe you, too, know how I feel. My feelings have not changed over the brief time since we first met."

"In one way or another, I have dedicated myself to the overthrow of the Cabal, their ilk, and those like them. I can only express my thanks that I have been lucky enough to find companions in whom my desires may reach fruition. I do not fully understand what has changed in you, what your master told or showed you, and that I would like to know. Aside from that, if we are not to continue toward Tellanon, we must consider what our next steps will be and how we can best go about reaching our desired individual and party outcomes, goals I feel we share in our efforts against the Cabal and their agents of Darkness."

There was a long pause before Wrindanneth filled in the silence, several emotions readily apparent as they crossed his face in a rush, each battling for expression as he glanced intently from Yip to the others. "You know I'm in it for the excitement, the opportunity to learn of new magics and artifacts, the chance for the development of new powers, and for recognition from and for my liege Maeth Onai. Wherever this quest takes us, I'm sure that we will reap many rewards for our good deeds and explorations."

Eyes directed downward, Wrin went on, "Besides, Maeth is always looking for gifts, and I haven't exactly had many offerings to make of late, so staying together seems like as good a path as any."

Clearing his throat, Wrin continued somewhat reluctantly, "And… ahem, well, I think I'm starting to like you all…"

He finished with a smile, "Just don't get any ideas, Slate."

Yip's smile was all he needed to tell his new friends. They would remain together as they moved forward working to eradicate the Cabal, however that may be. "Thank you, my friends, for your trust, dedication, and efforts both past and future."

Appearing slightly embarrassed, Wrin started again, "Before we go on together, perhaps it is time you learned a little of my story, Yip. Maybe then you'll understand what I mean, why I am the way I am, and why this whole situation, our chance for fellowship, is actually perfect for me."

Before starting, Wrindanneth's mind flashed back to his childhood and his first steps toward priesthood. Lost in memory, collecting his thoughts, he paused a few moments before beginning.

Wrindanneth felt his breath was a bit heavier in the cold morning air than usual.

Feeling the cool air rising off the lake caressing his cheeks, he wondered if perhaps this were a sign. Perhaps today would be the day the gusts swirling about him playfully tugging the hems of his robes would wipe all his troubles away and carry him to a new, gloriously promising future.

The sound of pebbles crunching beneath his feet brought him out of his reverie and back to the task at hand—his uncle's business and his own.

As he looked around his small village, he noticed others hurrying about doing their morning business and chores. Mothers tending children hung freshly washed clothes on lines angled most advantageously to catch the same breeze he had just been enjoying. Teams of fishermen hefted boats and tackle, heading off to the deep inland lakes which supplied his village with meat and provender. Goat herders and grain farmers prepared for the grueling tasks that comprised their day, moving stock from one wind-shorn hillside to the next or plying soil too tired to yield much sustenance.

Not that much could grow in the harsh mountain climate that the gods had been kind enough to bestow upon them. Little sun showed through the clouds here, and everyday life was, in his estimation, gloomy, menial, and tedious.

Although he did not know it at the time, the rest of the world did not suffer from such dearth. He lived in one of the few dead zones on Ea'ae, although the term dead was perhaps a bit too strong.

His village and the surrounding areas were deliberately muted, their magic dampened to hide the presence and power of one who lived nearby. Even simple villages elsewhere in the world had access to magics and charms that made life more productive, eased labor's toil, and helped mend the sick and broken. Those with magical talent in his village would experience a great awakening when they ventured a day's journey beyond the horizon. Unfortunately for them, most never made that choice, or rather a certain heaviness and weariness set in whenever they ventured too far from their native home. This languor remained until they finally returned to the village.

To those outside the lake and its village, the land was thought to be cursed and rumored to be the home of a powerful sorcerer whose power drained the very land on which he trod. In the sparsely inhabited northlands, rumors abounded that any that dared enter his domain gradually felt their strength and vitality lessen.

Carrying his uncle's newly mended net on his back, working under other burdens than the knowledge of his region's ills, he was ready to free himself of the encumbrance looped over his shoulders and the life that his load symbolized. Orphaned before he had a chance to know or love the parents who sired him, he had been taken in by an uncle who cared more about the nets Wrindanneth wove and tended than the boy who made them. Even now as he stood waiting for what he hoped in his deepest heart to be a meeting with fortune, he was still weighed down by the ill luck of his condition, afraid to cast off the net of his own expectation and misery, and meet his destiny.

Resettling the net on his back, ready to appear busy and on his way home should his uncle see him, he hoped that would all change for today was the day that the old master from the tower on the heights overlooking the village would come down to claim a new apprentice, someone with whom he would share his power and knowledge.

He yearned with all his heart to be picked and lifted out of the dull life for which he was otherwise headed.

As he waited, a bit tired from standing in anticipation for so long, he let the weight of the net settle on the ground behind him. As he did so, he first massaged his hands where the coarse weave had cut into his palms and then the tops of his shoulders where the ropes had bitten into them.

Relieved of the netting, he looked around the dusty village commons at the other hopefuls jumbled about him. Some were dressed up in their festival finery, others seemed to be in the midst of errands or work like Wrindanneth himself, some were escorted by expectant parents with their families gathered together. Whether they huddled for support or to shield each other from the wind he could not say, but they all seemed dreadfully slow-minded and ill-suited as far as he was concerned.

As he finished surveying the crowd, there was a brief commotion at the edge of the tiny hamlet. A tall figure draped in robes moved slowly through the streets. Stillness followed in his wake as townsfolk ceased what they were doing to gaze on the newcomer, chores quickly forgotten in his long shadow.

Very little could be discerned about the individual beneath the robes as he made his way over to the gathered young men and women who were waiting with pent up anticipation for this very moment. Wrindanneth could barely breathe as the stranger, whose stature and bearing could only mean he was the master of the tower, wandered through the crowd of hopefuls, as he did once a generation, passing most by without so much as a glance or pause.

When the stranger faced his direction, time seemed to slow to a crawl. Slowly, the robed figured stalked over to him. He did his best to remain calm and poised, hiding all signs of excitement and anticipation.

To his eyes, it seemed as if a fantastic predator had emerged from the darkest shadows in search of suitable prey. He was enthralled. Time stopped for Wrindanneth then as the shadow of the master's arm reached out with a long, gloved finger and touched him on the forehead.

"You'll do..."

He heard this pronouncement usher from beneath the deeply cowled robe as if from a great distance, another world far away and full of possibility, simultaneously feeling his stomach sink to the soles of his feet.

With the master's decision, a collective sigh released from the crowd, some of the gathered hopefuls soughed in disappointment, some muttered in relief as if anticipating the difficulties in store for Wrindanneth in the long days ahead. None lingered too long, eager to be about their business and away from the cowled stranger.

Wrindanneth's attention snapped back to himself when the fleeting touch on his forehead passed. His heart thumping loudly in his chest as his new master turned to walk away, he hurriedly collected his belongings to follow, visions of grandeur and power flying through his thoughts like leaves blown from a tree in a windstorm.

As though his new pupil had spoken his thoughts aloud, the master paused briefly. Without warning, he spun on his heel. The cowl fell back to reveal a man much younger than anyone remaining in the commons expected. Dark eyes flashed with green light and a bolt of glowing energy shot from his hand to strike Wrindanneth full in the chest. The youngster flew stricken through the air and crashed into the side of a small house, his netting lying limp and

forgotten at the master's feet. He lay slumped to the ground, nearly uncon-
scious, as he struggled to regain his breath.

The master walked over to his new student purposefully, standing over
him just as he was about to pass from consciousness.

"Do not mistake me, boy," he said. "I did not say you would do well."

As Wrindanneth tried to blink away the white motes swirling before his
eyes, he heard the master's far-off voice. "I said only that you'd do..."

Then Wrindanneth succumbed to darkness.

He awoke in gloom, disoriented and confused, unable to move or see. A voice
he now recognized as his new teacher spoke from the blackness. "Ah, you are
awake. Now is the time to learn something of the path you have chosen to
tread."

Not that he cared but he wondered briefly whether or not his uncle knew
he was here. His uncle probably thought he had just disappeared.

Struggling against the nagging shreds of befuddlement, the residuals of
the spell cast upon him, he wondered for a moment if he was safe.

"Yours is not the position to wonder."

Startled, he realized the voice had been speaking in his mind!

"I...I'm sorry," *Wrindanneth thought to himself, in the confines of his*
mind to the outside observer.

"That's better," *said the voice. There was a brief pause.* "And yes on
both counts."

Unsure what to expect or think, he listened as he tried to regain his senses.

"Long ago, there was a sorcerer of incredible power named Maeth
Onai. He was considered to be one of the great masters of his time, but
instead of appreciating the praise of his peers, he felt limited by the
constraints of the arcane magic used by other sorcerers and wizards,
by the vessel of his own body. Through rigorous experimentation and
conditioning, not accepting the traditional boundaries imposed upon
themselves by other magicians, he found a way to channel the energies
of the divine through arcane ritual."

Uncertain of the many niceties of arcana, Wrindanneth only later grasped
the significance of this revelation. As his eyes adjusted to the gloom, he could
make out the dim outline of a hooded figure seated on a leather chair a few
paces away across a stone floor covered by thick rugs.

"When the extent of the powers Maeth had learned to control were discovered by others, he was first tested and later shunned as a blasphemer by both priests and wizards, so jealous were they that he could control energies that could be only partially controlled by them and even then, more often than not, only when under the mandate of divine intermediaries."

"He was considered to be a thief of the power of the gods by priests of organized religions and as a charlatan and rogue by arcanists who employed traditional magical invocations."

"This stigma follows his disciples to this day if they reveal their true power."

He cringed inwardly as understanding of his situation began to dawn on him.

Would he be an outsider for all time?

Would tutelage to this man ensure his position on the fringes of a society that had never accepted him?

Once again picking up the course of his thoughts, the voice echoing in his mind responded directly to him, "Your questions will be answered in time, as will your position in the world at large."

"Know, however, that futures are made, not granted."

His teacher made a short gesture with his hand and the room lit up with a soft illumination as he sensed that his pupil's eyes were ready to receive more light.

Blinking briefly, focusing once again on the words flowing through his mind, he listened as his teacher continued his lesson.

"We must strive for power and knowledge for its own sake and not be clouded by others' prejudices. We must not be hampered by personal conceptions of such things as good and evil, right and wrong, for truth is often in the eye of the perceiver. Balance and equanimity must be achieved to truly master the teachings of Maeth Onai."

His master paused and looked directly at Wrindanneth under the room's new brightness, his eyes piercing deep into Wrindanneth's heart. "You will learn this if you are to live."

"To succeed, you mean?" replied Wrindanneth weakly, his voice breaking after long disuse, beneath his master's pointed consideration.

"To those of our order, failure and death all too often go hand in hand," replied his teacher.

Still lost in remembrance, his thoughts moved forward many years later, to a time when he had grown powerful in mind as well as tall of stature. The people of his former village showed him much respect now that in their eyes he had become a powerful sorcerer, but he also sensed a healthy amount of fear from them as well.

So much the better, he thought. Had they known his true path, they would likely shun him altogether, if not burn him as a heretic.

When he returned from acquiring supplies from the town, his master met him at the door.

"It is time you went out into the world, boy—time you saw something of civilization, time you began learning by your own experience, time you began to repay the debt you owe to Maeth Onai."

"You can learn nothing more from me."

It was odd, thought Wrin, that after all these years his master had never given his name, nor had he addressed Wrin by his own given name.

"I would not presume to be so arrogant as to think there is nothing more you can teach me, master," Wrin replied. "I intend to stay until I have gleaned all of your knowledge that I can comprehend."

An all-too-familiar bolt of energy flew from his master's hand toward him, but now things were different. He extended both hands and exerted his will, and the bolt crashed against a hastily erected energy shield.

"If you are trying to test my resolve, master, surely you can do better than that," said Wrindanneth in reply.

"I'm not trying to test you, boy! I am trying to be RID of you!"

Months passed and Wrindanneth was pleased with himself. He had endured every torment imaginable, from crockery smashed over his head while meditating, to his food flying off the plate as he sat down to eat, to dealing with minor denizens of the void left unexpectedly in his bed or boots. Still, he continued on with his studies despite these perturbations.

His master seemed frustrated with him to the point of distraction, but he was certain that it was merely for show, that his teacher would someday soon guide him to the next plateau of knowledge, to the next realm of understanding.

One clear fall night, just after bedding down for the evening after yet another day of ceaseless torment, he heard a massive explosion outside the rough-hewn tower in which he and his master resided. Before he had managed to get out of bed to investigate, the first explosion was followed by a second and the sound of a great beast roaring in pain or anguish as magical discharges flashed and lit up the night.

Fearing his master needed his aid, he rushed out of the tower.

He pulled up in shocked silence before the round oaken door leading outside, discovering his master locked in a ferocious contest with a hideous four-limbed Daemon from the netherworld. The black, vaguely humanoid form was slamming its great mass against a barrier his master had erected, teeth and claws drawing sparks as it surged and battered against the magical wall.

His teacher chanced a brief glance in his direction, turning to where he still stood motionless, stunned.

"I cannot defeat this being and neither can I hold him for long," his master labored under the intensity of the assault, the stress of maintaining the barrier sapping his will. "You must flee at once!"

"But, master, I can help..." Wrindanneth's limbs seemed weighed down by terrible, adrenaline pumping fear.

He was not sure that he actually could help.

"Get on your horse and flee!" His master shouted at him in desperation as the barrier flickered, wavering briefly. "Find your place in this world, Wrindanneth, before it is taken!"

Wrindanneth, shocked almost as much by his master's use of his name as he was with his master's surprising inability to handle the clawed nightmare caught in the energy field, ran over to his horse and jumped on without a second thought. Fleeing into the night, he pushed his horse until its sweat and lather had soaked his leggings.

Only then did he take a moment to wonder why the horse had been already outfitted for travel, and why the saddlebags were heavy with what he later discovered to be his tomes of arcane and divine lore.

Back by the tower, unbeknownst to Wrindanneth, after his apprentice was long out of sight, Maeth Onai waved his hand in a gesture of dismissal. The shrieking horror from the void disappeared almost instantly.

"That one may do well," Maeth said to himself as he slowly turned and walked back to his tower.

MAETH ONAI

Water's susurration
singing softly to the moss.
Only birds share the chorus.

"Wrindanneth, are you all right?"

He looked up to find Aroganji's hand on his shoulder.

"'Tis too early fer dreams," said Slate as he eyed his friend carefully, quickly masking the concern in his eyes lest anyone notice.

Shaking his head free from the murky cobwebs of memory, Wrindanneth turned to his friends, summarizing his thoughts, training and upbringing as best he could.

The time for his tale had come.

Clearing his throat, he began, "I serve a god who was once a man."

Wrindanneth studied his friends for but a moment, unsure what reaction to expect or hope for before continuing onward. Lost still in recollection, he said, "In ages long past, Maeth Onai ascended to divinity through sheer force of will, an apotheosis forged through the accumulation of hidden arcana and mystical formulae after millennia of questing for power."

"Through his searching, he learned the secrets of channeling divine energy into his spells, bolstering his abilities by fusing his knowledge of arcane energies as used by mundane mages with the divine powers used by gods. The result was power such as few men have dreamed."

"Maeth's ascension through the use of divine energy is the same goal shared by those few of us in his priesthood on this plane."

"At first I thought I was the only one who served him other than my teacher, but now I know better. Not only do these others seek Maeth Onai's favor, they wish to follow him into the heavens at whatever cost. Such an ascension is no mean feat, for the self-serving priests of my sect do not make it any easier for others who would follow his path."

"This lust for advancement often undermines the aim they seek."

"Maeth's priests, and those few who follow him, are generally egotistic and self-serving. Their lust for Maeth Onai's power clouds their vision and drives them to ever greater efforts to extend their power. In this way, they are very much like the Cabal."

"I say 'they' because I try to maintain a perspective not shared by my brethren though my aim is no different."

"You see, Maeth's priests are not out for fame, riches, or success in the normal sense, we are after magic, artifacts, spells, items of power, talismans, anything that can further our quest for arcane knowledge, anything that could be of interest to ourselves and our god, Maeth Onai. Priests are prodded, urged, forced, and cajoled to expand their magical talents in the interest of furthering not just their own interests but those of Maeth Onai."

"Those who fail in their efforts to gain greater power and glory for themselves and Maeth do not find an easy end. Either they die from their own shortcomings or enemies, are ostracized and then hunted down, are culled early from the ranks, or die at the hands of those who covet their power. Some directly face the wrath of their teachers and have their powers stripped, others meet an end at the hands of one of Maeth's avatars, or in extreme cases Maeth himself intervenes directly."

"The path of a Priest of Maeth Onai is as dangerous as it is rewarding, but once started, one can never leave. Our search for knowledge is as much a prison as our priesthood."

A look of sorrow accentuated the shadows on his face. "Why in the world would a sane man put himself in such a position you may ask? Well, oftentimes it is not the man's choice, for many are brought up as children to be priests and they know no different, or they foolishly make a choice to study like I did not knowing fully what that decision entails. However, a reckless few seek out Maeth Onai for the abilities he grants and the knowledge they can glean from his service."

"Sad as it may seem to some, or as exciting and grand as it may appear to others, I was brought up in the tradition by my choice and do not wish to know any different. Despite the hardships and expectations, Maeth Onai is generous to those who would follow in his footsteps, for they are granted power and knowledge unknown to most men."

"Maeth's priests represent a truly unique phenomena on this world, much like the special talents found only in your order, Yip. We are unlike any I have encountered in all my travels throughout Ea'ae, for we have access to both divine and learned magics."

Unsure if his friends truly understood, Wrindanneth added, "That is to say, Maeth Onai's priests can cast spells granted both by their deity, like a normal priest, and those that they learn, like a normal mage. We can channel divine energies through ourselves to cast both divine and mundane magics. We can infuse divine power into our spells to boost their effectiveness."

Slate whistled in appreciation. "And here I thought all ya were good fer was eatin' Aroganji's leftovers."

Ignoring this comment, Wrindanneth went on, "In return for this arcane knowledge and power, I get beaten, scolded, jibbed, berated, insulted, and otherwise forced to continue questing for arcana lest I lose access to the abilities granted to me as a priest."

"Maeth speaks to me, demands ever more from me, in dreams."

"Those who enter Maeth Onai's service do not leave. Mine is a journey that can never end, lest I lose all I have worked for and desire in this world."

Addressing his friends directly after his personal revelation, he asked honestly, "So why would I leave your side when the fun is just about to begin? Why would I leave before any have collected the rewards for our efforts?"

"Much in the way of opportunity lies in the future of those who would seek to overthrow powers such as the Cabal and their underlings."

Wrindanneth stared deeply into the cookfire. "The life of one such as I is not easy, as the rewards are brief, for power seeks power ever more and greed is a monster sated but briefly. In my quests, bitterness has become my friend, a knife that cuts into my back and steers me forward, for who can I trust when even my teacher would strike me down seeking his own ends? Focus has become my path, brooking no interference, for one must survive to succeed and always strive onward to achieve one's aims."

Lifting his gaze from the fire, he continued, "Time spent in a group such as this is a welcome relief to one accustomed to loneliness, exclusion, and seeking such as I have known. If rewards can be had among friends, then I am happier for it."

Finished, he looked at Yip, a rare, genuine grin on his face. "Perhaps when we're done, if I need some help with another priesthood, you will still be available."

As Wrindanneth once again settled into silence, the other party members were left to look at each other in turn, interpreting Wrin's words as best they could in the quiet that resettled over them like the mantle of partial darkness shrouding the far reaches of the great cavern.

LORD SARUGAUTH

The Dragon breathes deep,
its nostrils alight in flames—
blazing petals that
never reach the ground.

Later that evening, the silence and cool air of the cavern light on their shoulders, Yip once again broached the topic of their next destination, first giving his friends a brief formal bow showing his appreciation and esteem.

"I must say that it warms my heart to know that you will be with me as we continue onward together. I have been alone for quite some time and your company has been most welcome. Together, with our varied talents, I feel that we will, with time, become a formidable adversary for the Cabal and other agents of Darkness."

"We must now decide if we should pit ourselves directly against Darkness at this time and continue forward, or if we will seek to position ourselves to learn more before we strike out. I think that we can do both."

"How do you mean, Yip?" asked Aroganji.

"We have not ventured far from the Drake Spires in our journey toward Tellanon. When I was in the Spires with the Yerens, I learned of the great Dragon Sarugauth who forced the Shapers from their home high in the heart of the peaks. If we so choose, we could seek this Dragon out and see what we can learn from him."

"A Dragon! Yip, I'd rather confront a legion o' Orcs with a wooden mallet than confront an ancient wyrm." Slate shook his head fervently.

"How do Men survive when they continually hatch foolish Gnomish ideas like this? I'm all fer adventure, but this hardly counts! I know ya humans don't live long, but ya shouldn't seek ta cut yer lives any shorter!"

Aroganji looked at Yip closely, trying to gauge the conviction and thought behind his intent. "Yip has survived much in his time abroad and away from his fellows, Slate. I do not think his suggestion would be poorly reasoned."

Wrindanneth was next to speak up, his long red hair falling loosely before his eyes as he spoke, "I have told you why I am here. Knowledge and power are hoarded by Dragons as much as gold. I have long wanted to test my mettle against an intelligence that has seen the Ages of Man pass like the steam and smoke of its foul breath."

Yip shook his head dismissively before speaking. "My new abilities are quite limited. I do not propose that we directly confront a Dragon, much less an ancient one who has worked magics for millennia, one who has access to powers that may make some deities tremble."

"We know that Sarugauth is in league with the Cabal. In fact, his ties with the Cabal are the only connection I know of that exist materially and that are on open display on this world. Even if we cannot defeat him in combat, perhaps we can learn something of the Cabal's workings by going to his valley."

He looked earnestly at his friends. "I can see and read much when given the chance for careful observation. Perhaps I can learn something of use if we go."

An expansive gesture followed his hopeful suggestion. "Right now, this is our only faint trail that may lead to the Cabal. Though we may learn much in Tellanon, the information there is not certain. No leads are guaranteed."

He added, "Though there may be much opportunity in Tellanon, I am unfamiliar with the place and its ways. I would rather not attract the attention of those from whom I have been running in a place where information passes more freely than the exchange of coin. Perhaps when we are a bit better informed and have established ourselves a little more, we will be in a better position to search out clues there and follow them where they lead."

"Most importantly, we may also be in a position to restore the Yerens to their former home should we seek this wyrm out and learn of its habits and potential weaknesses."

Stroking his fingers through his beard, Slate glowered first at Yip and then at the others in the party intently. "As long as ya don't go chargin' inta his lair like some darn fool Northern berserker, I'll go along. But know this, caution is as much in tha hearts o' Dwarves as is bravery, and I will not spend my life needlessly."

No one else voiced any disagreement.

The next morning Yip informed them that the day had dawned even though no such light penetrated the dark recesses of the cavern.

The time had come to move on.

With an adroitness coming from long practice, the party made short work of breaking camp and removing the visible traces of their stay.

As they walked out of the cavern and back into the valley, Yip told them what he knew of Sarugauth the Red, the scourge of the Yerens and claws of the Cabal.

"From the beginning of their tale to the end, the Yerens imparted much insight and emotion to me. Although they are a peaceful people, their hearts know the depths of despair and the fires of hatred. Such are the unwanted gifts bestowed by the Cabal and those who accompany them."

"Sarugauth cloaks himself in darkness and Dragon fear. Gleaming red and gold, his scales are invulnerable to mundane weapons. With claws longer than spears and a head larger than a wagon, his great maw and claws can rend and tear armor as easily as flesh. The cloud of darkness that radiates out from him can make the stoutest heart tremble and cause the strongest spells to evaporate quicker than fog on a summer day. Leathery wings that span the heavens beat with such force as to generate gales strong enough to blow fully armored men and their mounts through the air and send them scrabbling across the ground in great clouds of dust and debris. Steaming bowels generate magical fires of such intensity as to melt the hardest mithril and the strongest adamantium. His intellect can shape magics and sigils undreamed by the most learned archmages..."

Slate broke in before Yip could continue further. "Enough o' tha encouragement, Yip! By Brendle's forge! I'm already dreadin' this enough. Yer words do little ta strengthin' my resolve!"

"I only speak truly, my friends."

"And truth does not always help one's cause," finished Wrindanneth. "Look, we know we are heading toward a foe we cannot hope to defeat, Yip. You don't need to make us feel worse about it."

"I am sorry. I did not realize that my words would cause such turmoil. I only wish for us to be prepared, not discouraged. I have faith in you, my friends, just as I have faith in myself."

"If not, why continue forward?"

"We may not be able to defeat a foe like Sarugauth with strength of arms, but our hearts and minds will provide a way. Remember, we are not setting out to fight a Dragon, just learn what we may of the Cabal for ourselves and for the Yerens. By being prepared, even if only in our minds, we will be ready for what the Dragon may have in store for any who may seek him out."

Aroganji nodded. "Wrindanneth and I can cloak ourselves in shadow or invisibility, although the eyes of a Dragon can see truly through such guises. To remain safe, we will have to stay well out of his sphere of influence and remain diligent for the traps and magical defenses that he will have established in his time lurking in the valley while waiting for the Cabal's return to this plane."

"Think of the treasures and artifacts this beast must have, Slate! A Dwarf such as yourself must dream of hoards like his from youth to old age," Wrindanneth's eyes sparkled as he had the opportunity to tease his friend.

Slate's eyes shone in return. "Aye, great gleamin' piles o' gems and jewels, eldritch armors and weapons stolen from fallen heroes and tha coffers o' Elves and Dwarves, talismans from races and cultures stamped out beneath his shadow and from those he conquered. A Dwarf could build a kingdom with lore and treasure such as that!"

Slate began to slowly wash his hands as they hiked up the hillside toward a ridgetop from which they could teleport toward the distant mountain fastness of the Spires.

Turning to Yip, Wrindanneth whispered, "Leave it to gold and greed to distract a Dwarf."

Overhearing, Aroganji raised an eyebrow, showing his disapproval.

"Don't raise your eyebrow at me, you robe-wearing ninny!"

Wrindanneth poked Yip in the ribs with his elbow, always happy to create camaraderie through discord.

A vigorous hike through the wood brought the party to the crest of the ridge around early mid-morning, well before the full heat of the day. A lush, predominantly green panorama spread outward around them. Flourishing mountains and verdant valleys caught the sunlight beneath the cloudless sky. Far away to the east, several week's journey by foot, the high rocky, snow-capped Drake Spires clawed their way heavenward—sharp crags as yet unbroken and unworn by the elements, completely unlike the much older rounded mountains of the Green Run at their feet.

Framed against the sky and the looming mountains ahead, the motley party seemed insignificant, almost too small for the tasks at hand, but their hearts did not falter at the thought. As was their way, they made light of their situation when possible and rose to the occasion as circumstances dictated.

"Aroganji?"

"Yes, Yip?"

"You said that you could only far-travel with a group a few times a day?"

"Yes."

"And that you could only port so far as you can see with clarity?"

"That is correct."

"Are you looking for another lecture on magic, Yip? Because, if so, you're talking to the right person," Wrindanneth smirked. "Aroganji is always ready to convene class and hold a lesson."

Ignoring Wrindanneth's jibe, Aroganji responded, "Why do you ask, Yip?"

"I have an idea that may get us around the limitations of your current spells. I cannot yet give you my energies to boost your powers, but I can share my conceptions."

"Don't you think that mages would have thought of alternatives, Yip, in all the time they have been practicing magic? Besides, with a bit more knowledge, experience, and time, we will be able to teleport and won't need to far-travel."

Addressing Wrindanneth directly, Yip countered, "Wrin, I do not doubt what you say, but much knowledge is kept secret, only to be revealed at a certain time when a person is ready. I know this from my own tradition, and I am certain the same is true in yours. Also, much of value in an idea or technique is not in the technique itself, but in how it is applied."

"Perhaps those who share spells are more willing to share new applications. I am not a wizard, so I must ask if what I think is possible."

Aroganji addressed Wrindanneth. "As Yip indicates, we should always be open to each other's ideas."

"And what would you suggest, Yip?" asked Aroganji.

"Perchance you or Wrindanneth has a type of far-seeing spell?"

"Maybe one of you can see like a great hawk or refract the atmosphere like an ocular used to watch constellations? If so, then perhaps one of you could cast that spell to look at a much farther spot while the other casts his far-traveling spell. Then we could reach the Drake Spires much quicker and more easily. We would save quite a bit of time and energy in our efforts to reach Sarugauth."

"Hmm..." Wrindanneth thought Yip's idea over quickly. "Yip, I think that's an idea that would make Maeth Onai proud! I know an eagle eye spell that multiplies the limits of my vision by a factor of ten! If I cast that on myself or Aroganji before we cast the far-traveling spell, we could reach the Drake Spires in perhaps a single cast!"

"Excellent, Yip! That makes far-traveling almost as good as a tele-port!" Aroganji was just as excited as Wrindanneth.

Slate sniffed. "We Dwarves thought o' such things long ago. We're just bright enough ta keep 'em quiet."

Wrindanneth could not contain himself after that suggestion and burst out laughing. "Why in the world would a Dwarf even need to far-travel underground in the first place? And, even if they did, where would they go?"

"Teleporting between enclaves I can understand, but far-traveling? You may hoard ideas and Craft like you hoard gold, but that is one statement I'll never believe."

Slate smiled. "Maybe we Dwarves are smarter than ya think."

"And maybe I don't get sunburned in the summer sun."

As if to offer proof, Wrindanneth showed Slate his pale white arm.

"Looks like ya could use a little sun, methinks," retorted Slate as he sat down on a rock waiting for his companions to get about their business.

Looking along the range from south to north and back again, Aroganji asked, "Do you have any idea where in the Drake Spires Sarugauth makes his home, Yip?"

"Unfortunately, I do not. Once we get closer, you may have to try to scry out his location if I cannot sense it. The visions I beheld when I heard the Yerens song implied that their old valley was northward toward the heart of the mountains, in the shadows of the greatest peaks. I have traveled both north and west through them but never passed through the range's heart."

"Aye," said Slate, "fer tha heart o' tha Drake Spires lies a few hundred leagues northward well past tha last o' tha Dwarven outposts delvin' inta tha mountains' depths. 'Tis rough country there and Dragons may be tha least o' what we find. Foul creatures breed like Orcs in those peaks, mark me."

"I think your spring fresh scent marks you well enough, thank you," retorted Wrindanneth.

Growling as he reached for his axe, Slate said, "I've had about enough o' yer foul humor, Northman!"

Aroganji intervened quickly, used to their bouts of anger and deliberate teasing of each other. "We have no time for this foolishness. The time is come to be off and you two dawdle like school children! Perhaps I will convene class, Wrindanneth, and teach the both of you a lesson."

"Gentlemen, perhaps we could be about that spell?" quietly watching the festivities from the sidelines, Yip was now ready to be off as well.

"Aye," said Slate, "and none too soon!"

"*Nostus ocularius egalum!*" with a wave of his hands, Wrindanneth completed the eagle's vision spell on the group in a fount of glimmering force.

Yip watched energy shower about their heads as Wrindanneth's spell took hold. With newfound clarity, each rediscovered the miracle of sight and the joy it bestows.

"I can see clear ta tha horizon!" burst out Slate as he spun around in joy.

"We need to focus on a single spot together now," began Aroganji as he pointed to a spot on the side of one of the now clearly visible peaks in the Drake Spires to the east and north. "We aim for the cleft between these two peaks."

With a forceful invocation and a few gestures, the party disappeared.

Caught between the strokes of Slate's hand on his beard, in the space between the blink of Wrindanneth's eyes, amidst the rustle of Yip's robe, before Aroganji's hands settled completing the motions invoking his spell, the party appeared perched on a rocky scree located precariously on the side of one of the great gray mountains formerly many long leagues distant.

"Remarkable!" said Yip taking in the panorama with joy in his heart as his mind soared with the clouds breaking against the buttresses of the peaks.

Cold air greeted them in an unwelcoming wall, a forceful reminder of the extremity of their condition.

Aroganji rubbed his hands along his arms. "Perhaps some warmth is in order?"

Wrindanneth nodded. "I'll take care of it."

Cloaking them in magic once more, Wrindanneth summoned a blanket of heat to envelop them through the day.

Satisfied, he washed his hands together proudly, enjoying the sensation of warmth flowing across his skin. "Where to next, Yip?"

"I am not entirely sure. I just know that the Yerens implied their home was far to the north and west from the Drake Spires' eastern peaks. Perhaps one of you could perform a scrying to give us a clue?"

As he spoke of the Yerens, Yip's hand strayed to the amulet at his neck in remembrance of his brief time spent with them in their wondrous, shifting caverns. The stone glowed red and warm in his grip, a reassuring pulse beneath his palm.

"Maeth Onai allows the invocation of prescience at times, but I may not have earned the favor of his ear since last we spoke," said Wrin. "But I can try."

Wrindanneth slipped to the far side of the clearing and settled down into his robes, his rangy figure huddled as if to protect itself from a strong wind. With his back to the party, Wrindanneth began to rock back and forth, muttering to himself.

As Wrin rocked, the air around him began to crackle with static electricity. The hair on the back of Yip's neck stood on end in the charged air. As he looked around the small shelf, Slate's beard stood on end as if drawn along some invisible current toward Wrindanneth's chanting. Surrounded by a large halo of dusky orange hair, Wrindanneth continued unaware of the party's new stylish demeanor.

After a few more minutes of muttering, Wrindanneth stood, appearing lost and forlorn as he walked back to his companions.

"Maeth Onai does not hear me. I have not earned his favor."

Yip had never seen Wrin so visibly distraught.

"Perhaps he will listen to your call next time, Wrin."

"I have done nothing to prove my worth to him in months. He is not happy with me."

"Too much resting on your laurels, eh? A little too self-satisfied perhaps?" Slate smirked at Wrindanneth.

Wrindanneth's lack of a response spoke volumes of the degree of his depression.

"Maeth Onai asks that we prove ourselves."

"Are you not trying to?" asked Yip.

"Aye."

"And do your efforts not have value?"

"To Maeth or me?" answered Wrin.

"Should you wish to be satisfied with yourself, then you. Should Maeth Onai wish you to be successful in your endeavors in his name, then Maeth. Should you wish to be happy, then us."

Wrin smiled vaguely, but without much conviction.

"Perhaps if we teleport once more to the northeast toward the heart of the range we will be in a better position to judge," said Yip gazing northward, magically enhanced eyes lost in the distance.

"I am spent for now," said Wrindanneth. "Aroganji, can you manage another port?"

"That will not be a problem. I have had time to recover."

Spreading his arms widely, he said, "Gather round and look northward with me to the large split double peak above the cloudbank. We will arrive in the pass below the two peaks. Ready?"

"Aye," said Slate looking resolutely into the distance, his woven beard highlighted in shades of reds in the bright sun.

For the second time that day, the party warped forward over the space of several weeks' journey by foot instantly.

With a sudden distortion of the atmosphere, the four companions arrived a bit disoriented in the rocky valley between the peaks. Their breath steaming in the cool air, snow lingered in the shadows at this altitude. Not far above, snow covered the face of the mountains all the way to their caps.

Reaching beneath his robes a second time, the Heart of the Yerens felt warmer under Yip's touch.

Thinking of his first time crossing the Spires, he remembered the talisman's warmth as he looked deep into the heart of the mountains. Perhaps the talisman's time had come! Suddenly sure of himself, he smiled brightly and said to his friends, "I think I have found a way to gauge our distance from Sarugauth's lair!"

"Have ya suddenly become a mage too, Yip?" asked Slate.

"Yes, Slate, and you had better take a few steps backward before I release a powerful curse against sarcasm!"

Caught unawares by Yip's attempt at humor, Slate's hands quickly found his stomach as he tried somewhat successfully to suppress a laugh.

Wrindanneth's head jerked upward in surprise. "Was that humor, Yip?" He looked at Slate incredulously, lost for a moment in stunned silence.

Aroganji smiled. "Perhaps you will get better with practice, friend."

Yip responded in kind.

"When I first crossed the Spires and wondered where Sarugauth lay hidden, the gem warmed slightly to the touch when I looked to the northwest toward the heart of the mountains. I feel that it may remember the way home."

Placing his hand on the stone, he continued, "The gem given by the Yerens appears to emit a bit more warmth after this last port. Perhaps its heat will grow the closer we get to the Yerens' old home."

"Your theory will have to wait until tomorrow, Yip, for I cannot cast another spell of the far traveling's difficulty today."

Wrindanneth answered similarly. "Between communing with Maeth Onai, the heat envelop, and the eagle's vision spells, I, too, am spent. If we need one, I can muster enough magic for a few low-level spells."

Smiling, he added, "Would anyone like me to light a campfire or release some pyrotechnics?"

"I've plenty o' flint fer tha likes o' that," muttered Slate. "Perhaps ya could make yerself useful and summon some firewood?"

Slate woke up with the sun early the next day to find Yip not staring off into the distance, doing some strange dance-like exercises, or tied up in a strange seated position as was the norm, but walking slowly with deliberate precision around the large ledge.

In a soft Dwarven whisper, which as it turns out was more than loud enough to wake up Wrindanneth and Aroganji, Slate asked, "What in tha name o' Freyda's beard are ya doin', Yip?"

With a yawn and a stretch, Wrindanneth blinked blearily at Slate. "You'd think that beard of yours would at least muffle the sound of your trap. Is it time to be up already?"

"Aye. Ya've slept half tha day away. Up with ya!" Slate took pleasure in teasing his friend and causing him minor discomfort.

Though Dwarves show their affection in strange ways, if their positions were reversed, Wrindanneth would have acted similarly.

Yip walked slowly back toward his reclining friends. Slate was busy wiping the morning's condensation from his mail, perhaps the remnants of his exhalations, Aroganji was slowly stirring, and Wrindanneth was preparing a small cookfire.

"I had hoped to see if the stone would give an indication as to which direction Sarugauth's lair may be found, but I have had no such luck walking around the camp. I do feel that it will help guide us, I just cannot tell any difference in its warmth by walking only a hundred paces or so."

"Why don't we see what we can learn after another port?" asked Wrindanneth.

"We can hike up to this ridgeline to get a better view of the interior of the range and port from there," suggested Aroganji.

"Let's be about it then. Too much skulkin' about in one spot makes a Dwarf surly when there's business ta be done."

"And no ale to be had?" offered Wrin.

"Aye," replied Slate creasing his brow and stroking his beard, looking a bit sad at the thought.

The party made the top of the snow encrusted ridgeline in little more than an hour's time. Yip was the first to crest the ridge and feel the cool rush of air hit his cheeks, the wind's movement no longer obstructed by the sheltering rock walls and pinnacles of the higher peaks. Opening before him as he looked east and north spread the sharp irregular peaks of the Drake Spire range as far as he could see. Distant peaks appeared lost and cut off in a haze of clouds and snow only to have their crests loom above the cloud line with clear authority farther up their slopes.

With the crisp air lightly filling his lungs and tingling the surface of his cheeks, he soaked in the world spread before him—the beauty, the vibrancy, the inherent perfection.

Holding his hand up to the sky, his fingers spread, catching the sunlight from the heavens, limned in brightness, he watched the shimmer of the snow packs on distant ridges, the glean of the many icy facets reflecting on the streaked granite slopes beneath his feet. He listened to the wind rustle his robes and the muted beat of his heart. Enveloped in the perfection of the moment and place, he stood transfixed between breaths not yet departed on their journey to rejoin the clouds beneath his feet.

Crunching through the snow and gravel behind him, his heavy mailed boots leaving their deep mark under his tread, Slate muttered throatily, "'Bout time we reached a place ta sit. I think I've got a rock in my boot."

Perhaps not everyone appreciates the innate perfection of being, thought Yip with a smile to himself as he turned toward his friends who were now joining him on the ridge.

"Some hike! The air's so thin, I can hardly talk!" said Wrindanneth with a slight wheeze.

"And that's a bad thing?" retorted Slate.

Intervening before either could get too excited, Aroganji said, "I think we should head toward the center of the range to the northeast and evaluate from there." Without waiting for comment, he began preparations for a spell similar to Wrindanneth's eagle vision spell.

Within just a few minutes, following Aroganji's direction and subsequent invocations, the companions found themselves standing on yet another slightly snowier but much steeper, mountainside.

"The Yeren's stone is warmer to the touch!" said Yip excitedly.

"We are on the right track!"

Over the course of the next few days, the party jumped back and forth across the mountaintops, chilled by the heights and thin air but exhilarated with the chase, triangulating toward their destination as best they could. One moment might find Yip studying the flight of a solitary eagle drifting on the thermals in search of prey; his eyes following the graceful leaps of a six-legged rotal bounding along ledges no mountain goat would dare; or perhaps pondering a herd of large, hairy quadrupedal kilodons grazing on alpine vegetation, their heads appearing to be weighed down to the grasses by two pairs of gigantic ridged horns. The next dizzying moment may revolve around trying to secure footing on the surface of a glacial flow many leagues distant; determining which direction would be safe for the next step on a new mountainside; or which direction they had just come from.

Given the limitations imposed by their ability to cast energy intensive higher order spells, the party's progress was restricted to a few ports each day but their spirits were quite high because they believed their destination was close. Teleporting from spot to spot also kept them out of any potential dangers from fast moving storms or encounters with potentially threatening mountain denizens. Although Yip had not detected any signs of pursuit, he was quite certain that their hopscotching would befuddle any agents of the Cabal seeking to track the group.

When, on the fifth day of porting in the mountains, the Yerens' stone felt like a small ingot direct from a forge in his palm, Yip knew they were close.

From his vantage on the ridgetop, to the east laid a rocky jumble of peaks stretching off and upward into the clouds lost in the distance. Immediately below them, a wide, desolate rock-strewn valley stretched for many leagues in both directions. From the heights above, the cliffs dropped precipitously down over largely vertical rock faces to a charred, granitic cleft in the valley below.

The steep slopes fell away beneath the party's feet for leagues on end before reaching the scoured surface of the gorge below. Although dry now, the valley floor appeared to have been weathered and worn by the action of glaciers long past, their only remnant the occasional pile of loose rocks and layered shale. Largely devoid of vegetation, dust swirled and clouded the air on the valley floor as winds swept down from the peaks above.

"My friends, this must be the Yerens' ancestral home for the Heart of Yere burns like a flame in my palm."

"Looks like a nice place to call home," muttered Wrindanneth. His tone was entirely unconvincing.

"'Bout time we got here! All this jumpin' to and fro is about as disorientin' as walkin' across a ship's deck in a full storm. Dwarves weren't meant fer travel such as this." Slate's gruff expression and sunburnt cheeks shone with a fervent intensity. His beard only partially masked his chapped lips as he spoke.

Looking at Slate's face as he ranted, Wrindanneth said, "Altitude agrees with Dwarves about as well as it does with Northmen it seems, Slate. I can grant you that at least." His fair skin had not fared much better under the thin atmosphere with the reflective snow along the ridgetops of the high peaks heightening the sun's damage.

Flashing back to the song inspired imagery from his time spent with the Yerens, Yip remembered the green valley in the heart of the mountains they once called their own. Green terraces rich in crops and myriad trees, verdant grasses waving in the breeze as much as to their Song, rock and earth steadily shifting beneath their urging and need, small gently sloping hills interspersed throughout the valley floor housing open-aired dwellings formed entirely of the interwoven branches of aspens and firs, Aeryn and Neana, all held the small civilization of the Yerens in its fold.

Superimposing his memory with the vista ahead, he said, "Although far from the wonder of the vision I remember, I think that the valley below us looks like a likely spot to have once held the Yerens' home. I do not sense the presence of an ancient Dragon, or any other real manifest power to speak of for that matter. Let me examine the area a bit more closely."

He turned away from the party to survey the valley yet again.

Casting his mind out far and wide, he sensed little in the way of life within the valley. The gorge appeared scarred, damage from past conflicts left raw, never allowed to fully heal. Ancient, residual magics lay thick upon the landscape as well interfering with his ability to fully discern any underlying subtleties that might otherwise be apparent.·

Much like his descent from the K'un Lun before the Jenyuan Shulin, all he sensed of living creatures were the traces of mosses and lichens along the wind-swept rocks and over the barren, recessed ghylls. These alcoves and outcroppings were only partially covered with sparse, low-lying vegetation. Intermittent nesting spots for birds and warrens for burrowing mammals were interspersed sporadically across the landscape. Though poor, the soil at least held a vibrant population of microorganisms diligently working to restore the earth's fertility and their living environs.

Settling down on the rocks, he let his mind drift with the breeze, caught in the energetic emanations from the earth. He could sense how the valley and its habitats had been marked, damaged, and changed over time by the presence of events long past. The Yerens with their gentle ways and soft songs would not have left the valley barren and empty, so what he felt must be the aftereffects of Sarugauth's scarring and burning. Though he could sense the workings of magics long past, of the beast's presence, he could feel no remaining trace.

"I would think that I could sense the presence of a being, a Dragon, as powerful as Sarugauth from afar. But I feel nothing of the sort. This valley is quite large, however, and my senses are limited. The many layers of old magics here interfere with my impressions as well."

"If here, he may be distant, the mass of the mountains may mask his presence, or he may be using some means of magical camouflage unknown to me, but I do not think he is present, for his presence seems mainly left in the past."

"Ya mean we've been traipsin' all through tha wilderness and he may not even be here? Why in tha world do I let myself be dragged on these darn fool Gnomish-inspired expeditions?"

Aroganji took a stern tone with Slate. "You know as well as I, that there could be something of interest here, Slate. You also know that you are here to do what is good and right and to help those who may need assistance while learning as much as we can. We will have the opportunity to glean more in relative safety if the valley is abandoned. If the Dragon is in fact truly gone, then the Yerens will be able to return home in peace, although I am sure that they could sense far better than you or I when it is safe to return."

After a significant pause, he added enticingly, "Besides, if the Dragon has left, that doesn't mean he took his treasure with him."

The twinkle in Aroganji's eyes spoke volumes to Yip and Wrindanneth. Apparently, it spoke even louder to Slate.

"Aye. 'Tis a good thing he's gone! Better fer him ta have left when he had tha chance! I was ready ta sharpen my axe on tha scales o' his coat! Perhaps he was in such a rush when he heard o' my comin' that he left a little coin fer me in his stead!" Slate was all in a huff, his show of bravado largely for his own benefit.

Slate's excitable nature was often evident in such mercurial displays. The thought of gold, or treasure in a larger sense, ale, or any other form of spirits, appeals to his ego and worth, or any praise or jibe aimed at his quality or heritage, all were enough to get him started on a rant or tirade. He loved to puff up and strut about whether he felt happy and self-satisfied or angry and complaining. There was little in-between along his emotional spectrum as long as the situation was not serious. When the situation did turn, however, he shed the foolish, light-hearted comicality and became as solid and resolute as a mountain and as implacable as an avalanche.

Slate liked to joke and perform, to play upon Dwarven images, perceptions, and reputations. Like an actor in a play or a bard at a feast, he was ready to perform at the slightest notice. That was one way he had learned to relate to the Men with whom he found himself. That way, he could feel free to joke and laugh, protected and insulated from emotional harm or upset as he was hidden behind a caricature of himself while keeping difficult situations as light and friendly as possible. On another level, since his actions quite often reflected his underlying true feelings, despite his play and pretense, his act was often as serious as it was fun.

With smiles all around for Slate's antics, the party began to discuss their options. Yip was first to speak. "Wrindanneth and Aroganji, do you sense the workings of any magics that may hide the presence of some danger or that could possibly mask the presence of a Dragon of Sarugauth's stature? Can you tell if this valley has seen any activity for some time?"

Aroganji cleared his throat. "My divination skills are rather weak, Yip," replied Aroganji, "and I don't think that Wrin will be much help in this department either since he is not exactly in Maeth Onai's good graces at the moment."

"That's true," said Wrindanneth, "but I can think of a few ways we can help. One of us could morph into a bird and scout the valley using the eagle eye spell to see what we find. A bird settling to the ground to inspect something of interest should not draw too much attention and would have access to points of view which we currently do not."

"Another option would be to cast a third-eye that can read the signs of magical spells and constructs and see items hidden to normal vision. With our background in magic, this may help us interpret what we see a bit more than what you would normally observe, Yip. We may be able to use the third eye in conjunction with the eagle eye spell."

"Either one of us could also scout the valley using an invisibility spell. This may not hide us completely from a Dragon's sight, but it would cover us from most other eyes that could possibly be in the valley."

"Or, I could charge inta tha valley like a crazed Northman and see if I get zapped," suggested Slate with a face as stoic as the stone.

"Sounds like a good plan to me," said Wrindanneth. "I love it when you show some initiative."

Slate smacked Wrindanneth firmly on his back with his flat, callused palm. "Anythin' fer a friend!"

"Perhaps if you scan the valley from here, you can fly in to investigate anything that may be of interest?" asked Yip.

"Aye, and then I'll charge it." Slate looked quite serious. "My axe needs a bit o' tunin'. She hasn't seen much use o' late."

Working together, Wrindanneth and Aroganji quickly cast their vision enhancement spells and began to scan as much of the valley as they could easily see.

"There appears to have been much magical activity here in the past," said Aroganji. "I can still see the weavings and tracery of many old spells, but they are mostly on the far side of the valley near that large outcropping and jumble of fallen boulders."

Aroganji pointed to a spot far away on the gorge's floor where the rocks appeared strewn, folded, a bit scorched, and somewhat melted, although those details were lost to those who did not have the eyes of eagles.

"Aye, there appears to have been much energy wielded and expended in this place over time, although we are far from the primary spots of usage. A few leagues farther away, there are rock formations that still seem to hold significant amounts of magical residue, but I cannot decipher the energies' meaning or usage from here even with the eyes of an eagle. I cannot tell if those are spells that are currently active or just their ethereal after-effects."

Yip stared intently into the distance. "The point of which you speak is well beyond my current range to feel and read. There is too much interference between here and there. Even in this desolate place, the touch of life, its associated energies, and layers of old magics are too complex for me to discern details that far away."

Following Yip's gaze into the distance, Aroganji took the opportunity to ask Yip a question. "So what are you looking for when you look out across the valley, Yip?" Taking the pause as a chance to resolve a bit of his curiosity, Aroganji did not hesitate to ask the question.

"I read, or try as best I can to read, and feel the *chi* flowing over and through the land," he answered while continuing to look down across the canyon for more details.

Wrindanneth turned to Yip curiously, following up on Aroganji's question. "What is it like to see *chi*, Yip? How does it look and feel? Does it resemble the magic Aroganji and I can see through our spells?"

Slate looked up from his perch as well, as if watching Yip directly would give him a more accurate or complete answer.

For his turn, Yip continued staring off into the distance, thinking how best to respond. After a time, he answered, "I remember what it was like long ago when I was young to not be able to see and feel *chi* coursing and flowing all around, but even so, describing it is difficult to explain."

"I do not know how you perceive, as I am not you, but seeing the energy of magic and seeing the energy of life should be similar, since one gives rise to the other. In effect, the two are very much the same, one being the expression of the other."

Reflecting for a moment, he added, "I can watch and interpret the energies in use and the effects of that use while a mage casts spells, so your perception may be close. Perhaps the difference is in the matter of depth, sensitivity, and what one can derive from the experience. I cannot say for sure."

Smiling he shrugged, saying, "Or maybe the difference is merely semantics."

He took a moment to try to convey himself with more clarity. "Your question is one I have thought of quite extensively, Wrindanneth, but, being as sheltered as we were in the mountains cut off from the rest of Ea'ae, I never had the chance to talk with those about the experience who perceived the world differently than I."

"Being able to see *chi* is perhaps a bit like being able to see the sun's light reflecting off the moon on a cloudless night. One cannot see the origin of life in the energy of its reflection, but one can see the manifestation and expression of that origin."

Smiling brightly and shaking his head in wonderment at the experience, he went on, "Seeing, feeling, *chi* is akin to being immersed in the shimmering gauze of creation at all times and realizing that the unfolding of creation actualizes continuously about and within."

"One learns to see and feel all around without one's eyes and read what one feels as if it were an extension of one's self." Yip laughed. "As your perception deepens, so, too, does your appreciation for the naturalness, interconnection, and beauty of the world within and without."

Ending with a sigh, he finished as he looked sadly, almost accusingly, down at his hands. "Which makes acting without compassion all the more difficult."

Aroganji bowed, thankful of his friend's consideration and always interested in learning the ways others interacted with energy. "Thank you, Yip, for opening your heart and mind to the curious."

"Maeth will be pleased to learn of this talent as well, Yip." He smirked. "Perhaps enough so that I will return to his good graces."

Aroganji nodded sympathetically. "Perhaps, my friend."

Wrindanneth's curiosity was not fully sated, however. "If magic and *chi* are basically one and the same, with one a part of, giving rise to, or one being an expression of the other, how is what you do with *chi* different than what a magician does with magic?"

Yip could not help but laugh, thinking back to many such conversations with his master, his own curiosity, and his own unending streams of questions. "An excellent question, my friend! Your question is too large to easily answer, Wrindanneth. How can words act as a surrogate for experience?"

He gestured broadly, intending to give a very simplified answer. "The differences are subtle and perhaps vary by the energy's expression, how the energy is put into practice, the intent behind the energy's usage, the purpose behind the practitioner's application, the adherent's view, and his ultimate aim."

"On the most basic level, speaking very generally, a wizard manipulates the energy around himself with his internal strength, his imagination, his formulae, and his focus. The stronger he becomes, the clearer his vision and purpose, the more energy he is able to manipulate and control."

"A Priest of the K'un Lun watches and learns from the energy within and without. He manipulates and internalizes these ambient energies both for greater understanding and as a natural part of the act of self-discovery and transformation. The gradual augmentation and strengthening of his abilities is a natural result of this process."

"Whereas energy control, the expression of will, and power may be the goal of some along the magical path, such desires are not the goal of the priest for those trappings do not necessarily lead to understanding, transformation, and insight."

"The two paths I have so briefly and unceremoniously generalized are actually many. Each approach can manifest itself in as many forms as can be imagined by human perception and ingenuity. These two general ways of interacting with the world can parallel or diverge by intended goal and application."

"Much of this perceived difference is a matter of perspective and intent, informed by culture and training. For, in truth, we all interact with the same reality."

He bowed. "Over time, perhaps, we can explore the differences and similarities."

"I would like that opportunity very much, Yip," answered Wrindanneth, glad for the ready opportunity to learn more of the ways of magic and its varied expression.

"As would I," finished Aroganji, "with many thanks."

Aroganji's heartfelt thanks and Wrindanneth's appreciation were followed by a snort. "'Tis well and good ta discuss tha finer points o' magic and energy before those o' us who cannot see, but what I want ta know is if it's safe ta go down?"

"I see your time with us has taught you much in the customs of patience and discernment, Slate," laughed Aroganji.

"Aye," grumbled Slate, ready to be on the move, even if it led to a bit of unexpected excitement.

"We should be safe if we port down to the valley bottom along the wall near the rock formation. I doubt that our slight magics will be detected from this far away," suggested Wrindanneth.

Aroganji raised one hand. "Just one moment please."

Knowing that ravens enjoy cavorting on mountains breezes, and being one of the few birds that he knew that would not seem too out of place here, Aroganji grasped the hems of his cloak, twisted his arms downward with a snap of his wrists and invoked his transformation after visualizing his change. *"Cambias mallum aviatrix ravenum!"*

With the proper mental imagery, energy expended, invocation and will, he was quickly flying away along the air currents, the magic of his spell aiding his transition to the new form.

Yip, Slate, and Wrindanneth watched as Aroganji slowly disappeared into the distance, hoping that he would come back with good news, that the valley was clear of traps and hostile magic.

Slate grinned. "Tha least he could've done was give us fair warnin'!"

Settling down for a long wait, Yip sat in silent meditation away from the cliff's edge so as to remain unseen by any potential threats in the ravine below. Left to their own devices, and with no obvious reason to start an argument or tease one another, Wrindanneth and Slate were somewhat at a loss as to what to do.

Wrindanneth began a series of exercises intended to build up his ability to channel divine energy into arcane spells, an exercise he had learned from his teacher before leaving to find his destiny. The air crackled about his arms and his hair stood on end as magic of one sort transformed into another, an ability that gave him access to a much wider range of spells than a normal magician.

For an observer inexperienced in the technique, Wrindanneth appeared to be playing with crackling azure bands of energy. To Yip's wonderment, Wrindanneth appeared to be transforming *yuan-chi*, the celestial or divine *chi*, into the *chi* created and maintained by living creatures.

Such a skill represented a very high level of attainment.

While Wrindanneth worked, after his complaints that his axe was growing dull and unused had gone unheeded, Slate began work of his own. First, he carefully sharpened his blade, his hands moving back and forth with a steady competency. Then, after he was satisfied with the results, he stood up and began to work through a series of forms with his axe intended to hone his skills and abilities in combat. Great swinging arcs of his blade led into graceful rolls and tumbles, upward thrusts with the butt of his handle or flat, stunning blows with the axe's face.

Stopping to watch after he had finished his exercises, Wrindanneth showed his appreciation. "You know, you almost look like you know what you're doing, Slate." Slate's concentration was too intense to be broken by Wrin's offhand comment. When he did not garner the normal, intended response, Wrindanneth took the time waiting for Aroganji's return to relax and catch a short nap.

Sweat dripping down his brow, the rivulets eventually lost in his beard, his face sheening in the sun, Slate gradually slowed down and then refastened his axe to his back.

Finally, walking over next to Wrin, he looked down and answered, "Aye," before sitting down to rest, his chest rising and falling in deep breaths as he recovered from his exertions.

After a time, Yip stood up slowly and walked over to Slate. He sat down next to the now dry Dwarf, the arid mountain atmosphere quickly erasing any signs of Slate's efforts, and offered a compliment.

"Your efforts are quite skillful, Slate, very natural and fluid. I am impressed. A wise foe would give you a wide berth."

"We Dwarves are not all drinkin', smithin', and name-callin'," answered Slate, his voice slow and even, well recovered from his previous exertions.

"May I offer a suggestion?" asked Yip.

Yip's soft tone and calm demeanor always struck Slate as odd, somehow very foreign, as though he were somehow at peace in every moment and movement when any sane Dwarf knew each moment should be grasped and wrung for all it was worth. But Yip was not a Dwarf, nor was he even a Man like these other two. He was as different from them as they were from a Dwarf.

Or at least he had become so.

"Aye, just be straight and short with it."

"Your movements are precise and natural with the axe, I have little to offer there. Your skills will refine with continued time and effort, although, again, I must say you are already very skillful. You could improve, however, on your breathing."

"My breathin'? Breathin' is as natural ta a Dwarf as is drinkin' ale. How could I change that?"

"As you move through your forms and extend your arms with your strokes, roll and feint, and respond to attacks, I noticed your breathing patterns could be better."

"Though your motion is constant and fluid, your breath is not. The breath must be maintained at all times lest you lose power and build up tension. The breath may respond as the situation dictates moving fast or slow, shallow or deep, but it should never stop."

Slate thought for a moment, visualizing his routine in his mind, the nuances of his movement and his responses, before nodding. "I can see yer point. There were times I was holdin' my breath or not breathin' at tha proper tempo fer my movements."

"I was not natural nor fully at ease. I'll work on it."

Slate raised two thick furrowed brows. "Anythin' else?"

Yip smiled. "You breathe from your chest when your center of balance should be in your stomach, centered near your navel, or, better yet, extended through your whole body. Keeping your breath and energy focused in your upper torso reduces your balance, your ability to respond, and reduces your power while heightening your tension and limiting your ability to remain at ease and persevere."

"Try breathing through your stomach. Let your inhalations sink all the way to your torso and beyond instead of expanding and holding the air in your chest. When all your energy, power, and focus are united with your breath as you move, Dragons will know fear when they see you approach."

Offering Slate a quick bow as he stood, Yip returned to his spot to resume sitting leaving Slate to his musings on his practice.

Closing his eyes, he heard Wrindanneth say quietly to Slate, "Pretty interesting chap, huh?"

"Aye, interestin' is tha least o' it."

With his eyes scanning the valley, Wrindanneth was the first to notice Aroganji's return.

"He's heading back this way!" Wrindanneth's pointing hand served as a guide for Slate to begin tracking Aroganji's return. "Hopefully we can get started."

With a ruffling of his feathers and the wind beneath his wings, Aroganji landed on the rocks with much more grace than when he took off.

Still shaped like a bird, he spoke to the party, his voice surprisingly unimpeded by his avian form, "The valley appears to be quite clear and safe for us to descend."

"Glad ta hear," said Slate. "I'm looking forward ta pokin' about in that Dragon's cave!"

"Which brings me to my next point," Aroganji cocked his small, feathered head, his dark eyes sparkling in the sunlight. "A little way past the jumble of disturbed rocks we can see from here, around the feet of the mountain, there is a cave."

Slate thought it odd that Aroganji's voice seemed so normal coming as it was from a small bird while his mannerisms suited the form.

"Excellent! At least we know we're on the right track and can move forward!" Wrindanneth felt the thrill of the chase and the nearness of opportunity.

"That is not all," said Aroganji, his voice firm, but somehow uneasy. "There is heat along with smoke rising from the cave's entrance."

Slate stroked his chin. "Ya think it's from a fumarole or tha like?"

Aroganji shook his dark, feathered head.

Slate feigned innocence. "Somethin' more interestin', perhaps?"

Aroganji nodded.

No longer restraining himself, Slate exclaimed, "A Dragon! This trip is finally gettin' excitin'!"

Slate was almost bouncing with enthusiasm, a far cry from his prior expressions of concern. After a moment's exuberance, he stopped just as suddenly, his mood turning as quickly as it started once the reality of the situation fully sank in.

"How will we deal with a Dragon? We've no Dreadnaughts!" For they did not have the mighty Dwarven Baera'Dur to provide them with implacable support.

"We will have to come up with a plan as I said before," said Yip coolly. "One need not always match one's brawn directly against a Dragon's. Oftentimes appeals to their vanity and cunning suffice. We are not looking for a direct physical confrontation then, but a battle of wits. Since we are only after information at this point and could not overcome a Dragon of Sarugauth's stature, that is our best option."

Slate raised an eyebrow. "And ya have experience in this?"

Yip smiled. "No."

"Assuming there is a Dragon down there, you'd like to trick it into revealing its secrets to you?" said Wrindanneth.

"Yes," replied Yip, his face resolute and intent as he met the gaze of his friends. "Is not that the very stuff of adventure?"

Slate snorted. "Sounds more like tha essence o' idiocy."

After a brief pause, ignoring Slate's derision, Wrindanneth's laughter broke the silence. "It is indeed, Yip! You and I have more in common than once I thought. How often does one get the opportunity to match wits against a Dragon?"

Grumbling under his breath, Slate muttered, "I fer one would still prefer ta match wits against a tankard o' ale. At least that's a battle I can hope ta win!"

"How do you propose to hold his interest, Yip?" asked Aroganji, all business as usual. "With what do you intend to bargain? For Dragon's always want something in return for their patience."

"I hold ransom that which Sarugauth failed to take the first time he was here, the heart of the people he sought to overthrow and destroy. I hold the symbol of his failure strung about my neck. If that is not Sarugauth in the cave, perhaps his successor will show similar interest."

"Perhaps," said Wrindanneth suddenly grave. "But don't you think it even more dangerous to point out his failure than confront him directly in combat?"

"That's just my point, Wrindanneth," said Yip, his voice firm in the crisp mountain air. "I will not point out his failure, I will appeal to his vanity. If he can defeat a lowly human in a battle of wits, I will return that which he lost when first he came to this valley so long ago. If he cannot, he will reveal what he can about the Cabal's doings on this plane after their long absence and perhaps shed light on what they are ultimately after besides destroying old enemies and gathering objects of power in exchange."

"If that is not Sarugauth in the cave, then earning the Heart of Yere will certainly prove his worth and add to his status."

"And how d' ya know that a Dragon will keep its word and not just destroy ya outright?" asked Slate who was the most skeptical of the group.

Wrindanneth answered for Yip. "A Dragon always keeps its word, though he may later seek to destroy the one to whom he originally gave it or twist the truth of his original intent. And you should know that given the opportunity to prove themselves, a Dragon's vanity often overrides good sense."

"Aye," said Slate forlornly, echoing Wrin's thought. "Tha fun never stops with you lot, that is if it can ever be said ta start."

Their discussions at an end, Wrindanneth ported the party down to the base of the mountain around the bend from the cave, out of sight from the entrance and hidden from prying eyes amidst the tangled jumble of rocks, about a league distant from the cave's mouth.

No hostile magics triggered upon their arrival. No enemies burst forth to attack them as soon as they set foot in the valley. No curses or threats fell upon them. Standing just a short distance away from the cave, they were met only by the unbroken silence of a vast, impoverished valley.

Surveying the location, Wrindanneth pointed out a suitable spot and said, "We will rest overnight here before entering the cave tomorrow so that our energies will be fresh and restored for the trials ahead."

"We must be careful, lest we alert the Dragon to our presence," said Aroganji. "I am puzzled as to why I did not sense more in the way of magical defenses or wards outside the cave, so we must be wary of any traps and subterfuge."

"This close to the cave, we should keep our magic usage to a minimum. A Dragon may not be able to catch us port in, but they will certainly smell new magics cast in their vicinity." Wrindanneth's concern was shared by those he advised. No one wished to bring down the wrath of a Dragon while unprepared.

With the sun gradually setting over the valley's edge, Yip quickly told his friends that he would see if he could find out anything about the cave that lay ahead before they embarked on their journey in the morn.

To his eyes, the air was thick with the residue of long-abandoned magics. Though no longer gathered for a particular purpose, some of the magics' power remained nonetheless. He could feel the presence of these energies intensely. That these forces yet persisted told him of the amount of power that must have been gathered and expended so long ago.

While the party made ready in preparation for the next day, he spent a significant amount of time in meditation before sending his mind out to explore the immediate area. As his mind passed over the weathered rocks and past the ruined slag near the cave's entrance, he felt great power laying nascent in the rocks alongside the remnants of forces expended that had changed the valley so long ago. Within these stones, he also sensed the faint motes and traces of a powerful being whose essence had deeply marked the valley and to a much larger extent, the cave ahead.

His mind adrift, scoping the cave and trying to make sense of what he found inside, pushing inward, he could sense the presence of a being of great power below in its depths, one whose *li* exhibited extreme complexity. But what he felt was not what he expected to find.

The traces of the being he sensed, the mighty one who had dwelt here in ages past, and the one who dwelt here now were not the same.

His friends' preparation done, Aroganji already settled in for bed, Yip opened his eyes suddenly, though his gaze still seemed lost in the distance. Refocusing quickly, he turned to his friends, pronouncing earnestly, "Sarugauth is gone!"

"What?" blurted Aroganji sitting up alertly. "I saw the smoke! That has to be from a Dragon's fire. I can smell its heat even from here. No normal flame or molten flow would put off such a vitriolic stench."

"I did not say the cave was empty, Aroganji. I just know that the great Dragon that terrorized this place is gone," his face shadowed in the moonlight, Yip tried to address his friends' need for clarity. "There still is something powerful in the cave, but its heart is not a dark void as was Sarugauth's. I can sense its intricacy even from here without casting my mind out now that I know what to look for."

"Can ya be a little clearer fer a Dwarf, Yip? I might have been dropped once or twice too many times as a wee lad. Should we be ready fer a Dragon?"

Yip shook his head. "I do not know, Slate. I am not sure what the patterns of Dragons are like as I have never seen or felt one alive. We may face a dangerous situation ahead, for the soul ahead is very complex and wields great energy. But I can say with certainty that it is not evil."

"'Tis good news indeed then, Yip! I can sleep a bit easier now knowin' that if I'm rent ta shreds by a Dragon tomorrow, at least it won't be an evil one." With that pronouncement, Slate closed his eyes and rested his head on the crook of his arm in preparation for sleep.

"At least the situation is not as grave as we once thought," said Aroganji looking at Slate's silhouette shadowed beneath the rocks.

"But we must still be prepared for the morn," said Wrindanneth before Yip could issue any more dire warnings or grave pronouncements.

More at ease than they had been for the past few days, the party slept soundly, each taking his turn at watch, before the morning of their attempt.

As they made ready for the day ahead, Aroganji spoke to the party with some conviction. "We may confront a foe today well beyond our abilities and fortitude. Caution and good sense must be our guide, although I fear that such wisdom has long since departed from the hearts of those like us considered as adventurers. Wrindanneth and I will do our best to protect and guard against potential injury should we face a confrontation, but, should events lead to that, I feel all hope will be lost. We must therefore keep our wits about us and move forward in strength and cunning."

"There is more to be said," Yip's focus rang as loud as his words. "As you know, a Dragon is immune to mundane weapons and only the strongest spells can breach its defenses. We have neither magic weapons, nor the strongest of spells. But we do have our cunning and tools that can help us win should our attempt go astray."

"We must attack where our enemy is weak should the situation dictate and opportunity arise. Do not let your fear cloud your abilities. We may not have spells powerful enough to harm him directly, but there are ways around magical resistance. Effects directed nearby an opponent can sometimes be just as effective as those cast directly on them. Pain, confusion, blindness, and lack of mobility are all options that we can use to create an opportunity should the need arise. Even if those options fail us, we may get lucky and one of our spells could get through his defenses."

"Never fear, there is always hope where wisdom can see it."

Slate shook his head, grumbling, "And I fear wisdom has never been fer tha likes o' any us ta see."

Before leaving the camp, Wrindanneth and Aroganji made ready to protect each of the party members with as many wards and spells as they could afford while still having some energy held in reserve for the day. Gathering themselves, they showered waves of magical protections upon each, layering defenses as best they could.

In order to be protected from fire, everyone walked toward the cave under the aegis of Wrindanneth's spell Fleurstil's Flameshield, although it was only partially effective against magical fires like those of a Dragon's breath. So, while they may not be able to survive a direct blast from the Dragon's fire, they would be free from harm should they be on the periphery of the blaze.

To help protect against the Dragon's claws, tail, and wings, they each received the mad mage Menarfus's Inverted Aura, a rare spell unearthed by Aroganji recently in his travels. The shielding made melee attacks reverse speeds as they passed through the translucent barrier, so a deadly blow from a great sword may be slowed sufficiently as to render it ineffective. One had to be careful in the application of the Aura, however, should one have it up for protection and not be in the thick of battle, even a soft pat on the back from a friend could turn into a fatal blow. The barmy Menarfus must have relished the thought of the confusion and chaos resulting from friends being more concerned about each other than their enemies on the field of battle when developing and applying this spell.

Wrindanneth also protected them with Langwelia's Bravura of Bravery, a magical tune to inspire their strength and fortitude that intoned quietly in time with their footsteps. Although there was no bard present to bring out the song's true power, the ditty bolstered their hearts and would help protect against the Dragon fear.

In order to help them see any magical wards or protections on the path ahead and to help anticipate the Dragon's spells, Aroganji cast Lo Chun's Perspicacity on everyone except Yip. The spell enabled them to see what was hidden, read magical resonances, and decipher something of the meaning behind various spells, traps, and wards.

Wrindanneth also cast the minor cantrip Myrna's Muffling to dampen the sounds of their footfalls and mask their approach. Any advantage granted by surprise and timing could play to their advantage.

Finally, Aroganji cast Alysha's Etheric Enervation, a spell that served to weaken their foe with each attack while strengthening the weapon's wielder with the life force siphoned away. The Etheric Enervation had the added benefit of allowing their weapons to hit creatures immune to mundane weapons. Although this ward provided a way around the Dragon's resistance to non-magical weapons, they would still have to brave its fury to overcome the strength of its scales before actually landing any damaging attacks.

Walking forward, feeling his auric body covered as it was in layers of glyphs, runes, and wards, Yip felt new tinglings and sensations of energy swirl and eddy about him, as if he had put on new layers of clothing only visible in the mind's eye.

Their confidence bolstered and their defenses strong, the party made its way cautiously toward the mouth of the great cave little more than a league distant. Rocks and thawed, refrozen snow crunched beneath their feet as they made their way forward in silence.

No birds sang in the valley to greet the day. No insects hummed in hidden recesses amongst the sparse vegetation. About them lay a land rocky and desolate, scarred and blighted long ago by the works of an agent of great evil.

After about half an hour of steady walking, Yip first discerned the broken jumble of boulders laying cast aside and reshaped after being melted at the feet of the great peaks marking the near edge of the great cavern that had once been Sarugauth's home. Although they could not yet see it, the cave's entrance was marked by a thin, black stream of acrid smoke billowing infrequently from the mouth of the cavern, as if the earth's breathing was laced with some dark, smoky pox.

Looking to his friends a few paces back, he asked, "How do you fare? Any signs?"

"Nothing as yet, although I read much of what you described in the valley's history," said Wrindanneth.

"Aye, ya must be a bit addled in tha head havin' all these images come at ya all tha time, Yip. If this is in any way how you see, that is."

"Addled is a nice way to put it, Slate. Thank you." Yip turned away with a smile on his face as he walked a few paces ahead in the vanguard.

Turning to Wrindanneth, Slate whispered, "See! He is crazy!"

With a scowl on his face, Wrindanneth hissed back, "Shut up, Slate."

Scurrying as quietly as mice in the hayloft of an old barn, the party scrabbled first over the fallen boulders and then the frozen wall of formerly molten slag next to the cave's entrance. Weapons and spells held at the ready, the party cautiously crested the rocks and descended the short distance to the cave's entry.

Ahead, partially deformed by awful heat, the entrance to the massive natural cavern loomed, its walls caught in time midway through a liquid transformation. The stones leading forward along the ground and walls of the cavern were still burnt, glassy, and blackened from the heat of its fiery past.

Yip motioned for the others to stay back as he walked forward on feet as silent as the wind. Moving ahead, his nose stung with the acrid smell of sulfur seeping up from the recesses of the cavern; he had to blink to keep his eyes from burning. Peering carefully around the edge of the entrance, he could see the rocky path gradually curve downward into the silent depths below.

Signaling that all was safe, he motioned his companions forward, each crouching low to the ground to minimize their profile. Once they had all safely gained the entrance, he whispered, "Do you sense anything? I can feel the beast's presence as a sleeping hulk far below. To my mind, however, it seems as though most of the magic that once filled this place was stripped away with Sarugauth's passing."

"I can see a thin tracery of spells about the entrance, but they are too fine to decipher and do not appear to indicate any real danger," said Aroganji looking intently past the party to the mouth of the cave, trying to make sense of the smoky symbols he found hovering loosely within the cave.

"I, too, see the remnants of spells long past, but I also get the impression of something else...a vision perhaps? I cannot say," finished Wrindanneth, clearly disappointed with his inability to read more. "It is a magic I am not familiar with. But I sense no real threat."

Slate scratched his beard. "All I see are quite a few bright streamin' lights and pretty colors."

"Then your visions are as insightful as mine," said Yip. "Forward then?"

"Aye, let's be about it."

"Yes," said Aroganji who looked to Wrindanneth for his nod.

Stepping carefully toward the darkness, the party slowly inched forward ill at ease in the silence of anticipation.

Crossing the threshold into the gloom, before anyone could react, a tremendous resounding voice boomed out of the cavern as a giant disembodied Dragon head appeared before them.

Taken aback, the party stared directly at the face of sheer terror embodied before them—great blackened horns jutted upward along a bony ridge above glaring yellow eyes; huge, stained teeth held at bay a long, snake-like tongue that slavered and danced amidst the flickering flames visible deep inside its great maw; dark, blood-red scales shimmered in the half-light, reflecting their worst fears and doubts in the gleamings of its impenetrable mail.

With a voice that shook the mountain and reverberated into their very bones, the Dragon roared, "Who dares enter the lair of Sarugauth the Red? Speak now and know your doom!"

Inadvertently taking a few steps back, their hands thrown up before them in surprise, dismay, and protection, the party only lost a moment before responding.

Had this been an actual Dragon intent upon their destruction, such a delay would have cost them dearly.

After recovering themselves, the party's response was as simple as it was elegant. Ignoring the illusion, they walked bravely forward into the darkness ahead. As they passed beneath the Dragon's head, Slate muttered, "Sarugauth is no more!" and brandished his axe with a great thump of his chest.

The flames in his heart now kindled, fire burst from Slate's hand to dance along the length of his axe in readiness for the trials ahead, the legacy of Brendle's forge made manifest through the heart and will of a Bor'Banna.

Wrindanneth's red hair flashed in a beam of sunlight as he turned to his friends. "There goes our opportunity for surprise."

He sighed.

Another slightly angrier outburst followed, as the terrible wyrm bellowed, "Quaver in fear before me, mortals, and know that you face your doom!"

No longer breaking stride, the party continued onward unperturbed.

What followed was as confusing as it was comical.

As they began to move forward following the curve ahead and downward leaving the daylight behind them, they could still hear the illusionary head yelling at them, its deep voice no longer issuing dour threats, instead sounding almost petulant. "Wait just a minute!"

There was an angry pause for a few moments. "Don't walk away from me! You face Sarugauth the Red!"

Its sense of command and surprise lost, the voice continued in a state of bemused annoyance and petulance, "What are you doing here? Answer me when I speak to you!"

As the companions rounded the bend and walked out of its line of sight, the beast roared, "Hey wait! Don't go!"

Slate could not contain himself any longer. "Ya'd think a Dragon would have a bit more dignity than that!"

With the great head left to rant unheard behind them, the party advanced unaccosted through the cavern.

Slate's Dwarven sight allowed him to see subtle variations in heat flow through the cavern, the warm air rising from the depths commingling with the much cooler air from the valley behind as the currents moved upward. As the cavern became darker, he could also make out the differences in surface temperatures on the rocks they passed, a very helpful skill to have for a people often wedded to a forge. Although he could no longer clearly make out his friend's faces in the dark, he could still tell who was whom by their various heat signatures and characteristic walking patterns even without the additional layer of information provided by his magically enhanced sight.

To Yip, the darkness of the cavern was lit up by the energies of his friends and the ambient energies around him. The rare lichens, bats, and insects all provided small constellations of brightness for him to mark their progress through the cave. The subtle etheric energies supporting the life around him provided shape and form to his surroundings. Although the halo of his sight was brightest in the radiance given off by his friends, the cavern provided ample energy for him to see unaided by torch or spell.

To Aroganji and Wrindanneth, guided by their spells, the darkness of the cavern was filled with energies they often wielded but seldom saw. Although confusing at first, seeing the forces they used for the creation of their spells lent a certain comfort and reality to their training. Wrindanneth, in particular, began to consider how being able to continually see the energy around him would certainly aid in his efforts to direct and manipulate spells in both divine and arcane energy channeling.

"Do you have any idea what lies ahead, Yip?" asked Aroganji. "Sarugauth may be gone, but someone or something at least would like us to think he is still here."

Yip glanced back briefly to the radiance that was Aroganji from his position at the front of the group while carefully examining the smooth walls and floor of the hallway as he moved ahead. "There is a being of power here. Perhaps it is a Dragon, I cannot say. But the magnitude of its power is nowhere near that of what I would expect for Sarugauth or any ancient wyrm."

He paused a moment as if remembering or trying to recall something of import. "And it's a juvenile."

"Are ya tellin' me that whatever's down here is a child?" burst out Slate, his skepticism a brief flash, a change of color, in his aura to Yip's senses.

"Just because it has not reached maturity does not in any way make it childish or immature. I could be wrong, but, if I am right, we may be able to use its inexperience to our advantage."

"How's that, Yip? Do we have some treats ta give him?" asked Slate as he continued to survey the walls and floor with his Dwarven eyes, searching for signs of traps and pitfalls.

"It may be naïve, lonely, and looking for companionship, or unused to dealings with the minds of other races. We will have to see, my friend. All will unfold well, I am sure."

"Or it may be hungry and look ta us fer an easy meal!"

Yip smiled, a gesture that was almost lost to his friends in the darkness. "You're too tough to make an easy meal, Slate. Besides, as I have said, whatever manner of creature it is that awaits us, it is basically good, even if, from our perspective, a bit misguided."

"Humph." Slate had no comment, or rather, thought little of the generosity and inherent goodness of others.

As they walked carefully onward, at this point there was no real reason for stealth since they had been found out by magic before they even truly started their journey inward, Slate ran his hand along the oddly smooth walls of the cavern.

"That Dragon almost melted tha entire mountain in its fury, it seems. 'Tis a wonder any o' those Yerens survived when that fool wyrm tried ta bring tha whole peak down on their heads in one great molten slag."

"If you have ever experienced the Yerens' skill in song and in the manipulation of matter, you would understand how a Dragon would have to melt quite a bit of rock to even reach them if they chose to close him out. In fact, I would not doubt that they could sing an entire mountain down on Sarugauth's head, if they so chose, or open a new passageway to escape quite easily. Surprise did them in that night aided as it was by the added might of the Cabal."

"That Dragon must've put quite a bit o' energy inta sculptin' tha tunnel ta his likin' then, fer I cannot find any trace or remnants o' tha original native cavern formations as we move."

"Seems to me more like he blasted this whole place to slag," offered Wrin.

"Aye, that too," replied Slate moving on resolutely through the gloom.

"I am a bit surprised that there is not even a trace of henchman or guardians. It is almost as if the place were abandoned and only recently reclaimed," suggested Aroganji, his eyes following the traceries of energy around him as much as his friends and the hallway.

"No one else has been here in a long time." Yip's voice was as distant as his thoughts.

"After that welcome, I was expectin' a bit more hospitality," said Slate, his hand straying to his axe.

"How far down do we have to go, Yip?" a slight undertone of tension in Wrindanneth's voice indicated his eager readiness.

"Some distance," said Yip. "There is quite a bit of strain in our host, so we must be on guard. Can you feel the gathering power?"

Yip paused and motioned to his friends with his hands. "We must use extreme vigilance! Stay to the side of the tunnel in case he releases his breath toward us in the confines of the passage. If we stay to the side, Wrindanneth's flameshield spell should protect us."

"Assuming it's a Dragon," said Wrindanneth.

"Aye." Slate's focus was more on the tunnel and the cavern ahead. "Hold friends. Put yer hands on tha wall." Slate paused a moment for his companions to feel the warm rock beneath their hands. "Tha walls're heatin' up. We're gettin' closer ta tha heart o' its lair."

Inching their way cautiously onward, time slowed for the group as they measured their progress by the increasing heat radiating off the walls. Within the space of just a few short minutes, Slate was wiping sweat from his brow.

"I thought we were in tha mountains! Where're tha cool temperatures?" he whispered jokingly to Yip who was close to him in the lead. "I feel like I'm back at tha forge!"

"If you'd shave your beard, chest, and back, your pelt might not be quite as thick as a bear's, Slate," Wrindanneth kept his own more pressing concerns about their vulnerability in the open passageway to himself.

"We must be ready for anything now." Yip paused, verbally echoing Wrindanneth's concern, extending his senses forward.

"We are close. I can feel the creature in the distance as intense as a great flame." A few seconds passed while Yip sought to read its essence, to glean something from its presence. "It is large and inhuman." He could feel its power radiating outward through the cave. "If it is a Dragon, it has not yet reached its full growth. I think it is quite unhappy with the way we treated its greeting."

"We're not exactly here to make friends," said Wrindanneth, his concern on their success, not the well-being of a potential foe.

Before they had traveled much farther down the tunnel, Yip held his hands outward for his friends to stop and hissed, "Hold!"

"What?" barked Slate who was closest to him.

"Onto the wall!" shouted Yip. Before he had finished his sentence, Yip had grabbed Slate and thrown him against the smooth stone wall.

Just a few moments later, a thundering roar reverberated through the passage.

Looking forward, the party drew back against the warm stone in terror as a faint shimmering of flame in the distance rapidly rushed and surged toward them, licking and burning the walls of the passage as it tumbled ahead in a liquid wall of plasmic destruction.

For the briefest moment, the flames outlined a large cavern in the distance before filling the tunnel with a roiling tumult of amorphous devastation.

"Hellfire!" Wrindanneth's voice echoed the apprehension felt by Aroganji and Slate clinging to the sides of the cavern.

Briefly before his vision was lost in heat and light, Yip could see his friends flattening their bodies against the raw rock.

"Hope the spell holds!" yelled Aroganji before the air in the tunnel was vaporized in the seething inferno.

Aroganji's faith was tested before his words reached his friends on the far side of the cavern, his wishes burnt away in the violent roar of the blazing conflagration, never reaching the ears of his companions.

A great wave of heat preceded the flames as scorching air rushed ahead of the blast in a tumult, sweeping the tunnel clean of small rocks and debris, singing the hair exposed on their arms and heads and burning their lungs as the hellish calefaction sucked the wind from their lungs. Arms covering their faces, heads hovering close to the wall, the party braced for the worst, their world suddenly disappearing in an awful haze of blinding white flames, as they were instantly transported to the surface of the sun, no void of space between them and the heat to cool the stellar intensity.

Lost under the brilliant heat, the party's Spellshields incandesced and sparked beneath the Dragon's hellflame, the smallest of barriers protecting their fragility, burnt away with the passage of the torrent.

Gasping for breath, their exposed hair completely burnt from their bodies, their lungs heaving after an empty eternity, robbed of life-giving air by the fires, each strove to make peace with the demands and pains of their bodies as they rejoiced in the life to which they still clung.

"Gods in tha heavens!" Slate gasped, his voice the first to return, well-trained after years of living by the forge.

"Maeth be praised that the Flameshield held, Wrin," gasped Yip, much of his clothing lying in ashes smoldering on the glowing hot floor, only partially protected by the spell, all the moisture burnt from the now dry air. Wiping the soot from his brow along with the remnants of his scorched hair, Yip's bald scalp made him look more like an initiate in his order than he had since he first fled the monastery.

"We'll need another one, Wrin," gasped Aroganji, hands on his knees heaving as his seared lungs screamed in pain with each breath.

"Nice haircut, Wrin. I like ya with tha bald look," said Slate, breathless as he eyed his friend whose long red hair laid in burnt ashes far down the tunnel.

"And you look nice clean-shaven, Dwarf!" replied Wrin as he prepared another Flameshield spell to protect his friends should a second blast follow the first.

Shocked, Slate reached quickly to stroke his beard. "My beard!"

Tears falling down his cheeks only cleaned part of the soot from his face. Slate was too proud to cover his eyes to hide his shame from his companions, as much of his Dwarven honor had been burnt away before their eyes. "Ya could've at least protected my beard, Northman! By Great Durin's ghost, there'll be a reckonin' fer this!"

His concern for Slate now evident, if rarely shown, Wrindanneth replied sincerely, "Don't worry, Slate, when we get out of here, I will restore the damage done to your beard."

Focusing on the task at hand, Yip added, "Your beard will regrow, Slate. Do not fear. All will be right in time." Looking to his friends in the dusky glow of the rock walls, he said, "We must wait for the rock to cool before we can move any farther," as much to let his friends recover as to protect them from the heat of the resolidifying rock.

"If everyone's welcomed like this, then I'm surprised the tunnel isn't as smooth blown glass," said Wrindanneth, offering his good humor to help bolster his friends' spirits.

The party waited.

"Any suggestions on how best to move forward?" asked Aroganji. "Now that we know that we face a Dragon, we make an easy target coming down this tunnel only partially protected. If it couldn't see through invisibility spells, we could hope to sneak up on the beast."

"We need a wall o' stout shields ta charge in ahead o' us, a few more strong arms, and spears at the ready ta take tha monster down," said Slate his hand reaching unconsciously to stroke the beard that was no longer there. "Where are tha Dreadnaughts when ya need 'em?"

"I will go by myself," said Yip, taking his friends' concerns upon himself. "I would not risk your lives further for this."

His look of consideration was clearly visible to his friends in the heat haze from the still-glowing stones. "I should be able to mask my essence from the eyes of even a Dragon for a time, giving me the opportunity to approach undetected, distract his attention should he attack, and approach with steps lighter than snow falling on the limbs of firs. I will send for you when it is safe to come forward."

"Utter foolishness! We can think of an alternative to get us all going in at once!" said Wrindanneth. "We have time before we move forward."

"Wrin, I can think of several options to help get us all in, but they involve risks that surprise and opportunity can avoid."

"Why not offer palaver?"

"Slate, I fear the time to talk is done though it may arise once more."

"Trust us ta help! We didn't come this far on yer fool quest just ta sit back and watch!" Slate stroked his axe, comforted in its shine now that his beard no longer offered any solace. "My axe is ready ta make a new acquaintance!"

"We can come in behind you once you have it distracted, Yip. Even though it knows we're here, we can be ready to keep it off balance in that regard." Acquiescing, changing tack, Wrindanneth's argument was as reasonable as it was sincere.

"You will have plenty of opportunity to help, friends. I am honored by your concern and will always look for your aid. With our surprise gone, I do respect your counsel. Give me the chance to move onward and engage the Dragon. If you hear sounds of a struggle, you can rush in and hopefully gain some element of surprise. With any luck, that will not be necessary and you can await my signal to join us."

"Aroganji, if you can mask my body's heat signatures, I would appreciate the added protection from Dragon sight."

Breaking off further discussion, understanding Yip's resolve, Aroganji said, "I am able and will," adding, "Good luck, Yip," in acceptance, wishing that his friend did not have to take this risk in the first place.

"Aye," Slate's sure pat directed toward his back gave Yip as much reassurance as any words. Before contact, however, Yip stepped lightly forward lest Slate's kindness invoke the power of Menarfus's Inverted Aura.

Smiling with delayed understanding, to Slate's heat sensitive eyes, Yip stood out clearly before him in the gloomy passageway as the rocks slowly cooled and dimmed while the Dragon's heat faded. With the completion of Aroganji's incantation, even these thermal cues disappeared.

To Aroganji and Wrindanneth, each using the magical sight granted by their spells, viewing the energies shining in the passageway, the bright filigrees from the Dragon's fire etched the air and stone and merged with the intense aura around their companion as his energies blended and mixed with the other ambient energies in the heat haze. As they watched, one moment Yip appeared clear and distinct standing with them, the next, his energy signatures were gone as quickly as the dust blown ahead of the Dragon's fire.

Yip quickly centered himself, gathered his intent, and then spread his essence as thinly as the soot lining the walls of the cave, blending his distinctive elements with the surrounding energies of the passage. Although still visible to the naked eye in normal light, the gloom helped mask his presence from the eyes of his friends, and, coupled with Aroganji's spell, would help hide him from the eyes of a Dragon capable of seeing the heat of his body and the magic in his aura in the absence of full light.

Set in motion, he sped down the tunnel on feet as light as the dust that was gradually resettling after the turbulence on the floor of the cavern. To his friends, he was there one second and gone the next. Slate, unable to hear him leave, watched for his friend's infrared heat signature gliding down the passage, though such traces were lost even to his eyes.

Although not yet able to move with the speed and lightness of his teachers, Yip's feet barely touched the tunnel's floor as he burst from the passageway into a great open cavern lit entirely to his eyes by the great presence within.

Laying in guarded repose at the far end of the cave, its scales gleaming a rich burnished golden red reflecting the iridescent flames burning in the depths of its nostrils, its great head resting calmly on clawed feet the size of horses, its eyes fixed intently on the entrance to its lair, the menace of the Dragon was palpable in the air even before he reached the sulfurous air of its den. To the naked eye, the wyrm filled the cavern, its great bulk heaving with each fiery breath, smoke burning the air with each exhalation.

To Yip's eyes, the story was entirely different.

Momentarily bemused and thrown off-balance as he raced into the opening, Yip stopped abruptly in confusion as he made sense of the vision that lay before him. Quickly recovering himself lest he lose his advantage, he quietly ran to the side of the cave away from the surety and safety of the exit to the passageway leading to his friends.

Lying sprawled before him on the far side of the cavern was in fact a Dragon, but what he saw was not at all what he expected. To his inner vision, shimmering about the Dragon was an intense haze of magical energies mimicking the shape and form of an ancient wyrm. Inside this illusionary haze was a much younger Dragon hiding behind the image of an older, more powerful creature. For those who believed in the magic of the illusion and accepted its reality, there was in fact an ancient, massive Dragon lying in wait ready to strike in the heart of the cave. For those who disbelieved the illusion and saw the reality, there was a young Dragon relying on the fear and reputation of an ancient wyrm to keep it safe and out of harm's way.

Perhaps only fifteen to twenty paces in length, its body no thicker than the height of a man at its widest, even a young Dragon represented a being of enormous power worthy of much caution and respect. Power radiated from its form in waves as the Dragon drew in magic from the mountain to sustain its growing body—a luminous being from the heavens alight on Ea'ae.

Being able to see through this disguise and disbelieve the reality of the illusion would be a significant advantage when the Dragon did not know its ruse had been fully penetrated.

Its great nostrils sniffing in the gloom, an imposing voice boomed out before Yip could decide on how best to proceed. "Who dares intrude upon the lair of Lord Sarugauth the Red, ruler of the Drake Spires, sovereign of the roof of the world?"

"I am Yip Chi Chuan of the K'un Lun." Yip's voice was small and insignificant in the open air of the expansive grotto as he moved cautiously about in comparison to the vast sound of the Dragon's bellowing.

"You show great hubris intruding upon my lair, manling!" The Dragon's great flashing eyes burned like torches in the gloom searching him out.

If the Dragon could see his body's heat signatures or magical aura, there was no sign.

"I come in open-handed, true to myself and you before me," said Yip, suddenly appearing before the beast on the opposite side of the cavern, hands open and extended, palms toward the Dragon, his demeanor a model of peace and serenity.

"And you will die for your pride mortal!" With a great heave of its chest, flames exploded out of its vast maw, melting the very rock upon which Yip stood.

His motions quicker than the eyes of the Dragon, Yip was away and out of harm's way before the hellfire had ever left the Dragon's gullet. "I am not the one who shows pride and lives in falsehood, Dragon! You deceive yourself and those who would help you. Saru-gauth is gone and you will follow in his stead if you do not change your ways!"

"Begone, miscreant, before I blast you to nothingness!" The great eyes on the illusionary Dragon swiveled to and fro, following Yip as he paced back and forth on the far side of the cave.

"Your illusion does not fool me, Dragon. I come in peace, unarmed, seeking your aid, nothing more. I come to learn of Sarugauth's passing and the Cabal with whom he held allegiance."

A change came over the Dragon, he read the transition in its essence beneath the illusion it presented to his normal eyes. "Do I have your word that you sue for peace?" asked the Dragon.

"You have my word and my name freely given. I also speak for my friends. I will call to them if you wish."

"Tell them to come with open arms and to remain clearly visible at the passage mouth." The Dragon's eyes gazed intently at Yip, unable to scry anything from his posture or his newly revealed magical aura, unlike most humans he had met who were easily read.

"Aroganji, Wrin, Slate, it is safe! Come to the cave with arms open and unarmed," his yell echoed along the passageway.

"How do you think I can help you?" The intensity of the Dragon's stare through its great illusionary eyes was mirrored in the aura around the much smaller form hidden beneath its magical deception.

"You may know something of Sarugauth that could be of use to us, of the Cabal, his allies, in particular. We know very little of their dealings on this plane." Yip offered honesty in the face of its deception.

"And what do you have to offer me in exchange for my aid, should I choose to give it?" asked the Dragon, its concern and self-serving motives now readily apparent in word as well as deed.

"I may be able to offer you some measure of safety," said Yip watching the Dragon's reactions keenly.

A great laugh resounded through the cavern. "And why do you think a Dragon such as I would need protection?"

"You have answered your own question. You already hide behind another's image and reputation."

"It is only a matter of time before some adventurers seeking fame, fortune, or glory, in pursuit of some misguided ideals or seeking to right imagined wrongs seeks you out while you pose as Sarugauth."

"Perhaps this will not happen. Perhaps the Cabal will discover that one is using their name and notoriety for its benefit and will retaliate. I know from my own experience that those who get in the Cabal's way are destroyed relentlessly and without remorse. There are other eventualities than these that I am sure you have imagined."

The Dragon paused, the warm radiance of its exhalations stopped, the stove fires in its breast temporarily banked. "How are you able to aid one such as I?"

"I cannot," said Yip, again offering his honesty. "But I know those who can, and the fit would be to both your likings and benefit, I would imagine."

"You see, before Sarugauth claimed this valley as his own, it belonged to the Yerens, masters of song and shapers of stories made real. I am certain they would welcome your aid in protecting the valley, should you drop your pretense. Those who would seek out a Dragon for personal gain would be ill-advised to confront the Singers. Together, you would also present quite an intimidating face to the Cabal should they choose to seek either of you out. I am also certain you could learn much in the ways of magic from them as well, but of that I cannot say nor is such knowledge mine to give."

Before it could further consider or respond to his proposition, there was a commotion at the entrance to the cave as Yip's friends arrived in all their sooty, bedraggled glory.

"Brendle's bane! Look at that!" said Slate. Apparently seeing the illusionary form before him as opposed to the true form underneath, Slate was lost in awe at the Dragon's presence filling the cavern engaged as it was with his friend Yip.

"Look closely, friends. What you see before you does not represent the reality beneath the illusion. See the Dragon for what it is."

Wrindanneth's laugh pierced the pregnant calm. "A Dragon in drag! Never have I heard of such a thing."

Once they all saw through the falsity of the illusion and disbelieved its ruse, the great Dragon shimmered before them and the much smaller version resolved itself.

Before anyone could interfere, Slate burst out as he marched forward, reassured now that the Dragon had reached a much more manageable, if still imposing, scale, "Ya took my beard, ya great scaly lizard! I'll have yer hide fer this!"

The Dragon laughed then, finally at ease in Yip's eyes. "And what do you intend to do about this travesty, Dwarf? My belly could use a good scratching, if you're proposing to use your axe."

Slate huffed, "That does it! Ya've taken my pride, fool, and I will have it back!"

Before Slate took even the slightest step, the Dragon's voice boomed out, "Know this, Dwarf!" its voice filled the cavern even now that its illusion had dropped. "What you do to me will be known to any Dragons that would choose to listen. Your life will be plagued not just by your attempt on my life, but by the anger of all my kind. Your life will be as unpleasant as it will be short should you somehow overcome me."

Slate paused, his determination wavering. "How's that? Speak truly or I'll have yer great forked tongue!"

Again the Dragon laughed, his sides shaking, flames shooting from his nostrils as it spoke. "You are quite a character, Dwarf. Yip, you I cannot read, but your friend's intentions are as translucent as yours are opaque. In him I can see one whom I can trust, even if he is as stubborn as the stone on which he stands!"

The Dragon turned back to Slate, its good heart and humor now readily apparent to those who could not read its aura. "We Dragons are of one mind, Dwarf. Our thoughts are seldom our own until we mature and learn to close the others of our kind out and not to listen to their words, ruses, and deception. Although we may not agree with one another, if we so choose, we can share our counsel with any of our kind who would listen."

"Then yer kind'll know tha wrath o' a Dwarf!" Slate still refused to back down and drop his bluster now that the Dragon had abandoned its deception.

"Hold, Slate!" said Yip, his voice steeped in command. "End this foolish banter! We are here to discuss matters of more importance than your pride, friend."

Slate huffed back to his companions by the cavern's exit, his anger melting in the heat of the cave and his friend's intensity.

Yip was quite intrigued by the Dragon's revelation. Though inexperienced, he had never imagined Dragons had this capability. Being able to share knowledge directly explained much of the Dragons' abilities and magical development through time. As a race, this aptitude would afford much advantage. In fact, if it weren't for their legendary greed and selfishness, he was certain they hoarded knowledge as much as they hoarded gold, the world could easily be entirely under their dominion.

Turning back to the Dragon, he asked, "So you may be able to tell us something of Sarugauth, his dealings with the Cabal, and his purpose here."

The Dragon shook its great head, still quite capable of swallowing one of them whole should it choose. "Sarugauth is no more. He has left this plane behind in his ascension. I came here in the past year and found this cave empty and abandoned, shrouded in dust as much as by Sarugauth's legacy, but knowing as I did that word of his passing had not reached the ears of any save we Dragons."

Slowly surveying the companions, it continued, "Do you think a youngling such as I would dare pose as the preeminent Lord Sarugauth if he were still alive? Although this may be good news to you, his void has left much turmoil among my kind as many good and just Dragons vie once again with their brothers of darker heart to reestablish something of a balance of power. Given my stature, I have chosen to remain well out of the fray."

"Ascension?" asked Aroganji, unfamiliar with the lore of Dragons, since, as a race, they kept so much of themselves hidden. In fact, Aroganji thought that this youngling might have slipped in giving its revelation, for an older Dragon would not even reveal that much.

"When a Dragon dies, we ride the currents to Heaven, mortal. Your destiny is no different. For us, however, there is a choice. We can sometimes remain on this plane in a newer, more powerful guise given the proper preparations, whereas your human form is left to the dust."

"So an ancient Dragon like Sarugauth could remain alive in a certain sense here, should he so choose?" asked Wrindanneth for clarification.

"Aye. One of a dark heart like Sarugauth could don any number of guises, but his counsel would be well-hidden from someone as untried as I. Sarugauth was among the oldest of our kind and few could rival his power. Only Auros the Golden, Uzsanthal the Grim, and Glaudron the Many Hued could rival his strength of those who still dwell on this plane in their hatched form. Others may exist whose motives, actions, and histories are hidden from the ken of the hatchlings."

Yip looked meaningfully to Aroganji and Wrindanneth. He would not think that Sarugauth would pass willingly from this plane given his dealings with the Cabal and their motivations for ever greater power on this world and others.

The Dragon then turned back to Yip as Slate was still digesting more information than he had wanted to hear. "What is your proposition then, and how do I know you can truly impart what you proffer?"

Yip walked slowly forward. "Look to my chest. This talisman I bear is the Heart of Yere."

He held out the stone for the Dragon's magic sensitive eyes to read and understand. "For reasons beyond my understanding, the Yerens have given me their trust. I am sure they would listen to our proposition to return home and rejoice in Sarugauth's demise while cultivating a guardian and friend such as yourself."

"Together you could form quite a mutually beneficial alliance."

Walking toward the Dragon, he felt a sudden surge in magic as a quick image flashed inside the Dragon, then it abruptly changed form. Where first there had been an image of an immense golden-bronze and scarlet wyrm, imposing and vast, then a much smaller shiny Gold Dragon underneath, growing into the fullness of its power, now stood a young boy just out of his teens, a Dragon in a much less intimidating form.

Gently taking the stone in his small, now human hands, the Dragon in a boy's guise carefully examined the burning red stone dangling from Yip's neck.

Standing directly in front of Yip, the boy's eyes still gleaming with the internal fires of a Dragon's flame, he said, "You appear as good as your word, Master Chuan. Candor is a quality much admired, if often neglected, by Dragons. I do have one request before I accept the sincerity of your agreement."

He sensed his friends listening intently behind him, waiting for the catch.

"What is your concern?" To Yip, the Dragon's aura was so complex that it was very difficult to grasp in totality, much less read and accurately interpret, when its primary emotions were not readily apparent or understood.

"I know that you can read my emanations. That much I can see in you, but you are as hidden from me as I am open to you. I would have you open yourself to me to read. I would glean something of your character as you have done with mine."

Yip nodded, his interior as tranquil as his friends' were turbulent, concerned as they were that this was some kind of trick on the part of the Dragon, a race known for their guile and craftiness.

Limpid, pellucid, his calm as deep and clear as one of the nearby glacial lakes fed entirely by pure snowmelt, he removed the mask covering his essence, bringing his energies back into his body, forces that had been left to blend and merge with the radiance surrounding them in the cavern.

A growl too loud and deep to come from such a small boyish figure issued in apparent surprise from the Dragon, for to his eyes a figure of great lustrous white stood shimmering before him.

Unaccustomed to the subtle nuances associated with a human face, the party waited with bated breath as a series of unreadable expressions crossed the Dragon's young visage. Finally, his face finally relaxed and assumed a semblance of a smile. "I can see that you are a being worthy of my trust and respect, Yip, if I may call you by your familiar name. I am honored to have met you and that you have been so patient with an impetuous youth."

A bit taken aback, unused as he was to open praise, Yip was too humbled at first to respond. "You give me too much credit."

He smiled, adding, "I only hope that you and the Yerens can prosper together, for you have both shown great faith and sincerity in one as untried as I."

From the far side of the cavern, Slate cleared his throat to draw attention before speaking up again. "What shall we call ya Dragon?"

The Dragon turned his attention toward the Dwarf. "I am glad to hear that Dwarves know something of good manners, Slate. I do apologize for any harm I have caused you, but you can understand how you and your kind would respond similarly if someone entered your kingdom, ignoring your attempts to parlay, and rushed brazenly into your home threateningly."

The Dragon in a boy's body paused as if considering before continuing, "Do not fear, Slate, if Yip's proposition does yield fruit, I will recompense you for the loss of your beard."

A bit mollified, wondering how a Dragon could ever possibly repay a Dwarf for the loss of his beard, Slate answered, "Aye, perhaps tha hearts o' Dragons and Dwarves are not unalike, fer we both relish tha heat o' tha forge."

Again the Dragon's great laughter filled the cavern, even though it now incongruously issued from the small, boyish figure in front of them. "Aye, Slate, although I know more about the heat of a forge than its use. I am known among my kind as Azaelle the Golden, for those of my line are as good as gold, pure and valuable to our kind—traits not often associated by outsiders with my race. Although you may not believe it after my earlier deception, I am as true to my word as you are." Strange as it was to the companions, small flames licked the Dragon's lips as it talked in its human guise, still needing some practice to master its ability to change forms and manipulate its expressions.

Slate turned to his friends. "Yip ya've met properly. The red-haired goon from tha Northlands is Wrindanneth." Wrin's sniff cut any further descriptions short, but his primary focus was on the Dragon now carefully inspecting him, not Slate's banter.

"Aroganji hails from lands not too far from Yip's, so they share several odd habits." Aroganji did not deign to respond as he was used to Slate's frivolity.

"Ah…your friends must hold you in high esteem for such warm sentiments, Slate." Azaelle's sarcasm was a bridge easily crossed, one Slate understood all too well.

"Indeed they do," answered Slate with a half-smile.

Before Slate could share any more good cheer, Yip spoke again. "I will send to the Yerens tonight and will give you their word in the morning." Sharing a bit of his counsel, perhaps to repay the Dragon after his openness, Yip continued, "I sincerely hope that the Yerens will consider my offer and you both can thrive together."

"A gesture of good will for you, my friends, before you leave to allay your fears," with a short sweep of his small hand, Slate's beard was restored to fullness. "I will see you in the morn," uttered Azaelle with a slight bow, his voice still far too large for his body.

"Until then," said Yip with a bow.

With that farewell, the party turned and cautiously left the cave, heading out to the refreshing, open air and cool breezes of the valley beneath the crisp mid-day sun.

As they walked back up the tunnel, slowly leaving the cloying, sulfurous air of the Dragon's sanctum behind, Slate asked, "Can we trust a beard-burnin' creature with a crooked, two-forked tongue?" Apparently he still held reservations about the Dragon's trustworthiness, even after it had taken the effort to restore what it had destroyed.

Wrindanneth looked to his cantankerous friend. "I know as much as anyone how to look after myself, Slate. Just because a Dragon does the same by looking after its own interests, doesn't make it all bad. We're all motivated by our own concerns to some extent. Are you any different?"

Slate's harrumph was answer enough.

"We should find a relatively safe spot to camp, should the Dragon prove duplicitous," said Aroganji still concerned about their vulnerability.

"Agreed," said Yip. He added with surety, "The Dragon's heart is good, of that I am sure."

"But one can never be too cautious," finished Wrindanneth ever wary.

The party camped that evening on the ridgeline away from the Dragon's cave, in clear sight of the entrance should he choose to leave or try anything untoward.

While Aroganji, Wrindanneth, and Slate took turns taking watch, Yip slept.

He dove into sleep with a purpose, ready to restore a culture lost, to provide safety to a youngling seeking a start and to a society in need of opportunity, and hoping to foster a relationship that would see both to a prosperous future. Shedding his thoughts as he would cumbersome clothes, masking his presence from those who would look, he drifted through the ether as action shed of thought in search of a Song.

Floating in darkness, moving through a landscape with no landmarks or scenery, no color or sound, the dreamscape only varied from his mind cleared of thought and consideration in that he knew his consciousness was outside his body, somehow adrift in a mindscape created by the psyches of people the world over, a universe of those whose minds remained open. Mind without body, thought without form, he let his awareness find its way toward the Yerens and the dreamworld created by their collective unconscious.

After time uncounted, his focus found its reward on the far side of the mountains as his soul echoed with the first tones of a people whose dreams were lifted in song.

Meeting the Yerens the first time had been an experience as wondrous as it was confusing. Finding a people of such majesty hidden in caves of ice, capable of expressing the language of the world through song, was a joy that he was as incapable of expressing as the Yerens were apt. Although his conscious mind could not fully comprehend the story of which they sang, his essence resonated with the truth and vibrancy of their efforts.

Adrift, heart lifted, mind soaring, he once again felt the familiar vibrancy of the Yerens' Song, the undercurrents of the heavens given voice through the notes of a people whose purpose seemed to be that very expression.

Rich, fluid, and vital, his universe hummed as he moved through a world dictated not by what he saw or imagined, but what he felt resounding through his heart. All around, individual songs and notes, hymns and choruses, merged into a great symphony of expression as foreign and beautiful to him as the sky was familiar. So complex and integrated were the chords and notes, lyrics and fugues, that he could not separate one sound from the next, one group from one another, one Yeren from the next.

In a world filled with danger and dissonance, his heart knew solace appreciating that those like the Yerens were able to survive and thrive despite all the risks inherent in their way of life while sharing their Light amidst the often deadly tumult.

Lost in a world of song, he did not know how to proceed, whom to address or how. Immersed in a kaleidoscope of sound, his awareness filled with music, he waited.

Time passed unmarked, patiently drifting, engrossed in harmonies. Nothing happened. No recognition, no insight, no response. For a moment he felt as though he was swimming with a pod of whales, deep in an ocean of sound, small and insignificant, surrounded by alien music, part of a conversation he was not meant to hear, one that he could not hope to comprehend.

Then he began to sing.

His small tune transported only by his mind and intent, his lungs and voice left far behind in the high peaks, he began his tale, interweaving the account of his journey with the threads of sound about him, doing his best to blend and build upon the music that passed through and around him.

He sang of his trip from the mountains to find his new friends and of his return. He sang of his teacher and his hopes. He sang of his search and of their rediscovered homeland. He sang of lessons learned and prospects unfolding. He sang of the Dragon gone and opportunity to come. He sang of trust and faith repaid. He sang of restoration and the future.

He sang not with his voice and tongue, but with his mind and heart, transporting thought and intention as best he could, limited as he was by the unfamiliar milieu with which he worked.

As he finished his song, its echoes and choruses losing cohesion in the distance, so caught up was he in his music that he did not notice his voice settled into complete calm. Quietude extended around him as deep and vast as the space between the stars. The silence following his song echoed in the ears that had given him his audience, that had listened to his proposal, and had given him their full attention.

Ever so slowly, the dreamspace around him began to fill with sound. He listened in wonder as the notes around him began to rebuild and regain cohesion, surging and adding intricacy, much like birds greeting and calling to a new day in ever greater numbers, building in volume and complexity. Great swells of song engulfed him then as the entire population of the Yerens lifted their hearts in joy at his news.

Fading into the background, calmly drifting back to sleep, a fugue whose time had passed, he left the Yerens to their celebration and dreams, happy to have helped those who had supported him so much in his journey.

Far away, his body returning to normal rest and ease, he smiled.

The Yerens would come.

What had been unmade would be restored.

THE DRAGON'S GATE

Crouched beneath a pine,
I watch the full moon, pondering
the shadow beneath my feet.

Murmurs of excitement woke him from sleep. His friends were relaxed and energized in the chill morning air, gathered around a small fire simmering a breakfast of dried meats and bread.

After a successful confrontation and negotiation with a Dragon, they are entitled to feeling a mixture of relief and elation, thought Yip. Inside, his heart shared their lightness.

His happiness reflected his aspirations for his order. Although not yet realized, the Yerens would soon have back their home and a much more secure future for themselves and their children now that Sarugauth was truly gone. With Azaelle's help, their prosperity would be assured as the Dragon came into the fullness of his power and as their prominence was restored. He could only hope for the same opportunity for his order, should they manage to overcome the Cabal.

"Good morning, my friends. I trust sleep left you well and replenished?"

"Aye. Orcs fell like rain last night," said Slate whose dreams obviously differed significantly from those of a priest.

"Any luck, Yip?" asked Aroganji as he finished putting away the cook pots.

"The Yerens will come and the valley will be restored." A slight smile cracked Yip's face, his emotions and expressions understated as usual.

"If Azaelle continues his cooperation," muttered Slate still smarting over the treatment of his beard, forgetting the fact that they had ignored the Dragon's initial, if deceptive, attempt to parlay and the fact that Azaelle had made it right in the end, perhaps understanding the significance of a Dwarf's beard.

Prior to breakfast, Slate had spent the better part of the morning first braiding and then restoring his Kazzak to their rightful places in his beard. At least none of them had been lost or damaged beyond recognition in the Dragon's hellfire.

"Excellent news!" said Wrindanneth as he finished repacking his bedroll. "I'm ready to return to Tellanon once this is done and find out what adventures await us there."

"Aye, too much talk and not enough action, I say. I've spent more time sharpenin' my axe than usin' it. Where's tha fun in that?"

Yip sniffed. "One should not joke about such things, Slate. All life is precious and of value, even if we do not see it."

"Aye, especially mine!" answered Slate, his clean, shiny beard so out of place against his sooty face, the grime serving as a reminder of his fragility.

"Shall we port down to the valley?" asked Wrindanneth, the rocks crunching beneath his feet as he stood to look over the precipitous cliffs and down to the boulder strewn valley below.

Aroganji nodded in readiness.

A terse, powerful incantation followed by a point of Wrindanneth's hand brought the party safely to the bottom of the valley.

For the second time, the party climbed over the partially melted rockfall next to the cave entrance. This time as they entered the empty darkness, the roof of the cave high above their heads, bright explosions of light greeted their first footsteps into the cave proper.

"Brendle's bane! What foolishness is this?" yelled Slate as he bound unexpectedly backward as the multicolored lights continued to flash overhead.

Wrindanneth turned uncharacteristically in wonder, his arms held wide as if to catch a welcome breeze, watching the pyrotechnics dance and shimmer above following their passage down the great hallway, a smile on his face. "Reminds me of the festivals we had celebrating the catch in the summer. My master and I put on shows for the village to express our appreciation for their support and to bring a bit of cheer to their arduous lives plying the waters with only the most rudimentary use of magic and spells, although my teacher and I helped bolster their equipment when we could."

Wrindanneth's eyes were lost in remembrance. He sighed. "One of the few fond memories from my childhood." Then he paused, adding, "This is quite a show."

A vast voice boomed out, "Would you expect anything less?"

It was Aroganji who answered, "I would expect nothing less from a Dragon who by his heritage is a master of Light and sound."

Azaelle laughed, his levity evident in his tone, even though a Dragon's laughter was still a bit disquieting to those unused to its force and depth. The Dragon's true form of burnished gold appeared above them frolicking amidst the bursting lights. "I trust you come with good tidings?"

"You truly are blessed, my friend," said Yip. "The Yerens will come if you are still willing."

"Excellent!" The cavern walls shook with his voice. "I will make ready for them!"

Yip went on as his eyes followed Azaelle's image frolicking overhead. "You will make an unusual pair, Azaelle. Your differences will become a great strength. You will have much to learn and to teach each other."

"Aye," broke in Slate. "Ya may know how ta put on a show o' lights, but next time I'm here I want ta hear a grand sonata with all tha vocal skills ya've learned from tha Singers!"

Turning to his friends, slapping both palms on his stomach to hold in laughter, he added, "Now that's a tale that would even impress tha Thane—Dragon song!"

"We wish you all the best together, free of any more incursions from the Cabal, and a bright destiny of untold potential," said Yip bowing before the Dragon's illusion overhead with both hands placed palms together before him.

A slight tone of confusion passed through Azaelle's voice. "You're not leaving so soon are you? We must celebrate our success together! I would show my appreciation for my newfound allies! Thanks to your thoughtfulness, I may actually have a future."

Azaelle sighed, his voice not localized to the illusion above. "Most Dragons do not live past adolescence. Such an unfortunate fact—those that do are often consumed with rage for those that persecute them."

Aroganji looked to Yip as if unsure how to proceed.

Azaelle went on, "Besides, I have to keep my side of the bargain. I may not know much of the Cabal and their dealings or the destiny of Sarugauth after his passing, but I do have some tokens to show my appreciation."

Slate washed his hands, the thought of treasure piquing his interest. "Now that's about tha first good suggestion I've heard all day, Dragon!"

Yip nodded and continued down the passage. "We will accept your hospitality and thanks, Azaelle."

"Follow tha dancin' Dragon!" said Slate as he watched Azaelle's illusion cavort amidst the lights above, a veritable rainbow shimmering on his burnished scales.

Wrindanneth turned to Slate. "Surely you cannot hope to make friends acting like that, Slate. Is your charm limited to sarcasm and contrarianism?"

"Funny, I do not see you acting very differently," said the Dwarf, fire gleaming in his eye.

"The difference is that I know when and where humor and sarcasm have their place, and this is not it, Slate."

Before Slate could respond, Yip put his finger to his lips. "Compose yourselves, gentlemen." As the pyrotechnics continued to explode overhead and light their passage to Azaelle's lair, he whispered, "Have some consideration for who may hear our words and how they reflect upon us."

After his words sank in, Yip continued just as quietly, "Our future is not secure yet as our negotiations may not be done."

A few minute's passage brought them from the smooth, fused stone walls of the large passage to the smoldering Dragon's den. Reclined on the far side of the large, ruddily lit cavern, Azaelle smoldered as much as the dim fires interspersed throughout the cave. As the party entered the cave, Yip's concerns were allayed as he sensed the Dragon's positive presence radiating through the cave.

"Greetings, friends!" Azaelle's great horned head rose toward the cave's roof as he stirred and stood on his massive hind legs to greet them. "You have helped assure my destiny and I would help guarantee yours." His pride left behind after their first meeting, Azaelle tilted his head in sincere respect and gratitude.

Yip was the first to respond to his greeting. "In the course of events, one must be guided by what is right and true, friend. We are glad that you have benefited from our small kindness."

"You are far too gracious, Yip! Without your aid, who knows how long I would have lasted impersonating Sarugauth? Chances are, within a few seasons, if my ruse had held, I would have met an untimely end. For that I owe you my life debt, and such a gift cannot be repaid. You have also given me not just my life but a bright future, one unique among all Dragons! For that you have my unending gratitude. You will be welcome to seek me out at any time or to send for my aid. If I cannot give you my assistance directly, you will always be welcome to my counsel."

"We do what we must, Azaelle, as do you," responded Wrindanneth. "We may look to you for support in times to come as we close upon the Cabal, if you are able to give it."

"With the Yerens' help, I may be in a much better position to offer assistance," Azaelle chuckled, flames licking upon his scaly lips. "Perhaps I will come to be known as something of a minstrel among my kind—Azaelle Wyrmtongue, Invoker of the Flamesong!"

Wrindanneth laughed with him. "Now that is an image! A skald among the Dragons!"

Yip laughed as well. "The Yerens have much to teach about the nature of our world and magic. The medium they use is song, but you should use whatever method is natural to you to internalize and express that knowledge."

"I would also show my appreciation for your efforts through a few trifles that you may find of value." Azaelle turned and reached behind where his tail lay against the wall of the cavern covering a small hidden nook.

"First and foremost, for Slate the Grim, I have a token worthy of a Dwarven hero. Come forward, Slate." As Slate walked somewhat dazedly forward, a bit unsure of what to expect, Azaelle produced a finely wrought, rune-etched axe held in a sturdy leather shoulder harness. In the dim light of the cave, the axe glowed with a soft blue radiance.

"Slate, I give to you Adrael's Curse, called Duraeleon, the axe wielded by Ithilieon in long ages past before Elves gave up their axes for swords. This blade smote the black wyrm Adrael deep in the heart of his lair. This piece was one of the chief endowments in my inheritance, but such treasures are of little use to me. If you ever encounter Auros and he sees this in your possession, tell him it was a gift freely given. He will know the truth in your words."

Watching the gleaming axe held in the Dragon's great paw, Slate could see why this weapon would be of little use to Azaelle unless he was changed into human guise. Even though he had not yet reached the fullness of his adult girth, the axe appeared as no more than a toothpick, perhaps useful to cut his great claws if nothing else. As he took the proffered axe, Slate bowed in heartfelt gratitude for, although finely forged, his own axe was not a weapon of Power.

With a blade like Ithilieon's he would be able to engage supernatural foes on even footing. This gift was a sign of deep trust. He was now honor-bound to Azaelle for letting pass a weapon of known power that had been used against Dragons in the past. As much as anything else, this cemented the reality of Azaelle's trustworthiness in his eyes.

"Through time and practice, you will be able to unlock more of the blade's power." Azaelle looked at Slate keenly then, his great head within arm's reach of Slate's shiny ruddy cheeks. "Be forewarned, Slate. With a blade like Ithilieon's, your tongue will be kept busy for tales of bravery are not all that follow in its wake."

As he bowed his head, Slate said, "Know that ya have a friend in tha Dwarves should tha need ever come, Azaelle." With a glint in his eye, Slate continued, "I fer one will sing yer praises once ya teach me how!"

"Begone, Dwarf!" Fire flashed quickly in Azaelle's eyes, but Slate knew that all was well.

Azaelle then turned to Aroganji and Wrindanneth. "Come forward Aroganji and Wrindanneth."

As they walked cautiously forward, Slate hurried back toward the cave's entrance already lost in his efforts trying to decipher the eldritch runes on the axe's surface. "For my seekers of knowledge, I have a gift worthy of your continued practice and developing lore. The archmage Ydrael Faer'Leirn met his end at the hands of my sire Auros as he tried to wrest an object of Power from beneath my sire's slumbering form. My sire was none too happy to be awoken by a pilfering thief. Unfortunately, the only thing that survived his fire was this book of spells and incantations the wizard had collected. I hope they are of some use to you in your journeys."

From across the cavern Yip saw Azaelle pass Wrindanneth a small, slightly travel-worn tome. This grimoire glowed with the traceries of arcane forces.

Wrindanneth tilted his head in thanks while Aroganji bowed in appreciation.

"I will put this to good use, Maeth willing," said Wrindanneth. "The time has come to learn a few new tricks. Your gift will do much to help our efforts."

The note of sarcasm in his tone with his thanks went unremarked by his friends. While his companions slept this night, he would pour over the tome granted by Azaelle, surveying the lost knowledge of Ydrael, seeking after secrets that may be hidden from or as yet unknown by his master. Although unlikely to hold mysteries concealed from his master, Maeth's insatiable thirst for knowledge spurned his followers to seek ever after lost and newly discovered lore, all in the attempt to further his own divine might.

As begrudging as his servitude was, at least he received the benefit of such understanding in turn for, unlike Maeth, much of the contents of Ydrael's tome was likely to be new to him.

Willingly or not, if he did not share in the lore as prescribed, his powers may be stripped.

Maeth would see all in his dreams.

As he finished his bow, unaware of Wrindanneth's train of thought, Aroganji also offered his thanks. "My fellow Fang Shih will be proud to know that I continue my studies under the tutelage of great teachers and friends."

As Wrindanneth and Aroganji walked away, Azaelle's eyes rested at last on Yip, still threadbare after his earlier encounter with the Dragon's fire.

"Unfortunately, Yip, I am out of trinkets that could be of use to you, though if I learn more of the Cabal, I will send for you."

"While you were gone, I sent to Auros to see if he could help answer your concerns about Sarugauth or the Cabal and their activities on this plane. His reach and experience are vast, Yip, and I trust his counsel above all others. Although he was quite glad to hear of the opportunity you have granted me, he warned me above all else to steer clear of any dealings with the Cabal. Although their base is not on this world, their presence here is growing as is their ability to gather information and resources. If you let it be known that you are looking for them or publicly show an interest in them, they will find you."

"My advice to you would be not to do so until you are absolutely ready. You can continue to hunt them down and be hunted in turn, or you can prepare and let what you would know and do come to you through the fullness of time."

Azaelle gestured to Yip to come closer and take a spot by his side near where Slate had stood directly in front of him. "The lore of the Dragons is as wide as the skies and just as deep. This is not pride for my kind and our lore, for such heights often lead to even greater falls, but knowledge at times does have its advantages. After describing you and your abilities, at least those that I could decipher to Auros, he told me something of your nature and history, priest."

"You and your kind may not know it as you have long been lost to the outside world, but there are those among the Dragons who hold the Order of the K'un Lun in high regard. We still remember the times in ages past when deeds worthy of legend were done together as allies. Auros for one recalls those days for he was alive to see them and take a hand in their shaping. Those times of alliance may come again now that you are back on this world even as you seek to rebuild."

"Know that your deeds have not been forgotten among the Dragons."

Much of this was news to Yip as he was as new to the order as it was old, and although he appreciated Azaelle's offer, he was too humble and in no position to take advantage of it. "I will do my best to keep your trust, Azaelle."

As Yip bowed, fist cupped in open hand to show his offer of peace, Azaelle continued, "You already have it, Yip, for you have given me a future as much as we Dragons would help restore yours should the time come. Auros also told me something of your kind's abilities with intrinsic energies, so, although I may not have a gift for you to hold, I may have something from which you can learn."

His long neck curling through the air, partially encircling Yip's vulnerable form as he watched, Azaelle said, "Watch. Look inward."

Turning his eyes from the Dragon's massive spiked and horny crown to his shimmering trunk, his great scaly sides moving slowly in and out with each breath as if working the bellows feeding a great internal furnace, Yip watched as Azaelle filled the cavern with light and Dragon's fire. Eyes on his stomach, Azaelle's sides within arm's reach or a short step, he observed with his inner vision as a star was born inside the Dragon's gullet, as energy was created, pulled in and concentrated, from the void, and then ignited by the magical energies ambient to the place that Azaelle had stored deep in the pit of his stomach.

Matter and anti-matter collided unleashing untold energies, a great wash of heat and light surged upward from Azaelle's gullet and atomized the very air through which it passed as hellfire surged through the room—a star born grounded, unable to reach the heavens.

"You offer too much my friend," said Yip, for he was overwhelmed by the opportunity and trust this Dragon had given him along with the many others who continued to place their faith and goodwill in his hands throughout his journey.

From Azaelle, he learned the secret of the Dragon's Gate, the way of energy concentration, creation, and direction.

Yip's head swirled with possibilities and applications, opportunities and abilities, as he considered the magnitude of Azaelle's gift. Azaelle had shown him the secret of a Dragon's power. Concentrating ambient energies while generating power from nowhere, from the seamless void of potential, then manipulating and modifying the form and function of those energies, sparking the fires of life itself with those of possibility, the ways of the Dragon magnified the potency of their nature beyond conception. Coupled with the teachings of his master and the Aeryn D'al, the array of skills he had to cultivate, practice, and ultimately master would daunt even the staunchest heart. Given the limitations of time and the urgency of his predicament, the pressure to learn was even greater.

Before he could consider the potentialities and ramifications of this newly revealed treasure any further, the time for leave-takings had come.

He bowed to Azaelle once more. "The Yerens will come from the far side of the mountains and other isolated places through the Drake Spires. I cannot say how soon they will come, if they will all come at once, gradually, gather and come en masse, or send a delegation."

"I will be honored to help restore their home, our home, to its former glory," said Azaelle, his eyes traveling slowly from one party member to the next, the great orbs simmering in apparent happiness as each appreciated his gifts.

"Until we meet again, Azaelle," Yip bowed humbly a final time. "May the light of a new dawn guide your steps."

"And may your shadow dance with each tread, for you and your kind deserve joy and peace as much as mine."

Excited and ready to move on toward a brighter future, the party once again left the great Dragon Sarugauth's cave, no longer a haunt for his wretched memories now that the original residents would return to sing of its luster and grace while restoring the cavern and the valley that cradled it to their former vibrancy.

Lost in reverie after the wonderment Azaelle's gift, only when they were far down the passage out of the brightness of Azaelle's presence, did Yip realize they were not alone. A bit puzzled, he looked around the cavern instinctively searching for someone or something hiding in the shadows.

His conscious mind initially interfered with and confused the obvious information presented by his mind's eye. Attached on Slate's back, the richly ensorcelled blade hanging in its holster not only radiated its own light, but its own presence. Bemused once again, he had never before encountered such a marvel.

As an object of power, his pendant effused energy and force in the subtle dimensions, but the axe Duraeleon was a thing of another sort. Not only did it radiate power, it shone with sentience, a presence like a person, a being with a soul. To his eyes, as he gazed in curiosity at the blade held closely in the wrought leather holster, the axe glowed with a deep yellow green inside its outer magical radiance—the light of a mind lay cradled within.

"That is quite an axe you bear, Slate," Yip said as they slowly picked their way closer to sunlight through the sulphurous haze of the Dragon's smoke.

"Aye. When we get outside and I have a little room ta limber up, I'm goin' ta test its heft and feel. Never have I seen its match wrought by hand o' Dwarf or Elf, but, ta be sure, there're many treasures ta be had that I've neither seen nor touched."

"There must be more than power to such a blade, Slate. Perhaps we will learn more of its history on our travels." Yip did not want to ruin the surprise he felt must await for his friend.

As they blinked under the early afternoon sun, eyes as yet unaccustomed to the full brightness of the day after the smoky haze of the cave, Slate excitedly unsheathed his axe in a single fluid stroke ready to watch it glimmer and test its heft in the shimmering sunlight.

"Ah!!! Free at last!"

Shocked, his lips slack, his mouth hanging agape, Slate nearly dropped the axe in mid-motion as he unsheathed it, taken aback that his new beautiful prize had spoken. "'Bout time you let me outta' that straight jacket. Do you know how long I've been locked up and stifled in that holster?"

"Don't just stand there like you've just seen a basilisk you great bearded ninny! Time's awastin'! We've got lots of adventurin' to do before the sun sets."

"Ah, treasures to unearth, monsters to slay, rights to wrong, bandits to rob, err, bring to justice, myths to make, lies to debunk, and falsehoods to rectify. The sky's the limit if you stick with me!"

Then the axe started to hum, before briefly bursting into the refrain, "A huntin' we will go, a huntin' we will go, high ho' the merry o' a huntin' we will go..."

The axe stopped in mid-refrain as if surveying the party and their reactions, although it did not have any means of sight that any of them could see. "What're you lookin' at? Has that Dragon given me over to a band of addled mutes?"

"I've a mind to march right back in there and tell him a thing or two..."

"Oy, Dwarf! Can I get a hand here? I can't do everythin' on my own, you know. I'm gonna need your help! Come on!"

"We've got an upstart Dragon to deal with!"

It was Wrindanneth's snicker that snapped Slate out of his stupor and back to his current predicament.

"'A gift worthy of a Dwarf', he says," Slate muttered, grumbling. "I've a mind ta march back in there and give that Dragon a taste o' my fist!"

When he realized that was exactly what the axe had suggested, Slate reconsidered. "What kind o' gift are ya? More like a curse! If I wanted nonstop talkin' and lecturin', I'd go ask my Gram fer her opinion on tha wisdom o' puttin' up with a talkin' axe!"

The tenor and timbre of the axe changed as a strident voice boomed out, "Lowly Dwarf! Behold! You gaze upon the great Ithilieon's blade, Duraeleon, the Light Bringer, bane of Adrael the Black, born in ages when your kind had not yet crawled out from under the rocks to see the light of day! It is you who should question your worthiness to wield me!"

The axe seemed to pause a bit as if in introspection before rambling on again. "Of course, I couldn't talk back then and Ithilieon never really had much to say..."

"What in tha world are ya babblin' about?" Apparently Slate had had enough banter for the day. "I can't believe I have ta put up with a talkin' axe! As if this great red-headed scarecrow weren't enough!"

"I'll have you know..." Slate cut the axe off mid-sentence as he slammed it back into the finely wrought leather scabbard.

Wrindanneth chuckled. Interrupting, he snickered, "Looks like now I won't be the only one who sees the need to put you in your place a bit, Slate."

"At least you have a gift worthy of a Dwarf!" chortled Aroganji.

"Shall we continue toward Tellanon?" asked Yip, ready to be on his way and not wishing to bring further difficulty upon his crestfallen friend.

"Aye, hopefully tha trip'll be a little less excitin' than this," sulked Slate, still a bit disappointed that his treasure came with an unwelcome twist.

They could still hear the axe's muffled exhortations and exclamations as it tried to give Slate a piece of its mind throughout the rest of the day while they ported from mountain top to mountain top, moving westward toward Tellanon.

THE SHRIKE

Praying mantis sways,
perched atop a wooden post,
to the breeze's tune.

Retracing their passage far-traveling westward, the party once again took in the grandeur of the Drake Spires, their soaring peaks, their vast rocky escarpments and snow-capped summits, the wide-ranging vistas, the open air, and the sense of unmitigated freedom.

Yip, however, did not share his fellows' sense of elation or their feelings of accomplishment. True, they had helped the Yerens reclaim their home and gained a powerful ally in Azaelle, thereby undermining some of the destruction wrought by the Cabal. However, although he had not yet sensed their pursuit, the Cabal was out there somewhere plotting against his order, wreaking havoc on innocents while pursuing their nefarious purposes.

Though time was short and their next encounter with the Cabal was imminent, he had been given many gifts and advantages since he fled the monastery many nights ago. If he were to be successful in his efforts against the Cabal, then he must capitalize on these gifts and continue his practice and cultivation in preparation.

Jumping from mountaintop to mountaintop, he took the opportunity to mask their passage, trying to extend the limits of his abilities beyond just hiding his own presence to include the energetic signatures of his friends, expanding upon the energy harmonization techniques he had learned from the Aeryn D'al. Porting from one rock-filled pass to the next, there was no better time to cultivate this veiling than now because pursuit from his foes was highly unlikely as the process of teleportation and random movement would make direct tracking by the Cabal nearly impossible.

Concentrating on his task, he let the actions and comments of his friends fade into the background as the day passed before his focus. With each settling, as the reality of their presence snapped in from the void of teleportation, the energy of their existence and the magics they wrought reverberated through the air creating ripples and currents in the ether, as visible to his mind's eye as a cascading avalanche of great rocks crashing through the still mountain air.

Watching this explosive current with each port, he reached out as best he could and smoothed their transition, taking the forces of the transfer into himself as he would the air he breathed or the ambient *chi* around him, internalizing the energy and presence, circulating the signatures through his greater heavenly cycle as he had done with the Zhan Zhuang exercise with the Aeryn D'al. Then he gently released this power, letting the reality of their presence settle easily over the rocks as smoothly and naturally as the cool mountain air.

As the day passed into evening and the silhouette of the Drake Spires faded into the haze of distance and sunset, he knew that with time and practice, their passage would be as soft as a spring breeze, as light as the snow, and as undetectable as the space between seconds.

After a full day teleporting for distance to the northwest, the party had over a hundred leagues between themselves and the heart of the mountains, a distance that would have been much greater if the sight of the peaks themselves had not limited the extent of some of their ports.

Lost in concentration, the sound of snapping fingers brought his attention back to the group.

"Oy, Yip!" Slate's bearded face appeared close to his own, the look of concern in his eyes as obvious as his newly regrown hair. "Ya okay, lad?"

Slate glanced to his friends who were looking up from where they were unpacking beneath some trees nearby. Turning back to Yip, he said, "We're done fer tha day. Perhaps ya'd like a bit o' brew before headin' ta sleep?"

"I am sorry, Slate, I was just practicing a bit of *chi gung* to help facilitate our passage."

"I don't care about yer witchery. I'm askin' about food and a meal, surely ya must be ready ta eat? Tha day is fast approachin' night and Wrin and Aroganji are exhausted after spendin' themselves gettin' us here. They may even need ta take tomorrow off after goin' so far in one day."

He looked around in a daze beyond Slate. Where once solid rock and great craggy peaks had loomed, rolling green forested foothills undulated toward the horizon. To those who had not just left the precarious heights of the Drake's Spires, these, too, would be considered mountains.

"Some tea would be very much appreciated, Slate." He bowed at the courtesy his friend offered. "I, too, could use a rest."

"Rest? Ya've been starin' off inta space hypnotized all day!" Slate shook his head. "If that's not rest, I don't know what is!"

"The reality you see and the reality you live are not always the same, friend Slate."

"I don't have time fer yer foolishness right now, priest. We've got a camp ta set up and some well-earned rest ta claim!"

With that Slate trundled off toward the cookfire. As he did so Yip's eyes shifted from following the Dwarf to watching the gray plume of smoke roil upward toward the orange sky, shifting and swirling amidst the currents.

Following his friend toward the smell of wood smoke, Aroganji looked up from unpacking his bundle. "Back with us, Yip?"

Yip bowed. "I, too, have been busy. I apologize if I have been too distant to be of help."

Wrindanneth smirked. "What've you been up to? If you've been as busy as Slate while we traveled, then I have little sympathy for your efforts."

"I have been trying to learn how to completely mask the presence of our passage, the footprint of our beings, from those who would follow us much as I have been endeavoring with my own. It is difficult to describe, but I am working to blend the presence of our life force and the magics we wield with the ambient energies all around us to cover our traces from those who would seek us."

Slate snorted as he bent over a cook pot filled with boiling water to which he was adding dried meat and seasoning. "He's been daydreamin'! Don't let him fool ya!"

"Perhaps we can walk a bit tomorrow instead of porting, my friends. I know the passage will be slow going, but Slate tells me you are both spent after traveling so far. A little exercise and air will do us good."

Wrindanneth chewed slowly on some old bread. "If Aroganji and I take the morning off, we should be well-replenished after a good night's rest. There's only so much casting we can do before we burn up all our stores and capacity without proper recovery."

"If we continue to cover ground like this, we should arrive at Tellanon within the week." Rummaging through his pack, Aroganji brought out the tome Azaelle had given them to study. "Maybe Wrindanneth and I can devote some time to learning a few useful spells from this grimoire in the morning."

"Aye, a silence spell for Slate and his axe would be nice," said Wrin as he moved over to help Slate with their meal. His initial review of the tome had shown much promise for his own improvement.

He doubted such was the case for Maeth.

Braemen was the first to notice the smoke plume drifting up from a distant ridge to the north and over a few intervening ridgelines. He and his crew had had quite a journey on their airship through these mountains, and, although his hold was now almost completely full of stolen cargo and other contraband, he could always use a little more coin to fatten his coffers before finding another trade route to skim.

As long as his crew got their cut, they would be quite happy with a little extra take after journeying so far off their normal routes. Besides, he could use a bit more gold to repair the *Shrike* after his last skirmish with those foolish Skaelian traders.

Who were they to try to prevent him from taking his fair share of their cargo? Did they not know and fear the wrath of the R'yn Daer?

"Verakesh! Head north toward that smoke!" As the cool wind rustled through the long white feathers of the noble R'yn Daeran wings furled behind his back, Braemen yelled through the wind to the cowled mage whose arcane energy fused with the airship giving it both power and direction. "Keep us to the valley bottom out of sight! I've a feeling we have a few hens nearby to fry!"

A slight nod from the pale-skinned mage was all the answer Braemen needed.

"Thaelos! What can your eyes tell me?" Braemen waited for the archer's answer as he lithely made his way up from belowdecks at the aft of the ship. What looked like a blurry tree-lined ridge some leagues distant would unfold in crystalline detail before the archer's magically enhanced eyes.

His long flowing golden hair tied back with a short leather strip to free his vision from the wind, the archer's padded footsteps brushed as light as the breeze upon the deck as he made his way to Braemen.

"There is too much foliage for me to see much in the way of detail, sir."

Braemen always did like the respect this one accorded him. Unlike the mage or the surly armsman, he could be trusted fully. Little could be left to chance in the life of a pirate, especially one's choice of friends and allies, should they be needed.

Joining them above decks, his presence noted by the creaking planks beneath his heavy tread fall, the eminent armsman Göerden strode up from below, his massive shoulders barely fitting through the doorway from the hold, the hilt of his great rune graven claymore just visible behind his shaggy head and pleated beard.

"What news?" Göerden asked, his booming voice resonating like thunder across the deck.

Braemen looked at him briefly before returning his attention to the archer. "We may have a bit more quarry before heading home."

"Try looking from the mast before we drop too low to have a clear vantage." With that command, the archer quickly skirted the railing from the captain's position at the aft of the ship and climbed the spar with an alacrity only possible by Elves and, in the case of Thaelos, Elf-kin—those raised and trained by Elves and granted something of their magic.

Perched atop the mast, sails billowing around him, Thaelos surveyed the mountaintop carefully for any signs of movement that would draw his eye and allow him to divine the presence of their quarry.

Several minutes of studied concentration passed before the archer called down to Braemen, "There are four. They appear unaware or unconcerned with our presence."

"Excellent!" Braemen could barely contain his building excitement with the first thrills of the hunt. "Wizard! Drop us down and out of sight! We will come upon them in the first blush of the morn!"

Swooping gracefully through the valley, at just over twenty rugged paces from stem to stern, the *Shrike* had prey on the horizon.

While the others prepared their meals, Yip realized he was not at all hungry. Although spiritually spent very much like his friends, apparently his new efforts at energy accumulation and dissipation did more than just hide their presence or refine his metabolism.

Normally, he would take a few herbs and slivers of dried vegetables with his tea.

Today, he felt no need.

While his friends ate around the campfire, their faces backlit against the glowing orange light of the fire, he wondered at this new change. Perhaps with a bit more practice, he would not need any sustenance like his teachers, or rather the land, the sky, and the energy around him would provide him with all the energy he needed. Inwardly shaking his head ruefully, he would never give up the refreshing depths of good, aged Chang Sen tea!

"When we get to Tellanon, what's your plan, Yip?" Aroganji's question brought Yip out of his reflection.

"Aye, we'll need ta know how ta proceed once we get there," continued Slate.

"I do not know the area or its customs," said Yip. "So we will have to observe and see what there is to learn. Perhaps we should frequent a few pubs and inns to see what we can overhear there and in the streets. Or one of your contacts, someone worthy of trust, like Hoyt, may have information of use. With so many trade routes passing through the city, I am sure we will learn something of import."

He shook his head. "Our current physical and social isolation does not help our search."

"And ya tryin' ta fit in at a bar won't either!" laughed Slate, the bright humor in his eyes caught dancing with the firelight.

"Perhaps the people of Tellanon are used to strangers and they will pay a small, bald man no notice?"

"'Tis true," said Slate with a half-smile. "But yer social manner doesn't exactly make people want ta talk, if ya take my meanin'."

"Slate, I do not need to talk, merely listen, and that, I can assure you, I am good at. Besides, I will have your help and together we will bring many skills to bear on the search I am sure."

"In that you are correct, Yip. Maybe some of the people I know there will have information they will share to help get us started. As long as we don't interfere in their interests, many of the people in Tellanon should be more than willing to help. If we're lucky, they may even share it for free," offered Wrindanneth as he, too, joined in a bit of Slate's humor.

Yip turned his eyes from his friends by the fire to the deep velvety sky and stars above, small dustings of light set in a deep sea of indigo blue.

Where were the Cabal now and what were they doing?

What plans were they hatching?

How many worlds knew their taint?

How many lives were the Cabal destroying or ruining even as they sat here enjoying a peaceful meal?

The people of Ea'ae were lucky in that the Cabal's interests were primarily elsewhere, their efforts partially thwarted by Ea'ae's seals, for if the Cabal chose to exert their will here, this planet would be an entirely different place.

As his eyes shifted from the heavens to the ridges below, his heart skipped in wonderment, instantly lightening as his gloomy ruminations scattered with the sparks from the popping flames.

"Faery fire!" His exclamation brought his friends' heads up from their conversation by the fire.

"Great Brendle's ghost! 'Tis a rare treat indeed!" effused Slate clapping his hands with child-like exuberance. "I haven't seen tha like in many years wanderin' these woods!"

"True," said Wrin as his eyes, too, shone with glee, as though he were transported back to a fair or celebration from his youth in his cold northern village. He paused. "The faeries normally only come out when there are no mortal eyes to see their cavorting."

"Or as a warning to each other," said Aroganji. In Chang Sen the Fang Shih read the sighting of faeries as an entirely different omen. "The faeries' intentions are benevolent to those of good heart and true spirit."

"Do you think they are telling us something?" Yip knew little of the ways of the fey folk, and the faeries that he could sense within the scope of his abilities to try to read and interpret divulged little.

"Or each other," said Aroganji. "We should stay alert."

"If something has startled the fey creatures of this wood, then we, too, should be cautious," agreed Wrindanneth.

Before bedding down warily, the party took some time to watch and appreciate the panorama spread out before them.

All around from ridgetop to valley bottom, the stars from the sky had taken refuge in the wooded hills. If he had not seen the woods in broad daylight, Yip would have thought that seated as he was in the darkness on the mountaintop, they were surrounded all around by torch lit towns and cities almost as far as the eye could see—lights danced and sparkled on the ridges and mountainsides in shades of deep greens, bright yellows, azures, argents, and burning oranges.

Overcome by the beauty and majesty of the land around him, there was much to be done before he could truly rest. There was too much beauty in the world to fall under the Cabal's sway.

The fragile innocence of this place and others like it were his to protect.

The next morning while his friends slept, Yip woke with the sun as he began his morning exercises, meditations, and energy work. He first started practice on a cosmic scale, interacting and equilibrating with the subtle traceries and pulling of the sun and moon, the constellations above, and the planets around. Much as he internalized the cool, humid pre-dawn air, he took the energies of the stars and planets that bathed him—radiant and gravitational, particle and light—and then circulated that which he was able through his heavenly meridians. Starting from his navel, the celestial energies passed upward along his spine, through his arms, through his crown, back down to his navel and through his legs, before returning upward along his spine in a gentle orbit reestablishing harmony with the subtle bodies around and above.

To the eyes of a priest, the obvious separation between an individual and their environment blurred and merged with arrangements and potentials beyond normal ken and interpretation. The body of a priest reflected these natural, macrocosmic energy patterns and emergent processes on a microcosmic scale through the mirroring and interpenetration of stellar cycles, while reflecting the beauty and complexity of natural relationships, and ultimately the unity of Heaven and Earth, man and the divine.

"'Tis a nice sunrise indeed," said Slate with a slight yawn as he shifted out of bed and watched Yip's seated figure facing the sunrise overlooking the valley slowly emerging from the purple and black morning shadows. The first rays of orange sunbeams alighted on the ridgetops and lit the morning fog in a pearlescent white while leaving the recesses of the valley bottoms still cloaked in shadow.

When Yip did not respond, Slate headed over toward the leavings of last night's cookfire, ready for breakfast. "Lemme know what, if anythin', ya want fer breakfast when tha time comes, Yip."

Yip joined Slate by the lively popping fire a short time later. "Yes, it is a wonderful sunrise, Slate," he said picking up on Slate's earlier comment. "I am glad we are here to see it together."

"Aye. 'Tis good indeed ta be out amidst tha rocks and trees, ta feel tha earth's firmament and surety below."

Dwarves' natural affinity for the land was often overlooked by other races who generally esteemed their industry and skill at arms as the most important and therefore the primary facets of their characters. Never having met a Dwarf before his travels, Yip did not share that prejudice. Slate went on, "Ya think that Wrin and Aroganji will wake up rested after so much portin' yesterday?" A look of brief concern briefly flashed across Slate's weather-wrought features.

Turning to examine his friends, Yip said, "Their spirits seem well. In the brief time I've known them, their facility with magic has increased significantly. Pushing themselves to their limits these past few days seems to have expanded their boundaries and capabilities further."

He let out a smile as bright as the newly minted sun. "Perhaps soon they will be able to cast that group teleport spell I've heard so much about."

"T'would be nice. After a day bouncin' from ridge ta ridge, I feel as disoriented as a Dwarf tryin' ta' navigate tha high seas."

The last bit of morning shadows highlighted the mixture of humor and real anxiety on Slate's face. Yip's eyes shifted from his friend to the far side of the small clearing where his other companions slept beneath the branches of an old, gnarly weather-bent oak.

"Any day we see is a gift, Slate, whether we're on the high seas or level ground. I only wish the sea ahead could be counted on to travel as smoothly."

Slate grunted as he stirred the oats in his pot.

"How many more leagues do these mountains run toward Tellanon?"

"Another hundred or so would be my guess. Then we'll be in tha rollin' hills o' Var'Kera. There'll be quite a bit more habitation there."

Yip's eyes followed Slate's as he looked over the tree enshrouded ridges toward the northwest.

"What can you tell me of the place? Lands such as these are only mysterious stories in my memory—thin and wispy, ready to burn off beneath the rising sun like the fog in the valley below."

"Hmm…Var'Kera is a land of many civilizations—Man, Elf, Gnome, and Dwarf, tha seat o' civilization in tha West, a cradle between tha mountains we now tread and tha vast Ayle'ine Sea. Tha lands o' Var'Kera are a focal point o' trade and ingenuity, a foray point fer expeditions and exploration tha world over and ta places beyond. Tha wonder o' Var'Kera is that so many diverse civilizations live in peace together fosterin' relationships ta each other's mutual benefit."

Yip's brief nod of acknowledgement was the last action he took before the sky exploded in tumult.

Without thought, before conscious action, Yip grabbed Slate and leapt away from the fire. As he rolled, he shouted to his still-sleeping friends, "'Ware the skies!!!"

He just caught the faintest trace of a warning and the impression of a few individuals at the limits of his perception as the firepit exploded beneath a blast of concussive force delivered from the fore of their distant vessel. The raining torrent of dirt and ash rocketing upward through the air from a large, smoking pit in the ground was all that was left of the spot he and Slate had just vacated.

Coming up from his crouch, Slate prone but rolling forward to stand, Yip saw the air shimmer and blur as a sleek wooden ship appeared in the bright morning sunlight swooping through the air toward them with reckless abandon. At the same time, he sensed Aroganji and Wrindanneth struggling for cover beneath the trees on the far side of the clearing. At least the first blast had not been meant for them, perhaps the ship's pilots had not yet seen Wrindanneth and Aroganji's sleeping forms at the clearing's edge or maybe they wanted to take care of Slate and him before the others were properly prepared and wakened.

He called out again, "Head for cover!"

Aroganji and Wrindanneth had already made the trees, but he and Slate still had some ground to cover before reaching the relative protection of the surrounding hardwoods.

He pushed Slate hard in the small of the back to help speed his progress toward the forest.

"I'm hurryin'!" Slate shouted back. He muttered, "Dwarves were built ta fight, not run!"

Turning for one last look at the ship before he made cover, Yip saw the captain of the vessel staring intently down at the clearing, large white wings held tightly against his back, looking for targets through the thick dust and ash left by the blast. A massive Northman stood at his shoulder calmly surveying the destruction disinterestedly as if at a poorly directed play or carnival show. From the back of the ship, he also saw an archer, long braided hair pulled taut, smoothly reach behind his back and draw and arrow.

All three radiated power both internally and from equipment they bore.

Once again, he shouted, "Arrows incoming!" His call had the intended effect as the archer's attention quickly jumped to him. With all the smoothness and grace of an Elf, the archer reached, threaded, and released his arrow with supernatural alacrity. As the arrow left his bowstring, the end burst into a blazing green flame, fueled by some facility Yip had never encountered.

To his eyes, the sure flight of the arrow through the air was akin to the struggle of an ant through amber. Before the arrow had left the string, his hands lit up and burned a deep blue.

True to its mark, the arrow sped right at Yip's heart where he stood paused next to the border of the wood. Having never encountered a Priest of the K'un Lun, the accomplished archer had never seen a being quicker than an Elf, faster than the reaction of hand or eye. Before the bowman registered the result, Yip caught the burning arrow and sent it speeding back toward the archer as he reached for another.

He never managed a second.

Yip said a silent prayer as the archer's limp form fell and lay in the center of the clearing beneath the hovering ship.

As they gained the wood, another blast from the ship's fore sent roots and foliage flying through the air as a tree to Yip's left exploded, its fragments uprooted, and ripped to flinders. He heard Wrindanneth's muffled curses a bit farther in as Aroganji shouted, "Regroup!"

Motioning for Yip to follow, Slate hissed incredulously, "How in tha name o' Freyda's frock did ya manage that bit o' witchery?"

Moving farther into cover he whispered back, "There is a long moment of time between the instant when a man decides to fire and his actually firing."

"Brendle's bane, man! That doesn't tell me anythin' nor does it explain yer speed!"

Answering calmly, he said, "I read his intention. *Chi* enlivened my actions. Now let's move!"

Slate nodded shortly and ducked through the branches.

By this time Slate had freed his axe from its scabbard. Yip heard a steady stream of invectives coming from Duraeleon, adding to the noise and confusion. "Of all the nerve!"

"To hit a man while he's down!"

"Some way to welcome a new day!"

"We'll give 'em what for, Granite! Stick with me and you'll learn the true power of Duraeleon the Bright!"

"Slate! Ya stupid axe! Slate, if ever my Nan spoke my name true!" Slate had little time to argue with his weapon, to correct his own name, as he looked to make sure Yip was following.

"Hush! Ya fool thing, lest ya draw their attention ta us!"

Slightly quieter now, Yip heard it continue in a soft whisper, "Don't you think Granite would be a bit better? After all, it's a bit sturdier than Slate. Slate is rather brittle, not at all a good quality in a warrior if you ask me..."

The axe's voice and Slate's reply faded as they made the wood.

As he, too, moved deeper through the underbrush, Yip knew that unless they found cover and hid, outran their foe, or found a way to disable the ship and engage the crew on more even footing that the day would be quickly lost.

Despite all that seemed to have happened after the ship first arrived, less than half a minute had passed since the attack commenced.

Casting his mind out, he located where Wrindanneth and Aroganji were hiding as he motioned shortly for Slate to follow from his deeper cover beneath the trees. Moving toward his other friends, he called out, "We need to find a way to disable the ship!"

A few feet away, he heard Wrindanneth reply glumly under his breath, "And I need to fasten my trousers!"

Following behind him, Yip heard the axe's pithy reply. "We all need something, don't we, Marble?"

Within a few seconds, he and Slate had reached Aroganji and Wrin where they huddled beneath a large tree. "Can you make them disembark so we can fight them on the ground? Otherwise we're just targets until they finally manage to hit us."

"Aye, my legs are meant fer chargin' not runnin'!"

"And your gums are meant for flappin'!" was his axe's retort.

Wrindanneth spared a second for a bit of sarcasm. "Ah, good morning to you and your side-kick, Slate. Every good hero needs one!"

Aroganji looked at Wrindanneth sternly. "Gentlemen, please!" He paused, adding, "I could cover the deck in ice, but we'll have to be careful. There is also a mage somewhere on that ship powering it. We can't know what tricks he may have accessible."

Wrindanneth responded, "Piloting the ship will hold most of his attention unless he lands. We'll just have to watch out for those force blasts he's raining down on us. I'll make their stay above decks interesting."

Looking back toward the clearing through the leaves, they could see the airship holding steady above the opening, its sail slowly riffling in the breeze, as the crew gazed intently through the trees.

"Do you think they're bounty hunters?" asked Aroganji.

"Bounty hunters or no, they've picked tha wrong Dwarf's breakfast ta interrupt." Slate's wicked smile reflected in the gleaming surface of his axe.

From his side, Duraeleon continued its steady train of witticisms. "Don't worry, Shale, you could spare to miss a breakfast or two, or maybe even three!"

Slate merely growled in response.

"I'll draw their attention," said Yip. "I can react before they hit me." Looking at Aroganji and Wrindanneth, he added, "You and Wrin take your shots when you get the chance."

As Slate moved toward the edge of the wood, he said, "I'll be waitin'!"

Yip ran back to where he had exited the clearing away from his friends and quickly sprinted out from cover. He leapt into a dive roll as another concussive blast met his return. Regaining his feet, a wave of cold air blasted up from behind him as Aroganji let loose his spell, freezing the air in a crystalline arch from his spot on the edge of the clearing to the decking of the ship with a sharp invocation and the successive etching of a series symbols for ice, water, and wind with his hand.

Looking up, Yip saw that the entire ship was covered in a layer of ice and frost, the water in the air collecting and hardening around every open foot of decking, mast, rigging, and sail. A few feet to Aroganji's right, he heard Wrindanneth shout his evocation as he covered the ship's deck in some kind of slippery viscous oil, adding further difficulty for the crew.

As his mage flailed about above decks trying to regain his balance and his armsman crashed through the railing to land with a bone-crunching *thud* on the ground overburdened as he was by his heavy armor, the captain made his move. With one firm stride, the captain leapt from the edge of the ship's railing and soared into the air, powerful wings unfurling from his back as he took to the skies as only a R'yn Daeran could—effortlessly and at ease, free of the need for incantation. Swooping in a sure arch by his ship, he banked quickly above the clearing gathering momentum for a strike.

From the side of the clearing behind Yip, Slate burst out, "Come down and fight ya coward! By Brendle's bones, I'll have yer head!" while brandishing his now silent axe threateningly.

Before Slate could act on his challenge, another great blast of concussive energy shot out from the ship. After the initial counterattack, the mage had managed to recover himself, enveloping Slate in a wave of destruction. Looking over, Yip watched in amazement when he saw the energy of the blast bend and bow about a great bubble of force as Slate held forth the scintillating axe Duraeleon. All about him dirt and leaves exploded into the air from the impact.

Untouched and unfazed by the blast, the heat of Brendle's forge now rushing through his veins, flames leapt from Slate's hands to flit along Duraeleon's length as the Dwarven Bor'Banna yelled, "Ya'll have ta do better'n that ya cowards!"

His axe must have muttered more than just insults this morning for Slate to have been so sure of his protection. Perhaps it had told him more than Slate had let them know about its capabilities on their journey from Azaelle's cavern. Or perchance Slate had not told them everything of the ways of the Ur'Daena. Regardless, his blood boiling, flames licking along his axe's length, Slate ran to the center of the clearing to make sure the massive armsman lying prone on the ground was finished after his fall from above the trees, brandishing his flaming axe burning as bright as the sun.

With a great beat of his wings, the force of their stroke blowing dirt across the clearing, the captain banked above Yip, even with the tree line, and yelled, "Die now fools! The breath of the R'yn Daer claims you!"

Holding forth both of his hands, arms together, palms flat, a massive swirling gray-white vortex of air lashed out into the clearing, smashing into Slate, who had dropped his shield to engage the North-man, throwing him like a toy into the trees as Yip leapt to the side and was flung dazed into the trunk of a tree as he rolled to lessen the impact.

Breathless, his ribs cracked and burning in his side, Yip jumped back into the clearing as Wrindanneth rained a sheet of fire on the ship, igniting the oil he had used to coat its surface. While the decks steamed from the melting ice, the mage Verakesh leapt from the ship to join his companion hovering in the air, twin bolts of lightning exploding from his hands as he flew into the sky, leaving the ship to smolder as the melting ice slowly put out the flames.

A great *boom* filled the dell, echoing off the surrounding hills, and sparks flew as Aroganji lifted his arms warding off the crackling blue bolts. Where his captain flew with the grace of a native, his grand white feathered wings sure and steady, the mage hovered in place by force of will, his face a studied mask of concentration as he rekindled his inner fires in preparation for his next attack after releasing the crackling bolts.

As the captain turned to look briefly in dismay at his ship after

Wrindanneth's attack, for the life of a R'yn Daer was forfeit, less than worthless, should he lose the skies or his ship, Yip struck.

With two great strides, he lifted his *chi* up and out from his *tan t'ien* in a sudden release of force, a spring violently let loose from its mooring. The effort rendered him temporarily weightless as he sped through the air—a missile seeking its mark.

As the captain turned back toward the clearing to where Yip had been, ready to release another elemental blast, he now instinctively banked back in fear bringing his hands up in self-protection as the small wiry man rocketed toward him swinging a blow to his temple, blue hands shimmering in the sunlight. With an audible *crack*, the captain went limp and fell to the dirt joining the archer, the armsman, and the leavings of the party's now pitiful camp.

Before Aroganji's firebolt released and hit its mark, just as Yip landed lightly on the ground, he sensed the expression of a spell and heard the mage yell, *"Jeras ül vialon!"* With a loud *pop* of air the mage was gone, saving his own skin rather than risking further loss.

A few seconds later, the smoking airship settled down light as a feather opposite them in the clearing.

Panting from the center of the clearing after his exertions, Wrindanneth cursed. "The cur had better run!"

As soon as his feet hit the ground, Yip sprinted to where Slate lay unconscious, his axe lying just out of reach. Hands still alight, he closed his eyes and gently placed them on Slate's temples while he plumbed the depths of Slate's injuries. Heartened by what he felt, he sent a burst of life-giving *chi* to his friend's battered ribs, lungs, and kidneys, overjoyed with the knowledge that his friend should fully recover, guiding the energy to flow into and restore Slate's injuries.

As the *chi* left his hands, the diffuse blue light went out and he turned to Wrin and Aroganji. "All will be well."

Relief flashed across Aroganji's face and Wrindanneth let out a short sigh. Bending over, he propped Slate's head up with his cloak and rested his axe by his side. As he placed the axe on the ground, he heard it whisper, "You have more in common with an armadillo than a Dwarf."

Slate's eyes fluttered briefly before closing again. Under his breath, Slate grumbled, "Yip, doesn't he have a muzzle?"

Wrindanneth, gladdened by the news and Slate's good humor, replied, "Sometimes it's good to refuse to take your armor off even for sleep. The rest of the time, we can smell that decision all day."

With a tenderness belying their normal harsh verbal interplay, Wrindanneth laid his hands gently on Slate's chest as he, too, explored the depths of Slate's injuries. Uttering an incantation, he then sent soothing, healing energies along Slate's wounds and into his ribs to help them bind and recover. With the invocation, brilliant white divine Light flashed briefly along Slate's skin as his cuts and abrasions quickly sealed beneath Wrindanneth's touch.

Opposite Wrindanneth where he knelt by Slate's side, Yip gave a brief note of approval. "Very well done, Wrindanneth! He will sleep for a time before waking."

Pausing briefly as he looked from Slate to the ship and back, Yip added, "At least we won't have to teleport any time soon, my friend."

While Yip and Wrindanneth knelt over Slate, tending his wounds and settling him in place, Aroganji used another invocation to quench the fires on the ship with a strong dowsing of rain.

He wanted the ship and its cargo unharmed.

Looking over at Aroganji and Wrindanneth who were now working on the ship, Yip asked, "Can either of you fly one of these airships?"

Aroganji shook his head.

After a pause, Wrindanneth cleared his throat. "I grew up sailing boats and fishing on large inland lochs. Navigation and boat craft are almost second nature to me. I'd imagine sailing in the air isn't much different than plying the water."

"That is good news. It may be a few days before Slate is comfortable moving on his own. Hopefully you can get familiar with the ship in that time."

Bent over his friend, making certain Slate was stable, Yip sighed as the *chi* resettled throughout his body and his adrenaline-induced tension began to dissipate. His cracked ribs responded in violent protest to his sigh, hot metal spikes in his side. The protections *chi* afforded him were also fading with his strength and concentration. He would have to rest and replenish himself soon to speed the recovery process. Standing up, he salvaged a bit of the scraps left of his bedroll, laid them out on the ground, and sat down in preparation for some rest.

Before Aroganji and Wrindanneth began to board the ship and look through its hold, he said, "I, too, must recover a bit, friends. I am injured. If you need me, just tap my shoulder."

If only he could harness *chi* from an unending well like his teachers without reducing his ability to use it! Despite all his improvements in capabilities these last few months, despite being able to harness ever greater amounts of *chi*, despite being able to replenish his store of *chi* rapidly and efficiently, he could still only use so much before his flame was spent, a small candlelight sputtering out in its own wax unable to burn all the way to the quick.

While he was wishing for the impossible, he might as well dream that men's greed would not force them to act so rashly or violently.

Wrindanneth called out over his shoulder, breaking his train of thought, "You don't even want to take a look?"

"The ship will be there when I am well."

"Are you all right, Yip?" asked Aroganji, his eyes full of concern.

"I am fine. Some of my ribs are cracked after hitting that tree. I need to gather the energies necessary for healing."

"Do you need anything for the pain? I can brew a potion for you."

"Pain comes and goes. It is something we all live with. I will be fine." Yip laid down on his bedroll and closed his eyes, ready to begin his focused healing. Cracking his eyes slightly, he said lightly, "Thank you for your consideration, Aroganji."

"Would you like me to work on it, Yip?" Wrindanneth called down from the ship, his voice also filled with concern.

He smiled, anticipating Wrindanneth's excitement to begin cataloging the ship's cargo. "Let me see what I can do first."

Eager to get on the ship and explore, Wrindanneth looked down from the charred decking. "If you need anything or change your mind just call!"

Waving his hand dismissively in Wrin's direction, Yip motioned for his friends to carry on before closing his eyes again. "You will be more interested in what you find inside anyway. Happy hunting!"

While his friends rummaged through the hold and took care of the ship's former occupants, Yip sank into darkness.

Following the slow, even rhythm of his breath, he left the tension of combat and the pain of injury far behind. With each intake of air, he zeroed in on the hitch in his side where his ribs had been cracked in two places. With his mind relaxed, gently probing the source of his pain, he began the process of healing.

Directing the *chi*, the life energy, stored in his *tan t'ien* to the source of his pain, a soft, warm suffusion of energy gradually encapsulated his discomfort and injury. With his spirit mobilized around the injury, he let his *chi* begin the process of healing and restoration. In order to speed the progression, he watched the *chi*'s cleansing light with his mind's eye and visualized his bones reforming under its warm nurturing touch. With his mind and spirit mobilized in tandem, his body began to heal and rebuild itself, restoring what had been harmed in a matter of hours instead of weeks.

By the time he finally opened his eyes, day had almost become night and spring's evening cool had settled over the ridgetop. Sitting by the beginnings of a fire, Aroganji and Wrindanneth had amassed a pile of goods from the ship for inspection. Scanning the clearing, they had also picked up the limbs and debris left after the attack and buried the crewmen.

As Yip slowly stood, gingerly inspecting his ribs to make sure all was in fact well, Aroganji said, "Welcome back to the land of the living, Yip."

He stretched slowly before sitting down next to his friends. "Has Slate stirred?"

"We gave him some water and bread an hour or so ago, then he fell back asleep," Aroganji offered mildly.

Reading the surety of Slate's breath and the solid strength in his aura, he responded, "Then all is well. He will sleep until the morning and should be almost completely recovered by then." Looking from his friends to their new pile of goods, he asked, "Do you think it wise to stay here? That mage could come back—if not for revenge then for his belongings."

"Oh I don't think he'll be coming back anytime soon," said Wrindanneth.

"Why is that, Wrin?"

"Aroganji's blast might have missed, but I threw a little twist into his spell that should have sent him quite a bit off course. If he's still alive, it will be some time before he rights himself and works up the nerve to find his way back. With the misdirection I cast on him, for all I know, he might have ended up buried in a mountain or at the bottom of the sea."

Even Aroganji was impressed with that feat.

"How did you manage that?"

"Sometimes being raised by a god has its perks."

After exchanging a quick glance with Aroganji, Yip commented on the changes he noticed in the clearing—branches taken away, leaves cleared, belongings recovered and resettled. "Looks as though you have been busy cleaning up the clearing and wreckage. Where are the crewmen?"

It was Wrindanneth who answered, "Aroganji insisted that we bury them properly. We made some cairns a ways back in the woods to be out of the way and not to disturb us while we were here."

"Aye," continued Aroganji. "One must be ever respectful of the dead, Wrin, lest their spirits curse us."

"Bah! Living or dead, an enemy is an enemy and I'll be ready to handle them."

"One shouldn't look to make more enemies than one has to," answered Aroganji.

Changing the subject for further argument would not be of benefit, Yip asked, "How do these airships work?" His time in the monastery had left him quite isolated from most forms of both pure and applied magic.

Wrindanneth answered again, "The ship you see here is a fine craft worthy of the open skies and even the heavens above, Yip. We've given it a thorough inspection and I must say that I am quite impressed. There are a few things I don't fully understand yet, but that will come soon enough. Basically, the power of the mage piloting the ship drives it—the mightier the mage, the more powerful, agile, and effective the ship."

He went on, "The true beauty of the airship is the actual relationship between the pilot and the ship itself. There's a symbiotic fusion that takes place when the pilot places his hands on the control sphere at the pilot's station. In a very real way, the mage actually becomes the ship, as it channels and stores his energy. I know firsthand because I tested it while you were asleep. It's almost as if I could see out of the ship in all directions and feel the limits of the ship as the limits of myself."

"The responsiveness and sensation are extraordinary!"

And on, "I'm not sure yet about its direct capabilities—its speed, how to fire the cannon that fool kept bombarding us with, whether it is suitable for interdimensional travel, how to protect us from the elements and provide a comfortable atmosphere at height or in hostile environments, but, like I said, that will come. I can tell you that having a ship like this is a treasure beyond counting. I can see why that R'yn Daer was so concerned about it."

"Is that so? You do go on at times, professor," teased Aroganji.

Ignoring his friend's quip, Wrindanneth shook his head in appreciation. "If only I had had a ship like this to ply the waters, or the skies above it, as a child!"

Interrupting Wrindanneth, Yip asked excitedly, "So you think it may be capable of *faerviage* then, Wrin?"

"*Faerviage*? Like I said, it could be. Interdimensional and interstellar travel are presently beyond our abilities by ourselves, much less with a ship, Yip."

"Perhaps the ship will make it easier for you?"

"Truth be told, Yip, much of what we cannot do is related not just by how much power we can wield, but what spells we have learned and memorized. Mages tend to guard their secrets about like Slate holds coin—very tightly."

Nodding, Yip replied, "There is much my teachers never showed me as well. In time we will be ready. Having a ship capable of *faerviage* would help us go after the Cabal when the time comes. If we could find them, we could use it to strike at their heart."

"That's a long way off yet, Yip," said Wrin.

Shaking his head sadly, Yip agreed. "Unfortunately, yes, but that, too, will change with time. Before that occasion comes, if we can learn to use it, perhaps we may consider traveling to the homeworld of the H'era. Their land and all its inhabitants were destroyed by the Cabal. We may be able to learn something of how the Cabal drains the life from the land and how to stop them by going there."

"If we found out where their planet is located and learn how to teleport the ship, then that would be an option," answered Wrindanneth.

"Perhaps I can find out from the H'era or the Yerens," answered Yip.

"If you have a strong enough visual image from your dream voyage to the H'era's world, then we may be able to use that as a target for interdimensional travel," added Aroganji.

"Now we just need to find out how to use the ship's full capabilities, assuming it can teleport, and generate enough power to tear the fabric of space and time to get us there. I certainly cannot actualize that amount of power right now!" added Wrin with a bit of exasperation.

Returning to the ship after looking over to Slate for a moment, Wrin finished his earlier thought. "It really is a marvel. Our travel will go so much easier without having to teleport all the time, especially when we reach flatter ground where our porting range will be significantly reduced."

Turning to Aroganji, Yip asked, "What did you find on board? Were there any more crew?"

"There were no more crew, but the ship is loaded with goods. Slate will be happy to hear that we will turn quite a profit once we sell it."

"You mean after we see if we can find the rightful owners and donate our fair share to those in need," answered Yip.

"You can't be serious!" Wrindanneth was up on his feet. "These fools tried to kill us for our coin and goods and you suggest that we are not entitled to their holdings?"

"Wrindanneth, people died here. These ruffians have probably killed others. Families depended on those who lost their lives at these people's hands. These people, these families, will need redress. At the minimum, if we cannot find the rightful owners, then we should donate some of the proceeds to those agencies who would help families like those bereaved at their hands. Whether right or wrong, the people piloting this ship probably had families too. What will they do without their fathers? Should their families be denied a future?"

"If what you say is true, and their hold has so much goods and coin, then there is probably a bounty on these bandits' heads. At the least you will get a reward for that should no one step forward to claim their goods. Given Slate's penchant for coin, I am certain that he can negotiate to keep some articles we've found once we've paid proper redress for their deeds."

Wrin was absolutely flabbergasted, rendered speechless for one of the few times in his adult life. Croaking and sputtering like a frog that forgot to swallow a cricket, he turned to Aroganji, seeking an ally, someone with whom he could find common cause against such silliness. "He can't be serious! We make our living doing this, Aroganji!"

"Yip has a point, Wrin. If we just take what we get, then how are we different from them?"

"But they tried to kill us!"

"There are lives involved here, Wrin, futures at stake. We need only take what we require."

Spinning in a circle, his eyes wide, Wrindanneth called out hopelessly, "Slate! Wake up, Slate! I'm surrounded by crazy people! Yip and Aroganji have lost their minds!"

Yip stood and placed a calming hand on Wrin's shoulder. "I cannot make you do the right thing, Wrindanneth. If you choose not to return what these miscreants stole, that is your decision."

Aroganji spoke up. "Honestly, Wrin, much of true value on these pirates is probably unclaimable, magical goods and artifacts that they purchased with previous earnings or stole long ago. If the authorities at Tellanon have nothing on them, then all this is ours by right of salvage anyway. No matter what, we can claim the ship as a reward for ridding the skies of their violence."

"Do not worry, Wrin, all will be well." Turning from his stammering friend, Yip asked Aroganji calmly, "So what else did you find?"

Surveying the pile laid out beside the ship, many of the items glowed with power, bright internal lights sparking and dancing announcing their worth to his mind's eye, their make-up bolstered and reinforced by magic, forged and wrought with spells.

"Well," said Wrindanneth, the beginnings of a plan already forming in his mind, "there is this." He held up a flat silver disc etched with the outlines of continents. "I noticed that when the ship is engaged, this device hovers up from the floor and lights up. If you think about your positioning, a three dimensional projection of your ship and the surrounding environment appears above the disk. Floating within this image, locational and atmospheric information about the vessel's current positioning are also shown. This topographic information will allow travel by night and in unfamiliar territories."

Aroganji nodded. "There is also this. Much of the gear worn by the crew is magical—a couple of cloaks that may confer some protection against magic, a few rings of unknown purpose including one ring on the captain that appeared to have an unusual aura, and some potions I do not care to sample."

Looking at Slate, thinking back to his episode turning into a chair after imbibing an unknown potion thinking it was his ale, he offered, "Maybe Slate will be willing to take a nip for us to find out!"

Wrin continued the joke. "Yeah, he'll be so thankful we don't have to teleport around all the time I'm sure he'd be willing to try a few for us!"

"Especially after he gets his sea legs," finished Aroganji smiling.

Shaking his head, Yip said, "It's a wonder you three can still call yourselves friends!"

"Who said we're friends?" asked Wrin in all seriousness.

When Wrin's comment did not elicit a reaction from Yip, Aroganji knew that the jokes had run their course and that Yip's stony impassivity was not to be broken by their attempts at humor. Aroganji then went back to the task at hand. "The warrior's great sword and armor are magical but we cannot yet divine their power. The archer's bow and boots are also magic. From what I can decipher, the boots ease the burden of motion on the body and help one move faster. I have no idea what the bow does, but it is Elven in origin."

Yip was particularly intrigued by the Elven bow. Turning it over in his hands, the bow was warm to the touch and radiated energy like a living thing. The delicate ivory surface was inlaid with twisting vines and limbs that appeared molded and formed rather than cut or hewn. Whoever had made this bow had put much of himself or herself together with the spirit of the tree into its fashioning, he thought. The magic of the joining of their spirits coursed strongly through the wood and radiated outward in a soothing wave.

Turning his attention to the boots, he felt their heft and weight and the suppleness of their weave. The boots were not made of leather like most boots worn in this part of the world. They appeared to be woven and intermeshed from some form of plant much like many types of clothing from his home were made of woven bamboo fibers. The texture of the weave was so fine that Yip could barely differentiate individual strands in the fabric. Feeling the weave under his hand, he was reminded of the finest silks reeled and spun from caterpillars in Chang Sen. The boots, too, radiated energy and vivacity like the bow.

Elven magic, it seemed, involved the infusion, suffusion, and blending of spirits between the maker and the made, creating something new from the merging of two life forces. This characteristic was but a small part of Elven Craft, for much of what Man knew of magic derived from the Elves.

While Yip examined the magical items, Wrindanneth added, "Besides the boots, the cloaks, and the rings, there is not much that is of use to us here that does not apply to the ship, although these items will hold quite a bit of value to the right buyer. The armor is too big for Slate and none of us uses a bow or great sword."

"We also found two spell books in the mage's quarters and some coin in the captain's room. Our collection of spells and lore is steadily growing. With any luck, there are a few spells that Wrin and I can learn in the tomes," added Aroganji brightly.

Wrin gave a begrudging nod. One could never be certain, but the caliber of magician indicated that the spells within may be of marginal use…at least to him. His review, when it came, would suffice for Maeth as well.

Then the Dream Stealer would have his due and take the lore that suited him.

To his friends, Wrindanneth said, "This ship has sacked quite a few other tradesmen for the hold is full of tapestries, silks, and paintings. There may be a reward on their return."

Yip was suitably impressed. "One could probably retire to a small manor on the proceeds and live comfortably for some time." Seeing his friends nod, catching the bait, he went on, "I am sure that my share will help quite a few charitable organizations do a bit more good than they anticipated this year."

Wrindanneth just sighed in response.

While Yip went over to Slate to tend his wounds, secure his bandages, and give him another small jolt of life-engendering *chi*, Wrin motioned Aroganji close. "Next time, let's try not to reveal everything we find. If all he wants to do is give everything away, then why adventure?"

He paused, considering before adding, "I did find this in a scabbard on the captain's belt." He held out a gem-encrusted dagger etched in eldritch runes toward Aroganji. The air around the blade actually hummed with power, a small dynamo vibrating within the scabbard. The sheath itself was also finely wrought and appeared completely new, untouched by use, sturdy and rugged in order to hold the blade's pulsing energies in check.

When Aroganji whistled in appreciation, Wrin went on in a low voice, making sure that Yip was not close, "This is quite a find. I've never seen a blade so fine. I am not certain if the captain unleashed its power on us in the clearing or if he used a spell, but I think his tornado came from the blade. I have not determined its story, but this dagger is an item of high quality and power. This blade would serve me well in close-combat." Wrindanneth placed the dagger carefully back under his cloak.

"I agree, perhaps it would be wise to be a bit more selective in what we reveal, Wrin. But remember, we can't hide something like that from him. Yip can see the power in that dagger you're hiding. He will notice it as something new about your person. To him the thing probably burns like a torch. You will not be able to conceal it."

Sighing only in partial defeat, Wrin said, "I will claim it as my reward or as my part of the split then. He cannot argue that!"

"Perhaps," said Aroganji with a smile while shaking his head. "He can also make you feel worse for keeping it."

Pausing but a moment, Aroganji offered, "Remember that we, too, must be well outfitted if we are to have any success against the Cabal. Yip would not argue against that point."

Aroganji did not discuss the issue any further with his friend for he knew that the dagger would be put to good use in Wrin's possession. Having it ultimately would do more good than losing it. Aroganji was content that he had given Wrindanneth pause to think and fully consider his actions. After all, their decisions should always serve the greater good, looking out for each other and checking each other's actions would help things happen as they should.

He smiled as his thoughts continued. Once Slate found out that Wrindanneth had claimed the dagger, Wrin would never hear the end of how he had already claimed more than his fair share of the value of their findings before it had been properly accounted for, divided, or sold.

Two more days passed before Slate was up on his feet and ready to travel, tromping around the camp bemoaning Yip's suggestion that they donate their earnings, wishing the warrior's armor was his size even if it was not Dwarven wrought, mumbling to himself about foolish ascetics and what Dwarves did with people who could not hold their coin. If not quite ready for battle, he certainly was ready to voice his opinion. In that time, Wrindanneth and Aroganji made the ship ready for travel with Yip's help, going over the vessel from stem to stern for signs of damage and weakness after their fight. Luckily, most of the damage had been cosmetic since they had not been trying to destroy the ship.

Wrindanneth also took the time to apologize to Yip in private while they worked on the rigging, wishing that he had been able to help more with Slate. While tying knots securely on the mast in preparation for their departure, he told Yip, "As I learn to harness divine energies with a bit more skill and subtlety, once my powers mature, I will be able to cast more potent healing magics to help aid in the party's recovery from injuries."

Perched above him a few feet on the ladder, climbing upward along the mast toward the crow's nest, Yip paused and looked down at his friend. "That is good news indeed, Wrin. Who knows when such skills may be needed? Should I get hurt, I am glad to hear that we will have someone else with us who can help mend the injuries we endure more effectively than I am able. Your aid will be most welcome even if the damage is not."

As he climbed a bit higher on the rigging below the look-out to double-check a few of their knots tied the day before, light white clouds floating lazily past in the clear blue pool of the sky above, he asked Wrin, "Have you made a decision about the new dagger you carry, Wrin?" To Yip, the new blade glowed like a small constellation, its power vibrating through the clearing from where it was cradled on Wrindanneth's waist.

Wrindanneth swallowed self-consciously, his Adam's apple taking one quick stuttering step up and down in his throat before settling, finally ready to talk.

Before Wrin answered, Yip went on, holding up his hand before turning back to his knot, "Perhaps you should keep it, Wrin, we will be better off with the dagger in your custody." As he continued upward on the ladder tugging rope, checking its moorings, he reassured Wrindanneth, assuaging some of his guilt, "We are here in this journey together, Wrin. The steps we take now and the decisions we heed could be of great import as we move forward toward our ultimate goals. Above all, we should be ready for what is to come. We must grow and mature if we are to be ready to face the Cabal. Although giving away to those in need is often the right thing to do, we must always keep our eyes toward our confrontation with the Cabal. Being ready for that day is as right as it is practical."

Letting out the breath he had been holding subconsciously, Wrindanneth smiled, for this was the very same thing Aroganji had told him. He did not want his friends to think he was dipping too deeply for himself into the fishing net, taking more than his fair share of the catch.

"Thanks, Yip," he said. "I appreciate that. I've given it much thought and honestly think keeping the dagger is the right thing to do. After all, we face enemies much greater in stature than ourselves. If we aren't ready when the time comes, then we will lose as surely as Maeth desires power."

Nodding, Yip said, "Just remember, Wrin, we do not desire power like your Maeth. Power is but a tool of which we should be ever wary. We desire what is right, what is best." Before Wrin could respond, he finished his thought with a chuckle, "Just be ready to hear Slate's concerns for *equitable* distribution when you tell him about your find."

Sharing Yip's light mood, Wrin called out as he climbed back down to the deck, at ease with his decision to keep the dagger, sure that his choice was as sound as the fastenings he had helped secure above, "Oh, don't worry about that. Slate dips into coin like a bear dips into honey. He's already gotten his fair share of our take and I'll be more than happy to point that out."

TOWARD TELLANON

Sails billowing white
within a cloudless blue sky.
Where does the horizon end?

On the morning of the third day after the attack, the party boarded the airship, ready to continue their journey toward Tellanon. They could have moved on earlier with Slate injured and recovering on board, but everyone agreed that should another attack occur, having Slate's axe at the ready would be of more benefit than a few days lost.

The day of their departure dawned bright and clear, quickly warming up in the lively spring sun just hinting at the warmth and vibrancy that would arrive with the oncoming summer. Yip, always up with the birds, made sure that his friends were roused and ready to go. He spent most of the time he had remaining before they left concealing the energetic patterns of their presence in the clearing, although hiding their energy emanations completely was about as difficult as stopping ripples traveling through a still pond.

Later, with Slate's help, they scoured the clearing hiding as many other signs as they could, but many visible tracings, much of the damage from the battle and the subtle energetic permutations indicating lives lost were beyond their current skills and time limitations to cover.

Yip doubted anyone would intentionally be able to locate their camp after teleporting here without leaving a trail. Even with the Cabal's uncanny ability to follow the traceries of the living, the remnants left from their teleporting were too old to track. He knew that he should stop worrying, that taking to the air would make tracking all but impossible, but being prepared was as much a part of his training as staying alive. Life on the run had honed his awareness as much as it had his paranoia.

Although he was from deep in the heart of the K'un Lun Mountains where trade was often handled as much by foot as by cart, he could still appreciate the beauty of the ship floating before him in the clearing as he did his final survey of the party's camp while the others waited for him onboard. After Wrin and Aroganji cleaned off the soot and other remnants of the attack, the wood gleamed in the sunlight, the grain crisp and well-defined, catching the light with a soft golden lambency. The unfurled sails held the air full and firmly in the breeze, their fabric a clean white as yet unsullied by the rigors of travel.

If he were a sailor, he would be proud to own such a vessel. Many would work a lifetime and never be able to afford its equivalent. As events stood, he was just happy to have access to a craft as marvelous as this for their journey. Seeing his friends standing on board waiting for him, the sparks of their beings as bright and light as the smiles on their faces, he was glad to be part of their fellowship and happy to be about his quest with them.

Breaking his reverie, Wrindanneth called out from the rear of the ship where his hands were held easily over the floating silver disk that controlled the ship's movements. "Are you going to stop gawking and climb aboard or do I have to send the Dwarf down to get you?"

"Can he even climb the rope without your help?" Yip called back knowing that he could tease his friends without hurting their feelings or breaking their fellowship.

"With or without a levitation spell?" Wrin yelled back.

Both hands clutching the railing, the whites of his knuckles visible even to Yip from the ground beneath the ship, his grip tight as much for balance as his taut emotion, Slate growled back, "When I regain tha surety o' tha earth beneath my boots I've a feelin' I may be sharpenin' my axe on a couple o' stone headed buffoons."

Yip could not help but laugh as he walked the last few steps to the rope ladder hanging from the airship as much with excitement as at his friends' repartee.

Climbing aboard the ship hovering lightly on a cushion of air a few feet above the wind-blasted edge of the clearing, the rope of the ladder coarse and rough beneath his hands, thinking forward as he felt the cords sway beneath his feet, he was glad of the hours he had spent practicing his balance and centering as part of his training at the monastery. All the time spent doing pole work atop sturdy wooden beams hammered into the rocky mountain soil avoiding attacks while leaping from pole to pole, working on his footwork moving from post to post dodging spear thrusts and thrown objects, running along ropes suspended between the beams would be an asset while traveling through the skies. Maintaining his balance and equilibrium on a moving object like this ship would be a challenge even for the most surefooted under difficult maneuvers in aerial combat or bad weather. Hopefully his friends were as well-prepared as he had been—certainly Wrindanneth at least would be ready with his time spent aboard skiffs on the open water.

Turning to his friends beaming with excitement, the anticipation and excitement soaring all around, the morning air crisp on his cheeks, he knew this was right, that his friends, even though just newly acquainted, were true, that the group's potential was as bright as the day and would only grow stronger with time.

As always, as if directly in tune with his emotions, Wrindanneth, their effusive captain, called out to him again, "If you smile any more, the top of your head is going to fall off, baldy!"

Feeling the ship rock gently beneath his feet, his high emotion and opinion only reinforced by their banter, Yip motioned for Wrin to get started, ready to usher in the next phase of their journey.

As the ship reached altitude, speeding along above and through the clouds, he marveled at the beauty of the land and its environs as they

unfurled beneath them—the weathered rounded green-topped mountains, soft spring leaves a vivid, dappled yellow-green, tinted with the
rainbow hues of magical symbioses, the expansive, open blue skies
with clouds seeming so close that you could reach out to touch and, if
you were exceedingly careful, perhaps walk, repose, or even jump on.

Such a trip would spark any child's fancy…or an adult who still in
some ways fancied himself a child.

To fly in the clouds, light and effortless, free and soaring above all
that he knew and imagined was akin not to his flights of imagination
or even the dreams of his youth but to his time spent deep in meditation with his body planted firmly on the ground, his mind unfettered
within.

His friends each enjoyed the voyage in a way befitting of their character. Slate, at first cautious, skeptical, and a bit fearful of not just the
ship, but of the idea of flight, had opened up after the first few short
hours aboard and now relished the speed and freedom traveling on a
ship afforded. Aroganji, ever curious, considered how the ship could
be utilized and modified, wondered what could be gleaned from the
ship's function, and pondered at the ship's mechanisms, the magic
behind them, and the significance of their function within the larger
realm of the magical noosphere. Wrindanneth, ever the seeker, thought
of the ship not just as a literal conveyance, but also as a vehicle to his
desires, a means to realize his destiny as a great and powerful
immortal archmage.

Each and every one felt that they shared in something special, not
just a magical ship or as part of a group, but in the potential for great-
ness, for success, for opportunity in each other's company. On the
almost subconscious level in which group dynamics and synergies
occur, each felt that their friends reinforced the essential and positive
in themselves and in each other, that their efforts were not just for
themselves, the group, or even their deepest desires, but for something
right, true, and worthwhile. Although none could probably put their
feelings fully into words, they all knew that this common cause bound
them together, guided their course, and would steer them throughout
their quest.

Some hours passed before Slate walked up to where Yip stood

looking out at the blue skies and green hills sliding by below watching the old verdant mountains gradually give way to large rolling hills and wide valleys broken by iridescent rivers and streams. Without turning his head, Yip asked, "Have we passed anywhere near your home, Slate?"

"Nay. Even if we had, ya'd only know it fer tha worn stone roads connectin' tha thanedoms ta nearby tradin' villages and tha great carved statuary at tha gates ta our caves. Our lands are much like these —rocky and hilly. Some thanedoms are covered in trees while others're perched atop peaks much like tha Drake Spires ya've already seen. We make our homes in tha heart o' tha hills where tha minerals are rich, tha metals are abundant, and tha gems decorate tha mineshafts like strands o' sunlight."

"Sounds beautiful, Slate. Perhaps if we are lucky, someday we can visit."

"Aye. My heart yearns fer my people and our land, my hands pine fer tha heat and surety o' tha forge, my mind wishes fer tha thoughts and comfort o' my kin, but deep down I know that my time o' wanderin' is not at an end, that I can serve my people and my Thane best out here 'neath tha skies instead o' under tha stone."

"Our hearts are very much in tune, my friend. The day will come when we know peace, when we can return home. Until then, the mountains will abide without us."

"Aye..." Slate's voice sounded somehow fragile and concerned to Yip's ear.

"What is it Slate? You seem troubled."

"Well..."

Slate paused a moment as if gathering himself. "I'll be straightforward." Yip nodded in acknowledgement, waiting for Slate to go on. "I've been stayin' up late at tha forge tryin' ta work this out, thinkin' things through since our encounter with Azaelle. I even took tha time ta try and talk ta that deranged red-headed scarecrow ta help sort things out but his line of thinkin' and mine match up about as well as oil and water or beer and Elves."

Slate harrumphed to himself as if this had taken an act of supreme effort, an act of will beyond the abilities of a normal man or Dwarf, and also with a bit of rueful humor. "What I'm getting' at is, if tha real Dragon, tha one we had come lookin' fer, had been there hunkered down in that cave, I don't think we would be here ta have this conversation."

He looked at Yip intently as if expecting a response. When none came, for Yip wanted him to express the fullness of his concern, he opened his heart, expressing the core of his worry. "Is this a foe we can handle, Yip? Are tha Cabal beyond us?"

Slate paused again and looked at his feet—in regret for having to ask and in remorse for the implications made by his questions.

"Is this a fool's errand, Yip?"

Yip sensed Slate's tension release after he got this last bit out. He also felt Slate's eagerness to move forward to help smooth out any hurts he may have caused by asking.

Before Yip could answer, Slate continued in a subdued tone, "My people have tales o' them from long ago, from time beyond tellin' when tha hills were young. Tha stories say tha Cabal and their league o' dark sorcerers and fell allies were destroyed in ages past through an alliance o' Man, Elf, Gnome, Dragon, and Dwarf that we may enjoy tha relative peace we've had since their demise. Those same tales say tha Cabal could bend tha will o' Man and Daemon, that they could turn day inta night, call meteors from tha sky, and walk between tha stars and beyond."

"Can we stand against their like?"

"Ta my eyes, our success thus far has largely been a matter o' luck. Are their recent incursions here signs that they're truly comin' back? Must we take this task upon ourselves?"

The answer to his friend's concerns was important. Bolstering his spirit would do much to help their cause. Wrin and Aroganji were also watching, gauging the conversation. Slate, in his brusque, up-front manner, had assuredly revisited the issue several times with Aroganji and Wrin. Now they wished to see the outcome of this discussion.

His answer would be as much for them as for Slate who now spoke from the heart.

He answered honestly with a heavy shrug of his shoulders. "Men and Dwarf rise to their potential as opportunity and necessity unfold,

Slate. They are not born with it. Given the right circumstances, the most humble person can perform miracles."

Maintaining Slate's gaze, he said, "Do I doubt your heart and courage?"

"No."

"Do I doubt your ability?"

"No."

"Will we be in danger as we move forward?"

"Yes."

"We are lucky, Slate, for your stories are true. The Cabal has been gone from this world for a long time. That they are now endeavoring to come back to their birthplace only shows their true power, their real motivations, the reach of their influence, and the weakness of our ancient defenses."

"Who has ever undertaken any worthwhile endeavor without hardship, without questioning their motivations, without introspection, or without self-doubt and personal assessment? What great deed has ever been done without commensurate risk?"

"I am but a mortal like you, my friend, and, after careful consideration, I believe we have some chance for success—for belief is as much the beginning of opportunity as is effort."

Taking Slate's measure, he continued on revealing more, "Let me share something with you I have not yet shared with the others. Aroganji's tale of the Cabal's incursion to his school told much, Slate, much that most stories of the Cabal omit or have forgotten. Our planet was saved from the Cabal's devastation long ago. That they have not come back before now was not because they were eradicated, or that they have not desired to return, or that they have been afraid to come back. They have not returned because they were banished—outcast after defeat. The seals erected in that time to protect this world from their return are breaking, or rather being broken."

"The Cabal's minions stole into Aroganji's learning institution not just to achieve an item of power, but to break one of the seals protecting this world from them and their ilk. That assault is further evidence that the Cabal's agents are still quite active on Ea'ae without their masters, that those who escaped banishment and death have worked long and hard to ensure the Cabal's return."

"Only the thinnest of barriers now protects our world from their invasion. Untold worlds in this plane and in others not so protected may not have been so lucky. The story of the H'era, the loss of their world and its life, are one sad example of a fate that may have befallen many others. I do not know how much life has been lost at their hands, how many worlds may have been ravaged, but I do know that their time must come to an end before they drain our world, its people, and all its life into a husk."

"Imagine the skies torn open, rent asunder, great roiling blackness spewing out across the land, evil permeating all that you know and hold dear, spirits ripped from the living without thought only to fuel the void wielders' power. Or, envision the vitality slowly stolen from the land, our people and the life on this world wasting away in slow torment, drained away solely for some group's despicable lust for power. That is our future if we do not stop their return."

Yip turned from the railing where he had been staring out at the sky to look directly at Slate.

Eyes filled with deep sadness, he went on, "My people, too, have been banished, outcast as much as the Cabal. Even though memory of the Cabal lingered, our story lost its luster through the time since their passing. Now very few know of us as more than ghosts."

"Our exile was self-imposed partly as restitution for my order's failings when we did not completely destroy those who betrayed us and then corrupted all we held dear and partly for the overarching guilt we felt for giving rise to something as evil and insidious as the Cabal. Even so, on occasion, we still ventured out from our place of exile to make certain Ea'ae was yet safe from their machinations and to help replenish our priesthood. After long ages in seclusion, our brief time of freedom reached a sudden end with their attack on our monastery, just as we had thrown off this cloud of personal darkness and guilt, within only a few short years of our return to the world at large as we undertook to reclaim our place on Ea'ae."

HiYip's voice grew firm with rising conviction, his face hardened with deep, rarely expressed emotion while gazing intensely into Slate's eyes. "The Cabal will be back and few will stand before them when they return. My order is yet strong, but we will not be able to hold them at bay if they come to our world in force as we did in the time of eld."

"Where others of my order wish to rebuild and grow strong again in our mountain fastness in preparation, I seek to strike out and cut the Cabal off at the source, wherever their stronghold may be, sundering the vine off at the root before it can branch out and encroach any further. I would fight them on their own ground where they least expect it."

"Although I am ill-prepared for the task, I feel that my cause is grounded in the right heart and mind. Where many may fail in a direct confrontation here, one may succeed given surprise and the right opportunity. Who would expect a lowly acolyte, one they have forced to flee in terror, chased and driven to quiet desperation, to seek out the greatest evil this world has ever seen?"

"I will fight for the land that I love not on the fertile grounds of Ea'ae beneath its glistening skies or on its lustrous hills but in dimensions dark and alien, on blasted planes stripped of life and resources, in environs as foreign as these are friendly."

"Do not mistake me, there will be battles to fight here on Ea'ae as the Cabal's power and influence grows. Many will rise to battle against them once they break open the interdimensional gates and summon beasts from the nether regions to overrun all we know and hold dear. Although I may be able to help during that time, my ultimate battle will lie elsewhere. If I am lucky, and all goes well, my efforts may even prevent such an end."

He looked at Slate in all seriousness, for this was the crux of his argument. "The decision to stay and fight on this world or join me and seek out the Cabal is yours to make. If we split at Tellanon or sometime thereafter, I will count myself fortunate for having had your help along the way. If we stay together, I will be proud to keep your company. Either way, the decision is not mine to make. You must do what you feel is right."

Yip's look of deep concern melted away as his taut eyebrows lifted and relaxed, releasing the tension in his brow as he hoped to ease his friend's concern. "Luck is a matter of making the most of opportunity. While the Cabal readies itself to strike, we have an opportunity to help restore accord in Heaven and Earth and set my order's ancient failings right. Given the urgency and immediacy of the Cabal's threat, we must make the most of the prospects that present themselves to us, and, while I cannot presume to make choices for you, Wrin, or Aroganji, I can say that we are doing what is right and just, what needs to be done."

Some seconds passed before Slate showed any sign of response, letting Yip's message settle inward. He, too, took some time to stare off into the clouds and the sunny spring sky so ripe and full of opportunity as Yip had been doing before his approach. "Aye. Most o' my luck has been hard-earned at tha forge. 'Tis is in tha nature o' a Dwarf ta do what needs doin', Yip." He paused a moment, thinking. "Aroganji and Wrin do not doubt what we're about, but I do not know if they grasp tha magnitude o' what they're in fer on tha road ahead."

After a few more moments spent in reflection, lost in the inner workings of his mind as much as the view, he offered Yip a callused hand. "Fer what it's worth, ya'll have Slate Flintforge's axe at yer service ta tha bitter end."

As Yip gladly took Slate's firm hand in his own, Slate said, "Aroganji's motives are true, o' that I can say without a doubt. His hatred o' tha Cabal runs deep and I am sure he too will see you ta tha finish." With a few reflective strokes of his beard, he added, "That fool Northmen would rather eat raw slugs and smell o' fish oil than miss a chance at adventure, power, and possible fortune. He'll stay with ya just fer tha chance at glory, reward from tha effort, and tha possible accolades from Maeth Onai ta be sure. Nonetheless, I feel it's my duty ta talk ta 'em all tha same."

Nodding, Yip answered simply, "That is all that can be expected of a friend, Slate."

Having complicated the issue more than he had probably wished, Yip turned back to watch the sky and their destiny arise with the approaching horizon.

Having had his say, Slate returned to the pilot's station to explain to his friends the full enormity of the endeavor they had decided to join.

DRAGON FLIGHT

A solemn oak waits
alone in the valley trough,
untouched by the rustling grass.

The party landed in a large, saddle-shaped valley strung between two small ridges after the first day's travel in the airship. Long, verdant green grasses and wildflowers blew beneath the wind in waves, their motion accentuated by the shadows rippling along the tips of their verdant blades, their fronds caressing the bottom of the ship's hull as it hovered just a few feet above the rich mountain soil that had collected in the small valley trough over time. Framed by large oaks, Senea, and hickories farther up and down the slope, the valley formed a small, protected glade inviting the party to rest and enjoy its comforts. Slightly below the crest where the ship rested, a large red oak laid solitary claim to the glade's center, a kind old lord holding court with the wind, sky, and grasses.

Climbing lightly over the ship's railing, Yip looked around the valley fondly. Although anxious to be about the journey to Tellanon, hopeful that they could find some information on the Cabal's current interests, he would miss the silence of the open skies, the peace of the woods, and the quietude of the wilderness that he had known these past few months.

Less than one day's journey, only fifty or so leagues distant, lay the realms of Var'Kera. From what he understood from his friends, the lands of the west were not as populous as the lands about the great cities of the Empire in Chang Sen, but once again being among people instead of running from them would be an adjustment to him after spending so much time pursued and alone.

As soon as he set his feet on the ground, he started quickly down the slope away from the ship, basking in the vibrancy and feel of the valley—its complexity and flavors, the interactions of its myriad inhabitants. Before he had gone more than a few paces downhill, he heard Slate call out from behind him, "Where're ya goin' in such a hurry?"

Chuckling, he asked, "Heedin' nature's call, wild man?"

Raising his hand slowly, bent at the elbow, his arm perpendicular to his shoulder, Yip kept walking without looking back. "Yes! There is a tree here that needs to make my acquaintance."

"Ya sure ya're not a druid? Ya seem ta spend an awful lot o' time with trees!" Yip could almost see the Dwarf shaking his head in mock consternation.

Calling back, he replied, "Perhaps you should take the time to spend a little more yourself."

A short walk farther down the hillside, grass brushing lightly against his robes, earth giving slightly beneath his feet, brought him directly in front of the old oak he had seen as they moved in toward the valley. Although no trees were like the Aeryn D'al, all trees shared something of their majesty, vibrancy, and energy.

Reaching his palm out and placing it gently on the tree's rough, furrowed bark, the tree sung with life; the air hung taut and hummed with vibrancy. Pausing for an instant in appreciation, he took in the place, let the valley soak into and through him. From the microbes in the soil, up the blades of grass, and along the tree's limbs reaching toward the sky, each being's medley joined together and bathed him in the greater movement of life cascading and coruscating throughout the tree, its shade, the valley, and beyond.

Whether or not the Aeryn D'al were the parents of all trees, he could not say, but he did know that trees were almost without exception good for sitting. Underneath, near, reclining against, perched high in their branches, partaking of their shade, or on the cool earth beneath them, trees were always a welcome partner to his meditations. So, after a long day flying through the sky under luminous white clouds on a ship powered in part by the magic of his friends, he took the time to sit beneath the boughs and protection of a friend of another sort.

Looking up through the soft green serrated leaves, a light dusting of lustrous crystalline magical symbiotes upon the surface, his robes settling softly on a cushion of wildflowers and bent grasses while his back rested gently against the striated gray trunk of a tree older than some kingdoms, his mind drifted back to the K'un Lun, to a time when he was young and just taking his first steps along the path of priesthood.

Once again sitting outside beneath an old tree, this one a weathered fir, its branches gnarled and curled inward upon itself to help protect against the biting mountain winds, he and Master Wei were holding his first lesson on meditation.

"Master, why do the priests sit?" He tilted his head uncertainly. "What is meditation? It certainly looks uncomfortable and boring, all the huffing and puffing in the same position for long periods of time without pause."

Master Wei chuckled before answering and brushed his hand across the broad landscape revealed as the mountain fell away below them. "Just as life expresses itself in the many forms around us, there are many types of meditation, each with a purpose dictated by its development and intent. The K'un Lun bring many of these approaches together into a complementary whole."

"What is it I am to see, master? What will this process reveal? Why spend all this time in one place just sitting?"

"Meditation is the process of revealing your true nature, Yip. At first contemplation may seem like toil and hardship, work spent without reward or insight, but with time the effort becomes effortless and wisdom unfolds as naturally as a new day. This meditation is tso-wang. *Insight-wisdom, living compassion, and right livelihood are its fruits."*

"Meditation is also seeing the reality of the world around you and moving within its currents and truths. Many of the paths to this goal are learned

through the ways of nei gung. Nei gung *is also fundamental to your spiri-*
tual development and safety. Nei gung *involves working with the living*
energies within and without, cultivating the chi, *accepting, exploring and*
understanding the natural order, and undergoing the process of internal
alchemy whether sitting, standing, or through martial practice."

"How does this process unfold? What am I to do?"

"Patience will be your guide. You must be with yourself without distrac-
tion to realize your true nature, to see the naturalness of your existence, to
gain insight into yourself and the world around you."

"Stillness and serenity will light the way."

"I do not understand, master. I just sit and listen to my thoughts, observe
my sensations, and feel my aches and pains for extended periods of time to
glean wisdom?"

Once again his teacher laughed as lightly as the cool breeze brushing
across his cheeks, before gazing deeply into Yip's eye. "Yip, you are not your
thoughts—seeing that is the beginning of wisdom."

Yip settled down into his robes, seated cross-legged beneath the old
oak while Aroganji and Wrindanneth tethered the airship a few
hundred paces away and Slate set up the evening's cookfire. With his
back resting against the deeply etched gray bark, the patterns of
decades revealed in the intricate gray whorls, he rested his palms
together in his lap in the *dhyana mudra*, palms up, his left hand placed
on top of his right, his thumbs lightly touching above as if holding a
very small, fragile egg. Leaning slightly forward, he rocked from side-
to-side a few times until his balance was fully settled in the center of
his pelvis directly below his spine.

He then drunk in the late spring air in several full extended
breaths, filling both his chest and abdomen with life-giving air as he let
his eyes close slowly to soft slits, still slightly open, looking at the
ground a few feet beyond his legs where his feet were tucked in front
of his trunk, soles lightly touching his thighs. While his lungs and
stomach filled with air, his awareness sank gradually to his navel along
with his breath.

With each inhalation, his mind moved and expanded with his
stomach, contracting rhythmically with each exhalation. Light and

expansive as dew settling over a spring field just breaking from bud to bloom, his awareness rested gently in his center—simultaneously aware of the intake of air cooling his nostrils, the firm pulse of his beating heart, the birdsong landing with soft wings upon his ears, the firm coolness of the ground beneath his legs and buttocks, the soft breeze caressing the hairs on his forearms and neck—a bright moon above and untouched, reflecting light to the world below and all around.

Thoughts of the Cabal, their journey to Tellanon, the difficulties lying in wait ahead, the party's shortcomings and their need to grow as their quest continued, the plight of his fellow monks, initiates, and acolytes among the K'un Lun, all fell away. These thoughts, silvery-gray clouds backlit in the soft white-gold light of the moonlit mind, briefly but only temporarily obscured the glow of the moon, before his awareness once again hung bright and unobscured in, above, and among the verdant green clearing while his friends bustled busily in the distance.

Shrouded in silence, encompassed by emptiness, permeated by peace, the world fell away into unity.

Time passed from moment to moment as his objectless awareness floated quietly in the clearing before gradually resettling into his *tan t'ien* on the wings of his deepening breath. Several more deep breaths helped his awareness recoalesce and settle before gradually opening his eyes. Once again swaying back and forth several times, this time to ensure looseness, he bowed in appreciation for his teachers' guidance, for his friends, and for all sentient beings in whom the light of freedom and awareness shone. Brushing his robes before standing, he turned and bowed to his sitting partner, the venerable old oak who had provided him with temporary, but much valued, shelter.

With the sounds of his friends' laughter and the smells of food wafting down the hillside, he quickly scanned the ground and gathered up a few worn stones. Walking a few paces beyond the tree's shade, he carefully piled them up into a tenuous stack.

His robes rustling as he walked back once again to stand under the tree's shade, he turned and faced the pile of rocks. Gathering himself and the energies about him, he took several deep, steadying breaths before centering his awareness in his *tan t'ien* and then directed *chi* to flow freely along his arms and up to his hands.

His hands glowing a soft almost imperceptible blue as he had been shown by Master Wei, he moved with a suddenness beyond thought, letting his life energy burst toward the stack of stones, directed with surety by his mind's eye just as the Dragon Azaelle had shown him.

Time stopped.

His awareness contracted to a point, no longer encompassing the clearing as his stomach fluttered with the briefest twinges of anxiousness.

Walking toward the stones in a fog, dazed and skeptical of the evidence his eyes and ears showed him, he wondered aloud, "Had the stones moved?"

Reaching the pile after a silent eternity, he bent over and the truth sank in—the soft thump of the stone hitting the soil muffled by the thick carpet of grasses, the rapid flight of the top rock through the air after an explosive impact, all assuaged his disbelief. For, beyond all doubt, the solid, unyielding stone lay fractured and buried in two clean pieces in the soft earth beyond the tree's reach.

In utter surprise, he burst into smile as he bent over and gathered up his token. He then turned back to the tree in thanks for its calm and assurance, letting the oak reclaim its solitary place at the center of the clearing as he walked back up the hill toward his friends.

Still incredulous, far from mastery or even learning its nuances, he had succeeded in unleashing the Echoing Fist guided as it once was by the lion Shakyamuni's illusion shattering palm.

As he reached the ship, the two fragments of rock still held in his hand, Wrindanneth looked at Yip curiously and asked archly, "Why the skip in your step, Yip?"

Yip held out his hand, showing Wrin the stone split cleanly down the middle.

"Are you starting a rock collection?"

Yip laughed. "No, Wrin, although that sounds like a novel idea. The last thing an Acolyte of the K'un Lun needs is to be weighed down by rocks."

"Well, there's always our pouch with a pocket dimension. You could store quite a few rocks in there. Slate certainly does."

"Yes and they would get lost along with all of Slate's potions and coin."

"Well then?"

"I finally managed to project my intent after many, many failed attempts."

"For once, Yip, can you just answer my question directly?"

He gave Wrin a short bow. "Although far from mastery, or even competence, I finally managed to express the rudiments of the Echoing Fist—the fist that can echo through the chambers of an opponent's mind and heart granting them the opportunity to make a choice between right and wrong, the past and the future."

"The fist is sometimes called Shakyamuni's Palm because a master can cut through falsehood and reveal the truth hidden beneath illusion. The fist is also called the Pai-lien Touch because, like the white lotus, the fist can grant the recipient a chance to be reborn and remade. With the proper discipline, a priest can project his intent, his life energy, to heal or harm, to force a foe to confront the summation of their atrocities, and be reborn."

"Hmm…sounds quite powerful." Wrin gave a short nod.

"Of course all I managed to do was crack a rock. Hardly the stuff of legends." He laughed again as did Wrin. "Your first cantrip was probably more effective than the summation of all my attempts after years of rigorous physical and mental discipline!"

"Well…" Wrin smiled. "We all have to start somewhere I suppose."

"Yes, but my beginnings seem to take a bit longer and are more arduous perhaps than most."

"One person's beginning is another's end… Your patience will serve you well in time, I am sure."

Yip smiled. "How many days flight before we make Tellanon?"

Wrin brought up his index finger quickly, as if to remind himself of something he had forgotten. "Oh! While you were adding to your rock collection, I found out how to use the navigational projection system to change position and location and to plot our coarse. I don't know if I will be able to use the system for an autopilot, but that may be an option in the future. Based on what I've seen from the imaging system, we should arrive at Tellanon within the week."

"Excellent!"

As the ship headed west, flying as gently upon the thermals as a dandelion seed adrift on a summer breeze, the lands gradually flattened and the hazy green mountains and shadowed valleys of the Green Run became rolling hills and dales. Streams and rivers hidden at the bottom of valleys under leaf and dappled shadows turned and meandered more plainly for the eye to see. As the days passed with the setting sun, at first the sky was largely populated by clouds—few other flying craft were visible. As Tellanon drew nearer, more and more craft were visible. However, unlike their earlier encounter with a flying vessel, no ships came close or made any aggressive maneuvers. Luckily for the inexperienced crew, the nearness of civilization appeared to bring more civil behavior.

From a safe distance then, Aroganji, Wrin, Slate, and Yip could see the many shapes and forms human ingenuity could imbue in a functional vessel. From fearsome Dragons to shimmering dragonflies, from meticulously formed owls to sinister insects, from sleek, otherworldly vessels of sculpted metals and aerodynamic corsairs as fearsome in flight as battle to hodge-podge assemblages of Gnomish Paratechnology, from massive Dwarven war mountains to ethereal Elven visions, the many ships, animals of flight, and the occasional flying wizard peppered the horizon.

On their third night after leaving the grassy hollow, while the ship rested lightly for the evening in the center of a grassy clearing, Yip called his friends up to the main deck where he kept watch.

Pointing toward the moon's soft white luminescence overhead, he urged, "Look!"

Slightly disgruntled from being woken in the middle of the night, Slate grumbled, "Wha—?" before cutting off his exclamation in midsentence.

Although too far to hear the beat of their mighty wings, a Dragon flight moved effortlessly above backlit by the moon's silvery opalescence. Great shadows made small by vast distance soared on thermals, buoyed by the magic so fundamental to their nature. Scales flashed in the soft moonlight as tails lashed back and forth and necks undulated up and down in time with the beat of each awesome wing.

To Yip, the Dragons themselves gleamed brighter than the moon or any constellation overhead—shooting stars held in orbit by the power of their inner fires arching gracefully across the horizon.

Standing together in silence, the party watched rapt as the majestic giants disappeared in the distant darkness.

Unwilling to break the tableau, they all remained on the deck in hopes of one last glimpse.

Finally, after a large cloud obscured the moon and all hopes of seeing the Dragon flight again, Aroganji bowed to Yip. "Thank you, Yip."

"Thankee, Yip." Slate's normally blustery tone was softened by the awe he felt for the spectacle of the Dragons.

"Aye, thanks, Yip." Wrindanneth turned with a flourish, smiling as his robes snapped in the wind. "And now for dreams more glorious than Dragons."

TELLANON

Bees about a hive
move with frenetic purpose,
in search of nectar.

As they flew westward, where before only streams and rocky outcroppings broke the sea of green, now the occasional trail and road wandered across the countryside. Small hamlets and cultivated fields began breaking through the deep forests and shrouded valleys. As the wilderness was gradually reshaped under the guidance of human ingenuity, much of the land kept its original vibrancy and luster. With magic coursing richly through the land, crops yielded richly all year round. Small patches of farmland were able to supply the needs of the majority of the populace with minimal disturbance to the surrounding wild lands. As a result, even in the heart of human civilization, wilderness, and many of the fey creatures associated with it, co-existed peaceably with man.

Standing with Wrindanneth where he now deftly piloted the ship, Yip had spent much of their time together of late lost in silent thought, wondering what course of action would be to their best advantage.

Turning to his friend, whose face was lit up by the projection of the land beneath them while his hands rested carefully above the silvery pilot's disk, Yip asked Wrindanneth, "What can you tell me of the lands of Var'Kera?"

Moving hands and fingers with the preternatural dexterity of those skilled in spell weaving and casting, Wrindanneth manipulated and rotated the imagery before him, showing Yip their present location relative to their destination as the ship automatically charted their course.

Nodding, Wrindanneth maneuvered the focus of the topology. "As you can see"—here Wrindanneth pointed to a small valley in the hills behind them—"we have left Shady Vale and the Green Run far behind us."

Moving his finger westward and across the holographic image over the rolling hills and woodlands between, he pointed to a spot along the coast not too distant from their present location. "Along this coastline, Tellanon floats heavenward, tethered and guided by ancient magics much like our ship's own."

Sweeping his hand across the general area along the coast and inland, he finished, "Herein lies Var'Kera, the ancient seat of Men of old, home of Dwarves and Men to the north, Elves to the south and east, and many in between."

"Do the people of this land come together in council, are the regions independent, or are they largely united through a leader or governing body?"

Wrindanneth smirked. "Can you imagine a Northman calling a Dwarf liege when it's hard enough to call one a friend? Or an Elf kneeling before anyone, especially a lowly mortal Man?"

Yip shrugged. "I do not know the ways of those here, Wrin, I am merely curious. Necessity and common interest can make friends of enemies as sure as the moon and sun trade space in the heavens."

Now Wrindanneth shrugged. "The roots of these kingdoms' histories are as long and deep as their lineages and loyalties to their own kind. The kingdoms here come together for trade in goods and ideas but not much more. Individuals freely cross borders and leave realms, as we are doing now, but the majority gladly stay in place with those of like mind and view."

Wrindanneth waited patiently for the next question from his small friend. When none was forthcoming, he added, "The people of these realms are free to choose where and how they live so long as they abide by the local laws set down by the kingdom they call home." Begrudgingly, he added, "Ages spent together with or in close proximity to diverse cultures has taught the people of Var'Kera how to live with each other peaceably, with at least some modicum of respect."

Hearing the reluctant, self-referential tone in his answer, Yip smiled and asked, already knowing the answer, "Present company included?"

"Aye," was Wrindanneth's curt answer as he studiously examined the horizon and the approaching clouds.

The next few days westward passed quietly on the ship. Yip spent much time in quietude visualizing the movements of different forms and feints, combat sequences and responses, honing his body and mind from within to respond instantly and naturally as needed without.

While Yip sat or stood, Slate rolled and tumbled, grunted and heaved, honing his skills with his axe nearby. Calling on elemental energies, his axe snapped and crackled, sizzling through the air, its constant banter an unending challenge to Slate's concentration.

Aroganji spent long periods on the ship's aft, feeling and gauging the wind, manipulating and channeling its energies, creating small gusts and squalls, vortexes and eddies, transforming its potential from one form into another.

For his part, Wrindanneth spent much of his time at the helm learning how to use his energies to augment and interact with the capabilities of the ship. Through dedicated practice, he had learned how to control the ship's movements while away from the control disk. He had also learned how to free the control disk from its moorings on the deck, letting the disk follow behind him so that he could use its full capabilities wherever he chose. Using either technique, he could navigate, manage, and pilot the ship from any spot aboard the vessel. Although he had yet to test the limits of his control via the disk, Wrindanneth thought that with practice he may even be able to control the ship while not aboard.

Working together with Aroganji, Wrindanneth had learned how to supplement the ship's functionality by tapping into the energies and abilities of the crew. He had also deciphered how to set a target by marking a specific location on the hologram projection. This target location could then be used as a destination that the ship would automatically fly toward, constantly scanning, updating, and moving based on the surrounding terrain as the ship progressed toward the designated goal.

He had discovered one other thing thanks to Aroganji's help. When worn, the captain's ring gave access to the ship's log and records stored magically within the control disk. Through it, he learned of the *Shrike*'s violent history, of the many lives and spoils claimed by the crew, and the plans and plots laid out by the former captain. Although he would not admit it openly, Wrindanneth felt some pride knowing that he and his friends had helped bring reprobates like these to justice.

Perhaps there would even be a reward for the deed when they arrived in Tellanon.

He also wished to erase this vile log and start anew at the earliest convenience.

When the air began to cool, laced with moisture from the western sea as it blew about his face and shoulders bringing a faint tingle to the backs of his hands as they rested on the ship's rail, Yip knew Tellanon was close. In the short time since he had left home a distant continent away, so much had transpired. Even so, he still felt far from any tangible success. He knew not where the Cabal hid, what they planned next, how to reach them, or, and this truly pained him, what he would do if he did know more since he was as yet capable of so little.

Lost in thought, he barely noticed when Wrindanneth called out from behind where he stood at the aft of the ship looking out toward the continent's interior.

With a whoop, he heard his friend yell, "Tellanon ho!!!"

Turning to catch his first glance of the fabled island city in the sky, Yip studied the horizon but could, at first, make out nothing that would indicate its presence. Following the currents of his subtle senses, however, he did not look in confusion for long.

Far out in the distance, beyond his ability to see with the naked eye, he felt a shimmering diamond of potential, a nexus of untold forces floating high aloft in the air above Ea'ae. This radiant jewel beckoned to his inner senses with a power and allure that he could never recall experiencing.

So wondrous was Tellanon that he did not have to lay eyes upon her surface to know the depths of her beauty and glamour.

Amazed, he then walked over to where Wrindanneth, Slate, and Aroganji stood by the helm staring together in the same direction as he had been gazing.

The air in front of his friends shimmered and glistened as he walked toward them from the side, almost as though a translucent piece of glass slowly coalesced to hang suspended in the air in front of them. Coming even with his friends, looking over Aroganji's shoulder, he saw that a translucent projection did in fact hover in the air over the floating navigation globe.

"Ah...fair Tellanon with Illdrassil at her heart." Slate seemed lost in reverie at their approach.

"Illdrassil?"

"Take a look." Slate indicated the projection. "Illdrassil is tha heart o' Tellanon where tha High Council holds court." He chuckled. "Like most o' Tellanon, she's not entirely all there."

Turning from Slate to peer inward, Yip asked, "How do you mean?"

"Many parts o' Tellanon are visible and accessible from within and around tha island but do not lie directly on tha island itself. They're part o' spaces linked ta tha island, but not entirely part o' tha island, if ya take my meanin'."

Wrindanneth nodded. "Extradimensional pocket realities, stretched and modified space, attenuated dimensions, much of what you see resides elsewhere both for security purposes and space limitations although it all appears as one island."

For clarification, or further obfuscation, Aroganji added, "But

Illdrassil resides upon Tellanon as much as she resides anywhere for she binds and holds everything together."

Gazing intently into the projection's depths, Yip could see the traceries of a floating island draped in lush greenery overtopping tall stone walls in verdant profusion, vines hanging in the air, swaying in the wind, tall trees framing buildings that merged and blended with the fine-spun buildings arrayed as the meandering hills atop its surface dictated. Toward the island's craggy bottom, wrapped around the island's underside like a series of intertwined threads spun and brought together through a loom, lay a series of interlinking docking ramps and loading stages, bulwarks and ramparts, mediating and controlling the movement, loading and unloading of ships and conveyances of every imaginable description.

Rising up from the greenery and lanes meandering across the island's surface, chimerical structures flitted with the limits of human conception. Chief among these, at the island's center, an ethereal, crystalline tower rose skyward, branching archways, limbs, and open-aired chambers radiating outward from the tremendous central stem, shimmering with all colors of the rainbow held within its heart—Illdrassil—a celestial tree finding refuge in the sky.

The air about the island buzzed with the vehicles of commerce—the swarming of bees about a hive, lively and vibrant, each moving with a chaotic but directed purpose. The air thrummed with magic of every shape and sort from arcane powered ships to magically controlled and monitored docking stations. Energy moved along the stony ramparts nestled beneath to the city perched on the island's crown, upward and through the air, culminating in what appeared to his eyes as a giant scintillating force field encompassing the island's totality. The field about the island glinted and coruscated—a glimmering bubble of soap forever trapped floating beneath the reflective rays of the sun.

Slate and Wrindanneth were right. The island, if indeed it were fractured, appeared blended and connected in a natural, seamless whole.

The island's true complexity and majesty, however, resided on an entirely different level.

Materially, though wondrous and multifarious beyond imagining, the city's physical appearance was but a pale shadow of her true reality.

Multi-layered, intricate without measure, a coruscating vision in the overarching sky, Tellanon shimmered with a sophistication that dwarfed his comprehension. Intertwined and interwoven, complex tapestries of magical force, the expression of countless generations, flowed through and around the city, the energetic manifestations of myriad minds and imaginings, thoughts and ideas, uncounted and uncatalogued. All centered, flowing to and from, the celestial grandeur of Illdrassil's resplendent bole and boughs.

Within Illdrassil, this overwhelming totality was concentrated, distilled, and focused—the limpid vibrancy expressing the birth of whole galaxies of stars, the germination of untold ideation and living potential.

So overwhelmed was he by the wonderments he beheld, the beauty and majesty of a city that expressed the magical niceties and lives of races and realities from the macroverse's far borders that, but for a moment, he forget to breathe.

No sooner had he begun to peer through the viewing projection and explore the island's richness, becoming lost in her details, than a deep voice loudly interjected, simultaneously speaking to them in their native tongues from within the confines of their minds.

"Approaching vessel, halt forward progress." In response to the voice, Wrindanneth began feverishly working his fingers, manipulating the course, speed, and motion of the ship. *"Prepare for aural scanning and imprinting."*

A diffuse glow settled over the ship like translucent fog. Yip felt his skin tingle. Only a few short seconds passed before the luminescence lifted.

Within mere moments, they were given a response. *"Warship Shrike, you have been prohibited access to Tellanon. Proceed no farther."*

Wrindanneth paled and appeared crestfallen.

He then began speaking to the commanding voice.

Quickly.

"Our tracking stones indicate our identities, access levels, and residence status. Only one passenger has yet not been granted provisionary access to Tellanon. We have taken the *Shrike* in fair combat and wish to lay claim to any rewards for its capture. We request a security escort to the city for confirmation of our stated intent."

"Confirmed. Preliminary scans indicate all but one passenger maintains residence on Tellanon."

A few moments passed before the voice answered Wrindanneth. *"Request granted."*

"Maintain position for a security escort."

Yip watched as several unmanned security drones floating around the periphery of the island's force field adjusted trajectory and whipped rapidly toward them.

As the drones approached, the automated voice continued, *"Confirm names and profession, cargo and intent."*

With a thump of his chest, Slate answered, "Slate, Bor'Banna o' tha Flintforge Clan, at yer service. Returnin' home and claimin' reward."

Wrindanneth cocked his head, lifting his chin haughtily. "Wrindanneth, Priest of Maeth Onai. Claiming the *Shrike*'s cargo by right of salvage. Returning home and claiming reward."

Aroganji answered softly, "Aroganji, Yuan Ser of the Fang Shih, originally of Chang Sen. Returning home and preparing for our next voyage."

Yip bowed in turn, opening his hands for all to see. "Yip Chi Chuan, friend of Aroganji, Wrindanneth, and Slate. Empty of hand and purse. Preparing for further journeys."

As the drones zipped into position, rotating around the ship cautiously, each shiny metallic orb bristling with wicked protrusions and manipulative arms, the voice continued, *"Mr. Chuan, hold for imprinting."*

A bright green light scanned back and forth making several passes over his body. He felt the light's energy at work from the surface of his skin to the deep recesses of his spirit, recording, imaging, and storing comprehensive information about his corporeal and etheric bodies.

"Imprinting complete."

"Yip Chi Chuan has been granted provisionary access to the city. Yip Chi Chuan will be required to hold and maintain a tracking stone upon docking.

This tracking stone must be worn or held at all times while visiting the city until further nonprovisional access is granted."

"Any physical violence, prohibited spellcasting, unlawful, or reprehensible behavior will result in immediate teleportation to the docks for disciplinary action. A full listing of prohibited activities will be made available at the dock or through direct access on your ship's command sphere. All activities while in the city will be monitored. Failure to hold or maintain the stone will also result in immediate teleportation to the docks for disciplinary action."

In a chipper tone, the voice finished warmly, *"Enjoy your visit to Tellanon!"*

Yip turned to Wrindanneth. "What was that?"

"The voice?"

When Yip nodded, Wrindanneth answered, "That was the Construct, a magical intelligence created to interact with all arriving vessels, manage and protect the city, and facilitate information flow and development. Among other duties, it guides and organizes the routes of all incoming and outgoing ships, controls the security drones around the island's perimeter, and also creates portals for *faerviage* should a ship not be capable of far-traveling on its own power."

"All the island's logistics and security are moderated and overseen by the Construct. If the Construct detects something out of order, it immediately notifies and brings to bear Tellanon's defenses. The Paratechnologists oversee and maintain the Construct and act as a mediary between its proper functioning, city operations, and city defense. As we move in, you will see many of their creations and innovations."

"The Construct also helps facilitate and coordinate activities and information movement throughout the city. In this regard, its primary functions cover a wide range from assisting with research and study, investigation, and analysis of issues on the forefront of Paratechnological discovery to promoting the day-to-day functioning of the populace. With the Construct and its various ancillary support systems, Tellanon remains an intergalactic model of ingenuity and efficiency."

As they flew in, Yip saw shimmering silvery disks forming in the air, the physical manifestation of *faerviage* as ships flew in and out of portals through and across multi-dimensional space. Portals materialized by the dock for departures concluding business on the island and outside the shielded zone for arrivals ready to commence activities in the city. Wrindanneth told him that these portals were all created or allowed to be created under the Construct's guidance. For those wishing to *faerviage* to Tellanon, a return stone was necessary. Even with a return stone or a built-in equivalent on a ship, no arrival portals opened within the shielded zone immediately around the island. Furthermore, with few exceptions, personal teleportation was prevented within the shielded zone around the island. Similar but less stringent protections extended across the entirety of Ea'ae due to the seals protecting its space from potential invaders and large-scale attack.

Looking at these shimmering disks, Yip watched the energy of his world flow briefly into other worlds and dimensions spread throughout the macroverse. Turbulent eddies rushed and collided as the *yuan-chi* existing in this world pushed past and against the *yuan-chi* on the other side of the portal. To his eyes, each portal seemed to mediate and bring into focus the collision of multiple flowing streams of forces traveling through a temporary hole in the sky. In the end, the universal energy that departed his world seemed to be replaced by the energy that had arrived.

Both along the dock and at prominent positions on the ramparts around the city, Yip could see vast, almost crystalline concentrations of energy. The light in these locations burned far brighter than the sun in the sky above. So bright were the energy foci, he could not see what physical manifestation held the force.

Pointing along the ramparts to these spots, he asked, "What are those?"

"You mean the cannons?" asked Aroganji.

"Yes."

"Each contingent of Paratechnologists channels a portion of their power into cannons located along the island's defensive perimeter. The energy is stored and then amplified until needed for defense."

"Aye," added Wrindanneth. "I think the wizards even channel some of the energy from the docked ships to maintain the island's defenses."

Shielding his eyes, Yip could sense the vague outlines of massive cannons backlit by the enormous energies stored within. He could not imagine the types of targets so much power would be directed against. Perhaps ships as large as or larger than the island itself plying the depths of deep space had made unwelcome appearances at Tellanon in the past.

Only Illdrassil burned brighter.

As the *Shrike* moved through the island's force field, the energies along its surface rippled and spread, thinning enough to allow the ship to pass slowly through. While the vessel moved through the field of concentrated force, Yip felt the energy move gradually through his system. The sensation felt quite a bit like diving through a sheet of very dense, cool water. Perhaps the localized thinning and rippling of the field reduced the force needed to pass across the barrier much like ripples in water alter the surface tension and ease with which objects move over.

There were so many novel things to keep track of, he lost count.

His eyes darted from one curiosity to the next, losing track of one point of interest to follow another. He watched energy beams pull in large cumbersome ships toward the docks without calamity. He observed cargo unloaded without rope or pulley, as goods were lifted, cataloged and transported magically under the guidance of Paratechnologists and drones. He beheld beings materializing out of thin air, ready to be about their business. He saw crews disembarking from alien vessels—enormous humanoid lizards shuttled steaming cauldrons from a ship that looked like a giant slab of rock; bulbous gelatinous beings encased in what looked like spheres of amber colored crystal floated out of a sleek metallic ship that seemed to soak up, rather than reflect sunlight; Gnomes covered in mechanical contraptions happily cavorted and skipped down from a steaming ship that seemed to be made as much from random pieces of scrap as well-formed materials; two beings of pure energy glided out of a ship that appeared to be made of clear molten glass—at the vessel's core a small sun burned with bright, endless power. Amid the thronging activity, a pair of crystalline intelligences hovered across the bulwark, one appearing to be made of a single, large sapphire of a deep indigo, the other akin to a vibrant crimson ruby. Neither appeared to have any appendages, so he imagined that these beings interacted with the world via telekinesis or magic. Around both a vibrant cloud of energy emanated.

Despite all the liveliness, all the forces at play, each and every arrival had a drone and Paratechnologist or other official waiting to meet them when they reached the docking station.

That all this enterprise, communication, and cultural exchange flowed freely and without incident was a wonder beyond his imagining.

After a few more minutes of flight, the *Shrike* gently glided to dock, guided by Wrindanneth's sure hand from the bridge. As Slate prepared to disembark at the gangway, eager to be off the ship and back on firm ground, he patted the magical bag tied securely to his belt that held the party's shared belongings and then checked again to make sure his axe was tied securely behind his back. From across the deck, Yip could hear Duraeleon's muffled humming as Slate made adjustments to its sheath, scolding the blade to remain quiet while he spoke, before lowering the small gangplank to the dock.

Where the wooden plank touched down on the stone berth, a Paratechnologist stood waiting patiently to greet the crew. He appeared to be a man with typical western Dharian features—tall and sure with piercing gray-blue eyes used to gazing in the full intensity of the sun crowned by close-cropped black hair peppered white at the temples. Examining the figure closely, Yip noted that in lieu of metal armor, the wizard shone in the sunlight, encased in some kind of clear flexible force field that conformed to the contours and movements of his body.

Over his left eye a translucent green ocular floated of its own accord. Perhaps the eyepiece provided a visual overview of the entirety of the docking ships. Maybe the lens allowed him to watch and interact with the Construct or take visual cues from it. Perchance he used the ocular to plan and guide his activities. With so many new magics and technologies, Yip had little understanding or grounds to make evaluations of the myriad objects and procedures he witnessed while disembarking.

Hovering behind the shielded wizard, another drone waited

silently, its metal a dull unreflective gray in the sunlight, small arms and appendages moving slowly at its sides. Watching the drone's movements, he thought the assorted limbs moving in place seemed quite similar to the studied movements of an insect delicately sampling the air with its antennae all the while holding what seemed like several short barbed wands trained at each of his friends.

Both the Paratechnologist and his drone radiated power held at the ready.

Other Paratechnologists walking along the docks and waiting for other ships appeared to wear a wide variety of defensive armaments, each uniquely designed and fitted for the owner. He saw graceful Elves moving lithely in shimmering metallic robes and clothing that flowed as loosely as the wind about their shoulders. Several Men and Dwarves rumbled by encased in metallic exoskeletons, holding large barreled cannons loosely in their arms. One Gnome Paratechnologist waiting for a ship to unload nearby appeared to be wrapped entirely in flames.

Yip shook his head in wonderment, trying to wake up from a dream.

Tellanon certainly did not welcome its guests with open arms, he thought as he followed Slate moving down the gangway. Instead, cautiously guarded but cordial efficiency was the primary operative principle on the docks. Following behind Slate and Yip, Wrindanneth held the ship's navigation orb loosely in his right hand, not wishing to leave the *Shrike* pilotable in his absence. Aroganji followed closely behind Wrindanneth, returning the plank to its moorings on the ship with the flick of a finger after he set foot on the solid stone of Tellanon.

The Paratechnologist bowed genially as the party gathered around him. "Welcome back to Tellanon Aroganji, Slate, and Wrindanneth." He looked at each party member in turn as he offered the greeting. Turning his attention to Yip, he added, "Do you have any questions or concerns you would like addressed before you enter the city, Mr. Chuan?"

He bowed to the wizard in response. "Thank you for welcoming us to your wondrous city." Waiting a brief moment, he asked, "With whom should we speak to alert the authorities that the crew of the *Shrike* is no more?"

"This way. I will guide you." The wizard extended his arm forward along the dock where it gently arched and sloped upward toward the city above curving around a monolithic wall of raw rock.

Falling in behind the wizard, the group moved along the stone walkway past the many travelers and tradesman traveling to and fro about the polished stone concourse. As they walked, Yip took time to survey the engines of commerce busily at work transporting goods and materials from one destination to another. Based on what he could see, the mode of transport and handling varied by the value of the goods transferred and the wealth of the conveyer. Most goods were levitated from ships as they arrived and were then escorted to stone buildings that served as staging areas butted up against the solid rock firmament of the island itself. This seemed to be the standard operating procedure. Some goods materialized at staging areas via teleportation, so he could not guess which ships those came from, or even if the ships docked. He conjectured that many goods were transported directly to their intended destination, but, given the amount of security around their arrival, he was unsure of the level of clearance needed to have direct magical access to the city.

Coming from a secluded mountain retreat to a crowded, bustling transdimensional metropolitan cultural and economic center was quite the juxtaposition for him. Moving from a place where little if any trade occurred or was needed, a place where most things of value were given freely, where the outside world was oftentimes only the faintest of memories, to a place where every manner of good and service was available, where beings traveled freely across space and through dimensions, where almost anything imaginable appeared possible, brought a bittersweet smile to his face. All this activity, ingenuity and possibility were exactly what he and his friends needed to work so hard to protect.

A short walk farther brought them to a beautifully formed stone building set against the monolithic rock wall. An engraved sign above the door read, "Magistrate".

He blinked and did a quick double-take. The sign was written in the ideograms of his home in Chang Sen! Chuckling under his breath, he had almost missed the magic of this place at work, so prevalent was its weaving. Of course signs and official postings would conform to the knowledge of the visitor, otherwise business and trade would be hampered.

Before they entered, the Paratechnologist handed Yip a tracking stone. "Please keep this on your person while in the city."

The Paratechnologist then guided them in to a space much larger and more spacious than the small exterior would have indicated. Light poured in from windows that looked directly out over the sky and the land below the island. The large stone concourse was nowhere to be seen.

"How may we be of service today, Adar?" asked a well-modulated disembodied voice.

"The…" Here Adar paused briefly before answering, turning to Wrindanneth as the ship's captain for clarification. "What do you wish to call your party?"

Wrindanneth answered, "The liberators of the *Shrike.*"

Adar nodded. "The liberators of the *Shrike* come on official business."

Here the voice answered quizzically, "And what business may that be?"

Adar made a broad motion indicating that the party was free to speak.

Yip stepped forward, bowing slightly at the waist. "We have come to you after being waylaid by the erstwhile crew of the *Shrike*…"

Before he could finish, the voice cut in, "Erstwhile?"

Yip continued, unperturbed, "The crew is no more."

"And do you have proof?"

Yip nodded shortly. "Proof can be provided."

"In due course," answered the voice.

Here Yip pushed the conversation to follow his own concerns as opposed to the speaker's. "I am not here to provide proof of conquest or for reward. I am here to find out if you have records of any families whose loved ones were lost or harmed by the *Shrike* and its crew."

"Files of the *Shrike*'s atrocities are on hand, but are not held in the public domain."

"If I may, once proper claim is established, I would like to donate my portion of the goods held on the ship, that is, those articles whose rightful owners cannot be found, to the families and survivors of those harmed by the *Shrike* and its crew. There must be those who are in need of succor after losing family members at the hands of brigands."

He heard Slate huff in disagreement with his gesture.

"That can be arranged, Mr. Chuan."

Here the voice paused. "The city and people of Tellanon note your generosity. Return when you have disposed of the goods on the ship and the proceeds will be distributed to those who come forward and provide proof of relationship. I can tell you that there will be many, so your gesture may not have the impact you would wish, but it will be appreciated nonetheless."

Yip bowed again. "Thank you for the assistance."

"Do you wish to give your portion of the reward for the ship's capture as well?"

Before Yip could answer, Wrindanneth stepped forward. "Reward?"

The magistrate's voice took on an official tone, as if reading a document held before him. "Whosoever shall destroy, capture, or confiscate the *Shrike* and its crew shall be entitled to first claim of ownership of all goods and materials aboard said vessel and her crew; shall be entitled to ownership of said vessel and its contents should it be salvaged or salvageable; will be awarded full citizenship to the city of Tellanon with all the attendant rights and privileges associated thereunto; and shall be granted full ownership of a fifth order demesne, should such an estate become available on Tellanon proper with no claimants thereunto, including the receipt of tithe in proportion to such station."

Wrindanneth's mouth hung open while Slate washed his hands, eyes glassy with anticipation in response to this pronouncement. Evidently the *Shrike* had caused far more loss, damage, and turmoil than any of them had realized during its many destructive forays into and around Var'Kera.

Yip's answer snapped both Wrindanneth and Slate out of their reverie. "Yes. I shall give my portion of the reward and annual allotment to the families of those harmed by the actions of the *Shrike*, such as that recompense may be."

"And will you lay claim to the title and ownership of the land?"

"My friends can claim ownership of the land. If citizenship on Tellanon aids in my travels, then I will take that as sole reward."

"So be it," said the voice.

And it was so.

"Please wait while we update the central records."

A bright light shone about each of their shoulders in turn. Yip felt his essence scanned once again.

"You have been given full access to Tellanon as afforded to a citizen of the fifth order. Be advised that citizenship is a privilege that may be revoked at any time should your actions be inappropriate, illegal, or jeopardize the larger city, its interests, or populace at large."

Yip bowed again, saying only, "Thank you," before stepping outside while his friends continued to talk to the magistrate.

A short while later Adar led his friends from the building. Wrindanneth and Slate were practically beaming with pleasure from the recognition and future guarantees.

Adar waved Yip over as they began the climb up toward the city proper. "You have done a good thing, Yip. Your deed will be remembered."

"Master, I have heard it said that some men are high and some are low, that some are holy and others base, that some are saints and some sin, that some are heroes and others rogues."

"What does this mean? Are we not all men?"

Master Wei gazed at him carefully, his eyes looking deeply into Yip's heart. "A man is a man, neither high nor low, the same and both."

"Our lives merely express the choices we make."

He pointed to the dizzying cloud enshrouded peak of Fay Long, the Celestial Courtyard, the highest peak in the K'un Lun, soaring above all the mountains marching toward the horizon beyond the rim of their valley.

"A mountain such as old Fay Long stands tall and proud, soaring above its peers, challenging even the heavens above, but what of his future?"

"What will happen when he is laid low by the passage of time, worn down beneath the unceasing movements of the elements, and he can no longer reach for the sky? What will the people say when he is not even a hill over which to tread? Will the people still speak of his majesty?"

"What is a mountain without relationship to its peers? What is a mountain when it is a hill? Is the mountain low? Or is a mountain just a mountain?"

Turning back to his pupil, Master Wei said, "Reality is for you to see, truth is for you to find, Yip."

Yip gave a slight bow as he walked. "My name and deed need not be remembered. Such honor should be reserved for those who have passed or those who wish the recognition. I want only peace"—and here he paused with a playful glint in his eye as if making a keen joke —"and quiet."

"Unfortunately heroes get little of that, Yip."

"True. And I am glad I am not a hero, just a man, like any other."

Adar looked at him aporetically.

Wrindanneth and Slate sauntered over, their pride evident in their gait. "Full citizenship, a home, a reward, and an annual stipend ta boot!" chortled Slate happily.

"Sometimes good deeds do pay off," added Wrindanneth with a smirk.

Yip looked at his friends. "We are lucky to be alive. Killing those who wished us harm makes us little better."

"Let them enjoy the moment, Yip. It's been a long trip. They deserve some joy, don't you think?" Aroganji's sober tone got Yip's attention.

Recognizing that he had no right to impose his will upon others, Yip assented, agreeing with Aroganji's sentiment. "I, too, am glad that I am here to see the sun rise and set, that we walk together."

Their journey up to the city gates took them past many more ships and oddities amidst the frenzied activity. Yip examined each one closely wondering if any may hold some clue or key to his understanding of what the Cabal planned, where they were hidden, and what he could do to stop them.

Not expecting the rewards discussed inside the magistrate's office to bear fruit so soon, Slate was surprised when Adar spoke next.

"I will take you to your new home. If you will, please hand me your tracking stones. As full citizens, they are no longer needed. The Construct will monitor your comings and goings only as needed."

Slate's face lit up in anticipation. He had not expected to have a new home waiting as part of the reward. He had thought it a mere possibility contingent upon availability. The *Shrike* must have been wreaking havoc for much longer than he had anticipated for the reality to happen so soon.

Ahead of them lay a colossal shimmering gate, its edges limned in blue light, shielded in black stone etched with eldritch runes. Yip could vaguely see buildings and motion on the other side, but discerning details was quite difficult. Looking through the portal was very much like trying to gaze through heat haze on the horizon or trying to peer out from underwater at objects beyond the surface in the distance. The energy signatures of people moving through what he assumed was a large boulevard looked very much like the reflections of light on the surface of a rippling pond—wavy and distorted, flickering and faint. He could only get the vaguest idea of what lay ahead.

The gate, however, was an entirely different matter. Complex, self-referential energy patterns flowed through and across its surface, reinforcing and augmenting its purpose. Powerful magics lay rooted deep within the stone, constantly refreshed and gathering more energy from the limitless wellspring of the island itself.

He had never seen its like.

"Follow me forward. As citizens, you no longer need the stones to pass through the Scimerian Gate to reach the city proper."

Together they walked forward following Adar's lead. As Adar strode through, Yip saw the Gate's surface ripple and reverberate sparking subtle energetic resonances whirling and fluctuating across its surface. Moving through in what appeared to be slow motion, he watched as Adar's distinctive energy patterns became less and less distinct as first his leading boot and hands, then his torso and back, and finally his trailing boot passed through until he, too, became hazy and indistinct on the far side.

With each motion forward, he observed as the magic of the Gate interacted with Adar's essence, ensuring the veracity of his form and the safety of his fellows.

When his turn finally came after following all his friends' crossings, Yip moved forward slowly and ran his hand over the Gate's rippling surface. Energy danced to his touch feeling cool, offering only the slightest resistance. With a sure step, he walked forward feeling the energy rush over his shoulders as if his whole body had dipped through the surface of a cool mountain stream only to reemerge completely dry, skin tingling from the cold.

On the other side, a whole new world opened to his purview.

If the dock had held wonders beyond his expectations, the city beyond the veil offered a total shock to his system.

Looking around in amazement, he gazed upon buildings molded and sculpted from living stone. So vibrant and alive, the architecture seemed to be caught, only fleetingly, in solid form as though the stone had become liquid, briefly frozen in a particular form, and was ready to resume flow at any time. Stonework was lovingly molded to resemble intricate vines and leaves with boughs and stems climbing over and around the many brightly lit shops and residences. The stonework blended beautifully and naturally with the surrounding vegetation in such a way that the built and the grown appeared to have happened together of their own accord. Large trees, bushes, vines, and flowers framed the boulevard in an overhanging tapestry of green, yellow, gold, lavender, and orange.

Everywhere there were lights—the Lights of the many spirits embodied in humanoid form strolling through the streets and alley-ways, the lights of homes and shops suffusing and blending with the white light of the sun, the light from floating globes hanging suspended in the air below the verdant natural trellises framing the faces of those who walked below in many shades and hues.

He felt the currents of all these rich forms and beings thrill through his system in complex waves of shimmering energy. What he felt was, if possible, more beautiful than what he saw.

So much Light, so much life!

So beautiful was Tellanon, its people, and environs that he heard his friends, who had already been here and lived here for a time, gasp in amazement and admiration at the sights.

Watching the reactions of his charges, Adar smiled with their pleasure.

"Let me show you the way to your new home," said Adar in measured tones as he guided them, wending through the traffic.

Moving through the crowds, Yip took the opportunity to learn what he could of Paratechnology, the city's operative mode of function. "What is Paratechnology, Adar? How does it differ from other magics?"

Magical tradition and application varied across cultures, each way of being resulting in unique expressions of arcana, individuals and societies manipulating and interpreting the energy of life based on worldview, ideology, history, and technologies. The various forms and approaches manifested by the human spirit and creativity never ceased to amaze him. Whenever he had the opportunity, even if he could not personally apply the techniques, he tried to learn as much as he could about other ways of interacting with and experiencing the world.

There were magical methods and applications based on causal, logical scientific method, discovery, and systematic practice, those based on spiritual insight and mystic revelation, practices based on faith and divine intervention from higher planes, many involved the interpretation and incarnation of native ancestral wisdom and shaman-istic ritual, while others relied upon tradition and familial knowledge.

Within the broader framework of how magical practice was approached and interpreted, the actual expression of magic ranged just as widely as the views behind its creation. There was magic expressed in song, in dance, in semantics and prestidigitation, through direct communion, channeling, visionary experience, formulae, and elaborate ritual. Magic was embodied in different objects, traditions and schools, in arts of Light and Darkness, in artifacts and symbols, in magical branches and schools like alchemy, thaumaturgy, evocation, divination, in religion and theology, philosophy, epistemology, philology, and ontology, along with many other approaches beyond counting. The manifold forms and expressions of magic were only limited by the scope of the imagination.

He waited for Adar's response, patiently observing the passersby as they walked with their guide while slowly navigating through the bustling streets past the magically formed shops, homes, and green spaces.

"Paratechnology is, I think, a phenomenon relatively unique to Ea'ae, excluding its spread beyond our bounds by our agents and influence."

"Unlike many other planets, magical tradition and lore run deep in our world and are native to this place. Growing and evolving in magical environs, our people developed great skill and knowledge of the surrounding world through time, manipulating the external and internal directly via magic. However, as we branched out from our home and began to explore the wider cosmos, early pioneers came to realize that there are many other ways to interact with and interpret the world around them. Paratechnology is an offshoot of this unending ideological cross-pollination."

"There are whole societies, worlds, and empires spread throughout the macroverse that know nothing of magic. However, many of these same people are capable of feats that would astound even the most powerful of archmages through their applied knowledge of the world around them and its governing laws. Despite not being able to directly manipulate and command the fundamental forces encompassing their existence through will, these people manage to prosper and thrive."

"Paratechnology brings the wisdom of these non-magical cultures, those based on the direct and indirect application and understanding of physical law, together with magical understanding capable of the direct manipulation and interaction with physical existence, into a profoundly capable and flexible system of practical, applied knowledge."

Occasionally glancing at Yip as they walked, Adar continued, "Although our world historically knows little of science without magic, Paratechnology is a marriage of magic and science. Throughout its existence, Tellanon has served both as a repository for our knowledge and as a staging area for our explorations throughout the multiverse. The continued growth of commerce and cultural transfer on Tellanon over time has also fostered our knowledge and development."

"Paratechnology is the logical outcome of this growth."

When Adar finished, Yip gave a truncated bow, not wishing to break stride as they headed along one spiraling road after another following the massive wall surrounding the edge of the city. "You and your kind have brought much to Ea'ae, Adar. I wish you continued prosperity and hope that your gifts continue to benefit and enrich the lives of all the people of Ea'ae."

"Thank you, Yip."

Again, he offered a short bow.

Much of the land around the city's perimeter alternated between green space, gardens, and open formal plazas for congregation and enjoyment. Marvels continued to abound in these areas as well. Many of the open spaces were actually much larger than the land would allow. Paratechnologists bent, molded and expanded the fabric of existence, at times creating full pocket dimensions and at others expanding the defined limits of space within certain contexts, to make significantly more room than would otherwise have been available. As a result, the city grounds were open and expansive despite the limitations in spatial extent imposed by the island's original geography. Quite a few of these open areas were terraced and dedicated to growing plants of every form and variety. So large were some of these spaces that, as Yip passed by, he had the impression of walking by a large pastoral vista ready to be explored. He could, however, see the traceries of magic holding the formations in place lest normal space rush to reassert itself.

Walking past one such particularly intriguing natural area, complete with a gurgling stream flowing into a pond surrounded by rolling hills, large trees, and picnicking families, he asked, "How do you mold and separate space in such a way as to maintain a stable arrangement?"

He was quite curious, perhaps not for the reasons Adar might think, but he was curious nonetheless. Until now, he had thought only masters of his own tradition were capable of molding, separating, and reforming space in such a way on Ea'ae. Dividing and reforming space was largely how the K'un Lun had deliberately isolated themselves over the centuries.

"As you are aware," Adar said, framing the statement in such a way since he was in fact not sure whether Yip or his companions were in fact aware, "both the world around us and the universe at large are composed of many dimensions. Space, the very fabric of existence, is in fact composed of three primary elements—space itself which on a microcosmic scale is constantly reforming, reemerging, and reconfiguring itself from the possible, or magic; magic, which binds together, delineates, guides, and expresses the potential, that is space, time, dimensionality, and all of existence; and time which provides a demarcation for the passing of events and marks the relative degree of dimensional curvature in multidimensional space. There are, of course, other dependent dimensions, variables, and possibilities that constitute and give rise to other expressions of reality within this broad framework."

At this point, Yip noticed Slate give Wrindanneth a look of complete befuddlement, but otherwise, he made no comment.

Unaware, however, Adar went on, "So the areas you see are normally composed or defined by a certain spatial extent. Magic itself binds that space together as it moves and shifts microcosmically with time. Concurrently, magic can be used to both expand the extent of the spatial arrangement and bind it together through time in a new stable configuration."

"Ah," said Slate nodding with certainty when the look in his eyes said anything but. "'Tis all clear ta me now."

Wrindanneth managed to hold back both a snort and a laugh with an iron will.

Aroganji did not manage to hold back the glare he directed at Slate.

A few minutes later, after entering a residential area composed of small, well-tended cottages, cobbled paths, and natural gardens, the street overhung by stately trees of every shape and sort, Adar said, "Here we are!" as they stopped in front of a tidy two-story home surrounded by a low cobbled wall covered with hanging plants and multicolored lichens. Sheltered by mature trees and a lush garden, the cottage nestled within the folds of its environs, a welcoming abode of wood and stone.

Yip felt that the house itself had been empty for some time. He sensed few traces of living activity inside, although the surrounding lawn and the cleanliness of the exterior belied those feelings.

"Let me show you inside!" With a flick of his wrist, Adar opened the door by a quick motion of his hand. As he crossed the threshold, a warm, feminine voice intoned, "Welcome, Adar! I see my new owners have arrived!"

As the voice began its welcome, Yip heard Slate exclaim, "What th—?"

By way of answer, Adar responded, "Your house, like all the others, is tied directly into the Construct. You need not worry about being monitored. As citizens you are protected from regular surveillance at home. Your house and its Aspect will be able to answer most questions you may have about the city and its goings on. You need only inquire."

Slate cleared his throat. "Is there a way ta turn it off? I prefer my house simple and quiet. Besides, I already have one inanimate object constantly talkin' ta me. I don't need another."

"Aye," Adar nodded. "Like most of the Construct's functionality, you need only ask."

Here Wrindanneth chimed in, directing a wicked grin toward Slate, "Besides, if we have an automaton or a simulacrum to constantly answer all of our questions, what would there be to bicker about? Without it, we can all be right all the time, and never agree on anything!"

Slate merely grumbled in reply.

While Adar began showing them around the house, Yip heard Slate mutter, "If I wanted a talkin' house I would've shacked up with a clan o' singin' and dancin' faeries!"

The house had an appealing open layout, filling the lower rooms with rich, vibrant natural light and affording multiple views of the surrounding greenery. There was a study, ready to be stocked with Aroganji's and Wrindanneth's many books, a small kitchen, and a living area on the first floor. Off the living room, on the side of the house perpendicular to the road, a small solarium looked out on a small cloistered garden framed by a stone wall separating their cottage from the next. Out of the kitchen window, Yip could see a small porch overlooking a laboratory and greenhouse nestled between flowering plants and trees. The upstairs was simple, with three small bedrooms large enough to hold small cots and a few accessories along with a common wash room at the end of the hall.

"You will not need to bolt or clean your home, nor will you need to carry a key or tend the lawn unless you so choose. Otherwise, the Aspect will coordinate the day-to-day functioning and maintenance of the house."

Here Slate's mood shifted. "Now ya're talkin'! I'm beginnin' ta like tha sound o' this system!"

Aroganji laughed. "More free time is always welcomed. Eh, Slate?"

Slate joined Aroganji in laughter, the sound echoing from deep inside his trunk. "More free time means more time fer beer! Brewin' and drinkin' are their own rewards, I say!"

Wrindanneth smirked. "Maybe you can use the laboratory in the back for your brewing experiments, lest we all suffer the consequences of your work."

"And risk contaminatin' my brew with yer foul concoctions? I'd rather drink toad venom!"

"You'd probably be better off, Slate," was Wrindanneth's deadpan answer.

Changing the subject, concerned that his friends would persist in their bickering, Yip broke in, "I am sure Adar has many other responsibilities to attend. We should let him finish his business here."

Aroganji nodded while Wrindanneth and Slate made a temporary truce in their war of words.

Holding back his own smile, Adar continued his instructions. "Should you need to reach anyone for information or assistance, you need only ask the Aspect to contact the party in question for you directly. In addition to providing information about almost any facet of the city and its store of knowledge, the Aspect can also update you on its core functionalities and features should you inquire."

As he turned to leave, Adar added, "Should you need assistance from me or any other Paratechnologist, you have only to ask."

"Thank you for help and generosity," said Yip bowing at the waist.

"You have been most helpful," echoed Aroganji.

"Ya're welcome ta come over an' have a beer anytime, friend!" added Slate enthusiastically.

"Aye, just be sure to bring your own for your own safety!" finished Wrindanneth.

Slate's growl was his only reply.

With a nod of his head and a final wave of his hand, Adar stepped out of the house with a smile and shut the door behind him.

Standing alone once more after coming so far, their next steps uncertain, Aroganji suddenly felt quite empty-handed, as though they needed direction. After a moment reorienting himself, he said, "If this is going to be our home, we should get started making it feel like we live here."

"Slate, why don't you, Yip, and Wrindanneth go and gather our things from the old home and bring them here so we can get started moving in? Once we get our possessions unloaded from your bag, Slate, we can also see about selling the goods from the *Shrike* we have stored in there as well. I will use the Aspect to contact our landlord and let her know that we will no longer need the space."

Before going on, he spoke aloud to the Aspect, "Aspect, resume dormancy."

"As you wish, Aroganji," was the happy reply.

"That thing is a bit disconcerting," said Wrindanneth. "I don't like the idea of something watching our every activity, even if what we do is not monitored or reported."

"If I wanted ta be watched all tha time, I'd stay at home with my Mum!"

Aroganji made a quick gesticulation and incantation, shielding them from being overheard. "Perhaps we can find out more information about the Cabal when we go talk to Hoyt about selling the magic items from the crew of the *Shrike*."

Slate nodded matter-of-factly. "If anyone here can help, it'll be Hoyt."

Wrindanneth laughed. "If he doesn't send us on a wild goose chase to start!"

Only knowing of him as a friend and contact of Aroganji, Wrindanneth, and Slate, Yip asked for clarification, "Who exactly is Hoyt?"

"Hoyt is a dealer in oddities, junk, and assorted *found* objects, if you take my meaning," answered Wrindanneth.

"Hoyt owns a shop by the docks where he buys, sells, and trades treasures from all over the known universe, and some places beyond as well." Here Wrindanneth chuckled.

"He also keeps his ear to the ground. Oftentimes, he hears news before the crew members docking a ship even disembark."

"And, last but not least, any trip to Hoyt always leads to some type of adventure!"

"Aye." Slate's face broke into a wide grin, barely visible beneath his thick beard. "If ya're lookin' fer somethin' ta do or want ta know about somethin' that needs doin', talk ta Hoyt. He'll set yer feet on tha right path."

"They are correct, Yip," added Aroganji. "If we hadn't followed Hoyt's tip to track down those bandits, we never would have met you. So our friendship is due, at least in part, to Hoyt's advice."

"I owe him my gratitude," said Yip gravely. "Hoyt certainly sounds like an individual I should meet," he added, eager to be moving forward in any way he could after the Cabal.

Slate laughed again, his mood still light. "He's a wily one that Hoyt. Ya'd never guess it ta talk ta him, but he has more tricks up his sleeve than a troupe o' carnival magicians!"

As evening fell about their new home, the dusk's gloaming providing soft interludes between the brightly lit posts marking their new street, Yip, Slate, and Wrindanneth returned just after the last of the sun's rays fell beneath the ramparts of the massive wall surrounding the city.

Opening the door first, Slate was glad to hear that the Aspect no longer greeted their entrance. Apparently Aroganji had maintained that detail while they were away. Perhaps he had quieted the thing down for good.

Slate could always hope. Once the Aspect was reactivated, maybe he could ask the Aspect how to quiet his axe. Then there would be two less talking objects floating around.

A Dwarf needed his peace and quiet after all.

As Yip walked in the door, Aroganji's voice greeted them energetically. "Welcome! I spoke with Joanna. I just have to settle up with her tomorrow and we will be rid of our rental."

"Good riddance," muttered Slate. "'Bout tha only thing that place was good fer was losin' money. What sound minded Dwarf ever rented property?"

Quick to seize the opportunity, Wrindanneth retorted, "What Dwarf has a sound mind?"

"Enough, you two," Aroganji admonished matter-of-factly. "We need to get our gear together before the morning so we can be about our business."

"Aye. Let's be about it then," nodded Slate in agreement as he quickly forgot Wrin's teasing.

The party spent the next few minutes unpacking their belongings from Slate's bottomless bag. Surprisingly enough after an hour of continual unpacking, the house appeared almost as empty as it had before their arrival. None of them had any furniture to speak of since they were constantly on the move. What furniture they needed had been provided as part of their rental.

In lieu of sharing a cramped room, Yip offered to sleep in the solarium so that each of his friends could have a place to themselves. While Wrindanneth, Aroganji, and Slate each claimed a bedroom upstairs and prepared for sleep, he laid out his bedroll beneath the clear glass, enjoying the feel of warmth the room radiated after a full day's exposure to the sun. Standing back up after adjusting his blankets, he gazed up through the arching glass framework, taking in the many stars scattered throughout the heavens, their silvery light providing an ethereal luminescence to the house's sheltered garden.

If ever he had the time, he could come to like it here.

Yip woke with the birds as the sun crested the horizon, purple shadows and long ochre rays commingling across the city. While his friends made ready for their trip to see Hoyt for more information regarding the Cabal, he sat watching the play of light and shadow on the grass and leaves, the plants and flowers, and the lichen and rocks in the garden, his breath as still as the shadows, letting the energy of the new day flow through and around him.

Rich smells of frying meat and sautéing onions finally drew Aroganji and Wrindanneth from their bedrooms and into the kitchen where Slate prepared a hearty breakfast. Yip joined them, ready to begin the day in earnest, hoping that he would learn some information that would aid them in their quest.

"Will Hoyt's shop be open this early in the morning?" asked Yip.

"Ta be honest, I don't think I've ever seen Hoyt leave his shop," replied Slate. "I know he beds in tha back. He seems as much a part o' tha place as his wares."

Wrindanneth nodded, his mouth full of eggs and sausage. "Seems like the things Hoyt needs come to him."

Yip nodded sagely, a slight smile on his face. "A man who lives in accord, needs little and wants less. All his desires are met because he has none. All his needs are met because he has few."

Wrindanneth arched an eyebrow, taking a moment between bites. "I think that is the most apt description of Slate I've ever heard!"

More concerned with his meal than his friend's taunts, Slate responded flatly as he chewed on a loaf of bread, "A Dwarf's happy if he has an axe in his hand and an enemy ta slay." Reaching over his shoulder and patting Duraeleon firmly, he looked at Wrindanneth significantly and added, "Both can be arranged."

"Hurry up and finish, you two. We need to get moving," Aroganji was in no mood for their usual bickering.

"Off to save the world!" Wrindanneth popped up from his stool, wiping his robes of crumbs.

"Aye and ta make some coin ta boot!" added Slate, patting the bag with the items from the *Shrike* hanging at his side.

They left the house together, eager to be off and about their business, the air of excitement and adventure leaving them heady with anticipation as they made their way toward the trade quarter. On the way,

Slate and Wrindanneth discussed their bargaining strategies—how to present their wares, what they expected to get for prices, and what they should keep. Yip shared in their enthusiasm, if not their intent, hoping to glean some information to help them track down and defeat the Cabal. Aroganji, too, joined in the group's exhilaration, but he held his excitement in check knowing that they had not fully identified the magical items they had recovered and therefore and no real indication of their true worth.

Walking through the streets past the sculpted buildings and lush greenery, Yip watched the faces of those he passed, reading their *li*, feeling their health and state of mind wash over him like a gentle breeze. By and large, the beings here, for people would be too limited a term for the many races that abided and traded on Tellanon, lived in peace and happiness relatively untroubled by their day-to-day concerns and stresses. To be sure, along the way to Hoyt's shop he passed many beings of power, many hardened warriors and mages whose time between and among the stars had been anything but peaceful, but almost all walked and carried themselves hopefully, confident in their futures, knowing the morrow would bring a bright, secure day.

This outlook told him that these residents had not yet encountered or knew of the Cabal.

Hoyt's shop was situated on the edge of the trade quarter near the docks, a location that afforded ready access to both information and goods. Many of the buildings nearby appeared to be warehouses— some derelict, others in use. Hoyt's building was therefore a bit out of the way relative to other businesses dealing in direct client trade in the quarter, but Yip felt that was probably how Hoyt wanted it.

The store itself blended in perfectly with the various structures and trade activity moving in and around the buildings. That is to say, with the exceptions of a faded, tilting sign over the door reading, "Hoyt's – Oddities, Found Goods, and Sundries" and a few assorted items laying on the ground beneath the eaves of two large oak trees shading the storefront, namely a rusty wagon wheel, a few potted plants, some stacked crates, and an oaken water barrel, the shop could have been an old office or outbuilding for one of the neighboring warehouses. The windows appeared dusty and full of cobwebs which struck him as out of place in a city where almost everything appeared to receive significant attention. Walking forward, he could see that the front entry was left ajar behind a screened door that appeared neglected and in need of paint, angling slightly off true, barely held on its hinges.

"Ah! Brings a tear ta my eye, she does," Slate commented to no one in particular as they made their way toward the dilapidated front door.

Yip heard a muffled snort from Duraeleon in its holster.

"Let's see where Hoyt leads us today!" Wrindanneth was obviously excited as well.

Moving ahead, Slate whispered to Yip, "Ya never can tell what ya'll get outta a meetin' with Hoyt, or where ya'll end up!"

Aroganji went in first, the screen door protesting the affront on its repose. Yip took up the rear, following Slate and Wrindanneth.

As his eyes adjusted to the gloom, for little light seemed to make it through the dust and cobwebs, Yip heard a slow drawl issue from behind the counter to his left.

"Well if it ain't tha Four gracin' my establishment!"

Turning to the sound, Hoyt's features appeared nondescript in the gloom—slightly unkempt brown hair framed a face on the trailing end of middle-age, smile lines surrounded eyes as brown as the burnished wooden display case beneath his hands. On first inspection, Hoyt appeared to be the most ordinary item in a space filled with oddities from the world over and beyond.

Such impressions were anything but true.

Yip could feel well-hidden power burning beneath the small man's exterior, like the sun on a sweltry summer day waiting for a break in the clouds to shine forth. Even so, power shone out from behind the veil.

All around, complex weavings of spells and arcana laced the air. The myriad expressions of magical goods and curiosities added multiple layers to the shop and its owner's intrinsic mystery.

"Aroganji, Wrindanneth, and Slate, good ta see ya back so soon! And you must be Yip! Welcome, welcome!"

Yip bowed. "I have heard much of you, friend Hoyt."

"And I you!"

Yip flicked his eyes briefly toward his friends, not sure how Hoyt would have heard of him.

Hoyt chuckled. "Don't worry. I haven't been keepin' tabs on ya. Y'all've been all over the Projections these past couple o' days."

"Projections?" asked Yip still confused.

Hoyt waved a hand and a three-dimensional representation of a scene showing the arrival of several diplomats to Tellanon appeared above his counter. "The news, daily updates, and what not. Y'all've gained quite a bit of notoriety by bringin' the *Shrike* ta justice!"

Here Hoyt smiled slyly. "Whether ya wanted it or not, I reckon."

Yip performed a mental shrug. The last thing he wanted was more attention drawn to himself lest he and his cause be discovered. At least there would be no information available linking him to being a priest.

"So what brings ya ta my fine establishment today?"

Here Aroganji stepped forward. "We have goods to trade and information to seek."

Hoyt nodded, washing his hands in anticipation. "Let's see 'em. Then we'll see ta yer questions."

Slate spent the next few minutes rummaging through his bottomless bag until the counter was eventually covered by the odds and ends they had retrieved from the *Shrike* and deemed of some value. The cloak, the Elven boots, the archer's bow, the rings, some potions, and a few other oddities covered the majority of Hoyt's counter.

Finally, heaving in effort as he pulled out the fallen warrior's armor and claymore from his bag, Slate wiped his hands in satisfaction. "That about does it!"

"Oh! Almost forgot!" Reaching into a small pouch on his belt, Slate put down a crumpled piece of parchment containing the list he and Wrindanneth had compiled of all the other trade goods found on the ship.

Hoyt raised an eyebrow. "Looks like a king's ransom ya got there! Anythin' else?"

There was a momentary pause while everyone waited before Wrindanneth reached under his cloak and laid the R'yn Daer's dagger on the counter as well.

"This is not for sale. I want you to tell me what you can of it, its history, and its powers."

Lifting his eyes appraisingly at the finely wrought workmanship and obvious power of the blade, Hoyt let out a shrill whistle. "That's a mighty fine dagger ya got there, Wrindanneth, mighty fine indeed!"

Wrindanneth nodded curtly. "Aye."

"Ya're sure you don't want ta part with it?"

Wrindanneth's answer remained the same. "Aye."

Hoyt shook his head. "A pity. Ya could fetch a small fortune with tha right buyer."

Wrindanneth shook his head. "I'm sure I could."

Seeing Wrindanneth's reluctance to change his position, Hoyt washed his hands eagerly and began. "We'll start with the trade goods. I'll have ta see 'em in person mind ya, but I should be able to give ya a general estimate."

Before Hoyt began his counting, Yip spoke up. "A portion of those goods' availability, or value, is contingent upon whether or not the families of the rightful owners and heirs can be found to claim them."

"Tryin' ta do the good deed, eh?" Hoyt nodded. "That's always welcome. Rights of salvage say they're yours, however, if not taken illegally or without justification."

Yip nodded. "Families may depend upon the return of these items as well."

"The return of your portion," Slate amended.

"The return of their portion," Yip asserted.

Muttering to himself and counting on his fingers, while the party ironed out their differences of opinion, Hoyt began his tally. "Three faerie spun Androsian rugs…twelve kegs of honeyed dew nectar and assorted spirits…a stack of Dragon, basilisk, terala, gryphon, manticore, and various other beast and monster skins…"

He paused momentarily to ask, "I'm assumin' y'all'll keep the gold and gems?"

"Aye," answered Slate. "Tha list is just a full accountin'. We intend ta keep tha currency and any magical items o' worth." Here he looked at Yip. "Unless someone comes forth ta claim their portion, or we decide ta trade fer somethin' else o' course."

"Of course," replied Hoyt. "Let's see, a box of ancient Flannish imperial texts…several crates of fine spices and herbs…assorted Dwarven forged armor and weapons…"

Here Hoyt mumbled off into incoherence while continuing his summations.

A few minutes later, he looked up brightly, done with his brief appraisal. "The goods alone appear ta be worth roughly two and a half million imperials."

Slate whistled. "That's enough coin ta ransom a Thanedom!"

Wrindanneth smiled in delight.

"Perhaps kingdoms *were* ransomed for such riches!" Yip then added, "The families of those harmed by the *Shrike* will know at least some security."

Lifting his eyebrows again, for he seldom knew of adventurers to so willingly part with their earnings, Hoyt said nothing.

"And the magical artifacts?" prompted Aroganji.

"Ya've got quite a collection there I must say. If their gear is any indication, the lot ya ran in with must've been formidable, formidable indeed."

"Ya missed a rousin' good fight, Hoyt! I was laid out fer days!" Slate's pride at his injuries struck Yip as rather odd, but he was a Dwarf after all.

"Sounds like it. Maybe y'all can fill me in after we finish our business?"

"Gladly," Wrindanneth relished the thought.

Hoyt stood up straight, clearing his throat as he pulled out a thick, gnarled ebony wand he had stuffed through the cord he had tied tightly around his waist.

To Yip's eyes, the wand was alive with power, almost blindingly incandescent, though its strength, like Hoyt's, was masked.

With a slow wave of his wand back and forth over the items, Hoyt began examining the gear.

Once again, he started mumbling to himself as he worked, "Oh…I see… That's odd… Aha!" One observation followed the next until his divinations were complete.

"As I said, quite a collection ya got there! Quite a collection!"

"And?" asked Wrindanneth eager as a boy at a Midsummer festival.

Hoyt picked up one of the rings; the band was etched in arcane runes and sigils and appeared to be made of a translucent green stone.

Yip thought it was the one worn by the captain, but he could not recall.

"This little gem magnifies the strength and effect of whatever spell the wearer casts." Here Aroganji and Wrindanneth turned to each other in excitement, as if they had won their childhood's delight at the fair.

Hoyt nodded appreciably. "This other ring"—he picked up the ebony band that seemed to drink the ambient energies radiating around them—"appears ta lessen the effects of spells cast upon tha bearer. I would guess that it absorbs a portion of whatever fell magics are cast, but the full mechanism o' how it functions is unfamiliar ta me."

Slate harrumphed while Wrin and Aroganji looked at each other again; each thinking of how the two rings could be put to good use.

"The armor and sword seem ta help guide the wearer's actions in combat so that his movements are more deft and accurate. The sword is also heavily enchanted ta harm creatures immune ta mundane weapons."

"Too bad tha armor's big enough ta fit an ox," grunted Slate.

Hoyt smiled. "Perhaps we can work out a trade then. I have some enchanted Dwarven forged armor that should fit ya with only slight adjustments. It doesn't help guide yer movements, but it adds a bit o' strength ta yer blows and helps shield ya from hostile strikes, charms, and spells. It'll also grant ya freedom o' movement as though ya weren't wearin' any armor at all."

"Please! Don't put such terrifying visions in my mind!" Wrindanneth's wicked grin begged Slate to respond.

All business, ignoring Wrindanneth's insult, Slate nodded, ready to begin haggling. "Aye. Per'aps."

Wrindanneth shook his head. "And perhaps he'll never take it off to clean himself, either!"

Slate ignored him.

"This bow is a wonder, although I would not recommend keepin' it. Bows like this are intended only fer Elves and their kith and kin. If an Elf saw ya usin' it, there may be a bit o' confusion until ya sorted things out, if ya take my meanin'."

Hoyt looked at them gravely as he said this, the seriousness of his tone not lost on the group. "It appears ta channel the user's energy inta magical projectiles ta great effect."

Yip nodded, remembering the archer's prowess.

"None o' us use a bow anyway, Hoyt." Slate grinned, adding, "I prefer ta meet my enemies face ta face, if ya take my meanin'."

Hoyt nodded. "Then I'd recommend y'all take it ta the Elven embassy. There may be a bit o' reward fer it there."

"The potions are nothin' too interestin'. A few healin' tonics, a couple of mana regeneration potions, and several draughts intended ta mask or disguise the wearer. Looks like one creates the guise ya wish via illusion, one polymorphs the drinker inta another humanoid form, and the last turns the drinker inta an inanimate object of yer choosin'."

Nodding sagely, he continued as he held up the finely wrought boots. "The boots give the wearer the alacrity and dexterity o' an Elf."

Noting Slate's shaggy eyebrows raised in interest, he added with a smile, "Which could be o' some use ta a Dwarf."

"This cloak acts very much like the ring, protectin' the bearer from magical attacks. I think it also helps the wearer avoid other types of damage as well."

Looking around, Hoyt said, "I think that's the lot."

"Whoa, whoa!" protested Wrin pointing to his dagger.

Hoyt smiled again, knowing full well Wrindanneth's excitement and ready to have a bit of sport with it.

"Oh, that. Hmm..."

He paused again, teasing Wrindanneth with his delay. "What ya have there is quite the artifact, Wrindanneth. Seems ta me that this item was made by a bein' of some power. Seems extraplanar ta me. If ya decide ta keep it, I'd take care ta make sure the original owner doesn't come back and try ta reclaim it!"

Warning given, he continued, "From what I can tell, the dagger draws on the elemental power of air and water ta strike down foes.

The dagger holds its secrets tightly, however. From my readin', the power o' the dagger grows with the stature o' the bearer. As formidable as it is now, it'll get more so over time."

He laughed, adding, "Assumin' ya do."

Only raising an eyebrow, too eager to hear more or play into Hoyt's hands, Wrindanneth remained silent.

"I think some of its powers are triggered by key words or gestures. If ya remember how it was used against ya in that battle, ya may have yer first clue as ta how ta unlock its secrets."

Wrindanneth could barely contain his excitement, which brought a smile to Yip's face unused as he was to Wrin's outward displays of happiness. "Thank you, Hoyt. Thank you!"

"Nothin' ta thank me fer, ya're the one who earned it."

Hoyt gazed at them each in turn. "Seems ta me that much o' this gear could be quite useful ta those in yer vocation. If y'all ain't interested, I can think o' several folks who'd pay a pretty coin fer some o' these items, myself included. As usual, I'm also willin' ta trade if there's somethin' ya're after."

"Gives us a minute to decide what we'd like to do," replied Aroganji.

They walked back outside together to discuss their options and choose what was the best course to take.

Wrindanneth leaned against one of the rickety crates, Slate stood by the door eager to go back in and take a look at Hoyt's wares, while Yip and Aroganji stood out of the sun beneath the shade of the two broad trees.

Wrindanneth was the first to speak. "I plan on keeping the dagger, if there was ever any doubt about it, even if there is some risk to owning it."

Yip nodded. "You should. We will need what aid we can find in the times to come. For my part, I feel these items have seen and, more likely than not, created much suffering and dismay. I would be glad to know that we could put them toward a positive end. Whatever you feel you need or that will help us in our quest, we should keep and use or trade for items that will aid us in our efforts."

Slate nodded. "I'd like ta keep tha boots. If puttin' on boots that make me prance like an Elf can help guide my axe, then so be it. I'd also like ta see what Hoyt has in tha way o' armor fer trade. I'm keen ta learn a bit more about tha enchanted Dwarven armor he mentioned. With Duraeleon at my side," he said, patting his axe, "I don't need tha warrior's great sword."

"Although Wrindanneth could make use of them as well, if no one objects, I will take the rings," said Aroganji knowing he needed improvements in equipment and protection as well.

Wrindanneth nodded in agreement, having taken more than his fair share.

"Anything for you, Yip?" asked Aroganji.

Yip shook his head.

Slate spoke up, "That leaves us with tha archer's bow, tha arms man's sword, tha potions, and tha protective cloak."

Yip added, "One of you should take the cloak. Wrindanneth or Slate could use its protection since Aroganji's ring seems to offer similar affects." Yip's primary concern was that his friends be as well protected and effective as possible.

Slate spoke then. "If this armor does as Hoyt says, then perhaps ya should take tha cloak, Wrin. After all, all ya have ta protect yerself is yer own skill." Slate smirked, adding, "We all know how much that'll aid ya! At least I have my armor."

Wrindanneth scoffed, "Which shows the difference in our relative levels of skill."

"We will trade the sword then and return the bow to the Elven embassy," said Yip.

"Since none o' us is a thief, we should keep tha potions as well. I'm about as sneaky as a boulder rollin' downhill." Slate's words rang true and brought a smile to his friends' faces with the thought of Dwarven clandestine activities.

"Agreed," replied Wrindanneth, heading back in to the shop through the squeaky door.

Hoyt greeted them with his usual smile, not because he smiled for everyone, but because over time he had genuinely come to like these three, now four, and wanted them to remain safe and do well. He remembered his younger days when he had traveled far and wide in search of adventure and fortune. Although his storefront belied it, he had been quite successful at both.

"Y'all make up yer minds?"

Wrindanneth answered for the group. "We have. We're going to keep everything except the sword and armor. On your advice, we'll return the bow. Slate wants to inspect the armor you mentioned for trade."

Wrin asked, "What do you consider fair value on the sword? What do you have to trade that you think could be of use to us?"

"Well, that depends on where ya're goin' and what ya're doin'. Let me show Slate this armor and we'll discuss yer options. I'll be right back."

Hoyt turned around and walked through a door and into the back of his store. Yip assumed he used the area as a storage and living space judging by what little he could see and sense through the open door shielded as it was magically. A few minutes later, Hoyt returned with a bulky bundle wrapped in white cloth held lightly in his arms.

"Here we are!" He unwrapped the cloth to reveal a brightly burnished suit of armor that appeared to have a weight and solidity to its presence that contradicted the ease with which Hoyt handled the bundle.

Yip felt the air around the armor condense in the set's presence and power.

Stepping forward, Slate lovingly ran his fingers over the pieces of plate laid out before him after Hoyt fully unwrapped the bundle. "A real jewel this is, Hoyt."

Slate spent some time examining the markings and decorations etched in the armor's surface, going over each piece, judging the weight and feel, and appreciating its quality. "Tha runes on this tell quite a tale, Hoyt. Dagron Iron Beard himself made this in tha pit o' Amakar!"

Incredulous, Slate shook his head in confusion. "Ya're offerin' this as trade fer tha warrior's armor? That's more a gift than a trade!"

Hoyt smiled. "I seldom get Dwarves in here ta trade. Perhaps y'all can make use o' it instead."

Slate's voice rang with sincerity and emotion as he answered,

"Though I doubt yer claims, fer I've heard many a Dwarf speak o' yer merits, my clan would be honored ta hold such a treasure, Hoyt."

"I've got a feelin' ya may need somethin' like this in due time, friend."

Seeing Slate's heartfelt response, Aroganji spoke up. "Perhaps we should include the sword in the trade as well?"

"Nonsense!" Hoyt puffed up. "That thing was just gatherin' dust in the back. No one even bothered ta inquire about it in all the time I've had it!"

He neglected to mention he had yet to bring it out or speak of having it since he had uncovered the set some years ago.

He really did have a feeling these boys were going to need all the help they could get. He had never seen someone quite like their new friend, but he had heard tell of folks who might be like him, that is if his memory served him right and it usually did.

"Will you take the sword as a gift then?" asked Aroganji.

"I've offered fair trade fer that armor, don't ya think?"

"More than fair," answered Aroganji. "Your advice and guidance have always been welcome as well. You have always treated us fairly, more than fair, in fact. We would like to show the same consideration to you. Even with the sword, we still are in your debt and you know it."

While Aroganji bartered with Hoyt to take the sword, Slate was lost in reverie. A piece of armor from a Dur'kazak! How could he have gotten so lucky? Surely Hoyt understated the piece's capabilities.

When Slate finally recovered himself and the room returned to focus, he put his fist across his chest and bowed to Hoyt formally from the waist. "Ya've done us a great service, Hoyt. Returnin' a treasure like this ta tha Dunédâne is an honor without tellin'. Tha sons o' my sons shall know yer name and deeds."

Hoyt chuckled. "Maybe y'all send 'em ta my shop ta check out my wares, then!" Brushing off further comment, he said, "Let's see that sword."

Slate passed the greatsword over the counter to him, its blade easily two-thirds Hoyt's height.

"Seems ta me the only one here in need o' gear is you, Yip," said Hoyt matter-of-factly.

Yip bowed. "I have too much as it is, Hoyt. Thank you for the kindness of your attention. All I seek from you is information."

"What're ya after?"

"I seek to find and destroy an enemy beyond my reach, beyond my skill to defeat, and save all I hold dear in so doing."

Hoyt nodded matter-of-factly, as if such things were easily attained, common matters of everyday concern. "Sounds simple enough. What're ya after?"

"The Cabal." Yip knew from his friends and by reading Hoyt's *li* that he was one who could be trusted with this information as would be his response. Even if he heard quite a bit, Hoyt did not pass all of what he heeded on to other ears.

Hoyt whistled. "Y'all're gonna need more than that armor ta help yer cause then!"

"What can you tell me about the Cabal, Hoyt? Do you know where they hide, to whom they give their counsel, or how to defeat them?"

Hoyt spat, "The sun has burned brighter every day since that lot was banished from our world."

Yip nodded. "But the light of many other stars has grown dim since their departure. The time has come to root them out and cleanse the universe of their foul taint. Even now they seek to break the seals that keep our world safe. They have already mustered the strength necessary to briefly overcome the seals for a time and sow their revenge on my home. I fear what comes next."

Hoyt nodded, muttering, "I've heard that very thing said myself. Incursions left unchallenged, death and destruction in their wake."

"What can we do, Hoyt? How shall we proceed?"

"I can't tell ya how ta destroy the Cabal, Yip. We couldn't do it fully long ago, and I don't think we could do it now. Many o' Ea'ae's champions no longer call this world home. Whole armies came together ta stem their strength, forces from many nations and races united against their evil, and still they were not destroyed completely. I don't know how one man"—here he surveyed the party—"or four, could do what whole legions could not."

"Is there nothing you can recommend?" asked Yip imploringly.

"Hold yer horses there, friend." Hoyt's voice was resolute, his face firm. "I don't know how ta defeat them, nor where they're hidin', nor what they're up ta besides no good, but I may be able to start ya on the right path if y'all'll hear me out. Yer chances may not be good, but the life o' adventure's always a gamble."

Yip nodded.

"How d'ya defeat an enemy, Yip?"

Yip paused, unsure what direction Hoyt was taking. "By turning their strength to weakness; by converting their greatest asset into their greatest liability; by countering and redirecting their energies and the forces around them against them when the opportunity presents itself, acting when they do not move in accordance with the energies of creation."

"And what is tha Cabal's greatest strength?"

"They can bend and warp the energy of life to serve their own ends by turning its power in upon itself, drawing *chi* away in ever greater amounts and then use this power for their own ends."

"Then ya need to find out how ta counter this process, Yip." Hoyt's answer was simple, direct and absolutely correct.

"How will I go about this task, Hoyt?"

"Ya have ta find out how they do it, Yip. Ya have ta see how's it done and figure out how ta neutralize it ta defeat 'em."

Yip, too, was resolute, having thought very much the same thing but glad for the confirmation. "Then we must go to the world of the H'era and see for ourselves what their evil brings and how it works."

Hoyt nodded.

"How can we get there? I have no idea where this world is, Hoyt."

"Y'all have a mighty fine ship there, Yip. Even if y'all aren't strong enough yet ta *faerviage* under yer own power, there are other ways ta teleport long distances. Tha city itself uses tha portal disks ta send people hither and yon through tha nether fer commerce, travel, and trade. Y'all could pay fer transport and a return stone through tha city's portals. As long as yer destination ain't shielded and y'all can accurately visualize yer destination, *faerviage* can take ya just about anywhere. If ya can't return under yer own power, tha return stone can give ya safe passage home when used with yer onboard navigation system."

Yip bowed. "Thank you, Hoyt. Your guidance has confirmed my feelings about our course. I am honored by your assistance and counsel."

Hoyt nodded again, saying, "I'll be honored and heartened myself if y'all succeed and come back in one piece. I'll see what I can do ta help yer cause on this front. There are still a few out there who would be loath ta see the Cabal's return. Those who don't know of 'em won't be too keen on havin' 'em around here either."

He then looked at Slate. "Let's get yer armor fitted. Ya're gonna need it."

Waving his wand deftly, the Dwarven armor floated gently up in the air, while Slate's current armor set floated off over his head and shoulders, unfastening and untying from his legs and arms as well.

In short order, Slate was covered from head to toe in fearsome, burnished silvery armor, the reflections of his friends clearly visible on the wicked surface of his eldritch Dwarven-wrought plates. With a few more waves of Hoyt's wand, the armor cinched and tightened itself, adjusting to Slate's form until he wore a nearly weightless second skin.

When Hoyt was done, Slate stared in wonderment flexing his gauntlets, feeling the armor bend and move with the subtlest of his motions. So perfect was the fit, Slate swore that he could feel through the armor's protective surface as he stroked his beard in amazement.

After feeling his beard through the armor, Slate could not contain himself. "It's almost as if I'm not wearin' anythin' at all!"

Wrindanneth grunted, "Thank goodness for us you are!"

Ignoring his friend's joke, Slate brought his hand close up to his face to examine the gloves. "I'd swear that I can feel my breath through tha metal!"

"I wouldn't be surprised if ya did, Slate, not in the slightest." Hoyt smiled happily knowing this was the first of many surprises for his friend.

"Tell ya what, lemme see what I can do fer tha sword. It's a mighty fine weapon. I'd like ta give a bit o' thought ta what may be o' use t'ya in the future against the Cabal."

Interjecting soberly, Yip said, "Why don't you hold on to the sword for us? If any of the families harmed by the *Shrike* come forward in the future, we can use its value to repay them even after the goods are sold."

"Either way, it all adds up ta about the same."

"Fair enough. We know you will take care of us as you always do." Aroganji would be glad if Hoyt forgot all about the sword and kept it without recompense for they were already exceedingly in his debt.

The party left a few minutes later after finalizing a time for the inspection and transfer of the ship's goods, pending word from the embassy on claims by victims' families. After talking with Hoyt, they were ready to visit the Elven embassy and finish their errands prior to making preparations to leave for Al'Marr, the homeworld of the H'era.

YENARIA

Scattered moonlight falls
on dewdrops of purest rain
formed by dreams of Elves.

Wrindanneth led the way through the city toward the Elven legation, unsure what would happen once they arrived, not worried about how they would be received upon delivering a cultural artifact that was probably illegally taken and certainly used against its intended purpose.

He was more concerned with unraveling the continued puzzle that was his dagger. He could feel the blade's power thrum at his side. Like Slate with his new armor, he was eager for the opportunity to practice channeling its power.

He had waited to try using the dagger's enchantments until he had someone else confirm that it was safe. Now that Hoyt had outlined the risks and he had an idea of the best way to start investigating how to tap its powers, he thought back to the fight with the R'yn Daer. He had played the battle over and over in his mind looking for the key to its usage.

The only phrase he had heard when the captain summoned forth the swirling blast of air was the invocation, "The breath of the R'yn Daer claims you!" The captain had also brought his hands together palms outward. Perhaps the spell he cast was not entirely his own. Perhaps one or both of these invocations were needed to summon forth the dagger's power or a similar intent.

He would find out soon enough.

Slate practically skipped down the street in his new armor, feeling both a newfound sense of strength and a lightness to his movements that he was unaccustomed to relative to his old cumbersome set. If there were not passersby, he would have whipped out Duraeleon and wielded it ferociously through the streets whooping and hollering through his forms as he practiced with the fires he felt. As it was, he pranced like a schoolboy elated to be out of school with the prospect of a full summer ahead, ready to get home and play.

In his case, however, play meant feeling the heft of his axe and armor moving together in deadly harmony.

Aroganji went through the mental lists of items they would need to outfit a voyage to another world, working through the necessities for an extended journey without potential to replenish stores on a depleted and diminished planet. There were contingency items they would require should he or Wrindanneth not be able to summon what they needed.

There were many questions to answer prior to leaving.

Would the ship be able to provide atmosphere should they arrive in a place without air suitable to breath? He could only maintain breathable air for so long. Could the ship stock itself summoning food and water as needed to supplement what he and Wrin could manage? To what extent would the ship's defense rely on Wrindanneth and his abilities directly?

Perhaps he could have Hoyt walk through the ship to help Wrindanneth figure out these and other subtleties when they transferred the ship's cargo.

Once they finished with the Elves, he also had to determine how exactly one undertook *faerviage*. He would use the Aspect at the cottage to help answer his questions, determine how to register for *faerviage*, and arrange for travel after double-checking on the status of any claims against the *Shrike*'s stolen cargo.

Yip was lost in excited rumination as well. They were finally moving forward toward information that would be crucial to the success of their cause!

For one trained in calm, whose actions and reactions were carefully tempered by full awareness of his activity and intention, he, too, practically whooped like Slate was doing off and on as they made their way through the wondrous city. If they made Al'Marr and were successful in learning how to undo the Cabal's strength, what would they do next?

What would they learn? How would they apply that knowledge?

He would certainly have to alert the H'era to the current status of their world. If successful, he would have to risk another contact with his master as well.

"We're almost there. Follow my lead when we get in. I've a natural affinity fer Elves," Slate chuckled to himself, knowing that he had anything but a natural affinity for Elfkin or Elves. Elves and Dwarves often ended up on the same side in many conflicts and each respected the natural world deeply in their own ways, but each race also had contrary and sometimes contentious differences of opinion as well.

A soft exhalation from Aroganji turned Yip's attention from Slate to the view ahead as they rounded a corner and entered a large outdoor common area.

The city disappeared.

Instead of a cobbled boulevard, a tree-lined street, or a park, a wooded glade spread out before them blending in and transitioning from the nearby city buildings seamlessly. Straight-trunked trees with shimmering silvery boles and boughs soared overhead surrounded by coruscating golden leaves, their canopies lost in the heavens. Shafts of sunlight highlighted by dust motes illuminated small openings beneath the trees where small fountains, trails, and meeting areas merged in with the lush undergrowth and a few passersby wandered amidst the beauty. In the distance, suffused with light, Yip could see two intricately carved ivory trees arching through the air gracefully forming a natural gateway over a faint trail wandering through the wood. As he watched, the stone trees of the archway rustled softly in the breeze, mirroring the motions of the massive trees above from which their likeness was derived.

While his friends moved along the path to the archway, he stopped to take in the unique beauty and flavor of the place. After spending time in the city proper with all its busyness and activity, the myriad races and expressions of life all vividly and starkly apparent, here the diversity of life held a completely different flavor. The richness and beauty, the variety and miscellany, were all here in profusion but with a single difference.

Here all the life in its many forms and expressions blended together in a continuous whole.

"Come on, Yip!" Wrindanneth called back from far ahead where the party stood beneath the free-flowing carven archway, breaking Yip's absorption.

"If we're gonna save tha world, we don't have all day!" Slate's eagerness to get going was readily apparent even though he made a joke of it to help cover his desire to be done with the Elves and move forward on their quest.

Even though his friends were keen to press on, Yip took his time moving through the eldritch wood. He felt the vibrant energy of the place rush through him as he walked, the presence of the trees very much like a shadow, a diminished version of the Aeryn D'al from which they so closely resembled.

As of yet, he picked up no traces of the Elves.

When he finally caught up with his friends, they were none too happy. "Watchin' tha grass grow?" Slate snuffed. "Maybe ya need ta spend more time with tha Elves than just droppin' off tha bow allows."

"We really must be moving on, Yip. There is much to be done before we can leave."

Yip nodded in agreement. Walking through the glade brought so many memories of the Aeryn D'al to the fore of his consciousness. He wondered how the seed he had given Master Wei was doing. Hopefully it had been planted and was already sprouting in a nurturing location.

"Let's be about it then." Slate stepped forward through the gates and disappeared.

"What?" Wrindanneth was as surprised as everyone else, never having visited the home of the Elves and their embassy on the island, so he had not known what to expect. Nor was he particularly happy that Slate went through first.

"There's only one thing to do," said Yip, moving through the gate after Slate, leaving Aroganji and Wrindanneth on the other side.

Passing through the portal, Yip nearly walked into Slate where his friend stood rapt, transfixed by the panorama ahead. Yip stopped in his tracks as well after he lifted his attention from avoiding his friend. Standing immediately beyond the gateway transfixed, he, too, was nearly run over by Aroganji and Wrindanneth as they materialized behind him.

Ahead, a scene unlike any other unfolded before them in choate fullness.

Yip blinked.

Could this be real?

He marveled, knowing that in fact what he was seeing was real. He could sense the presence of his friends by his side, feel their breath and solidity.

The reality ahead stood in stark contrast.

The world of the Elves spread before them.

Buildings, chambers, and rooms with only the vaguest of distinguishable forms, sculpted of purest sunlight, columns and walkways formed by shafts of refulgence, the light of the stars in the heavens framed and lit rooftops, motes of dust and moonlight defined archways and bridges spanning the boughs, all solidified and shaped by the shadows of leaves and clouds, intertwined through stately silver trees—spider webs of diaphanous sunshine. The city, town, or meeting place ahead, for he did not know what to call such a place, breathed and moved with Life as much as the trees anchoring it in place and the Elves defining its form framed its living presence.

Motion and lambency defined the place as much as Elven imagination.

Even though the area ahead was only a small outpost of the Elven Empire, the feeling of the place was open and capacious, a space without border or definition. Casting his mind out, there was no sense of an end to the expanse from where they stood. For all he knew, they might have stepped directly into an Elven city far removed from Tellanon. Perhaps they ventured onto another world entirely.

Moving toward them, gliding as lightly as wisps of fog over a moonlit stream, an Elf approached, his robes flowing loosely in his wake, his skin shimmering with the light of a harvest moon.

The Elf was tall and lithe, much taller than Yip but not the height of Wrindanneth, his skin an iridescent silver much like the forest giants beneath which they stood. His piercing golden eyes sheltered warmth and kindness, radiating wisdom and compassion. In his right hand he held a great staff molded from flaxen wood that shone with the light of the sun at its apex. His robes rustled and swirled of their own accord, dancing with an invisible wind where he now stood calmly before them.

He was a being from another world.

"Welcome, travelers, to Yenaria, home to hopes and dreams."

Slate snapped his slack jaw shut, composing himself. Wrindanneth blinked his eyes for clarity. Aroganji removed the hand he had been holding by the side of his face.

Speaking with the echoes of rustling leaves, of the sound of raindrops pattering on branches, and the memory of seasons past with hope for the future, the Elf introduced himself with a fluid bow. "I am Alderan and bid you greetings and peace."

Recovering himself, Yip bowed introducing each of his friends in turn. "I am Yip Chi Chuan and these are my friends and allies Slate, Wrindanneth, and Aroganji."

While his friends offered their greetings, Yip studied the Elf carefully. He had lived in such isolation in the monastery that he had never before met one of their kind. To his eyes, Alderan was unreadable, his *li* indistinguishable from the place, as much a part of his surroundings as a distinct presence. His essence blended and merged with the forest in the same way the sunlight lost itself in the air—helping to fill and define the totality of the place without center or edge. Looking around, he could see other Elves gliding through the wood, their presence as much a part of the place as Alderan's—undifferentiated from the ground on which they trod and the air through which they moved, only their physical form hinting at the spirit within and without.

While Men learned to live with and shape the magical energies within and without, magic, the energy of life, was native to the Elves, part of their history, heritage, and evolution, shaping their existence long before the rise of Men. So long had they bathed in its presence that their essences were no longer distinguishable from the living energies flowing within, through, and around them. Although he could read little of the Elf's mind and could therefore guess little of his outlook, the Elves he could see, their spirits moving so naturally, in accord, free of distinction from the ebb and flow of the *yuan-chi*, reminded Yip of the Chih-jen, those who have realized unity with the Ultimate and move free of all concepts and limitations.

He wished he had more time to spend with the Elves for he could learn much of the flow of energy and moving in peace from them. If he were to mirror the Elven harmony with the intrinsic energies of life, he would need to learn to fully open his energy gates and let the *yuan-chi*, the universal energy, flow freely through and around him—buoyant as a dandelion seed on the breeze and as open as the eyes of a child.

"What brings you four to the Elves of Yenaria on this day?"

Ending his study, Yip stepped forward and bowed. "We come to return an item that we believe was wrongfully taken from your kind. We wish to see it in its rightful place."

The Elf brought both hands that he held loosely at his waist apart in a slow outward arch leaving his palms open face up at the end of his gesture. Unable to read him, Yip assumed this meant he was to continue.

"We were waylaid by a band of thieves while traveling to Tellanon. One of them wielded this bow..." Yip brought his arm out gesturing toward Slate.

Opening his pouch at his side, Slate dove down to his shoulder and began rummaging through the bag. "I know ya're in here somewhere. Ah ha!!!" Pulling the lovingly shaped ivory bow from the bag by the top of the bowstave, he presented it to Alderan resting on the flats of his hands.

Nodding, Alderan lightly took the bow in hand, caressing its surface slightly. Yip could see the faintest tracery of energy passing back and forth between the bow and Alderan's fingers and palm.

After a time, Alderan gave a slight genuflection. "You have done the Elves a great service by returning this artifact." He nodded slightly, adding, "You are correct in that the bow was in the hands of one who could not rightfully claim ownership or possession to its true heritage. The one for whom this bow was attuned has long since passed from this world. I cannot say how the one who assailed you came to possess an item such as this, only that it resisted his usage and loathed his touch."

Here he gave a grim smile and stated matter-of-factly, "Had he been in full command of the bow's powers, I doubt that I would have the pleasure of your present company. Regardless, we are honored and gladdened that you have returned this"—and here he used the Elven term—"*lianel* to its rightful home."

Yip bowed. "It is only proper."

Alderan shrugged and again motioning broadly. "If only everyone felt as you, the history and lineage of my people would not be held in the hands of so many usurpers." Yip saw a bit of ire in his eye. "But what is wrongfully taken invariably finds its way home."

"The merit of your deed shall not go unnoticed. The Elves of Yenaria shall call you friends from this day forward." Pulling his robes out slightly at the side, he bowed more fully. "You are welcome to share our Lights at any time."

Yip, too, bowed again. "You are most gracious, Alderan. We would be honored to call you and your kind friends as well."

"Will you partake of our hospitality?" Alderan indicated back from whence he came, offering an invitation to join him.

"Perhaps another time. There is much we must do in preparation for an impending journey."

Alderan gave a slight nod. "What would you have of the Elves to show our fellowship?"

Yip spoke for his companions. "The knowledge of your goodwill and your friendship should suffice, Alderan. Your kindness and thanks are their own reward."

Alderan inclined his head, his bright eyes gleaming, piercing in their intensity as though he were reading currents denied their mortal eyes, examining patterns outlining the details of their lives and their need. "Wait here," he said turning as silently as the breeze, drifting away beneath the trees.

"An odd bird, that one," muttered Slate.

"I don't know," answered Wrindanneth. "I think you two got along pretty well together. Maybe you should spend more time with the Elves. You'll blend right in with your new boots."

Slate harrumphed.

"Elves are very difficult to read," said Aroganji, mirroring Yip's feelings. He paused silently for a few moments. "They are the essence of goodness in many ways, but their goodness is ineffable, empyrean. They are like the stars. Their light is welcome and bright, but distant and far removed."

Wrindanneth glanced at Slate, muttering, "I think Aroganji has been hanging around our priestly friend too much. The two are rubbing off on each other."

Slate nodded. "They're like stones in a river, abradin' against each other, wearin' themselves smooth and round until they're hard ta tell apart."

Wrindanneth laughed. "Now they both just need clean-shaven heads!"

Yip smiled, both at the jokes and at the observation. "Such is the way of monasticism at times, my friends."

The ambassador came back with a small wooden chest held lightly in his hands. The box itself was covered in elaborate filigrees that glowed with faint energy to Yip's eyes.

Holding the box out before him, Alderan opened the lid to reveal two shining golden bracers. In the center of each band, graceful Elven characters floated on the surface, ready to take flight like a flock of birds or drift away like feathery clouds.

Yip sensed that the two bands seemed tied together, made of the same substance and being. He felt the magic in the bands flow freely between each bracer, intertwining and interconnecting their power.

Alderan presented the box to Aroganji and Wrindanneth. "You have earned the esteem of the Elves by the simple act of your good faith. I would have you take these bracers that your spirits will support one another as you have supported my people."

Gesturing to the etching, he said, "The engraving reads –

One will sundered in twain,
Shall be made whole again.

Two minds apart,
Together thou art."

"These are the bands of the Elven twins Aerdos and Aerlyn. Their bond saw them through many hardships."

As Aroganji and Wrindanneth began to gingerly examine the exquisitely wrought metal Alderan smiled and added, "If I may, I would offer a suggestion. Perhaps you should each wear one."

While Wrindanneth gave his thanks, Aroganji bowed, carefully placing the box and the bracers in his robes.

"My Dwarven friend, your deeds, too, deserve some recompense. Is there anything the Elves can do for you or your kin?"

Slate stroked his beard briefly. "No, Alderan. Just seein' where ya live has been gift enough fer my eyes. Thank ya."

Alderan smiled. "Of that I am glad to hear, Slate. You, too, have earned the esteem of the Elves." He added with a slight tilt of his head, "You have also earned the boots on your feet and may wear them proudly."

Slate blushed having completely forgotten that he had been wearing Elven goods without proper entitlement; much like the archer had held the bow.

"And you, Yip? Is there anything I can do to aid you in return for the kindness you have shown the Elves?"

Yip bowed, as was his custom. "I have all that I need, Alderan. You have already shown my friends too much kindness. We are now in your debt."

"Are you sure? The life of adventure leads to many hardships."

Yip paused for a moment. "There is one thing you can do for me, Alderan." His tone became serious. "Give word to your people that the Cabal may soon walk again upon Ea'ae."

Alderan bowed gravely. "Your warning will be heeded and is appreciated, my friends."

With that they turned and left Alderan to make preparations for the voyage to Al'Marr.

AL' MARR

The dusty wind whips
grit and sand onto dry eyes.

Obscuring a view
no man should ever behold.

Stepping back into the glade from the portal, Slate sighed. "Even a Dwarf could get used ta that!"

Their thoughts of the embassy, if such a word could be used to describe the empyrean place after having visited, were short-lived. Hovering before them, flitting in the air like a will-o'-the-wisp, a small light danced back and forth. Inside, Yip could see a small image of Hoyt standing behind his counter.

"Hallo!" The projection spoke to them affably. "Thought I'd find ya here. All is ready for the transfer o' goods if ya want ta come over and supervise. I've notified the magistrate per yer request that everythin' is in order as ya claimed and that the crew o' the *Shrike* has indeed been accounted fer and laid ta rest."

Wrindanneth nodded. "Thanks, Hoyt. We'll be over shortly. If you're willing, I'd like for you to help us learn a bit more about the ship's capabilities while we're there as well. We'll need every advantage we can get on the journey ahead."

"Not a problem!" Hoyt's voice rang through the clearing.

Yip smiled in response to Hoyt's clarion answer. Apparently Hoyt had forgotten how well his voice projected through his creation.

The little wisp winked out of existence soon after Hoyt's words reached their ears.

Aroganji spoke up to clarify his agenda. "I'll return to the house to arrange for travel via *faerviage* and plan for the voyage's necessities while you meet with Hoyt."

Yip gave his assent. "Wrindanneth and Slate won't need my help." He knew that, if anything, he would only get in their way. "I'll return to the magistrate to ensure that the transfer of funds has been taken care of and see if any more information about the affected families is available."

Aroganji replied, "I may contact the magistrate before you get there so that you can get the portal stones Hoyt described, if that's possible."

Yip nodded.

Addressing Wrindanneth and Slate, Aroganji continued, "Be sure to see what Hoyt can tell you of the ship's ability to maintain atmosphere, its ability to summon provisions, and any other capabilities that may serve us on an extended journey. We still don't know much about its weapon systems or defenses." Aroganji's tone sounded a bit like the admonishments of a schoolteacher.

Realizing that, he added placatingly, "Finding out will help with my, our, preparations."

"Aye," Slate was ready to be off.

"Let's go," said Wrindanneth, untroubled by Aroganji's thoroughness, as he turned and walked away from Yip and Aroganji.

As his two friends left the clearing, Aroganji offered, "I will let you know what I find out."

"May the day fall lightly on your shoulders," answered Yip, turning and leaving Aroganji to his business.

The docks were just as Yip had last seen them—alive and awash with energy as beings from all over the multiverse bustled about their myriad tasks and assorted errands.

The magistrate's building stood in stark relief against the sheer rock wall soaring upward behind it, a building commanding attention while maintaining an aesthetic subtle enough to blend in with the immensity of the rock face and thronging activity.

He hoped good news awaited within.

Moving through the airy entry, he felt his essence scanned, the sensory forces tingling from the crown of his head down to his sandaled feet.

"Welcome back, Mr. Chuan!"

He bowed to the disembodied voice.

"How may I be of service today?"

"I have come to see how the needs of those affected by the *Shrike* are being met."

"News of your deed has spread quickly. Many have come forward." The voice paused as if consulting records. "Thankfully, Hoyt has transferred your portion of the proceeds into our custody as you requested. We will begin disbursement of funds after giving some allowance for all claims to be processed and corroborated. We will hold some funds in reserve for those who have not come forward as promptly as others. Your annual tithe will be disbursed equally between all claimants. We will continue to update and divide the tithe among those who have valid claims over time."

He bowed again, knowing that any words he offered would not fill the voids left in the lives of those lost to the *Shrike*. "Thank you."

"It is you who should be thanked. Your generosity has been duly noted. Many have requested information about you to express their thanks."

The voice continued, "We continue to respect your right to privacy, however."

He gave a slight nod.

"Aroganji has contacted us regarding a trip you intend to take to the Sythaeran Quadrant to the planet known as Al'Marr. Our records have no indication of such a world. If you are to *faerviage* there and return via travel stone, we will need suitable temporal and spatial imagery of the place to allow us to facilitate your port there."

"What do I need to do?"

"Do you know what the world looks like, or has looked like in the past?"

"Yes, I have seen it in visions."

"Good, then your trip should be possible. Open your mind to us. Bring images of Al'Marr to the fore of your consciousness. We will use these images to translocate your possessions and essences through space-time to your intended destination when your ship moves through its portal."

Yip relaxed and did as requested, bringing images shared with him by the H'era of their world to his mind. Again, a slight tingling registered, as when his essence was scanned, this time the sensation only lit upon his brow.

"Excellent. That should suffice. You may open your eyes."

Floating in the air before him, a small, opalescent stone vibrated lightly in the air. Resembling a multi-hued pearl, the stone blazed with incandescent light to his inner vision, representing the concentration and materialization of enormous amounts of force.

"When you are ready, hold this stone in hand and visualize Tellanon. Your ship and its crew will return home."

"Aroganji has already arranged for a departure time tomorrow. Your memory will guide your ship to its intended destination when you pass through the fey gate."

Yip nodded.

"We have no current record of Al'Marr in our databases. Do you wish for this destination to be made available in the public domain?"

"I do not understand."

"Would you like for others to be able to *faerviage* to Al'Marr via the portals?"

"That is not for me to decide," answered Yip.

"You have made the information available and have every right to dictate how and if that knowledge can be used. There is no pressing reason at this time to override that privilege."

Yip paused. "Al'Marr is the home of the H'era. Access to their world should be decided by the H'era."

"So you would give access only to the H'era?"

"Until they say otherwise, yes."

"Do you wish to retain the right to travel to Al'Marr?"

"Yes," answered Yip.

"You have retained the right to visit the homeworld of the H'era. When you are ready to transport tomorrow, you need only communicate your desire to the Paratechnologists."

Yip nodded, saying, "Again I thank you."

"And I you."

Knowing that his friends were occupied, Yip took the time to venture into one of the large public parks to reflect prior to their departure on the morrow.

Wandering slowly through the streets of the city, he strolled until he found a park amenable to his needs. The public space he found was bordered by an aged winding wall of rounded stacked stones, covered in moss and lichen with little flowers and plants growing from the gaps between the rocks. A small weathered wooden gate allowed entrance into the tract, its iron hinges creaking as he opened its oaken door.

Rolling hills framing a small bubbling stream spread out before him. In the distance, he could see a few beings of different shapes and sizes basking in the soothing light in small grassy green clearings below the trees, their energies commingling with those of the valley. Insects flitted on the breeze, creating a faint hum as the wind carried their sounds to his ears.

Making his way upon the pebbled path bordered by set stones beyond the gate, he meandered beneath the verdant trees until he found an out-of-the-way clearing that should allow for time without disturbance.

Taking a position in the glade, the grass swaying about him at shoulder height as he sat, he placed his hands lightly together beneath his navel.

In repose, he relaxed into his breath, letting his shoulders drop, feeling the warmth of the sun on his skin. Sitting dispassionately, he watched the *chi* circulate naturally along his macrocosmic orbit, moving through the open energy gates, continually replenished with each breath.

Time passed, awareness held.

He did not sit down to meditate, however.

He sat down to think and wonder.

Watching patiently, he let his thoughts arise and come together, converging and coalescing like clouds passing in the night sky.

The amount of energy he could channel and allow to flow through his body was limited by the amount of *chi* he could let pass through each open energy gate. This energy, in turn, limited his ability to direct and focus toward an intended aim.

After watching the Elves move through and in the world, even so briefly, he realized something very troubling, but at the same time potentially liberating.

A few minutes within the presence of the Elves told him that his whole framework and mode of interacting with the intrinsic energies around him was flawed.

His preconceptions about himself and the macroverse around him limited both his capabilities and potential to understand and move forward, or, rather, his preconceptions about how energy moved through and around him and others limited his continued development.

He had always worked toward feeling, channeling, and then storing the ambient and intrinsic energies within and without, in part because he felt that was what his training, so recently begun in earnest before fleeing the monastery, was about. With more practice and effort, through more open energy gates, more energy could be moved and stored.

He had seen and learned much since beginning his training and after leaving the monastery. His current understanding of the way *chi* moved and passed within and along meridians had served as a useful framework on which to build, but what he had seen and learned thus far had been colored and defined by his own limited understanding.

Despite all his insights and abilities, he was wrong.

Completely and utterly.

His framework, his foundation, and all that he had built upon it, were flawed.

He should have known how deeply he was mistaken after watching the Aeryn D'al move energy so effortlessly, unbounded by internal restraints.

Moreover, and more dramatically, he should have sensed his error after watching Azaelle generate energy and power from the void of potential, standing beside the Dragon, feeling the force move through its body, but he had missed the connection. So enraptured had he been by the Dragon's ability to actually create energy to strengthen his blaze, he had missed the spark needed to augment that fire. Prior to the act of creating energy to fuel his breath, Azaelle drew energy in.

Azaelle did not store energy, trying to build it up internally, nor did he move energy strictly through energy gates associated with different parts of his body as Yip would have if he were in the Dragon's position. Azaelle opened himself up completely and then gathered in ambient energies to react with the energy he generated inside for transformation upon need.

Despite his failings and misunderstandings, he felt total, utter gratitude for the opportunity to learn of his misapprehension.

For finally, after yet another opportunity, he had seen.

The Elves moved through the world in a way he could not fully see, only feel and appreciate. The Elves harnessed and flowed with the universal energy of life as effortlessly as the stars moved through the sky above, as easily as Ea'ae orbited the sun and just as naturally. They did not appear to pass energy through gates or channels nor did they store and pool energy within. Energy flowed through them, completely, totally, through their whole beings.

The Elves' only limits were their skill and understanding and, perhaps, their will and belief.

He smiled as the totality of his framework, the entirety of his life's effort thus far, crumbled before his mind's eye.

There are no gates.

There are no meridians.

There is no need to store energy.

Energy can be created and allowed to flow freely.

There is no limit to the flow of energy.

The only limits are one's capabilities and imagination.

After all this time, and all his efforts, his practice had not even begun.

He spent some time wandering through the park before returning home, letting his thoughts come into order.

Unfortunately, knowing and doing were not always the same.

He had not decided exactly how he would change his approach and alter his practice. He still had yet to determine how to go beyond or outside his current techniques of interacting with *chi*. Perhaps, if he relaxed his energy gates, they would slowly open more over time, and, if relaxed enough, the gates, along with his conceptions, would open fully of their own accord and then dissolve. Or, perhaps he needed to try and forget the whole idea of energy channels and gates and just let the energy flow naturally without conception or will. Perhaps he would have to follow the way of the watercourse and let the natural energies flow and find their path within and through him in order to improve, constantly changing with the energy's direction and expression. Perchance he should continue on the path outlined by Master Wei for it could lead to the result he desired. Maybe Master Wei's approach would reshape his body allowing him to change the way in which he interacted with *chi*. Possibly Dragon and Elven constitutions and their makeup were so different from his own that he could never hope to replicate their approaches. Perhaps he would have to find another way entirely.

The possibilities and questions were endless.

As was his determination.

Whatever the method, he would ultimately be successful if for no reason other than he had to be.

He had to find another way. If his world were to survive, he had to become more adept, learn new techniques, open himself more fully to growth and understanding to continue developing, to push himself forward in order to overcome the Cabal.

He had to be more than he was, become more than he imagined. If not, his world's future would exist only as a shadow.

Before he left the reserve to return home, he walked down the trail to the small brook he had observed upon entering the park. After reaching its banks, he examined the area carefully.

Interlacing tree branches above softened the sunlight warming the stream's depths. The lapping of water along the banks and murmuring over submerged stones blended with the sound of birds and insects celebrating a beautiful day. The soil along the stream's edge was dark, rich in moisture and nutrients. Reflecting this abundance, the organisms within the soil's surface and profile suffused the loam with a subtle luminescence. Moss and lichen clung to the surface of the worn rocks that framed the water by his feet.

Bending over, he picked up one small, mottled gray-green rock from the bank along with a handful of soil and a small pile of fresh leaves. He then reached into the rill's cool water and selected a slick, palm-sized rock covered in green algae. Placing the soil and lichen-encrusted rock carefully in a waterproof bag and the algae covered rock along with some of the stream's water in another, he set the bags and their contents in the small pouch hanging at his waist.

Yip finally returned home to find his friends enjoying a raucous meal about a garish table Wrindanneth had summoned to fill the space in the kitchen. From the looks of it, Wrindanneth had conjured the table of a nobleman who had more money than discernment, taste, or propriety.

Or from a raucous carnival.

Wherever the table was from, it would not be missed.

"Welcome, Yip!" Slate managed a greeting around a churning mouthful of food.

"I trust you had a productive afternoon?" Aroganji asked.

He nodded.

"And?" asked Wrindanneth.

"I took a walk in a park."

"We're about to fly across the known universe, into who knows what kind of reception, potentially facing the K'un Lun's sworn enemies, and you took a walk in the park?"

Apparently Wrindanneth had a different view on how time was usefully spent.

"Yes," he answered, smiling slightly. "It was quite enjoyable. And you?"

Wrindanneth's tone was curt, even if his answer was not. "We learned what we had to. The ship will support us. We can summon food and water, maintain atmosphere, and navigate through uncharted regions. Hoyt also showed us what he could of the ship's weaponry and defenses and offered a few pointers on how to pilot more effectively, especially in combat, should we engage an enemy."

Yip nodded, reaching into his robes. "The magistrate gave me this." He held out the nacreous return stone to Wrindanneth who took it carefully. "You can use it to teleport us home after we are done on Al'Marr."

"So your afternoon was not entirely a walk in the park?"

Smiling with the jest, Yip answered, "No. There is some good news. The families affected by the *Shrike* are coming forward and receiving succor. I can only hope that their futures are easier than their pasts."

Aroganji nodded in agreement. "We are scheduled to leave tomorrow. I suggest we get a full night's sleep in preparation for our departure early in the morning."

Unworried about the risks ahead, ever concerned about the bottom line, Slate asked, "How much did *faerviage* cost us?"

"Nothing. It was free."

"Free?" Slate was skeptical. "How could travel across tha known universe be free?"

"The magistrate said our generosity deserved repayment in kind."

Wrindanneth glanced at Yip, his gaze complimentary. "Sounds like a fruitful walk in the park."

Yip shrugged, adding, "There is much yet to be done. Of that I am all too aware."

"Is there anything else we need to do in preparation to depart?" Aroganji had organized the majority of their preparations thus far and wanted to ensure that their expedition went well.

Yip took a moment before speaking. "I am unsure exactly what to expect when we approach the planet Al'Marr, but I would have you prepared and understanding the difficulties ahead."

"I do not know how the Cabal worked their evil on that world, draining it slowly of its energy and life. We are going to find out, to learn what they did and how to counteract it, and to prevent the same fate from happening to our world and others. Whatever the Cabal did to drain the living energy from an entire planet will certainly have dire consequences for us if we are unprotected."

"As we draw near Al'Marr, I will have to read the energy currents and patterns to decide how best to protect us from harm and how to proceed forward."

Here he paused as he studied his friends, taking the opportunity to give them more understanding of the situation they faced and the world they lived in. "The living energy around us is, in actuality, a spectrum, an unending well with many sources, layers and interactions, universal and vibrant. At their most fundamental level, prior to emerging from the primordial source, the primal absolute of the Wuji, the ambient energies permeating existence are deep and vast, cosmic in scale and breadth, all-embracing and encompassing. This energy serves as the firmament of our existence."

"In my tradition, we call this force the *yuan-chi*, the celestial or primordial *chi*. From this heavenly *chi*, many other energy sources and types arise and come to being through further refinements and interactions. Fundamentally, this is the energy of life and everything."

"Our *chi* as individuals is but one small, refined aspect of this universal force. The *chi* around us, the living energy that pervades and enlivens all living things, finds its source in the *yuan-chi*. Above the limitless depths of the *yuan-chi*, existing as infinitesimal motes in the universal Light, living beings create and strengthen this *chi* by their very existence and thus return to and replenish the source. On the most surficial level, this *chi* is the source of all magic, just as the *yuan-chi* is the source of all *chi*. Magicians, sorcerers, and alchemists interact with and draw from this *chi* on many levels for their power. Living beings depend upon its energy for their existence."

"Even if the Cabal has learned how to drain away the *chi* created by all living beings on a planet, then the well of celestial *chi* should still be available to drink from and vivify us. Even if the *yuan-chi*, the primordial potential, is being destroyed or siphoned off, however difficult it may be to garner, its unbounded reserves should be accessible to enliven and empower us. That is, if I can make the energy available to sustain our bodies, minds, and spirits."

Slate raised a thick eyebrow questioningly. "What d'ya mean, if ya 'can make the energy available'?"

"I cannot say what we will see and what circumstance we will face, Slate. If the energies are too thin, or draining too rapidly, I may not be able to guide and manipulate them as we get nearer to the source of the disturbance. The same may hold for you as well. In fact, the closer we get to the source of the Cabal's disturbance, the less control we may have, the more energy may be pulled from us, putting our lives at greater and greater risk. Not knowing what lies ahead gives me little opportunity to understand how best to handle the situation."

"I s'ppose that's fair enough," grumbled Slate not sure exactly that it was fair or enough, or even if he fully understood what exactly in Brendle's name Yip was babbling on about.

"If we have to, I can explore the planet's surface on my own without risking your health, assuming we can land or teleport safely. We shall see what must be done when the time comes."

"If the ship's shielding holds in atmosphere, would it not hold our *chi* in as well?" Wrindanneth's question was one Yip had not considered and was most perceptive.

"I do not see why it would not help contain the personal *chi* we generate and transfer from our *shen*, our spirits. The *yuan-chi*, however, knows no bounds and thus would not be constrained by a shield, in the same way that *yuan-shen*, primordial consciousness, would not be constrained by such a barrier. So even if the shield does not confine our *chi*, celestial *chi* should still be available."

"Either way, at least we have a backup. With your guidance, we will know how far we can safely proceed." Wrindanneth sounded slightly more certain now that he had some confirmation that they had a contingency option that would provide them with energy either to live on from Yip's perspective or magic to cast spells from his.

After having spent quite some time around Yip, Wrindanneth still was not at all sure about this whole *chi* phenomenon, much less how life depended on it, but he did understand and believe in magic in multiple levels from the universal, divine to the personal energies. If *chi* and magic were roughly synonymous, and magic was as critical to life as life was to magic, then there was much to be concerned about if the Cabal could drain an entire world of its magic.

He could also relate to the thought of magic, or *chi*, as both being created by and sustaining living beings on one level while at the same time having a universal generative component. From his point of view, and this was but a crude approximation, based on his training in both divine and mundane magics as a Priest of Maeth Onai, the universal magic typically employed by priests of a given deity derived primarily from divine energies while the mundane magics generally used by wizards were drawn mostly from natural earthly energies that the casters themselves could manage internally.

Of course, there was significant crossover between the two traditions depending on the types of spells and energies worked with and cast. Otherwise, magicians would not be able to perform arcana in areas devoid of life unless they drew upon other energy sources, for example, but the metaphor generally held.

After his friends' discussion, Aroganji could contain himself no longer, having held the impending reality of their venture in check for so long. As an explorer and adventurer seeking knowledge and new horizons as much as thrill and reward, the thought of his first voyage between the stars held no end of excitement. As a young boy he had watched and admired the stars from the gardens of his home, wondering if one day he would ever explore their reaches.

The time had almost come!

He shared his exhilaration with his friends. "We are finally going to be off and exploring the cosmos! The universe is opening its gates for us to venture forth and discover!"

"Aye," Slate grunted. "Let's hope those gates don't slam shut behind us before we get back or in our faces as we're tryin' ta leave!"

"What are you talking about, Slate?" Wrindanneth had no idea if

Slate was making a joke, was concerned about their safety, or was alluding to something else entirely.

"I'd hate ta travel halfway across tha universe and never come back. A Dwarf likes solid ground 'neath his feet, or safely over his head, after all. And he prefers ta have tha key ta any gate he encounters."

Wrindanneth snickered. "If you're anxious now, then you're going to be worried the rest of the time we're together. I don't see things getting any easier from here on, especially after the Cabal notices that we've plugged their little *chi* drain on Al'Marr."

Aroganji nodded in agreement with Wrindanneth. "Exploration has as much to do with risk as reward."

"And a Dwarf's axe likes ta know what and where it needs ta cut. I'm just echoin' Yip's concern and offerin' a bit o' caution ta temper yer excitement."

Yip heard a muffled curse from Duraeleon, as the axe shrugged and struggled loose from its holster, while Slate spoke. Finally, its words partially muffled around its sheath, Duraeleon managed, "I'd rather not have to cut at all, thank you, especially given how infrequently you clean me or how well you seem to guide me toward targets."

Wrindanneth laughed, glad that all was normal, at least for the time being.

For his part, Slate reminded himself to make sure he had firmly strapped his axe in place in the future.

The shadows of evening still gathered in cool pools throughout the city streets as the band made their way toward the docks. Wrindanneth and Aroganji carried small packs slung loosely over their shoulders, readily available supplements to the items Slate stowed in his magic bag. Yip, too, carried his small traveling kit looped over the loose robes covering his shoulders, eager to be on his way.

Despite his reluctance to leave the ground, Slate was positively skipping with anticipation to be on their way. His voice raised in song, keeping time with his steps, Slate chanted,

"Through blood and tears,

We fight our fears,
The journey's just begun.

O'er wearisome years,
We lose those dear,
And despair that we're done.

With axe in hand,
We form a mighty band,
Until tha battle's won!"

While Slate's voice echoed off the still-silent homes and storefronts, Wrindanneth merely shook his head in silence where he walked behind his stocky companion. Instead of commenting on Slate's verse as was his wont, he held his tongue, preferring to let his friend revel in his excitement, preparing in his own way for the tribulations to come, for the journey ahead would be long and trying.

By the time they reached the Scimerian Gate, the early morning shadows had faded with the birdsong as the city and its inhabitants woke in preparation for the coming day. The gate's swirling surface parted easily before them as they made their way forward toward the docks, hurrying over the smooth stone toward the *Shrike* docked well below.

Walking down the bulwark, Yip looked beyond the stonework, past the gentle sweep of marble arching down to the ship's landing, past the portals shimmering suspended in the air, through the massive shield encircling the island, to the land bathed in umbral gloom far beneath Tellanon. Watching the city's great shadow pass slowly across the earth below as the island moved overhead, darkening the fields and trees in temporary dusk, his eyes gazed backward to where the trailing darkness gave way to the rapidly advancing sun.

Observing the interplay of light and dark flitting behind them, his thoughts turned to the events ahead.

He only hoped that the coming darkness would be as brief for Ea'ae.

Wrindanneth's heart swelled with pride as he beheld his ship, for he already considered the *Shrike* his after so short a time piloting her. The bond only deepened with the connection he felt as he piloted her, his senses racing along her length and breadth, filled with keen awareness of her every detail. After Hoyt's instruction and a bit more time spent guiding her, he was confident that he would be able to maintain as much control over the ship as he could with his own body. Every moment with the ship only improved his ability and capacity to learn more.

Standing by the ship waiting for them, a Paratechnologist who resembled nothing more than a humanoid bronze-hued Dragon hailed their approach. His face was elongated and tapered just like a Dragon's, ending in a jagged maw filled by sharp teeth. Several large horns framed his head while spines ridged his back and tail. Large taloned wings that folded behind his shoulders were held in place by powerful shoulder and pectoral muscles. His hind legs bent sharply at the knee, ending in clawed feet expertly crafted for leaping and tearing. Burnished scales glimmered warm honey and golden hues in the early morning light. Despite his small size, for he stood only a head taller than Yip, the wizard presented a formidable appearance.

Walking closer, Yip could sense how the wizard had modified the subtle energy structures of his body, gradually remolding his appearance and capabilities under the constant crucible of magical spell and ritual. The relentless influx of magical energies had completely altered his structure and metabolism on all levels from cellular to system.

To his eyes, the wizard now appeared to be a creature entirely of magic, granted power and improved control over arcane energies at the expense of his humanity. Only his non-reptilian eyes with their round pupils belied the overall impression, bespeaking of his now lost past.

When Wrindanneth neared, bowing slightly, the Paratechnologist asked, "Is there any way I may be of assistance prior to your departure?"

Shaking his head Wrindanneth answered, "I think we're all set. Yip tells me our destination has been arranged. I trust the Construct will guide us to the proper portal for *faerviage*?"

His scales making only the slightest susurration as he nodded, the wizard replied, "Aye. If you prefer, the drones can lead you to the appropriate portal or we can remotely guide your ship for you."

Eager to feel the ship under his control again, Wrindanneth declined the offer. "We should be able to manage. Thank you."

Nodding in acquiescence, the Paratechnologist said, "The people of Tellanon wish you safe journeys. You have but to use the provided return stone when you wish to come back."

"Thank you," answered Wrindanneth in turn, moving toward the ship past the wizard as he went aboard.

Calling over his shoulder to his friends as they crossed the gangplank and boarded, Wrindanneth yelled, "Enjoy the stone underfoot while you can, you lubbers! You may not feel anything under your boots but the planks of the *Shrike* for some time!"

Slate blanched and grasped his belt firmly, as if a tighter grip would help secure his footing and his future.

Aroganji laughed at Slate's response, knowing full well that he was capable of handling himself adroitly on the ship. "Let's move, Slate!"

"Argh! I'm movin'! Can't a Dwarf savor his last bit o' freedom before bein' confined ta tha decks?"

Aroganji laughed again. "When has being confined ever bothered you?"

By the time they dropped off their bags and settled into position onboard, Wrindanneth had pulled the ship away from the mooring and had the ship rotated and reoriented to move away from the island. Crossing the polished wooden deck to stand by Wrindanneth, Yip could see a three-dimensional holographic projection of the island and the surrounding ships floating in the air in front of his friend. Tellanon glowed in the hologram's half-light, radiating activity and energy like a bustling hive as ships and drones moved to and fro rapidly.

The voice of the Construct broke into Wrindanneth's graceful maneuverings. "Crew of the *Shrike*! Modify your heading by thirty-seven degrees east and twenty-four degrees north. Incline your altitude by sixty-three degrees. Your portal will be ready in five minutes and counting."

Wrindanneth reacted instantly, his hands moving over the hovering silver steering disk frenetically. Marking the position on the projection where their portal awaited, a golden light flashed periodically in the upper right quadrant.

Though the ship rapidly gained altitude, Wrindanneth's quick adjustments did not cause any jostling or discomfort amidships. Yip likened the rapid corrections more to the drifting of a cloud than the jarring motions of a swiftly adjusting horse or wagon. Moving forward, the crisp morning air felt brisk and invigorating.

Looking toward where he thought the portal awaited, Yip eventually saw a shimmering disk hovering in the air about a league or so distant. The morning sunlight limned the disk's rim presenting an annulus, a view akin to an eclipse where the moon hides the majority of the sun behind its body. As they neared, the light behind the disk became brighter and more visible, highlighting the portal's edges in a scintillating silvery gold corona.

He stared transfixed by the beauty of the sight.

"Four minutes until portal activation!" The Construct's voice quickly brought him out of his reverie.

"Amazing," he heard Aroganji's muttered exclamation mirroring his own sentiments after the Construct's warning ended.

He caught Aroganji's eye and smiled.

Slate sauntered over, walking carefully despite the steady planks beneath their feet, squinting ahead toward the awaiting gate. "Reminds me o' tha times we used ta climb ta tha top o' tha peaks ta watch eclipses with me Dam."

He chuckled. "'Twas so long ago, my beard was unbraided and unadorned."

"You've always had a beard?" Yip had never seen a young Dwarf.

Slate cocked his head and looked at Yip curiously.

Before he could answer, the voice of the Construct called out, "Three minutes until portal activation! Maintain current heading."

After the Construct quieted, Slate answered, "Male Dwarves start growing their beards upon birth with tha rest o' their hair. By tha time o' our rights o' passage inta manhood, our beards have grown long and thick. If we successfully enter inta manhood, we braid our beards."

"Some o' my people place tokens and talismans o' honor and power inta tha folds o' their hair, called Kazzak in tha tongue o' my people, while others leave their hair unadorned, feelin' tha braids themselves are decoration enough."

Yip nodded, examining Slate's neatly braided beard with its bangles, metal adornments, bones, and yellowed teeth marking his past accomplishments. All signs of soot and ash from Azaelle's fires had long since been cleaned.

"Two minutes until portal activation!"

Wrindanneth's hands steadied now, resting lightly over the navigation disk. With a quick mental command, the air shimmered briefly about the ship, encasing the entirety of the vessel and some of the surrounding atmosphere within a faintly glimmering shield.

Smiling a bit grimly, Wrindanneth offered, "If it weren't for Hoyt showing me that little maneuver, this trip wouldn't be possible."

Yip sensed the shield encircling them as a dense, responsive bubble. The surface felt firm and unyielding to the magical energies and atmosphere within the ship, serving as a filter and barrier between the atmosphere within and without. Even though he sensed the barrier as unresponsive and unyielding to most energy and molecules, he knew that physically objects could pass through with ease. The tiny membrane he probed would be their shield against the vast, empty void of space on the far side of the portal.

"One minute until portal activation! Prepare for transport!"

The portal loomed ahead, the dark pit of its interior swirling in stark contrast to the bright sunlight fracturing and dispersing along its edges. Despite having no discernible physical depth when viewed at an angle, the interior of the portal seemed to lose itself in incalculable distance.

Wrindanneth brought the ship into position directly in front of the portal, the *Shrike*'s shield hovering just in front of the portal's inky surface—one shimmering surface juxtaposed against another.

"Portal activated! Enter the gate and prepare for *faerviage*!" The Construct's voice commanded quick action.

Wrindanneth eased the *Shrike* forward, the shimmering shield contacting the portal's surface prior to the ship itself. His mind cast forward with the shield, Yip felt his consciousness torn between two locations unimaginably far apart. As the ship drifted ahead more and more of his consciousness was torn in twain, encompassing both Ea'ae and somewhere else, until he stood directly in front of the depthless surface of the portal itself.

Closing his eyes, he felt his existence interminably, in the faintest sliver between seconds, briefly in the lifetime of stars, being torn apart, annihilated and scattered to the interstellar winds, unified in consciousness throughout the cosmos, before vertiginously collapsing back to a single point within his body. Opening his eyes, he realized they were now through and on the other side of the portal.

His consciousness once again knew the confines of his own body in but a single location in space.

Turning his head quickly in the direction from whence they came, the portal was no more. Inky darkness and the eternity of interstellar space caught his gaze in the impartial light of countless stars.

THE LAND BENEATH ONE SKY

Dust and grit choke lungs
struggling for breath,
a lone shadow on the plains.

Directly in front of the prow of the ship, within its own swirling atmospheric shield, lay the dusky brown orb of Al'Marr, the homeworld of the H'era, a living testament to the evils of the Cabal and their ilk.

Looking forward through the void of space toward Al'Marr, Yip saw an unending well of wonder. Where his friends saw limitless inky blackness interspersed with various stars and interstellar bodies, he felt the fullness of emptiness, the unending currents and energies of creation. A luminous gauze, the softest of lace, suffused the darkness with a subtly variegated radiance as far as he could feel, see, or imagine.

Extending his mind out, eyes closed, reaching as far as he possibly could, Yip scanned space between the ship and their destination. Lighter than the thinnest cloud, softer than the finest silk, he could feel the currents of the celestial *yuan-chi* encompassing and moving around them. Waiting patiently, sensing its presence, he began to notice a slight direction in its movement. The *chi*, even in the space so far removed from the planet below, drifted slowly, inexorably to the world ahead. Bringing his mind back to the ship, he could feel how these currents swirled around the *Shrike*'s shield, marking its extent easily in his mind's eye, simultaneously coming into and out of existence within and outside the protective barrier's confines.

Sending his mind out once more, first to his left and then to his right to try and determine the direction of the energy's flow, he felt the *chi* moving around them steadily toward Al'Marr, gaining an understanding of its directionality. Bringing his awareness back toward the ship, he briefly noticed a slight anomaly, as if many powerful minds lay shielded behind a carefully disguised barrier. Before he could investigate further, the sensation quickly disappeared.

Opening his eyes, he heard Slate curse. "I wouldn't wish that experience on my worst enemy. Seems ta me like they're a few kinks in this whole *faerviage* business!"

He snorted. "Nothin' 'fair' about it. Tha next time I want ta be scattered ta tha winds o' creation is on my funeral bier amidst flowin' ale and sooty smoke!"

Wrindanneth smirked. "You know we have to go back don't you?"

Aroganji added, "And who knows where else this quest will take us?"

Slate blanched.

Yip filled the silence left by Slate's conundrum, ready to move ahead and share his observations. "I have cast my mind out about the ship and read the subtle energy currents. I think that I should be able to determine the location of the source of the disturbance created by the Cabal on this world by studying the movements of the energies around us."

"Energy?" asked Slate. "We're in space! There's nothin' here! Look around ya, Yip! Only tha scattered sparks and embers from Brendle's forge light tha darkness, tha heat from his fires have grown dim!"

"Embers?" Now it was Aroganji's turn to be confused.

"Tha stars o' course! Stars are tha smolderin' embers from Brendle's forge." Slate appeared a bit flummoxed by his friends' lack of even the most basic understanding of cosmology. How had humans managed to get into space not knowing something as simple as that?

Who else cast the universe if not Brendle?

Where else but with his anvil and forge?

"Slate, there is energy around us at all times and in all places. If not, how would the magic of this ship and its protections persist?"

"Outside of magic and the manifestations of *chi*, these embers as you call them, constantly bath us in light, in energy, as well. What you call the heat of Brendle's forge yet remains around us as well. This is the Light, the *yuan-chi*, that sustains and governs all life and magic."

"So yes, there is energy here, boundless energy, in fact, and I can read its presence as it arises and returns to infinity."

Slate shook his head, opened his mouth, and muttered sheepishly, "I stand corrected. I wasn't even thinkin' o' tha heat from tha first forge. Tha universe is not yet cast in its final form nor is all her heat lost!"

Smiling somewhat ruefully, embarrassed, he realized Men were not the only ones with a thing or two to learn.

"What are you thinking, Yip?" Aroganji was ready to move onward with their quest.

"If we slowly circle the planet, I should be able to more readily discern how the *chi* flows to the source of the Cabal's disturbance and quickly pinpoint its location."

"Sounds promising to me." Wrindanneth trusted Yip's ability to locate and neutralize the source of this planet's destruction. After all, weren't priests meant to discover and heal what was broken?

"How long will you be able to maintain the shield around us without replenishing our atmosphere, Wrindanneth?" Yip needed to know how much time he had before the ship and its crew would be opened to the same inexorable pull that had doomed the H'era's world.

Wrindanneth's confidence shone forth in his answer. "As long as I have to. Between the power source for the ship and our food stock, including, our ability to summon more, I would wager that we would run out of food before the ship will run out of power."

"Good." Yip nodded in satisfaction. "One more thing."

"What's that?" asked Wrindanneth.

"We're not alone."

"What?" Slate was incredulous. "What're tha odds someone else would visit a dead world?"

Aroganji answered in all seriousness. "Very slim. The Cabal may have set up guardians. Even though a world is extinguished, that does not mean it is not without interest. There are those who would harvest its resources whether the world is living or dead. There are also secrets the Cabal may wish to remain hidden."

Slate nodded reluctantly. "Plenty o' ore ta be had, methinks, if it's safe enough ta try now. Maybe artifacts ta find as well."

"We'll be on guard." Wrindanneth was eager to try a few of the tricks Hoyt had shown him now that he knew how to pilot the ship somewhat competently.

Yip nodded in agreement. "When I locate the source of the Cabal's evil, Wrindanneth, you and Aroganji will have to port me down to the surface. I will try to mend what the Cabal ruined while there."

"What if ya can't?" asked Slate, concerned.

"Then we get to go home," answered Wrindanneth matter-of-factly.

"And you will be safe, should I fail. If I succeed, you will know. If I fail, you will have to tell Master Wei that I was unable to cure the ill that the Cabal may bring to our world."

"Aye," answered Slate grimly for both Aroganji and Wrindanneth.

Wrindanneth turned his eyes to the dusty world ahead. "Let's move forward then and see if we can discover the source of the Cabal's witchery."

While Slate left and went to his room belowdecks, Yip took advantage of the time to talk further with Wrindanneth and Aroganji.

"Aroganji, I will need you to cast a spell to let me communicate with you directly while I am on the planet's surface. Otherwise, you will have to wait for me to gather myself to try and communicate across the void between us. Given the potential energy I anticipate needing, I may not be able to gather more or have time to do so."

"That should not be a problem, Yip. There are several spells in the wizard's books that we recovered that should work well."

"I would ask for more in the way of protection, but I fear that any spells you may cast upon me will be torn away to no avail."

Addressing Wrindanneth then, he added, "Wrindanneth, whatever I sensed when trying to locate the source of the disturbance was not friendly. I could not tell much more, only that whatever beings are out there with us are fully capable of shielding themselves mentally and physically while also masking their presence. You and Aroganji will need to be prepared for the worst."

Nodding, Aroganji said, "I will lay wards and traps to prepare for an assault should we come to that while Wrindanneth pilots."

"I may add a few tricks to Aroganji's weavings as well," added Wrindanneth menacingly.

"Be sure to do what you can to protect yourselves from mental assaults and beguilements. I do not know how to give words to the sensation I had, but whatever I contacted felt...unctuous, mentally adroit and well-accustomed to and prepared for psychic activity."

"Aye, aye, Cap'n." Wrindanneth half-smiled in reply.

Yip laughed.

The next few days were spent steadily searching above Al'Marr's surface, flying counter to the direction of planetary rotation to take advantage of the planet's natural motion for added search speed while using the planet's gravitational field along with the ship's velocity to maintain a steady distance orbiting above the planet's atmosphere. While they moved toward their target, following the energy currents toward their terminus, Wrindanneth gradually shifted from a polar to an equatorial orbit based on Yip's impressions of the directions of strongest energy flow.

When not reading the flow of energies around them, Yip stared somberly at the gritty surface of the planet below. Aided by visual enhancement spells from Aroganji, he watched dusty clouds and plumes move over what appeared to be a landscape strewn with loose dirt and debris, few anchors were available to stop the silt's continual drifting. With the exception of well-embedded rocks and mountains, the terrain below seemed to be in a state of random, disordered flux, covered in the dregs and leavings of the wind. Occasionally, more permanent structures rose up briefly from the tableau, haunting memories of times long past, eroded by the wind and elements.

Based on the lands the *Shrike* flew over, Al'Marr appeared to have changed quite drastically since the H'era had been forced to flee. The lands appeared much hotter and drier than they had been in his visions with most of the surface moisture no longer visible on the ground. Without living creatures to regulate and replenish the air, the atmospheric composition had begun a steady, inevitable change to ever more inhospitable environs. Similarly, without living beings to anchor the soil, much that was once held in place was now free to drift and flow.

After time spent scrying the elements and patterns of change below, Aroganji told him that the planet's atmosphere had not yet degraded to such an extent that it no longer contained breathable air or held completely untenable weather conditions. However, without normal biogeochemical cycles to replenish the soil and atmosphere, the world the H'era once knew and loved would remain a distant memory.

Passing so swiftly high above the mountains and plains below, Yip found significant difficulty in resisting the desire to imagine the lands below as they had been prior to the Cabal's ravaging energy drainage. In his mind, he could see fertile green plains spreading to the horizon, lush forests blanketing the mountains and hills, full rivers and streams draining into rich alluvial fans, herds of wild animals roving the land, and flocks of birds sweeping through the sky—the full width and breadth of living beings spread in a glorious tapestry beneath the vault of Heaven.

"We are close."

Yip felt the increased turbulence, the more rapid and volatile movement of living energies below and knew their target was fast approaching. Even from here, far above the planet's surface, he felt the growing tug of the Cabal's evil on his senses, extended as they were beyond the *Shrike*'s shield.

Aroganji, Wrindanneth, and Slate all turned their questioning eyes upon him.

"Our destination grows near. Our search will soon be at an end."

Slate felt a surge of adrenaline building within his chest, eager to be about something, anything, other than scouring the heavens and Earth.

No longer content to read the lay of the land from afar, passively staring at the barren lifeless world from on high, he made his thoughts and feelings known. Standing alongside Wrindanneth, Aroganji and Yip at the helm, he said, "We've come this far together. Why not go a bit farther?"

"What would you do, Slate?" Wrindanneth's acerbic voice cut through the air disapprovingly as though the suggestion of additional action were presently offensive, counter to the plan they had already discussed.

"While it's still safe enough, if it's still safe enough, I'd have us put some boots on tha ground ta get a feel fer what's been done, what's been lost, and how tha world's changed. We all can't read tha energy currents with tha facility o' Yip, but we can get a direct understandin' o' tha enormity o' what's been lost."

Summarizing his argument succinctly, he finished, "While we're scoutin', let's scout!"

Aroganji gave a considering nod of his head. "You would have us all teleport down to the ground to see what has been done?"

Slate nodded shortly. "Aye. That or send astral projections o' ourselves down ta do it if ya think our bodies would be in too much risk."

Finally, after some time in thought, Aroganji answered Slate's request with one of his own. "If you feel the risk is worth it and the tale of the experience will aid in our cause, then I am for it. But this cannot be done unless Yip feels it is a venture safe enough for us to undertake without risk of compromising the mission."

Yip gave a short bow of his head. "There is no certainty in such a venture. We should remain far enough from the source of the Cabal's evil to avoid most of its affects and be safe so long as we do not linger overlong."

Wrindanneth was more cautious. "And the others you sensed? They are not presently a threat?"

Yip shook his head. "I have not felt their presence for some time. We should be safe to visit the surface briefly and return to the ship."

Slate grinned excitedly. "Let's go!"

Wrindanneth shook his head. "Not so fast, Slate. Let me perform a few confirmatory scans before we jump headlong into a situation we may or may not be prepared for."

Turning to Yip, he asked, "Is this worth the risk? Is there enough magical energy available to harness on the ground to return us to the ship should we have to do so quickly?"

Yip's response was as clear as it was chilling. "I cannot be certain. We must act as though there is none and any available may be stripped from us."

He then added, "We should prepare such spells ahead of time to be assured of our return. The *chi* is thin on the planet's surface, not replenished by living creatures. The *yuan-chi*, even here, is drawn and pulled, attenuated by the planetary disturbance."

"This close, we should also shield ourselves to ensure that we are not at risk from having our life forces drained from us."

Emphasizing the seriousness of what they were about to attempt, he said, "These will need to be your strongest spells of shielding."

While Aroganji and Wrindanneth considered, looking beyond his friends to the empty world below, he finished, "I feel the Cabal's blight as an ever-growing tide pulling, drawing, ambient energies into its ravenous maw. We must avoid falling victim to its hunger."

Aroganji gave a short, understanding nod. "Then we will make our preparations now."

Yip turned his eyes back to his friends. "If we are to do this, so close to the source of the Cabal's evil, then I would feel its presence as intimately as possible that I may understand its workings before attempting more."

Echoing Wrindanneth's concern, he asked gravely, "Is this a risk you would undertake?"

The ship's deck fell into an uneasy silence as his friends considered, the weight of this decision heavy on their minds. Finally, Aroganji spoke. "With knowledge there is risk. We came to achieve and transform, not to observe."

"Aye. I'll not sit by and watch while ya have all tha fun!" Slate's furrowed brow indicated his resolve, but the ready smile that came over his face indicated his enthusiasm and attitude.

Wrindanneth gave a brief half-smile. "What's adventure without excitement?"

Aroganji gave his assent. "Let us begin!"

Yip quickly went belowdecks to place the Heart of Yere within the folds of his bedroll along with his magical teaching scrolls and personal effects. If he was to feel the Cabal's evil directly, he did not want the Heart of Yere's protections interfering with the sensations that would come. Neither did he wish to risk the magic of his scrolls or the Yeren's artifact should they inadvertently venture too far and have the magic stripped from them.

Hurrying back to the deck, he joined Slate where he stood beside Aroganji and Wrindanneth at the helm, their preparations just begun.

Slate held back and watched while his friends worked their wonders, filling the air with light and sound, energy manifest and transformed.

Slate had come in search of adventure and soon would have it! The thrill of the hunt, the heady rush of adrenaline coursing through his veins, heightened his mood. He had to resist the urge to bounce from Elven boot to boot in anticipation.

Though he would not be meeting his foe on the field of battle, he would soon have the chance to see his enemy's handiwork on the leavings of one—a planetary wasteland destroyed and impoverished by war.

No longer able to hold back any longer, he barked into a lull in his friends' casting. "Are ya about done?"

Wrindanneth scoffed disparagingly, "Only if you want to be!"

Returning Wrin's insult with a glare, Slate held his tongue. He would wait, albeit reluctantly. Under the circumstances, it would not be wise to anger his friend and risk being stranded in the forlorn wastes below.

Instead, tapping his foot, he counted out the seconds until Aroganji and Wrindanneth were done.

Finally, when so much time had passed that he felt certain his beard must have grown enough to need a new knot, Wrindanneth announced that he was finished.

Looking to Wrindanneth, Aroganji said, "Would you like to do the honors?"

Wrindanneth nodded shortly in reply. "Certainly."

Drawing on the energies of the ship to strengthen his effort, with several waves of his hands and a brief invocation, the world shifted and was gone.

Unimaginably vast forces moved and shifted around him.

Ahead through the grit, past low-slung dunes, and over the barren rocky ground, Yip sensed the disturbance he sought in the massive flow of the ambient energies. Farther on in the desert, the remnants of the pervasive celestial *chi* seemed even more muted and fleeting—the last remnants of fog burning off in the fullness of the mid-morning sun, evaporating as quickly as it manifest.

Still farther, the land appeared devoid of substance, bleak and still. Blinking rapidly, lest the dust in his eyes, the foreign matter flying through the air, confuse his sight and inner vision, he could neither see nor feel energies arising to suffuse the land beyond a certain point, as if the *chi* created by and sustaining life had reached a high tide mark and progressed no farther, drawn away into some nether abyss.

Around this invisible point of demarcation, immense amounts of energy swirled and gathered, pooling before oblivion.

He shook his head in the torridity, unsure if what he sensed before him was an illusion in the heat haze, a wispy mirage created and filled in by his imagination or true and actual. Despite the unlikelihood, in spite of his rational confusion, he felt that his inner vision remained unclouded and ahead laid a land completely devoid of life-fulfilling ambient energies. Or, to be clear, any life giving forces that moved in or arose were siphoned away as quickly as they were generated from the boundless continuum of possibility.

Checking carefully given the risks, the shield of radiant force surrounding his body remained unbroken. His friends remained similarly protected.

Reassured, he pointed forward, indicating this horizon to his friends. "The generation of *chi* grows ever thinner as we move forward. Ahead it grows so thin as to be almost imperceptible, its movements becoming more and more rapid toward the source of the Cabal's evil."

"I would feel this transition directly."

Aroganji nodded. "I will take us there."

Slate voiced his concern quickly. "Will we be able ta return ta tha ship if we jump forward?"

Aroganji gave a brief nod.

Satisfied, Slate grunted and indicated his assent with a nod of his own.

Wrindanneth remained cautious as he asked, "Will the pull of these increasing currents risk our protections?"

Yip replied as honestly as he could. "Our magic should abide a while yet though it will not hold for its full duration. Soon the pull will be too strong."

Wrindanneth gave a curt nod. "Then let's be quick about this."

Yip pointed onward. "Take us to that ridgeline next to the great rounded stone."

Summoning the magic he had set aside once more, Aroganji shaped his intent and the world fell away.

They stood within the center of a tidal wave. Powerful forces moved imperceptibly around them, drawn inexorably ahead and away.

His awareness sound, extending outward and untouched by the rush, Yip felt the encompassing wash of forces as though he were a point of stability anchored amidst a storm, a single mote floating in place within a flood.

He indicated the way forward. "I would go a bit farther for the transition, the point of no return, is near. Stay here and await my return."

Aroganji and Wrindanneth looked at each other in alarm.

Shaking his head, a common unvoiced concern shared between them, Aroganji said, "We must stay together. If we have to leave, I will not be able to transport us if we are apart. We will follow a short distance behind you, ready as needed."

He gave a brief nod of acceptance.

Aroganji was right.

He could not risk such poor decisions this close.

Coming here might already be one.

He must do better.

He must be better.

"We have but a short distance to go. Follow me."

As his tread drew him steadily onward toward the demarcation, over land layered in dust, his friends following slowly some distance behind, moving downward along the sere, dust-strewn slope, the surreality of the situation grew and grew, becoming more and more oppressive, as if the sun itself were bearing its full weight on his shoulders. As the universal *chi* about him thinned and wavered, drawn out from the wellspring of potential, the *chi* within and around him implacably pulled away even through his shield, his awareness of himself shrunk smaller and smaller, forced further inward upon itself as the extended energies of his body were pulled away into the unseen abyss.

So long had he felt and identified with the halo of ambient energies moving around his body, that he considered them part of himself. This sphere of energetic awareness and sensation was an extension of his essence, a continuation of his own mind-body. Now almost completely absent, a part of himself, the majority of what he felt enlivened and empowered his existence, had disappeared, ripped away, gone beyond the reach of his mind's eye.

He walked forward as but a shadow of what he once was.

He could sense his friends weakening behind him. Though their protections yet held, he perceived the magic holding the shields together gradually fraying and unraveling. The degradation would only accelerate as they moved forward and the pull of the abyss grew greater. Their vitality would leave just as quickly.

The risk of moving ahead was too great. Ready to tell his friends to stop, that the danger was too much, he lurched to an abrupt stop, his world reeling and distorted.

Caught like an insect in amber, his normally easy breath frozen and cold in his chest, he held rigid in mid-stride, his shadow as still as the beating of his heart. Overhead, the once soft white clouds seemed to give up their light, swift passage and linger in the same confusion felt deep in his heart.

Why had he risked this?

For a moment, he lost track of the sky and sun, the earth and horizon, as his world fell in pieces, small shards of glass left destitute and broken in the dust beneath a forgotten sun.

Unable to find his bearings, his center lost, his connection to the world around him shorn, he floundered.

Time stopped for him then.

Slowly ever so slowly, he reclaimed his sense of self and union with the space around and within.

What had happened?

Feeling empty inside, bereft of his essence, he had lost touch with the *chi*, the life force that normally bathed and sustained him.

Gone!

The living energies were being pulled from him quicker than he could gather or regenerate!

The *yuan-chi* vanished faster than it was replenished!

His shield was no longer holding!

He stood atop an eagre, a tsunami of force, watching energy surge past but unable to grasp, his mind bereft of the strength necessary to reach outward and restore the connection he always maintained.

Awesome tides of force raged past him faster than he could touch or feel. He could not hold them before they slipped away.

He was alone and powerless amidst immensity.

So used to being awash in the life-sustaining energies of creation, he had forgotten the feel of their absence. There had been a time when he was not aware of the presence of *chi*, but never before had he known its complete absence.

He had reached a line of demarcation.

Proceeding forward, he would quickly diminish as the energies of life were pulled from him.

Moving farther back, he could yet replenish himself from the seething stores of *yuan-chi* pulled inexorably forward and into the insatiable pit of the Cabal's *chi* void.

If he were to free this world of the Cabal's blight, it was forward and into this madness that he must tread.

Letting his mind sink deeply into calm, empty of worry and concern, open and spacious, fighting the suffocating urge to breathe, to find safety and replenishment, to retreat, he waited, an island of peace amidst the confusion, practicing patience.

As the urgent seconds passed interminably, devoid of seeking or aim, he waited.

He would have to hold as would his friends.

He felt it!

Slow and elusive, soft and yielding, distant yet pervasive, the *yuan-chi*, the universal force, the source of the energy of life, still flowed hidden in the depths of Wuji, the primal Absolute, the infinite Emptiness giving rise to manifold existence that underlies normal consciousness. At the very edges of his awareness, at the far bounds of his perception, past any limits he had ever thought to experience, he could feel its faint arising from the boundless potential all around just as he could feel its passage.

He could touch the Source once more.

Given the strength of the pull of the Cabal's atrocity, he knew not how long he would be able to maintain this tenuous connection if he proceeded forward without sufficient preparation.

Letting out a deep sigh of relief, he let his heel finally return to the ground over which it had hovered while he was lost in inner turmoil.

Why had this happened?

How could the energies of life be disturbed so profoundly?

If righted, how long would it take before the universal energy repaired the damage that had been wrought and allowed life to reflower and reassert its potential?

These questions and more flashed through his mind as the clouds overhead once again seemed to regain their motion as he considered the enormity of the Cabal's evil.

Similar feelings were not lost to his friends. Pulled from his thoughts by Wrindanneth's voice from where his friends stood transfixed behind him, he heard his companion bemoan, "The magic is gone!"

Aroganji responded in kind. "The life energies of creation are silent!"

To which Slate added, "Brendle's forge has dimmed! My axe is quiet!"

"What has happened?" asked Wrindanneth, the sound of his weakening voice calling Yip to caution, wondering aloud the question they all felt in their hearts.

Yip gave silent witness to the atrocity displayed before them. The life energies of this place had been stripped—culled—drained for a purpose. He did not yet fully know how, but he knew the source.

This affront could not be allowed to persist.

The creators of this vortex required a similar fate.

He reiterated these truths to himself, a reminder of the Cabal's evil and of the fact that they, like the horror of their creation, must be dealt with if all was to be made right.

Only the most insidious, twisted beings in all of creation, those well versed in the ways of life, its energies and generation, could see how to twist their knowledge so deeply and force such a wondrous gift down such a dark path.

With this affirmation, his reality reordered itself and, with it, his sense of identity.

Anger welled up deep and unbidden as he expressed his rejection of the abomination before him, an evil that even now sought to pull his very life force from within along with that of his friends. "The Cabal has drained this place, sucked the life and marrow from its essence and left but a hollow shell."

He voiced what they already knew, what they had known and feared, but now experienced.

Though the magnitude of this evil had been discussed many times before on the way to Al'Marr and in the planning of their mission, when faced with the stark, unrelenting enormity of the perversion, the memory, the actuality of such discussions were lost.

Only the most fundamental questions remained in the face of reality.

Unbelieving, Aroganji gave voice to just such a one. "Why?"

Yip did not answer. Instead, he stated flatly, compellingly, "We must return to safety." Watching the strength of his friends' magics fade and their vitality along with it, he urged them back toward safety. For now, there was no other choice.

Aroganji gave a nod of understanding, feeling the toil of the place wearing him down, sensing that his protections would not hold much longer. Drawing forth on the reserves he had set aside once more, he called upon the last spell left to him, the rest of his magic drained even while they stood in shock.

In the space between moments, the world shifted and was renewed.

Standing safely on the deck of the *Shrike* once more, the horrors of Al'Marr still far too tangible before him, Yip said, "I do not understand how the Cabal could harness such unimaginable amounts of energy, or to what ends they would put them, but they have tried to do this to our world in the past and will do so again in the future."

Gathering himself, he went on, for the thought pained him deeply, "I know they have done this elsewhere on other worlds, only the alliances of old prevented such a fate from befalling Ea'ae. Even now, having just touched the ground of Al'Marr, having seen its fall in visions, I cannot fully imagine experiencing the doom of a planet when its essence is slowly drained, its magic lost."

Unbidden, tears of compassion welled in his eyes as the reality of the H'era's fall washed through him.

He understood what would happen to the people of such a world.

He knew how civilizations would fare when the life and magic sustaining them fled, torn from between their grasping fingers.

He mourned at the lives and knowledge that would disappear along with the magic as the living energies were shorn from the planet.

He saw how difficult it would be for life to take hold in such a place once more after it had been drained and sullied.

And then the deepest blow fell, one that shook him to his center. He could not help but utter his lament out loud as his world seemed to collapse inward, giving voice to his misery.

The one undeniable connection he yet held to Al'Marr's fall and the H'era's doom was far too much to hold in.

He floundered in the anguish of the thought; the experience on Al'Marr was too much. "And to think, my order gave rise to this. We gave it birth and were powerless to stop it."

A mixture of pity, loathing, fear, and compassion commingled fiercely within him for a time before he let those feelings pass and refocused on the present—his friends, their quest, and the need to right the failures of his spiritual forebears.

His order had let this evil loose on the universe.

How many worlds had fallen before them?

How many other Al'Marr's lay hidden within the tapestry of the stars?

Despite his order's best intentions, how much suffering had his kind indirectly created?

Although Priests of the K'un Lun may have found a path to an end to personal suffering, one that could relieve the ills of others, his brethren had inadvertently visited torment upon countless innocents despite all their noble intentions.

"We cannot let this happen again." His voice cracked as he met the eyes of his friends through tears flowing freely down his dusty cheeks.

"Aye. This'll end with us or we'll die in tha effort." Slate's beard bristled with conviction.

His eyes locked on the view of the planet below, his own future, Yip took in every bit.

He would not turn away just as he would not be diverted.

This wrong would be righted—one among many, a stepping stone on the path to redemption and restoration.

ARIGHT

Stardust strewn lightly
scattered across the heavens—
ash to ash, all is dust.

After their trip to Al'Marr's desolate surface, Yip was resolute in his determination to right the travesty visited upon this once vibrant world. Letting his feelings guide him, he voiced his thoughts to Wrindanneth at the helm of the *Shrike*. "The time has come to move against this pit of Darkness."

Aroganji and Slate turned to Yip to listen.

Pointing in the direction he felt the energies flowing into the heart of the vileness they had touched on Al'Marr's surface, Yip watched Slate, Wrindanneth, and Aroganji's gazes follow his gesture. "We set our target there."

Wrindanneth nodded. "I will call up a detailed image."

Wrindanneth muttered a few words under his breath and the air in front of them churned and thickened, eventually settling into an opalescent lens. Looking through the translucent disk, they stared down at a landscape filled with dry ragged peaks, shorn and blasted gorges, desolate and forlorn.

In a forgotten valley, windswept and sere, some leagues beyond the hills they had so recently braved, Yip's eyes found their mark.

Even after recovering for some time, after experiencing the actuality directly, after taking part in the H'era's vision, after mentally preparing himself for what the Cabal had done, the reality, the depth of the evil presented before him, still left his mind shaken. His stomach dropped, his mind reeled and recoiled in remembrance, and he felt his heart sink beneath the weight of the atrocity he sensed waiting below.

What awaited would be far worse than what he had already experienced.

Despite a wrenching emotional desire to push himself away from the truth he found, he simultaneously felt compelled to reach out in response to the pain, in sympathy and compassion for those harmed, for the plight of the once living land.

Despite the intensity of his unease and shock, the extent of his disgust, these seething emotions served to strengthen his resolve. He would do whatever was necessary to prevent the Cabal's evil from spreading farther. He would do whatever was required to make right what the Cabal had wronged.

"What do you see, Yip?" Noting the depth of emotion on his friend's face, where feeling was seldom shown, Wrindanneth's question held many layers of concern.

Wrindanneth's query fell on deaf ears, however.

Yip watched as power seethed and flowed, roiling in a turbulently surging whirlpool, spiraling around and around in frothing chaos. In the center of the madness, almost lost amidst the violence and confusion, was what he and his friends had journeyed so far to see, the end of their journey, the beginning of their quest.

The maelstrom whose edge they had just touched waited on the ground below.

An absolute void persisted in the center of the turmoil. Inky blackness, or rather the impression of darkness, for nothing escaped from within the center of the mayhem, lay in wait.

This pit held sway over the vortex—an invisible abyss that siphoned off the lifeblood of an entire world.

Despite his impression of darkness lying in wait at the center of the void, he could only infer the presence of the singularity based on the continual passage of *chi* around it, for no energy, no light, emerged from within the awful depths. The sensation of the nihility, however, was so strong to his senses that he felt it to have form and solidity.

His future lay within the heart of that insanity.

With an effort, Yip managed to pull his gaze away from the *chi* funneling riotously below.

"What is it, Yip? What do you see?" This time, Aroganji asked the question that both he and Wrindanneth wanted answered for they knew not if something had changed since their visit to the surface.

Letting his feelings of sadness and despair slip away, Yip answered as best he could based on what he saw and felt. "I do not rightly know. It is as if the Cabal has punched a hole through the very fabric of existence, forcing all the *chi*, all the ambient living energies, to drain away with no hope of escape."

He had explained his impressions before. But now he tried to convey what these impressions meant and signified.

Glancing toward the anomaly, he added, "There is a point I cannot see or feel beyond, a point of demarcation from which nothing emerges. It is beyond this point, within this void, that I must go."

Wrindanneth remained silent for some time, thinking on Yip's words and their recent foray to Al'Marr. "You will be torn apart, Yip. The lifeblood that flows through you will be ripped from your grasp as surely as grains of sand slip through open fingers."

Remembering back, Slate bellowed, "Ya'll die there, Yip!"

Nodding solemnly, he answered them both, "Perhaps."

They had all felt the inexorable pull on Al'Marr's surface.

Regardless of the outcome, he must make the attempt to seal the rift or die trying. For why else had they come?

To allay his friends' fears, he said, "I will seal the energy gates of my body to hold the *chi* within while I work. Do not fear for my safety, my friends."

"Are you certain this is the wisest course?" Aroganji's concern was evident in his tone. If they had almost perished at the void's periphery, how would Yip survive within it?

Yip answered calmly, for he had given this much consideration after their return from Al'Marr's surface, "Who else is here to do what I must? How else can we learn to overcome this evil? Should I fail, I will meet my destiny sooner rather than later."

"I must prepare carefully for the coming test. While I make ready, Aroganji, I will need you to cast your communication spell on me that I may let you know how I fare."

With a smile, he added, "Assuming it holds."

Aroganji nodded. Not only would he listen, he would watch and be ready.

"Wrindanneth, I need you to be prepared to port me down to the surface below as we did when crossing the mountains of the Green Run. If you cast a farseeing disk like you did to see the Cabal's disruption, that should allow me to select the proper spot to arrive at via teleportation."

"You should have ample time to fly directly over the site of the disturbance while I prepare."

"As soon as I stand from my sitting posture, I will need the teleportation ready. Sealing my energy gates, cutting off the living energies within, will be like holding my breath under water. I will only be able to survive without the life force circulating within and without for a very short time."

Wrindanneth nodded grimly.

"I will leave everything but the clothes on my back here on the ship lest the energies below and the pull of the vortex damage the magic contained in the items. Should you need to find them, I have placed these items in my bedroll for the time being. If I fail, I leave it to you to return the Heart of Yere to the Yerens and my teaching scroll to Master Wei."

Leaving Slate and Aroganji to their thoughts and letting Wrindanneth maneuver toward the disturbance, Yip walked over to the ship's fore and sat next to the railing to prepare for the trial ahead. He sat down slowly, folding his legs gracefully beneath his trunk, letting his loose clothing settle where it may. Placing his hands on his knees, he opened himself up to the surrounding *chi* as fully as he could, letting the vitality course through his open gates, passing through his open energy centers, suffusing his meridians with light.

Then he began to carefully seal each primary energy gate, each Wu Xin, where the internal *chi* interacted and mingled with external *chi*. Starting with his navel at the *tan t'ien*, moving downward to the soles of his feet at the Yongquan points, then traveling upward to the center of his palms and the Laogong points of his hands, until finally reaching and sealing the entry points on his face, he closed the main energy inlets to his body. With the primary inlets closed, he let his awareness settle lightly over his skin, sealing the energy apertures of his pores, for he had been taught Fu Xi, skin breathing, to allow energy to diffuse through the openings in his skin as well. Then, directing his attention inward, he moved along each of the twelve primary energy meridians and through the eight energy vessels, one by one, until each and every segment and point of the *chi* circulatory and storage system was fully sealed and isolated.

While Yip prepared, Wrindanneth and Aroganji discussed their safeguards and arrangements.

"I worry that we will not be in a position to help Yip should he fail or succeed. If his efforts fall short, you will be in no state to return his spirit to his body if the energy void remains in place. If he succeeds, I fear a similar outcome for we may not react quickly enough to come to his aid should the effort to undo the Cabal's evil prove too arduous. In either case, the violence of the magical energies below will render my communication spell ineffective, so we will have difficulty discerning and reacting to the outcome, be it for good or ill."

Wrindanneth agreed. "We will be at least partially protected by the ship's shield should we need to try to get closer to try and rescue"— here Wrindanneth paused—"or recover him. If he is successful, I will port down as soon as he is done to heal him should he need my assistance. Be ready to bring us back if I am unable."

Aroganji nodded. "We will watch and make ready."

Aroganji paused. "I had almost forgotten! We've been so busy, I never thought to give this to you."

He reached into his robes and brought out the beautifully engraved wooden box Alderan had given them. "We should be prepared for any eventuality as there may be no time for errors. From what Alderan implied, the bands of the Elven twins Aerdos and Aerlyn should serve us well in this regard."

Gingerly sliding the box open, Aroganji reached in and brought forth the two finely wrought aureate bracers. Each shone brightly with an inner light, twin constellations captured incandescing inside. Handling the bracers in his palm, the metal striking together chimed softly with an eldritch music. Cautiously placing one over his wrist, Aroganji handed the second to Wrindanneth.

Watching Aroganji's reaction carefully, Wrindanneth donned his bracer as well.

Both waited.

Nothing happened. The metal felt slightly warm on their wrists, but that was the extent of the impression given by donning the bracers.

"That's odd," Aroganji thought, expecting something more.

"Yes it is," commented Wrindanneth.

They both stopped in place, stunned.

Neither had spoken aloud. Making direct eye contact, each peered deeply into the other's eyes.

"You know what I'm thinking," thought Wrindanneth.

"Yes I do."

They both burst into laughter.

Aroganji had briefly seen Wrindanneth imagining himself, tall and lanky, all limbs, knees and elbows, dressed in long underwear standing abashedly in the center of a very busy town square for all to see. Aroganji thought it perhaps an image from the kind of dream one had as a young adult coping with the awkwardness and vicissitudes of maturation.

For his part, Wrindanneth had seen Aroganji imagining himself in a very large, dimly lit chamber. Aroganji had been shifting his eyes back and forth circumspectly, quickly reacting to the feeling of being watched by unseen eyes. Wrindanneth thought Aroganji's response rather sedate given the fact that someone shared the confines of his mind, or met somewhere in the middle.

Now that each was aware of the other, they both noticed a slight, very light presence, analogous to someone watching, unbidden, over their shoulder but strangely within the confines of their minds. This slight awareness was the other within their mind. Experimenting, they quickly discovered that the magic only let them explore and share the current contents of their consciousness. Neither one could delve deeply into the other's consciousness nor could they intrude unless allowed.

Reassured, they both quickly came to appreciate the opportunities wearing the bracers afforded.

Aroganji walked over to where Yip sat. Taking a moment, he wove a spell that would allow his friend to communicate with him verbally or directly through mental imagery. Then, thinking about his decision carefully, for he was about to do something Yip had not requested, he began moving his hands through an intricate series of patterns in the air, scribing a spider's web with his gestures.

The air about Yip congealed, coalescing into a scintillating skin, covering Yip in shimmering dew drops of coalesced mana.

As the energy for the spell left him, Aroganji swayed on his feet and stumbled. Caught by surprise at how much the effort to cast the intricate spell had drained him, compounded by how incomplete his recovery from the ordeal on Al'Marr must have been, he had been unprepared for the toll its magic exacted.

This particular spell had been scribbled in the margin near a particularly esoteric section on subtle energy manipulation near the end of Ydrael Faer'Leirn's spell book. Above the instructions and diagrams for the incantation had been written, "Mana, mana burning bright, no magic shall touch me on this night."

Forgetting the bond now shared between them, Aroganji was surprised when Wrindanneth's supporting hand caught his arm before he fell unsteadily to the deck.

"That was quite a risk you just took, Aroganji." Wrindanneth's stern gaze was betrayed by his friend's pride at Aroganji's success in casting such a difficult spell.

"We need to save our energy for the journey ahead." Smiling grimly to his friend, Wrindanneth jokingly added, "If Yip is right, we'll also need your energy should we be beset by psychotic psychics."

Aroganji could barely manage a nod, much less a smile.

"Slate!" Wrindanneth's call was quickly answered by the sound of Slate's boots coming up from belowdecks where his exposure to open space and the sensation of flight were minimal.

"Would you help Aroganji to bed? He needs to rest and recover."

Slate nodded, having quickly assessed his friend's state before arriving by Wrindanneth's side. Picking Aroganji up as though he weighed little more than a child, Slate carried his friend gingerly to his quarters where he laid him down on the small tatami mat and tubular *makura* style buckwheat hull pillow that were his sleeping preferences.

His eyes already closed, lost in the seamless depths of sleep, Aroganji did not know that Slate had taken him to bed.

Emerging above, Slate walked over to Wrindanneth. "Is he all right?"

"Aye. He cast a spell that I would have imagined being well beyond his limits. He took a steep risk, but I am proud of him for mastering the spell."

Unused to praise coming from Wrindanneth, Slate raised an eyebrow. "What exactly was he tryin' ta do?"

"He was trying to shield Yip from the violence of the magical energies below. I do not know if Aroganji's spell will work, but it may give Yip the time and opportunity he needs to be successful."

Glancing toward Yip, Slate asked, "Yip's still makin' ready fer his attempt below?"

"He's 'sealing his energy gates' to help protect him from the disruptive forces below. We'll port him down once he's finished. We should arrive over the site of the disturbance any moment, hopefully before Yip is done. If Aroganji is not up and almost recovered by then, I'll need your help on deck."

"I'll get some food ready fer him and be right back."

"Good."

"Need me ta help keep watch?"

Wrindanneth shook his head. "With the ship's navigation system, I should be able to anticipate any concerns. Just be ready when I call for you. We'll want everyone we can have on deck when Yip ports below."

Slate nodded in response and left Wrindanneth standing by himself on deck, his tall figure accentuated by the faint luminescence of the ship's energy shield against the immense darkness between the stars.

Opening his eyes, Yip looked out upon the world through finite, human eyes. The light of universal *chi* no longer illuminated the emptiness between the stars, bathing the cosmos in limitless potential. Bereft of his senses, closed to the energies around and within him, he no longer felt the Light of Life caressing his mind and body as his world had contracted to the limits of his physical form. Given his newfound perspective, the boundaries of his physical embodiment suddenly, violently came into sharp focus—just as they had so unwelcomingly on the surface of Al'Marr such a short time ago.

At least this time he had some experience.

Shrugging off his feelings of isolation, of limitation, he stood, feeling weak and cumbersome, his actions no longer empowered by the *chi* circulating around or stored within. Turning toward Wrindanneth, where Aroganji now stood unsteadily by his side, he nodded his head and made ready to transport below.

The air in front of him slowly gathered upon itself, congealing into a steady, translucent disk as Wrindanneth worked the magic of his spell. Gazing through the magical lens, he quickly surveyed the land below for the distinctive features he had committed to memory upon first viewing Al'Marr's surface. Without the benefit of his ability to read and feel the patterns of *chi* moving around him, his search took longer than he would have hoped. Already, he could feel his legs tightening, slowly weakening as he drew upon physical reserves bereft of proper replenishment and sustenance.

Finally finding the scattered rocks and boulders that marked the epicenter of the Cabal's disturbance, he motioned to Wrindanneth that he was ready to teleport below.

Focusing on the exact spot he had noted before, he waited for Wrindanneth's magic to take hold of him.

A few seconds later, on Wrindanneth's word, he stepped into chaos.

Yip disappeared.

This was a mistake.

He knew it as soon as he committed himself to the act, but he had stepped forward through the portal anyway because there was, as far as he could determine, no other choice. If he did not find a way to neutralize or circumvent the Cabal's destructive capabilities, then there may not be another opportunity for Ea'ae. Events could quickly spiral out of control beyond any hope of possible recovery, exactly as they had on Al'Marr.

Before he had time to think, feel, or react, the colossal, violent movements of energy stripped him bare, ripping his defenses to tatters, exposing him, utterly, inexorably to the forces of the tides rushing into the void.

The gates he had worked so arduously to seal blasted open, his body left helpless before the torrents raging through and around him.

Collapsing, an incomprehensible avalanche of force tore through him, surging through his meridians, his entire body, indomitably, setting his essence aflame. He felt his life force evaporating, rent from body by the fires of the heavens.

No effort to hold on to his essence, no effort to replenish his internal energies, no struggle to seal and protect himself from the flood, could hold off the inevitability of his doom.

Only the briefest exposure to the furor saw him huddled on hands and knees shuddering in unending torrents of pain, crouched amidst absolute bedlam, poised on the brink of an abyss, his life collapsing to a diminishing point of darkness.

In desperation, recklessly drawing upon what little energy he could capture as it rent through and past him, what little energy was left to him, he fell forward and through the brightest of argent lights, tumbling into darkness, into oblivion.

UMBRAGE

Some shadows persist
during the brightest of days.
What of those that arise in the Night?

In the darkness between dimensions, a Shadow stirred.

Scattered—stars in the distance—small pinpricks of Light defined the limits of Its confinement.

A bleak and utter absence, depthless, fathomless, insatiable, and wholly malevolent, the incalculable Void lashed out, raging at the confines of Its prison as one of the luminous points winked out.

Darkness seethed.

The universe shuddered.

THE GYARXON

A fly in amber,
entombed in golden resin.

Wings no longer free
to stir with the wind.

With Aroganji standing wearily by his side, Wrindanneth watched as Yip blinked away.

"Slate!" Because he had to react swiftly, Wrindanneth had not had time to summon Slate abovedecks once more prior to Yip's departure.

Aroganji ran forward unsteadily toward where the shimmering disk still hovered in the air above the planks, fading slowly with its sustaining magics.

Reaching the deck, Wrindanneth heard Slate call out, "He's gone?"

Nodding to Slate, making ready to join Aroganji by the viewing lens, Wrindanneth noticed a slight blip on the ship's sensory projection —close, very close. Quickly circulating his energy throughout the ship's systems, Wrindanneth powered up the defensive shields as Hoyt had shown him. As he did so, a faint bluish tinge briefly surrounded the *Shrike*'s atmospheric shell.

Though the other vessel had caught them off-guard at their most vulnerable, he would not let them be unprepared!

Simultaneously, he heard Aroganji shout, "Yip has fallen!"

Visible in the dust below, Yip lay motionless on the ground.

"Bring him back!" Wrindanneth left it to Aroganji to use one of the new, more difficult, direct teleportation spells that they had learned from Verakesh's tomes to transport Yip back up, if at all possible.

Though Aroganji was still weak and recovering, there was no alternative.

Just as suddenly as the alien craft materialized and Yip fell, violent shock waves tore through the ship. The *Shrike* rocked up and down and side-to-side, pitched about in the midst of a ferocious storm, buffeted by terrible waves of force roiling through and past the hull.

As quickly as Wrindanneth had put them up, the shields were down. The blast waves had somehow rent their ship's magical shielding away.

Wrindanneth cursed.

At least their atmosphere and magical wards still held.

"What in blazes is that?" Slate yelled, steadying himself on the handrail at the top of the stairs.

"No idea! Ship incoming! Be ready!" Still berating himself, Wrindanneth had no idea how he had missed it, but the other vessel had materialized on his navigation system within easy targeting range. With a ship so close, he had no time to worry about the violent disturbance that was beyond his control or restoring their supplemental defenses now.

As suddenly as they began pitching about, the *Shrike* wrenched, lurching beneath their feet, abruptly discontinuing all motion. Both the rocking from the radiating waves of force and their trajectory orbiting above the planet below, tracking with the planet's rotation to remain immediately above where Yip lay prone on the ground stopped.

Reacting instinctively, Wrindanneth gave the mental command to surge away from the other ship's location.

Nothing happened.

Trying a diagonal away from the ship, Wrindanneth channeled the ship's drives to move.

Again no response.

Looking over his shoulder, he saw a formidable ship wavering, semi-translucent behind them. Matte gray, barely reflecting any light, the vessel appeared entirely alien, a form not cast or imagined by human hands and minds. Although roughly the shape of a smooth, inverted boomerang, both wings of which currently pointed toward the *Shrike*, subtle features along the ship's surface implied an abstract geometry not fully revealed in three dimensions.

Wrindanneth got a headache just looking at the thing.

Trying another tack, Wrindanneth gently tried to bring the ship backward, toward the alien vessel.

The *Shrike* shifted almost imperceptibly.

Smiling grimly while easing back on the ship's propulsion, he had the workings of a plan, should he need it.

Across the deck, nodding in agreement with his idea, Aroganji smiled as well through the weavings of his spell.

"We're caught!" Wrindanneth yelled out for Slate's benefit since he could not share directly in Wrindanneth's thoughts and impressions. "We won't be able to move to help Yip unless we manage to break free!"

He would have to wait to spring his counter to the vessel's trap, however, lest he lose his opportunity. Unfortunately, Yip may not have the luxury of the extra time.

He had to wonder how long the ship had been monitoring their activities undetected.

Since their arrival?

Since Yip first noticed their presence?

For the ship to time its appearance immediately after Yip disappeared indicated that not only had the vessel been observing the *Shrike* but that the crew had been waiting for the most favorable opportunity to strike.

Aroganji agreed.

Their actions on the ground may have also elicited or aggravated the response.

Aroganji did not argue against that point either.

Opening the communication channels, Wrindanneth hailed the alien vessel using magic to frame his words so that his intent would be clear to any beings on the other ship regardless of language. "Alien vessel, this is Wrindanneth, Captain of the *Shrike*. We mean you no harm. Please discontinue your restraint of our vessel. We have a crew member in need of immediate assistance on the surface of the planet."

"I repeat, we must be allowed to come to our crew member's aid! If you do not discontinue your restraint, we will be forced to consider your actions as hostile and will respond accordingly."

By Maeth, there could be no doubting their actions were hostile. If his friend's life were not at risk, he never would have considered parlaying. As the situation stood, he just wanted to buy some time for Aroganji to come to Yip's aid.

He waited as patiently as he could for a response. A minute passed interminably without any indication of understanding.

The alien ship's only reply could be felt in the steady pull of the *Shrike* toward the other vessel's immensity.

In the back of his mind, he felt Aroganji's concentration growing as he gathered power through the connection, his spell taking hold, and his attempt to summon Yip nearing completion. Waiting to see if Aroganji had in fact brought Yip back, he extended the time he had originally intended to grant a response, resisting the urge to take further action against the aggressive alien ship.

Aroganji had done it!

He had brought Yip back!

Simultaneous to his thoughts, he heard a small *pop* of air as Yip's limp, unconscious form materialized on the deck.

Yip must have been successful! Otherwise Aroganji's magic would not have been able to retrieve him. Nor would they have been able to see him to perform the summons.

He would not let any other reason or fear come to mind.

Maintaining his control over the ship, he rushed over to where Slate and Aroganji hovered over their friend.

"How is he?" Concern was etched deeply on Slate's creased face.

Muttering under his breath, Wrindanneth cast a quick diagnostic spell checking for injuries and infirmities.

Staggering back, he was overwhelmed by pain, unrelenting, unimaginable pain surging through Yip's body and mind.

Miraculously, Yip seemed otherwise physically intact with no signs of injury. Composing himself, scanning Yip's body further, he could not locate the source of Yip's affliction. Despite the calm guise on Yip's face, Wrindanneth felt as though his friend had been burned traumatically internally, his essence yet ablaze while flames consumed him from within. With these internal, all-consuming fires, Yip radiated excruciating agony from head to toe.

He knew not how to quench the conflagration.

Bending over and lightly brushing Yip's brow, he cast a spell inducing deep, untroubled stupor. He hoped a spell meant to soothe and alleviate pain and tension could ease his friend's travails for he could do nothing else to help him.

After ensuring that Yip was as healthy and comfortable as he could make him, he warded Yip's body with protective energies since neither he nor Aroganji would be with Yip for a time while he recuperated belowdecks.

Answering Slate's question at last, Wrindanneth said, "He is in great pain, but I can see no signs of physical damage. I fear the magical energies below may have burned him up somehow, consuming him. Let us just hope Yip yet remains somewhere within."

"Slate, take him belowdecks and make him as comfortable as you can then return to us. We may be in for a little more fun ahead."

While Slate rushed Yip's limp form away, cradling his friend gently in his arms, Wrindanneth returned to the helm to continue his efforts to communicate with the other ship one last time.

Although risky, he decided to use the *Shrike*'s capabilities to project his mind across the distance between the two ships in an effort to communicate directly with the alien vessel.

Taking a few deep steadying breaths to prepare himself, he let his mind fully merge with the ship, feeling it as a part of and as an extension of himself. Taking direct control of the communications system, he launched forward projecting his mind outward, oddly simultaneously aware of his body still standing on the deck of the ship while his cognizance hurtled forward.

He closed the space between the two ships in less than a fraction of a second.

Stopping abruptly, he probed the ship floating before him, encountering a shield of some type that prevented his mind ready access to the vessel. Pushing his awareness forward probingly, trying to move beyond the resistance he felt, his consciousness reeled, forcing him to drop to his knees in pain as his awareness lurched back violently to his body.

The alien vessel's mental assault tore the *Shrike*'s patchwork mental shields and wards to ribbons, blasting Wrindanneth and Aroganji in successive waves of unrelenting misery.

Hunched over on the *Shrike*'s deck, a powerful migraine pulsing excruciatingly through body and mind, the *Shrike* once again lurched. This time the ship began moving rapidly toward the alien vessel, accelerating faster and faster unlike the steady motion of before. The closer the *Shrike* got to the other ship, the more intense and debilitating the pain became, throbbing with such intensity that he thought his blood vessels might burst.

Aroganji, too, squatted on the deck clutching his head in both arms where Yip had rematerialized just moments before toward the fore of the ship.

Apparently the occupants of the other vessel did not appreciate his attempts to breach its defenses.

With his ship moving out of control beneath his feet, feeling as though jagged shards of glass had decided to take up residence within his skull, turning molten as the pain spread throughout his body, he glared at the other ship, spittle drooling unnoticed down his chin.

He was pissed.

And there was little he could do about it.

By the time Slate returned to the deck, holding Duraeleon gleaming at his side, the *Shrike* was held suspended and vulnerable immediately in front of the other looming craft.

Barely noticing how insignificant the *Shrike* appeared now that it was juxtaposed almost directly against the alien craft, Slate quickly noticed his friends huddled on the deck in obvious torment. Sprinting over to Wrindanneth, Slate hoisted him up by the arm asking, "What's wrong? What's happened?"

As soon as the Dwarf got within a few feet of Wrindanneth, he felt the cool, blissful waves of clarity return to his mind.

"We've got to get to Aroganji!"

Running over, Aroganji, too, felt instant relief as soon as Slate approached.

"How in the wide world did you manage that, Slate?" asked Wrindanneth, his thinking still a bit fuzzy. "I knew you were hardheaded, but never imagined the true extent!"

Recovering himself, Aroganji blurted, "Duraeleon!"

With an oddly smug tone, the axe responded, "You rang?"

Turning to glare at his axe, Slate snapped, "I thought we'd agreed that ya would only speak when spoken ta!"

"Was I not the subject of an observation? Although not addressing me for explicit communication, I was, in fact, referred to directly as the object of Aroganji's intent."

"Quiet, you two! There's no time for this!" Wrindanneth would let them sort their differences out at some other, more favorable, time.

"Duraeleon's shield protects you from mental as well as physical assault! Quite the weapon!" Aroganji was impressed, a little addled, the remembrance of frenetic waves of volcanic pain still radiating in waves through his body, but appreciative nonetheless.

"Is that not what a weapon is for? Protection?" Duraeleon was not going to be left out of this conversation, especially after Slate had prevented its communication for so long.

"We will have to stay near Duraeleon to prevent further attacks then. We need to return to the helm."

"Your shield prevents all mental encroachment, Duraeleon?"

"Aye, aye, Cap'n!" answered Duraeleon slipping back into character. "Ahoy mateys!" Duraeleon pointed its blade toward the other ship of its own accord.

Directing their attention to the other vessel, they all stared in awe at the enormity of the ship before them. Whereas the *Shrike* appeared to be a vessel that would normally ply the seas for trade, the type of craft one might see at any port, albeit of superb craftsmanship, unusual lines, and able to fly, the ship before them was an entirely different matter. The vessel, the cruiser, was obviously intended to traverse the void between the stars for extended journeys lasting for substantial periods of time. Floating before the alien spacecraft, the *Shrike* appeared barely larger than the observation viewing window of the craft's control room immediately before them.

Standing by the *Shrike*'s control disk, floating before a thick, semi-translucent dome mounted on the fore of the carrier, Wrindanneth, Aroganji, and Slate stared directly into the helm of the alien craft. Inside, almost a dozen tall, gangly humanoid creatures with hairless heads and armored torsos stood watching them impassively.

Examining the figures standing only a few stone throws away, Wrindanneth noted their elongated limbs and digits, attenuated torsos, and fine skeletal structures. This race had been living and moving in space under low gravity conditions for some time. Based on the work-manship of their shimmering armor and assorted instrumentation, their level of technical sophistication with material objects was well beyond the capabilities of most visitors to Ea'ae without access to significant magic.

The creatures inside the other ship did not register the same shock, excitement, or upset that Wrindanneth felt coursing through his body. After ignoring and mistreating them, the other crew still did not deign to recognize or acknowledge the *Shrike*. Instead, they merely held her locked in place, neutralized, for some unknown purpose.

"Now that we are protected by Duraeleon's aegis, should I try one last time to contact the other vessel?" Although his sensibilities grated against doing so, Wrindanneth wanted to make sure that he gave the other ship every opportunity to grant the *Shrike* her freedom before he took control of the situation.

As much as he hated to admit it, their mercy might be the only path to the *Shrike*'s freedom.

Aroganji looked back and forth between the two ships gravely. "We should always try to do what is right even if we are not afforded the same opportunity. Especially when it may be our only hope."

Slate grunted, "I say skin 'em and use their scrawny little teeth fer necklaces. Assumin' they have teeth that is!"

"If my broadcast doesn't work, be prepared to board the other ship. We may have to take command of the enemy vessel."

Slate glanced back and forth between the two ships. He had no idea how many crew members the other ship had or their capabilities, but there were certainly many more of the aliens than the three of them. He also did not know what capabilities the other ship had, but if it could hold them in place and pull them in from leagues distant, then he was sure that the *Shrike* was no match for it. "Am I missin' somethin' here? How d'ya plan ta do that?"

Wrindanneth grinned wickedly. "Just stay close. We'll need your shield."

Wrindanneth stepped slightly forward, once again opening communication with the alien cruiser using the *Shrike*'s control disk.

"Alien vessel, we have retrieved our comrade. He is in desperate need of medical attention beyond our current capabilities. We request that you allow us our freedom to return home to seek further aid."

He had no idea if the return stone would allow them to transport back to Ea'ae if used under the influence of the other vessel's gravity well. As such, he did not want to risk their ability to return. Even if it did work, he would prefer not to have to use the return stone since Yip may need to go back to the surface once he recovered.

If he recovered.

He grated his teeth while the creatures on the other vessel watched impassively, giving no further response.

Turning to his friends, he smiled archly. "Are you ready?"

Aroganji was ready and understood full well his plan, eager to move despite his own weakness. Slate gave a curt nod, tightening his grip on Duraeleon's handle as the white fires of Brendle's forge engulfed the length of his glowing axe. For its part, Duraeleon called out, "Bring 'er alongside and we'll blow the men down!"

Wrindanneth assumed the creatures controlled their ship through their mental commands in much the same way as he did with the

Shrike. If so, he would have to be swift and decisive, giving little time for them to react or counter. Either way, he would find out soon enough.

Bracing his feet, he turned to his friends as if engrossed in deep conversation, all the while maintaining a keen focus on the command center of the other vessel. With a faint wave of his hand and a resolute mental directive, he thrust all of the *Shrike's* power into propulsion, aiming directly toward the alien ship's center of command.

The *Shrike* lurched, wood grinding and grating but steadily gaining speed against the forces holding her in place. Smiling grimly, he noted that a few of the alien creatures even managed to act alarmed after remaining so aloof before, but it was too late. They had reacted too slowly to his counter maneuver.

The aliens had made the mistake of pulling the *Shrike* inside the barrier that had barred his earlier mental advance. He did not know why they drew his ship so close. Perhaps they did not detect any weapons that they felt could threaten their vessel. Maybe they wanted to study a craft so different from their own within the confines of their own ship. Perchance they viewed the lack of technical sophistication apparent on the *Shrike* as a sign of weakness. Whatever the cause, the creatures on the other ship would pay dearly for their blunder. He would close the distance between the two vessels before the psychics could escape or halt his progress.

Launching forward, rapidly closing with the other ship, the *Shrike's* prow aimed directly for the clear viewing window the creatures had used to observe and manipulate his ship. He could feel resistance building rapidly as the *Shrike* bridged the short gap between the two vessels.

Pushing more of his energy into the ship than he would have cared to, he deliberately propelled the *Shrike* forward and against the same force that had been used to pull them in. This time, however, the *Shrike* had managed to gain some momentum prior to the application of the alien control beam.

Drones launched into space, fanning about defensively around the other ship in response to the *Shrike's* advance. Volleys of multicolored energy shot out in rapid pulses from mounted turrets arrayed along the alien vessel's wings, arching through space with deadly accuracy. Maintaining his attention on the impending impact, Wrindanneth watched as the *Shrike*'s wards flared and sparked with the impact of the aliens' counter assault. Pieces of wood shattered and flew through the air within the atmospheric shield as some of the beams breached the *Shrike*'s defenses.

A second volley of cannon fire took aim on the *Shrike* as it advanced, launching a steady barrage of inky black energy beams almost indistinguishable from the dark void of space. Somehow, these shadowy rays bypassed the ship's shielding and wards without even registering the *Shrike*'s defenses.

Striking with uncanny accuracy, these beams obliterated the ship wherever they impacted, annihilating wood and fabric, slicing through the hull and decks, leaving the ship perforated and shredded by hundreds of cuts. Were the *Shrike* not held together and strengthened by magic, powered by the energies held within the control disk, then the hull would have disintegrated beneath the assault, its structure and vital mechanisms destroyed. With the disk shielded and no machinery to be damaged by the alien's onslaught, the *Shrike* continued its advance unimpeded.

In the back of his mind, he felt Aroganji scrambling to fend off the attacking drones, sending coruscating balls of explosive flames to intercept and counter their erstwhile captor's defenses. Fragments of molten metal from blasted drones pelted the ship, shattering through portions of the decks leaving gaping, smoldering rents from the impact. Small burning holes appeared in the rigging overhead as beams of light and shrapnel found their way through the *Shrike*'s defenses.

Slate maintained a solid grip on Duraeleon's hilt, grunting with the force of impacts from multiple beams and bolts raining down around them, directly buffeting against Duraeleon's shield, blasts intended for the three standing clearly visible on the ship's deck.

With a savage shudder, the prow of the *Shrike* shattered through the crystalline enclosure protecting the aliens onboard from the harsh vacuum of space, sending a cloud of iridescent shards into orbit about the ship along with all the atmosphere in the control room.

Simultaneous to the impact, Wrin clapped both hands together and shouted, "The breath of the R'yn Daer claims you!" as he whipped out the dagger from his side and channeled the energy of the blade through the *Shrike*, commingling its power with that of the ship.

The resulting tornadic blast tore through the scrambling creatures with massive concussive force, hurtling them bodily into the interior walls of the control room, and sent them ricocheting out into the cold recesses of space. Scattering the ship's atmosphere in the swirling cone of destruction, the detonation tore equipment and chairs in the room from their moorings, and rended the two sealed, protective bay doors leading out of the room from their housings. Along with the portals and equipment, the ship's remaining atmosphere rushed into space.

With the alien ship pierced by prow of the *Shrike*, its debris orbiting in a cloud, Wrindanneth shouted, "Now it is the *Shrike* that hunts!"

Anticipating the coming impact, two of the creatures launched themselves upward into the air gracefully, their shimmering silhouettes indicating some type of shielding in the half-light of the surrounding stars. One of the two arched through the void above the *Shrike* firing barrage after barrage of molten plasma at the *Shrike*'s crew, vaporizing large portions of the *Shrike*'s deck around Duraeleon's shield. The other creature loped off fluidly along the curving surface of the ship's exterior disappearing from view before either Wrindanneth or Aroganji could react.

With a quick flick of his wrist, Aroganji screamed out a violent incantation as scorching white sunfire shot out from his fingers, evaporating the alien's shield, incinerating the creature.

Turning to his friends, Wrindanneth yelled, "We must hurry while we have the advantage should the other creature be fleeing to alert more of the crew on the ship or others come to its aid!"

With a wave of his hand and a muttered incantation in preparation to disembark, Wrindanneth gathered some of the air from the *Shrike*'s atmosphere in a swirling cocoon about each of them, protecting the party from the chill void of empty space.

Pocketing the ship's control disk lest one of the remaining creatures return, Wrindanneth settled the hull of the *Shrike* directly above the other ship's demolished control room and locked her into position.

Before proceeding, Wrindanneth hurriedly cast a spell to modify his vision to help detect the presence of other living creatures, even if hidden. His vision flashed briefly with white light upon the spell's culmination. Glancing toward his friends, he could see that each was surrounded by a variegated halo of light.

He did not know exactly what could be inferred from this light's color and intensity, for Verakesh's spellbooks left little in the way of description, but, given the glow, Aroganji and Slate's presences were certainly obvious.

Blinking rapidly, water coming to his eyes in response to a series of bright flares emanating directly from Aroganji, Wrindanneth watched the halo around his friend dance and flicker as Aroganji completed a spell intended to help protect them from the effects of the creatures' energy beams should one of the group not be fully protected by Duraeleon's shield.

Waiting a moment to recover his vision, Wrindanneth urged them forward, shouting, "Let's move!" while motioning for his friends to follow him down to the floor of the other ship.

Grabbing the gangplank affixed to the side of the *Shrike*, he slid the wooden plank through the railing and sprinted down, wary for more of the creatures. Slate reached the floor of the control room close on Wrindanneth's heals, huffing to stay within shield range to protect his friend.

Surveying the room quickly, Wrindanneth noted that besides the jagged remnants of the crystalline viewing material overhead, the rest of the room seemed to be a burnished gray color with little decoration or differentiation. Rubbing the palm of his hand over the material along one wall, he noted that the entire room appeared to be made of a single piece of seamless metal. Tapping the material beneath his feet, the flooring gave a faint hollow resonance, of a timbre indicating a very light or thin substance. He had no idea what the ship was made out of or how it was crafted but its level of sophistication appeared astounding.

Floating immediately in front of them, positioned in the center of the room between themselves and the crumpled automatic doors, a crystalline orb of many hues commanded his attention. He could only imagine that the sphere served a similar function as the control disk he now carried in his pocket. Whether or not it operated on equivalent principles and through a similar fashion, he could not say. Perhaps the Paratechnologists could decipher its function.

Without voicing a word, Aroganji assented, noting in particular the value of the knowledge this race may have stored within the orb's confines, especially if it held copious amounts of information in a similar fashion to Tellanon's Construct.

Wrindanneth would try to bring the orb aboard the *Shrike* after the alien vessel was secured.

Speaking aloud, he said, "Any preference on which hatchway we take?"

"I didn't see anyone escape through one, so either's fine by me. Tha sooner we're done, tha sooner I can stow my axe."

Duraeleon echoed its master's sentiments. "Whichever one leads to more of those vermin!"

Nodding, Wrindanneth strode forward cautiously, taking the doorway to the left. A well-lit hallway of the same sleek metallic material curved away from them, presumably toward the tips of the ship's wings.

Before having the opportunity to examine the passage further, Wrindanneth yelled, "Get back!"

He pulled his friends out of the hallway as soon as they entered.

A brief flicker of light indicated the presence of one of the inimical creatures around a corner down the passage. Just as they ducked around the corner adjacent to the hall's entry hatch, a silvery haze roiled out of the hatchway. The mist drifted languidly, sparkling under the light of the surrounding stars. Wherever the haze settled on the alien metal, bright flashes heralded a sinister reaction that left portions of the metal vitiated, spongy and porous, eaten through and riddled with holes.

"'Ware the door!" Wrindanneth sensed the rapid approach of the creature sprinting down the hall.

With a simple, quick incantation, Aroganji thrust his hands outward and down toward the floor in front of the hatchway, coating the ground in a layer of slick, oily material.

Immediately after Aroganji's spell took effect, one of the creatures leapt through the doorway, limned in shimmering, translucent armor that protected it from the corrosive presence of the haze, a glowing, crystalline blade gripped firmly in one hand held menacingly over-head, and an irregular orb held in the other. At its waist, a bright gem glowed with a white light, perhaps providing or channeling the power for the creature's aura. Before landing, it shot a beam of light from the orb in its hand toward them. Duraeleon's shield absorbed the energy without effect. Simultaneously, the creature swung the blade in its other hand a blazing arch, slicing through a portion of Duraeleon's shield.

"Argh! Keelhaul that scallywag!" Duraeleon shook angrily in Slate's hand, quickly refreshing its sundered shield, lest its charges become susceptible to the creature's mental assault.

All grace left the creature as it landed, sliding limbs akimbo, across Aroganji's oily magical slick.

As soon as the creature began to slide, Wrindanneth followed Aroganji's spell with a gout of green flame, igniting the entire column of oil in a magical conflagration that burnt without need for air.

Recovering itself, carefully stepping off the slick, the alien being stood, its long limbs accentuated by the burning flames covering the length of its oil-coated body. Crystalline sword and orb held ready, the creature charged, its mental armor having protected it from the effects of the flame and heat.

Reacting instinctively, Aroganji lashed out with a bolt of lightning, hoping that electricity would travel through the creature's shielding. He knew that visible light would cross the creature's barrier because his sunfire spell had penetrated the shield and he could currently see the creature, though the efficacy of both could just be temporary. Perhaps lightning would be effective as well.

The crystal at the creature's waist changed color slightly as the bolt impacted, flashing bright blue light around its silhouette. As the bolt struck, the creature was lifted bodily off the ground from the force of the impact, smashing into the chamber's far wall. Dazed, the creature rose wobbly to its feet, reaching unsteadily for the object held at its side, the same object that had spewed forth the acidic haze and the beam of light.

Alarmed, Aroganji asked Wrindanneth mentally, faster than words could travel, *"Any thoughts?"*

Clapping both hands together, dagger drawn, Wrindanneth yelled his summons once more as a great concussive blast issued forth from between his hands, radiating outward in a deadly cone. The creature smashed into the wall again, this time with significantly more force. Leaving an impression of its shield imprinted in the wall, the creature fell forward, unconscious, its armor blinking out of existence as it lost consciousness.

In answer to Aroganji's question, Wrindanneth noted the color change in the creature's translucent gem, the one he assumed powered the shield, indicating that it had somehow adjusted to and absorbed or deflected the bolt's energy. "The creature's armor may have deflected the bolt, but it did not absorb the force of the impact."

Flames kindling along the length of Duraeleon's resplendent blade, Slate ran over and quickly finished the supine creature before returning to his friends to offer the protection of Duraeleon's shield.

"We have to be careful. Those things' mental shields, if that's what they are, are an effective counter to most of our attacks. If their blades can slice through Duraeleon's protective barrier, we'll have to be doubly careful." Wrindanneth wanted to leave nothing to chance. After the haze settled and the fire dimmed, he looked up and down both corridors for signs of life.

There was nothing he could discern.

Slate grunted, "Hopefully that was tha last of 'em."

"It's all clear for now, Slate."

"Lemme check this one out."

Slate walked over to the alien humanoid, followed closely by his friends, carefully inspecting its sculpted features and long, lissome limbs. To Slate, the creature looked something like a delicate marionette. So fine were its features that he could easily imagine strings suspended from the joints to hold the humanoid in place to prevent it from falling over. Bending down, he gingerly placed the crystalline sword, the energy and haze projecting orb, and the glass-like apparatus on the creature's belt in his magical pouch.

From where he crouched at the alien's side, he said with a grin, "Adar may have a use fer these items."

Slate assumed the crystalline device somehow channeled the creature's mental energy to form a shield in the same way its sword appeared to harness its psychic power. He had no idea how the blaster worked.

Before standing, Slate inspected the rest of the creature's uniform. The airy gray clothing draped lightly over its limbs appeared to glimmer faintly, akin to fine silk. There were no pockets or seams visible to Slate's eye, so he would not be able to find anything else of use on the creature's corpse. Turning his attention to the creature's breast, Slate hissed, pointing for his friends to see.

Emblazoned in faint black markings barely distinguishable from the clothing's reflective finish, a very small glaring lidded eye stared out menacingly from the fabric.

"Tha Cabal!"

Wrindanneth and Aroganji crowded close.

"Well that answers that question," grumbled Wrindanneth. "The Cabal sent these poor fools to watch over their handiwork."

He chuckled wryly. "We had to cross half the known universe just to find these miscreants and we weren't even looking when we did!"

Aroganji cut him off. "We should leave as quickly as possible. Perhaps the ship alerted the Cabal to our presence when they were monitoring us after our arrival."

Aroganji doubted they would be so lucky in another confrontation. "They might have been holding us until their allies arrived."

"I fer one would at least stay until we clean this ship o' tha rest o' those creatures. If we don't, then they'll be in touch with their masters fer sure." Slate had rooted out many Orc dens in his day. The last thing you ever did with a nest of buggers like that was leave it uncleaned.

"Agreed. We can't afford to leave just yet. We also don't know what Yip would have us do. Any number of things are possible. For all we know, he may not have fully succeeded down below. He may need more time. And even if he did succeed, there may be more he wants to do. I cannot say. After we clean the ship, we can focus on getting Yip better or finding help for him if we can't. If his condition doesn't improve or more ships arrive, we may be forced to leave regardless."

Wrindanneth hoped Yip had finished so they would not have to go through any more travails before returning home. The *Shrike* could not take another encounter like this last one without some serious repairs. Nor did he think that they would survive another encounter if a ship like the alien's cruiser acted aggressively with the intent to destroy them from the outset.

Aroganji agreed.

"Let's finish down the left hall way. Then we can try the right."

"Are ya not concerned that we may be flanked and our own ship attacked?" Slate did not want Yip left alone for too long, even if he was warded.

"To be honest, I don't think there are any more here, Slate. A ship like this is probably almost entirely automated. I think most were on the bridge when we struck and killed them. I think the one runner who survived lies dead on the floor in front of us. I cannot imagine these creatures would run off and hide, abandoning their fellow crewman during an attack."

Slate grunted and then said, "Let's be quick about this."

They spent the next hour carefully wandering the ship with Wrindanneth scanning ahead looking for signs of life, all to no avail.

Much of the ship appeared unadorned, smooth walls and floors with no visible furniture or decoration. Wrindanneth speculated that seats and bedding for the crew must retract from the walls and floors upon command. However, he could find no signs of slots or other openings for these basic appointments in the chambers they visited. Interestingly, several rooms were coated in large crystalline accretions, the shards glowing with bright, multicolored light emanating internally with a soft, diffuse radiance. He was unsure if these structures were the source of the crystals used for the crewman's weaponry and armor, if they somehow served to power the ship and its weaponry, or if they had some other function.

When they had finished their survey, Aroganji, Wrindanneth, and Slate returned to the control room.

If any of the psions had survived, they were no longer on the ship.

"Ready?" Slate was eager to board the *Shrike* and leave the barren carrier behind. Even when the creatures were alive and working inside the vessel, he imagined it must have been a rather bleak, depressing place, not at all like the well-lit caves and warrens of home. After his brief encounter with the pallid aliens, he did not suspect the walls lit up with color and vibrancy with use. The structures probably remained as cold and lifeless as their prior occupants.

Wrindanneth projected his thoughts toward Aroganji. *"I'll need your help on this, if you still have the strength. I'm not sure if this ship's control console is tethered to the ship or not. I'm going to have you help me create a containment field to try and break its ties to the ship if it is tethered and prevent it from interacting with the Shrike and any other vessels while aboard."* Wrindanneth cautiously reached out toward the ship's control crystal.

Aloud for Slate's benefit, he said, "One last thing then I'll be ready."

Reaching out, extending his faculties forward, he encountered no resistance to his spell as he had when he had approached the ship. Reassured, he gradually projected his enchantment in a diaphanous web around the crystalline orb at the command room's center, first weaving a net and then, building layer upon layer until completion, creating a cocoon of eldritch radiance around the ship's control sphere. Drawing upon Aroganji's power as much as he was able, he reinforced the cocoon's layers, over and over, until the panel was encased in folded lamina of crystallized force.

Placing his hands gently upon the ensorcelled navigation orb, Wrindanneth sighed gently and guided it toward him through the air. "Now I'm ready!"

"Is that thing safe?" The last thing Slate wanted on the ship was any more excitement. They would have enough just trying to nurse Yip back to health.

"I think the spell we have placed on it will isolate it and protect us from anything it may be capable of independently."

"Ya think?" Slate did not like the sound of those words.

Wrindanneth grinned. "I am almost certain. I will use energy from the *Shrike* to sustain the shielding."

Walking toward the gangplank, preferring that answer, Slate asked Wrindanneth, "What d'ya plan ta do with it?"

"After our fruitless efforts to trace the Cabal to their source, to garner any information on their activities and plans, this orb may hold the key to the information we've sought. Even if we fail here, this orb may be of value in our quest."

"I doubt that I can crack the orb's defenses, nor would I want to risk the endeavor, but Adar or one of the other Paratechnologists may be able to. I am certain they have encountered and reverse-engineered many such systems in their explorations. I would imagine that the Construct itself would be ideally suited to such a task."

Wrindanneth chuckled. "Besides, one of Maeth's cardinal rules is never to leave empty-handed. The information stored in these crystals may be more valuable than a horde of Dragon's gold. Don't you think?"

A gleam in his eye, Slate answered, "Aye," already thinking of untold riches and opportunity awaiting their fingertips. He patted the bag at his side now housing the other alien devices—even more riches and opportunity were within reach.

REPRIEVE

The first rays of dawn
adumbrate a horizon
steeped in darkest night.

Pain.

Unending waves of pain.

All-consuming agony.

The heat of a thousand suns consumed him before the shreds of his fleeting awareness were obliterated in absolute darkness.

Over and over he awoke to unrelenting torment, to agony beyond measure, before succumbing, exhausted to the void—emptiness before thought, before awareness, before sensation, complete cessation, Wuji.

How many times he struggled for wakefulness, grasping for the light and life beyond his sealed eyes, he could never say, nor fully remember.

Each time he woke to anguish, his conscious awareness recoiled, separating from the sensations raging through his body of necessity, the light of his consciousness only flickering momentarily before the effort to maintain mindfulness evaporated with his dwindling energies amidst the cataclysm of suffering. As his energies failed, so did his detachment, so did his strength, and so did his distance from total nigritude.

Pain marked the beginning and end of his universe, his rebirth to each moment and his death.

Each waking instant, each exposure to the pain consuming his existence, became a forge, a crucible—both a trial and a reformation—recasting his consciousness over and over, redefining his limits and tolerances anew.

Surely stars were born and died in the time he suffered, for if the universe were vast enough to contain such pain, it had to be spread throughout eternity.

Eventually, gradually, after countless cycles of rebirth, death, and reincarnation, awareness and oblivion, the pain, the blazing heat, began to diminish, first cooling and then, later, much later, finally becoming nourishing and replenishing beneath the gaze of his impassive attention. So subtle was the transition, however, that he actually did not notice the lessening in his agony for a very long time. Rather, he noticed an increase in the clarity and constancy of his awareness, an increase in his ability to maintain sustained attention before losing himself once more to darkness.

Long before the pain left him, as his awareness steadied, stabilizing in lucidity, realization dawned before him. Even though he still could not yet open his eyes, he wept in joy, laughing at the cruel irony. The unending torrent of pain raging incessantly through his body, consuming all his faculties and every fiber of his being, lashing him into extinction, was caused by his very lifeblood, the *chi* that nurtured and sustained all beings.

In the ceaseless darkness, the limitless expanse between moments, he gradually began replenishing what had been lost, examining how he had changed, and restoring his health and vivacity.

Eyes flickering, burning and tearing, he tried and succeeded, albeit briefly, to open his eyes. The darkness and shadows of the room were still too much for his eyes.

He had to close them again immediately.

He felt tears falling down his cheeks as his eyes watered in response to the tortuous glare.

How many times had he tried and failed to open his eyes?

How many tears remained unshed?

Far away, so very far away, muffled footsteps and muttered voices responded to his efforts.

A cool towel was placed on his forehead and a firm hand rested on his shoulder. He opened his mouth but no sounds came out.

He tried again.

Cool drops of water landed on his parched lips, dribbling with excruciating torpor into his mouth.

Soft words in his ear, "Welcome back, Yip."

Aroganji.

Time passed and more water came before he was finally able to speak in the faintest of whispers, "Thank you."

A muttered incantation, vibrant energies coursing through his body in a cool wave leaving him cleansed and refreshed—Wrindanneth.

"'Bout time. Thought ya were gonna hibernate through tha winter."

Slate.

Sure of himself now, he sat up slowly, testing his limits, and managed a brief smile.

"Are you well?" Aroganji's simple question held many others hidden underneath.

He gave a slight nod, his voice a whisper, foreign to his ears. "As well as I could hope."

"Were you completely successful? Are you ready to return home or must we wait here in hiding longer for another attempt?" Wrindanneth's voice held an urgency that his line of questioning did not clarify or explain.

He did not know how to explain what happened, or, rather, he did not know how to explain what he thought had happened, but he would try. "Al'Marr is now safe."

Soft exhalations, sighs of relief, from his gathered friends. "You were right to be concerned. I was foolish and unprepared. I am lucky to be alive. We are lucky that I succeeded."

He shrugged, adding, "Coincidence and fortune saved me as much as any preparation."

Thinking back, the blinding silver-white flash before the darkness consumed him was not an act of protection provided by the Heart of Yere for he had left it in his friends' keeping.

What then?

What had saved him?

He looked blearily at Aroganji through lidded eyes. Luck, as much as anything else had given him the briefest instant to act. Were it not for the boon of Aroganji's protective spell and the act of sealing his energy gates, his life force would have been wrenched away from his body before even the briefest time to react. His preparations, working in conjunction with Aroganji's spell had given him the slightest opportunity—a moment's time.

"Thank you for your protection, my friend."

Aroganji smiled. "We are thankful for your return."

"How long was I unconscious?"

Aroganji answered flatly, "Nearly two weeks. We had decided to return to Tellanon earlier but feared a return journey to Al'Marr may be difficult if we left. More importantly, we wanted to make certain that everything had been completed here before we returned home."

Yip nodded, ready to try and answer his friends' questions.

"I will try to describe what happened as best I can."

He paused for a moment before commencing. "As soon as I appeared below, the energy of my body left me, rent from my grasp and through all of my protections as surely as sand passing through open outstretched fingers. With my feet not yet settled on the ground, before I could consciously react, I fell forward into the void, the abysm draining away all of the living *chi* within and around me, the chasm draining the life from this world."

"I do not know exactly how or what happened then. As I said, I felt the life force leaving my body as I fell, rapidly losing consciousness and vitality, toward and through the heart of the terrible singularity.

Somehow, as the locus of the disturbance passed through my body, I internalized its field, spontaneously"—here he struggled for a word, an idea to express what he felt happening within as the central point of the turmoil passed through his *tan t'ien*—"inverting its presence, healing the Cabal's wound. In that instant, all the remaining power trapped or channeled within and through that point lashed back, radiating outward in an unimaginably powerful pulse."

"I was but a slight sliver of driftwood within a tsunami tossed about by tidal waves surging through an impossible ocean of force."

"Lost before this fury, I could not hold and knew only darkness."

Thinking back, he remained silent for some time. Finally, he added, "I think perhaps that it was Azaelle's gift that saved me."

"How so?" Aroganji's curiosity would not let him remain silent.

"As I fell forward, I knew that I was dying. I think that as the energy left my body, I somehow instinctively created *chi* as Azaelle had shown me in return for our favor. I think it was this energy, or rather, this act of creation that somehow disrupted and canceled the *chi* void the Cabal created."

Silence held for some time in response.

"Then perhaps we have a weapon to use against the Cabal," added Aroganji thoughtfully.

"Perhaps." Yip was not so sure, just as he was still unsure of his new abilities.

When Yip and Aroganji finished, Slate grunted, "That explains tha violent shakin' right before we were caught in those buggers' net."

"Net?" Now it was Yip's turn to ask a question.

"In due time." Wrindanneth cut off Yip's question. "Is there more you would do here before we leave? Our time may be short. The Cabal may be coming for us!"

Yip answered patiently, although now he, too, had questions.

The Cabal!

Here? Now? How?

"There is one more thing I would do. Then we can go. But first, you must tell me more. The Cabal is here?"

Wrindanneth summarized their encounter with the alien vessel and the subsequent revelations as quickly as he could. "Immediately after you left us, the alien ship you sensed before materialized. They did not respond to our attempts to hail them or give us the opportunity to come to your aid. We were trapped by some kind of restraining beam that first held us in place and then drew us toward the ship."

"After our attempts at direct communication failed, I tried mentally circumventing their trap to speak with them directly. That's when I found out that the crew of the other craft were psychics for their vessel was shielded from my attempts. As soon as my mind encountered their barrier, they locked both Aroganji and myself in the throes of mortal physical and mental agony. Luckily, Duraeleon's ward protected Slate from the psionic assault and he came to our aid."

Here Wrindanneth broke into a wicked grin. "They were foolish enough to bring us in close, thinking us trapped and ineffectual."

He laughed throatily. "Unsuspecting, we seized the moment and countered. I rammed directly into their command deck! Those wretches learned the true measure of the *Shrike*!"

"We blasted the aliens on the bridge into space, boarded the ship, and cleansed it of the remaining blackguards. That's when we found out the crew of the vessel owed its allegiance to the Cabal by the insignia on their uniforms. We claimed some of their weaponry for the Paratechnologists to examine in addition to their ship's command orb."

"Hopefully the vessel's command sphere will have information regarding the Cabal's whereabouts and activity, that is, if the Paratechnologists can safely divulge and decipher the information."

Here Wrindanneth turned to the less positive news. "Unfortunately, we do not know if this ship was in direct communication with the Cabal or if its presence will be missed. Given the amount of time you have been incapacitated with no response or sign from the craft's allies, I would say that the vessel only communicated with others occasionally, but we cannot be sure. Even if the ship did not communicate directly with its associates, the explosion of magical energy, for that is what I assume was released after you sealed the energy hole, may have been detected."

Yip nodded. "I doubt the Cabal would leave their handiwork guarded by a single sentry. Even though I do not know exactly what, if anything, they did with the energy they siphoned off or how they harnessed what power they withdrew, their reaction will be quick once they find out what happened."

Wrindanneth nodded in turn. "We have hidden ourselves in a valley on the opposite side of the planet from the site of their taint. Our isolation has bought us time, for I, too, am sure they are on the hunt."

Yip nodded, imagining the sky opening with portals to dark realms better left unconsidered as it had when Aroganji's school had been assaulted and his monastery waylaid, the land filling with seething masses of dark creatures intent upon hunting them down and destroying them. "I do not think that they will be able to recreate another void quickly with so much excess *chi* in the vicinity to disturb their work. Nor do I think this planet is a desirable location for another energy void since all the living creatures they would draw power from have already perished."

"Let me complete one small task and then we can return home. Is there water near?"

Aroganji nodded. "There is a small arroyo down the hillside from where our ship rests beneath the escarpments of the valley we hide in."

Yip stood up slowly, his body protesting violently, weak and unused to movement after having remained motionless for so long. "I will be back within the hour."

He walked unsteadily out of the small chamber where his kit had lain these past two weeks, absorbing his feverish heat and sweat, taking the stairs to the deck deliberately as his strength recovered. A dusty brown sky overhead masked the afternoon sun from view. The ship itself floated above the floor of a sere valley perhaps a league across at its top. Sheer, striated cliffs sloped down to a shaded basin almost as wide at the bottom.

The ship itself looked to have barely survived significant violence. The deck appeared riddled with holes, shorn open in places with sizable gashes throughout. From where he stood, there were many spots where he could look down through the deck and out onto the ground below.

He could tell that Wrindanneth had been gradually channeling his energy through the craft to fix the damage for most of the holes he noticed appeared to have regular, smooth edges without signs of stress or blemish as if the mars and gashes were growing back toward central points. Even so, Wrindanneth still had much work ahead of him, however. Most of the ship appeared to be held together as much by luck as by structural integrity.

Casting a rope ladder over the side of the railing, he scrambled carefully down to the valley floor, setting down amid a puff of orange dirt. Each step he took left a trail of dust floating in his wake. He followed the gentle slope of the valley downward through an area he assumed was once a floodplain until he finally reached the bed of what must have been a river. Walking slowly across the river's channel, he noticed that the soil here appeared slightly darker than on the plain above and did not puff into the air so readily.

By the time he reached what he judged to be the former river's center, the soil was obviously moist to the touch. Bending over, he dug a small trench and was happy to find that it slowly filled with water. Working carefully, he widened and deepened his hole until it gradually filled with enough liquid to form a small pool.

Taking out the bags of organic material that he had retrieved from the park on Tellanon, he gingerly placed the rock with algae inside the pool beneath the collected water, adding the water from the cool stream to the pool as well. He then placed the lichen-covered rock along with the soil and leaf litter below the lip of the trench he dug, immediately adjacent to the water, intermingling the soil from Tellanon with the soil of Al'Marr.

Although not a proper pond, he hoped it would be a start.

With a deep breath, he let *chi* flow both through him and directly from his body, channeling the energy around and within him into the small pool, suffusing it with energy and vivacity. Then, with a deep breath drawn from the soles of his feet and exhaled into the pool, he sent densified *chi* into the water and soil so that his energy would remain in this place long after he left.

Although he could not right the Cabal's evils, he could do his best to offer a new beginning.

He had been transformed, transformed by the energies tearing his essence apart, by internalizing the *chi* void's expanse, by the explosion of forces released in the aftermath of the void's implosion, and by the time spent reforming his consciousness under the effects of the *chi* radiating so strongly around the former void's center.

Feeling the *chi* move through him now, he felt entirely different than he had prior to the ordeal. Meridians, the energy channels he had spent so long opening up and cultivating, nurturing and strengthening through the years, were gone—blasted away into the halls of memory.

Whereas meridians had served to guide the *chi* through his body before his transformation, now he felt the energy move through his whole being, flowing and radiating in waves. Similarly, he no longer needed to gather *chi* in particular reserves located throughout his body for practice, health, or use. He could utilize, store, and manipulate energy within and around himself much more freely, without regard to a particular location, framework, or pathway. Furthermore, *chi* no longer entered solely through the Wu Xin, the energy gates. Instead, energy entered his body from everywhere. In fact, the energy of his body, the *chi* that he generated and the energy flowing around him, energy that he could harness, were no longer separable.

Before his trials, he saw and experienced much of the world as unified, as a totality intrinsically integrated through the all-pervading *chi*. At the same time, physically he felt paradoxically both separate from and a part of the energies moving within and without, as if only the thinnest of distinctions existed between himself, his body, and the world around him. In many ways, he felt that his consciousness, or what he identified as his self, had existed on this finest of margins between the interior and exterior worlds—an almost invisible presence serving as an intermediary between the internal and external realms, between the limitless *chi* circulating without and the energies flowing within.

Now he felt no such distinctions between himself and the *chi* flowing and moving all around him. The bounds of his being, due to the broadened extent of his interaction with the unlimited potentials around him, were blurred so strongly that he had to consciously focus on his physical being to feel bounded, to feel limited by the confines of his own skin. In a very real sense, the ordeal had burnt much of what he had considered fundamental to himself and to his prior existence, his previous confines, his sense of self, away.

Despite his wonder at the changes he felt within, despite the heightened potential he felt the ordeal had unlocked, and even after two weeks of gradual healing, he still had a long journey ahead to make a full recovery. He would have to spend just as much time and effort harnessing and training with his new abilities as he had when he worked on opening his meridians.

He wondered how different he would be when he returned to full health and had time to cultivate his abilities. He wondered if he would actually have the time and the opportunity to do so.

All these thoughts and feelings flashed through his mind as he gradually stood above the pool, watching his wavering reflection in the rippling water, hoping that the seeds of life he brought to this world would eventually take hold and transform the planet. In time, the H'era might return and hasten the process, but that decision was theirs to make and not his.

With a purposeful step, he retraced his path to the ship, eager to return to Tellanon to see what clues the Paratechnologists could pry from the alien device.

By the time he reached the *Shrike*, everyone was on deck ready to depart. Slate threw the rope ladder back down to him and he climbed up, the coarse fibers of the rope reminding him of the immediacy of the moment and the opportunity unfolding with each breath.

"Did you finish what needed to be done?" asked Aroganji.

"I hope so," answered Yip. "When we return I will let the H'era know what we have done. Perhaps, in time, they will wish to return home and reseed their world."

Aroganji smiled, his face bright with optimism.

"I hate to break up the party but is everyone ready to go?" Wrindanneth stood poised and eager at the ship's helm, the silvery navigation disk floating directly in front of where he stood. He was ready to put Al'Marr in the past along with the risks it posed to their futures.

Slate laughed and replied sardonically, "Sure ya do, Wrin. Sure ya do. I'd imagine there's not much that would make ya happier'n spoilin' other folks' enjoyment."

Wrindanneth shared a half-smile with his friend. "You may have a point there but only just."

"Let's be on with it then!"

When Aroganji and Yip nodded in agreement with Slate, Wrindanneth reached into his robes and brought out the pearlescent return stone, cupping it in his hands delicately. Channeling the ship's energy through its facets, unraveling its concentrated energies, he felt the stone warm slightly to the touch. In an instant, this heat exploded into a torrent of power, enveloping the ship.

Then the world expanded into Light and they were gone.

ALSO BY JOSEPH J. BAILEY

Out of the Box

Zombies Forever

The <u>*Unlikely Heroes*</u> series:

Master of the Flying Broom - Sword Saint in Training

Demon Hunter - The Misadventures of a Fallen Holy Knight

Gnomegeddon – The Adventures of an Untried Gnome

Joe is also working on something else but really cannot say more on the matter at present.

HELP SPREAD THE WORD!

I hope you have enjoyed reading this book as much as I enjoyed writing it.

Whether these words transported you to another place, one you enjoyed wholeheartedly, or pushed you away without lasting impression, I would welcome your review wherever you may choose.

If you truly did appreciate this book, feel free to spread the word to your friends, family, and random acquaintances. I would also love for you to visit me at either my website or like me on my Facebook Author's Page.

If you would like to learn about future book releases, please consider signing up for my book announcement newsletter. I promise to use this information judiciously.

Many thanks and happy reading!

— Joseph J. Bailey

GLOSSARY OF TERMS
PEOPLE, PLACES, AND THINGS

Abyss – a general name often used for extradimensional regions home to Daemonic creatures of Darkness and despair. Also called nether realms.

Adamantium – an exceedingly strong magical metal.

Acolyte – an Initiate of the K'un Lun that has shown some attainment but has not yet been accepted as a priest.

Adar – a Paratechnologist from Tellanon.

Adrael the Black – an ancient Black Dragon slain by Ithilieon while wielding Duraeleon.

Aerdos and Aerlyn – Elven twins and heroes from ages long past.

Aerie – a name commonly used for the peaks and summits claimed by Dragons as their homes.

Aeromancy – the study of the air and its currents, the manipulation of its energies, and the fashioning of airships.

Aerya – literally, 'Light' or 'air.' An Elven term for the living energy of the universe. The concept of Aerya encompasses all forms of magical energetic expression in a single totality from the universal source to the personal creation—both *chi* and *yuan-chi*. See also *yuan-chi* and *chi*.

Aerya'ana – literally, 'those who bring the Light.' An elite Elven contingent named in honor of Yip Chi Chuan, trained in the ways of Light discovered and shared by Yip, commissioned to spread knowledge and sanctity across the cosmos.

Aerya'anan – literally, 'Light Bringer' or 'one who brings the Light.' An Elven name for Yip Chi Chuan.

Aerya Etherum – literally, 'highest air' or 'highest breath.' Alternatively, 'first breath' or 'source of breath.' An Elven term for the source of the Aerya, the formless, boundless Void, source of limitless potential. See also Wuji.

Aeryaology – the study of living creatures that utilize magical energies as the basis of their constitutions.

Aeryasynthetic – a general term used to refer to those entities that utilize magical energies as the basis for their metabolism.

Aeryn – 'tree' in Elven. Also, a large, silver-boled tree named after the legendary Aeryn D'al for its similar, if diminished, appearance.

Aeryn D'al – literally, 'tree lord' in Elven. Also a derivation of 'magic lord' or 'Light lord.' A legendary, highly accomplished race of sentient trees. Original teachers of the Elves on Ea'ae.

Aeryn Sh'al – literally, 'tree heart' in Elven. Also a derivation of 'magic heart.' Enchanted wood sung from the heart of trees by Elven Iyela and fashioned into implements ranging from bows, swords, and armor to household goods like furniture, utensils, and living structures. Stronger than adamantine and able to carry powerful enchantments, the material of choice for Elven-wrought magical artifacts. Sometimes called Witchwood or Weirding Wood by Men.

Afternoon's Shade Inn – an inn in Shady Vale.

Age – any extensive period of time. Typically thought of as representing one thousand years though events of particular significance may also define its limits.

Airship – magically powered ships in as many shapes as the mind can imagine found plying the air currents and trade routes throughout Ea'ae and beyond. See also aeromancy.

Alaeron – a junior Paratechnologist on Tellanon.

Alain Ar'laen – member of Tellanon's guiding Protectorate, leader of the Home Guard, Tellanon's Master-at-Arms and principal defender, general and Champion. Once a man and a famed warrior, now a synthetic being joined with the Construct whose form and presence are owed as much to his imagination and will as his original physical form. First and foremost of the NUMEN. Also called Brightblade.

Aldael – the Indural's name for the Green Run.

Alderan – a guide, ambassador, and lorekeeper of the Elves of Yenaria.

Aleron – Elven noble and lorekeeper. Father to Llyewia. Husband of Nydia.

Allomorph – a being capable of taking on various shapes and guises, potentially augmenting its own intrinsic abilities, while retaining its primary core awareness, sense of self, and intelligence. The Jira S'al Alann are one such example.

Al'Marr – the homeworld of the H'era.

Aluran – literally, 'Green Glade.' The jungle village of the H'era Al'Marr.

Amakar – an ancient volcano located in the Drake Spires.

Anjali mudra – a gesture of salutation with both palms together at the chest.

Anubaraëthi – literally, 'Spawn of the Shadow,' or 'Shadow made manifest.' A general Elven name for greater sentient Daemons. Sometimes called Dread Lords.

Anubavaeri – literally, 'Spawn of the Flame,' or 'Spawn of the Fire.' An Elven name for powerful Daemons of flame.

Anuvaerya – literally, 'Children of the Light.' An Elven name for those Elves who have willingly left the bounds of the body to explore the realms of the mind and spirit. The existence of Anuvaerya is a closely guarded secret, known only to a few Elf-Friends outside the Elven people.

Anuvatali – literally, 'Children of the Dawn,' or 'Children of the New Morn.' An Elven name for the half-Elven children of Men and Elves born on Ea'ae.

Anuvatari – literally, 'Children of the Sun.' An Elven name for those Elves who first came to Ea'ae.

Anuvatari'aliana– literally, 'of one voice with the Children of the Sun' or 'friend-kin of the Children of the Sun.' An Elven name for those people of any race taken in by the Elves and taught something of their ways or those who are trusted and respected as Elf-kin.

Archaeus – the holy sword of Eidelion, forged from the rarified light of the sun, glows white when wielded by one of pure heart. Also known as the White Sword and the Bright Blade. Originally called Erudhaerya by the Elves.

Archfiend – a general name for a Daemon, particularly in reference to powerful Daemons that have usurped dominion over lesser representatives of their own kind.

Archlich – a particularly powerful Lich, often a powerful deceased practitioner of magic. See Lich.

Archmage – a highly accomplished or powerful magician.

ARMED – Allomorphic Recombinatorial Multidimensional Extravehicular Drones. A flexible, multi-faceted, shapechanging drone system invented by Spreesprocket. Also called sentry drones.

Aroganji – a Fang Shih from the lands of Chang Sen. A practitioner of magical proscriptions and formulae and friend to Yip, Wrindanneth, and Slate. Member of the Four.

Ar'thas – literally, 'Black Mountain Orcs.' A tribe of evil Orcs and their allies, hidden deep in the heart of the Drake Spires.

Aruene – desolate continent to the west of Dharia.

Aspect – a fragment of the Construct. Used to perform specialized duties for the larger Construct in Tellanon. Like a hologram, an Aspect is a smaller, self-aware representation of the whole functionality of the Construct contained entirely within the larger system but granted broad freedom, flexibility, and independence. Often given to and used extensively by citizens of Tellanon. Also called a Fragment.

Aurana – the deep-seated mental link shared between the H'era and the H'era D'ur.

Auros the Golden – along with Uzsanthal the Grim and Glaudron the Many Hued, one of the most powerful benevolent Dragons in all of Ea'ae. Father of Azaelle.

Ayle'ine Sea – the western boundary of Dharia. A vast expanse of open water dotted with wild, isolated islands.

Azaelle the Golden – a young golden Dragon of Auros's brood.

Azagothe – a Daemon lord of the nether abyss.

Baërn – literally, 'Berserker's Bane.' A magical ring given to Slate by Hoyt.

Baera – 'Brendle the All-Father' in the tongue of the Dwarves.

Baera'Dur – literally, 'Brendle's bulwark' in the tongue of the Dwarves. Called Dreadnaughts by Men.

Baeradun – a legendary Dwarven hero known to burst into flames.

Ba Duan Jin – the Eight Pieces of Brocade. A widely practiced and highly respected series of *qigong* movements with many associated benefits to health.

Bang tui – leg ties used to secure pants or stockings.

Barnaby Bilantré – a famous craftsman, aeronaut, and world-class aeromancer. Also known as Barney Black Eyes.

Beast Riders of Al'Marr – name for the feline beast riders of the Forlorn Forest who count their mounts as their brothers. Called the H'era in their own tongue.

Beyond – a general term for other dimensions in the multiverse, often in reference to the nether realms. See Abyss.

Blade Master – a highly proficient teacher of hand-to-hand combat in the Home Guard.

Blade Singer – see Caer'collas.

Blaeken Wode – literally, 'dark, bleak, or black wood' in the tongue of Men. An ancient forest on the continent of Kilaeron. Within its reaches, the Keep of Garen Muer houses the seal of Weis'liuhath.

Body of Light – another term for the *jalü*, celestial body, or rainbow body.

Bor'Banna – literally, 'bearded demon.' A name for the Dwarven masters of the axe, imbued by the remnants of power from Brendle's fire.

Borus – Head Magistrate, lead Justicar, and Adjudicator for the city of Tellanon. Member of the Protectorate and famed invoker.

Bot – short for robot, particularly with regard to Paratechnological clockwork devices made by Tinkerers that may or may not manifest synthetic intelligence capable of independent thought.

Braemen – captain of the airship *Shrike*, member of the nomadic R'yn Daer.

Brendle – The All-Father. Dwarven god of the forge and, in the eyes of the Dwarves, the creator of the known universe. More often than not, the brunt of Slate's curses. Called Baera in the tongue of the Dwarves.

Brendle's Flame – see Brendle's Spark.

Brendle's Spark – the remaining embers from Brendle's original flame and forge when Brendle first wrought the universe under hammer, anvil, and flame. The remaining embers even now bring forth life and magic into the universe. Also, the fires at the heart of the Daer-daana'Duin, the Bor'Banna's highest known skill, where the exponent merges directly with Brendle's flames. Also called Brendle's Flame. An analogue to Aerya and *yuan-chi* in Dwarven cosmology.

Brendle's Tears – the finest of Dwarven ales. Reputed to be so wondrous and flavorful that Brendle himself cries tears of joy and amazement with each sip.

Brightblade – see Alain Ar'laen.

Byear – literally, 'heart of flame.' Magical robe once worn by Mandros Gray Beard, famed archmage, now worn by Aroganji. Able to deflect a blade as well as allow full spellcasting, among other wardings.

C^3 – the Cogitation Clarifying Cap. A Gnomish Paratechnological device capable of reading and analyzing both simple and higher-order thought processes. Much more complex, convoluted, and cumbersome than using mind reading spells, the C^3 benefits from a certain Gnomish style and sense of eccentricity. Because of its complexity, convolution, and cumbersomeness, the C^3 is sometimes referred to as the C^6 or, more often, the C^0.

The Cabal –A sinister alliance of dark mages, fallen priests, extradimensional beings, and other creatures of might bent not only on domination but power. Known by many other names including the Order of the Lidded Eye, the Fallen, the Light Fallen, the Order of the Burning Eye, and the Order of the Hooded Gaze. Called Liúxīng Làngrén by the Priests of K'un Lun. Often symbolized by a blazing sigil of a closed eye.

Caelebeor – literally, 'Shadow's Grace' in the tongue of the Elves. A magical ring given to Slate by Hoyt.

Caer'collas – a Q'sharian blade master. Often called Blade Singers by those who watch their masterful interplay of magic and blade work.

Celestial body – see rainbow body, body of light, or *jalü*.

Cersaegian – Liege and eldest of the Fiersayne. Keeper of the Ghrem Weard. An ancient Black Dragon abiding in northern Maeron.

Champion of Light – a general honorific for those who have earned great esteem fighting the forces of Darkness. Also, a title for one of great accomplishment within the Dalaren Ka.

Master Chang – an exalted teacher of the K'un Lun.

Chang Sen – an ancient land of empire and intrigue home to unique ways and traditions found nowhere else in Ea'ae. Homeland to Aroganji and the Fang Shih along with Yip Chi Chuan and the K'un Lun.

Chen-jen – a true human being. Seen as the ideal figure in philosophical and religious Taoism. Chen-jen refers to someone who has apprehended the truth within herself and thereby attained the Tao.

Chi – *Qi*; breath, air, or vapor of particular significance in Taoism and Eastern medicine. From a Taoist perspective, the *chi* is the vital energy or life force that enlivens and pervades all things. *Chi gung—chi kung* or *qigong*—are exercises to build and strengthen *chi* flow. Along with *shen* and *ching*, one of the Three Treasures essential to human life. A less subtle and refined form of the *yuan-chi*, the universal potential. The fire that does not burn.

Chih-jen – a perfected human being. Another term describing an ideal person. A Chih-jen has realized unity with the Tao and is free of all concepts and limitations.

Ching – *Jing*; the germ or source of life. Along with the breath or vital energy (*chi*) and the mind or consciousness (*shen*), one of the life forces essential for the preservation and prolongation of life in the Taoist view.

Chuan – *Quan*; Fist.

Chutefunnel Knobwhistle – member of Tellanon's governing Protectorate, head of higher learning, intercollegial understanding, cross-communication, and numenal exchange, facilitator of intellectual prosperity, and citizen enlightenment.

Ciërna – literally, 'vision of the world to be' in the tongue of the Elves. An expression encompassing and embodying both how one would hope the world will unfold and arise, either individually or as a collective, and what may be required for the realization and actualization of this reality.

Circle – a powerful ritual magic employed by the leaders of Tellanon as a last resort. Used to invoke the Loel'dara.

Class M Fire – a general fire category used by Paratechnologists to describe fires of magical origin. There are multiple subtypes depending upon source, intensity, and required quenching response.

Cletus – Hoyt's pet Fairy Dragon.

Clockwork – a general name for a particular branch or type of Paratechnology focusing on magically animated contraptions of any shape, size, and function often resembling machines and robots but not limited to any specific shape. A particular specialty of Gnomish Paratechnological Tinkerers.

Coerdaerya – literally 'partner in Light' in the tongue of the Elves. A term used to describe two individuals bound together inextricably by *ciërna*, common vision, and common love.

COG – the Construct Organization Group on the island of Tellanon. The Paratechnologists in COG have direct responsibility over the Construct and its attendant artificial intelligence subroutines including the various Aspects and other specialized intelligence engines in addition to the management of the Construct's subordinate functions.

Common – see Common Tongue.

Common Tongue – a universal language used across Ea'ae to facilitate nonmagical communication. Also called Common.

The Construct – a powerful, centralized, multi-faceted sentient intelligence created by the Paratechnologists used to oversee, understand, envision, and facilitate activities in Tellanon. Administered and overseen by COG.

The Council – a secretive, informal band of wizards, priests, druids, and other wielders of arcane power from many different races focused on ensuring Ea'ae's continued safety and prosperity. Sometimes called the Council of Light.

Although an entirely different body, the ruling Protectorate of Tellanon is also referred to as the council or High Council.

The Council of Light – see the council.

Cozy Cabbage Inn – an inn in Tellanon known for its Gnomish delicacies.

Craft – higher magical skills. An umbrella term inclusive of various branches of magic including unique talents and abilities native to particular races, guilds, and tribes.

Cycles – the Elven equivalent for the lunar year. Based as much on the turning and changing of seasons and the ebb and flow of life as Ea'ae's revolution around the sun. Called Soerlyn in the tongue of Elves.

D'al – 'Lord' in Elven.

Daeja – a trade city in central Var'Kera.

Daemon – a general name for extradimensional creatures with hostile intent or for those otherworldly creatures that feed and prey upon the energies of the living. Also called Infernals.

Daerdros – lieutenant of the Home Guard and Master at Arms. A Caer'collas, a Q'sharian blade master.

Daerdaana'Duin – literally, 'to become the heart of fire' or 'to become the heart of the forge.' One of the highest skills of the Bor'Banna, wherein the practitioner wreaths himself in the flames of Brendle's forge, becoming a direct manifestation of Brendle's power and one with its heat, energy, and vitality. In times of old, these warriors cloaked themselves in flames, striking down foes directly with Brendle's might. See Brendle's Spark.

Daer'Duin – literally, 'heart of fire' or 'heart of the forge.' Given Dwarven name for Slate Flintforge.

Dagron Iron Beard – a famous Dwarven Dur'kazak of old.

Dalare – 'Light' or 'One Light' in the tongue of Tol Aeron.

Dalaren Ka – the 'Knights of the One Light.' A chivalrous order whose members follow the ways of the Dalaren Mere, the Light's Path. Guardians of the Star of Elendial.

Dalaren Mere – the 'Light's Path.' The way of chivalry, faith, and the sword through the expression of the Light of Life.

Darkness – a general term for those beings opposed to the Light and Life it engenders and who would subvert, pervert, or otherwise mar Its presence and manifestation. Also a general term for the corruption of the energy of life, the Light, itself.

Dauren'Kas – 'the Bringers of Light.' A name taken by those Shau-r'Daus who bring forth the Light of creation to negate the energy voids and Darkness brought forth by Ur'Daus and Its minions.

Dawrac di Gaydial – an alien Paratechnologist resembling an Ogre composed largely of stone and crystal.

Delving – a general name for any Dwarven city or outpost. See also undermount.

Deur Spricken Sprack – Gnomish for 'the Omnispark.' See also Phlogiston and Omnispark.

Dharia – the largest continent on the world of Ea'ae.

Dharma – cosmic law or truth.

Dhwer'werde – literally, 'Fate's Door' or 'Fated Forest.' A cursed forest surrounding the lands of Taerris'thule.

Dhyana mudra – a meditation *mudra*. To form the *mudra*, two hands are placed on the lap, right hand on left with fingers fully stretched and the palms facing upwards.

Diaspora – a general name for the large-scale exodus of various races of humanity from Ea'ae with the development of *faerviage*. Although not native to Ea'ae, Elves participated in these departures alongside Men, Dwarves, Gnomes, and other sentient races of Ea'ae. Many of those people who left have since reestablished contact with Ea'ae thereby encouraging interstellar trade.

DISCO – Daemonic Irradiating Stroboscopic Catastrophe Orb. A multifaceted Paratechnological orb capable of emitting multiple streams of high intensity magically amplified light suitable for the destruction of extradimensional creatures of Darkness...and dancing

Dizzywig Paddlepulley – member of Tellanon's Protectorate, Gnomish Paratechnologist extraordinaire, and leader of the Sliced Bread Society.

Doerdaana'Duin – literally, 'the dance of the heart of fire' or 'to dance in the heart of the forge.' One form of Dwarven axe work known for its fluid strikes and counters, commonly used by particularly adept Bor'Banna.

D'orauk managua al'zurka – literally, 'may your blood flow strong and pure.' A Dracodaeran expression of well-wishing for health and vitality, strength, and power. Often expressed at times of parting.

Dracodaera – a race of humanoid Dragon-kin. Hunters of Daemons and other creatures of Darkness. Originators of the Shaur'Daus.

Dracodin – an extraplanar being of some power resembling a humanoid Dragon.

Dragonflight – a group of Dragons living and moving together.

Dragons – along with the Aeryn D'al, one of the oldest races of Ea'ae. Steeped in magic and power, Dragons are feared by all who cross their path. As complex as they are storied, Dragons are as diverse as their characters and can wield power only rivaled by the gods themselves.

The Dragon's Gate – the way of energy creation, concentration, and direction taught to Yip by Azaelle the Golden.

Drake – Dragon.

The Drake Spires – also the Spine of the World. A series of lofty peaks running down the center of the Dharian continent. Named after the many Dragon lairs and aeries scattered throughout its heights. Ancestral home of the Yeren people.

Dread Lord – a general name for higher order, more powerful Daemons granted intelligence and power far beyond their peers. Called Anubaraëthi, Children of the Shadow, by Elves.

Dreadnaught – a Dwarven warrior specializing in heavy combat. Utilizing enchanted, rune-etched full plate armor along with two-handed axes, hammers, and maces, Dreadnaughts earn their place at the fore of the battlefield by fighting against the most implacable foes. Famous as much for their rallying battle cries and songs along with their fear inducing chants and dirges as their blades. Called Baera'Dur in the tongue of Dwarves.

Dread Steed – the otherworldly flying steeds of the Fyrskal.

Dream Stealer – Wrindanneth's own name for Maeth Onai. A reference to Maeth coming to Wrindanneth in dreams to partake of the choicest lore uncovered or discovered during his travels and research.

Drogu – an Orcish commander.

Drothman – a famous Dwarven hero.

Druids – protectors of the wilds, guardians of nature, and lovers of freedom. First students of the Indural.

Dunédâne – literally, 'deep delver.' Name for the Dwarves among their own kind and the Karadüm.

Dûnedar – a Dwarf from Slate's hold.

Duraeleon – 'The Light Bringer,' bane of Adrael the Black, ancient axe of Ithilieon. Wielded by Slate Flintforge.

Durden – literally, 'valiant heart.' A Dwarven rune that serves to protect against fear and indecision when properly enchanted.

Durin – a famous Dwarven hero from times of yore.

Dur'kazak – literally, 'fire shaper.' A Dwarven master smith skilled in the art and craft of metallurgy, elemental magics, and rune crafting known as Karaduen.

Durnok – literally, 'possibility reader.' One skilled in the reading and interpretation of possibility and chance, probable futures, cause and effect, and the outcomes of events. Often used as trackers, mercenaries, bounty hunters, and assassins.

Duuna'Dan – literally, 'rocks of the father.' The Dwarven name for the Green Run. The old, rounded hills, worn mountains, and boulders of the Duuna'Dan are thought to be the original handiwork of Brendle as he formed Ea'ae from the Void with the careful molding of his hands. Although no longer under their control, many Dwarven mining communities and outposts still dot the wilds in this region.

Duurn'Laden – a large northern Dwarven delving known for the depths and richness of its mines, the skill of its Dur'kazak and the quality of their craftsmanship.

Dwarves – along with Elves, Gnomes, and Men, one of the four most prominent races on Ea'ae. Dwarves are short, hearty, and solidly built and known for their ability to work metal. They excel at reading the earth and mining. Their keen knowledge of metals and runes allows for the creation of powerful works of Craft. Also called Dunédâne.

Ea'ae – 'The world.' Home to magical creatures and races of many shapes, cultures, and forms.

Echoing Fist – see Pai-lien Touch.

Ectoplasmic Reconnaissance Goggles – Gnomish Paratechnological visual enhancement device allowing the viewing and analysis of supernatural energies. Commonly referred to as ERG's.

EGAD – see the Every Gnome's Anti-Intelligence Device.

Eidelion – knight-captain and officer of the Tellanon Home Guard, leader of the Light's Guard, paladin of the Light, initiate of the Dalaren Ka, bane of the wicked, and wielder of Archaeus the White Sword. Known as Night's Bane, True Heart, and Dawn's Light.

Eiryna – a particularly fleet and agile Elven airship.

El'alen – literally, 'old home.' The Elven name for the Green Run. Named after the ancestral homes of their allies of old, the Dwarves.

Eldre'gheu – literally, 'old god.' One of the fourteen seals protecting Ea'ae from extradimensional incursion. Also the temple to the god once serving as the focal point of Taerris'thule.

Elf-friends – see Elf-kin or Anuvatari'aliana.

Elf-kin – Those people of any race taken in by the Elves and taught something of their ways. Sometimes called Elf-friends or Anuvatari'aliana in the tongue of the Elves.

Elixir field – energy fields in the body. See *tan t'ien*.

Elves – a fey race at home among the trees and dells of Ea'ae. Elves are a race of great Craft and knowledge that made peace with the land long before the coming of Men and Dwarves and many other sentient races. It is said that magic is the lifeblood of the Elves. Often called Lords of the Wood or Tree Singers by Men, although not all Elves are indeed Iyela. Those Elves on Ea'ae are the Anuvatari.

Embodied Cloven Crystallization of Refined Essence – A sentient crystalline entity with significant psychic ability. Also a well-respected Paratechnologist.

EMMA – a NUMEN serving Tellanon. Short for Energetic Mapping, Monitoring, and Analysis. EMMA's specialization is developing predictive models to visualize the magical energy currents flowing across Ea'ae.

Empen Wastes – coastal wetland wilderness of west-central Dharia composed of bogs, fens, swamps, lowland forests, and associated rivers, deltas, islands, and lakes. A vast, largely uninhabited region home to fey creatures and unusual beasts.

The Enemy – Ur'Daus, the Darkness between dimensions. Also known as the Creeping Shadow, Destroyer of Light, the Umbral Lord, the Devourer of Worlds, among many other names and curses.

ENNIS – see Epistemic Noetic Numenetic Integrating Summator.

Epistemic Noetic Numenetic Integrating Summator – a multifunctional Gnomish device with capabilities ranging from measurement and systematic evaluation of phenomena, data analysis, computation, and communication to independent reasoning, learning aid, and thought transference. Also called ENNIS for short.

Éremon – Exarch of Tellanon, august Consul of the ruling Protectorate, Fifth of Thirteen.

ERG – see Ectoplasmic Reconnaissance Goggles.

Erudhluin – literally, 'Heaven's Home.' One of many sacred groves tended and held sacred by Elven Iyela.

Erudhaerya – literally, 'Heaven's Light' in the tongue of the Elves. One of many names for the White Sword Archaeus.

Essence – the essential energies. The energies of life and magic and the source of their origination, especially when viewed wholistically.

Eyrdeas – the White Blade of Morn. The storied sword of Maeven D'lanaran. Called Taliaerya, Morning's Light or Dawn's Light, among the Elves.

Every Gnome's Anti-Intelligence Clandestine Apparatus version 3.1, Corvette Class – see the Every Gnome's Anti-Intelligence Device. Also EGAD.

Every Gnome's Anti-Intelligence Device – a Paratechnological defensive system suitable for espionage, surveillance, and camouflage added to items ranging in size from personal armor to airships. The Every Gnome's Anti-Intelligence Device replicates the surrounding environmental variables and superimposes them over the object protected by the defensive system rendering it indistinguishable from its surroundings. Sometimes referred to as EGAD or, more specifically and to add to the general air of confusion around Gnomish devices, as the Every Gnome's Anti-Intelligence Clandestine Apparatus version 3.1, Corvette Class.

Faerviage – magical voyage. A name for the magical ships capable of interdimensional and interstellar travel. Ships vary in form and function based on magical technology, need, and culture.

Fa jin – also sometimes called '*fa jing*'; a sudden wave of energy that surges through the exponent's body and into an opponent. A spontaneous energy release; to issue and discharge power.

Fallen – the Cabal or Liúxīng Làngrén.

Fang Shih – literally, 'a master of prescriptions'; a magician in Chang Sen. Traditionally, the precursor of Taoist sages and priests skilled in the use of various supramundane arts including astrology, astronomy, spirit healing, prophecy, geomancy, arts of love, the use of talismans and drugs, exercises for prolonging life, and enlisting the aid of gods.

Fang Shu – magical arts, especially as practiced by the Fang Shih.

Far travel – see traveling.

Fay Long – the Celestial Courtyard, highest peak in the K'un Lun.

Fiersayne – the brood and broodmates of Cersaegian.

The Fists – see the Flaming Fists.

Fizzlemiz – a Gnomish Paratechnologist. One of the foremost experts on alien technologies among the Paratechnologists.

The Flaming Fists – an honorific name granted to the adventuring band composed of Aroganji, Wrindanneth, Slate, and Yip. Sometimes called the Four, the Fists, the Four of the Flaming Fists, among other honorifics.

Forlorn Forest – the Emerald Jungle. A vast wilderness adjacent to Jenyuan Shulin and the Drake Spires. A region largely unknown and unexplored by most races. Home to the H'era.

Four Lands – a general reference to the four principle continents of Ea'ae. Although there are many smaller islands and land masses scattered across Ea'ae, Dharia, Maeron, Aruene, and Kilaeron are the largest and most prominent.

The Four – see the Flaming Fists.

Fraeü – literally, 'shadow's heart.' Magical robe once worn by Mandros Gray Beard, famed Archmage, now worn by Wrindanneth. Able to deflect a blade as well as allow full spellcasting, among other wardings.

Fragment – another name for an Aspect. A personalized portion of the Construct assigned to and intended to assist citizens of Tellanon in various capacities.

Freyda – Brendle's wife. Known for her patience and virtue.

Fria al'Othra – literally, 'eyes of true vision.' An Elven term for the universal perspective of the Iyela.

Fu – literally, 'return.' Returning to the root or source, the Tao. In Taoist meditative practice this return is synonymous with realization. The perception of the firmament from which the dynamic energy processes of *chi* flow, emerge, and return. An experience of the primal Emptiness or spacious void expressing the fundamental unity and equality of all things. See also Wuji and Taiji.

Fueron Mountains – a range of southern mountains near the city of Taerris'thule.

Fu-lu – Magical talismans, especially strips of paper, metal, or bamboo inscribed with symbols for protection employed by the Fang Shih.

Fyrskal – Guardians of the seal of Mihtig'leht and founders of Morowen. A chivalrous order of ages past that held to the ways and teachings of the Light.

Gaesia – sea-covered homeworld of the Jira S'al Alann.

Garen Muer – an ancient keep located in the heart of the Blaeken Wode.

Ghrem Weard – a common name for the nearly impenetrable northern cliff boundary of Maeron.

Gideon Goldsprocket – Flight Master of Tellanon. A Paratechnologist skilled in the ways of *faerviage*.

Gil-alan – a member of the Home Guard.

Gilaethe – literally, 'the light born.' Son of Nienael and a Wyaera of Tueran.

Gnomes – a race of short stature but of broad mind known for their creativity, imagination, and Paratechnological aptitude. Originators of Paratechnology, famed Tinkerers, often unable to leave well enough alone. Distant relatives of Dwarves.

Gnomeproof – a Dwarven colloquialism for foolproof.

Goran – a forest giant skilled in the ways of the Indural.

Gorthäk – a shaman of the Ar'thas.

Göerden – an armsman of some repute aboard the *Shrike*.

Grast – an evil Orcish tribal leader.

The Green Run – Man's name for the wilds of old, rounded mountains and ancient deciduous forests spanning the region from the western feet of the Drake Spires to eastern Var'Kera. Untamed and largely unsettled, this region is home to ruins, outposts, and creatures of every description. Called Duuna'Dan by the Dwarves, Aldael by the Indural, and El'alen by the Elves.

Gristnast – an Orcish sentry in the desolate wastes of Maeron.

Gromdek – a tribe of Orcs known for their skilled magic-wielding shaman.

Gruendan Weirndan – Champion of the Gleaming Blade, knight and commander of the Fyrskal.

Gründen – Thane of the Flintforge Clan. Kinsman of Slate.

Guai Lo – a Lung-wang, or Dragon king, from Chang Sen's past. Many artifacts of power have been made from his remains as well as his horde.

Guàn – monastery.

Guernden – a magical Dwarven hand cannon similar in appearance to an ornate rifle. Sometimes referred to as Dragon's Gullets for the fire contained in their bellies.

Günda – literally, 'Dwarf excrement.' An Orcish curse.

Guor' Uenaqe – literally, 'forge of our spirits.' Name for the harsh, volcanic homeworld of the Dracodaera.

Gyarxon – a race of psychic warriors who use their mental powers to travel interdimensionally seeking conquest.

Halls of Choosing – special locations spread throughout Tellanon that allow the visitor to select the pocket dimension of their choice to visit.

The Heart of Yere – a blazing red stone talisman that protects and guides its bearer. An artifact of the Yerens' and a piece of their heart and home.

Hellforge – a Daemonic smithy capable of producing fell items of great power.

Hellforged – a reference to Daemonic items made in a Hellforge. Most commonly weapons, armor, or arcane artifacts.

Henosis – a theurgical practice whose ultimate aim is unification with and expression of the Divine Light.

H'era – short for H'era Al'Marr.

H'era Al'Marr – the name of the beast riders of Al'Marr in their own tongue. H'era means 'children of the twin skies,' a reference both to the green canopy of their jungle home beneath the blue skies of Ea'ae and in remembrance of their homeworld of Al'Marr. Al'Marr means 'green sea.' Taken together, their name shows how the H'era find their compass and direction somewhere between the earth below and sky above their home—current and remembered.

H'era D'ur – 'Brother of the H'era.' Name of the sentient cat mounts with whom the H'era share a deep mental affinity, the so-called Aurana. Treated with much honor and respect, these mounts are an integral part of the H'era family groups and are considered an equal member in H'era society.

High Conservator – leader of the Dalaren Ka.

High Council – Tellanon's governing body of thirteen Paratechnologists and citizen representatives. Sometimes referred to as the council. See also Protectorate.

Holder of Secrets – a keeper of esoteric knowledge within the Home Guard. Also Keeper of Secrets.

The Home Guard – elite squadron of Tellanon's defenders and champions led by Eidelion.

The Home Reach – the fortress of the Home Guard located in Tellanon's center, part of Illdrassil.

Homeworld – planet of origin or primary habitation for a race, species, or group.

Hoyt – shop owner, gossip, and guide in Tellanon. Purveyor of fine goods, staples, information, and oddities. Wizard of some repute. Most often seen in his store, Hoyt's – Oddities, Found Goods, and Sundries.

Hröthe – literally, 'divine healing.' A Dwarven Karaduen offering a one-time boon of healing from a grievous or debilitating wound.

Hsiang Lung – a lush mountain range in eastern Chang Sen bordering the Q'ia Shan Sea. Home to Xian Shi, the school of the Fang Shih.

Hui-yin – an energy center located at the perineum called the Gate of Mortality and the Door of Life and Death. The seat of *ching*, the generative reproductive energy.

Human – see humanity. A general name for all sentient races on Ea'ae.

Humanity – a general name for all humanoid races on Ea'ae. Men,

Dwarves, Gnomes, Indural, and other sentient races of Ea'ae are included under this broad description. As a naturalized race, Elves, too, are considered part of humanity although they are genetically distinct from the other humanoid races.

Humbol – a traveling merchant and airman. Friend and former adventuring partner of Hoyt. Captain and owner of the airship the *Rare Aer*.

Hürn – literally, 'evil's bane.' A Dwarven rune used for protection from evil.

Iera – literally, 'brother of the heart' in the tongue of the H'era. Uuraja's H'era D'ur.

Ilidian – Watcher of the Drake Spires.

I'ldaerya J'al Ishentaré – literally, 'the art of unbroken change.' An art unique to the Jira S'al Alann that encompasses an unending range of physical and magical transformations in response both to an opponent and the energies expressed by past and present teachers and adversaries.

Illdrassil – literally, 'Spire of the Heavens' or 'Tree of Heaven' in the Old Tongue of Men. The home of the High Council, Tellanon's ruling body and the Home Guard. A vast repository of magical energies that empowers the city in the sky.

Illendial – the North Star in the tongue of the Elves. Sometimes used as an invocation to guide and protect the spirit from assailment.

Imperial – centralized unit of currency used in many lands across Ea'ae.

Incirrinaen – highly intelligent cephalopodic organisms widely known for their heightened cognitive and mental abilities.

Indural – one trained in the magic, lore, and woodcraft of the forest giants.

Infernal – a Daemon.

Initiate – an ascetic just accepted into the K'un Lun.

Irielia – an Elven city in south central Dharia.

Ithil'alen – literally 'elden home' or 'eldritch home.' Elven territory in northeastern Dharia.

Ithilieon – a legendary Elven hero. Wielder of Duraeleon and slayer of Adrael.

Iyela – an Elven lorekeeper, wonder worker, tree singer, and shaper. Known for their ability to commune with the spirit of trees and request the boon of their heartwood, the Aeryn Sh'al. Called Tree Singers by Men.

Jae'elthos – member of Tellanon's Protectorate, Iyela, Lorekeeper of the Anuvatari, the Children of the Light.

Ja'lal – literally, 'dearest one' in the tongue of the H'era.

Jalü – a rainbow body. A spiritual attainment allowing for the direct transition and ascendancy of the body to Light and Mind. Also called celestial body, rainbow body, or body of light.

Jarvis Jenkins – a tailor of some repute in Tellanon known for his functional clothing, craftsmanship, and ability to meet his customers' expectations for unique garment properties.

Jenkins – a trader and merchant from Shady Vale.

Jenta – literally, 'to call' in the tongue of the H'era. To call oneself is *jentara*. To call a group or a people is *jentaro*.

Jenyuan Shulin – literally, 'forbidden garden forest.' The Forbidden Forest, ancestral home of the Aeryn D'al. See also Noes Al'amroth.

Jian Lu – one of Aroganji's teachers at the arcane institution Xian Shi in Chang Sen.

Jin – literally, 'power.' Also an opponent's experience of the energy manifest by another.

Jing – *ching*; literally, 'essence.' Along with *qi* and *shen*, it is considered one of the Three Treasures. *Jing* provides the material basis and fuel for the body and transmits genetic heritage.

Jing luo – the invisible system of channels or pathways through which *qi* circulates throughout the body. Also sometimes referred to as vessels and collaterals, conduits or meridians.

Jira S'al Alann – literally, 'People of the Imagining.' A race of changelings able to shift their guise and abilities depending upon their magical development and attunement. See also allomorph.

Jueran'al – literally, 'brothers-in-living-ideation' or, more simply, 'brothers in ideals' in the tongue of the Jira S'al Alann. The term refers to a particularly organic way of looking at those who share a common ground of thought and ideation created by shared goals and ideals reinforced through each other's commitment and communication to the continual development and expression of these underlying intentions.

Ka – 'Knight' or 'Paladin' in the tongue of Tol Aeron.

K'an and Li and the esoterica that follow – literally, 'water and fire.' In some schools of internal alchemy the interchange of *k'an* and *li* represent a combination of *yin* and *yang* whose interchange corresponds to the functioning of the Tao, both the macrocosm and microcosm, within an individual. After completing the large heavenly cycle represented by the microcosmic orbit and the fusion of the five elements, thereby opening all the energy channels within the body, the Taoist adept is ready to begin the process of energy sublimation of *k'an* and *li*.

Through various stages, the *ching*, the generative energy, is converted into *chi*, the life force energy. The power of the reproductive hormones is thereby transferred into the whole body and brain. The process is similar process to the yogic awakening of the Kundalini, except in the Taoist process the resulting energy is directed throughout the body continuously along the meridians instead of being directed solely upward to the head.

During the initial stages (lesser enlightenment of the *k'an* and *li*) this interchange focuses on the cultivation of the root, the *hui-yin* or perineum, and the heart *chakras* while the *ching* energies are transformed at the navel.

The next stage, Ta K'an Li (greater enlightenment of the *k'an* and *li*), involves increasing the amount of energy drawn up through the body while bringing the energy up to the solar plexus. The increased energy in this stage results from the adept drawing energy directly from Heaven (Yang, above) and Earth (Yin, below) while adding the elemental powers to those of the adept's body.

The following stage, T'ai K'an Li (greatest enlightenment of the *k'an* and *li*), involves further mixing of the *yin* and *yang* powers at a higher energy center in the heart.

From here the adept has several potential stages to follow. The adept goes through a process of sealing the five sensory organs to prevent energy loss. The *chi* is then converted into mental energy (*shen*), or the energy of the soul, to preserve and purify the body and spirit while controlling the emotions.

There are still other formulae available for the adept to practice. Among these are the congress of Heaven and Earth immortality. At this stage, the adept mixes *yin* and *yang* energies at the crown of the head to preserve and cultivate the body to allow the spirit to achieve immortality. As the energies circulate, the body, soul, and spirit mingle and unite with the universe. The spirit thereby returns to nothingness or the source.

Finally, one last formula in the adept's development is the reunion of man and Heaven resulting in a true immortal man. At this stage, the internal alchemist has overcome reincarnation, developed an immortal spirit and an immortal body to house the spirit and soul, and is reunited with creation.

Karaduen – a Dwarven word meaning 'Light's ward' or 'Light's seal.' Special Dwarven runes and symbols often employed by Dur'Kazak and Kor'Dannan in the crafting of artifacts and the creation of spells and enchantments.

Karadüm – a type of particularly powerful stone giant in tune with the ebb and flow of the land's development and unfolding; usually guardians of a particular sacred place. Distant kin of the Indural.

Kazarhan the Stout – Dwarven lieutenant of the Home Guard, Kor'Dannan, and Dur'kazak. Wielder of the great hammer Raurdros. Master of Karaduen.

Kazzak – literally, 'marks of honor' in the tongue of the Dwarves. Symbols, tokens, and items of repute woven into a Bor'Banna's beard as badges of honor and accomplishment. Also common among other Dwarves.

Keep of Terraboer – the Citadel of Light. Home to the Dalaren Ka, the Knights of the One Light, and the Star of Elendial.

Keeper of Secrets – a select group of the Home Guard charged with guarding and maintaining Tellanon's secrets, hidden lore, and artifacts of repute. Also Holder of Secrets.

Khuerkanna – a famous Dwarven general known for his triumphant last stand against the Orcs and their allies in the Battle of the Broken Blade.

Kiervos – a large city-state in the plains of Var'Kera.

Kilaeron – wild continent to the east of Dharia.

Kiloboulder – a Gnomish unit of force, energy output, and weight.

Kor'Dannan – Dwarven Priests of Brendle given the keeping and wisdom of his fires, Brendle's Spark. Fierce warriors equally adept at healing and providing succor.

Koerdian Cave Bear – a species of gigantic cave bear particularly respected by Dwarves for their strength, perseverance, and indomitable spirit.

Kordas – Orcish blood beer.

Ku – pants.

K'un Lun – a mountain range often portrayed as a Taoist paradise, home to immortals. Home to the Priests of K'un Lun.

The K'un Lun – mystical priests from high in the mountains of Chang Sen. Also the Priests of K'un Lun.

Lael'darnael – literally, 'mission-view-survival-path' in the tongue of the Jira S'al Alann. A shared view and purpose developed organically together from the dictates and exigencies of the requirements for survival and success for an entire group providing the basis and direction for future action.

Landeiss – a large island nation to the south of Dharia.

Liao Qua – a large city in Chang Sen.

Li – literally, 'principle'. The expression of potential in form; the manifestation of inherent order distinct to each and every thing; the order of flow; the Tao in motion. Also pattern.

Lianel – literally, 'bowyer's heart.' A bow crafted by a master bowyer of the Elves melded and formed from his spirit and the spirit of a willing tree.

Lich – undead beings sustained by twisted magical energies.

Life – all living beings taken as a whole.

The Light – the ambient energy of the universe; the energy of Life enlivening all of existence. Considered holy, sacred, and heavenly. See also Aerya, *chi, ching, dalare,* Deur Spricken Sprack, Omnispark, Phlogiston, *shen,* Brendle's Spark, and *yuan-chi.*

Light Fallen – the Cabal or Liúxīng Làngrén.

Light's Grace – theurgical religious group on Tellanon led by

Magdalia Miera whose activities focus on henosis, unification with and expression of the Divine Light on Ea'ae and beyond.

The Light's Guard – an elite force within the Home Guard led by Eidelion.

Light's Swath – the brilliant center of the galaxy encompassing Ea'ae.

Lightwell – the spontaneous, self-sustaining creation of life-giving energies formed through deft manipulation of the Dragon's Gate and the spontaneous creation of Light from limitless potential.

Master Liu – a revered teacher of the K'un Lun.

Liúxīng Làngrén – literally, 'falling star vagrants.' More figuratively, 'those fallen or straying from Heaven's path'. The Cabal, and those fallen priests associated with it, that have strayed from the path of Life, as referenced by the Priests of K'un Lun.

Llyewia L'oerllana – literally 'spring's first breath' or 'first breath of spring.' A lieutenant of the Home Guard. Elven Iyela, lorekeeper, and ambassador.

Loel'dara – literally, 'the Light's shadow beckons.' Tellanon's weapon of last resort and final line of defense.

Loesia – a cold, rugged region of lakes and mountains in the heart of the Northlands. Home to Wrindanneth and seat of Maeth Onai.

Loess – literally, 'Heaven's shielding.' A protective Dwarven rune meant for use against supernatural forces.

Master Loquan – a respected teacher of the K'un Lun.

Lords of the Wood – see Elves.

Lotus – see Pai-lien.

Lueciane Sea – the sea to Dharia's south. Lying directly between Dharia and Maeron, it surrounds the island nation of Landeiss.

Luereal – literally, 'troll's bane' or 'evil's bane' in the tongue of the Elves. The black wand of Q'ia'Li. Once in the possession of Hoyt, given to Aroganji. An exceedingly rare Anuvaeryan wrought artifact of witchwood.

Luerdan – literally, 'troll dung' in the tongue of the Dwarves.

Lung – a Dragon in Chang Sen.

Lung-hu – literally, 'Dragon and tiger,' symbolic of *yang* and *yin* respectively, and the fusion of *k'an* and *li* in the Taoist alchemical tradition which leads to the realization of the Tao. The Dragon rises from the fire and is therefore associated with *li* while the tiger arises from the water and is therefore associated with *k'an*.

Lung-hu-i tao – literally, 'way of the Dragon and tiger.' A colloquial description by exponents of other alchemical traditions for the mystical traditions practiced by the priests of the K'un Lun.

Lung-wang – Dragon kings; mythological Taoist figures. Dragons (*lung*) also correspond to the *yang* principle in Taoist iconography.

Macrocosmic orbit – the energy path encompassing both the internal and external energy paths. Completion of the macrocosmic orbit is signified by opening the energy gates completely to the passage of *chi* which ultimately leads to unification with the energies of creation.

Macrocosmos – see macroverse.

Macroverse – the totality of multi-dimensional existence, inclusive of all planes, alternate universes, and extradimensional regions. See multiverse. Also megacosm or macrocosmos.

Maeglan – a Dwarven Dur'kazak of the Flintforge clan. Uncle to Slate.

Maer'Din – a loremaster of the H'era. Keepers of the tribe's dreams, aspirations, and history. Their knowledge is brought to life through the dance of the Seura.

Maeron – a largely tropical continent on the southern side of Ea'ae.

Maeth Onai – a god of magic. Wrindanneth's exemplar and ultimate guide. Depending on his mood, sometimes referenced privately as the Dream Stealer by Wrindanneth.

Maeven D'lanaran – a champion of the Dalaren Ka and exemplar of the Light.

MAFS – see Magical Air Foam System.

Magdalia Miera – member of Tellanon's ruling High Council, eminent Theurgist, and leader of the Light's Grace congregation.

Mage armor – enchanted armor for magic users that allows the freedom and flexibility to cast spells while also offering some protection against physical or magical assault. Often made from robes or clothing typical of a given magical tradition.

Magic – the translation of the possible into the actual, the imagined into the real. The three primary components of magical practice are often understood as belief, faith that an individual can take an active part in universal creation; intent (or will), the shaping of this belief can guide in creation; and imagination, the vision or desired outcome made possible by belief and shaped by intent.

The wellspring of magic is universal energy. Depending upon the tradition, this source is known as *yuan-chi*, Brendle's Spark, Phlogiston and the Omnispark, Aerya, and Light among others. This universal energy is often understood as the source and fuel of life, the *chi*. Sometimes broken into greater and lesser magics referencing the differentiation between the universal source energy—*yuan-chi*, Phlogiston, Aerya, Light, and celestial or divine magics—and the intrinsic ambient energies of life—the *chi*.

See also *yuan-chi*, *chi*, Brendle's Spark, Phlogiston and Omnispark, Aerya, and Light.

Magical Air Foam System – a magical Gnomish Paratechnological fire extinguishing foam. Particularly effective against Class M magical fires. Also known as MAFS.

Magnus Flintforge – a distant relation of Slate. Innkeeper of the Afternoon's Shade Inn located in isolated Shady Vale.

Major and Minor Shielding – a complex combination of spells serving to protect the recipient from arcane damage and hostile spells, the Major Shield, while also guarding against physical damage, impacts, blows, cuts, and the like, the Minor Shield.

Mandros Gray Beard – a once renowned archmage known for his great enchantments and wondrous Craft.

Mantaed – a massive mantid native to Landeiss. One of the preferred mounts of the Wyaera.

Mazithras – a leading Paratechnologist.

Megacosm – see multiverse or macroverse.

Men – the youngest and most prolific race of Ea'ae. Native flexibility and intuitiveness allows Men to excel in many fields, progressing quickly through their chosen arts.

Mere – 'Path' or 'Way' in the tongue of Tol Aeron.

Meridians – see *jing luo*.

METS – see Multidimensional Examination Tracker Survey.

Microcosmic orbit – the primary channel for the circulation of *chi* within the body. From the perineum, the pathway follows the spine up the back, over the crown of the head, past the brow, across the tongue, down the throat, past the solar plexus and navel, back to the perineum. This energy meridian passes through several major energy points or *chakras* along its route.

The microcosmic orbit is divided into two primary channels. The governor channel runs from the perineum along the back up the spine to the crown and down to the roof of the mouth. The tongue touching the roof of the mouth serves as a bridge between the two channels. The functional channel continues downward from the mouth through the throat, the heart, the navel, until ending in the perineum.

When energy flows freely along the microcosmic orbit joining the two primary energy routes, the practitioner has completed the small heavenly cycle. When the circuits along the arms and legs are open and flowing in conjunction with the small heavenly cycle, the practitioner has then completed the large heavenly cycle.

See also *jing luo* and macrocosmic orbit.

Mihtig'leht – literally, 'mighty light.' One of the fourteen seals protecting Ea'ae from extradimensional incursion. Housed in a bastion in the far reaches of Aruene in the keep of Morowen.

Mithril – a particularly light, yet strong, magical metal.

Molly Flintforge – Magnus's wife and co-owner of the Afternoon's Shade Inn.

Morowen – the bastion protecting the seal of Mihtig'leht. Keep of the Fyrskal.

Mudra – literally, 'seal or sign.' A spiritual gesture and an energetic seal of authenticity. A physical posture or symbolic gesture meant to connect outer actions with spiritual concepts. In Mahayana and Vajrayana Buddhist cosmography, *mudra* help actualize certain inner states, anticipating their bodily expression, creating a connection between the practitioner and the Buddha or experience visualized in meditation.

Mui Fa Jong – literally, 'plum flower poles.' Vertical poles used in martial practice to train balance, focus, coordination, relaxation, and agility.

Multidimensional Examination Tracker Survey – an active evaluation and classification system for the type and origin of energies used by Gnomish Paratechnologists. Also known as METS.

Multiverse – the entirety of multidimensional space inclusive of alternate universes, planes, and dimensions. Also macroverse and megacosm.

Neana – a rainbow-hued magical tree species whose glimmering, diamond-flecked trunks soar to the heavens.

Negentropy cannon – a Paratechnological cannon that locally reverses the process of energy dispersal associated with a given object's entropy at the cost of localized energy injection into the targeted system. In essence, the targeted object explodes into a highly energized cloud of superheated plasma. Sometimes referred to as the Energy Accumulator or the Particulate Plasmifier.

New Unified Mental-Energetic Noesis – NUMEN. A synthetic Paratechnological being of great mental and physical capacity able to take on many shapes, forms, and functions. An extension of the Paratechnology developed in the TAMERS units without need of an operator as the NUMEN is guided by its own intelligence. Also, a play on words among Paratechnologists for their magical-technological creations that may one day supersede them.

Nether realms – extradimensional planes home to Infernals and other fiendish creatures. See Abyss.

Nienael – a lord of Tueran. Father of Gilaethe.

Noeldri – literally, 'flowing water.' A Dwarven rune granting grace and agility both physically and mentally.

Noes Al'amroth – 'the land where tears do not dry.' Elven name for the home of the Aeryn D'al. Called Jenyuan Shulin by the people of Chang Sen. Bordered by Ithil'alen, the ancient homeland of the Elves on Ea'ae.

Noosphere – the realm of the mind, the collective consciousness, or the sphere of thought. A general name for the metamagical plane allowing for the shared existence and interaction both within and between various synthetic intelligences. A Paratechnological creation of the highest order. Also references the sphere of thought, mind, or knowledge itself.

Noumel – member of the Protectorate of Tellanon. The city's chief diplomat, head of interspecies and interstellar diplomacy and trade.

Novice – an aspirant not yet accepted into the priesthood. Upon acceptance into the K'un Lun, the novice becomes an initiate.

Nüaerblun – literally, 'Dragon dung' in the tongue of the Dwarves. Often used as a Dwarven insult.

Nüaer'Daer – literally, 'life's heart.' A Dwarven term for Dragons.

Nüaer'Duin – literally, 'Dragon fire' or 'life's fire' in the tongue of the Dwarves. Among the Dwarves, Dragon fire is respected for its magical properties and power so like the heat of Brendle's forge.

NUMEN – see New Unified Mental-Energetic Noesis.

Nydia – Elven noble and Iyela. Mother to Llyewia. Wife of Aleron.

Oedenara – literally, 'Daemon's heart.' A crystalline gem found at the heart of some Daemons with powerful magical properties and of much practical use.

Omnispark – Gnomish conception of the ignited or expressed source of life unending, ever-changing and evolving, fueled by Phlogiston. Deur Spricken Sprack in Gnomish. Also called *yuan-chi*, magic, Aerya, Brendle's Spark, and Light, among other terms, by other races.

Orcs – a large, prolific evil race spread through the wilds and caverns of Ea'ae. Orcs are strong, aggressive, and full of guile, a race of warriors and shaman. Working in league with Trolls and Ogres, Orcs often lead their slower-witted brethren on the field of battle.

Oroende – Paratechnologist, member of the Protectorate, and Ueralen, leader of the Thelios.

Orogast – one of the lieutenants of the Home Guard under Eidelion. A Jira S'al Alann, able to change shape and form at will. Also known as Orogast the Elder.

Quju – a type of *shenyi* worn primarily by women

Pai-hui – crown energy center corresponding to the Sahasrara *chakra* in some yogic practices. The Yellow Palace. The spirit door.

Pai-lien – White lotus. The lotus is a significant symbol in the Buddhist and Hindu cosmologies. The lotus can represent a symbol of beauty; the various centers of consciousness (*chakras*) located throughout the body; the lotus floating in water can be seen as a symbol for non-attachment—as the lotus floats in the water and remains dry, the spiritual seeker lives in the world and remains unaffected by it; in Buddhism the lotus is also a symbol of the true nature of beings.

Pai-lien Touch – White Lotus Touch. A method of intervention developed within the Priests of K'un Lun that gives the recipient a chance to reform and remake themselves by granting visions of the summation of their experience, akin to a near death experience. Also called the Echoing Fist because the energies of the Touch echo through the chambers of the recipient's mind. Also called Shakyamuni's Palm because a master can use the Touch to cut through falsehood.

Paladin – a holy warrior dedicated to and empowered by the Light, vanquishers of evil, banishers of the unholy, adjudicators and arbiters, healers and almsmen. Many variants exist, some dedicated to particular deities and powerful entities, each with different talents, specialties, and ethos. The Dalaren Ka are one such group.

Paratechnology – literally, 'beyond technology.' The study of making the imagined real and actualizing the impossible. The art and science of applied magic and magical technologies. Paratechnological apprehension is shared across many races, however, the Gnomes' natural curiosity and creativity have brought Paratechnological expertise to its current refined state and have helped to spread its knowledge throughout the cosmos.

Pattern – the unique movements and shapes of *chi*, of limitless potential, indicative of the particular life force of an individual—the fingerprints of the soul. See also *li*.

Peran – Vicar of the High Lord Éremon.

Perfectly Polished Particulate Propeller – Beta Naught Mark Seven – a Gnomish frictionless toothpick invented by Spreesprocket.

Phlogiston – called Deur Spricken Sprack in the tongue of Gnomes. In Gnomish reckoning, the invisible spark of life pervading the universe akin to an invisible metastate of gaseous energetic conductance. Once ignited, Phlogiston fuels all life as the Omnispark. When manipulated by will, the Phlogiston gives rise to magic. Also called *yuan-chi*, magic, Aerya, Brendle's Spark, and Light, among other terms, by other races and traditions.

Plane – one of many distinct layers of existence in the larger macro or multiverse. Often synonymous with universe or dimension.

Plains of Kadoor – open grassy plains on the western section of Dharia. Part of Var'Kera.

Pocket dimension – a miniature space or reality created expressly for a specific purpose. In the case of the myriad pocket dimensions of Tellanon, these represent miniature universes intimately connected to Tellanon itself, extending its breadth and depth. More often, pocket dimensions are used to extend space within a given region, for example, to make the space within a bag or room larger.

Port – a shortened term for teleport.

Powers – beings of great might, often extradimensional in origin.

Priest – one who has been accepted fully into the Order of the K'un Lun. See Priest of K'un Lun.

Priest of Maeth Onai – an order of magicians from the cold Northlands that practices a unique blend of mundane and divine magics whereby divine energies are channeled to perform traditional and inimitable spells.

Priest of K'un Lun – an order of mystics dedicated to the practice of various esoteric and martial traditions found nowhere else on Ea'ae. The way of the priest is geared toward continual transformation and development within and without through the evolving practice of internal alchemy, meditation, and physical cultivation.

Projection – a general term for a multi-dimensional representation of an object. A magical hologram or depiction. Also a reference to life-like, immersive news feeds displaying current happenings and items of worth.

Protectorate – Tellanon's governing body composed of thirteen elected Paratechnologists and other citizen representatives governing matters of security, trade, diplomacy, research, and city form and function. Also called the High Council or council.

Current members include Éremon, Oroende, Rowena Bowspirit, Dizzywig Paddlepulley, Jae'elthos, Vaendoer Thunderhammer, Whirlygig Sparksocket, Magdalia Miera, Borus, Noumel, Salia Proventure, Chutefunnel Knobwhistle, and Alain Ar'laen.

Psion – a being gifted mentally and psychically.

Psionics – psychic mental powers and abilities as expressed by a psion.

Qì – *chi*.

Q'ia'Li – a highly regarded Elven magician of great power that transitioned to Anuvaerya in order to defeat an exceedingly powerful Anubaraëthi in single combat. Creator of Luereal.

Q'ia Shan Sea – eastern border of Chang Sen. A vast and sometimes turbulent body of tropical water dotted by islands and many atolls.

Qigong – literally, '*chi* work' or 'life energy work.' Generally, exercises to build and strengthen *chi* flow.

Qìxīnquán – literally, 'life essence-mind boxing' or 'life energy-mind boxing.' Another term often ascribed to the martial style of the K'un Lun.

Q'shar – A kingdom in far southern Dharia known for its fierce nomadic warriors.

Quai-lo – A widespread race of semi-intelligent insectoid predators. Large and ferocious, they resemble nothing more than vicious humanoid mantises.

Radok – war chief of the Ar'thas, the Black Mountain Orcs.

Rainbow body – a body of pure Light, a celestial or energy body. Called a *jalü* in esoteric tradition. See also *jalü*.

Rare Aer – Humbol's airship.

Rakshasa – a race of powerful feline Daemonic sorcerers in league with the Cabal.

Raour'Saqan – a Dracodaeran Shaur'Daus. Lieutenant of the Home Guard.

Raurdros – literally, 'evil's bane.' The great rune-etched hammer of Kazarhan, forged by Dwarven smiths of old, empowered by ancient runes of power, Karaduen, and other workings of enchantment.

Return stone – a magical crystal of concentrated energy used to transport the bearer to a predefined location—generally the starting point of a journey. Often used with airships to allow passage home without a portal.

Rhyllia – literally, 'the Mother Tree.' An ancient tree in the grove of

Erudhluin held sacred by the Elves. One of the few surviving Aeryn D'al beyond the borders of Jenyuan Shulin.

Rócí – literally, 'pliant or soft poetry.' A simple three-lined poem consisting of five to seven syllables per line. Meant to capture the essence of a moment or the central character of an event, a few words to capture the entirety of an impression. Oftentimes, but not always, the final line heightens the moment of clarity provided by the poem through a sudden, unexpected transition, change, or image.

Rowena Bowspirit – Tellanon's foremost Aeromancer and fleet commander, member of the Protectorate, master pilot and craftswoman.

Ruena O'reine – archmage nonpareil, a principal magical instructor of the Home Guard, and a Holder of Secrets.

Ruen'elde – a name for the cadre of Archliches ruling Garen Muer.

R'yn Daer – a people at home in the skies as much as on the land. Native fliers, swashbucklers and rogues, they wander the skies of Ea'ae in search of fame and fortune.

Saedeus – Lich king, ruler of Garen Muer. Formerly an archmage of great repute and guardian of the seal of Weis'liuhath.

Salia Proventure – member of Tellanon's ruling Protectorate, citizen advocate, and voice of the community and its concerns.

Sarugauth the Red – a primeval Red Dragon allied with the Cabal. Bane of the Yerens.

SAVERS – see Self Actuated Variable Emergency Response System.

SBS – see Sliced Bread Society.

Sceaduwulf – literally, 'shadow wolf.' A spectral wolf.

Scierdyas – literally, 'Spectral Dragons.' Energetic beings very similar in appearance to Dragons summoned from the unholy nether realms of the darkest abysms.

Scimerian Gate – literally, 'Shimmering Gate.' A magical portal allowing entry into Tellanon proper from the loading docks. Also known as the Weirding Gate.

Seals – fourteen magical wards of untold power scattered equidistant across the planet forming a magical barrier protecting Ea'ae from extradimensional incursion and extraplanetary attack.

Seiza – a sitting position commonly used in Buddhist meditation along with the lotus and half-lotus positions. The practitioner sits on her knees with feet tucked under the buttocks.

Self-Actuated Variable Emergency Response System – a Paratechnological clockwork emergency response bot of Gnomish invention capable of independently responding to, assessing, and reacting to multiple life-threatening situations. Called SAVERS for short.

Senea – a massive, thickly trunked forest giant. Its magically reinforced wood is among the strongest on Ea'ae.

Sentry drones – a general name for Paratechnological defensive drones. See also ARMED.

Seura – the 'dance of dreams unborn.' A form of moving knowledge and history transmitted by the Maer'Din of the H'era.

Shade – a nebulous creature of Darkness.

Shadow – a general term for creatures of Darkness and their ilk. Those opposed to the energy of Life in all its manifestations and who seek to subvert, pervert, consume, or otherwise destroy the Light in all its manifold expressions.

Shadowkin – a general term for creatures of Darkness. See Shadow.

Shady Vale – a small hamlet in the western wilds of Dharia deep in the heart of the Green Run.

Shakyamuni – literally, 'sage of the Shakyas.' The historical Buddha Siddhartha Gautama, born into the Shakya, or Lion, clan before realizing the Four Noble Truths and discovering the Eightfold Path as a means to end suffering.

Shapers – see Yerens.

Shaur'Daus – literally, a 'Stalker of Darkness' in the tongue of the Dracodaerans. Draconic warriors wreathed in the fires of Heaven that do battle against the creatures of Darkness across the cosmos and beyond.

Shen – a deity or spirit; also the personal spirit or mind of an individual. One of the three essential life energies of man along with *chi* (*qi*) and *ching* (*jing*). In the Taoist meditative tradition, *shen* refers to both *shih-shen* and *yuan-shen*. Shih-shen refers to ordinary consciousness—thoughts, feelings, perceptions, and the senses. In contrast, *yuan-shen* refers to the spiritual consciousness that exists before birth and is part of the energy that pervades the entire universe (the *yuan-chi*). Meditation, or inner-alchemy, allows the Taoist practitioner to reestablish contact with her spiritual consciousness while eliminating the influence of the ordinary day-to-day consciousness.

Sheng-jen – a sage or saint. Taoist terms for an ideal man who has achieved perfection.

Shen-jen – a spiritual man. Another term used to describe an ideal man, a person who has realized the Tao.

Shen Po – master of the void palm, one of the fallen founding fathers of the K'un Lun, member of the Cabal, and one time teacher of Master Wei.

Shenyi – a long garment of Chang Sen much like a full-body robe with flowing sleeves tied by a sash at the waist. *Zhiju* are worn by men. *Quju* are worn women.

Master Shi – T'ien-shih of the K'un Lun.

Shih – master or expert.

Shrike – airship of Braemen, later of the Fists.

Shuǐ lù xiàn – literally, 'the way of the water course or water's path.' An inner teaching of Xīnyìquán embodying *wu wei, wu bu wei*, and non-resistance, the effortless passage and redirection of force and intent.

Singers – see Yerens.

Skael – a people of nomadic traders who travel the skies in airships plying their wares.

Slate Flintforge – a Dwarf of the land, Bor'Banna, and adventurer of some renown. Friend of Yip, Aroganji, and Wrindanneth. Member of the Four. In the tongue of Dwarves, known as Daer'Duin.

Sliced Bread Society – a Paratechnological think tank dedicated to furthering the depth and breadth of magical and material knowledge and understanding whose study spans the breadth and depth of the mundane and mystical. Driven by the motto, "It doesn't get any better!" Also called the SBS.

Soerlyn – Elven years. See Cycles.

Span – a unit of distance roughly equivalent to a league.

Spreesprocket Goldpulley – a lieutenant of the Home Guard, Gnomish Paratechnologist, and warrior nonpareil.

Squarepeg Springwidget – highly skilled Gnomish Paratechnologist of Tellanon.

Star of Elendial – a magical artifact of great power housed in the Keep of Terraboer. One of the fourteen seals protecting Ea'ae from extradimensional incursion.

Star of Illdrassil – small crystalline fragments of Illdrassil that grant magical boons to members of the Home Guard.

Stasis box – a magical storage box, often enclosing a pocket dimension for added storage space that ensures the freshness of stored food.

Super sack – a magical Gnomish bottomless bag. Super sacks are often cluttered, disorganized, and very difficult to retrieve items from within, especially within a short, highly critical period of time.

Synthetic intelligence – a Paratechnological term for the sentience resulting from the merger of two different intelligences. Typically, one intelligence is natural and the other is artificial, one is organic and the other is disembodied or a metamagical complex arising from technical sophistication, or one intelligence is formed explicitly to merge with and augment another. Far different from the Abstract and Construct's relationship with citizens, for example, wherein one intelligence serves another directly and indirectly, synthetic intelligences are the result of a complete union between two disparate awarenesses, the resulting union having complete access to the knowledge and capabilities of both. Most typically, one intelligence is created explicitly to merge with and augment another, extending the field of sentient consciousness into directions and dimensions only limited by the imagination.

Also a reference to any created intelligence.

Sythaeran Quadrant – a region of space containing the planet known as Al'Marr.

Taerris'thule – literally, 'old home.' Formerly a religious city and home to the seal of Eldre'gheu. Sometimes referred to as the City of the Fallen Gods.

Taiji – alternatively, Tai chi or T'ai chi. Literally, 'supreme ultimate' or 'great absolute.' Undifferentiated or unlimited potential. The source of existence. The primordial state of emptiness from which potential and existence arose and returns. The great, undifferentiated beginning. The wellspring and return of possibility.

Taliaerya – literally, 'Morning's Light' or 'Dawn's Light' in the tongue of the Elves. Known as Eyrdeas, the White Blade of Morn among the Dalaren Ka. The storied blade of Maeven D'lanaran.

TAMERS – see Transmorphic Actionable Multidimensional Exo-Robotic System.

Tan t'ien – an elixir field. The primary energy centers of the human body located at the navel, chest, and forehead. Often a specific reference to the elixir field near the navel. The seat of the *shen*. Alternatively, *dantian*.

More generally, *tan t'ien* can also refer to various energy centers throughout the body through which energy is successively refined. Depending on the alchemical system, the number and purpose may vary. Typically, one *tan t'ien* is located at the navel, another is found at the heart, and one is situated between the eyebrows. Most commonly, the lower *tan t'ien* at or below the navel transforms sexual essence, or *jing*, into *chi*. The middle *tan t'ien* in the center of the chest transmutes *qi* energy into *shen*, or spirit. Finally, the higher *tan t'ien* at the forehead, or on the top of the head, transforms *shen* into Wuji, the infinite space of void.

Tao – literally, 'Way.' Also refers to the way of Nature or Heaven. The mysterious, elusive source and guiding principle behind the phenomena of the universe. The unnamable spring from which *chi* and all existence flow. Also Dao and Wuji.

> *The Tao that can be told is not the eternal Tao;*
> *The name that can be named is not the eternal name.*
> *The nameless is the beginning of Heaven and Earth.*
> *The named is the mother of ten thousand things.*
> *Ever desireless, one can see the mystery.*
> *Ever desiring, one can see the manifestations.*
> *These two spring from the same source but differ in name;*
> *This appears as darkness.*
> *Darkness within darkness.*
> *The gate to all mystery.*[5]

Tao-Shih – a Taoist priest in religious as opposed to philosophical

Taoism. Supervisors of various religious rituals and ceremonies, leaders of congregations, and scholars.

Tellanon – literally, 'Heaven's Landing' in the Old Tongue of Men. A spectacular floating island city in the sky, a center of commerce and diplomacy, and a starting point for both interstellar and interdimensional travel. Home of Illdrassil, the Home Guard, and Paratechnologists on Ea'ae.

Temple of Eldre'gheu – see Eldre'gheu.

Terala – a massive, sentient man-eating spider.

Thaelos – an Elven-trained archer aboard the *Shrike*. Braemen's second.

Thaiel Lui'nost – Elven lorekeeper and sage.

Thane – traditional leader of a Dwarven clan.

Thelios – a guild of Paratechnologists focused on material transformation and alteration led by Oroende.

Therion – an ancient hero known for many exploits including cleansing the seal of Eldre'gheu.

The Thirteen – euphemism for the council.

The Three Pillars – a code of ethics or core tenets of the K'un Lun which guide and support their actions and activities. These moral pillars fall into three general categories reflective of the three primary regions of human endeavor: morality of deed, morality of mind, and morality of spirit.

Furthermore, within each ethical pillar, actions are elucidated by additional secondary tenets. Morality of deed includes expressing humility, loyalty, respect, righteousness, and trust in all actions. Morality of mind entails evincing courage, endurance, patience, perseverance, and will in thought. Morality of spirit includes internalizing, manifesting, and actualizing contemplation, insight, compassion, wisdom, and serenity through freedom of thought and expression.

Three Treasures – the three essential substances of the human body. The three treasures are *jing* (*ching*), the material essence; *qi* (*chi*), the vital energy; and *shen*, the spirit or soul.

The Thunderhammer Clan – a clan of Dwarves residing upon Tellanon known for their technical expertise and cooperative working partnership with Gnomish Paratechnologists.

T'iao chi – harmonizing the breaths. A Taoist breathing technique that serves as preparation for further Taoist development exercises.

T'ien – celestial; Heaven.

T'ien Ming – the celestial mandate or mandate of Heaven. The right to rule granted by Heaven to just emperors.

T'ien-shih – celestial master. Also a title borne by the leaders of some schools of Taoism.

Tinkerers – Paratechnologists focusing on clockwork devices melding magic and technology in forms often resembling complex mechanical devices. Most often associated with Gnomish Paratechnologists due to their strong imaginative mechanical tendencies.

Tol Aeron – a lush, temperate mountainous island far to the south and west of Tellanon off the western coast of Dharia. Birthplace of Eidelion, home of the Keep of Terraboer, the Citadel of Light and the Dalaren Ka, the Knights of the One Light.

Transmorphic Actionable Multidimensional Exo-Robotic System – A multi-functional, transforming exoarmor system created by Spreesprocket. Also known as TAMERS.

Traveler – a magic user capable of teleportation.

Traveling – teleportation or any other form of instantaneous travel whether inter- or intradimensionally.

Tso-wang –meditation characterized by objectless attention or pure awareness coupled with inner and outer stillness—the universe expressing its own enlightened true nature. One of many contemplative approaches employed by the K'un Lun.

Tueran – a largely Anuvatali city that is also home to humans, Dwarves, Gnomes, and Elves located on the southern island nation of Landeiss.

Tuio Shou – literally, 'pushing hands.' A name for the two-person training routines utilized in some internal martial arts.

Tyraethe – homeworld of the Tyraethians.

Tyraethian – reptilian humanoids originating from the planet Tyraethe known for their extreme physical prowess, highly developed code of honor, cultivated ethical systems, and complex moral conduct.

Ueralen – title for the leader of the Thelios, a band of Paratechnologists focused on transmutation and alteration of matter.

The Umbral Lord – see the Enemy or Ur'Daus.

Undermount – a general name for any Dwarven city or a Dwarven occupied region. Typically located in the bedrock beneath mountains. Dwarven fastnesses and attendant halls and byways that grow within the roots of the hills. Also called delvings, though delvings are typically smaller in scale.

Ungar – literally, 'earthen might.' A Dwarven rune granting physical strength and endurance.

Uraera Al'on – literally, 'strengthener of intent' or 'gatherer of will.' A form of magic practiced by the Anuvatali that weaves webs of enchantment around allies, augmenting and expanding upon strengths and abilities.

Ur'Daena – literally, 'the axe's lament.' The uniquely Dwarven art of the axe. Many styles and forms are known, each generally ascribed to a specific family, clan, or thanedom. Variations in styles from the use of great two-handed war axes taller than a man suited to the openness of the battlefield to forms of double-bladed combat better suited to the close quarters of a mineshaft are all practiced with distinctly Dwarven fervor.

When practiced by a master, a Bor'Banna, these styles rely as much on channeling the remnants of Brendle's original creation magic through the axe as physical prowess for their efficacy. When wielded by a true master, the axe of the Bor'Banna is said to glow with the light and heat of Brendle's original forge.

Ur'Daus – literally, 'The Darkness.' Also known as the Enemy, the Creeping Shadow, the Devourer of Worlds, the Umbral Lord, the Great Devourer, and many others. A fathomless Light consuming Darkness trapped between dimensions in ages long past.

Urduen – large Dwarven-fortified city-state of north central Dharia.

Uuraja – leader of the beast riders of Al'Marr, feline lords of the Forlorn Forest. Father of Uuraru.

Uuraru – young son of Uuraja, hereditary lord of the Al'Marr. Named Evensong for his skill in weaving music and magic.

Vaellorea – a grand Elven tree of wondrous form and silvery hue. Kin to Aeryn D'al.

Vaendoer Thunderhammer – member of Tellanon's ruling Protectorate, Dur'kazak, and thane of the Thunderhammer clan.

Vanduen – literally, 'divine regeneration.' A Dwarven Karaduen that enhances healing capacities, speeding recovery and repair from exhaustion and injury.

Vapor of Golden Quintessent Life – a sentient gaseous Paratechnologist with significant psychic ability.

Var'Kera – a land of open grasslands and rich, rolling forests, home to many great kingdoms, and the typical mooring below Tellanon.

Verakesh – a mage in Braemen's employ, pilot of the airship the *Shrike*.

Vöer – Troll in the tongue of the Dwarves.

Vöerdan – literally, 'Troll saliva or spittle.' A Dwarven insult.

Void – the wellspring of creation. The limitless potential underlying all existence. Source of the Tao and *yuan-chi*. Also Wuji.

Void palm – an unassailable attack directly upon the life force of an opponent.

Vorath – an amorphous, mist-like intelligent predator that reads the thoughts of its prey and feeds on their essence.

Vradek – Orcish gruel made from ground bones simmered in blood.

Vyaera – literally, 'wanderers along the path.' An Elven term for those sharing the same path, quest, purpose, or journey.

War of Shadows – one name for the first war with the Cabal and their dark allies waged on Ea'ae in the distant past.

Warren – a general name for the complexly convoluted and often interconnected structures typical of Gnomish homes. Also a name for large, extended Gnomish families.

The Watcher – elusive denizen of the Drake Spires; Ilidian.

Master Wei – an accomplished teacher of the K'un Lun. Yip's primary instructor and guide through the ways of the priesthood. Teacher of the Five Excellencies, master of the Moonlit Mind, keeper of the Echoing fist, and Sheng-jen.

Weirding Gate – see Scimerian Gate.

Weirding Wood – see Aeryn Sh'al.

Weis'liuhath – literally, 'wise light' or 'light of wisdom.' One of the fourteen seals protecting Ea'ae from extradimensional incursion. Housed in a fastness secluded in the lost forests of Kilaeron in the keep of Garen Muer.

Whirlygig Sparksocket – member of the Tellanon Protectorate, Paratechnologist, and lead Designer and System Administrator of COG, the Construct Organization Group.

Wieru S'al Alann – literally 'Way of the Imagining,' 'Way of the Imagined,' or 'Way of Imagining.' The path of self-transformation and actualization taken by the Jira S'al Alann. This way encompasses the techniques, knowledge, and skills necessary to live, survive, adapt, and change in a mutable world.

Witchwood – see Aeryn Sh'al.

Worgs – massive wolves used by Orcs as mounts in lieu of horses.

Wrindanneth – friend of Yip, Aroganji, and Slate. Priest of Maeth Onai. Member of the Fists.

Wu – literally, 'nonbeing; emptiness.' The fundamental characteristic of the Tao. Also refers to a Taoist imbued with the Tao so that he has become free of all passions and desires (empty). Also the absence of qualities perceivable by the senses.

Wu bu Wei – literally, 'not left undone.' The creative completion and natural accompaniment to wu wei. Knowing when and how to act and not to act in intuitive harmony with the Tao. The active, creative complement to the passive stillness of *wu wei*. Taken as a whole, by not acting, nothing is left undone.

Wuji – alternatively, Wu Chi. Literally, 'boundless,' 'ultimateless,' 'limitless,' or infinite. The Ultimateless, Void, or Infinite before the Great Ultimate, Taiji, before differentiation. Synonymous with Tao.

Denoted in Zhan Zhuang standing meditation *qigong* practice as the initial and fundamental stance for practice.

Wu Wei – literally, 'without action' or 'non-action.' A description of 'effortless doing,' 'action without action,' perfect equilibrium, or harmony with the Tao. The complement to *wu bu wei*, or 'not left undone'. Together, *wu wei* and *wu bu wei* form the creative, harmonious passivity and intuition needed to know when and how to act or not to act.

Wu Xin – literally, 'energy gates,' points in the body where internal and external *chi* come into contact. The five primary energy gates include the face, the center of the palms of the hands at the Laogong points, and the Yongquan points on the bottoms of the feet. Energy can also enter through the navel at the *tan t'ien* and through the skin at the pores through special *qigong* practices (i.e. via Fu Xi or skin breathing).

Wu-hsing – alternatively, the Wu Xing, literally 'the five movers,' 'the five elements,' 'the five virtues' (Wu-te). Also represent the five phases of transformation or the five energies that determine the course of natural phenomena. These 'elements' correspond to abstract forces and act as symbols or metaphors for basic characteristics, properties, and interactions of matter. The five symbolic elements are water, earth, fire, metal, and wood.

Master Wuping – a venerated teacher of the K'un Lun.

Wyaera – literally, 'wanderers along the sky,' or, more loosely, 'sky striders,' or 'cloud walkers.' The Riders of Tueran.

Wyrm – an ancient or powerful Dragon.

Xi Wue – a Fang Shih and respected teacher at Xian Shi.

Xian Shi – a school in Chang Sen dedicated to the arcane study of *fang shu* and *fu-lu* and the development of young Fang Shih. Located between the Hsiang Lung Mountains
and the Q'ia Shan Sea.

Xīnyì – literally, 'mind-to-mind,' 'mind to intent,' or 'mind to thought.' A higher order of teaching rarely employed by the Priests of K'un Lun in which a priest directly shares his knowledge and experience with another.

Xīnyìquán – literally, 'heart to mind fist,' 'mind to thought or intent boxing,' or, more loosely, 'mind-to-mind boxing.' The term used to describe a primary component of the martial tradition employed by the Priests of the K'un Lun. Not so much an internal or external martial style, practitioners read and feel the *chi*, the intention and spirit of their opponent, anticipating, redirecting, and manipulating their opponent's energies and intent before and during expression.

Yaozi – a term for 'kite' in Chang Sen.

Ydrael Faer'Leirn – a fabled archmage and author of a magical tome of high magics given to Wrindanneth and Aroganji by Azaelle.

Yenaria – literally, 'House of Dreams.' Elven city linked to Tellanon.

Yerens – a noble race of yeti-like creatures. Singers of the world-song. Called the Shapers of the True Song, Shapers, and Singers.

Yi – any open cross-collar garment worn by both men and women in Chang Sen.

Yin-T'ang – the gateway to Heaven; a primary energy center of the body. The point between the eyes along the brow corresponding to the Ajna *chakra*.

Yip Chi Chuan – an Acolyte of the K'un Lun. Friend of Wrindanneth, Aroganji, and Slate. One of the Flaming Fists. Called Aerya'anan, 'Light bringer,' by the Anuvatari.

Ylldel – literally, 'Mountain Father.' The Indural's name for the mountain home of the Karadüm in the Green Run.

Yrien Al'nori – member of the Home Guard, Anuvatali Uraera Al'on.

Yuan-chi – the primordial energy, the inherent unrealized potential, of the universe; the celestial or divine *chi*. In some Taoist cosmologies, the personal spirit *shen* is thought to arise from the union of *ching*, the essence, with the universal primordial energy of *yuan-chi*. The *shen*, the result of this union, enters the newborn infant with its first breath. The *shen* resides in the body in the *tan t'ien* (navel), where it determines thoughts and feelings until leaving the body at death.

Yuan Ser – a journeyman amongst the Fang Shih. Not yet a fully accomplished master or archmage in the rites and traditions of the *fang shu*.

Yuan-shen – universal, original, or primordial awareness, spirit, or mind.

Yu-jen – literally, 'feather man.' An alternative designation for Tao-shih.

Zabuton – a flat padded mat used for sitting. Sometimes positioned under a *zafu* in meditation.

Zafu – a round cushion used for seated meditation.

Zhan Zhuang – standing like a tree or post; a form of standing meditation used in various systems of *chi gung* (internal energy work).

Zhiju – a type of *shenyi* worn primarily by men in Chang Sen.

Zhiyuan – a term for kite in Chang Sen.

REFERENCES FOR MORE IN-DEPTH INFORMATION AND FURTHER STUDY

1. Blofield, John. *Taoism - The Road to Immortality*. Shambhala: Boston. 1978.
2. Chia, Mantak. *Awaken Healing Energy through the Tao*. Aurora: Santa Fe. 1983.
3. Chuen, Master Lam Kam. *The Way of Energy*. Simon & Schuster, Inc.: New York. 1991.
4. Cleary, Thomas (trans.). *Opening the Dragon Gate*. Tuttle: Boston. 1996.
5. Gia-Fu Feng & Jane English (translators). *Lao Tsu/Tao Te Ching*. New York: Vintage Books. 1972.
6. Liang, Master Shou-Yu and Wu, Wen-Ching. *Qigong Empowerment - A Guide to Buddhist Taoist Medical Wushu Energy Cultivation*. Dragon Publishing: East Providence. 1997.
7. Schuhmacher, Stephan and Woerner Gert (eds.). *The Encyclopedia of Eastern Philosophy and Religion*. Shambhala: Boston. 1989.
8. Suzuki, Shunryu. *Zen Mind, Beginner's Mind*. Shambhala: Boston. 1973.
9. Watson, Burton (trans.). *The Complete Works of Chuang Tzu*. Columbia University Press: New York. 1968.

ABOUT THE AUTHOR

Through such simple questions as, "What if we lived in a world where our beliefs were real, tangible, and actualizable?" Joe explores the possible through thought, fantasy, wit, and character.

Including influences such as Shunryu Suzuki, Tolkien, Krishnamurti, Iain M. Banks, Laozi, Stephen R. Donaldson, Philip Kapleau, Raymond E. Feist, Edward O. Wilson, Dan Simmons, and David Bohm, Joe creates existential fantasy filled with rich worlds, concepts, stories, and ideas.

Joe holds an advanced degree in environmental management from Duke University, where he also studied religion with a focus on meditative, experiential, and transformative traditions. Additionally, Joe graduated with (dubious) honors from the Tellanon Institute of Noetic Knowledge, Education, and Research (TINKER), but has yet to put this knowledge to good use.

When not at play with his family, he enjoys reading, writing, and relaxation. When he can, Joe also practices various martial traditions in which he has attained the victim level of proficiency.

Joe's website

ACKNOWLEDGMENTS

I would like to thank my wife for her patience, love, and support; my beta readers for their willingness to enter worlds unlike any other; my friends for listening to my all-too-frequent updates and ideas; Ashley Davis, my editor, for helping realize my vision; and all the readers who took a chance in reading my work.

Thank you!

SHADOW'S RISE SYNOPSIS

Yip Chi Chuan, a young martial and spiritual ascetic, must flee as the only home he has ever known, the ancient monastery of the Priests of K'un Lun, is destroyed by a newly ascendant extradimensional evil. Cast out and alone, Yip strikes out on a quest spanning the breadth of his home world of Ea'ae and into the greater macroverse beyond in an attempt to unseat an all-consuming Darkness rooted in his once vaunted order's distant past.

Will Yip, the last of his kind to walk the wide world beyond his fallen sanctuary, succeed where his mighty brethren failed in ages past?

Unfortunately for Yip, the answer appears all too clear... Without the guidance and teachings of his lineage, pursued by malevolent supernatural agents of the Cabal, unable to fully defend himself in a world steeped in magic, his quest may fail before it ever begins.

Unfazed by his limitations, guided by his inner vision and direct experience of the energies of life, the radiant *chi* suffusing and enlivening the world all around, he is determined to triumph where others have faltered.

To win forward, he will need help...but first he must survive.

A blend of Western fantasy and Eastern martial arts and mysticism, *Shadow's Rise* is the first book of the *Chronicles of the Fists*, an epic trilogy recounting Yip's adventures against all odds.

COPYRIGHT

www.ingramcontent.com/pod-product-compliance
Lightning Source LLC
Chambersburg PA
CBHW032251020726
47495CB00001B/58